KU-360-263

The Oxford India Paper Dickens, Complete Edition
With Illustrations by Cruikshank, ' Phiz,' &c.
In Seventeen Volumes

Great Expectations

This Edition of the

COMPLETE WORKS OF CHARLES DICKENS

Is issued in Seventeen Volumes.

——◆◆——

"WITH YOU—HOB AND NOB," RETURNED THE SERGEANT

Great Expectations

By

Charles Dickens

With Ten Illustrations

By Charles Green

London

Chapman & Hall, Limited; and

Henry Frowde

New York: Oxford University Press American Branch

29–35 West 32nd Street

Printed by HORACE HART,
University Press, Oxford

LIST OF ILLUSTRATIONS

CHARACTERS

OLD BILL BARLEY, a bedridden purser.

MR. RAYMOND CAMILLA, a toady, a relative of Miss Havisham's.

COMPEYSON, a convict.

BENTLEY DRUMMLE ("The Spider"), a proud, idle young man.

JOE GARGERY, a blacksmith.

MR. HUBBLE, a wheelwright.

MR. JAGGERS, a criminal lawyer of Little Britain.

ABEL MAGWITCH, *alias* PROVIS, an escaped convict.

DOLGE ORLICK, a journeyman employed by Joe Gargery.

PHILIP PIRRIP ("Pip"), the hero, an orphan.

HERBERT POCKET, a youth with "great expectations," a close friend of Pip's.

MR. MATTHEW POCKET, a relative of Miss Havisham's.

UNCLE PUMBLECHOOK, a well-to-do corn-chandler and seedsman.

MR. STARTOP, a lively young man, a fellow-boarder with Pip.

MR. TRABB, a prosperous tailor and undertaker.

TRABB'S BOY, an impudent young rascal, shop-boy to the preceding.

MR. JOHN WEMMICK, confidential clerk to Mr. Jaggers.

MR. WEMMICK, SENIOR ("The Aged"), father of the preceding.

MR. WOPSLE, a parish clerk, afterwards an indifferent actor.

CLARA BARLEY, daughter of Old Bill Barley.

BIDDY, an orphan, later Joe Gargery's second wife.

MRS. BRANDLEY, a widow lady at Richmond.

MRS. CAMILLA, wife to Mr. Raymond Camilla.

ESTELLA, the adopted daughter of Miss Havisham.

MRS. GEORGIANA MARIA GARGERY, wife to Joe Gargery.

MISS HAVISHAM, an eccentric lady, who adopts Estella.

MRS. HUBBLE, a sharp-eared little person.

MOLLY, housekeeper to Mr. Jaggers.

MRS. BELINDA POCKET, wife to Mr. Matthew Pocket.

SARAH POCKET, a little, dry old woman.

MISS SKIFFINS, a propertied lady, of uncertain age.

GREAT EXPECTATIONS

CHAPTER I

My father's family name being Pirrip, and my christian name Philip, my infant tongue could make of both names nothing longer or more explicit than Pip. So I called myself Pip, and came to be called Pip.

I give Pirrip as my father's family name, on the authority of his tombstone and my sister—Mrs. Joe Gargery, who married the blacksmith. As I never saw my father or my mother, and never saw any likeness of either of them (for their days were long before the days of photographs), my first fancies regarding what they were like, were unreasonably derived from their tombstones. The shape of the letters on my father's, gave me an odd idea that he was a square, stout, dark man, with curly black hair. From the character and turn of the inscription, "Also Georgiana Wife of the Above," I drew a childish conclusion that my mother was freckled and sickly. To five little stone lozenges, each about a foot and a half long, which were arranged in a neat row beside their grave, and were sacred to the memory of five little brothers of mine—who gave up trying to get a living exceedingly early in that universal struggle—I am indebted for a belief I religiously entertained that they had all been born on their backs with their hands in their trousers-pockets, and had never taken them out in this state of existence.

Ours was the marsh country, down by the river, within, as the river wound, twenty miles of the sea. My first most vivid and broad impression of the identity of things, seems to me to have been gained on a memorable raw afternoon towards evening. At such a time I found out for certain, that this bleak place overgrown with nettles was the church-yard; and that Philip Pirrip, late of this parish, and also Georgiana wife of the above, were dead and buried; and that Alexander, Bartholomew, Abraham, Tobias, and Roger, infant children of the aforesaid, were also dead and buried; and that the dark flat wilderness beyond the churchyard, intersected with dykes and mounds and gates, with scattered cattle feeding on it, was the marshes; and that the low leaden line beyond was the river; and that the distant savage lair from which the wind was rushing, was the sea; and that the small bundle of shivers growing afraid of it all and beginning to cry, was Pip.

"Hold your noise!" cried a terrible voice, as a man started up from among the graves at the side of the church porch. "Keep still, you little devil, or I'll cut your throat!"

A fearful man, all in coarse grey, with a great iron on his leg. A man with no hat, and with broken shoes, and with an old rag tied round his head. A man who had been soaked in water, and smothered in mud, and lamed by stones, and cut by flints, and stung by nettles, and torn by briars; who limped and shivered, and glared and growled; and whose teeth chattered in his head as he seized me by the chin.

"O! Don't cut my throat, sir," I pleaded in terror. "Pray don't do it, sir."

"Tell us your name!" said the man. "Quick!"

"Pip, sir."

"Once more," said the man, staring at me. "Give it mouth!"

"Pip. Pip, sir."

"Show us where you live," said the man. "Pint out the place!"

I pointed to where our village lay, on the flat in-shore among the alder-trees and pollards, a mile or more from the church.

The man, after looking at me for a moment, turned me upside down, and emptied my pockets. There was nothing in them but a piece of bread. When the church came to itself—for he was so sudden and strong that he made it go head over heels before me, and I saw the steeple under my feet—when the church came to itself, I say, I was seated on a high tombstone, trembling, while he ate the bread ravenously.

"You young dog," said the man, licking his lips, "what fat cheeks you ha' got."

I believe they were fat, though I was at that time undersized, for my years, and not strong.

"Darn Me if I couldn't eat 'em," said the man, with a threatening shake of his head, "and if I han't half a mind to't!"

I earnestly expressed my hope that he wouldn't, and held tighter to the tombstone on which he had put me; partly, to keep myself upon it; partly, to keep myself from crying.

"Now lookee here!" said the man. "Where's your mother?"

"There, sir!" said I.

He started, made a short run, and stopped and looked over his shoulder.

"There, sir!" I timidly explained. "Also Georgiana. That's my mother."

"Oh!" said he, coming back. "And is that your father alonger your mother?"

"Yes, sir," said I; "him too; late of this parish."

"Ha!" he muttered then, considering. "Who d'ye live with—supposin' you're kindly let to live, which I han't made up my mind about?"

"My sister, sir—Mrs. Joe Gargery—wife of Joe Gargery, the blacksmith, sir."

"Blacksmith, eh?" said he. And looked down at his leg.

After darkly looking at his leg and at me several times, he came closer to my tombstone, took me by both arms, and tilted me back as far as he could hold me; so that his eyes looked most powerfully down into mine, and mine looked most helplessly up into his.

"Now lookee here," he said, "the question being whether you're to be let to live. You know what a file is?"

"Yes, sir."

"And you know what wittles is?"

"Yes, sir."

After each question he tilted me over a little more, so as to give me a greater sense of helplessness and danger.

"You get me a file." He tilted me again. "And you get me wittles." He tilted me again. "You bring 'em both to me." He tilted me again. "Or I'll have your heart and liver out." He tilted me again.

I was dreadfully frightened, and so giddy that I clung to

him with both hands, and said, "If you would kindly please
to let me keep upright, sir, perhaps I shouldn't be sick, and
perhaps I could attend more."

He gave me a most tremendous dip and roll, so that the
church jumped over its own weather-cock. Then, he held
me by the arms in an upright position on the top of the
stone, and went on in these fearful terms:

"You bring me, to-morrow morning early, that file and
them wittles. You bring the lot to me, at that old Battery
over yonder. You do it, and you never dare to say a word
or dare to make a sign concerning your having seen such
a person as me, or any person sumever, and you shall be let
to live. You fail, or you go from my words in any partickler
no matter how small it is, and your heart and your liver
shall be tore' out, roasted and ate. Now, I ain't alone, as
you may think I am. There's a young man hid with me,
in comparison with which young man I am a Angel. That
young man hears the words I speak. That young man has
a secret way pecooliar to himself, of getting at a boy, and
at his heart, and at his liver. It is in wain for a boy to
attempt to hide himself from that young man. A boy may
lock his door, may be warm in bed, may tuck himself up,
may draw the clothes over his head, may think himself
comfortable and safe, but that young man will softly creep
and creep his way to him and tear him open. I am a keeping
that young man from harming of you at the present moment,
with great difficulty. I find it wery hard to hold that young
man off of your inside. Now, what do you say?"

I said that I would get him the file, and I would get him
what broken bits of food I could, and I would come to him
at the Battery, early in the morning.

"Say, Lord strike you dead if you don't!" said the man.

I said so, and he took me down.

"Now," he pursued, "you remember what you've under
took, and you remember that young man, and you get
home!"

"Goo-good night, sir," I faltered.

"Much of that!" said he, glancing about him over the
cold wet flat. "I wish I was a frog. Or a eel!"

At the same time, he hugged his shuddering body in both
his arms—clasping himself, as if to hold himself together—
and limped towards the low church wall. As I saw him go,
picking his way among the nettles, and among the brambles

that bound the green mounds, he looked in my young eyes as if he were eluding the hands of the dead people, stretching up cautiously out of their graves, to get a twist upon his ankle and pull him in.

When he came to the low church wall, he got over it, like a man whose legs were numbed and stiff, and then turned round to look for me. When I saw him turning, I set my face towards home, and made the best use of my legs. But presently I looked over my shoulder, and saw him going on again towards the river, still hugging himself in both arms, and picking his way with his sore feet among the great stones dropped into the marshes here and there, for stepping-places when the rains were heavy, or the tide was in.

The marshes were just a long black horizontal line then, as I stopped to look after him ; and the river was just another horizontal line, not nearly so broad nor yet so black ; and the sky was just a row of long angry red lines and dense black lines intermixed. On the edge of the river I could faintly make out the only two black things in all the prospect that seemed to be standing upright ; one of these was the beacon by which the sailors steered—like an unhooped cask upon a pole—an ugly thing when you were near it ; the other a gibbet, with some chains hanging to it which had once held a pirate. The man was limping on towards this latter, as if he were the pirate come to life, and come down, and going back to hook himself up again. It gave me a terrible turn when I thought so ; and as I saw the cattle lifting their heads to gaze after him, I wondered whether they thought so too. I looked all round for the horrible young man, and could see no signs of him. But now I was frightened again, and ran home without stopping.

CHAPTER II

My sister, Mrs. Joe Gargery, was more than twenty years older than I, and had established a great reputation with herself and the neighbours because she had brought me up "by hand." Having at that time to find out for myself what the expression meant, and knowing her to have a hard and heavy hand, and to be much in the habit of laying it upon her husband as well as upon me, I supposed that Joe Gargery and I were both brought up by hand.

She was not a good-looking woman, my sister; and I had a general impression that she must have made Joe Gargery marry her by hand. Joe was a fair man, with curls of flaxen hair on each side of his smooth face, and with eyes of such a very undecided blue that they seemed to have somehow got mixed with their own whites. He was a mild, good-natured, sweet-tempered, easy-going, foolish, dear fellow—a sort of Hercules in strength, and also in weakness.

My sister, Mrs. Joe, with black hair and eyes, had such a prevailing redness of skin, that I sometimes used to wonder whether it was possible she washed herself with a nutmeg-grater instead of soap. She was tall and bony, and almost always wore a coarse apron, fastened over her figure behind with two loops, and having a square impregnable bib in front, that was stuck full of pins and needles. She made it a powerful merit in herself, and a strong reproach against Joe, that she wore this apron so much. Though I really see no reason why she should have worn it at all: or why, if she did wear it at all, she should not have taken it off every day of her life.

Joe's forge adjoined our house, which was a wooden house, as many of the dwellings in our country were—most of them, at that time. When I ran home from the churchyard, the forge was shut up, and Joe was sitting alone in the kitchen. Joe and I being fellow-sufferers, and having confidences as such, Joe imparted a confidence to me, the moment I raised the latch of the door and peeped in at him opposite to it, sitting in the chimney corner.

"Mrs. Joe has been out a dozen times, looking for you, Pip. And she's out now, making it a baker's dozen."

"Is she?"

"Yes, Pip," said Joe; "and what's worse, she's got Tickler with her."

At this dismal intelligence, I twisted the only button on my waistcoat round and round, and looked in great depression at the fire. Tickler was a wax-ended piece of cane, worn smooth by collision with my tickled frame.

"She sot down," said Joe, "and she got up, and she made a grab at Tickler, and she Ram-paged out. That's what she did," said Joe, slowly clearing the fire between the lower bars with the poker, and looking at it: "she Ram-paged out, Pip."

"Has she been gone long, Joe?" I always treated him as a larger species of child, and as no more than my equal.

"Well," said Joe, glancing up at the Dutch clock, "she's been on the Ram-page, this last spell, about five minutes, Pip. She's a-coming! Get behind the door, old chap, and have the jack-towel betwixt you."

I took the advice. My sister, Mrs. Joe, throwing the door wide open, and finding an obstruction behind it, immediately divined the cause, and applied Tickler to its further investigation. She concluded by throwing me—I often served as a connubial missile—at Joe, who, glad to get hold of me on any terms, passed me on into the chimney and quietly fenced me up there with his great leg.

"Where have you been, you young monkey?" said Mrs. Joe, stamping her foot. "Tell me directly what you've been doing to wear me away with fret and fright and worrit, or I'd have you out of that corner if you was fifty Pips, and he was five hundred Gargerys."

"I have only been to the churchyard," said I, from my stool, crying and rubbing myself.

"Churchyard!" repeated my sister. "If it warn't for me you'd have been to the churchyard long ago, and stayed there. Who brought you up by hand?"

'You did," said I.

"And why did I do it, I should like to know?" exclaimed my sister.

I whimpered, "I don't know."

"*I* don't!" said my sister. "I'd never do it again! I know that. I may truly say I've never had this apron of mine off, since born you were. It's bad enough to be a blacksmith's wife (and him a Gargery), without being your mother."

My thoughts strayed from that question as I looked disconsolately at the fire. For, the fugitive out on the marshes with the ironed leg, the mysterious young man, the file, the food, and the dreadful pledge I was under to commit a larceny on those sheltering premises, rose before me in the avenging coals.

"Hah!" said Mrs. Joe, restoring Tickler to his station. "Churchyard, indeed! You may well say churchyard, you two." One of us, by-the-bye, had not said it at all. "You'll drive *me* to the churchyard betwixt you, one of these days, and oh, a pr-r-recious pair you'd be without me!"

As she applied herself to set the tea-things, Joe peeped down at me over his leg, as if he were mentally casting me and himself up, and calculating what kind of pair we practically should make, under the grievous circumstances foreshadowed. After that, he sat feeling his right-side flaxen curls and whisker, and following Mrs. Joe about with his blue eyes, as his manner always was at squally times.

My sister had a trenchant way of cutting our bread-and-butter for us, that never varied. First, with her left hand she jammed the loaf hard and fast against her bib—where it sometimes got a pin into it, and sometimes a needle, which we afterwards got into our mouths. Then she took some butter (not too much) on a knife and spread it on the loaf, in an apothecary kind of way, as if she were making a plaister—using both sides of the knife with a slapping dexterity, and trimming and moulding the butter off round the crust. Then, she gave the knife a final smart wipe on the edge of the plaister, and then sawed a very thick round off the loaf: which she finally, before separating from the loaf, hewed into two halves, of which Joe got one, and I the other.

On the present occasion, though I was hungry, I dared not eat my slice. I felt that I must have something in reserve for my dreadful acquaintance, and his ally the still more dreadful young man. I knew Mrs. Joe's housekeeping

to be of the strictest kind, and that my larcenous researches might find nothing available in the safe. Therefore I resolved to put my hunk of bread-and-butter down the leg of my trousers.

The effort of resolution necessary to the achievement of this purpose, I found to be quite awful. It was as if I had to make up my mind to leap from the top of a high house, or plunge into a great depth of water. And it was made the more difficult by the unconscious Joe. In our already-mentioned freemasonry as fellow-sufferers, and in his good-natured companionship with me, it was our evening habit to compare the way we bit through our slices, by silently holding them up to each other's admiration now and then— which stimulated us to new exertions. To-night, Joe several times invited me, by the display of his fast-diminishing slice, to enter upon our usual friendly competition ; but he found me, each time, with my yellow mug of tea on one knee, and my untouched bread-and-butter on the other. At last, I desperately considered that the thing I contemplated must be done, and that it had best be done in the least improbable manner consistent with the circumstances. I took advantage of a moment when Joe had just looked at me, and got my bread-and-butter down my leg.

Joe was evidently made uncomfortable by what he supposed to be my loss of appetite, and took a thoughtful bite out of his slice, which he didn't seem to enjoy. He turned it about in his mouth much longer than usual, pondering over it a good deal, and after all gulped it down like a pill. He was about to take another bite, and had just got his head on one side for a good purchase on it, when his eye fell on me, and he saw that my bread-and-butter was gone.

The wonder and consternation with which Joe stopped on the threshold of his bite and stared at me, were too evident to escape my sister's observation.

"What's the matter now?" said she, smartly, as she put down her cup.

"I say, you know!" muttered Joe, shaking his head at me in a very serious remonstrance. "Pip, old chap! You'll do yourself a mischief. It'll stick somewhere. You can't have chawed it, Pip."

"What's the matter *now?*" repeated my sister, more sharply than before.

"If you can cough any trifle on it up, Pip, I'd recommend

you to do it," said Joe, all aghast. "Manners is manners, but still your elth's your elth."

By this time, my sister was quite desperate, so she pounced on Joe, and, taking him by the two whiskers, knocked his head for a little while against the wall behind him: while I sat in the corner, looking guiltily on.

"Now, perhaps you'll mention what's the matter," said my sister, out of breath, "you staring great stuck pig."

Joe looked at her in a helpless way; then took a helpless bite, and looked at me again.

"You know, Pip," said Joe, solemnly, with his last bite in his cheek, and speaking in a confidential voice, as if we two were quite alone, "you and me is always friends, and I'd be the last to tell upon you, any time. But such a "— he moved his chair, and looked about the floor between us, and then again at me—"such a most uncommon bolt as that!"

"Been bolting his food, has he?" cried my sister.

"You know, old chap," said Joe, looking at me, and not at Mrs. Joe, with his bite still in his cheek, "I Bolted, myself, when I was your age—frequent—and as a boy I've been among a many Bolters; but I never see your bolting equal yet, Pip, and it's a mercy you ain't Bolted dead."

My sister made a dive at me, and fished me up by the hair; saying nothing more than the awful words, "You come along and be dosed."

Some medical beast had revived Tar-water in those days as a fine medicine, and Mrs. Joe always kept a supply of it in the cupboard; having a belief in its virtues corre-spondent to its nastiness. At the best of times, so much of this elixir was administered to me as a choice restorative, that I was conscious of going about, smelling like a new fence. On this particular evening, the urgency of my case demanded a pint of this mixture, which was poured down my throat, for my greater comfort, while Mrs. Joe held my head under her arm, as a boot would be held in a boot-jack. Joe got off with half a pint; but was made to swallow that (much to his disturbance, as he sat slowly munching and meditating before the fire), "because he had had a turn." Judging from myself, I should say he certainly had a turn afterwards, if he had had none before.

Conscience is a dreadful thing when it accuses man or boy; but when, in the case of a boy, that secret burden

co-operates with another secret burden down the leg of his trousers, it is (as I can testify) a great punishment. The guilty knowledge that I was going to rob Mrs. Joe—I never thought I was going to rob Joe, for I never thought of any of the housekeeping property as his—united to the necessity of always keeping one hand on my bread-and-butter as I sat, or when I was ordered about the kitchen on any small errand, almost drove me out of my mind. Then, as the marsh winds made the fire glow and flare, I thought I heard the voice outside, of the man with the iron on his leg who had sworn me to secrecy, declaring that he couldn't and wouldn't starve until to-morrow, but must be fed now. At other times, I thought, What if the young man who was with so much difficulty restrained from imbruing his hands in me, should yield to a constitutional impatience, or should mistake the time, and should think himself accredited to my heart and liver to-night, instead of to-morrow! If ever anybody's hair stood on end with terror, mine must have done so then. But, perhaps, nobody's ever did?

It was Christmas Eve, and I had to stir the pudding for next day, with a copper-stick, from seven to eight by the Dutch clock. I tried it with the load upon my leg (and that made me think afresh of the man with the load on *his* leg), and found the tendency of exercise to bring the bread-and-butter out at my ankle, quite unmanageable. Happily I slipped away, and deposited that part of my conscience in my garret bedroom.

"Hark!" said I, when I had done my stirring, and was taking a final warm in the chimney corner before being sent up to bed; "was that great guns, Joe?"

"Ah!" said Joe. "There's another conwict off."

"What does that mean, Joe?" said I.

Mrs. Joe, who always took explanations upon herself, said snappishly, "Escaped. Escaped." Administering the definition like Tar-water.

While Mrs. Joe sat with her head bending over her needlework, I put my mouth into the forms of saying to Joe, "What's a convict?" Joe put *his* mouth into the forms of returning such a highly elaborate answer, that I could make out nothing of it but the single word, "Pip."

"There was a conwict off last night," said Joe, aloud, "after sunset-gun. And they fired warning of him. And now it appears they're firing warning of another."

" *Who's* firing ? " said I.

"Drat that boy," interposed my sister, frowning at me over her work, "what a questioner he is. Ask no questions, and you'll be told no lies."

It was not very polite to herself, I thought, to imply that I should be told lies by her, even if I did ask questions. But she never was polite, unless there was company.

At this point, Joe greatly augmented my curiosity by taking the utmost pains to open his mouth very wide, and to put it into the form of a word that looked to me like "sulks." Therefore, I naturally pointed to Mrs. Joe, and put my mouth into the form of saying "her ? " But Joe wouldn't hear of that at all, and again opened his mouth very wide, and shook the form of a most emphatic word out of it. But I could make nothing of the word.

"Mrs. Joe," said I, as a last resort, "I should like to know—if you wouldn't much mind—where the firing comes from ? "

"Lord bless the boy ! " exclaimed my sister, as if she didn't quite mean that, but rather the contrary. "From the Hulks ! "

"Oh-h ! " said I, looking at Joe. "Hulks ! "

Joe gave a reproachful cough, as much as to say, "Well, I told you so."

"And please what's Hulks ? " said I.

"That's the way with this boy ! " exclaimed my sister, pointing me out with her needle and thread, and shaking her head at me. "Answer him one question, and he'll ask you a dozen directly. Hulks are prison-ships, right 'cross th' meshes." We always used that name for marshes in our country.

"I wonder who's put into prison-ships, and why they're put there ? " said I, in a general way, and with quiet desperation.

It was too much for Mrs. Joe, who immediately rose. "I tell you what, young fellow," said she, "I didn't bring you up by hand to badger people's lives out. It would be blame to me, and not praise, if I had. People are put in the Hulks because they murder, and because they rob, and forge, and do all sorts of bad ; and they always begin by asking questions. Now, you get along to bed ! "

I was never allowed a candle to light me to bed, and, as I went up-stairs in the dark, with my head tingling—from

Mrs. Joe's thimble having played the tambourine upon it, to accompany her last words—I felt fearfully sensible of the great convenience that the hulks were handy for me. I was clearly on my way there. I had begun by asking questions, and I was going to rob Mrs. Joe.

Since that time, which is far enough away now, I have often thought that few people know what secrecy there is in the young, under terror. No matter how unreasonable the terror, so that it be terror. I was in mortal terror of the young man who wanted my heart and liver; I was in mortal terror of my interlocutor with the iron leg; I was in mortal terror of myself, from whom an awful promise had been extracted; I had no hope of deliverance through my all-powerful sister, who repulsed me at every turn; I am afraid to think of what I might have done on requirement, in the secrecy of my terror.

If I slept at all that night, it was only to imagine myself drifting down the river on a strong spring-tide, to the Hulks; a ghostly pirate calling out to me through a speaking-trumpet, as I passed the gibbet-station, that I had better come ashore and be hanged there at once, and not put it off. I was afraid to sleep, even if I had been inclined, for I knew that at the first faint dawn of morning I must rob the pantry. There was no doing it in the night, for there was no getting a light by easy friction then; to have got one, I must have struck it out of flint and steel, and have made a noise like the very pirate himself rattling his chains.

As soon as the great black velvet pall outside my little window was shot with grey, I got up and went down-stairs; every board upon the way, and every crack in every board, calling after me, "Stop thief!" and "Get up, Mrs. Joe!" In the pantry, which was far more abundantly supplied than usual, owing to the season, I was very much alarmed, by a hare hanging up by the heels, whom I rather thought I caught, when my back was half turned, winking. I had no time for verification, no time for selection, no time for anything, for I had no time to spare. I stole some bread, some rind of cheese, about half a jar of mincemeat (which I tied up in my pocket-handkerchief with my last night's slice), some brandy from a stone bottle (which I decanted into a glass bottle I had secretly used for making that intoxicating fluid, Spanish-liquorice-water, up in my room;

diluting the stone bottle from a jug in the kitchen cupboard), a meat bone with very little on it, and a beautiful round compact pork pie. I was nearly going away without the pie, but I was tempted to mount upon a shelf, to look what it was that was put away so carefully in a covered earthenware dish in a corner, and I found it was the pie, and I took it, in the hope that it was not intended for early use, and would not be missed for some time.

There was a door in the kitchen communicating with the forge; I unlocked and unbolted that door, and got a file from among Joe's tools. Then I put the fastenings as I had found them, opened the door at which I had entered when I ran home last night, shut it, and ran for the misty marshes.

CHAPTER III

It was a rimy morning, and very damp. I had seen the
damp lying on the outside of my little window, as if some
goblin had been crying there all night, and using the window
for a pocket-handkerchief. Now I saw the damp lying on
the bare hedges and spare grass, like a coarser sort of
spiders' webs; hanging itself from twig to twig and blade
to blade. On every rail and gate, wet lay clammy, and
the marsh-mist was so thick, that the wooden finger on the
post directing people to our village—a direction which they
never accepted, for they never came there—was invisible to
me until I was quite close under it. Then, as I looked up
at it, while it dripped, it seemed to my oppressed conscience
like a phantom devoting me to the Hulks.

The mist was heavier yet when I got out upon the
marshes, so that instead of my running at everything, everything seemed to run at me. This was very disagreeable
to a guilty mind. The gates and dykes and banks came
bursting at me through the mist, as if they cried as plainly
as could be, "A boy with Somebody-else's pork pie! Stop
him!" The cattle came upon me with like suddenness,
staring out of their eyes, and steaming out of their nostrils,
"Halloa, young thief!" One black ox, with a white cravat
on—who even had to my awakened conscience something
of a clerical air—fixed me so obstinately with his eyes,
and moved his blunt head round in such an accusatory
manner as I moved round, that I blubbered out to him,
"I couldn't help it, sir! It wasn't for myself I took it!"
Upon which he put down his head, blew a cloud of smoke
out of his nose, and vanished with a kick-up of his hind-
legs and a flourish of his tail.

All this time I was getting on towards the river; but
however fast I went, I couldn't warm my feet, to which the
damp cold seemed riveted, as the iron was riveted to the leg
of the man I was running to meet. I knew my way to the
Battery, pretty straight, for I had been down there on

a Sunday with Joe, and Joe, sitting on an old gun, had told me that when I was 'prentice to him, regularly bound, we would have such Larks there! However, in the confusion of the mist, I found myself at last too far to the right, and consequently had to try back along the river-side, on the bank of loose stones above the mud and the stakes that staked the tide out. Making my way along here with all despatch, I had just crossed a ditch which I knew to be very near the Battery, and had just scrambled up the mound beyond the ditch, when I saw the man sitting before me. His back was towards me, and he had his arms folded, and was nodding forward, heavy with sleep.

I thought he would be more glad if I came upon him with his breakfast, in that unexpected manner, so I went forward softly and touched him on the shoulder. He instantly jumped up, and it was not the same man, but another man!

And yet this man was dressed in coarse grey, too, and had a great iron on his leg, and was lame, and hoarse, and cold, and was everything that the other man was; except that he had not the same face, and had a flat, broad-brimmed, low-crowned felt hat on. All this I saw in a moment, for I had only a moment to see it in: he swore an oath at me, made a hit at me—it was a round, weak blow that missed me and almost knocked himself down, for it made him stumble—and then he ran into the mist, stumbling twice as he went, and I lost him.

"It's the young man!" I thought, feeling my heart shoot as I identified him. I dare say I should have felt a pain in my liver, too, if I had known where it was.

I was soon at the Battery, after that, and there was the right man—hugging himself and limping to and fro, as if he had never all night left off hugging and limping—waiting for me. He was awfully cold, to be sure. I half expected to see him drop down before my face and die of deadly cold. His eyes looked so awfully hungry, too, that when I handed him the file and he laid it down on the grass, it occurred to me he would have tried to eat it, if he had not seen my bundle. He did not turn me upside down, this time, to get at what I had, but left me right side upwards while I opened the bundle and emptied my pockets.

"What's in the bottle, boy?" said he.

"Brandy," said I.

He was already handing mincemeat down his throat in the most curious manner—more like a man who was putting it away somewhere in a violent hurry, than a man who was eating it—but he left off to take some of the liquor. He shivered all the while so violently, that it was quite as much as he could do to keep the neck of the bottle between his teeth, without biting it off.

"I think you have got the ague," said I.

"I'm much of your opinion, boy," said he.

"It's bad about here," I told him. "You've been lying out on the meshes, and they're dreadful aguish. Rheumatic too."

"I'll eat my breakfast afore they're the death of me," said he. "I'd do that if I was going to be strung up to that there gallows as there is over there, directly arterwards. I'll beat the shivers so far, I'll bet you."

He was gobbling mincemeat, meat bone, bread, cheese, and pork pie, all at once: staring distrustfully while he did so at the mist all round us, and often stopping—even stopping his jaws—to listen. Some real or fancied sound, some clink upon the river or breathing of beast upon the marsh, now gave him a start, and he said, suddenly:

"You're not a deceiving imp? You brought no one with you?"

"No, sir! No!"

"Nor giv' no one the office to follow you?"

"No!"

"Well," said he, "I believe you. You'd be but a fierce young hound indeed, if at your time of life you could help to hunt a wretched warmint, hunted as near death and dunghill as this poor wretched warmint is!"

Something clicked in his throat as if he had works in him like a clock, and was going to strike. And he smeared his ragged rough sleeve over his eyes.

Pitying his desolation, and watching him as he gradually settled down upon the pie, I made bold to say, "I am glad you enjoy it."

"Did you speak?"

"I said, I was glad you enjoyed it."

"Thankee, my boy. I do."

I had often watched a large dog of ours eating his food; and I now noticed a decided similarity between the dog's way of eating, and the man's. The man took strong sharp

sudden bites, just like the dog. He swallowed, or rather
snapped up, every mouthful, too soon and too fast; and he
looked sideways here and there while he ate, as if he
thought there was danger in every direction of somebody's
coming to take the pie away. He was altogether too
unsettled in his mind over it, to appreciate it comfortably,
I thought, or to have anybody to dine with him, without
making a chop with his jaws at the visitor. In all of which
particulars he was very like the dog.

"I am afraid you won't leave any of it for him," said I,
timidly; after a silence during which I had hesitated as to
the politeness of making the remark. "There's no more to
be got where that came from." It was the certainty of this
fact that impelled me to offer the hint.

"Leave any for him? Who's him?" said my friend,
stopping in his crunching of pie-crust.

"The young man. That you spoke of. That was hid
with you."

"Oh ah!" he returned, with something like a gruff
laugh. "Him? Yes, yes! *He* don't want no wittles."

"I thought he looked as if he did," said I.

The man stopped eating, and regarded me with the keenest
scrutiny and the greatest surprise.

"Looked? When?"

"Just now."

"Where?"

"Yonder," said I, pointing; "over there, where I found
him nodding asleep, and thought it was you."

He held me by the collar and stared at me so, that
I began to think his first idea about cutting my throat had
revived.

"Dressed like you, you know, only with a hat," I explained, trembling; "and—and"—I was very anxious to
put this delicately—"and with—the same reason for wanting to borrow a file. Didn't you hear the cannon last
night?"

"Then, there *was* firing!" he said to himself.

"I wonder you shouldn't have been sure of that," I
returned, "for we heard it up at home, and that's further
away, and we were shut in besides."

"Why, see now!" said he. "When a man's alone on
these flats, with a light head and a light stomach, perishing of cold and want, he hears nothin' all night, but guns

firing, and voices calling. Hears? He sees the soldiers, with their red coats lighted up by the torches carried afore, closing in round him. Hears his number called, hears himself challenged, hears the rattle of the muskets, hears the orders, 'Make ready! Present! Cover him steady, men!' and is laid hands on—and there's nothin'! Why, if I see one pursuing party last night—coming up in order, Damn 'em, with their tramp, tramp—I see a hundred. And as to firing! Why, I see the mist shake with the cannon, arter it was broad day.—But this man;" he had said all the rest as if he had forgotten my being there; "did you notice anything in him?"

"He had a badly bruised face," said I, recalling what I hardly knew I knew.

"Not here?" exclaimed the man, striking his left cheek mercilessly, with the flat of his hand.

"Yes, there!"

"Where is he?" He crammed what little food was left, into the breast of his grey jacket. "Show me the way he went. I'll pull him down, like a blood-hound. Curse this iron on my sore leg! Give us hold of the file, boy."

I indicated in what direction the mist had shrouded the other man, and he looked up at it for an instant. But he was down on the rank wet grass, filing at his iron like a madman, and not minding me or minding his own leg, which had an old chafe upon it and was bloody, but which he handled as roughly as if it had no more feeling in it than the file. I was very much afraid of him again, now that he had worked himself into this fierce hurry, and I was likewise very much afraid of keeping away from home any longer. I told him I must go, but he took no notice, so I thought the best thing I could do was to slip off. The last I saw of him, his head was bent over his knee and he was working hard at his fetter, muttering impatient imprecations at it and his leg. The last I heard of him, I stopped in the mist to listen, and the file was still going.

CHAPTER IV

I FULLY expected to find a Constable in the kitchen, waiting to take me up. But not only was there no Constable there, but no discovery had yet been made of the robbery. Mrs. Joe was prodigiously busy in getting the house ready for the festivities of the day, and Joe had been put upon the kitchen door-step to keep him out of the dust-pan—an article into which his destiny always led him, sooner or later, when my sister was vigorously reaping the floors of her establishment.

"And where the deuce ha' *you* been?" was Mrs. Joe's Christmas salutation, when I and my conscience showed ourselves.

I said I had been down to hear the Carols. "Ah! well!" observed Mrs. Joe. "You might ha' done worse." Not a doubt of that, I thought.

"Perhaps if I warn't a blacksmith's wife, and (what's the same thing) a slave with her apron never off, *I* should have been to hear the Carols," said Mrs. Joe. "I'm rather partial to Carols myself, and that's the best of reasons for my never hearing any."

Joe, who had ventured into the kitchen after me as the dust-pan had retired before us, drew the back of his hand across his nose with a conciliatory air, when Mrs. Joe darted a look at him, and, when her eyes were withdrawn, secretly crossed his two forefingers, and exhibited them to me, as our token that Mrs. Joe was in a cross temper. This was so much her normal state, that Joe and I would often, for weeks together, be, as to our fingers, like monumental Crusaders as to their legs.

We were to have a superb dinner, consisting of a leg of pickled pork and greens, and a pair of roast stuffed fowls. A handsome mince-pie had been made yesterday morning (which accounted for the mincemeat not being missed), and the pudding was already on the boil. These extensive arrangements occasioned us to be cut off unceremoniously in respect of breakfast ; "for I ain't," said Mrs. Joe, "I ain't a going to have no formal cramming and busting and washing up now, with what I've got before me, I promise you!"

So, we had our slices served out, as if we were two thousand troops on a forced march instead of a man and boy at home ; and we took gulps of milk and water, with apologetic countenances, from a jug on the dresser. In the meantime, Mrs. Joe put clean white curtains up, and tacked a new flowered-flounce across the wide chimney to replace the old one, and uncovered the little state parlour across the passage, which was never uncovered at any other time, but passed the rest of the year in a cool haze of silver paper, which even extended to the four little white crockery poodles on the mantelshelf, each with a black nose and a basket of flowers in his mouth, and each the counterpart of the other. Mrs. Joe was a very clean housekeeper, but had an exquisite art of making her cleanliness more uncomfortable and unacceptable than dirt itself. Cleanliness is next to Godliness, and some people do the same by their religion.

My sister having so much to do, was going to church vicariously ; that is to say, Joe and I were going. In his working clothes, Joe was a well-knit characteristic-looking blacksmith ; in his holiday clothes, he was more like a scarecrow in good circumstances, than anything else. Nothing that he wore then, fitted him or seemed to belong to him ; and everything that he wore then, grazed him. On the present festive occasion he emerged from his room, when the blithe bells were going, the picture of misery, in a full suit of Sunday penitentials. As to me, I think my sister must have had some general idea that I was a young offender whom an Accoucheur Policeman had taken up (on my birthday) and delivered over to her, to be dealt with according to the outraged majesty of the law. I was always treated as if I had insisted on being born in opposition to the dictates of reason, religion, and morality, and against the dissuading arguments of my best friends. Even when I was taken to have a new suit of clothes, the tailor had orders to make them like a kind of Reformatory, and on no account to let me have the free use of my limbs.

Joe and I going to church, therefore, must have been a moving spectacle for compassionate minds. Yet, what I suffered outside, was nothing to what I underwent within.

The terrors that had assailed me whenever Mrs. Joe had gone near the pantry, or out of the room, were only to be equalled by the remorse with which my mind dwelt on what my hands had done.   Under the weight of my wicked secret, I pondered whether the Church would be powerful enough to shield me from the vengeance of the terrible young man, if I divulged to that establishment.   I conceived the idea that the time when the banns were read and when the clergyman said, "Ye are now to declare it!" would be the time for me to rise and propose a private conference in the vestry.   I am far from being sure that I might not have astonished our small congregation by resorting to this extreme measure, but for its being Christmas Day and no Sunday.

Mr. Wopsle, the clerk at church, was to dine with us; and Mr. Hubble, the wheelwright, and Mrs. Hubble; and Uncle Pumblechook (Joe's uncle, but Mrs. Joe appropriated him), who was a well-to-do corn-chandler in the nearest town, and drove his own chaise-cart.   The dinner hour was half-past one.   When Joe and I got home, we found the table laid, and Mrs. Joe dressed, and the dinner dressing, and the front door unlocked (it never was at any other time) for the company to enter by, and everything most splendid. And still, not a word of the robbery.

The time came, without bringing with it any relief to my feelings, and the company came.   Mr. Wopsle, united to a Roman nose and a large shining bald forehead, had a deep voice which he was uncommonly proud of; indeed it was understood among his acquaintance that if you could only give him his head, he would read the clergyman into fits; he himself confessed that if the Church was "thrown open," meaning to competition, he would not despair of making his mark in it.   The Church not being "thrown open," he was, as I have said, our clerk.   But he punished the Amens tremendously; and when he gave out the psalm—always giving the whole verse—he looked all round the congregation first, as much as to say, "You have heard our friend overhead; oblige me with your opinion of this style!"

I opened the door to the company—making believe that it was a habit of ours to open that door—and I opened it first to Mr. Wopsle, next to Mr. and Mrs. Hubble, and last of all to Uncle Pumblechook.   N.B. *I* was not allowed to call him uncle, under the severest penalties.

"Mrs. Joe," said Uncle Pumblechook; a large hard-breathing middle-aged slow man, with a mouth like a fish, dull staring eyes, and sandy hair standing upright on his head, so that he looked as if he had just been all but choked, and had that moment come to; "I have brought you as the compliments of the season—I have brought you, Mum, a bottle of sherry wine—and I have brought you, Mum, a bottle of port wine."

Every Christmas Day he presented himself, as a profound novelty, with exactly the same words, and carrying the two bottles like dumb-bells. Every Christmas Day, Mrs. Joe replied, as she now replied, "Oh, Un—cle Pum—ble—chook! This is kind!" Every Christmas Day, he retorted, as he now retorted, "It's no more than your merits. And now are you all bobbish, and how's Sixpennorth of halfpence?" meaning me.

We dined on these occasions in the kitchen, and adjourned, for the nuts and oranges and apples, to the parlour; which was a change very like Joe's change from his working clothes to his Sunday dress. My sister was uncommonly lively on the present occasion, and indeed was generally more gracious in the society of Mrs. Hubble than in other company. I remember Mrs. Hubble as a little curly sharp-edged person in sky-blue, who held a conventionally juvenile position, because she had married Mr. Hubble—I don't know at what remote period—when she was much younger than he. I remember Mr. Hubble as a tough high-shouldered stooping old man, of a sawdusty fragrance, with his legs extraordinarily wide apart: so that in my short days I always saw some miles of open country between them when I met him coming up the lane.

Among this good company I should have felt myself, even if I hadn't robbed the pantry, in a false position. Not because I was squeezed in at an acute angle of the table-cloth, with the table in my chest, and the Pumblechookian elbow in my eye, nor because I was not allowed to speak (I didn't want to speak), nor because I was regaled with the scaly tips of the drumsticks of the fowls, and with those obscure corners of pork of which the pig, when living, had had the least reason to be vain. No; I should not have minded that if they would only have left me alone. But they wouldn't leave me alone. They seemed to think the opportunity lost, if they failed to point the conversation at

me, every now and then, and stick the point into me.
I might have been an unfortunate little bull in a Spanish
arena, I got so smartingly touched up by these moral
goads.

It began the moment we sat down to dinner. Mr. Wopsle
said grace with theatrical declamation—as it now appears
to me, something like a religious cross of the Ghost in
Hamlet with Richard the Third—and ended with the very
proper aspiration that we might be truly grateful. Upon
which my sister fixed me with her eye, and said, in a low
reproachful voice, "Do you hear that? Be grateful."

"Especially," said Mr. Pumblechook, "be grateful, boy,
to them which brought you up by hand."

Mrs. Hubble shook her head, and contemplating me with
a mournful presentiment that I should come to no good,
asked, "Why is it that the young are never grateful?"
This moral mystery seemed too much for the company until
Mr. Hubble tersely solved it by saying, "Naterally wicious."
Everybody then murmured "True!" and looked at me in
a particularly unpleasant and personal manner.

Joe's station and influence were something feebler (if
possible) when there was company, than when there was
none. But he always aided and comforted me when he
could, in some way of his own, and he always did so at
dinner-time by giving me gravy, if there were any. There
being plenty of gravy to-day, Joe spooned into my plate, at
this point, about half a pint.

A little later on in the dinner, Mr. Wopsle reviewed the
sermon with some severity, and intimated—in the usual
hypothetical case of the Church being "thrown open"—
what kind of a sermon *he* would have given them. After
favouring them with some heads of that discourse, he remarked that he considered the subject of the day's homily,
ill-chosen; which was the less excusable, he added, when
there were so many subjects "going about."

"True again," said Uncle Pumblechook. "You've hit it,
sir! Plenty of subjects going about, for them that know
how to put salt upon their tails. That's what's wanted.
A man needn't go far to find a subject, if he's ready with
his salt-box." Mr. Pumblechook added, after a short interval of reflection, "Look at Pork alone. There's a subject!
If you want a subject, look at Pork!"

"True, sir. Many a moral for the young," returned

Mr. Wopsle; and I knew he was going to lug me in, before he said it; "might be deduced from that text."

("You listen to this," said my sister to me, in a severe parenthesis.)

Joe gave me some more gravy.

"Swine," pursued Mr. Wopsle, in his deepest voice, and pointing his fork at my blushes, as if he were mentioning my christian name; "Swine were the companions of the prodigal. The gluttony of Swine is put before us, as an example to the young." (I thought this pretty well in him who had been praising up the pork for being so plump and juicy.) "What is detestable in a pig, is more detestable in a boy."

"Or girl," suggested Mr. Hubble.

"Of course, or girl, Mr. Hubble," assented Mr. Wopsle, rather irritably, "but there is no girl present."

"Besides," said Mr. Pumblechook, turning sharp on me, "think what you've got to be grateful for. If you'd been born a Squeaker——"

"He *was*, if ever a child was," said my sister, most emphatically.

Joe gave me some more gravy.

"Well, but I mean a four-footed Squeaker," said Mr. Pumblechook. "If you had been born such, would you have been here now? Not you——"

"Unless in that form," said Mr. Wopsle, nodding towards the dish.

"But I don't mean in that form, sir," returned Mr. Pumblechook, who had an objection to being interrupted; "I mean, enjoying himself with his elders and betters, and improving himself with their conversation, and rolling in the lap of luxury. Would he have been doing that? No, he wouldn't. And what would have been your destination?" turning on me again. "You would have been disposed of for so many shillings according to the market price of the article, and Dunstable the butcher would have come up to you as you lay in your straw, and he would have whipped you under his left arm, and with his right he would have tucked up his frock to get a penknife from out of his waistcoat-pocket, and he would have shed your blood and had your life. No bringing up by hand then. Not a bit of it!"

Joe offered me more gravy, which I was afraid to take.

"He was a world of trouble to you, ma'am," said Mrs. Hubble, commiserating my sister.

"Trouble?" echoed my sister, "trouble?" And then entered on a fearful catalogue of all the illnesses I had been guilty of, and all the acts of sleeplessness I had committed, and all the high places I had tumbled from, and all the low places I had tumbled into, and all the injuries I had done myself, and all the times she had wished me in my grave, and I had contumaciously refused to go there.

I think the Romans must have aggravated one another very much, with their noses. Perhaps, they became the restless people they were, in consequence. Anyhow Mr. Wopsle's Roman nose so aggravated me, during the recital of my misdemeanours, that I should have liked to pull it until he howled. But all I had endured up to this time, was nothing in comparison with the awful feelings that took possession of me when the pause was broken which ensued upon my sister's recital, and in which pause everybody had looked at me (as I felt painfully conscious) with indignation and abhorrence.

"Yet," said Mr. Pumblechook, leading the company gently back to the theme from which they had strayed, "Pork—regarded as biled—is rich, too; ain't it?"

"Have a little brandy, uncle," said my sister.

O Heavens, it had come at last! He would find it was weak, he would say it was weak, and I was lost! I held tight to the leg of the table, under the cloth, with both hands, and awaited my fate.

My sister went for the stone bottle, came back with the stone bottle, and poured his brandy out: no one else taking any. The wretched man trifled with his glass—took it up, looked at it through the light, put it down—prolonged my misery. All this time Mrs. Joe and Joe were briskly clearing the table for the pie and pudding.

I couldn't keep my eyes off him. Always holding tight by the leg of the table with my hands and feet, I saw the miserable creature finger his glass playfully, take it up, smile, throw his head back, and drink the brandy off. Instantly afterwards, the company were seized with unspeakable consternation, owing to his springing to his feet, turning round several times in an appalling spasmodic whooping-cough dance, and rushing out at the door; he then became visible through the window, violently plunging and expectorating, making the most hideous faces, and apparently out of his mind.

I held on tight, while Mrs. Joe and Joe ran to him. I didn't know how I had done it, but I had no doubt I had murdered him somehow. In my dreadful situation, it was a relief when he was brought back, and, surveying the company all round as if *they* had disagreed with him, sank down into his chair with the one significant gasp, "Tar!"

I had filled up the bottle from the tar-water jug. I knew he would be worse by-and-by. I moved the table, like a Medium of the present day, by the vigour of my unseen hold upon it.

"Tar!" cried my sister, in amazement. "Why, how ever could Tar come there?"

But Uncle Pumblechook, who was omnipotent in that kitchen, wouldn't hear the word, wouldn't hear of the subject, imperiously waved it all away with his hand, and asked for hot gin-and-water. My sister, who had begun to be alarmingly meditative, had to employ herself actively in getting the gin, the hot water, the sugar, and the lemon-peel, and mixing them. For the time at least, I was saved. I still held on to the leg of the table, but clutched it now with the fervour of gratitude.

By degrees, I became calm enough to release my grasp, and partake of pudding. Mr. Pumblechook partook of pudding. All partook of pudding. The course terminated, and Mr. Pumblechook had begun to beam under the genial influence of gin-and-water. I began to think I should get over the day, when my sister said to Joe, "Clean plates— cold."

I clutched the leg of the table again immediately, and pressed it to my bosom as if it had been the companion of my youth and friend of my soul. I foresaw what was coming, and I felt that this time I really was gone.

"You must taste," said my sister, addressing the guests with her best grace, "you must taste, to finish with, such a delightful and delicious present of Uncle Pumblechook's!"

Must they! Let them not hope to taste it!

"You must know," said my sister, rising, "it's a pie: a savoury pork pie."

The company murmured their compliments. Uncle Pumblechook, sensible of having deserved well of his fellow-creatures, said—quite vivaciously, all things considered—"Well, Mrs. Joe, we'll do our best endeavours; let us have a cut at this same pie."

My sister went out to get it. I heard her steps proceed to the pantry. I saw Mr. Pumblechook balance his knife. I saw re-awakening appetite in the Roman nostrils of Mr. Wopsle. I heard Mr. Hubble remark that "a bit of savoury pork pie would lay atop of anything you could mention, and do no harm," and I heard Joe say, "You shall have some, Pip." I have never been absolutely certain whether I uttered a shrill yell of terror, merely in spirit, or in the bodily hearing of the company. I felt that I could bear no more, and that I must run away. I released the leg of the table, and ran for my life.

But I ran no further than the house door, for there I ran head foremost into a party of soldiers with their muskets: one of whom held out a pair of handcuffs to me, saying, "Here you are, look sharp, come on!"

CHAPTER V

THE apparition of a file of soldiers ringing down the butt-ends of their loaded muskets on our door-step, caused the dinner-party to rise from table in confusion, and caused Mrs. Joe, re-entering the kitchen empty-handed, to stop short and stare, in her wondering lament of "Gracious goodness gracious me, what's gone—with the—pie!"

The sergeant and I were in the kitchen when Mrs. Joe stood staring; at which crisis I partially recovered the use of my senses. It was the sergeant who had spoken to me, and he was now looking round at the company, with his handcuffs invitingly extended towards them in his right hand, and his left on my shoulder.

"Excuse me, ladies and gentlemen," said the sergeant, "but as I have mentioned at the door to this smart young shaver" (which he hadn't), "I am on a chase in the name of the king, and I want the blacksmith."

"And pray what might you want with *him*?" retorted my sister, quick to resent his being wanted at all.

"Missis," returned the gallant sergeant, "speaking for myself, I should reply, the honour and pleasure of his fine wife's acquaintance; speaking for the king, I answer, a little job done."

This was received as rather neat in the sergeant; insomuch that Mr. Pumblechook cried audibly, "Good again!"

"You see, blacksmith," said the sergeant, who had by this time picked out Joe with his eye, "we have had an accident with these, and I find the lock of one of 'em goes wrong, and the coupling don't act pretty. As they are wanted for immediate service, will you throw your eye over them?"

Joe threw his eye over them, and pronounced that the job would necessitate the lighting of his forge fire, and would take nearer two hours than one. "Will it? Then will you set about it at once, blacksmith?" said the off-hand sergeant, "as it's on his Majesty's service. And if my men can bear a hand anywhere, they'll make themselves useful." With that he called to his men, who came trooping into the kitchen one after another, and piled their arms in a corner. And then they stood about, as soldiers do; now, with their hands loosely clasped before them; now, resting a knee or a shoulder; now, easing a belt or a pouch; now, opening the door to spit stiffly over their high stocks, out into the yard.

All these things I saw without then knowing that I saw them, for I was in an agony of apprehension. But, beginning to perceive that the handcuffs were not for me, and that the military had so far got the better of the pie as to put it in the background, I collected a little more of my scattered wits.

"Would you give me the Time?" said the sergeant, addressing himself to Mr. Pumblechook, as to a man whose appreciative powers justified the inference that he was equal to the time.

"It's just gone half-past two."

"That's not so bad," said the sergeant, reflecting; "even if I was forced to halt here nigh two hours, that'll do. How far might you call yourselves from the marshes, hereabouts? Not above a mile, I reckon?"

"Just a mile," said Mrs. Joe.

"That'll do. We begin to close in upon 'em about dusk. A little before dusk, my orders are. That'll do."

"Convicts, sergeant?" asked Mr. Wopsle, in a matter-of-course way.

"Ay!" returned the sergeant, "two. They're pretty well known to be out on the marshes still, and they won't try to get clear of 'em before dusk. Anybody here seen anything of any such game?"

Everybody, myself excepted, said no, with confidence. Nobody thought of me.

"Well," said the sergeant, "they'll find themselves trapped in a circle, I expect, sooner than they count on. Now, blacksmith! If you're ready, his Majesty the King is."

Joe had got his coat and waistcoat and cravat off, and his leather apron on, and passed into the forge. One of the soldiers opened its wooden windows, another lighted the fire, another turned to at the bellows, the rest stood round the blaze, which was soon roaring. Then Joe began to hammer and clink, hammer and clink, and we all looked on.

The interest of the impending pursuit not only absorbed the general attention, but even made my sister liberal. She drew a pitcher of beer from the cask, for the soldiers, and invited the sergeant to take a glass of brandy. But Mr. Pumblechook said sharply, "Give him wine, Mum. I'll engage there's no Tar in that:" so, the sergeant thanked him and said that, as he preferred his drink without tar, he would take wine, if it was equally convenient. When it was given him, he drank his Majesty's health and compliments of the season, and took it all at a mouthful and smacked his lips.

"Good stuff, eh, sergeant?" said Mr. Pumblechook.

"I'll tell you something," returned the sergeant; "I suspect that stuff's of *your* providing."

Mr. Pumblechook, with a fat sort of laugh, said, "Ay, ay? Why?"

"Because," returned the sergeant, clapping him on the shoulder, "you're a man that knows what's what."

"D'ye think so?" said Mr. Pumblechook, with his former laugh. "Have another glass!"

"With you. Hob and nob," returned the sergeant. "The top of mine to the foot of yours—the foot of yours to the top of mine—Ring once, ring twice—the best tune on the Musical Glasses! Your health. May you live a thousand years, and never be a worse judge of the right sort than you are at the present moment of your life!"

The sergeant tossed off his glass again and seemed quite ready for another glass. I noticed that Mr. Pumblechook in his hospitality appeared to forget that he had made a present of the wine, but took the bottle from Mrs. Joe and had all the credit of handing it about in a gush of joviality. Even I got some. And he was so very free of the wine that he even called for the other bottle, and handed that about with the same liberality, when the first was gone.

As I watched them while they all stood clustering about the forge, enjoying themselves so much, I thought what terrible good sauce for a dinner my fugitive friend on the marshes was. They had not enjoyed themselves a quarter so much, before the entertainment was brightened with the excitement he furnished. And now, when they were all in lively anticipation of "the two villains" being taken, and when the bellows seemed to roar for the fugitives, the fire to flare for them, the smoke to hurry away in pursuit of them, Joe to hammer and clink for them, and all the murky shadows on the wall to shake at them in menace as the blaze rose and sank and the red-hot sparks dropped and died, the pale afternoon outside almost seemed in my pity-ing young fancy to have turned pale on their account, poor wretches.

At last, Joe's job was done, and the ringing and roaring stopped. As Joe got on his coat, he mustered courage to propose that some of us should go down with the soldiers and see what came of the hunt. Mr. Pumblechook and Mr. Hubble declined, on the plea of a pipe and ladies' society; but Mr. Wopsle said he would go, if Joe would. Joe said he was agreeable, and would take me, if Mrs. Joe approved. We never should have got leave to go, I am sure, but for Mrs. Joe's curiosity to know all about it and how it ended. As it was, she merely stipulated, "If you bring the boy back with his head blown to bits by a musket, don't look to me to put it together again."

The sergeant took a polite leave of the ladies, and parted from Mr. Pumblechook as from a comrade; though I doubt if he were quite as fully sensible of that gentleman's merits under arid conditions, as when something moist was going. His men resumed their muskets and fell in. Mr. Wopsle, Joe, and I, received strict charge to keep in the rear, and to speak no word after we reached the marshes. When we were all out in the raw air and were steadily moving towards our business, I treasonably whispered to Joe, "I hope, Joe, we shan't find them." And Joe whispered to me, "I'd give a shilling if they had cut and run, Pip."

We were joined by no stragglers from the village, for the weather was cold and threatening, the way dreary, the footing bad, darkness coming on, and the people had good fires indoors and were keeping the day. A few faces hurried to glowing windows and looked after us, but none came out. We passed the finger-post, and held straight on to the church-yard. There, we were stopped a few minutes by a signal from the sergeant's hand, while two or three of his men dispersed themselves among the graves, and also examined the porch. They came in again without finding anything, and then we struck out on the open marshes, through the gate at the side of the churchyard. A bitter sleet came rattling against us here on the east wind, and Joe took me on his back.

Now that we were out upon the dismal wilderness where they little thought I had been within eight or nine hours, and had seen both men hiding, I considered for the first time, with great dread, if we should come upon them, would my particular convict suppose that it was I who had brought the soldiers there? He had asked me if I was a deceiving imp, and he said I should be a fierce young hound if I joined the hunt against him. Would he believe that I was both imp and hound in treacherous earnest, and had betrayed him?

It was of no use asking myself this question now. There I was, on Joe's back, and there was Joe beneath me, charging at the ditches like a hunter, and stimulating Mr. Wopsle not to tumble on his Roman nose, and to keep up with us. The soldiers were in front of us, extending into a pretty wide line with an interval between man and man. We were taking the course I had begun with, and from which I had diverged into the mist. Either the mist was not out again yet, or the wind had dispelled it. Under the low red glare of sunset, the beacon, and the gibbet, and the mound of the Battery, and the opposite shore of the river, were plain, though all of a watery lead colour.

With my heart thumping like a blacksmith at Joe's broad shoulder, I looked all about for any sign of the convicts. I could see none, I could hear none. Mr. Wopsle had greatly alarmed me more than once, by his blowing and hard breathing; but I knew the sounds by this time, and could dissociate them from the object of pursuit. I got a dreadful start, when I thought I heard the file still going; but it was only a sheep bell. The sheep stopped in their eating and looked timidly at us; and the cattle, their heads turned from the wind and sleet, stared angrily as if they held us responsible for both annoyances; but, except these things, and the shudder of the dying day in every blade of grass, there was no break in the bleak stillness of the marshes.

The soldiers were moving on in the direction of the old Battery, and we were moving on a little way behind them, when, all of a sudden, we all stopped. For, there had reached us, on the wings of the wind and rain, a long shout. It was repeated. It was at a distance towards the east, but it was long and loud. Nay, there seemed to be two or more shouts raised together—if one might judge from a confusion in the sound.

To this effect the sergeant and the nearest men were speaking under their breath, when Joe and I came up. After another moment's listening, Joe (who was a good judge) agreed, and Mr. Wopsle (who was a bad judge) agreed. The sergeant, a decisive man, ordered that the sound should not be answered, but that the course should be changed, and that his men should make towards it "at the double." So we started to the right (where the East was), and Joe pounded away so wonderfully, that I had to hold on tight to keep my seat.

It was a run indeed now, and what Joe called, in the only two words he spoke all the time, "a Winder." Down banks and up banks, and over gates, and splashing into dykes, and breaking among coarse rushes: no man cared where he went. As we came nearer to the shouting, it became more and more apparent that it was made by more than one voice. Sometimes, it seemed to stop altogether, and then the soldiers stopped. When it broke out again, the soldiers made for it at a greater rate than ever, and we after them. After a while, we had so run it down, that we could hear one voice calling "Murder!" and another voice, "Convicts! Runaways! Guard! This way for the runaway convicts!" Then both voices would seem to be stifled in a struggle, and then would break out again. And when it had come to this, the soldiers ran like deer, and Joe too.

The sergeant ran in first, when we had run the noise quite down, and two of his men ran in close upon him. Their pieces were cocked and levelled when we all ran in.

"Here are both men!" panted the sergeant, struggling at the bottom of a ditch. "Surrender, you two! and confound you for two wild beasts! Come asunder!"

Water was splashing, and mud was flying, and oaths were being sworn, and blows were being struck, when some more men went down into the ditch to help the sergeant, and dragged out, separately, my convict and the other one. Both were bleeding and panting and execrating and struggling; but of course I knew them both directly.

"Mind!" said my convict, wiping blood from his face with his ragged sleeves, and shaking torn hair from his fingers; "*I* took him! *I* give him up to you! Mind that!"

"It's not much to be particular about," said the sergeant; "it'll do you small good, my man, being in the same plight yourself. Handcuffs there!"

"I don't expect it to do me any good. I don't want it to do me more good than it does now," said my convict, with a greedy laugh. "I took him. He knows it. That's enough for me."

The other convict was livid to look at, and, in addition to the old bruised left side of his face, seemed to be bruised and torn all over. He could not so much as get his breath to speak, until they were both separately handcuffed, but leaned upon a soldier to keep himself from falling.

"Take notice, guard—he tried to murder me," were his first words.

"Tried to murder him?" said my convict, disdainfully. "Try, and not do it? I took him, and giv' him up; that's what I done. I not only prevented him getting off the marshes, but I dragged him here—dragged him this far on his way back. He's a gentleman, if you please, this villain. Now, the Hulks has got its gentleman again, through me. Murder him? Worth my while, too, to murder him, when I could do worse and drag him back!"

The other one still gasped, "He tried—he tried—to—murder me. Bear—bear witness."

"Lookee here!" said my convict to the sergeant. "Single-handed I got clear of the prison-ship; I made a dash and I done it. I could ha' got clear of these death-cold flats likewise—look at my leg: you won't find much iron on it—if I hadn't made discovery that *he* was here. Let *him* go free? Let *him* profit by the means as I found out? Let *him* make a tool of me afresh and again? Once more? No, no, no. If I had died at the bottom there;" and he made an emphatic swing at the ditch with his manacled hands; "I'd have held to him with that grip, that you should have been safe to find him in my hold."

The other fugitive, who was evidently in extreme horror of his companion, repeated, "He tried to murder me. I should have been a dead man if you had not come up."

"He lies!" said my convict, with fierce energy. "He's a liar born, and he'll die a liar. Look at his face; ain't it written there? Let him turn those eyes of his on me. I defy him to do it."

The other, with an effort at a scornful smile—which could not, however, collect the nervous working of his mouth into any set expression, looked at the soldiers, and looked about at the marshes and at the sky, but certainly did not look at the speaker.

"Do you see him?" pursued my convict. "Do you see

what a villain he is? Do you see those grovelling and wandering eyes? That's how he looked when we were tried together. He never looked at me."

The other, always working and working his dry lips and turning his eyes restlessly about him far and near, did at last turn them for a moment on the speaker, with the words, "You are not much to look at," and with a half-taunting glance at the bound hands. At that point, my convict became so frantically exasperated, that he would have rushed upon him but for the interposition of the soldiers. "Didn't I tell you," said the other convict then, "that he would murder me, if he could?" And any one could see that he shook with fear, and that there broke out upon his lips curious white flakes, like thin snow.

"Enough of this parley," said the sergeant. "Light those torches."

As one of the soldiers, who carried a basket in lieu of a gun, went down on his knee to open it, my convict looked round him for the first time, and saw me. I had alighted from Joe's back on the brink of the ditch when we came up, and had not moved since. I looked at him eagerly when he looked at me, and slightly moved my hands and shook my head. I had been waiting for him to see me, that I might try to assure him of my innocence. It was not at all expressed to me that he even comprehended my intention, for he gave me a look that I did not understand, and it all passed in a moment. But if he had looked at me for an hour or for a day, I could not have remembered his face ever afterwards, as having been more attentive.

The soldier with the basket soon got a light, and lighted three or four torches, and took one himself and distributed the others. It had been almost dark before, but now it seemed quite dark, and soon afterwards very dark. Before we departed from that spot, four soldiers standing in a ring, fired twice into the air. Presently we saw other torches kindled at some distance behind us, and others on the marshes on the opposite bank of the river. "All right," said the sergeant. "March."

We had not gone far when three cannon were fired ahead of us with a sound that seemed to burst something inside my ear. "You are expected on board," said the sergeant to my convict; "they know you are coming. Don't straggle, my man. Close up here."

The two were kept apart, and each walked surrounded by a separate guard. I had hold of Joe's hand now, and Joe carried one of the torches. Mr. Wopsle had been for going back, but Joe was resolved to see it out, so we went on with the party. There was a reasonably good path now, mostly on the edge of the river, with a divergence here and there where a dyke came, with a miniature windmill on it and a muddy sluice-gate. When I looked round, I could see the other lights coming in after us. The torches we carried, dropped great blotches of fire upon the track, and I could see those, too, lying smoking and flaring. I could see nothing else but black darkness. Our lights warmed the air about us with their pitchy blaze, and the two prisoners seemed rather to like that, as they limped along in the midst of the muskets. We could not go fast, because of their lameness; and they were so spent, that two or three times we had to halt while they rested.

After an hour or so of this travelling, we came to a rough wooden hut and a landing-place. There was a guard in the hut, and they challenged, and the sergeant answered. Then, we went into the hut, where there was a smell of tobacco and whitewash, and a bright fire, and a lamp, and a stand of muskets, and a drum, and a low wooden bedstead, like an overgrown mangle without the machinery, capable of holding about a dozen soldiers all at once. Three or four soldiers who lay upon it in their great-coats, were not much interested in us, but just lifted their heads and took a sleepy stare, and then lay down again. The sergeant made some kind of report, and some entry in a book, and then the convict whom I call the other convict was drafted off with his guard, to go on board first.

My convict never looked at me, except that once. While we stood in the hut, he stood before the fire looking thoughtfully at it, or putting up his feet by turns upon the hob, and looking thoughtfully at them as if he pitied them for their recent adventures. Suddenly, he turned to the sergeant, and remarked:

"I wish to say something respecting this escape. It may prevent some persons laying under suspicion alonger me."

"You can say what you like," returned the sergeant, standing coolly looking at him with his arms folded, "but you have no call to say it here. You'll have opportunity enough to say about it, and hear about it, before's it's done with, you know."

"I know, but this is another pint, a separate matter. A man can't starve; at least I can't. I took some wittles, up at the willage over yonder—where the church stands a'most out on the marshes."

"You mean stole," said the sergeant.

"And I'll tell you where from. From the blacksmith's."

"Halloa!" said the sergeant, staring at Joe.

"Halloa, Pip!" said Joe, staring at me.

"It was some broken wittles—that's what it was—and a dram of liquor, and a pie."

"Have you happened to miss such an article as a pie, blacksmith?" asked the sergeant, confidentially.

"My wife did, at the very moment when you came in. Don't you know, Pip?"

"So," said my convict, turning his eyes on Joe in a moody manner, and without the least glance at me; "so you're the blacksmith, are you? Then I'm sorry to say, I've eat your pie."

"God knows you're welcome to it—so far as it was ever mine," returned Joe, with a saving remembrance of Mrs. Joe. "We don't know what you have done, but we wouldn't have you starved to death for it, poor miserable fellow-creatur.—Would us, Pip?"

The something that I had noticed before, clicked in the man's throat again, and he turned his back. The boat had returned, and his guard were ready, so we followed him to the landing-place made of rough stakes and stones, and saw him put into the boat, which was rowed by a crew of convicts like himself. No one seemed surprised to see him, or interested in seeing him, or glad to see him, or sorry to see him, or spoke a word, except that somebody in the boat growled as if to dogs, "Give way, you!" which was the signal for the dip of the oars. By the light of the torches, we saw the black Hulk lying out a little way from the mud of the shore, like a wicked Noah's ark. Cribbed and barred and moored by massive rusty chains, the prison-ship seemed in my young eyes to be ironed like the prisoners. We saw the boat go alongside, and we saw him taken up the side and disappear. Then, the ends of the torches were flung hissing into the water, and went out, as if it were all over with him.

CHAPTER VI

My state of mind regarding the pilfering from which I had been so unexpectedly exonerated, did not impel me to frank disclosure; but I hope it had some dregs of good at the bottom of it.

I do not recall that I felt any tenderness of conscience in reference to Mrs. Joe, when the fear of being found out was lifted off me. But I loved Joe—perhaps for no better reason in those early days than because the dear fellow let me love him—and, as to him, my inner self was not so easily composed. It was much upon my mind (particularly when I first saw him looking about for his file) that I ought to tell Joe the whole truth. Yet I did not, and for the reason that I mistrusted that if I did, he would think me worse than I was. The fear of losing Joe's confidence, and of thenceforth sitting in the chimney-corner at night staring drearily at my for ever lost companion and friend, tied up my tongue. I morbidly represented to myself that if Joe knew it, I never afterwards could see him at the fireside feeling his fair whisker, without thinking that he was meditating on it. That, if Joe knew it, I never afterwards could see him glance, however casually, at yesterday's meat or pudding when it came on to-day's table, without thinking that he was debating whether I had been in the pantry. That, if Joe knew it, and at any subsequent period of our joint domestic life remarked that his beer was flat or thick, the conviction that he suspected Tar in it, would bring a rush of blood to my face. In a word, I was too cowardly to do what I knew to be right, as I had been too cowardly to avoid doing what I knew to be wrong. I had had no intercourse with the world at that time, and I imitated none of its many inhabitants who act in this manner. Quite an untaught genius, I made the discovery of the line of action for myself.

As I was sleepy before we were far away from the prison-ship, Joe took me on his back again and carried me home.

He must have had a tiresome journey of it, for Mr. Wopsle, being knocked up, was in such a very bad temper that if the Church had been thrown open, he would probably have excommunicated the whole expedition, beginning with Joe and myself. In his lay capacity, he persisted in sitting down in the damp to such an insane extent, that when his coat was taken off to be dried at the kitchen fire, the circumstantial evidence on his trousers would have hanged him if it had been a capital offence.

By that time, I was staggering on the kitchen floor like a little drunkard, through having been newly set upon my feet, and through having been fast asleep, and through waking in the heat and lights and noise of tongues. As I came to myself (with the aid of a heavy thump between the shoulders, and the restorative exclamation " Yah ! Was there ever such a boy as this ! " from my sister), I found Joe telling them about the convict's confession, and all the visitors suggesting different ways by which he had got into the pantry. Mr. Pumblechook made out, after carefully surveying the premises, that he had first got upon the roof of the forge, and had then got upon the roof of the house, and had then let himself down the kitchen chimney by a rope made of his bedding cut into strips; and as Mr. Pumblechook was very positive and drove his own chaise-cart—over everybody—it was agreed that it must be so. Mr. Wopsle, indeed, wildly cried out " No ! " with the feeble malice of a tired man ; but, as he had no theory, and no coat on, he was unanimously set at nought—not to mention his smoking hard behind, as he stood with his back to the kitchen fire to draw the damp out : which was not calculated to inspire confidence.

This was all I heard that night before my sister clutched me, as a slumberous offence to the company's eyesight, and assisted me up to bed with such a strong hand that I seemed to have fifty boots on, and to be dangling them all against the edges of the stairs. My state of mind, as I have described it, began before I was up in the morning, and lasted long after the subject had died out, and had ceased to be mentioned saving on exceptional occasions.

CHAPTER VII

AT the time when I stood in the churchyard, reading the family tombstones, I had just enough learning to be able to spell them out. My construction even of their simple meaning was not very correct, for I read "wife of the Above" as a complimentary reference to my father's exaltation to a better world; and if any one of my deceased relations had been referred to as "Below," I have no doubt I should have formed the worst opinions of that member of the family. Neither were my notions of the theological positions to which my Catechism bound me, at all accurate; for I have a lively remembrance that I supposed my declaration that I was to "walk in the same all the days of my life," laid me under an obligation always to go through the village from our house in one particular direction, and never to vary it by turning down by the wheelwright's or up by the mill.

When I was old enough, I was to be apprenticed to Joe, and until I could assume that dignity I was not to be what Mrs. Joe called "Pompeyed" or (as I render it) pampered. Therefore, I was not only odd-boy about the forge, but if any neighbour happened to want an extra boy to frighten birds, or pick up stones, or do any such job, I was favoured with the employment. In order, however, that our superior position might not be compromised thereby, a money-box was kept on the kitchen mantel-shelf, into which it was publicly made known that all my earnings were dropped. I have an impression that they were to be contributed eventually towards the liquidation of the National Debt, but I know I had no hope of any personal participation in the treasure.

Mr. Wopsle's great-aunt kept an evening school in the village; that is to say, she was a ridiculous old woman of limited means and unlimited infirmity, who used to go to sleep from six to seven every evening, in the society of youth who paid twopence per week each, for the improving opportunity of seeing her do it. She rented a small cottage, and Mr. Wopsle had the room up-stairs, where we students used to overhear him reading aloud in a most dignified and terrific manner, and occasionally bumping on the ceiling. There was a fiction that Mr. Wopsle "examined" the scholars, once a quarter. What he did on those occasions was to turn up his cuffs, stick up his hair, and give us Mark Antony's oration over the body of Cæsar. This was always followed by Collins's Ode on the Passions, wherein I particularly venerated Mr. Wopsle as Revenge, throwing his blood-stained sword in thunder down, and taking the War-denouncing trumpet with a withering look. It was not with me then, as it was in later life, when I fell into the society of the Passions, and compared them with Collins and Wopsle, rather to the disadvantage of both gentlemen.

Mr. Wopsle's great-aunt, besides keeping this Educational Institution, kept in the same room—a little general shop. She had no idea what stock she had, or what the price of anything in it was; but there was a little greasy memorandum-book kept in a drawer, which served as a Catalogue of Prices, and by this oracle Biddy arranged all the shop transactions. Biddy was Mr. Wopsle's great-aunt's granddaughter; I confess myself quite unequal to the working out of the problem, what relation she was to Mr. Wopsle. She was an orphan like myself; like me, too, had been brought up by hand. She was most noticeable, I thought, in respect of her extremities; for her hair always wanted brushing, her hands always wanted washing, and her shoes always wanted mending and pulling up at heel. This description must be received with a week-day limitation. On Sundays she went to church elaborated.

Much of my unassisted self, and more by the help of Biddy than of Mr. Wopsle's great-aunt, I struggled through the alphabet as if it had been a bramble-bush; getting considerably worried and scratched by every letter. After that, I fell among those thieves, the nine figures, who seemed every evening to do something new to disguise themselves and baffle recognition. But, at last I began, in a purblind groping way, to read, write, and cipher, on the very smallest scale.

One night, I was sitting in the chimney-corner with my slate, expending great efforts on the production of a letter to Joe. I think it must have been a full year after our hunt upon the marshes, for it was a long time after, and it was winter and a hard frost. With an alphabet on the hearth at my feet for reference, I contrived in an hour or two to print and smear this epistle:

"mI deEr JO i opE U r krWitE wEll i opE i shAl soN B haBelL 4 2 teeDge U JO aN theN wE shOrl b sO gLOdd aN wEn i M preNgtD 2 u JO woT larX an blEvE ME inF xn PiP."

There was no indispensable necessity for my communicating with Joe by letter, inasmuch as he sat beside me and we were alone. But, I delivered this written communication (slate and all) with my own hand, and Joe received it, as a miracle of erudition.

"I say, Pip, old chap!" cried Joe, opening his blue eyes wide, "what a scholar you are! Ain't you?"

"I should like to be," said I, glancing at the slate as he held it: with a misgiving that the writing was rather hilly.

"Why, here's a J," said Joe, "and a O equal to anythink! Here's a J and a O, Pip, and a J-O, Joe."

I had never heard Joe read aloud to any greater extent than this monosyllable, and I had observed at church last Sunday, when I accidentally held our Prayer-book upside down, that it seemed to suit his convenience quite as well as if it had been all right. Wishing to embrace the present occasion of finding out whether in teaching Joe, I should have to begin quite at the beginning, I said, "Ah! But read the rest, Joe."

"The rest, eh, Pip?" said Joe, looking at it with a slowly searching eye. "One, two, three. Why, here's three Js, and three Os, and three J-O, Joes, in it, Pip!"

I leaned over Joe, and, with the aid of my forefinger, read him the whole letter.

"Astonishing!" said Joe, when I had finished. "You ARE a scholar."

"How do you spell Gargery, Joe?" I asked him, with a modest patronage.

"I don't spell it at all," said Joe.

"But supposing you did?"

"It *can't* be supposed," said Joe. "Tho' I'm oncommon fond of reading, too."

"Are you, Joe?"

"On-common. Give me," said Joe, "a good book, or

a good newspaper, and sit me down afore a good fire, and I ask no better. Lord!" he continued, after rubbing his knees a little, "when you *do* come to a J and a O, and says you, 'Here, at last, is a J-O, Joe,' how interesting reading is!"

I derived from this last, that Joe's education, like Steam, was yet in its infancy. Pursuing the subject, I inquired:

"Didn't you ever go to school, Joe, when you were as little as me?"

"No, Pip."

"Why didn't you ever go to school, Joe, when you were as little as me?"

"Well, Pip," said Joe, taking up the poker, and settling himself to his usual occupation when he was thoughtful, of slowly raking the fire between the lower bars: "I'll tell you. My father, Pip, he were given to drink, and when he were overtook with drink, he hammered away at my mother most onmerciful. It were a'most the only hammering he did, indeed, 'xcepting at myself. And he hammered at me with a wigour only to be equalled by the wigour with which he didn't hammer at his anwil.—You're a-listening and understanding, Pip?"

"Yes, Joe."

"'Consequence, my mother and me we ran away from my father several times; and then my mother she'd go out to work, and she'd say, 'Joe,' she'd say, 'now, please God, you shall have some schooling, child,' and she'd put me to school. But my father were that good in his hart that he couldn't abear to be without us. So, he'd come with a most tremenjous crowd and make such a row at the doors of the houses where we was, that they used to be obligated to have no more to do with us and to give us up to him. And then he took us home and hammered us. Which, you see, Pip," said Joe, pausing in his meditative raking of the fire, and looking at me, "were a drawback on my learning."

"Certainly, poor Joe!"

"Though mind you, Pip," said Joe, with a judicial touch or two of the poker on the top bar, "rendering unto all their doo, and maintaining equal justice betwixt man and man, my father were that good in his hart, don't you see?"

I didn't see; but I didn't say so.

"Well!" Joe pursued, "somebody must keep the pot a-biling, Pip, or the pot won't bile, don't you know?"

I saw that, and said so.

"'Consequence, my father didn't make objections to my going to work; so I went to work at my present calling, which were his too, if he would have followed it, and I worked tolerable hard, I assure *you*, Pip. In time I were able to keep him, and I kep him till he went off in a purple leptic fit. And it were my intentions to have had put upon his tombstone that Whatsume'er the failings on his part, Remember reader he were that good in his hart."

Joe recited this couplet with such manifest pride and careful perspicuity, that I asked him if he had made it himself.

"I made it," said Joe, "my own self. I made it in a moment. It was like striking out a horseshoe complete, in a single blow. I never was so much surprised in all my life—couldn't credit my own ed—to tell you the truth, hardly believed it *were* my own ed. As I was saying, Pip, it were my intentions to have had it cut over him; but poetry costs money, cut it how you will, small or large, and it were not done. Not to mention bearers, all the money that could be spared were wanted for my mother. She were in poor elth, and quite broke. She waren't long of following, poor soul, and her share of peace come round at last."

Joe's blue eyes turned a little watery; he rubbed, first one of them, and then the other, in a most uncongenial and uncomfortable manner, with the round knob on the top of the poker.

"It were but lonesome then," said Joe, "living here alone, and I got acquainted with your sister. Now, Pip;" Joe looked firmly at me, as if he knew I was not going to agree with him; "your sister is a fine figure of a woman."

I could not help looking at the fire, in an obvious state of doubt.

"Whatever family opinions, or whatever the world's opinions, on that subject may be, Pip, your sister is," Joe tapped the top bar with the poker after every word following, "a—fine—figure—of—a—woman!"

I could think of nothing better to say than "I am glad you think so, Joe."

"So am I," returned Joe, catching me up. "*I* am glad I think so, Pip. A little redness, or a little matter of Bone, here or there, what does it signify to Me?"

I sagaciously observed, if it didn't signify to him, to whom did it signify?

"Certainly!" assented Joe. "That's it. You're right, old chap! When I got acquainted with your sister, it were the talk how she was bringing you up by hand. Very kind of her too, all the folks said, and I said, along with all the folks. As to you," Joe pursued, with a countenance expressive of seeing something very nasty indeed: "if you could have been aware how small and flabby and mean you was, dear me, you'd have formed the most contemptible opinions of yourself!"

Not exactly relishing this, I said, "Never mind me, Joe."

"But I did mind you, Pip," he returned, with tender simplicity. "When I offered to your sister to keep company, and to be asked in church, at such times as she was willing and ready to come to the forge, I said to her, 'And bring the poor little child. God bless the poor little child,' I said to your sister, 'there's room for *him* at the forge!'"

I broke out crying and begging pardon, and hugged Joe round the neck: who dropped the poker to hug me, and to say, "Ever the best of friends; ain't us, Pip? Don't cry, old chap!"

When this little interruption was over, Joe resumed:

"Well, you see, Pip, and here we are! That's about where it lights; here we are! Now, when you take me in hand in my learning, Pip (and I tell you beforehand I am awful dull, most awful dull), Mrs. Joe mustn't see too much of what we're up to. It must be done, as I may say, on the sly. And why on the sly? I'll tell you why, Pip."

He had taken up the poker again; without which. I dcubt if he could have proceeded in his demonstration.

"Your sister is given to government."

'Given to government, Joe?" I was startled, for I had some shadowy idea (and I am afraid I must add, hope) that Joe had divorced her in favour of the Lords of the Admiralty, or Treasury.

"Given to government," said Joe. "Which I meantersay the government of you and myself."

"Oh!"

"And she ain't over partial to having scholars on the premises," Joe continued, "and in partickler would not be over partial to my being a scholar, for fear as I might rise. Like a sort of rebel, don't you see?"

I was going to retort with an inquiry, and had got as far as "Why——" when Joe stopped me.

"Stay a bit. I know what you're a-going to say, Pip; stay a bit! I don't deny that your sister comes the Mo-gul over us, now and again. I don't deny that she do throw us back-falls, and that she do drop down upon us heavy. At such times as when your sister is on the Ram-page, Pip," Joe sank his voice to a whisper and glanced at the door, "candour compels fur to admit that she is a Buster."

Joe pronounced this word as if it began with at least twelve capital Bs.

"Why don't I rise? That were your observation when I broke it off, Pip?"

"Yes, Joe."

"Well," said Joe, passing the poker into his left hand, that he might feel his whisker; and I had no hope of him whenever he took to that placid occupation; "your sister's a master-mind. A master-mind."

"What's that?" I asked, in some hope of bringing him to a stand. But Joe was readier with his definition than I had expected, and completely stopped me by arguing circularly, and answering with a fixed look, "Her."

"And I ain't a master-mind," Joe resumed, when he had unfixed his look, and got back to his whisker. "And last of all, Pip—and this I want to say very serous to you, old chap—I see so much in my poor mother, of a woman drudging and slaving and breaking her honest hart and never getting no peace in her mortal days, that I'm dead afeerd of going wrong in the way of not doing what's right by a woman, and I'd fur rather of the two go wrong the t'other way, and be a little ill-conwenienced myself. I wish it was only me that got put out, Pip; I wish there warn't no Tickler for you, old chap; I wish I could take it all on myself; but this is the up-and-down-and-straight on it, Pip, and I hope you'll overlook shortcomings."

Young as I was, I believe that I dated a new admiration of Joe from that night. We were equals afterwards, as we had been before; but, afterwards at quiet times when I sat looking at Joe and thinking about him, I had a new sensation of feeling conscious that I was looking up to Joe in my heart.

"However," said Joe, rising to replenish the fire; "here's the Dutch-clock a-working himself up to being equal to strike Eight of 'em, and she's not come home yet! I hope Uncle Pumblechook's mare mayn't have set a fore-foot on a piece o' ice, and gone down."

Mrs. Joe made occasional trips with Uncle Pumblechook on market-days, to assist him in buying such household stuffs and goods as required a woman's judgment; Uncle Pumblechook being a bachelor and reposing no confidences in his domestic servant. This was market-day, and Mrs. Joe was out on one of these expeditions.

Joe made the fire and swept the hearth, and then we went to the door to listen for the chaise-cart. It was a dry cold night, and the wind blew keenly, and the frost was white and hard. A man would die to-night of lying out on the marshes, I thought. And then I looked at the stars, and considered how awful it would be for a man to turn his face up to them as he froze to death, and see no help or pity in all the glittering multitude.

"Here comes the mare," said Joe, "ringing like a peal of bells!"

The sound of her iron shoes upon the hard road was quite musical, as she came along at a much brisker trot than usual. We got a chair out, ready for Mrs. Joe's alighting, and stirred up the fire that they might see a bright window, and took a final survey of the kitchen that nothing might be out of its place. When we had completed these preparations, they drove up, wrapped to the eyes. Mrs. Joe was soon landed, and Uncle Pumblechook was soon down too, covering the mare with a cloth, and we were soon all in the kitchen, carrying so much cold air with us that it seemed to drive all the heat out of the fire.

"Now," said Mrs. Joe, unwrapping herself with haste and excitement, and throwing her bonnet back on her shoulders where it hung by the strings: "if this boy ain't grateful this night, he never will be!"

I looked as grateful as any boy possibly could, who was wholly uninformed why he ought to assume that expression.

"It's only to be hoped," said my sister, "that he won't be Pompeyed. But I have my fears."

"She ain't in that line, Mum," said Mr. Pumblechook. "She knows better."

She? I looked at Joe, making the motion with my lips

and eyebrows, "She?" Joe looked at me, making the motion with *his* lips and eyebrows, "She?" My sister catching him in the act, he drew the back of his hand across his nose with his usual conciliatory air on such occasions, and looked at her.

"Well?" said my sister, in her snappish way. "What are you staring at? Is the house a-fire?"

"—Which some individual," Joe politely hinted, "mentioned she."

"And she is a she, I suppose?" said my sister. "Unless you call Miss Havisham a he. And I doubt if even you'll go so far as that."

"Miss Havisham up town?" said Joe.

"Is there any Miss Havisham down town?" returned my sister. "She wants this boy to go and play there. And of course's he's going. And he had better play there," said my sister, shaking her head at me as an encouragement to be extremely light and sportive, "or I'll work him."

I had heard of Miss Havisham up town—everybody for miles round, had heard of Miss Havisham up town—as an immensely rich and grim lady who lived in a large and dismal house barricaded against robbers, and who led a life of seclusion.

"Well, to be sure!" said Joe, astounded. "I wonder how she comes to know Pip!"

"Noodle!" cried my sister. "Who said she knew him?"

"—Which some individual," Joe again politely hinted, "mentioned that she wanted him to go and play there."

"And couldn't she ask Uncle Pumblechook if he knew of a boy to go and play there? Isn't it just barely possible that Uncle Pumblechook may be a tenant of hers, and that he may sometimes—we won't say quarterly or half-yearly, for that would be requiring too much of you—but sometimes—go there to pay his rent? And couldn't she then ask Uncle Pumblechook if he knew of a boy to go and play there? And couldn't Uncle Pumblechook, being always considerate and thoughtful for us—though you may not think it, Joseph," in a tone of the deepest reproach, as if he were the most callous of nephews, "then mention this boy, standing Prancing here"—which I solemnly declare I was not doing—"that I have for ever been a willing slave to?"

"Good again!" cried Uncle Pumblechook. "Well put!

Prettily pointed! Good indeed! Now, Joseph, you know the case."

"No, Joseph," said my sister, still in a reproachful manner, while Joe apologetically drew the back of his hand across and across his nose, "you do not yet—though you may not think it—know the case. You may consider that you do, but you do *not*, Joseph. For you do not know that Uncle Pumblechook, being sensible that for anything we can tell, this boy's fortune may be made by his going to Miss Havisham's, has offered to take him into town to-night in his own chaise-cart, and to keep him to-night, and to take him with his own hands to Miss Havisham's to-morrow morning. And Lor-a-mussy-me!" cried my sister, casting off her bonnet in sudden desperation, "here I stand talking to mere Mooncalfs, with Uncle Pumblechook waiting, and the mare catching cold at the door, and the boy grimed with crock and dirt from the hair of his head to the sole of his foot!"

With that, she pounced on me, like an eagle on a lamb, and my face was squeezed into wooden bowls in sinks, and my head was put under taps of water-butts, and I was soaped, and kneaded, and towelled, and thumped, and harrowed, and rasped, until I really was quite beside myself. (I may here remark that I suppose myself to be better acquainted than any living authority, with the ridgy effect of a wedding-ring, passing unsympathetically over the human countenance.)

When my ablutions were completed, I was put into clean linen of the stiffest character, like a young penitent into sackcloth, and was trussed up in my tightest and fearfullest suit. I was then delivered over to Mr. Pumblechook, who formally received me as if he were the Sheriff, and who let off upon me the speech that I knew he had been dying to make all along: "Boy, be for ever grateful to all friends, but especially unto them which brought you up by hand!"

"Good-bye, Joe!"

"God bless you, Pip, old chap!"

I had never parted from him before, and what with my feelings and what with soap-suds, I could at first see no stars from the chaise-cart. But they twinkled out one by one, without throwing any light on the questions why on earth I was going to play at Miss Havisham's, and what on earth I was expected to play at.

CHAPTER VIII

MR. PUMBLECHOOK'S premises in the High-street of the market town, were of a peppercorny and farinaceous character, as the premises of a corn-chandler and seedsman should be. It appeared to me that he must be a very happy man indeed, to have so many little drawers in his shop : and I wondered when I peeped into one or two on the lower tiers, and saw the tied-up brown paper packets inside, whether the flower-seeds and bulbs ever wanted of a fine day to break out of those jails, and bloom.

It was in the early morning after my arrival that I entertained this speculation. On the previous night, I had been sent straight to bed in an attic with a sloping roof, which was so low in the corner where the bedstead was, that I calculated the tiles as being within a foot of my eyebrows. In the same early morning, I discovered a singular affinity between seeds and corduroys. Mr. Pumblechook wore corduroys, and so did his shopman ; and somehow, there was a general air and flavour about the corduroys, so much in the nature of seeds, and a general air and flavour about the seeds, so much in the nature of corduroys, that I hardly knew which was which. The same opportunity served me for noticing that Mr. Pumblechook appeared to conduct his business by looking across the street at the saddler, who appeared to transact *his* business by keeping his eye on the coachmaker, who appeared to get on in life by putting his hands in his pockets and contemplating the baker, who in his turn folded his arms and stared at the grocer, who stood at his door and yawned at the chemist. The watchmaker, always poring over a little desk with a magnifying glass at his eye, and always inspected by a group in smock-frocks poring over him through the glass of his shop-window, seemed to be about the only person in the High-street whose trade engaged his attention.

Mr. Pumblechook and I breakfasted at eight o'clock in the parlour behind the shop, while the shopman took his mug of tea and hunch of bread-and-butter on a sack of peas in the front premises. I considered Mr. Pumblechook wretched company. Besides being possessed by my sister's idea that a mortifying and penitential character ought to be imparted to my diet—besides giving me as much crumb as possible in combination with as little butter, and putting such a quantity of warm water into my milk that it would have been more candid to have left the milk out altogether —his conversation consisted of nothing but arithmetic. On my politely bidding him Good morning, he said, pompously, "Seven times nine, boy?" And how should *I* be able to answer, dodged in that way, in a strange place, on an empty stomach! I was hungry, but before I had swallowed a morsel, he began a running sum that lasted all through the breakfast. "Seven?" "And four?" "And eight?" "And six?" "And two?" "And ten?" And so on. And after each figure was disposed of, it was as much as I could do to get a bite or a sup, before the next came; while he sat at his ease guessing nothing, and eating bacon and hot roll, in (if I may be allowed the expression) a gorging and gormandising manner.

For such reasons I was very glad when ten o'clock came and we started for Miss Havisham's; though I was not at all at my ease regarding the manner in which I should acquit myself under that lady's roof. Within a quarter of an hour we came to Miss Havisham's house, which was of old brick, and dismal, and had a great many iron bars to it. Some of the windows had been walled up; of those that remained, all the lower were rustily barred. There was a court-yard in front, and that was barred; so, we had to wait, after ringing the bell, until some one should come to open it. While we waited at the gate, I peeped in (even then Mr. Pumblechook said, "And fourteen?" but I pretended not to hear him), and saw that at the side of the house there was a large brewery. No brewing was going on in it, and none seemed to have gone on for a long time.

A window was raised, and a clear voice demanded "What name?" To which my conductor replied, "Pumblechook." The voice returned, "Quite right," and the window was shut again, and a young lady came across the court-yard, with keys in her hand.

"This," said Mr. Pumblechook, "is Pip."

"This is Pip, is it?" returned the young lady, who was very pretty and seemed very proud; "come in, Pip."

Mr. Pumblechook was coming in also, when she stopped him with the gate.

"Oh!" she said. "Did you wish to see Miss Havisham?"

"If Miss Havisham wished to see me," returned Mr. Pumblechook, discomfited.

"Ah!" said the girl; "but you see she don't."

She said it so finally, and in such an undiscussible way, that Mr. Pumblechook, though in a condition of ruffled dignity, could not protest. But he eyed me severely—as if I had done anything to him!—and departed with the words reproachfully delivered: "Boy! Let your behaviour here be a credit unto them which brought you up by hand!" I was not free from apprehension that he would come back to propound through the gate, "And sixteen?" But he didn't.

My young conductress locked the gate, and we went across the court-yard. It was paved and clean, but grass was growing in every crevice. The brewery buildings had a little lane of communication with it; and the wooden gates of that lane stood open, and all the brewery beyond stood open, away to the high enclosing wall; and all was empty and disused. The cold wind seemed to blow colder there, than outside the gate; and it made a shrill noise in howling in and out at the open sides of the brewery, like the noise of wind in the rigging of a ship at sea.

She saw me looking at it, and she said, "You could drink without hurt all the strong beer that's brewed there now, boy."

"I should think I could, miss," said I, in a shy way.

"Better not try to brew beer there now, or it would turn out sour, boy; don't you think so?"

"It looks like it, miss."

"Not that anybody means to try," she added, "for that's all done with, and the place will stand as idle as it is, till it falls. As to strong beer, there's enough of it in the cellars already, to drown the Manor House."

"Is that the name of this house, miss?"

"One of its names, boy."

"It has more than one, then, miss?"

"One more. Its other name was Satis; which is Greek, or Latin, or Hebrew, or all three—or all one to me—for enough."

"Enough House!" said I: "that's a curious name, miss."

"Yes," she replied; "but it meant more than it said. It meant, when it was given, that whoever had this house, could want nothing else. They must have been easily satisfied in those days, I should think. But don't loiter, boy."

Though she called me "boy" so often, and with a carelessness that was far from complimentary, she was of about my own age. She seemed much older than I, of course, being a girl, and beautiful and self-possessed; and she was as scornful of me as if she had been one-and-twenty, and a queen.

We went into the house by a side door—the great front entrance had two chains across it outside—and the first thing I noticed was, that the passages were all dark, and that she had left a candle burning there. She took it up, and we went through more passages and up a staircase, and still it was all dark, and only the candle lighted us.

At last we came to the door of a room, and she said, "Go in."

I answered, more in shyness than politeness, "After you, miss."

To this, she returned: "Don't be ridiculous, boy; I am not going in." And scornfully walked away, and—what was worse—took the candle with her.

This was very uncomfortable, and I was half afraid. However, the only thing to be done being to knock at the door, I knocked, and was told from within to enter. I entered, therefore, and found myself in a pretty large room, well lighted with wax candles. No glimpse of daylight was to be seen in it. It was a dressing-room, as I supposed from the furniture, though much of it was of forms and uses then quite unknown to me. But prominent in it was a draped table with a gilded looking-glass, and that I made out at first sight to be a fine lady's dressing-table.

Whether I should have made out this object so soon, if there had been no fine lady sitting at it, I cannot say. In an arm-chair, with an elbow resting on the table and her head leaning on that hand, sat the strangest lady I have ever seen, or shall ever see.

She was dressed in rich materials—satins, and lace, and silks—all of white. Her shoes were white. And she had a long white veil dependent from her hair, and she had bridal flowers in her hair, but her hair was white. Some bright jewels sparkled on her neck and on her hands, and

IN AN ARM-CHAIR, WITH AN ELBOW RESTING ON THE TABLE

some other jewels lay sparkling on the table. Dresses, less splendid than the dress she wore, and half-packed trunks, were scattered about. She had not quite finished dressing, for she had but one shoe on—the other was on the table near her hand—her veil was but half arranged, her watch and chain were not put on, and some lace for her bosom lay with those trinkets, and with her handkerchief, and gloves, and some flowers, and a Prayer-book, all confusedly heaped about the looking-glass.

It was not in the first few moments that I saw all these things, though I saw more of them in the first moments than might be supposed. But, I saw that everything within my view which ought to be white, had been white long ago, and had lost its lustre, and was faded and yellow. I saw that the bride within the bridal dress had withered like the dress, and like the flowers, and had no brightness left but the brightness of her sunken eyes. I saw that the dress had been put upon the rounded figure of a young woman, and that the figure upon which it now hung loose, had shrunk to skin and bone. Once, I had been taken to see some ghastly waxwork at the Fair, representing I know not what impossible personage lying in state. Once, I had been taken to one of our old marsh churches to see a skeleton in the ashes of a rich dress, that had been dug out of a vault under the church pavement. Now, waxwork and skeleton seemed to have dark eyes that moved and looked at me. I should have cried out, if I could.

"Who is it?" said the lady at the table.

"Pip, ma'am."

"Pip?"

"Mr. Pumblechook's boy, ma'am. Come—to play."

"Come nearer; let me look at you. Come close."

It was when I stood before her, avoiding her eyes, that I took note of the surrounding objects in detail, and saw that her watch had stopped at twenty minutes to nine, and that a clock in the room had stopped at twenty minutes to nine.

"Look at me," said Miss Havisham. "You are not afraid of a woman who has never seen the sun since you were born?"

I regret to state that I was not afraid of telling the enormous lie comprehended in the answer "No."

"Do you know what I touch here?" she said, laying her hands, one upon the other, on her left side.

v.   c

"Yes, ma'am." (It made me think of the young man.)

"What do I touch?"

"Your heart."

"Broken!"

She uttered the word with an eager look, and with strong emphasis, and with a weird smile that had a kind of boast in it. Afterwards, she kept her hands there for a little while, and slowly took them away as if they were heavy.

"I am tired," said Miss Havisham. "I want diversion, and I have done with men and women. Play."

I think it will be conceded by my most disputatious reader, that she could hardly have directed an unfortunate boy to do anything in the wide world more difficult to be done under the circumstances.

"I sometimes have sick fancies," she went on, "and I have a sick fancy that I want to see some play. There, there!" with an impatient movement of the fingers of her right hand; "play, play, play!"

For a moment, with the fear of my sister's working me before my eyes, I had a desperate idea of starting round the room in the assumed character of Mr. Pumblechook's chaise-cart. But, I felt myself so unequal to the performance that I gave it up, and stood looking at Miss Havisham in what I suppose she took for a dogged manner, inasmuch as she said, when we had taken a good look at each other:

"Are you sullen and obstinate?"

"No, ma'am, I am very sorry for you, and very sorry I can't play just now. If you complain of me I shall get into trouble with my sister, so I would do it if I could; but it's so new here, and so strange, and so fine—and melancholy——" I stopped, fearing I might say too much, or had already said it, and we took another look at each other.

Before she spoke again, she turned her eyes from me, and looked at the dress she wore, and at the dressing-table, and finally at herself in the looking-glass.

"So new to him," she muttered, "so old to me; so strange to him, so familiar to me; so melancholy to both of us! Call Estella."

As she was still looking at the reflection of herself, I thought she was still talking to herself, and kept quiet.

"Call Estella," she repeated, flashing a look at me. "You can do that. Call Estella. At the door."

To stand in the dark in a mysterious passage of an un-known house, bawling Estella to a scornful young lady neither visible nor responsive, and feeling it a dreadful liberty so to roar out her name, was almost as bad as playing to order. But, she answered at last, and her light came along the dark passage like a star.

Miss Havisham beckoned her to come close, and took up a jewel from the table, and tried its effect upon her fair young bosom and against her pretty brown hair. "Your own, one day, my dear, and you will use it well. Let me see you play cards with this boy."

"With this boy! Why, he is a common labouring-boy!"

I thought I overheard Miss Havisham answer—only it seemed so unlikely—"Well? You can break his heart."

"What do you play, boy?" asked Estella of myself, with the greatest disdain.

"Nothing but beggar my neighbour, Miss."

"Beggar him," said Miss Havisham to Estella. So we sat down to cards.

It was then I began to understand that everything in the room had stopped, like the watch and the clock, a long time ago. I noticed that Miss Havisham put down the jewel exactly on the spot from which she had taken it up. As Estella dealt the cards, I glanced at the dressing-table again, and saw that the shoe upon it, once white, now yellow, had never been worn. I glanced down at the foot from which the shoe was absent, and saw that the silk stocking on it, once white, now yellow, had been trodden ragged. Without this arrest of everything, this standing still of all the pale decayed objects, not even the withered bridal dress on the collapsed form could have looked so like grave-clothes, or the long veil so like a shroud.

So she sat, corpse-like, as we played at cards; the frillings and trimmings on her bridal dress, looking like earthy paper. I knew nothing then of the discoveries that are occasionally made of bodies buried in ancient times, which fall to powder in the moment of being distinctly seen; but, I have often thought since, that she must have looked as if the admission of the natural light of day would have struck her to dust.

"He calls the knaves, Jacks, this boy!" said Estella with disdain, before our first game was out. "And what coarse hands he has! And what thick boots!"

I had never thought of being ashamed of my hands before, but I began to consider them a very indifferent pair. Her contempt for me was so strong, that it became infectious, and I caught it.

She won the game, and I dealt. I misdealt, as was only natural, when I knew she was lying in wait for me to do wrong; and she denounced me for a stupid, clumsy labouring-boy.

"You say nothing of her," remarked Miss Havisham to me, as she looked on. "She says many hard things of you, yet you say nothing of her. What do you think of her?"

"I don't like to say," I stammered.

"Tell me in my ear," said Miss Havisham, bending down.

"I think she is very proud," I replied, in a whisper.

"Anything else?"

"I think she is very pretty."

"Anything else?"

"I think she is very insulting." (She was looking at me then with a look of supreme aversion.)

"Anything else?"

"I think I should like to go home."

"And never see her again, though she is so pretty?"

"I am not sure that I shouldn't like to see her again, but I should like to go home now."

"You shall go soon," said Miss Havisham aloud. "Play the game out."

Saving for the one weird smile at first, I should have felt almost sure that Miss Havisham's face could not smile. It had dropped into a watchful and brooding expression—most likely when all the things about her had become transfixed—and it looked as if nothing could ever lift it up again. Her chest had dropped, so that she stooped; and her voice had dropped, so that she spoke low, and with a dead lull upon her; altogether, she had the appearance of having dropped, body and soul, within and without, under the weight of a crushing blow.

I played the game to an end with Estella, and she beggared me. She threw the cards down on the table when she had won them all, as if she despised them for having been won of me.

"When shall I have you here again?" said Miss Havisham. "Let me think."

I was beginning to remind her that to-day was Wednesday,

when she checked me with her former impatient movement of the fingers of her right hand.

"There! there! I know nothing of days of the week; I know nothing of weeks of the year. Come again after six days. You hear?"

"Yes, ma'am."

"Estella, take him down. Let him have something to eat, and let him roam and look about him while he eats. Go, Pip."

I followed the candle down, as I had followed the candle up, and she stood it in the place where we had found it. Until she opened the side entrance, I had fancied, without thinking about it, that it must necessarily be night-time. The rush of the daylight quite confounded me, and made me feel as if I had been in the candlelight of the strange room many hours.

"You are to wait here, you boy," said Estella; and disappeared and closed the door.

I took the opportunity of being alone in the court-yard, to look at my coarse hands and my common boots. My opinion of those accessories was not favourable. They had never troubled me before, but they troubled me now, as vulgar appendages. I determined to ask Joe why he had ever taught me to call those picture-cards, Jacks, which ought to be called knaves. I wished Joe had been rather more genteelly brought up, and then I should have been so too.

She came back, with some bread and meat and a little mug of beer. She put the mug down on the stones of the yard, and gave me the bread and meat without looking at me, as insolently as if I were a dog in disgrace. I was so humiliated, hurt, spurned, offended, angry, sorry—I cannot hit upon the right name for the smart—God knows what its name was—that tears started to my eyes. The moment they sprang there, the girl looked at me with a quick delight in having been the cause of them. This gave me power to keep them back and to look at her: so, she gave a contemptuous toss—but with a sense, I thought, of having made too sure that I was so wounded—and left me.

But, when she was gone, I looked about me for a place to hide my face in, and got behind one of the gates in the brewery-lane, and leaned my sleeve against the wall there, and leaned my forehead on it and cried. As I cried, I kicked

the wall, and took a hard twist at my hair; so bitter were
my feelings, and so sharp was the smart without a name,
that needed counteraction.

My sister's bringing up had made me sensitive. In the
little world in which children have their existence, whosoever
brings them up, there is nothing so finely perceived and so
finely felt, as injustice. It may be only small injustice that
the child can be exposed to; but the child is small, and its
world is small, and its rocking-horse stands as many hands
high, according to scale, as a big-boned Irish hunter. Within
myself, I had sustained, from my babyhood, a perpetual
conflict with injustice. I had known, from the time when
I could speak, that my sister, in her capricious and violent
coercion, was unjust to me. I had cherished a profound
conviction that her bringing me up by hand, gave her no
right to bring me up by jerks. Through all my punishments, disgraces, fasts and vigils, and other penitential
performances, I had nursed this assurance; and to my
communing so much with it, in a solitary and unprotected
way, I in great part refer the fact that I was morally timid
and very sensitive.

I got rid of my injured feelings for the time, by kicking
them into the brewery-wall, and twisting them out of my
hair, and then I smoothed my face with my sleeve, and came
from behind the gate. The bread and meat were acceptable,
and the beer was warming and tingling, and I was soon in
spirits to look about me.

To be sure, it was a deserted place, down to the pigeon-
house in the brewery-yard, which had been blown crooked
on its pole by some high wind, and would have made the
pigeons think themselves at sea, if there had been any
pigeons there to be rocked by it. But, there were no
pigeons in the dove-cot, no horses in the stable, no pigs in
the sty, no malt in the store-house, no smells of grains and
beer in the copper or the vat. All the uses and scents of the
brewery might have evaporated with its last reek of smoke.
In a by-yard, there was a wilderness of empty casks, which
had a certain sour remembrance of better days lingering
about them; but it was too sour to be accepted as a sample
of the beer that was gone—and in this respect I remember
those recluses as being like most others.

Behind the furthest end of the brewery, was a rank garden
with an old wall: not so high but that I could struggle up

and hold on long enough to look over it, and see that the rank garden was the garden of the house, and that it was overgrown with tangled weeds, but that there was a track upon the green and yellow paths, as if some one sometimes walked there, and that Estella was walking away from me even then. But she seemed to be everywhere. For, when I yielded to the temptation presented by the casks, and began to walk on them, I saw *her* walking on them at the end of the yard of casks. She had her back towards me, and held her pretty brown hair spread out in her two hands, and never looked round, and passed out of my view directly. So, in the brewery itself—by which I mean the large paved lofty place in which they used to make the beer, and where the brewing utensils still were. When I first went into it, and, rather oppressed by its gloom, stood near the door looking about me, I saw her pass among the extinguished fires, and ascend some light iron stairs, and go out by a gallery high overhead, as if she were going out into the sky.

It was in this place, and at this moment, that a strange thing happened to my fancy. I thought it a strange thing then, and I thought it a stranger thing long afterwards. I turned my eyes—a little dimmed by looking up at the frosty light—towards a great wooden beam in a low nook of the building near me on my right hand, and I saw a figure hanging there by the neck. A figure all in yellow white, with but one shoe to the feet; and it hung so, that I could see that the faded trimmings of the dress were like earthy paper, and that the face was Miss Havisham's, with a movement going over the whole countenance as if she were trying to call to me. In the terror of seeing the figure, and in the terror of being certain that it had not been there a moment before, I at first ran from it, and then ran towards it. And my terror was greatest of all when I found no figure there.

Nothing less than the frosty light of the cheerful sky, the sight of people passing beyond the bars of the court-yard gate, and the reviving influence of the rest of the bread and meat and beer, could have brought me round. Even with those aids, I might not have come to myself as soon as I did, but that I saw Estella approaching with the keys, to let me out. She would have some fair reason for looking down upon me, I thought, if she saw me frightened; and she should have no fair reason.

She gave me a triumphant glance in passing me, as if she rejoiced that my hands were so coarse and my boots were so thick, and she opened the gate, and stood holding it. I was passing out without looking at her, when she touched me with a taunting hand.

"Why don't you cry?"

"Because I don't want to."

"You do," said she. "You have been crying till you are half blind, and you are near crying again now."

She laughed contemptuously, pushed me out, and locked the gate upon me. I went straight to Mr. Pumblechook's, and was immensely relieved to find him not at home. So, leaving word with the shopman on what day I was wanted at Miss Havisham's again, I set off on the four-mile walk to our forge; pondering, as I went along, on all I had seen, and deeply revolving that I was a common labouring-boy; that my hands were coarse; that my boots were thick; that I had fallen into a despicable habit of calling knaves Jacks; that I was much more ignorant than I had considered myself last night, and generally that I was in a low-lived bad way.

Whitewash on the forehead hardens the brain into a state of obstinacy perhaps. Anyhow, with whitewash from the wall on my forehead, my obstinacy was adamantine. I reflected for some time, and then answered as if I had discovered a new idea, "I mean pretty well."

My sister with an exclamation of impatience was going to fly at me—I had no shadow of defence, for Joe was busy in the forge—when Mr. Pumblechook interposed with "No! Don't lose your temper. Leave this lad to me, ma'am; leave this lad to me." Mr. Pumblechook then turned me towards him, as if he were going to cut my hair, and said:

"First (to get our thoughts in order): Forty-three pence?"

I calculated the consequences of replying "Four Hundred Pound," and finding them against me, went as near the answer as I could—which was somewhere about eightpence off. Mr. Pumblechook then put me through my pence-table from "twelve pence make one shilling," up to "forty pence make three and fourpence," and then triumphantly demanded, as if he had done for me, "*Now!* How much is forty-three pence?" To which I replied, after a long interval of reflection, "I don't know." And I was so aggravated that I almost doubt if I did know.

Mr. Pumblechook worked his head like a screw to screw it out of me, and said, "Is forty-three pence seven and sixpence three fardens, for instance?"

"Yes!" said I. And although my sister instantly boxed my ears, it was highly gratifying to me to see that the answer spoilt his joke, and brought him to a dead stop.

"Boy! What like is Miss Havisham?" Mr. Pumblechook began again when he had recovered; folding his arms tight on his chest and applying the screw.

"Very tall and dark," I told him.

"Is she, uncle?" asked my sister.

Mr. Pumblechook winked assent; from which I at once inferred that he had never seen Miss Havisham, for she was nothing of the kind.

"Good!" said Mr. Pumblechook, conceitedly. ("This is the way to have him! We are beginning to hold our own, I think, Mum?")

"I am sure, uncle," returned Mrs. Joe, "I wish you had him always: you know so well how to deal with him."

CHAPTER IX

WHEN I reached home, my sister was very curious to know all about Miss Havisham's, and asked a number of questions. And I soon found myself getting heavily bumped from behind in the nape of the neck and the small of the back, and having my face ignominiously shoved against the kitchen wall, because I did not answer those questions at sufficient length.

If a dread of not being understood be hidden in the breasts of other young people to anything like the extent to which it used to be hidden in mine—which I consider probable, as I have no particular reason to suspect myself of having been a monstrosity—it is the key to many reservations. I felt convinced that if I described Miss Havisham's as my eyes had seen it, I should not be understood. Not only that, but I felt convinced that Miss Havisham too would not be understood; and although she was perfectly incomprehensible to me, I entertained an impression that there would be something coarse and treacherous in my dragging her as she really was (to say nothing of Miss Estella) before the contemplation of Mrs. Joe. Consequently, I said as little as I could, and had my face shoved against the kitchen wall.

The worst of it was that that bullying old Pumblechook, preyed upon by a devouring curiosity to be informed of all I had seen and heard, came gaping over in his chaise-cart at tea-time, to have the details divulged to him. And the mere sight of the torment, with his fishy eyes and mouth open, his sandy hair inquisitively on end, and his waistcoat heaving with windy arithmetic, made me vicious in my reticence.

"Well, boy," Uncle Pumblechook began, as soon as he was seated in the chair of honour by the fire. "How did you get on up town?"

I answered, "Pretty well, sir," and my sister shook her fist at me.

"Pretty well?" Mr. Pumblechook repeated. "Pretty well is no answer. Tell us what you mean by pretty well, boy?"

"Now, boy! What was she a doing of, when you went in to-day?" asked Mr. Pumblechook.

"She was sitting," I answered, "in a black velvet coach."

Mr. Pumblechook and Mrs. Joe stared at one another—as they well might—and both repeated, "In a black velvet coach?"

"Yes," said I. "And Miss Estella—that's her niece, I think—handed her in cake and wine at the coach-window, on a gold plate. And we all had cake and wine on gold plates. And I got up behind the coach to eat mine, because she told me to."

"Was anybody else there?" asked Mr. Pumblechook.

"Four dogs," said I.

"Large or small?"

"Immense," said I. "And they fought for veal-cutlets out of a silver basket."

Mr. Pumblechook and Mrs. Joe stared at one another again, in utter amazement. I was perfectly frantic—a reckless witness under the torture—and would have told them anything.

"Where *was* this coach, in the name of gracious?" asked my sister.

"In Miss Havisham's room." They stared again. "But there weren't any horses to it." I added this saving clause, in the moment of rejecting four richly caparisoned coursers, which I had had wild thoughts of harnessing.

"Can this be possible, uncle?" asked Mrs. Joe. "What can the boy mean?"

"I'll tell you, Mum," said Mr. Pumblechook. "My opinion is, it's a sedan-chair. She's flighty, you know— very flighty—quite flighty enough to pass her days in a sedan-chair."

"Did you ever see her in it, uncle?" asked Mrs. Joe.

"How could I," he returned, forced to the admission, "when I never see her in my life? Never clapped eyes upon her!"

"Goodness, uncle! And yet you have spoken to her?"

"Why, don't you know," said Mr. Pumblechook, testily, "that when I have been there, I have been took up to the outside of her door, and the door has stood ajar, and she has spoken to me that way. Don't say you don't know *that*, Mum. Howsever, the boy went there to play. What did you play at, boy?"

"We played with flags," I said. (I beg to observe that I think of myself with amazement, when I recall the lies I told on this occasion.)

"Flags!" echoed my sister.

"Yes," said I. "Estella waved a blue flag, and I waved a red one, and Miss Havisham waved one sprinkled all over with little gold stars, out at the coach-window. And then we all waved our swords and hurrahed."

"Swords!" repeated my sister. "Where did you get swords from?"

"Out of a cupboard," said I. "And I saw pistols in it—and jam—and pills. And there was no daylight in the room, but it was all lighted up with candles."

"That's true, Mum," said Mr. Pumblechook, with a grave nod. "That's the state of the case, for that much I've seen myself." And then they both stared at me, and I, with an obtrusive show of artlessness on my countenance, stared at them, and plaited the right leg of my trousers with my right hand.

If they had asked me any more questions I should undoubtedly have betrayed myself, for I was even then on the point of mentioning that there was a balloon in the yard, and should have hazarded the statement but for my invention being divided between that phenomenon and a bear in the brewery. They were so much occupied, however, in discussing the marvels I had already presented for their consideration, that I escaped. The subject still held them when Joe came in from his work to have a cup of tea. To whom my sister, more for the relief of her own mind than for the gratification of his, related my pretended experiences.

Now, when I saw Joe open his blue eyes and roll them all round the kitchen in helpless amazement, I was overtaken by penitence; but only as regarded him—not in the least as regarded the other two. Towards Joe, and Joe only, I considered myself a young monster, while they sat debating what results would come to me from Miss Havisham's acquaintance and favour. They had no doubt that Miss Havisham would "do something" for me; their doubts related to the form that something would take. My sister stood out for "property." Mr. Pumblechook was in favour of a handsome premium for binding me apprentice to some genteel trade—say, the corn and seed trade, for

instance. Joe fell into the deepest disgrace with both, for offering the bright suggestion that I might only be presented with one of the dogs who had fought for the veal-cutlets. "If a fool's head can't express better opinions than that," said my sister, "and you have got any work to do, you had better go and do it." So he went.

After Mr. Pumblechook had driven off, and when my sister was washing up, I stole into the forge to Joe, and remained by him until he had done for the night. Then I said, "Before the fire goes out, Joe, I should like to tell you something."

"Should you, Pip?" said Joe, drawing his shoeing-stool near the forge. "Then tell us. What is it, Pip?"

"Joe," said I, taking hold of his rolled-up shirt sleeve, and twisting it between my finger and thumb, "you remember all that about Miss Havisham's?"

"Remember?" said Joe. "I believe you! Wonderful!"

"It's a terrible thing, Joe; it ain't true."

"What are you telling of, Pip?" cried Joe, falling back in the greatest amazement. "You don't mean to say it's——"

"Yes, I do; it's lies, Joe."

"But not all of it? Why sure you don't mean to say, Pip, that there was no black welwet co——ch?" For I stood shaking my head. "But at least there was dogs, Pip? Come, Pip," said Joe, persuasively, "if there warn't no weal-cutlets, at least there was dogs?"

"No, Joe."

"A dog?" said Joe. "A puppy? Come!"

"No, Joe, there was nothing at all of the kind."

As I fixed my eyes hopelessly on Joe, Joe contemplated me in dismay. "Pip, old chap! This won't do, old fellow! I say! Where do you expect to go to?"

"It's terrible, Joe; ain't it?"

"Terrible?" cried Joe. "Awful! What possessed you?"

"I don't know what possessed me, Joe," I replied, letting his shirt sleeve go, and sitting down in the ashes at his feet, hanging my head; "but I wish you hadn't taught me to call Knaves at cards, Jacks; and I wish my boots weren't so thick nor my hands so coarse."

And then I told Joe that I felt very miserable, and that I hadn't been able to explain myself to Mrs. Joe and

Pumblechook, who were so rude to me, and that there had been a beautiful young lady at Miss Havisham's who was dreadfully proud, and that she had said I was common, and that I knew I was common, and that I wished I was not common, and that the lies had come of it somehow, though I didn't know how.

This was a case of metaphysics, at least as difficult for Joe to deal with, as for me. But Joe took the case altogether out of the region of metaphysics, and by that means vanquished it.

"There's one thing you may be sure of, Pip," said Joe, after some rumination, "namely, that lies is lies. Howsever they come, they didn't ought to come, and they come from the father of lies, and work round to the same. Don't you tell no more of 'em, Pip. *That* ain't the way to get out of being common, old chap. And as to being common, I don't make it out at all clear. You are oncommon in some things. You're oncommon small. Likewise you're a oncommon scholar."

"No, I am ignorant and backward, Joe."

"Why, see what a letter you wrote last night! Wrote in print even! I've seen letters—Ah! and from gentlefolks!—that I'll swear weren't wrote in print," said Joe.

"I have learnt next to nothing, Joe. You think much of me. It's only that."

"Well, Pip," said Joe, "be it so, or be it son't, you must be a common scholar afore you can be a oncommon one, I should hope! The king upon his throne, with his crown upon his 'ed, can't sit and write his acts of Parliament in print, without having begun, when he were a unpromoted Prince, with the alphabet—Ah!" added Joe, with a shake of the head that was full of meaning, "and begun at A too, and worked his way to Z. And *I* know what that is to do, though I can't say I've exactly done it."

There was some hope in this piece of wisdom, and it rather encouraged me.

"Whether common ones as to callings and earnings," pursued Joe, reflectively, "mightn't be the better of continuing for to keep company with common ones, instead of going out to play with oncommon ones—which reminds me to hope that there were a flag, perhaps?"

"No, Joe."

"(I'm sorry there weren't a flag, Pip.) Whether that

might be, or mightn't be, is a thing as can't be looked into now, without putting your sister on the Rampage ; and that's a thing not to be thought of, as being done intentional. Lookee here, Pip, at what is said to you by a true friend. Which this to you the true friend say. If you can't get to be oncommon through going straight, you'll never get to do it through going crooked. So don't tell no more on 'em, Pip, and live well and die happy."

"You are not angry with me, Joe ? "

"No, old chap. But bearing in mind that them were which I meantersay of a stunning and outdacious sort— alluding to them which bordered on weal-cutlets and dog-fighting—a sincere well-wisher would adwise, Pip, their being dropped into your meditations, when you go up-stairs to bed. That's all, old chap, and don't never do it no more."

When I got up to my little room and said my prayers, I did not forget Joe's recommendation, and yet my young mind was in that disturbed and unthankful state, that I thought long after I laid me down, how common Estella would consider Joe, a mere blacksmith : how thick his boots, and how coarse his hands. I thought how Joe and my sister were then sitting in the kitchen, and how I had come up to bed from the kitchen, and how Miss Havisham and Estella never sat in a kitchen, but were far above the level of such common doings. I fell asleep recalling what I " used to do " when I was at Miss Havisham's ; as though I had been there weeks or months, instead of hours : and as though it were quite an old subject of remembrance, instead of one that had risen only that day.

That was a memorable day to me, for it made great changes in me. But it is the same with any life. Imagine one selected day struck out of it, and think how different its course would have been. Pause you who read this, and think for a moment of the long chain of iron or gold, of thorns or flowers, that would never have bound you, but for the formation of the first link on one memorable day.

CHAPTER X

THE felicitous idea occurred to me a morning or two later
when I woke, that the best step I could take towards making
myself uncommon was to get out of Biddy everything she
knew. In pursuance of this luminous conception, I mentioned to Biddy when I went to Mr. Wopsle's great-aunt's
at night, that I had a particular reason for wishing to get
on in life, and that I should feel very much obliged to her
if she would impart all her learning to me. Biddy, who
was the most obliging of girls, immediately said she would,
and indeed began to carry out her promise within five
minutes.

The Educational scheme or Course established by Mr.
Wopsle's great-aunt may be resolved into the following
synopsis. The pupils ate apples and put straws down one
another's backs, until Mr. Wopsle's great-aunt collected her
energies, and made an indiscriminate totter at them with
a birch-rod. After receiving the charge with every mark of
derision, the pupils formed in line and buzzingly passed a
ragged book from hand to hand. The book had an alphabet
in it, some figures and tables, and a little spelling—that is
to say, it had had once. As soon as this volume began to
circulate, Mr. Wopsle's great-aunt fell into a state of coma ;
arising either from sleep or a rheumatic paroxysm. The
pupils then entered among themselves upon a competitive
examination on the subject of Boots, with the view of ascer-
taining who could tread the hardest upon whose toes. This
mental exercise lasted until Biddy made a rush at them and
distributed three defaced Bibles (shaped as if they had been
unskilfully cut off the chump-end of something), more illegibly
printed at the best than any curiosities of literature I have
since met with, speckled all over with iron-mould, and having
various specimens of the insect world smashed between their
leaves. This part of the Course was usually lightened by
several single combats between Biddy and refractory students.
When the fights were over, Biddy gave out the number of

a page, and then we all read aloud what we could— or what we couldn't—in a frightful chorus ; Biddy leading with a high shrill monotonous voice, and none of us having the least notion of, or reverence for, what we were reading about. When this horrible din had lasted a certain time, it mechanically awoke Mr. Wopsle's great-aunt, who staggered at a boy fortuitously, and pulled his ears. This was under-stood to terminate the Course for the evening, and we emerged into the air with shrieks of intellectual victory. It is fair to remark that there was no prohibition against any pupil's entertaining himself with a slate or even with the ink (when there was any), but that it was not easy to pursue that branch of study in the winter season, on account of the little general shop in which the classes were holden—and which was also Mr. Wopsle's great-aunt's sitting-room and bed-chamber—being but faintly illuminated through the agency of one low-spirited dip-candle and no snuffers.

It appeared to me that it would take time to become un-common under these circumstances : nevertheless, I resolved to try it, and that very evening Biddy entered on our special agreement, by imparting some information from her little catalogue of Prices, under the head of moist sugar, and lending me, to copy at home, a large old English D which she had imitated from the heading of some newspaper, and which I supposed, until she told me what it was, to be a design for a buckle.

Of course there was a public-house in the village, and of course Joe liked sometimes to smoke his pipe there. I had received strict orders from my sister to call for him at the Three Jolly Bargemen, that evening, on my way from school, and bring him home at my peril. To the Three Jolly Barge-men, therefore, I directed my steps.

There was a bar at the Jolly Bargemen, with some alarmingly long chalk scores in it on the wall at the side of the door, which seemed to me to be never paid off. They had been there ever since I could remember, and had grown more than I had. But there was a quantity of chalk about our country, and perhaps the people neglected no opportunity of turning it to account.

It being Saturday night, I found the landlord looking rather grimly at these records, but as my business was with Joe and not with him, I merely wished him good evening, and passed into the common room at the end of the passage, where there was a bright large kitchen fire, and where Joe was smoking his pipe in company with Mr. Wopsle and a stranger. Joe greeted me as usual with "Halloa, Pip, old chap!" and the moment he said that, the stranger turned his head and looked at me.

He was a secret-looking man whom I had never seen before. His head was all on one side, and one of his eyes was half shut up, as if he were taking aim at something with an invisible gun. He had a pipe in his mouth, and he took it out, and, after slowly blowing all his smoke away and looking hard at me all the time, nodded. So I nodded, and then he nodded again, and made room on the settle beside him that I might sit down there.

But, as I was used to sit beside Joe whenever I entered that place of resort, I said "No, thank you, sir," and fell into the space Joe made for me on the opposite settle. The strange man, after glancing at Joe, and seeing that his attention was otherwise engaged, nodded to me again when I had taken my seat, and then rubbed his leg—in a very odd way, as it struck me.

"You was saying," said the strange man, turning to Joe, "that you was a blacksmith."

"Yes. I said it, you know," said Joe.

"What'll you drink, Mr. ——? You didn't mention your name, by-the-bye."

Joe mentioned it now, and the strange man called him by it.

"What'll you drink, Mr. Gargery? At my expense? To top up with?"

"Well," said Joe, "to tell you the truth, I ain't much in the habit of drinking at anybody's expense but my own."

"Habit? No," returned the stranger, "but once and away, and on a Saturday night too. Come! Put a name to it, Mr. Gargery."

"I wouldn't wish to be stiff company," said Joe. "Rum."

"Rum," repeated the stranger. "And will the other gentleman originate a sentiment?"

"Rum," said Mr. Wopsle.

"Three Rums!" cried the stranger, calling to the landlord. "Glasses round!"

"This other gentleman," observed Joe, by way of introducing Mr. Wopsle, "is a gentleman that you would like to hear give it out. Our clerk at church."

"Aha!" said the stranger, quickly, and cocking his eye at me. "The lonely church, right out on the marshes, with the graves round it!"

"That's it," said Joe.

The stranger, with a comfortable kind of grunt over his pipe, put his legs up on the settle that he had to himself. He wore a flapping broad-brimmed traveller's hat, and under it a handkerchief tied over his head in the manner of a cap: so that he showed no hair. As he looked at the fire, I thought I saw a cunning expression, followed by a half-laugh, come into his face.

"I am not acquainted with this country, gentlemen, but it seems a solitary country towards the river."

"Most marshes is solitary," said Joe.

"No doubt, no doubt. Do you find any gipsies, now, or tramps, or vagrants of any sort, out there?"

"No," said Joe; "none but a runaway convict now and then. And we don't find *them*, easy. Eh, Mr. Wopsle?"

Mr. Wopsle, with a majestic remembrance of old discomfiture, assented; but not warmly.

"Seems you have been out after such?" asked the stranger.

"Once," returned Joe. "Not that we wanted to take them, you understand; we went out as lookers on; me and Mr. Wopsle, and Pip. Didn't us, Pip?"

"Yes, Joe."

The stranger looked at me again—still cocking his eye, as if he were expressly taking aim at me with his invisible gun—and said, "He's a likely young parcel of bones that. What is it you call him?"

"Pip," said Joe.

"Christened Pip?"

"No, not christened Pip."

"Surname Pip?"

"No," said Joe; "it's a kind of a family name what he gave himself when a infant, and is called by."

"Son of yours?"

"Well," said Joe, meditatively—not, of course, that it could be in anywise necessary to consider about it, but because it was the way at the Jolly Bargemen to seem to consider deeply about everything that was discussed over pipes; "well—no. No, he ain't."

"Nevvy?" said the strange man.

"Well," said Joe, with the same appearance of profound

cogitation, "he is not—no, not to deceive you, he is *not*—my nevvy."

"What the Blue Blazes is he?" asked the stranger. Which appeared to me to be an inquiry of unnecessary strength.

Mr. Wopsle struck in upon that; as one who knew all about relationships, having professional occasion to bear in mind what female relations a man might not marry; and expounded the ties between me and Joe. Having his hand in, Mr. Wopsle finished off with a most terrifically snarling passage from Richard the Third, and seemed to think he had done quite enough to account for it when he added,—"as the poet says."

And here I may remark that when Mr. Wopsle referred to me, he considered it a necessary part of such reference to rumple my hair and poke it into my eyes. I cannot conceive why everybody of his standing who visited at our house should always have put me through the same inflammatory process under similar circumstances. Yet I do not call to mind that I was ever in my earlier youth the subject of remark in our social family circle, but some large-handed person took some such ophthalmic steps to patronise me.

All this while, the strange man looked at nobody but me, and looked at me as if he were determined to have a shot at me at last, and bring me down. But he said nothing after offering his Blue Blazes observation, until the glasses of rum-and-water were brought: and then he made his shot, and a most extraordinary shot it was.

It was not a verbal remark, but a proceeding in dumb show, and was pointedly addressed to me. He stirred his rum-and-water pointedly at me, and he tasted his rum-and-water pointedly at me. And he stirred it and he tasted it: not with a spoon that was brought to him, but *with a file*.

He did this so that nobody but I saw the file; and when he had done it, he wiped the file and put it in a breast-pocket. I knew it to be Joe's file, and I knew that he knew my convict, the moment I saw the instrument. I sat gazing at him, spell-bound. But he now reclined on his settle, taking very little notice of me, and talking principally about turnips.

There was a delicious sense of cleaning-up and making a quiet pause before going on in life afresh, in our village on Saturday nights, which stimulated Joe to dare to stay out half an hour longer on Saturdays than at other times. The half hour and the rum-and-water running out together, Joe got up to go, and took me by the hand.

"Stop half a moment, Mr. Gargery," said the strange man. "I think I've got a bright new shilling somewhere in my pocket, and if I have, the boy shall have it."

He looked it out from a handful of small change, folded it in some crumpled paper, and gave it to me. "Yours!" said he. "Mind! Your own."

I thanked him, staring at him far beyond the bounds of good manners, and holding tight to Joe. He gave Joe good-night, and he gave Mr. Wopsle good-night (who went out with us), and he gave me only a look with his aiming eye— no, not a look, for he shut it up, but wonders may be done with an eye by hiding it.

On the way home, if I had been in a humour for talking, the talk must have been all on my side, for Mr. Wopsle parted from us at the door of the Jolly Bargemen, and Joe went all the way home with his mouth wide open, to rinse the rum out with as much air as possible. But I was in a manner stupefied by this turning up of my old misdeed and old acquaintance, and could think of nothing else.

My sister was not in a very bad temper when we presented ourselves in the kitchen, and Joe was encouraged by that unusual circumstance to tell her about the bright shilling. "A bad un, I'll be bound," said Mrs. Joe, triumphantly, " or he wouldn't have given it to the boy! Let's look at it."

I took it out of the paper, and it proved to be a good one. "But what's this?" said Mrs. Joe, throwing down the shilling and catching up the paper. "Two One-Pound notes?"

Nothing less than two fat sweltering one-pound notes that seemed to have been on terms of the warmest intimacy with all the cattle markets in the county. Joe caught up his hat again, and ran with them to the Jolly Bargemen to restore them to their owner. While he was gone I sat down on my usual stool and looked vacantly at my sister, feeling pretty sure that the man would not be there.

Presently Joe came back, saying that the man was gone, but that he, Joe, had left word at the Three Jolly Bargemen concerning the notes. Then my sister sealed them up in a piece of paper, and put them under some dried rose-leaves in an ornamental tea-pot on the top of a press in the state parlour. There they remained a nightmare to me many and many a night and day.

I had sadly broken sleep when I got to bed, through thinking of the strange man taking aim at me with his invisible gun, and of the guiltily coarse and common thing it was, to be on secret terms of conspiracy with convicts—a feature in my low career that I had previously forgotten. I was haunted by the file too. A dread possessed me that when I least expected it, the file would reappear. I coaxed myself to sleep by thinking of Miss Havisham's next Wednesday; and in my sleep I saw the file coming at me out of a door, without seeing who held it, and I screamed myself awake.

CHAPTER XI

At the appointed time I returned to Miss Havisham's, and my hesitating ring at the gate brought out Estella. She locked it after admitting me, as she had done before, and again preceded me into the dark passage where her candle stood. She took no notice of me until she had the candle in her hand, when she looked over her shoulder, superciliously saying, "You are to come this way to-day," and took me to quite another part of the house.

The passage was a long one, and seem to pervade the whole square basement of the Manor House. We traversed but one side of the square, however, and at the end of it she stopped and put her candle down and opened a door. Here, the daylight reappeared, and I found myself in a small paved court-yard, the opposite side of which was formed by a detached dwelling-house, that looked as if it had once belonged to the manager or head clerk of the extinct brewery. There was a clock in the outer wall of this house. Like the clock in Miss Havisham's room, and like Miss Havisham's watch, it had stopped at twenty minutes to nine.

We went in at the door, which stood open, and into a gloomy room with a low ceiling, on the ground floor at the back. There was some company in the room, and Estella said to me as she joined it, "You are to go and stand there, boy, till you are wanted." "There" being the window, I crossed to it, and stood "there," in a very uncomfortable state of mind, looking out.

It opened to the ground, and looked into a most miserable corner of the neglected garden, upon a rank ruin of cabbage-stalks, and one box-tree that had been clipped round long ago, like a pudding, and had a new growth at the top of it, out of shape and of a different colour, as if that part of the pudding had stuck to the saucepan and got burnt. This was my homely thought, as I contemplated the box-tree. There had been some light snow, overnight, and it lay nowhere else to my knowledge ; but it had not quite melted from the

cold shadow of this bit of garden, and the wind caught it up
in little eddies and threw it at the window, as if it pelted me
for coming there.

I divined that my coming had stopped conversation in the
room, and that its other occupants were looking at me.
I could see nothing of the room except the shining of the fire
in the window glass, but I stiffened in all my joints with the
consciousness that I was under close inspection.

There were three ladies in the room and one gentleman.
Before I had been standing at the window five minutes, they
somehow conveyed to me that they were all toadies and
humbugs, but that each of them pretended not to know that
the others were toadies and humbugs : because the admission
that he or she did know it, would have made him or her out
to be a toady and humbug.

They all had a listless and dreary air of waiting somebody's
pleasure, and the most talkative of the ladies had to speak
quite rigidly to suppress a yawn. This lady, whose name
was Camilla, very much reminded me of my sister, with the
difference that she was older, and (as I found when I caught
sight of her) of a blunter cast of features. Indeed, when
I knew her better I began to think it was a Mercy she had
any features at all, so very blank and high was the dead wall
of her face.

"Poor dear soul!" said this lady, with an abruptness
of manner quite my sister's. "Nobody's enemy but his
own!"

"It would be much more commendable to be somebody
else's enemy," said the gentleman ; "far more natural."

"Cousin Raymond," observed another lady, "we are to
love our neighbour."

"Sarah Pocket," returned Cousin Raymond, "if a man is
not his own neighbour, who is ?"

Miss Pocket laughed, and Camilla laughed and said (checking a yawn), "The idea!" But I thought they seemed to
think it rather a good idea too. The other lady, who had
not spoken yet, said gravely and emphatically, "*Very* true!"

"Poor soul!" Camilla presently went on (I knew they
had all been looking at me in the mean time), "he is so
very strange! Would any one believe that when Tom's wife
died, he actually could not be induced to see the importance
of the children's having the deepest of trimmings to their
mourning? 'Good Lord!' says he, 'Camilla, what can it

"Now?" said she. "You little coarse monster, what do you think of me now?"

"I shall not tell you."

"Because you are going to tell up-stairs. Is that it?"

"No," said I, "that's not it."

"Why don't you cry again, you little wretch?"

"Because I'll never cry for you again," said I. Which was, I suppose, as false a declaration as ever was made; for I was inwardly crying for her then, and I know what I know of the pain she cost me afterwards.

We went on our way up-stairs after this episode; and, as we were going up, we met a gentleman groping his way down.

"Whom have we here?" asked the gentleman, stopping and looking at me.

"A boy," said Estella.

He was a burly man of an exceedingly dark complexion, with an exceedingly large head and a corresponding large hand. He took my chin in his large hand and turned up my face to have a look at me by the light of the candle. He was prematurely bald on the top of his head, and had bushy black eyebrows that wouldn't lie down, but stood up bristling. His eyes were set very deep in his head, and were disagreeably sharp and suspicious. He had a large watch-chain, and strong black dots where his beard and whiskers would have been if he had let them. He was nothing to me, and I could have had no foresight then, that he ever would be anything to me, but it happened that I had this opportunity of observing him well.

"Boy of the neighbourhood? Hey?" said he.

"Yes, sir," said I.

"How do you come here?"

"Miss Havisham sent for me, sir," I explained.

"Well! Behave yourself. I have a pretty large experience of boys, and you're a bad set of fellows. Now mind!" said he, biting the side of his great forefinger as he frowned at me, "you behave yourself!"

With these words he released me—which I was glad of, for his hand smelt of scented soap—and went his way down-stairs. I wondered whether he could be a doctor; but no, I thought; he couldn't be a doctor, or he would have a quieter and more persuasive manner. There was not much time to consider the subject, for we were soon in Miss Havisham's signify so long as the poor bereaved little things are black ? ' So like Matthew! The idea ! "

" Good points in him, good points in him," said Cousin Raymond ; " Heaven forbid I should deny good points in him ; but he never had, and he never will have, any sense of the proprieties."

" You know I was obliged," said Camilla. " I was obliged to be firm. I said, ' It will not do, for the credit of the family.' I told him that, without deep trimmings, the family was disgraced. I cried about it from breakfast till dinner. I injured my digestion. And at last he flung out in his violent way, and said, with a D, ' Then do as you like.' Thank Goodness it will always be a consolation to me to know that I instantly went out in a pouring rain and bought the things."

" He paid for them, did he not ? " asked Estella.

" It's not the question, my dear child, who paid for them," returned Camilla. " I bought them. And I shall often think of that with peace, when I wake up in the night."

The ringing of a distant bell, combined with the echoing of some cry or call along the passage by which I had come, interrupted the conversation and caused Estella to say to me, " Now, boy ! " On my turning round, they all looked at me with the utmost contempt, and, as I went out, I heard Sarah Pocket say, " Well, I am sure ! What next ! " and Camilla add, with indignation, " Was there ever such a fancy ! The i-d-e-a ! "

As we were going with our candle along the dark passage, Estella stopped all of a sudden, and, facing round, said in her taunting manner, with her face quite close to mine :

" Well ? "

" Well, miss," I answered, almost falling over her and checking myself.

She stood looking at me, and of course I stood looking at her.

" Am I pretty ? "

" Yes ; I think you are very pretty."

" Am I insulting ? "

" Not so much so as you were last time," said I.

" Not so much so ? "

" No."

She fired when she asked the last question, and she slapped my face with such force as she had, when I answered it.

room, where she and everything else were just as I had left them. Estella left me standing near the door, and I stood there until Miss Havisham cast her eyes upon me from the dressing-table.

"So!" she said, without being startled or surprised; "the days have worn away, have they?"

"Yes, ma'am. To-day is——"

"There, there, there!" with the impatient movement of her fingers. "I don't want to know. Are you ready to play?"

I was obliged to answer in some confusion, "I don't think I am, ma'am."

"Not at cards again?" she demanded with a searching look.

"Yes, ma'am; I could do that, if I was wanted."

"Since this house strikes you old and grave, boy," said Miss Havisham, impatiently, "and you are unwilling to play, are you willing to work?"

I could answer this inquiry with a better heart than I had been able to find for the other question, and I said I was quite willing.

"Then go into that opposite room," said she, pointing at the door behind me with her withered hand, "and wait there till I come."

I crossed the staircase landing, and entered the room she indicated. From that room, too, the daylight was completely excluded, and it had an airless smell that was oppressive. A fire had been lately kindled in the damp old-fashioned grate, and it was more disposed to go out than to burn up, and the reluctant smoke which hung in the room seemed colder than the clearer air—like our own marsh mist. Certain wintry branches of candles on the high chimney-piece faintly lighted the chamber; or, it would be more expressive to say, faintly troubled its darkness. It was spacious, and I dare say had once been handsome, but every discernible thing in it was covered with dust and mould, and dropping to pieces. The most prominent object was a long table with a table-cloth spread on it, as if a feast had been in preparation when the house and the clocks all stopped to-gether. An épergne or centre-piece of some kind was in the middle of this cloth; it was so heavily overhung with cob-webs that its form was quite undistinguishable; and, as I looked along the yellow expanse out of which I remember its seeming to grow, like a black fungus, I saw speckled-legged spiders with blotchy bodies running home to it, and

running out from it, as if some circumstance of the
greatest public importance had just transpired in the spider
community.

I heard the mice too, rattling behind the panels, as if the
same occurrence were important to their interests. But the
blackbeetles took no notice of the agitation, and groped
about the hearth in a ponderous elderly way, as if they were
short-sighted and hard of hearing, and not on terms with
one another.

These crawling things had fascinated my attention, and I
was watching them from a distance, when Miss Havisham
laid a hand upon my shoulder. In her other hand she had
a crutch-headed stick on which she leaned, and she looked
like the Witch of the place.

"This," said she, pointing to the long table with her
stick, "is where I will be laid when I am dead. They shall
come and look at me here."

With some vague misgiving that she might get upon the
table then and there and die at once, the complete realisation
of the ghastly waxwork at the Fair, I shrank under her
touch.

"What do you think that is?" she asked me, again
pointing with her stick; "that, where those cobwebs are?"

"I can't guess what it is, ma'am."

"It's a great cake. A bride-cake. Mine!"

She looked all round the room in a glaring manner, and
then said, leaning on me while her hand twitched my
shoulder, "Come, come, come! Walk me, walk me!"

I made out from this, that the work I had to do, was to
walk Miss Havisham round and round the room. Accordingly, I started at once, and she leaned upon my shoulder,
and we went away at a pace that might have been an imitation (founded on my first impulse under that roof) of Mr.
Pumblechook's chaise-cart.

She was not physically strong, and after a little time said,
"Slower!" Still, we went at an impatient fitful speed, and
as we went, she twitched the hand upon my shoulder, and
worked her mouth, and led me to believe that we were going
fast because her thoughts went fast. After a while she said,
"Call Estella!" so I went out on the landing and roared
that name as I had done on the previous occasion. When
her light appeared, I returned to Miss Havisham, and we
started away again round and round the room.

"WHAT DO YOU THINK THAT IS?"

If only Estella had come to be a spectator of our proceedings, I should have felt sufficiently discontented; but, as she brought with her the three ladies and the gentleman whom I had seen below, I didn't know what to do. In my politeness I would have stopped; but, Miss Havisham twitched my shoulder, and we posted on—with a shamefaced consciousness on my part that they would think it was all my doing.

"Dear Miss Havisham," said Miss Sarah Pocket. "How well you look!"

"I do not," returned Miss Havisham. "I am yellow skin and bone."

Camilla brightened when Miss Pocket met with this rebuff; and she murmured, as she plaintively contemplated Miss Havisham, "Poor dear soul! Certainly not to be expected to look well, poor thing. The idea!"

"And how are *you*?" said Miss Havisham to Camilla. As we were close to Camilla then, I would have stopped as a matter of course, only Miss Havisham wouldn't stop. We swept on, and I felt that I was highly obnoxious to Camilla.

"Thank you, Miss Havisham," she returned, "I am as well as can be expected."

"Why, what's the matter with you?" asked Miss Havisham, with exceeding sharpness.

"Nothing worth mentioning," replied Camilla. "I don't wish to make a display of my feelings, but I have habitually thought of you more in the night than I am quite equal to."

"Then don't think of me," retorted Miss Havisham.

"Very easily said!" remarked Camilla, amiably repressing a sob, while a hitch came into her upper lip, and her tears overflowed. "Raymond is a witness what ginger and sal volatile I am obliged to take in the night. Raymond is a witness what nervous jerkings I have in my legs. Chokings and nervous jerkings, however, are nothing new to me when I think with anxiety of those I love. If I could be less affectionate and sensitive, I should have a better digestion and an iron set of nerves. I am sure I wish it could be so. But as to not thinking of you in the night—the idea!" Here, a burst of tears.

The Raymond referred to, I understood to be the gentleman present, and him I understood to be Mr. Camilla. He came to the rescue at this point, and said in a consolatory and complimentary voice, " Camilla, my dear, it is well known that your family feelings are gradually undermining you to the extent of making one of your legs shorter than the other."

" I am not aware," observed the grave lady whose voice I had heard but once, " that to think of any person is to make a great claim upon that person, my dear."

Miss Sarah Pocket, whom I now saw to be a little dry brown corrugated old woman, with a small face that might have been made of walnut shells, and a large mouth like a cat's without the whiskers, supported this position by saying, " No, indeed, my dear. Hem ! "

" Thinking is easy enough," said the grave lady.

" What is easier, you know ? " assented Miss Sarah Pocket.

" Oh, yes, yes ! " cried Camilla, whose fermenting feelings appeared to rise from her legs to her bosom. " It's all very true ! It's a weakness to be so affectionate, but I can't help it. No doubt my health would be much better if it was otherwise, still I wouldn't change my disposition if I could. It's the cause of much suffering, but it's a consolation to know I possess it, when I wake up in the night." Here another burst of feeling.

Miss Havisham and I had never stopped all this time, but kept going round and round the room : now, brushing against the skirts of the visitors : now, giving them the whole length of the dismal chambers.

" There's Matthew ! " said Camilla. " Never mixing with any natural ties, never coming here to see how Miss Havisham is ! I have taken to the sofa with my stay-lace cut, and have lain there hours, insensible, with my head over the side, and my hair all down, and my feet I don't know where——"

(" Much higher than your head, my love," said Mr. Camilla.)

" I have gone off into that state, hours and hours, on account of Matthew's strange and inexplicable conduct, and nobody has thanked me."

" Really I must say I should think not ! " interposed the grave lady.

" You see, my dear," added Miss Sarah Pocket (a blandly vicious personage), " the question to put to yourself is, who did you expect to thank you, my love ? "

"Without expecting any thanks, or anything of the sort," resumed Camilla, "I have remained in that state hours and hours, and Raymond is a witness of the extent to which I have choked, and what the total inefficacy of ginger has been, and I have been heard at the pianoforte-tuner's across the street, where the poor mistaken children have even supposed it to be pigeons cooing at a distance—and now to be told——" Here Camilla put her hand to her throat, and began to be quite chemical as to the formation of new combinations there.

When this same Matthew was mentioned, Miss Havisham stopped me and herself, and stood looking at the speaker. This change had a great influence in bringing Camilla's chemistry to a sudden end.

"Matthew will come and see me at last," said Miss Havisham, sternly, "when I am laid on that table. That will be his place—there," striking the table with her stick, "at my head! And yours will be there! And your husband's there! And Sarah Pocket's there! And Georgiana's there! Now you all know where to take your stations when you come to feast upon me. And now go!"

At the mention of each name, she had struck the table with her stick in a new place. She now said, "Walk me, walk me!" and we went on again.

"I suppose there's nothing to be done," exclaimed Camilla, "but comply and depart. It's something to have seen the object of one's love and duty, even for so short a time. I shall think of it with a melancholy satisfaction when I wake up in the night. I wish Matthew could have that comfort, but he sets it at defiance. I am determined not to make a display of my feelings, but it's very hard to be told one wants to feast on one's relations—as if one was a Giant—and to be told to go. The bare idea!"

Mr. Camilla interposing, as Mrs. Camilla laid her hand upon her heaving bosom, that lady assumed an unnatural fortitude of manner which I supposed to be expressive of an intention to drop and choke when out of view, and kissing her hand to Miss Havisham, was escorted forth. Sarah Pocket and Georgiana contended who should remain last; but, Sarah was too knowing to be outdone, and ambled round Georgiana with that artful slipperiness, that the latter was obliged to take precedence. Sarah Pocket then made her separate effect of departing with "Bless you, Miss Havisham dear !" and with a smile of forgiving pity on her walnut-shell countenance for the weaknesses of the rest.

While Estella was away lighting them down, Miss Havisham still walked with her hand on my shoulder, but more and more slowly. At last she stopped before the fire, and said, after muttering and looking at it some seconds :

"This is my birthday, Pip."

I was going to wish her many happy returns, when she lifted her stick.

"I don't suffer it to be spoken of. I don't suffer those who were here just now, or any one, to speak of it. They come here on the day, but they dare not refer to it."

Of course I made no further effort to refer to it.

"On this day of the year, long before you were born, this heap of decay," stabbing with her crutched stick at the pile of cobwebs on the table but not touching it, "was brought here. It and I have worn away together. The mice have gnawed at it, and sharper teeth than teeth of mice have gnawed at me."

She held the head of her stick against her heart as she stood looking at the table ; she in her once white dress, all yellow and withered ; the once white cloth all yellow and withered ; everything around, in a state to crumble under a touch.

"When the ruin is complete," said she, with a ghastly look, "and when they lay me dead, in my bride's dress on the bride's table—which shall be done, and which will be the finished curse upon him—so much the better if it is done on this day !"

She stood looking at the table as if she stood looking at her own figure lying there. I remained quiet. Estella returned, and she too remained quiet. It seemed to me that we continued thus a long time. In the heavy air of the room, and the heavy darkness that brooded in its remoter corners, I even had an alarming fancy that Estella and I might presently begin to decay.

At length, not coming out of her distraught state by degrees, but in an instant, Miss Havisham said, "Let me see you two play at cards ; why have you not begun ?" With that, we returned to her room, and sat down as before ; I was beggared, as before ; and again, as before, Miss Havisham watched us all the time, directed my attention to Estella's beauty, and made me notice it the more by trying her jewels on Estella's breast and hair.

Estella, for her part, likewise treated me as before ; except that she did not condescend to speak. When we had played some half-dozen games, a day was appointed for my return, and I was taken down into the yard to be fed in the former dog-like manner. There, too, I was again left to wander about as I liked.

It is not much to the purpose whether a gate in that garden wall which I had scrambled up to peep over on the last occasion was, on that last occasion, open or shut. Enough that I saw no gate then, and that I saw one now. As it stood open, and as I knew that Estella had let the visitors out—for, she had returned with the keys in her hand —I strolled into the garden, and strolled all over it. It was quite a wilderness, and there were old melon-frames and cucumber-frames in it, which seemed in their decline to have produced a spontaneous growth of weak attempts at pieces of old hats and boots, with now and then a weedy offshoot into the likeness of a battered saucepan.

When I had exhausted the garden and a greenhouse with nothing in it but a fallen-down grape-vine and some bottles, I found myself in the dismal corner upon which I had looked out of window. Never questioning for a moment that the house was now empty, I looked in at another window, and found myself, to my great surprise, exchanging a broad stare with a pale young gentleman with red eyelids and light hair.

This pale young gentleman quickly disappeared, and re-appeared beside me. He had been at his books when I had found myself staring at him, and I now saw that he was inky.

" Halloa !" said he, " young fellow ! "

Halloa being a general observation which I had usually observed to be best answered by itself, I said " Halloa ! " politely omitting young fellow.

" Who let *you* in ? " said he.

" Miss Estella."

" Who gave you leave to prowl about ? "

" Miss Estella."

" Come and fight," said the pale young gentleman.

What could I do but follow him ? I have often asked myself the question since : but what else could I do ? His manner was so final and I was so astonished, that I followed where he led, as if I had been under a spell.

"Stop a minute, though," he said, wheeling round before we had gone many paces. "I ought to give you a reason for fighting, too. There it is!" In a most irritating manner he instantly slapped his hands against one another, daintily flung one of his legs up behind him, pulled my hair, slapped his hands again, dipped his head, and butted it into my stomach.

The bull-like proceeding last mentioned, besides that it was unquestionably to be regarded in the light of a liberty, was particularly disagreeable just after bread and meat. I therefore hit out at him, and was going to hit out again, when he said, "Aha! Would you?" and began dancing backwards and forwards in a manner quite unparalleled within my limited experience.

"Laws of the game!" said he. Here, he skipped from his left leg on to his right. "Regular rules!" Here, he skipped from his right leg on to his left. "Come to the ground, and go through the preliminaries!" Here, he dodged backwards and forwards, and did all sorts of things while I looked helplessly at him.

I was secretly afraid of him when I saw him so dexterous; but I felt morally and physically convinced that his light head of hair could have had no business in the pit of my stomach, and that I had a right to consider it irrelevant when so obtruded on my attention. Therefore, I followed him without a word, to a retired nook of the garden, formed by the junction of two walls and screened by some rubbish. On his asking me if I was satisfied with the ground, and on my replying Yes, he begged my leave to absent himself for a moment, and quickly returned with a bottle of water and a sponge dipped in vinegar. "Available for both," he said, placing these against the wall. And then fell to pulling off, not only his jacket and waistcoat, but his shirt too, in a manner at once light-hearted, business-like, and blood-thirsty.

Although he did not look very healthy—having pimples on his face, and a breaking out on his mouth—these dreadful preparations quite appalled me. I judged him to be about my own age, but he was much taller, and he had a way of spinning himself about that was full of appearance. For the rest, he was a young gentleman in a grey suit (when not denuded for battle), with his elbows, knees, wrists, and heels considerably in advance of the rest of him as to development.

My heart failed me when I saw him squaring at me with every demonstration of mechanical nicety, and eyeing my anatomy as if he were minutely choosing his bone. I never have been so surprised in my life, as I was when I let out the first blow, and saw him lying on his back, looking up at me with a bloody nose and his face exceedingly fore-shortened.

But he was on his feet directly, and after sponging himself with a great show of dexterity began squaring again. The second greatest surprise I have ever had in my life was seeing him on his back again, looking up at me out of a black eye.

His spirit inspired me with great respect. He seemed to have no strength, and he never once hit me hard, and he was always knocked down; but he would be up again in a moment, sponging himself or drinking out of the water-bottle, with the greatest satisfaction in seconding himself according to form, and then came at me with an air and a show that made me believe he really was going to do for me at last. He got heavily bruised, for I am sorry to record that the more I hit him, the harder I hit him; but he came up again and again and again, until at last he got a bad fall with the back of his head against the wall. Even after that crisis in our affairs, he got up and turned round and round confusedly a few times, not knowing where I was; but finally went on his knees to his sponge and threw it up: at the same time panting out, "That means you have won."

He seemed so brave and innocent, that although I had not proposed the contest, I felt but a gloomy satisfaction in my victory. Indeed, I go so far as to hope that I regarded myself while dressing, as a species of savage young wolf, or other wild beast. However, I got dressed, darkly wiping my sanguinary face at intervals, and I said, "Can I help you?" and he said, "No thankee," and I said, "Good afternoon," and *he* said, "Same to you."

When I got into the court-yard, I found Estella waiting with the keys. But she neither asked me where I had been, nor why I had kept her waiting; and there was a bright flush upon her face, as though something had happened to delight her. Instead of going straight to the gate, too, she stepped back into the passage, and beckoned me.

"Come here! You may kiss me if you like."

I kissed her cheek as she turned it to me. I think I would have gone through a great deal to kiss her cheek. But I felt that the kiss was given to the coarse common boy as a piece of money might have been, and that it was worth nothing.

What with the birthday visitors, and what with the cards, and what with the fight, my stay had lasted so long, that when I neared home the light on the spit of sand off the point on the marshes was gleaming against a black night-sky, and Joe's furnace was flinging a path of fire across the road.

CHAPTER XII

My mind grew very uneasy on the subject of the pale young gentleman. The more I thought of the fight, and recalled the pale young gentleman on his back in various stages of puffy and incrimsoned countenance, the more certain it appeared that something would be done to me. I felt that the pale young gentleman's blood was on my head, and that the Law would avenge it. Without having any definite idea of the penalties I had incurred, it was clear to me that village boys could not go stalking about the country, ravaging the houses of gentlefolks and pitching into the studious youth of England, without laying themselves open to severe punishment. For some days, I even kept close at home, and looked out at the kitchen door with the greatest caution and trepidation before going on an errand, lest the officers of the County Jail should pounce upon me. The pale young gentleman's nose had stained my trousers, and I tried to wash out that evidence of my guilt in the dead of night. I had cut my knuckles against the pale young gentleman's teeth, and I twisted my imagination into a thousand tangles, as I devised incredible ways of accounting for that damnatory circumstance when I should be haled before the Judges.

When the day came round for my return to the scene of the deed of violence, my terrors reached their height. Whether myrmidons of Justice, specially sent down from London, would be lying in ambush behind the gate? Whether Miss Havisham, preferring to take personal vengeance for an outrage done to her house, might rise in those grave-clothes of hers, draw a pistol, and shoot me dead? Whether suborned boys—a numerous band of mercenaries— might be engaged to fall upon me in the brewery, and cuff me until I was no more? It was high testimony to my confidence in the spirit of the pale young gentleman, that I never imagined *him* accessory to these retaliations; they always came into my mind as the acts of injudicious relatives of his, goaded on by the state of his visage and an indignant sympathy with the family features.

However, go to Miss Havisham's I must, and go I did. And behold! nothing came of the late struggle. It was not alluded to in any way, and no pale young gentleman was to be discovered on the premises. I found the same gate open, and I explored the garden, and even looked in at the windows of the detached house; but, my view was suddenly stopped by the closed shutters within, and all was lifeless. Only in the corner where the combat had taken place, could I detect any evidence of the young gentleman's existence. There were traces of his gore in that spot, and I covered them with garden-mould from the eye of man.

On the broad landing between Miss Havisham's own room and that other room in which the long table was laid out, I saw a garden-chair—a light chair on wheels, that you pushed from behind. It had been placed there since my last visit, and I entered, that same day, on a regular occupation of pushing Miss Havisham in this chair (when she was tired of walking with her hand upon my shoulder) round her own room, and across the landing, and round the other room. Over and over and over again, we would make these journeys, and sometimes they would last as long as three hours at a stretch. I insensibly fall into a general mention of these journeys as numerous, because it was at once settled that I should return every alternate day at noon for these purposes, and because I am now going to sum up a period of at least eight or ten months.

As we began to be more used to one another, Miss Havisham talked more to me, and asked me such questions as what had I learnt and what was I going to be? I told her I was going to be apprenticed to Joe, I believed; and I enlarged upon my knowing nothing and wanting to know everything, in the hope that she might offer some help towards that desirable end. But she did not; on the contrary, she seemed to prefer my being ignorant. Neither did she ever give me any money or anything but my daily dinner—nor even stipulate that I should be paid for my services.

Estella was always about, and always let me in and out, but never told me I might kiss her again. Sometimes, she would coldly tolerate me; sometimes, she would condescend to me; sometimes, she would be quite familiar with me;

sometimes, she would tell me energetically that she hated me. Miss Havisham would often ask me in a whisper, or when we were alone, "Does she grow prettier and prettier, Pip?" And when I said Yes (for indeed she did), would seem to enjoy it greedily. Also, when we played at cards Miss Havisham would look on, with a miserly relish of Estella's moods, whatever they were. And sometimes, when her moods were so many and so contradictory of one another that I was puzzled what to say or do, Miss Havisham would embrace her with lavish fondness, murmuring something in her ear that sounded like "Break their hearts, my pride and hope, break their hearts and have no mercy!"

There was a song Joe used to hum fragments of at the forge, of which the burden was Old Clem. This was not a very ceremonious way of rendering homage to a patron saint; but I believe Old Clem stood in that relation towards smiths. It was a song that imitated the measure of beating upon iron, and was a mere lyrical excuse for the introduction of Old Clem's respected name. Thus, you were to hammer boys round—Old Clem! With a thump and a sound—Old Clem! Beat it out, beat it out—Old Clem! With a clink for the stout—Old Clem! Blow the fire, blow the fire—Old Clem! Roaring dryer, soaring higher—Old Clem! One day soon after the appearance of the chair, Miss Havisham suddenly saying to me, with the impatient movement of her fingers, "There, there, there! Sing!" I was surprised into crooning this ditty as I pushed her over the floor. It happened so to catch her fancy that she took it up in a low brooding voice as if she were singing in her sleep. After that, it became customary with us to have it as we moved about, and Estella would often join in; though the whole strain was so subdued, even when there were three of us, that it made less noise in the grim old house than the lightest breath of wind.

What could I become with these surroundings? How could my character fail to be influenced by them? Is it to be wondered at if my thoughts were dazed, as my eyes were, when I came out into the natural light from the misty yellow rooms?

Perhaps I might have told Joe about the pale young gentleman, if I had not previously been betrayed into those enormous inventions to which I had confessed. Under the circumstances, I felt that Joe could hardly fail to discern in the pale young gentleman, an appropriate passenger to be put into the black velvet coach ; therefore I said nothing of him. Besides : that shrinking from having Miss Havisham and Estella discussed, which had come upon me in the beginning, grew much more potent as time went on. I reposed complete confidence in no one but Biddy ; but I told poor Biddy everything. Why it came natural for me to do so, and why Biddy had a deep concern in everything I told her, I did not know then, though I think I know now.

Meanwhile, councils went on in the kitchen at home, fraught with almost insupportable aggravation to my exasperated spirit. That ass, Pumblechook, used often to come over of a night for the purpose of discussing my prospects with my sister ; and I really do believe (to this hour with less penitence than I ought to feel), that if these hands could have taken a linchpin out of his chaise-cart, they would have done it. The miserable man was a man of that confined stolidity of mind, that he could not discuss my prospects without having me before him—as it were, to operate upon—and he would drag me up from my stool (usually by the collar) where I was quiet in a corner, and, putting me before the fire as if I were going to be cooked, would begin by saying, "Now, Mum, here is this boy! Here is this boy which you brought up by hand. Hold up your head, boy, and be for ever grateful unto them which so did do. Now, Mum, with respections to this boy!" And then he would rumple my hair the wrong way—which from my earliest remembrance, as already hinted, I have in my soul denied the right of any fellow-creature to do—and would hold me before him by the sleeve : a spectacle of imbecility only to be equalled by himself.

Then he and my sister would pair off in such nonsensical speculations about Miss Havisham, and about what she would do with me and for me, that I used to want—quite painfully—to burst into spiteful tears, fly at Pumblechook, and pummel him all over. In these dialogues, my sister spoke to me as if she were morally wrenching one of my teeth out at every reference ; while Pumblechook himself, self-constituted my patron, would sit supervising me with a depreciatory eye, like the architect of my fortunes who thought himself engaged in a very unremunerative job.

In these discussions, Joe bore no part. But he was often talked at, while they were in progress, by reason of Mrs.

Joe's perceiving that he was not favourable to my being taken from the forge. I was fully old enough now, to be apprenticed to Joe ; and when Joe sat with the poker on his knees thoughtfully raking out the ashes between the lower bars, my sister would so distinctly construe that innocent action into opposition on his part, that she would dive at him, take the poker out of his hands, shake him, and put it away. There was a most irritating end to every one of these debates. All in a moment, with nothing to lead up to it, my sister would stop herself in a yawn, and catching sight of me as it were incidentally, would swoop upon me with "Come ! there's enough of *you !* You get along to bed ; *you*'ve given trouble enough for one night, I hope !" As if I had besought them as a favour to bother my life out.

We went on in this way for a long time, and it seemed likely that we should continue to go on in this way for a long time, when, one day, Miss Havisham stopped short as she and I were walking, she leaning on my shoulder ; and said with some displeasure :

"You are growing tall, Pip !"

I thought it best to hint, through the medium of a meditative look, that this might be occasioned by circumstances over which I had no control.

She said no more at the time ; but, she presently stopped and looked at me again ; and presently again ; and after that, looked frowning and moody. On the next day of my attendance, when our usual exercise was over, and I had landed her at her dressing-table, she stayed me with a movement of her impatient fingers :

"Tell me the name again of that blacksmith of yours."

"Joe Gargery, ma'am."

"Meaning the master you were to be apprenticed to ?"

"Yes, Miss Havisham."

"You had better be apprenticed at once. Would Gargery come here with you, and bring your indentures, do you think ?"

I signified that I had no doubt he would take it as an honour to be asked.

"Then let him come."

"At any particular time, Miss Havisham ?"

"There, there ! I know nothing about times. Let him come soon, and come along with you."

When I got home at night, and delivered this message for Joe, my sister "went on the Rampage," in a more alarming degree than at any previous period. She asked me and Joe whether we supposed she was door-mats under our feet, and how we dared to use her so, and what company we graciously thought she *was* fit for? When she had exhausted a torrent of such inquiries, she threw a candlestick at Joe, burst into a loud sobbing, got out the dustpan—which was always a very bad sign—put on her coarse apron, and began cleaning up to a terrible extent. Not satisfied with a dry cleaning, she took to a pail and scrubbing-brush, and cleaned us out of house and home, so that we stood shivering in the back-yard. It was ten o'clock at night before we ventured to creep in again, and then she asked Joe why he had not married a Negress Slave at once? Joe offered no answer, poor fellow, but stood feeling his whiskers and looking dejectedly at me, as if he thought it really might have been a better speculation.

CHAPTER XIII

It was a trial to my feelings, on the next day but one, to see Joe arraying himself in his Sunday clothes to accompany me to Miss Havisham's. However, as he thought his court-suit necessary to the occasion, it was not for me to tell him that he looked far better in his working dress; the rather, because I knew he made himself so dreadfully uncomfortable, entirely on my account, and that it was for me he pulled up his shirt-collar so very high behind, that it made the hair on the crown of his head stand up like a tuft of feathers.

At breakfast-time, my sister declared her intention of going to town with us, and being left at Uncle Pumblechook's, and called for "when we had done with our fine ladies"—a way of putting the case, from which Joe appeared inclined to augur the worst. The forge was shut up for the day, and Joe inscribed in chalk upon the door (as it was his custom to do on the very rare occasions when he was not at work) the monosyllable HOUT, accompanied by a sketch of an arrow supposed to be flying in the direction he had taken.

We walked to town, my sister leading the way in a very large beaver bonnet, and carrying a basket like the Great Seal of England in plaited straw, a pair of pattens, a spare shawl, and an umbrella, though it was a fine bright day. I am not quite clear whether these articles were carried penitentially or ostentatiously; but I rather think they were displayed as articles of property—much as Cleopatra or any other sovereign lady on the Rampage might exhibit her wealth in a pageant or procession.

When we came to Pumblechook's, my sister bounced in and left us. As it was almost noon, Joe and I held straight on to Miss Havisham's house. Estella opened the gate as usual, and, the moment she appeared, Joe took his hat off and stood weighing it by the brim in both his hands: as if he had some urgent reason in his mind for being particular to half a quarter of an ounce.

Estella took no notice of either of us, but led us the way that I knew so well. I followed next to her, and Joe came last. When I looked back at Joe in the long passage, he was still weighing his hat with the greatest care, and was coming after us in long strides on the tips of his toes.

Estella told me we were both to go in, so I took Joe by the coat-cuff and conducted him into Miss Havisham's presence. She was seated at her dressing-table, and looked round at us immediately.

"Oh!" said she to Joe. "You are the husband of the sister of this boy?"

I could hardly have imagined dear old Joe looking so unlike himself or so like some extraordinary bird; standing, as he did, speechless, with his tuft of feathers ruffled, and his mouth open as if he wanted a worm.

"You are the husband," repeated Miss Havisham, "of the sister of this boy?"

It was very aggravating; but, throughout the interview, Joe persisted in addressing Me instead of Miss Havisham.

"Which I meantersay, Pip," Joe now observed, in a manner that was at once expressive of forcible argumentation, strict confidence, and great politeness, "as I hup and married your sister, and I were at the time what you might call (if you was any ways inclined) a single man."

"Well!" said Miss Havisham. "And you have reared the boy, with the intention of taking him for your apprentice; is that so, Mr. Gargery?"

"You know, Pip," replied Joe, "as you and me were ever friends, and it were looked for'ard to betwixt us, as being calc'lated to lead to larks. Not but what, Pip, if you had ever made objections to the business—such as its being open to black and sut, or such-like—not but what they would have been attended to, don't you see?"

"Has the boy," said Miss Havisham, "ever made any objection? Does he like the trade?"

"Which it is well beknown to yourself, Pip," returned Joe, strengthening his former mixture of argumentation, confidence, and politeness, "that it were the wish of your own hart." (I saw the idea suddenly break upon him that he would adapt his epitaph to the occasion, before he went on to say) "And there weren't no objection on your part, and Pip it were the great wish of your hart!"

It was quite in vain for me to endeavour to make him

sensible that he ought to speak to Miss Havisham. The more I made faces and gestures to him to do it, the more confidential, argumentative, and polite, he persisted in being to Me.

"Have you brought his indentures with you?" asked Miss Havisham.

"Well, Pip, you know," replied Joe, as if that were a little unreasonable, "you yourself see me put 'em in my 'at, and therefore you know as they are here." With which he took them out, and gave them, not to Miss Havisham, but to me. I am afraid I was ashamed of the dear good fellow —I *know* I was ashamed of him—when I saw that Estella stood at the back of Miss Havisham's chair, and that her eyes laughed mischievously. I took the indentures out of his hand and gave them to Miss Havisham.

"You expected," said Miss Havisham, as she looked them over, "no premium with the boy?"

"Joe!" I remonstrated; for he made no reply at all. "Why don't you answer——"

"Pip," returned Joe, cutting me short as if he were hurt, "which I meantersay that were not a question requiring a answer betwixt yourself and me, and which you know the answer to be full well No. You know it to be No, Pip, and wherefore should I say it?"

Miss Havisham glanced at him as if she understood what he really was, better than I had thought possible, seeing what he was there; and took up a little bag from the table beside her.

"Pip has earned a premium here," she said, "and here it is. There are five-and-twenty guineas in this bag. Give it to your master, Pip!"

As if he were absolutely out of his mind with the wonder awakened in him by her strange figure and the strange room, Joe, even at this pass, persisted in addressing me.

"This is very liberal on your part, Pip," said Joe, "and it is as such received and grateful welcome, though never looked for, far nor near nor nowheres. And now, old chap," said Joe, conveying to me a sensation, first of burning and then of freezing, for I felt as if that familiar expression were applied to Miss Havisham; "and now, old chap, may we do our duty! May you and me do our duty, both on us by one and another, and by them which your liberal present— have—conweyed—to be—for the satisfaction of mind—of—

them as never—" here Joe showed that he felt he had fallen into frightful difficulties, until he triumphantly rescued himself with the words, "and from myself far be it!" These words had such a round and convincing sound for him that he said them twice.

"Good-bye, Pip!" said Miss Havisham. "Let them out, Estella."

"Am I to come again, Miss Havisham?" I asked.

"No. Gargery is your master now. Gargery! One word!"

Thus calling him back as I went out of the door, I heard her say to Joe, in a distinct emphatic voice, "The boy has been a good boy here, and that is his reward. Of course, as an honest man, you will expect no other and no more."

How Joe got out of the room, I have never been able to determine; but I know that when he did get out he was steadily proceeding up-stairs instead of coming down, and was deaf to all remonstrances until I went after him and laid hold of him. In another minute we were outside the gate, and it was locked, and Estella was gone. When we stood in the daylight alone again, Joe backed up against a wall, and said to me, "Astonishing!" And there he remained so long, saying "Astonishing" at intervals, so often, that I began to think his senses were never coming back. At length, he prolonged his remark into "Pip, I do assure *you* this is as-TON-ishing!" and so, by degrees, became conversational and able to walk away.

I have reason to think that Joe's intellects were brightened by the encounter they had passed through, and that on our way to Pumblechook's, he invented a subtle and deep design. My reason is to be found in what took place in Mr. Pumblechook's parlour: where, on our presenting ourselves, my sister sat in conference with that detested seedsman.

"Well!" cried my sister, addressing us both at once. "And what's happened to *you*? I wonder you condescend to come back to such poor society as this, I am sure I do!"

"Miss Havisham," said Joe, with a fixed look at me, like an effort of remembrance, "made it wery partick'ler that we should give her—were it compliments or respects, Pip?"

"Compliments," I said.

"Which that were my own belief," answered Joe—" her compliments to Mrs. J. Gargery——"

"Much good they'll do me!" observed my sister: but rather gratified too.

"And wishing," pursued Joe, with another fixed look at me, like another effort of remembrance, "that the state of Miss Havisham's elth were sitch as would have—allowed, were it, Pip?"

"Of her having the pleasure," I added.

"Of ladies' company," said Joe. And drew a long breath.

"Well!" cried my sister, with a mollified glance at Mr. Pumblechook. "She might have had the politeness to send that message at first, but it's better late than never. And what did she give young Rantipole here?"

"She giv' him," said Joe, "nothing."

Mrs. Joe was going to break out, but Joe went on.

"What she giv'," said Joe, "she giv' to his friends. 'And by his friends,' were her explanation, 'I mean into the hands of his sister, Mrs. J. Gargery.' Them were her words; 'Mrs. J. Gargery.' She mayn't have know'd," added Joe, with an appearance of reflection, "whether it were Joe or Jorge."

My sister looked at Pumblechook: who smoothed the elbows of his wooden armchair, and nodded at her and at the fire, as if he had known all about it beforehand.

"And how much have you got?" asked my sister, laughing. Positively, laughing!

"What would present company say to ten pound?" demanded Joe.

"They'd say," returned my sister curtly, "pretty well. Not too much, but pretty well."

"It's more than that, then," said Joe.

That fearful impostor, Pumblechook, immediately nodded, and said, as he rubbed the arms of his chair: "It's more than that, Mum."

"Why, you don't mean to say——" began my sister.

"Yes, I do, Mum," said Pumblechook; "but wait a bit. Go on, Joseph. Good in you! Go on!"

"What would present company say," proceeded Joe, "to twenty pound?"

"Handsome would be the word," returned my sister.

"Well then," said Joe, "it's more than twenty pound."

That abject hypocrite, Pumblechook, nodded again, and said with a patronising laugh, "It's more than that, Mum Good again! Follow her up, Joseph!"

"Then to make an end of it," said Joe, delightedly, handing the bag to my sister; "it's five-and-twenty pound."

"It's five-and-twenty pound, Mum," echoed that basest of swindlers, Pumblechook, rising to shake hands with her; "and it's no more than your merits (as I said when my opinion was asked), and I wish you joy of the money!"

If the villain had stopped here, his case would have been sufficiently awful, but he blackened his guilt by proceeding to take me into custody, with a right of patronage that left all his former criminality far behind.

"Now you see, Joseph and wife," said Mr. Pumblechook, as he took me by the arm above the elbow, "I am one of them that always go right through with what they've begun. This boy must be bound out of hand. That's *my* way. Bound out of hand."

"Goodness knows, Uncle Pumblechook," said my sister (grasping the money), "we're deeply beholden to you."

"Never mind me, Mum," returned that diabolical cornchandler. "A pleasure's a pleasure all the world over. But this boy, you know; we must have him bound. I said I'd see to it—to tell you the truth."

The Justices were sitting in the Town Hall near at hand, and we at once went over to have me bound apprentice to Joe in the Magisterial presence. I say, we went over, but I was pushed over by Pumblechook, exactly as if I had that moment picked a pocket or fired a rick; indeed, it was the general impression in Court that I had been taken redhanded; for, as Pumblechook shoved me before him through the crowd, I heard some people say, "What's he done?" and others, "He's a young 'un, too, but looks bad, don't he?" One person of mild and benevolent aspect even gave me a tract ornamented with a woodcut of a malevolent young man fitted up with a perfect sausage-shop of fetters, and entitled, To BE READ IN MY CELL.

The Hall was a queer place, I thought, with higher pews in it than a church—and with people hanging over the pews looking on—and with mighty Justices (one with a powdered head) leaning back in chairs, with folded arms, or taking snuff, or going to sleep, or writing, or reading the newspapers—and with some shining black portraits on the walls, which my unartistic eye regarded as a composition of hard-bake and sticking-plaister. Here, in a corner, my indentures were duly signed and attested, and I was "bound;" Mr. Pumblechook holding me all the while as if we had looked in on our way to the scaffold, to have those little preliminaries disposed of.

When we had come out again, and had got rid of the boys who had been put into great spirits by the expectation of seeing me publicly tortured, and who were much disappointed to find that my friends were merely rallying round me, we went back to Pumblechook's. And there my sister became so excited by the twenty-five guineas, that nothing would serve her but we must have a dinner out of that windfall, at the Blue Boar, and that Mr. Pumblechook must go over in his chaise-cart, and bring the Hubbles and Mr. Wopsle.

It was agreed to be done; and a most melancholy day I passed. For it inscrutably appeared to stand to reason, in the minds of the whole company, that I was an excrescence on the entertainment. And to make it worse, they all asked me from time to time—in short, whenever they had nothing else to do—why I didn't enjoy myself? And what could I possibly do then, but say that I *was* enjoying myself—when I wasn't!

However, they were grown up and had their own way, and made the most of it. That swindling Pumblechook, exalted into the beneficent contriver of the whole occasion, actually took the top of the table; and, when he addressed them on the subject of my being bound, and had fiendishly congratulated them on my being liable to imprisonment if I played at cards, drank strong liquors, kept late hours or bad company, or indulged in other vagaries which the form of my *indentures* appeared to contemplate as next to inevitable, he placed me standing on a chair beside him to illustrate his remarks.

My only other remembrances of the great festival are, That they wouldn't let me go to sleep, but whenever they saw me dropping off, woke me up and told me to enjoy myself. That, rather late in the evening Mr. Wopsle gave us Collins's ode, and threw his blood-stain'd sword in thunder down, with such effect that a waiter came in and said, "The Commercials underneath sent up their compliments, and it wasn't the Tumblers' Arms." That, they

were all in excellent spirits on the road home, and sang
O Lady Fair! Mr. Wopsle taking the bass, and asserting
with a tremendously strong voice (in reply to the inquisitive
bore who leads that piece of music in a most impertinent
manner, by wanting to know all about everybody's private
affairs) that *he* was the man with his white locks flowing,
and that he was upon the whole the weakest pilgrim going.

Finally, I remember that when I got into my little bedroom, I was truly wretched, and had a strong conviction on
me that I should never like Joe's trade. I had liked it
once, but once was not now.

CHAPTER XIV

It is a most miserable thing to feel ashamed of home. There may be ..ck ingratitude in the thing, and the punishment may be retri...ve and we..ll deserved; but, that it is a miserable thing, I ca.. testify.

Home had never been ... .y pleasant place to me, because of my sister's temper. But, Joe had sanctified it, and I believed in it. I had believed in the best parlour as a most elegant saloon; I had believed in the front door, as a mysterious portal of the Temple of State whose solemn opening was attended with a sacrifice of roast fowls; I had believed in the kitchen as a chaste though not magnificent apartment; I had believed in the forge as the glowing road to manhood and independence. Within a single year all this was changed. Now, it was all coarse and common, and I would not have had Miss Havisham and Estella see it on any account.

How much of my ungracious condition of mind may have been my own fault, how much Miss Havisham's, how much my sister's, is now of no moment to me or to any one. The change was made in me; the thing was done. Well or ill done, excusably or inexcusably, it was done.

Once, it had seemed to me that when I should at last roll up my shirt-sleeves and go into the forge, Joe's 'prentice, I should be distinguished and happy. Now the reality was in my hold, I only felt that I was dusty with the dust of the small coal, and that I had a weight upon my daily remembrance to which the anvil was a feather. There have been occasions in my later life (I suppose as in most lives) when I have felt for a time as if a thick curtain had fallen on all its interest and romance, to shut me out from anything save dull endurance any more. Never has that curtain dropped so heavy and blank, as when my way in life lay stretched out straight before me through the newly-entered road of apprenticeship to Joe.

I remember that at a later period of my "time," I used to stand about the churchyard on Sunday evenings, when night

was falling, comparing my own perspective with the wind
marsh view, and making out some likeness between the
by thinking how flat and low both were, and how on bot
there came an unknown way and a dark mist and then th
sea. I was quite as dejected on the first working-day of m
apprenticeship as in that after-time : but I am glad to kno
that I never breathed a murmur to Joe while my indent
lasted. It is about the only thing I *am* glad to know o
myself in that connection.

For, though it includes what I proceed to add, all the
merit of what I proceed to add was Joe's. It was no
because I was faithful, but because Joe was faithful, that
I never ran away and went for a soldier or a sailor. It was
not because I had a strong sense of the virtue of industry,
but because Joe had a strong sense of the virtue of industry,
that I worked with tolerable zeal against the grain. It is
not possible to know how far the influence of any amiable
honest-hearted duty-doing man flies out into the world : but
it is very possible to know how it has touched one's self in
going by, and I know right well that any good that intermixed itself with my apprenticeship came of plain contented
Joe, and not of restless aspiring discontented me.

What I wanted, who can say? How can I say, when I
never knew? What I dreaded was, that in some unlucky
hour I, being at my grimiest and commonest, should lift up
my eyes and see Estella looking in at one of the wooden
windows of the forge. I was haunted by the fear that she
would, sooner or later, find me out, with a black face and
hands, doing the coarsest part of my work, and would exult
over me and despise me. Often after dark, when I was
pulling the bellows for Joe, and we were singing Old Clem,
and when the thought how we used to sing it at Miss
Havisham's would seem to show me Estella's face in the fire,
with her pretty hair fluttering in the wind and her eyes
scorning me,—often at such a time I would look towards
those panels of black night in the wall which the wooden
windows then were, and would fancy that I saw her just
drawing her face away, and would believe that she had come
at last.

After that, when we went in to supper, the place and the
meal would have a more homely look than ever, and I would
feel more ashamed of home than ever, in my own ungracious
breast.

CHAPTER XV

As I was getting too big for Mr. Wopsle's great-aunt's room, my education under that preposterous female terminated. Not, however, until Biddy had imparted to me everything she knew, from the little catalogue of prices, to a comic song she had once bought for a halfpenny. Although the only coherent part of the latter piece of literature were the opening lines,

> When I went to Lunnon town, sirs,
> > Too rul loo rul!
> > Too rul loo rul!
> Wasn't I done very brown, sirs?
> > Too rul loo rul!
> > Too rul loo rul!

—still, in my desire to be wiser, I got this composition by heart with the utmost gravity; nor do I recollect that I questioned its merit, except that I thought (as I still do) the amount of Too rul somewhat in excess of the poetry. In my hunger for information, I made proposals to Mr. Wopsle to bestow some intellectual crumbs upon me; with which he kindly complied. As it turned out, however, that he only wanted me for a dramatic lay-figure, to be contradicted and embraced and wept over and bullied and clutched and stabbed and knocked about in a variety of ways, I soon declined that course of instruction; though not until Mr. Wopsle in his poetic fury had severely mauled me.

Whatever I acquired, I tried to impart to Joe. This statement sounds so well, that I cannot in my conscience let it pass unexplained. I wanted to make Joe less ignorant and common, that he might be worthier of my society and less open to Estella's reproach.

The old Battery out on the marshes was our place of study, and a broken slate and a short piece of slate pencil were our educational implements: to which Joe always added a pipe of tobacco. I never knew Joe to remember anything from one Sunday to another, or to acquire, under my tuition, any piece of information whatever. Yet he would smoke his pipe at the Battery with a far more sagacious air than anywhere else—even with a learned air—as if he considered himself to be advancing immensely. Dear fellow, I hope he did.

It was pleasant and quiet, out there with the sails on the river passing beyond the earthwork, and sometimes, when the tide was low, looking as if they belonged to sunken ships that were still sailing on at the bottom of the water. Whenever I watched the vessels standing out to sea with their white sails spread, I somehow thought of Miss Havisham and Estella; and whenever the light struck aslant, afar off, upon a cloud or sail or green hill-side or water-line, it was just the same.—Miss Havisham and Estella and the strange house and the strange life appeared to have something to do with every-thing that was picturesque.

One Sunday when Joe, greatly enjoying his pipe, had so plumed himself on being "most awful dull," that I had given him up for the day, I lay on the earthwork for some time with my chin on my hand, descrying traces of Miss Havisham and Estella all over the prospect, in the sky and in the water, until at last I resolved to mention a thought concerning them that had been much in my head.

"Joe," said I; "don't you think I ought to pay Miss Havisham a visit?"

"Well, Pip," returned Joe, slowly considering. "What for?"

"What for, Joe? What is any visit made for?"

"There is some wisits p'r'aps," said Joe, "as for ever remains open to the question, Pip. But in regard of wisiting Miss Havisham. She might think you wanted something—expected something of her."

"Don't you think I might say that I did not, Joe?"

"You might, old chap," said Joe. "And she might credit it. Similarly, she mightn't."

Joe felt, as I did, that he had made a point there, and he pulled hard at his pipe to keep himself from weakening it by repetition.

"You see, Pip," Joe pursued, as soon as he was past that danger, "Miss Havisham done the handsome thing by you. When Miss Havisham done the handsome thing by you, she called me back to say to me as that were all."

"Yes, Joe. I heard her."

"ALL," Joe repeated, very emphatically.

"Yes, Joe. I tell you, I heard her."

"Which I meantersay, Pip, it might be that her meaning were—Make a end on it!—As you was!—Me to the North, and you to the South!—Keep in sunders!"

I had thought of that too, and it was very far from comforting to me to find that he had thought of it ; for it seemed to render it more probable.

"But, Joe."

"Yes, old chap."

"Here am I, getting on in the first year of my time, and, since the day of my being bound I have never thanked Miss Havisham, or asked after her, or shown that I remember her."

"That's true, Pip ; and unless you was to turn her out a set of shoes all four round—and which I meantersay as even a set of shoes all four round might not act acceptable as a present in a total wacancy of hoofs——"

"I don't mean that sort of remembrance, Joe ; I don't mean a present."

But Joe had got the idea of a present in his head and must harp upon it. "Or even," said he, "if you was helped to knocking her up a new chain for the front door—or say a gross or two of shark-headed screws for general use—or some light fancy article, such as a toasting-fork when she took her muffins—or a gridiron when she took a sprat or such like——"

"I don't mean any present at all, Joe," I interposed.

"Well," said Joe, still harping on it as though I had particularly pressed it, "if I was yourself, Pip, I wouldn't. No, I would *not*. For what's a door-chain when she's got one always up? And shark-headers is open to misrepresenta- tions. And if it was a toasting-fork, you'd go into brass and do yourself no credit. And the oncommonest workman can't show himself oncommon in a gridiron—for a gridiron IS a gridiron," said Joe, steadfastly impressing it upon me, as if he were endeavouring to rouse me from a fixed delusion, "and you may haim at what you like, but a gridiron it will come out, either by your leave or again your leave, and you can't help yourself——"

"My dear Joe," I cried in desperation, taking hold of his coat, "don't go on in that way. I never thought of making Miss Havisham any present."

"No, Pip," Joe assented, as if he had been contending for

that all along; "and what I say to you is, you are right, Pip."

"Yes, Joe; but what I wanted to say, was, that as we are rather slack just now, if you would give me a half-holiday to-morrow, I think I would go up-town and make a call on Miss Est—Havisham."

"Which her name," said Joe, gravely, "ain't Estavisham, Pip, unless she have been rechris'ened."

"I know, Joe, I know. It was a slip of mine. What do you think of it, Joe?"

In brief, Joe thought that if I thought well of it, he thought well of it. But he was particular in stipulating that if I were not received with cordiality, or if I were not encouraged to repeat my visit as a visit which had no ulterior object, but was simply one of gratitude for a favour received, then this experimental trip should have no successor. By these conditions I promised to abide.

Now, Joe kept a journeyman at weekly wages whose name was Orlick. He pretended that his christian name was Dolge—a clear impossibility—but he was a fellow of that obstinate disposition that I believe him to have been the prey of no delusion in this particular, but wilfully to have imposed that name upon the village as an affront to its understanding. He was a broad-shouldered loose-limbed swarthy fellow of great strength, never in a hurry, and always slouching. He never even seemed to come to his work on purpose, but would slouch in as if by mere accident; and when he went to the Jolly Bargemen to eat his dinner, or went away at night, he would slouch out, like Cain or the Wandering Jew, as if he had no idea where he was going, and no intention of ever coming back. He lodged at a sluice-keeper's out on the marshes, and on working days would come slouching from his hermitage, with his hands in his pockets and his dinner loosely tied in a bundle round his neck and dangling on his back. On Sundays he mostly lay all day on sluice-gates, or stood against ricks and barns. He always slouched, locomotively, with his eyes on the ground; and, when accosted or otherwise required to raise them, he looked up in a half resentful, half puzzled way, as though the only thought he ever had, was, that it was rather an odd and injurious fact that he should never be thinking.

This morose journeyman had no liking for me. When I was very small and timid, he gave me to understand that the Devil lived in a black corner of the forge, and that he knew the fiend very well : also that it was necessary to make up the fire, once in seven years, with a live boy, and that I might consider myself fuel. When I became Joe's 'prentice, Orlick was perhaps confirmed in some suspicion that I should displace him ; howbeit, he liked me still less. Not that he ever said anything, or did anything, openly importing hostility ; I only noticed that he always beat his sparks in my direction, and that whenever I sang Old Clem, he came in out of time.

Dolge Orlick was at work and present, next day, when I reminded Joe of my half-holiday. He said nothing at the moment, for he and Joe had just got a piece of hot iron between them, and I was at the bellows ; but by-and-by he said, leaning on his hammer :

"Now, master ! Sure you're not a going to favour only one of us ? If Young Pip has a half-holiday, do as much for Old Orlick." I suppose he was about five-and-twenty, but he usually spoke of himself as an ancient person.

"Why, what'll you do with a half-holiday, if you get it ? " said Joe.

"What'll *I* do with it ? What'll *he* do with it ? I'll do as much with it as *him*," said Orlick.

"As to Pip, he's going up-town," said Joe.

"Well then, as to Old Orlick, *he's* a going up-town," retorted that worthy. "Two can go up-town. Tain't only one wot can go up-town."

"Don't lose your temper," said Joe.

"Shall if I like," growled Orlick. "Some and their up-towning ! Now, master ! Come. No favouring in this shop. Be a man !"

The master refusing to entertain the subject until the journeyman was in a better temper, Orlick plunged at the furnace, drew out a red-hot bar, made at me with it as if he were going to run it through my body, whisked it round my head, laid it on the anvil, hammered it out—as if it were I, I thought, and the sparks were my spirting blood— and finally said, when he had hammered himself hot and the iron cold, and he again leaned on his hammer :

"Now, master !"

"Are you all right now ?" demanded Joe.

"Ah ! I am all right," said gruff Old Orlick.

"Then, as in general you stick to your work as well as most men," said Joe, "let it be a half-holiday for all."

My sister had been standing silent in the yard, within hearing—she was a most unscrupulous spy and listener—and she instantly looked in at one of the windows.

"Like you, you fool!" said she to Joe, "giving holidays to great idle hulkers like that. You are a rich man, upon my life, to waste wages in that way. I wish I was his master!"

"You'd be everybody's master if you durst," retorted Orlick, with an ill-favoured grin.

("Let her alone," said Joe.)

"I'd be a match for all noodles and all rogues," returned my sister, beginning to work herself into a mighty rage. "And I couldn't be a match for the noodles, without being a match for your master, who's the dunder-headed king of the noodles. And I couldn't be a match for the rogues, without being a match for you, who are the blackest-looking and the worst rogue between this and France. Now!"

"You're a foul shrew, Mother Gargery," growled the journeyman. "If that makes a judge of rogues, you ought to be a good 'un."

("Let her alone, will you?" said Joe.)

"What did you say?" cried my sister, beginning to scream. "What did you say? What did that fellow Orlick say to me, Pip? What did he call me, with my husband standing by? O! O! O!" Each of these exclamations was a shriek; and I must remark of my sister, what is equally true of all the violent women I have ever seen, that passion was no excuse for her, because it is undeniable that instead of lapsing into passion, she consciously and deliberately took extraordinary pains to force herself into it, and became blindly furious by regular stages; "what was the name that he gave me before the base man who swore to defend me? O! Hold me! O!"

"Ah-h-h!" growled the journeyman, between his teeth, "I'd hold you, if you was my wife. I'd hold you under the pump, and choke it out of you."

("I tell you, let her alone," said Joe.)

"Oh! To hear him!" cried my sister, with a clap of her hands and a scream together—which was her next stage. "To hear the names he's giving me! That Orlick! In my own house! Me, a married woman! With my husband

ORLICK WAS VERY SOON AMONG THE COAL-DUST

standing by! O! O!" Here my sister, after a fit of clappings and screamings, beat her hands upon her bosom and upon her knees, and threw her cap off, and pulled her hair down—which were the last stages on her road to frenzy. Being by this time a perfect Fury and a complete success, she made a dash at the door, which I had fortunately locked.

What could the wretched Joe do now, after his disregarded parenthetical interruptions, but stand up to his journeyman, and ask him what he meant by interfering betwixt himself and Mrs. Joe; and further whether he was man enough to come on? Old Orlick felt that the situation admitted of nothing less than coming on, and was on his defence straightway; so, without so much as pulling off their singed and burnt aprons, they went at one another, like two giants. But, if any man in that neighbourhood could stand up long against Joe, I never saw the man. Orlick, as if he had been of no more account than the pale young gentleman, was very soon among the coal-dust, and in no hurry to come out of it. Then Joe unlocked the door and picked up my sister, who had dropped insensible at the window (but who had seen the fight first, I think), and who was carried into the house and laid down, and who was recommended to revive, and would do nothing but struggle and clench her hands in Joe's hair. Then came that singular calm and silence which succeed all uproars; and then with the vague sensation which I have always connected with such a lull— namely, that it was Sunday, and somebody was dead—I went up-stairs to dress myself.

When I came down again, I found Joe and Orlick sweeping up, without any other traces of discomposure than a slit in one of Orlick's nostrils, which was neither expressive nor ornamental. A pot of beer had appeared from the Jolly Bargemen, and they were sharing it by turns in a peaceable manner. The lull had a sedative and philosophical influence on Joe, who followed me out into the road to say, as a parting observation that might do me good, "On the Rampage, Pip, and off the Rampage, Pip;—such is Life!"

With what absurd emotions (for, we think the feelings that are very serious in a man quite comical in a boy) I found myself again going to Miss Havisham's, matters little here. Nor, how I passed and repassed the gate many times before I could make up my mind to ring. Nor, how I de-

bated whether I should go away without ringing ; nor, how
I should undoubtedly have gone, if my time had been my
own, to come back.

Miss Sarah Pocket came to the gate.   No Estella.

"How, then ?   You here again ? " said Miss Pocket
"What do you want ? "

When I said that I only came to see how Miss Havisham
was, Sarah evidently deliberated whether or no she should
send me about my business.   But, unwilling to hazard the
responsibility, she let me in, and presently brought the sharp
message that I was to "come up."

Everything was unchanged, and Miss Havisham was alone
"Well ! " said she, fixing her eyes upon me.   "I hope you
want nothing ?   You'll get nothing."

"No indeed, Miss Havisham.   I only wanted you to know
that I am doing very well in my apprenticeship, and am
always much obliged to you."

"There, there ! " with the old restless fingers.   "Come
now and then ; come on your birthday.—Ay ! " she cried
suddenly, turning herself and her chair towards me.   "You
are looking round for Estella ?   Hey ? "

I had been looking round—in fact, for Estella—and I
stammered that I hoped she was well.

"Abroad," said Miss Havisham ;   "educating for a lady ;
far out of reach ; prettier than ever ; admired by all who see
her.   Do you feel that you have lost her ? "

There was such a malignant enjoyment in her utterance
of the last words, and she broke into such a disagreeable
laugh, that I was at a loss what to say.   She spared me the
trouble of considering, by dismissing me.   When the gate
was closed upon me by Sarah of the walnut-shell countenance, I felt more than ever dissatisfied with my home and
with my trade and with everything ; and that was all I took
by *that* motion.

As I was loitering along the High-street, looking in disconsolately at the shop windows, and thinking what I would
buy if I were a gentleman, who should come out of the book-
shop but Mr. Wopsle.   Mr. Wopsle had in his hand the
affecting tragedy of George Barnwell, in which he had that
moment invested sixpence, with the view of heaping every
word of it on the head of Pumblechook, with whom he was
going to drink tea.   No sooner did he see me, than he
appeared to consider that a special Providence had put

a 'prentice in his way to be read at; and he laid hold of me, and insisted on my accompanying him to the Pumblechookian parlour. As I knew it would be miserable at home, and as the nights were dark and the way was dreary, and almost any companionship on the road was better than none, I made no great resistance; consequently, we turned into Pumblechook's just as the street and the shops were lighting up.

As I never assisted at any other representation of George Barnwell, I don't know how long it may usually take; but I know very well that it took until half-past nine o'clock that night, and that when Mr. Wopsle got into Newgate, I thought he never would go to the scaffold, he became so much slower than at any former period of his disgraceful career. I thought it a little too much that he should complain of being cut short in his flower after all, as if he had not been running to seed, leaf after leaf, ever since his course began. This, however, was a mere question of length and wearisomeness. What stung me, was the identification of the whole affair with my unoffending self. When Barnwell began to go wrong, I declare I felt positively apologetic, Pumblechook's indignant stare so taxed me with it. Wopsle, too, took pains to present me in the worst light. At once ferocious and maudlin, I was made to murder my uncle with no extenuating circumstances whatever; Millwood put me down in argument, on every occasion; it became sheer monomania in my master's daughter to care a button for me; and all I can say for my gasping and procrastinating conduct on the fatal morning, is, that it was worthy of the general feebleness of my character. Even after I was happily hanged and Wopsle had closed the book, Pumblechook sat staring at me, and shaking his head, and saying, "Take warning, boy, take warning!" as if it were a well-known fact that I contemplated murdering a near relation, provided I could only induce one to have the weakness to become my benefactor.

It was a very dark night when it was all over, and when I set out with Mr. Wopsle on the walk home. Beyond town, we found a heavy mist out, and it fell wet and thick. The turnpike lamp was a blur, quite out of the lamp's usual place apparently, and its rays looked solid substance on the fog. We were noticing this, and saying how that the mist rose with a change of wind from a certain quarter of our marshes, when we came upon a man, slouching under the lee of the turnpike house.

"Halloa!" we said, stopping.   "Orlick there?"

"Ah!" he answered, slouching out.   "I was standing by, a minute, on the chance of company."

"You are late," I remarked.

Orlick not unnaturally answered, "Well?   And _you're_ late."

"We have been," said Mr. Wopsle, exalted with his late performance, "we have been indulging, Mr. Orlick, in an intellectual evening."

Old Orlick growled, as if he had nothing to say about that, and we all went on together.   I asked him presently whether he had been spending his half-holiday up and down town?

"Yes," said he, "all of it.   I come in behind yourself.   I didn't see you, but I must have been pretty close behind you. By-the-bye, the guns is going again."

"At the Hulks?" said I.

"Ay!   There's some of the birds flown from the cages. The guns have been going since dark, about.   You'll hear one presently."

In effect, we had not walked many yards further, when the well-remembered boom came towards us, deadened by the mist, and heavily rolled away along the low grounds by the river, as if it were pursuing and threatening the fugitives.

"A good night for cutting off in," said Orlick.   "We'd be puzzled how to bring down a jail-bird on the wing, to-night."

The subject was a suggestive one to me, and I thought about it in silence.   Mr. Wopsle, as the ill-requited uncle of the evening's tragedy, fell to meditating aloud in his garden at Camberwell.   Orlick, with his hands in his pockets, slouched heavily at my side.   It was very dark, very wet, very muddy, and so we splashed along.   Now and then, the sound of the signal cannon broke upon us again, and again rolled sulkily along the course of the river.   I kept myself to myself and my thoughts.   Mr. Wopsle died amiably at Camberwell, and exceedingly game on Bosworth Field, and in the greatest agonies at Glastonbury.   Orlick sometimes growled, "Beat it out, beat it out—Old Clem!   With a clink for the stout—Old Clem!"   I thought he had been drinking, but he was not drunk.

Thus we came to the village. The way by which we approached it took us past the Three Jolly Bargemen, which we were surprised to find—it being eleven o'clock—in a state of commotion, with the door wide open, and unwonted lights that had been hastily caught up and put down, scattered about. Mr. Wopsle dropped in to ask what was the matter (surmising that a convict had been taken), but came running out in a great hurry.

"There's something wrong," said he, without stopping, "up at your place, Pip. Run all!"

"What is it?" I asked, keeping up with him. So did Orlick, at my side.

"I can't quite understand. The house seems to have been violently entered when Joe Gargery was out. Supposed by convicts. Somebody has been attacked and hurt."

We were running too fast to admit of more being said, and we made no stop until we got into our kitchen. It was full of people; the whole village was there, or in the yard; and there was a surgeon, and there was Joe, and there was a group of women, all on the floor in the midst of the kitchen. The unemployed bystanders drew back when they saw me, and so I became aware of my sister—lying without sense or movement on the bare boards where she had been knocked down by a tremendous blow on the back of the head, dealt by some unknown hand when her face was turned towards the fire—destined never to be on the Rampage again, while she was the wife of Joe.

CHAPTER XVI

With my head full of George Barnwell, I was at first disposed to believe that *I* must have had some hand in the attack upon my sister, or at all events that as her near relation, popularly known to be under obligations to her, I was a more legitimate object of suspicion than any one else. But when, in the clearer light of next morning, I began to reconsider the matter and to hear it discussed around me on all sides, I took another view of the case, which was more reasonable.

Joe had been at the Three Jolly Bargemen, smoking his pipe, from a quarter after eight o'clock to a quarter before ten. While he was there, my sister had been standing at the kitchen door and had exchanged Good Night with a farm-labourer going home. The man could not be more particular as to the time at which he saw her (he got into dense confusion when he tried to be) than that it must have been before nine. When Joe went home at five minutes before ten, he found her struck down on the floor, and promptly called in assistance. The fire had not then burnt unusually low, nor was the snuff of the candle very long ; the candle, however, had been blown out.

Nothing had been taken away from any part of the house. Neither, beyond the blowing out of the candle—which stood on a table between the door and my sister, and was behind her when she stood facing the fire and was struck—was there any disarrangement of the kitchen, excepting such as she herself had made, in falling and bleeding. But there was one remarkable piece of evidence on the spot. She had been struck with something blunt and heavy, on the head and spine ; after the blows were dealt, something heavy had been thrown down at her with considerable violence, as she lay on her face. And on the ground beside her, when Joe picked her up, was a convict's leg-iron which had been filed asunder.

Now, Joe, examining this iron with a smith's eye, declared it to have been filed asunder some time ago. The hue and

cry going off to the Hulks, and people coming thence to
examine the iron, Joe's opinion was corroborated. They did
not undertake to say when it had left the prison-ships to
which it undoubtedly had once belonged; but they claimed
to know for certain that that particular manacle had not
been worn by either of two convicts who had escaped last
night. Further, one of those two was already re-taken, and
had not freed himself of his iron.

Knowing what I knew, I set up an inference of my own
here. I believed the iron to be my convict's iron—the iron
I had seen and heard him filing at, on the marshes—but my
mind did not accuse him of having put it to its latest use.
For I believed one of two other persons to have become
possessed of it, and to have turned it to this cruel account.
Either Orlick, or the strange man who had shown me the
file.

Now, as to Orlick; he had gone to town exactly as he
told us when we picked him up at the turnpike, he had
been seen about town all the evening, he had been in divers
companies in several public-houses, and he had come back
with myself and Mr. Wopsle. There was nothing against
him, save the quarrel; and my sister had quarrelled with
him, and with everybody else about her, ten thousand times.
As to the strange man; if he had come back for his two
bank-notes there could have been no dispute about them,
because my sister was fully prepared to restore them.
Besides, there had been no altercation; the assailant had
come in so silently and suddenly, that she had been felled
before she could look round.

It was horrible to think that I had provided the weapon,
however undesignedly, but I could hardly think otherwise.
I suffered unspeakable trouble while I considered and recon-
sidered whether I should at last dissolve that spell of my
childhood and tell Joe all the story. For months afterwards,
I every day settled the question finally in the negative, and
reopened and reargued it next morning. The contention
came, after all, to this;—the secret was such an old one now,
had so grown into me and become a part of myself, that
I could not tear it away. In addition to the dread that,
having led up to so much mischief, it would be now more
likely than ever to alienate Joe from me if he believed it,
I had a further restraining dread that he would not believe
it, but would assert it with the fabulous dogs and veal-cutlets

as a monstrous invention. However, I temporized with myself, of course—for was I not wavering between right and wrong, when the thing is always done?—and resolved to make a full disclosure if I should see any such new occasion as a new chance of helping in the discovery of the assailant.

The Constables, and the Bow Street men from London—for this happened in the days of the extinct red-waistcoated police—were about the house for a week or two, and did pretty much what I have heard and read of like authorities doing in other such cases. They took up several obviously wrong people, and they ran their heads very hard against wrong ideas, and persisted in trying to fit the circumstances to the ideas, instead of trying to extract ideas from the circumstances. Also, they stood about the door of the Jolly Bargemen, with knowing and reserved looks that filled the whole neighbourhood with admiration; and they had a mysterious manner of taking their drink, that was almost as good as taking the culprit. But not quite, for they never did it.

Long after these constitutional powers had dispersed, my sister lay very ill in bed. Her sight was disturbed, so that she saw objects multiplied, and grasped at visionary teacups and wine-glasses instead of the realities; her hearing was greatly impaired; her memory also; and her speech was unintelligible. When, at last, she came round so far as to be helped down-stairs, it was still necessary to keep my slate always by her, that she might indicate in writing what she could not indicate in speech. As she was (very bad hand-writing apart) a more than indifferent speller, and as Joe was a more than indifferent reader, extraordinary complications arose between them, which I was always called in to solve. The administration of mutton instead of medicine, the substitution of Tea for Joe, and the baker for bacon, were among the mildest of my own mistakes.

However, her temper was greatly improved, and she was patient. A tremulous uncertainty of the action of all her limbs soon became a part of her regular state, and afterwards, at intervals of two or three months, she would often put her hands to her head, and would then remain for about a week at a time in some gloomy aberration of mind. We were at a loss to find a suitable attendant for her, until a circumstance happened conveniently to relieve us. Mr. Wopsle's great-aunt conquered a confirmed habit of living into which she had fallen, and Biddy became a part of our establishment.

It may have been about a month after my sister's reappearance in the kitchen, when Biddy came to us with a small speckled box containing the whole of her worldly effects, and became a blessing to the household. Above all she was a blessing to Joe, for the dear old fellow was sadly cut up by the constant contemplation of the wreck of his wife, and had been accustomed, while attending on her of an evening, to turn to me every now and then and say, with his blue eyes moistened, " Such a fine figure of a woman as she once were, Pip! " Biddy instantly taking the cleverest charge of her as though she had studied her from infancy, Joe became able in some sort to appreciate the greater quiet of his life, and to get down to the Jolly Bargemen now and then for a change that did him good. It was characteristic of the police people that they had all more or less suspected poor Joe (though he never knew it), and that they had to a man concurred in regarding him as one of the deepest spirits they had ever encountered.

Biddy's first triumph in her new office, was to solve a difficulty that had completely vanquished me. I had tried hard at it, but had made nothing of it. Thus it was :

Again and again and again, my sister had traced upon the slate, a character that looked like a curious T, and then with the utmost eagerness had called our attention to it as something she particularly wanted. I had in vain tried everything producible that began with a T, from tar to toast and tub. At length it had come into my head that the sign looked like a hammer, and on my lustily calling that word in my sister's ear, she had begun to hammer on the table and had expressed a qualified assent. Thereupon, I had brought in all our hammers, one after another, but without avail. Then I bethought me of a crutch, the shape being much the same, and I borrowed one in the village, and displayed it to my sister with considerable confidence. But she shook her head to that extent when she was shown it, that we were terrified lest in her weak and shattered state she should dislocate her neck.

When my sister found that Biddy was very quick to understand her, this mysterious sign reappeared on the slate. Biddy looked thoughtfully at it, heard my explanation, looked thoughtfully at my sister, looked thoughtfully at Joe (who was always represented on the slate by his initial letter), and ran into the forge, followed by Joe and me.

"Why, of course!" cried Biddy, with an exultant face. "Don't you see? It's *him!*"

Orlick, without a doubt! She had lost his name, and could only signify him by his hammer. We told him why we wanted him to come into the kitchen, and he slowly laid down his hammer, wiped his brow with his arm, took another wipe at it with his apron, and came slouching out, with a curious loose vagabond bend in the knees that strongly distinguished him.

I confess that I expected to see my sister denounce him, and that I was disappointed by the different result. She manifested the greatest anxiety to be on good terms with him, was evidently much pleased by his being at length produced, and motioned that she would have him given something to drink. She watched his countenance as if she were particularly wishful to be assured that he took kindly to his reception, she showed every possible desire to conciliate him, and there was an air of humble propitiation in all she did, such as I have seen pervade the bearing of a child towards a hard master. After that day, a day rarely passed without her drawing the hammer on her slate, and without Orlick's slouching in and standing doggedly before her, as if he knew no more than I did what to make of it.

CHAPTER XVII

I NOW fell into a regular routine of apprenticeship life, which was varied, beyond the limits of the village and the marshes, by no more remarkable circumstance than the arrival of my birthday and my paying another visit to Miss Havisham. I found Miss Sarah Pocket still on duty at the gate, I found Miss Havisham just as I had left her, and she spoke of Estella in the very same way, if not in the very same words. The interview lasted but a few minutes, and she gave me a guinea when I was going, and told me to come again on my next birthday. I may mention at once that this became an annual custom. I tried to decline taking the guinea on the first occasion, but with no better effect than causing her to ask me very angrily, if I expected more? Then, and after that, I took it.

So unchanging was the dull old house, the yellow light in the darkened room, the faded spectre in the chair by the dressing-table glass, that I felt as if the stopping of the clocks had stopped Time in that mysterious place, and, while I and everything else outside it grew older, it stood still. Daylight never entered the house, as to my thoughts and remembrances of it, any more than as to the actual fact. It bewildered me, and under its influence I continued at heart to hate my trade and to be ashamed of home.

Imperceptibly I became conscious of a change in Biddy, however. Her shoes came up at the heel, her hair grew bright and neat, her hands were always clean. She was not beautiful—she was common, and could not be like Estella—but she was pleasant and wholesome and sweet-tempered. She had not been with us more than a year (I remember her being newly out of mourning at the time it struck me), when I observed to myself one evening that she had curiously thoughtful and attentive eyes; eyes that were very pretty and very good.

It came of my lifting up my own eyes from a task I was poring at—writing some passages from a book, to improve myself in two ways at once by a sort of stratagem—and seeing Biddy observant of what I was about. I laid down my pen, and Biddy stopped in her needlework without laying it down.

"Biddy," said I, "how do you manage it? Either I am very stupid, or you are very clever."

"What is it that I manage? I don't know," returned Biddy, smiling.

She managed her whole domestic life, and wonderfully too; but I did not mean that, though that made what I did mean more surprising.

"How do you manage, Biddy," said I, "to learn everything that I learn, and always to keep up with me?" I was beginning to be rather vain of my knowledge, for I spent my birthday guineas on it, and set aside the greater part of my pocket-money for similar investment; though I have no doubt, now, that the little I knew was extremely dear at the price.

"I might as well ask you," said Biddy, "how *you* manage?"

"No; because when I come in from the forge of a night, any one can see me turning to at it. But you never turn to at it, Biddy."

"I suppose I must catch it—like a cough," said Biddy, quietly; and went on with her sewing.

Pursuing my idea as I leaned back in my wooden chair and looked at Biddy sewing away with her head on one side, I began to think her rather an extraordinary girl. For, I called to mind now, that she was equally accomplished in the terms of our trade, and the names of our different sorts of work, and our various tools. In short, whatever I knew, Biddy knew. Theoretically, she was already as good a black-smith as I, or better.

"You are one of those, Biddy," said I, "who make the most of every chance. You never had a chance before you came here, and see how improved you are!"

Biddy looked at me for an instant, and went on with her sewing. "I was your first teacher, though; wasn't I?" said she, as she sewed.

"Biddy!" I exclaimed, in amazement. "Why, you are crying!"

"No, I am not," said Biddy, looking up and laughing. "What put that in your head?"

What could have put it in my head, but the glistening of a tear as it dropped on her work? I sat silent, recalling what a drudge she had been until Mr. Wopsle's great-aunt successfully overcame that bad habit of living, so highly desirable to be got rid of by some people. I recalled the hopeless circumstances by which she had been surrounded in the miserable little shop and the miserable little noisy evening school, with that miserable old bundle of incompetence always to be dragged and shouldered. I reflected that even in those untoward times there must have been latent in Biddy what was now developing, for in my first uneasiness and discontent I had turned to her for help, as a matter of course. Biddy sat quietly sewing, shedding no more tears, and while I looked at her and thought about it all, it occurred to me that perhaps I had not been sufficiently grateful to Biddy. I might have been too reserved, and should have patronised her more (though I did not use that precise word in my meditations), with my confidence.

"Yes, Biddy," I observed, when I had done turning it over, "you were my first teacher, and that at a time when we little thought of ever being together like this, in this kitchen."

"Ah, poor thing!" replied Biddy. It was like her self-forgetfulness, to transfer the remark to my sister, and to get up and be busy about her, making her more comfortable: "that's sadly true!"

"Well!" said I, "we must talk together a little more, as we used to do. And I must consult you a little more, as I used to do. Let us have a quiet walk on the marshes next Sunday, Biddy, and a long chat."

My sister was never left alone now; but Joe more than readily undertook the care of her on that Sunday afternoon, and Biddy and I went out together. It was summer-time and lovely weather. When we had passed the village and the church and the churchyard, and were out on the marshes, and began to see the sails of the ships as they sailed on, I began to combine Miss Havisham and Estella with the prospect, in my usual way. When we came to the river-side and sat down on the bank, with the water rippling at our feet, making it all more quiet than it would have been without that sound, I resolved that it was a good time and place for the admission of Biddy into my inner confidence.

"Biddy," said I, after binding her to secrecy, "I want to be a gentleman."

"Oh, I wouldn't, if I was you!" she returned. "I don't think it would answer."

"Biddy," said I, with some severity, "I have particular reasons for wanting to be a gentleman."

"You know best, Pip; but don't you think you are happier as you are?"

"Biddy," I exclaimed, impatiently, "I am not at all happy as I am. I am disgusted with my calling and with my life. I have never taken to either since I was bound. Don't be absurd."

"Was I absurd?" said Biddy, quietly raising her eyebrows; "I am sorry for that; I didn't mean to be. I only want you to do well, and be comfortable."

"Well, then, understand once for all that I never shall or can be comfortable—or anything but miserable—there, Biddy!—unless I can lead a very different sort of life from the life I lead now."

"That's a pity!" said Biddy, shaking her head with a sorrowful air.

Now, I too had so often thought it a pity, that, in the singular kind of quarrel with myself which I was always carrying on, I was half inclined to shed tears of vexation and distress when Biddy gave utterance to her sentiment and my own. I told her she was right, and I knew it was much to be regretted, but still it was not to be helped.

"If I could have settled down," I said to Biddy, plucking up the short grass within reach, much as I had once upon a time pulled my feelings out of my hair and kicked them into the brewery well: "if I could have settled down and been but half as fond of the forge as I was when I was little, I know it would have been much better for me. You and I and Joe would have wanted nothing then, and Joe and I would perhaps have gone partners when I was out of my time, and I might even have grown up to keep company with you, and we might have sat on this very bank on a fine Sunday, quite different people. I should have been good enough for *you*; shouldn't I, Biddy?"

Biddy sighed as she looked at the ships sailing on, and returned for answer, "Yes; I am not over-particular." It scarcely sounded flattering, but I knew she meant well.

"Instead of that," said I, plucking up more grass and

chewing a blade or two, "see how I am going on. Dissatisfied, and uncomfortable, and—what would it signify to me, being coarse and common, if nobody had told me so!"

Biddy turned her face suddenly towards mine, and looked far more attentively at me than she had looked at the sailing ships.

"It was neither a very true nor a very polite thing to say," she remarked, directing her eyes to the ships again. "Who said it?"

I was disconcerted, for I had broken away without quite seeing where I was going to. It was not to be shuffled off, now, however, and I answered, "The beautiful young lady at Miss Havisham's, and she's more beautiful than anybody ever was, and I admire her dreadfully, and I want to be a gentleman on her account." Having made this lunatic confession, I began to throw my torn-up grass into the river, as if I had some thoughts of following it.

"Do you want to be a gentleman, to spite her or to gain her over?" Biddy quietly asked me, after a pause.

"I don't know," I moodily answered.

"Because, if it is to spite her," Biddy pursued, "I should think—but you know best—that might be better and more independently done by caring nothing for her words. And if it is to gain her over, I should think—but you know best —she was not worth gaining over."

Exactly what I myself had thought, many times. Exactly what was perfectly manifest to me at the moment. But how could I, a poor dazed village lad, avoid that wonderful inconsistency into which the best and wisest of men fall every day?

"It may be all quite true," said I to Biddy, "but I admire her dreadfully."

In short, I turned over on my face when I came to that, and got a good grasp on the hair, on each side of my head, and wrenched it well. All the while knowing the madness of my heart to be so very mad and misplaced, that I was quite conscious it would have served my face right, if I had lifted it up by my hair, and knocked it against the pebbles as a punishment for belonging to such an idiot.

Biddy was the wisest of girls, and she tried to reason no more with me. She put her hand, which was a comfortable hand though roughened by work, upon my hands, one after another, and gently took them out of my hair. Then she softly patted my shoulder in a soothing way, while with my face upon my sleeve I cried a little—exactly as I had done in the brewery yard—and felt vaguely convinced that I was very much ill-used by somebody, or by everybody; I can't say which.

"I am glad of one thing," said Biddy, "and that is, that you have felt you could give me your confidence, Pip. And I am glad of another thing, and that is, that of course you know you may depend upon my keeping it and always so far deserving it. If your first teacher (dear! such a poor one, and so much in need of being taught herself!) had been your teacher at the present time, she thinks she knows what lesson she would set. But it would be a hard one to learn, and you have got beyond her, and it's of no use now." So, with a quiet sigh for me, Biddy rose from the bank, and said, with a fresh and pleasant change of voice, "Shall we walk a little further, or go home?"

"Biddy," I cried, getting up, putting my arm around her neck, and giving her a kiss, "I shall always tell you everything."

"Till you're a gentleman," said Biddy.

"You know I never shall be, so that's always. Not that I have any occasion to tell you anything, for you know everything I know—as I told you at home the other night."

"Ah!" said Biddy, quite in a whisper, as she looked away at the ships. And then repeated, with her former pleasant change, "Shall we walk a little further, or go home?"

I said to Biddy we would walk a little further, and we did so, and the summer afternoon toned down into the summer evening, and it was very beautiful. I began to consider whether I was not more naturally and wholesomely situated, after all, in these circumstances, than playing beggar my neighbour by candlelight in the room with the stopped clocks, and being despised by Estella. I thought it would be very good for me if I could get her out of my head with all the rest of those remembrances and fancies, and could go to work determined to relish what I had to do, and stick to it, and make the best of it. I asked myself the question whether I did not surely know that if Estella were beside me at that moment instead of Biddy, she would make me miserable? I was obliged to admit that I did know it for a certainty, and I said to myself, "Pip, what a fool you are!"

We talked a good deal as we walked, and all that Biddy said seemed right. Biddy was never insulting, or capricious, or Biddy to-day and somebody else to-morrow; she would have derived only pain, and no pleasure, from giving me pain; she would far rather have wounded her own breast than mine. How could it be, then, that I did not like her much the better of the two?

"Biddy," said I, when we were walking homeward. "I wish you could put me right."

"I wish I could!" said Biddy.

"If I could only get myself to fall in love with you—you don't mind my speaking so openly to such an old acquaintance?"

"Oh dear, not at all!" said Biddy. "Don't mind me."

"If I could only get myself to do it, *that* would be the thing for me."

"But you never will, you see," said Biddy.

It did not appear quite so unlikely to me that evening, as it would have done if we had discussed it a few hours before. I therefore observed I was not quite sure of that. But Biddy said she *was*, and she said it decisively. In my heart I believed her to be right; and yet I took it rather ill, too, that she should be so positive on the point.

When we came near the churchyard, we had to cross an embankment, and get over a stile near a sluice gate. There started up, from the gate, or from the rushes, or from the ooze (which was quite in his stagnant way), Old Orlick.

"Halloa!" he growled, "where are you two going?"

"Where should we be going, but home?"

"Well, then," said he, "I'm jiggered if I don't see you home!"

This penalty of being jiggered was a favourite supposititious case of his. He attached no definite meaning to the word that I am aware of, but used it, like his own pretended Christian name, to affront mankind, and convey an idea of something savagely damaging. When I was younger, I had had a general belief that if he had jiggered me personally, he would have done it with a sharp and twisted hook.

Biddy was much against his going with us, and said to me in a whisper, "Don't let him come; I don't like him."

As I did not like him either, I took the liberty of saying that we thanked him, but we didn't want seeing home. He received that piece of information with a yell of laughter, and dropped back, but came slouching after us at a little distance.

Curious to know whether Biddy suspected him of having had a hand in that murderous attack of which my sister had never been able to give any account, I asked her why she did not like him.

"Oh!" she replied, glancing over her shoulder as he slouched after us, "because I—I am afraid he likes me."

"Did he ever tell you he liked you?" I asked indignantly.

"No," said Biddy, glancing over her shoulder again, "he never told me so; but he dances at me, whenever he can catch my eye."

However novel and peculiar this testimony of attachment, I did not doubt the accuracy of the interpretation. I was very hot indeed upon Old Orlick's daring to admire her; as hot as if it were an outrage on myself.

"But it makes no difference to you, you know," said Biddy, calmly.

"No, Biddy, it makes no difference to me; only I don't like it; I don't approve of it."

"Nor I neither," said Biddy. "Though *that* makes no difference to you."

"Exactly," said I; "but I must tell you I should have no opinion of you, Biddy, if he danced at you with your own consent."

I kept an eye on Orlick after that night, and whenever circumstances were favourable to his dancing at Biddy, got before him, to obscure that demonstration. He had struck root in Joe's establishment, by reason of my sister's sudden fancy for him, or I should have tried to get him dismissed. He quite understood and reciprocated my good intentions, as I had reason to know thereafter.

And now, because my mind was not confused enough before, I complicated its confusion fifty thousand-fold, by having states and seasons when I was clear that Biddy was immeasurably better than Estella, and that the plain honest working life to which I was born had nothing in it to be ashamed of, but offered me sufficient means of self-respect and happiness. At those times, I would decide conclusively that my disaffection to dear old Joe and the forge, was gone, and that I was growing up in a fair way to be partners with Joe and to keep company with Biddy—when all in a moment some confounding remembrance of the Havisham days would fall upon me, like a destructive missile, and scatter my wits again. Scattered wits take a long time picking up; and often, before I had got them well together, they would be dispersed in all directions by one stray thought, that perhaps after all Miss Havisham was going to make my fortune when my time was out.

If my time had run out, it would have left me still at the height of my perplexities, I dare say. It never did run out, however, but was brought to a premature end, as I proceed to relate.

CHAPTER XVIII

IT was in the fourth year of my apprenticeship to Joe, and it was a Saturday night. There was a group assembled round the fire at the Three Jolly Bargemen, attentive to Mr. Wopsle as he read the newspaper aloud. Of that group I was one.

A highly popular murder had been committed, and Mr. Wopsle was imbrued in blood to the eyebrows. He gloated over every abhorrent adjective in the description, and identified himself with every witness at the Inquest. He faintly moaned, "I am done for," as the victim, and he barbarously bellowed, "I'll serve you out," as the murderer. He gave the medical testimony, in pointed imitation of our local practitioner; and he piped and shook, as the aged turnpike-keeper who had heard blows, to an extent so very paralytic as to suggest a doubt regarding the mental competency of that witness. The coroner, in Mr. Wopsle's hands, became Timon of Athens; the beadle, Coriolanus. He enjoyed himself thoroughly, and we all enjoyed ourselves, and were delightfully comfortable. In this cosy state of mind we came to the verdict of Wilful Murder.

Then, and not sooner, I became aware of a strange gentleman leaning over the back of the settle opposite me, looking on. There was an expression of contempt on his face, and he bit the side of a great forefinger as he watched the group of faces.

"Well!" said the stranger to Mr. Wopsle, when the reading was done, "you have settled it all to your own satisfaction, I have no doubt?"

Everybody started and looked up, as if it were the murderer. He looked at everybody coldly and sarcastically.

"Guilty, of course?" said he. "Out with it. Come!"

"Sir," returned Mr. Wopsle, "without having the honour of your acquaintance, I do say Guilty." Upon this we all took courage to unite in a confirmatory murmur.

"I know you do," said the stranger; "I knew you would.

HE BIT THE SIDE OF A GREAT FOREFINGER

I told you so. But now I'll ask you a question. Do you know, or do you not know, that the law of England supposes every man to be innocent, until he is proved—proved—to be guilty?"

"Sir," Mr. Wopsle began to reply, "as an Englishman myself, I——"

"Come!" said the stranger, biting his forefinger at him. "Don't evade the question. Either you know it, or you don't know it. Which is it to be?"

He stood with his head on one side and himself on one side, in a bullying interrogative manner, and he threw his forefinger at Mr. Wopsle—as it were to mark him out—before biting it again.

"Now!" said he. "Do you know it, or don't you know it?"

"Certainly I know it," replied Mr. Wopsle.

"Certainly you know it. Then why didn't you say so at first? Now, I'll ask you another question;" taking possession of Mr. Wopsle, as if he had a right to him. "*Do* you know that none of these witnesses have yet been cross-examined?"

Mr. Wopsle was beginning, "I can only say——" when the stranger stopped him.

"What? You won't answer the question, yes or no? Now, I'll try you again." Throwing his finger at him again. "Attend to me. Are you aware, or are you not aware, that none of these witnesses have yet been cross-examined? Come, I only want one word from you. Yes, or no?"

Mr. Wopsle hesitated, and we all began to conceive rather a poor opinion of him.

"Come!" said the stranger, "I'll help you. You don't deserve help, but I'll help you. Look at that paper you hold in your hand. What is it?"

"What is it?" repeated Mr. Wopsle, eyeing it much at a loss.

"Is it," pursued the stranger in his most sarcastic and suspicious manner, "the printed paper you have just been reading from?"

"Undoubtedly."

"Undoubtedly. Now, turn to that paper, and tell me whether it distinctly states that the prisoner expressly said that his legal advisers instructed him altogether to reserve his defence?"

"I read that just now," Mr. Wopsle pleaded.

"Never mind what you read just now, sir; I don't ask you what you read just now. You may read the Lord's Prayer backwards, if you like — and, perhaps, have done it before to-day. Turn to the paper. No, no, no, my friend; not to the top of the column; you know better than that; to the bottom, to the bottom." (We all began to think Mr. Wopsle full of subterfuge.) "Well? Have you found it?"

"Here it is," said Mr. Wopsle.

"Now, follow that passage with your eye, and tell me whether it distinctly states that the prisoner expressly said that he was instructed by his legal advisers wholly to reserve his defence? Come! Do you make that of it?"

Mr. Wopsle answered, "Those are not the exact words."

"Not the exact words!" repeated the gentleman, bitterly. "Is that the exact substance?"

"Yes," said Mr. Wopsle.

"Yes," repeated the stranger, looking round at the rest of the company with his right hand extended towards the witness, Wopsle. "And now I ask you what you say to the conscience of that man who, with that passage before his eyes, can lay his head upon his pillow after having pronounced a fellow-creature guilty, unheard?"

We all began to suspect that Mr. Wopsle was not the man we had thought him, and that he was beginning to be found out.

"And that same man, remember," pursued the gentleman, throwing his finger at Mr. Wopsle heavily; "that same man might be summoned as a juryman upon this very trial, and having thus deeply committed himself, might return to the bosom of his family and lay his head upon his pillow, after deliberately swearing that he would well and truly try the issue joined between Our Sovereign Lord the King and the prisoner at the bar, and would a true verdict give according to the evidence, so help him God!"

We were all deeply persuaded that the unfortunate Wopsle had gone too far, and had better stop in his reckless career while there was yet time.

The strange gentleman, with an air of authority not to be disputed, and with a manner expressive of knowing something secret about every one of us that would effectually do for each individual if he chose to disclose it, left the back of the settle, and came into the space between the two settles, in front of the fire, where he remained standing: his left hand in his pocket, and he biting the forefinger of his right.

"From information I have received," said he, looking round at us as we all quailed before him, "I have reason to believe there is a blacksmith among you, by name Joseph— or Joe—Gargery. Which is the man?"

"Here is the man," said Joe.

The strange gentleman beckoned him out of his place, and Joe went.

"You have an apprentice," pursued the stranger, "commonly known as Pip? Is he here?"

"I am here!" I cried.

The stranger did not recognise me, but I recognised him as the gentleman I had met on the stairs, on the occasion of my second visit to Miss Havisham. I had known him the moment I saw him looking over the settle, and now that I stood confronting him with his hand upon my shoulder, I checked off again in detail, his large head, his dark complexion, his deep-set eyes, his bushy black eyebrows, his large watch-chain, his strong black dots of beard and whisker, and even the smell of scented soap on his great hand.

"I wish to have a private conference with you two," said he, when he had surveyed me at his leisure. "It will take a little time. Perhaps we had better go to your place of residence. I prefer not to anticipate my communication here; you will impart as much or as little of it as you please to your friends afterwards; I have nothing to do with that."

Amidst a wondering silence, we three walked out of the Jolly Bargemen, and in a wondering silence walked home. While going along, the strange gentleman occasionally looked at me, and occasionally bit the side of his finger. As we neared home, Joe vaguely acknowledging the occasion as an impressive and ceremonious one, went on ahead to open the front door. Our conference was held in the state parlour, which was feebly lighted by one candle.

It began with the strange gentleman's sitting down at the table, drawing the candle to him, and looking over some entries in his pocket-book. He then put up the pocket-book and set the candle a little aside, after peering round it into the darkness at Joe and me, to ascertain which was which.

"My name," he said, "is Jaggers, and I am a lawyer in London. I am pretty well known. I have unusual business to transact with you, and I commence by explaining that it is not of my originating. If my advice had been asked, I should not have been here. It was not asked, and you see me here. What I have to do as the confidential agent of another, I do. No less, no more."

Finding that he could not see us very well from where he sat, he got up, and threw one leg over the back of a chair and leaned upon it; thus having one foot on the seat of a chair, and one foot on the ground.

"Now, Joseph Gargery, I am the bearer of an offer to relieve you of this young fellow, your apprentice. You would not object to cancel his indentures at his request and for his good? You would want nothing for so doing?"

"Lord forbid that I should want anything for not standing in Pip's way," said Joe, staring.

"Lord forbidding is pious, but not to the purpose," returned Mr. Jaggers. "The question is, Would you want anything? Do you want anything?"

"The answer is," returned Joe, sternly, "No."

I thought Mr. Jaggers glanced at Joe, as if he considered him a fool for his disinterestedness. But I was too much bewildered between breathless curiosity and surprise, to be sure of it.

"Very well," said Mr. Jaggers. "Recollect the admission you have made, and don't try to go from it presently."

"Who's a-going to try?" retorted Joe.

"I don't say anybody is. Do you keep a dog?"

"Yes, I do keep a dog."

"Bear in mind then, that Brag is a good dog, but that Holdfast is a better. Bear that in mind, will you?" repeated Mr. Jaggers, shutting his eyes and nodding his head at Joe, as if he were forgiving him something. "Now, I return to this young fellow. And the communication I have *got to make is*, that he has Great Expectations."

Joe and I gasped, and looked at one another.

"I am instructed to communicate to him," said Mr. Jaggers, throwing his finger at me sideways, "that he will come into a handsome property. Further, that it is the desire of the present possessor of that property, that he be immediately removed from his present sphere of life and from this place, and be brought up as a gentleman—in a word, as a young fellow of great expectations."

My dream was out; my wild fancy was surpassed by sober reality; Miss Havisham was going to make my fortune on a grand scale.

"Now, Mr. Pip," pursued the lawyer, "I address the rest of what I have to say, to you. You are to understand, first, that it is the request of the person from whom I take my instructions, that you always bear the name of Pip. You will have no objection, I dare say, to your great expectations being encumbered with that easy condition. But if you have any objection, this is the time to mention it."

My heart was beating so fast, and there was such a singing in my ears, that I could scarcely stammer I had no objection.

"I should think not! Now you are to understand, secondly, that the name of the person who is your liberal benefactor remains a profound secret, until the person chooses to reveal it. I am empowered to mention that it is the intention of the person to reveal it at first hand by word of mouth to yourself. When or where that intention may be carried out, I cannot say; no one can say. It may be years hence. Now, you are distinctly to understand that you are most positively prohibited from making any inquiry on this head, or any allusion or reference, however distant, to any individual whomsoever as *the* individual, in all the communications you have with me. If you have a suspicion in your own breast, keep that suspicion in your own breast. It is not the least to the purpose what the reasons of this prohibition are: they may be the strongest and gravest reasons, or they may be a mere whim. This is not for you to inquire into. The condition is laid down. Your accep-tance of it, and your observance of it as binding, is the only remaining condition that I am charged with, by the person from whom I take my instructions, and for whom I am not otherwise responsible. That person is the person from whom you derive your expectations, and the secret is solely held by that person and by me. Again, not a very difficult condition with which to encumber such a rise in fortune; but if you have any objection to it, this is the time to mention it. Speak out."

Once more, I stammered with difficulty that I had no objection.

stipulations." Though he called me Mr. Pip, and began rather to make up to me, he still could not get rid of a certain air of bullying suspicion; and even now he occasionally shut his eyes and threw his finger at me while he spoke, as much as to express that he knew all kinds of things to my disparagement, if he only chose to mention them. " We come next, to mere details of arrangement. You must know that although I use the term 'expectations' more than once, you are not endowed with expectations only. There is already lodged in my hands, a sum of money amply sufficient for your suitable education and maintenance. You will please consider me your guardian. Oh ! " for I was going to thank him, " I tell you at once, I am paid for my services, or I shouldn't render them. It is considered that you must be better educated, in accordance with your altered position, and that you will be alive to the importance and necessity of at once entering on that advantage."

I said I had always longed for it.

" Never mind what you have always longed for, Mr. Pip," he retorted, " keep to the record. If you long for it now, that's enough. Am I answered that you are ready to be placed at once, under some proper tutor ? Is that it ? "

I stammered yes, that was it.

" Good. Now, your inclinations are to be consulted. I don't think that wise, mind, but it's my trust. Have you ever heard of any tutor whom you would prefer to another ? "

I had never heard of any tutor but Biddy, and Mr. Wopsle's great-aunt ; so, I replied in the negative.

" There is a certain tutor, of whom I have some knowledge, who I think might suit the purpose," said Mr. Jaggers. " I don't recommend him, observe ; because I never recommend anybody. The gentleman I speak of is one Mr. Matthew Pocket."

Ah ! I caught at the name directly. Miss Havisham's relation. The Matthew whom Mr. and Mrs. Camilla had spoken of. The Matthew whose place was to be at Miss Havisham's head, when she lay dead, in her bride's dress on the bride's table.

" You know the name ? " said Mr. Jaggers, looking shrewdly at me, and then shutting up his eyes while he waited for my answer.

My answer was, that I had heard of the name.

"Oh!" said he. "You have heard of the name! But the question is, what do you say of it?"

I said, or tried to say, that I was much obliged to him for his recommendation——

"No, my young friend!" he interrupted, shaking his great head very slowly. "Recollect yourself!"

Not recollecting myself, I began again that I was much obliged to him for his recommendation——

"No, my young friend," he interrupted, shaking his head and frowning and smiling both at once; "no, no, no; it's very well done, but it won't do; you are too young to fix me with it. Recommendation is not the word, Mr. Pip. Try another."

Correcting myself, I said that I was much obliged to him for his mention of Mr. Matthew Pocket——

"*That's* more like it!" cried Mr. Jaggers.

—And (I added) I would gladly try that gentleman.

"Good. You had better try him in his own house. The way shall be prepared for you, and you can see his son first, who is in London. When will you come to London?"

I said (glancing at Joe, who stood looking on, motionless), that I supposed I could come directly.

"First," said Mr. Jaggers, "you should have some new clothes to come in, and they should not be working clothes. Say this day week. You'll want some money. Shall I leave you twenty guineas?"

He produced a long purse with the greatest coolness, and counted them out on the table and pushed them over to me. This was the first time he had taken his leg from the chair. He sat astride of the chair when he had pushed the money over, and sat swinging his purse and eyeing Joe.

"Well, Joseph Gargery? You look dumbfoundered?"

"I *am*!" said Joe, in a very decided manner.

"It was understood that you wanted nothing for yourself, remember?"

"It were understood," said Joe. "And it are understood. And it ever will be similar according."

"But what," said Mr. Jaggers, swinging his purse, "what if it was in my instructions to make you a present, as compensation?"

"As compensation what for?" Joe demanded.

"For the loss of his services."

Joe laid his hand upon my shoulder with the touch of a woman. I have often thought him since, like the steam-hammer, that can crush a man or pat an egg-shell, in his combination of strength with gentleness. "Pip is that hearty welcome," said Joe, "to go free with his services, to honour and fortun', as no words can tell him. But if you think as Money can make compensation to me for the loss of the little child—what come to the forge—and ever the best of friends!—"

O dear good Joe, whom I was so ready to leave and so unthankful to, I see you again, with your muscular black-smith's arm before your eyes, and your broad chest heaving, and your voice dying away. O dear good faithful tender Joe, I feel the loving tremble of your hand upon my arm, as solemnly this day as if it had been the rustle of an angel's wing!

But I encouraged Joe at the time. I was lost in the mazes of my future fortunes. and could not retrace the by-paths we had trodden together. I begged Joe to be comforted, for (as he said) we had ever been the best of friends, and (as I said) we ever would be so. Joe scooped his eyes with his disengaged wrist, as if he were bent on gouging himself, but said not another word.

Mr. Jaggers had looked on at this, as one who recognised in Joe the village idiot, and in me his keeper. When it was over, he said, weighing in his hand the purse he had ceased to swing:

"Now, Joseph Gargery, I warn you this is your last chance. No half measures with me. If you mean to take a present that I have it in charge to make you, speak out, and you shall have it. If on the contrary you mean to say——" Here, to his great amazement, he was stopped by Joe's suddenly working round him with every demonstration of a fell pugilistic purpose.

"Which I meantersay," cried Joe, "that if you come into my place bull-baiting and badgering me, come out! Which I meantersay as sech if you're a man, come on! Which I meantersay that what I say, I meantersay and stand or fall by!"

I drew Joe away, and he immediately became placable: merely stating to me, in an obliging manner and as a polite expostulatory notice to any one whom it might happen to concern, that he were not a-going to be bull-baited and badgered in his own place. Mr. Jaggers had risen when Joe demonstrated, and had backed near the door. Without evincing any inclination to come in again, he there delivered his valedictory remarks. They were these :

"Well, Mr. Pip, I think the sooner you leave here—as you are to be a gentleman—the better. Let it stand for this day week, and you shall receive my printed address in the meantime. You can take a hackney-coach at the stage-coach office in London, and come straight to me. Understand that I express no opinion, one way or other, on the trust I undertake. I am paid for undertaking it, and I do so. Now, understand that finally. Understand that !"

He was throwing his finger at both of us, and I think would have gone on, but for his seeming to think Joe dangerous, and going off.

Something came into my head which induced me to run after him as he was going down to the Jolly Bargemen, where he had left a hired carriage.

"I beg your pardon, Mr. Jaggers."

"Holloa !" said he, facing round, "what's the matter ?"

"I wish to be quite right, Mr. Jaggers, and to keep to your directions ; so I thought I had better ask. Would there be any objection to my taking leave of any one I know, about here, before I go away ?"

"No," said he, looking as if he hardly understood me.

"I don't mean the village only, but up town ?"

"No," said he. "No objection."

I thanked him and ran home again, and there I found that Joe had already locked the front door and vacated the state parlour, and was seated by the kitchen fire with a hand on each knee, gazing intently at the burning coals. I too sat down before the fire and gazed at the coals, and nothing was said for a long time.

My sister was in her cushioned chair in her corner, and Biddy sat at her needlework before the fire, and Joe sat next Biddy, and I sat next Joe in the corner opposite my sister. The more I looked into the glowing coals, the more incapable I became of looking at Joe ; the longer the silence lasted, the more unable I felt to speak.

At length I got out, "Joe, have you told Biddy ?"

"No, Pip," returned Joe, still looking at the fire, and holding his knees tight, as if he had private information that they intended to make off somewhere, "which I left it to yourself, Pip."

"I would rather you told, Joe."

"Pip's a gentleman of fortun' then," said Joe, "and God bless him in it!"

Biddy dropped her work, and looked at me. Joe held his knees and looked at me. I looked at both of them. After a pause they both heartily congratulated me; but there was a certain touch of sadness in their congratulations that I rather resented.

I took it upon myself to impress Biddy (and through Biddy, Joe) with the grave obligation I considered my friends under, to know nothing and to say nothing about the maker of my fortune. It would all come out in good time, I observed, and in the meanwhile nothing was to be said, save that I had come into great expectations from a mysterious patron. Biddy nodded her head thoughtfully at the fire as she took up her work again, and said she would be very particular; and Joe, still detaining his knees, said, "Ay, ay, I'll be ekervally partickler, Pip;" and then they congratulated me again, and went on to express so much wonder at the notion of my being a gentleman, that I didn't half like it.

Infinite pains were then taken by Biddy to convey to my sister some idea of what had happened. To the best of my belief, those efforts entirely failed. She laughed and nodded her head a great many times, and even repeated after Biddy, the words "Pip" and "Property." But I doubt if they had more meaning in them than an election cry, and I cannot suggest a darker picture of her state of mind.

I never could have believed it without experience, but as Joe and Biddy became more at their cheerful ease again, I became quite gloomy. Dissatisfied with my fortune, of course I could not be; but it is possible that I may have been, without quite knowing it, dissatisfied with myself.

Anyhow, I sat with my elbow on my knee and my face upon my hand, looking into the fire, as those two talked about my going away, and about what they should do without me, and all that. And whenever I caught one of them looking at me, though never so pleasantly (and they often looked at me—particularly Biddy), I felt offended: as if they were expressing some mistrust in me. Though Heaven knows they never did by word or sign.

At those times I would get up and look out at the door; for our kitchen door opened at once upon the night, and stood open on summer evenings to air the room. The very stars to which I then raised my eyes, I am afraid I took to be but poor and humble stars for glittering on the rustic objects among which I had passed my life.

"Saturday night," said I, when we sat at our supper of bread-and-cheese and beer. "Five more days, and then the day before *the* day! They'll soon go."

"Yes, Pip," observed Joe, whose voice sounded hollow in his beer mug. "They'll soon go."

"Soon, soon go," said Biddy.

"I have been thinking, Joe, that when I go down town on Monday, and order my new clothes, I shall tell the tailor that I'll come and put them on there, or that I'll have them sent to Mr. Pumblechook's. It would be very disagreeable to be stared at by all the people here."

"Mr. and Mrs. Hubble might like to see you in your new gen-teel figure too, Pip," said Joe, industriously cutting his bread with his cheese on it, in the palm of his left hand, and glancing at my untasted supper as if he thought of the time when we used to compare slices. "So might Wopsle. And the Jolly Bargemen might take it as a compliment."

"That's just what I don't want, Joe. They would make such a business of it—such a coarse and common business—that I couldn't bear myself."

"Ah, that indeed, Pip!" said Joe. "If you couldn't abear yourself——"

Biddy asked me here, as she sat holding my sister's plate, "Have you thought about when you'll show yourself to Mr. Gargery, and your sister, and me? You will show yourself to us; won't you?"

"Biddy," I returned with some resentment, "you are so exceedingly quick that it's difficult to keep up with you."

("She always were quick," observed Joe.)

"If you had waited another moment, Biddy, you would have heard me say that I shall bring my clothes here in a bundle one evening—most likely on the evening before I go away."

Biddy said no more. Handsomely forgiving her, I soon exchanged an affectionate good-night with her and Joe, and went up to bed. When I got into my little room, I sat down and took a long look at it, as a mean little room that

I should soon be parted from and raised above, for ever. It was furnished with fresh young remembrances too, and even at the same moment I fell into much the same confused division of mind between it and the better rooms to which I was going, as I had been in so often between the forge and Miss Havisham's, and Biddy and Estella.

The sun had been shining brightly all day on the roof of my attic, and the room was warm. As I put the window open and stood looking out, I saw Joe come slowly forth at the dark door below, and take a turn or two in the air; and then I saw Biddy come, and bring him a pipe and light it for him. He never smoked so late, and it seemed to hint to me that he wanted comforting, for some reason or other.

He presently stood at the door immediately beneath me, smoking his pipe, and Biddy stood there too, quietly talking to him, and I knew that they talked of me, for I heard my name mentioned in an endearing tone by both of them more than once. I would not have listened for more, if I could have heard more: so, I drew away from the window, and sat down in my one chair by the bedside, feeling it very sorrowful and strange that this first night of my bright fortunes should be the loneliest I had ever known.

Looking towards the open window, I saw light wreaths from Joe's pipe floating there, and I fancied it was like a blessing from Joe—not obtruded on me or paraded before me, but pervading the air we shared together. I put my light out, and crept into bed; and it was an uneasy bed now, and I never slept the old sound sleep in it any more.

CHAPTER XIX

MORNING made a considerable difference in my general prospect of Life, and brightened it so much that it scarcely seemed the same. What lay heaviest on my mind, was, the consideration that six days intervened between me and the day of departure; for, I could not divest myself of a misgiving that something might happen to London in the meanwhile, and that, when I got there, it might be either greatly deteriorated or clean gone.

Joe and Biddy were very sympathetic and pleasant when I spoke of our approaching separation; but they only referred to it when I did. After breakfast, Joe brought out my indentures from the press in the best parlour, and we put them in the fire, and I felt that I was free. With all the novelty of my emancipation on me, I went to church with Joe, and thought, perhaps the clergyman wouldn't have read that about the rich man and the kingdom of Heaven, if he had known all.

After our early dinner, I strolled out alone, proposing to finish off the marshes at once, and get them done with. As I passed the church, I felt (as I had felt during service in the morning) a sublime compassion for the poor creatures who were destined to go there, Sunday after Sunday, all their lives through, and to lie obscurely at last among the low green mounds. I promised myself that I would do something for them one of these days, and formed a plan in outline for bestowing a dinner of roast-beef and plum-pudding, a pint of ale, and a gallon of condescension, upon everybody in the village.

If I had often thought before, with something allied to shame, of my companionship with the fugitive whom I had once seen limping among those graves, what were my thoughts on this Sunday, when the place recalled the wretch, ragged and shivering, with his felon iron and badge! My comfort was, that it happened a long time ago, and that he had doubtless been transported a long way off, and that he was dead to me, and might be veritably dead into the bargain.

No more low wet grounds, no more dykes and sluices, no more of these grazing cattle—though they seemed, in their dull manner, to wear a more respectful air now, and to face round, in order that they might stare as long as possible at the possessor of such great expectations—farewell, monotonous acquaintances of my childhood, henceforth I was for London and greatness: not for smith's work in general and for you! I made my exultant way to the old Battery, and, lying down there to consider the question whether Miss Havisham intended me for Estella, fell asleep.

When I awoke, I was much surprised to find Joe sitting beside me, smoking his pipe. He greeted me with a cheerful smile on my opening my eyes, and said:

"As being the last time, Pip, I thought I'd foller."

"And, Joe, I am very glad you did so."

"Thankee, Pip."

"You may be sure, dear Joe," I went on, after we had shaken hands, "that I shall never forget you."

"No, no, Pip!" said Joe, in a comfortable tone, "*I*'m sure of that. Ay, ay, old chap! Bless you, it were only necessary to get it well round in a man's mind, to be certain on it. But it took a bit of time to get it well round, the change come so oncommon plump ; didn't it?"

Somehow, I was not best pleased with Joe's being so mightily secure of me. I should have liked him to have betrayed emotion, or to have said, " It does you credit, Pip," or something of that sort. Therefore, I made no remark on Joe's first head : merely saying as to his second, that the tidings had indeed come suddenly, but that I had always wanted to be a gentleman, and had often and often speculated on what I would do, if I were one.

"Have you though?" said Joe. "Astonishing!"

"It's a pity now, Joe," said I, "that you did not get on a little more, when we had our lessons here ; isn't it?"

"Well, I don't know," returned Joe. "I'm so awful dull. I'm only master of my own trade. It were always a pity as I was so awful dull ; but it's no more of a pity now, than it was—this day twelvemonth—don't you see!"

What I had meant was, that when I came into my property and was able to do something for Joe, it would have been much more agreeable if he had been better qualified for a rise in station. He was so perfectly innocent of my meaning, however, that I thought I would mention it to Biddy in preference.

So, when we had walked home and had had tea, I took Biddy into our little garden by the side of the lane, and, after throwing out in a general way for the elevation of her spirits, that I should never forget her, said I had a favour to ask of her.

"And it is, Biddy," said I, "that you will not omit any opportunity of helping Joe on, a little."

"How helping him on?" asked Biddy, with a steady sort of glance.

"Well! Joe is a dear good fellow—in fact, I think he is the dearest fellow that ever lived—but he is rather backward in some things. For instance, Biddy, in his learning and his manners."

Although I was looking at Biddy as I spoke, and although she opened her eyes very wide when I had spoken, she did not look at me.

"Oh, his manners! won't his manners do, then?" asked Biddy, plucking a black-currant leaf.

"My dear Biddy, they do very well here—— "

"Oh! they *do* very well here?" interrupted Biddy, looking closely at the leaf in her hand.

"Hear me out—but if I were to remove Joe into a higher sphere, as I shall hope to remove him when I fully come into my property, they would hardly do him justice."

"And don't you think he knows that?" asked Biddy.

It was such a provoking question (for it had never in the most distant manner occurred to me), that I said, snappishly, "Biddy, what do you mean?"

Biddy having rubbed the leaf to pieces between her hands —and the smell of a black-currant bush has ever since recalled to me that evening in the little garden by the side of the lane—said, "Have you never considered that he may be proud?"

"Proud?" I repeated, with disdainful emphasis.

"Oh! there are many kinds of pride," said Biddy, looking full at me and shaking her head; "pride is not all of one kind—— "

"Well? What are you stopping for?" said I.

"Not all of one kind," resumed Biddy. "He may be too proud to let any one take him out of a place that he is competent to fill, and fills well and with respect. To tell you the truth, I think he is: though it sounds bold in me to say so, for you must know him far better than I do."

"Now, Biddy," said I, "I am very sorry to see this in you. I did not expect to see this in you. You are envious, Biddy, and grudging. You are dissatisfied on account of my rise in fortune, and you can't help showing it."

"If you have the heart to think so," returned Biddy, "say so. Say so over and over again, if you have the heart to think so."

"If you have the heart to be so, you mean, Biddy," said I, in a virtuous and superior tone; "don't put it off upon me. I am very sorry to see it, and it's a—it's a bad side of human nature. I did intend to ask you to use any little opportunities you might have after I was gone, of improving dear Joe. But after this, I ask you nothing. I am extremely sorry to see this in you, Biddy," I repeated. "It's a—it's a bad side of human nature."

"Whether you scold me or approve of me," returned poor Biddy, "you may equally depend upon my trying to do all that lies in my power, here, at all times. And whatever opinion you take away of me, shall make no difference in my remembrance of you. Yet a gentleman should not be unjust neither," said Biddy, turning away her head.

I again warmly repeated that it was a bad side of human nature (in which sentiment, waiving its application, I have since seen reason to think I was right), and I walked down the little path away from Biddy, and Biddy went into the house, and I went out at the garden gate and took a dejected stroll until supper-time; again feeling it very sorrowful and strange that this, the second night of my bright fortunes, should be as lonely and unsatisfactory as the first.

But, morning once more brightened my view, and I extended my clemency to Biddy, and we dropped the subject. Putting on the best clothes I had, I went into town as early as I could hope to find the shops open, and presented myself before Mr. Trabb, the tailor; who was having his breakfast in the parlour behind his shop, and who did not think it worth his while to come out to me, but called me in to him.

"Well!" said Mr. Trabb, in a hail-fellow-well-met kind of way. "How are you, and what can I do for you?"

Mr. Trabb had sliced his hot rolls into three feather beds,

and was slipping butter in between the blankets, and covering it up. He was a prosperous old bachelor, and his open window looked into a prosperous little garden and orchard, and there was a prosperous iron safe let into the wall at the side of his fireplace, and I did not doubt that heaps of his prosperity were put away in it in bags.

"Mr. Trabb," said I, "it's an unpleasant thing to have to mention, because it looks like boasting; but I have come into a handsome property."

A change passed over Mr. Trabb. He forgot the butter in bed, got up from the bedside, and wiped his fingers on the table-cloth, exclaiming, "Lord bless my soul!"

"I am going up to my guardian in London," said I, casually drawing some guineas out of my pocket and looking at them; "and I want a fashionable suit of clothes to go in. I wish to pay for them," I added—otherwise I thought he might only pretend to make them—"with ready money."

"My dear sir," said Mr. Trabb, as he respectfully bent his body, opened his arms, and took the liberty of touching me on the outside of each elbow, "don't hurt me by mentioning that. May I venture to congratulate you? Would you do me the favour of stepping into the shop?"

Mr. Trabb's boy was the most audacious boy in all that country-side. When I had entered he was sweeping the shop, and he had sweetened his labours by sweeping over me. He was still sweeping when I came out into the shop with Mr. Trabb, and he knocked the broom against all possible corners and obstacles, to express (as I understood it) equality with any blacksmith, alive or dead.

"Hold that noise," said Mr. Trabb, with the greatest sternness, "or I'll knock your head off! Do me the favour to be seated, sir. Now, this," said Mr. Trabb, taking down a roll of cloth, and tiding it out in a flowing manner over the counter, preparatory to getting his hand under it to show the gloss, "is a very sweet article. I can recommend it for your purpose, sir, because it really is extra super. But you shall see some others. Give me Number Four, you!" (To the boy, and with a dreadfully severe stare; foreseeing the danger of that miscreant's brushing me with it, or making some other sign of familiarity.)

Mr. Trabb never removed his stern eye from the boy until he had deposited number four on the counter and was at a safe distance again. Then, he commanded him to bring number five, and number eight. "And let me have none of your tricks here," said Mr. Trabb, "or you shall repent it, you young scoundrel, the longest day you have to live."

Mr. Trabb then bent over number four, and in a sort of deferential confidence recommended it to me as a light article for summer wear, an article much in vogue among the nobility and gentry, an article that it would ever be an honour to him to reflect upon a distinguished fellow-townsman's (if he might claim me for a fellow-townsman) having worn. "Are you bringing numbers five and eight, you vagabond," said Mr. Trabb to the boy after that, "or shall I kick you out of the shop and bring them myself?"

I selected the materials for a suit, with the assistance of Mr. Trabb's judgment, and re-entered the parlour to be measured. For, although Mr. Trabb had my measure already, and had previously been quite contented with it, he said apologetically that it "wouldn't do under existing circumstances, sir—wouldn't do at all." So, Mr. Trabb measured and calculated me in the parlour, as if I were an estate and he the finest species of surveyor, and gave himself such a world of trouble that I felt that no suit of clothes could possibly remunerate him for his pains. When he had at last done and had appointed to send the articles to Mr. Pumblechook's on the Thursday evening, he said, with his hand upon the parlour lock, "I know, sir, that London gentlemen cannot be expected to patronise local work, as a rule; but if you would give me a turn now and then in the quality of a townsman, I should greatly esteem it. Good morning, sir, much obliged.—Door!"

The last word was flung at the boy, who had not the least notion what it meant. But I saw him collapse as his master rubbed me out with his hands, and my first decided experience of the stupendous power of money, was, that it had morally laid upon his back, Trabb's boy.

After this memorable event, I went to the hatter's, and the bootmaker's, and the hosier's, and felt rather like Mother Hubbard's dog whose outfit required the services of so many trades. I also went to the coach-office and took my place for seven o'clock on Saturday morning. It was not necessary to explain everywhere that I had come into a handsome property; but whenever I said anything to that effect, it followed that the officiating tradesman ceased to have his attention diverted through the window by the High-street, and concentrated his mind upon me. When I had ordered everything I wanted, I directed my steps towards Pumble-chook's, and, as I approached that gentleman's place of business, I saw him standing at his door.

He was waiting for me with great impatience. He had been out early with the chaise-cart, and had called at the forge and heard the news. He had prepared a collation for me in the Barnwell parlour, and he too ordered his shopman to "come out of the gangway" as my sacred person passed.

"My dear friend," said Mr. Pumblechook, taking me by both hands, when he and I and the collation were alone, "I give you joy of your good fortune. Well deserved, well deserved!"

This was coming to the point, and I thought it a sensible way of expressing himself.

"To think," said Mr. Pumblechook, after snorting admiration at me for some moments, "that I should have been the humble instrument of leading up to this, is a proud reward."

I begged Mr. Pumblechook to remember that nothing was to be ever said or hinted, on that point.

"My dear young friend," said Mr. Pumblechook; "if you will allow me to call you so——"

I murmured "Certainly," and Mr. Pumblechook took me by both hands again, and communicated a movement to his waistcoat, which had an emotional appearance, though it was rather low down. "My dear young friend, rely upon my doing my little all in your absence, by keeping the fact before the mind of Joseph.—Joseph!" said Mr. Pumblechook, in the way of a compassionate adjuration. "Joseph!! Joseph!!!" Thereupon he shook his head and tapped it, expressing his sense of deficiency in Joseph.

"But, my dear young friend," said Mr. Pumblechook, "you must be hungry, you must be exhausted. Be seated. Here is a chicken had round from the Boar, here is a tongue had round from the Boar, here's one or two little things had round from the Boar, that I hope you may not despise. But do I," said Mr. Pumblechook, getting up again the moment after he had sat down, "see afore me, him as I ever sported with in his times of happy infancy? And may I—*may* I——?"

This May I, meant might he shake hands? I consented, and he was fervent, and then sat down again.

"Here is wine," said Mr. Pumblechook. "Let us drink, Thanks to Fortune, and may she ever pick out her favourites with equal judgment! And yet I cannot," said Mr. Pumblechook, getting up again, "see afore me One—and likewise drink to One—without again expressing—May I—*may I*——?"

I said he might, and he shook hands with me again, and emptied his glass and turned it upside down. I did the same; and if I had turned myself upside down before drinking, the wine could not have gone more direct to my head.

Mr. Pumblechook helped me to the liver wing, and to the best slice of tongue (none of those out-of-the-way No Thoroughfares of Pork now), and took, comparatively speaking, no care of himself at all. "Ah! poultry, poultry! You little thought," said Mr. Pumblechook, apostrophising the fowl in the dish, "when you was a young fledgling, what was in store for you. You little thought you was to be refreshment beneath this humble roof for one as—Call it a weakness, if you will," said Mr. Pumblechook, getting up again, "but may I? *may I*——?"

It began to be unnecessary to repeat the form of saying he might, so he did it at once. How he ever did it so often without wounding himself with my knife, I don't know.

"And your sister," he resumed, after a little steady eating, "which had the honour of bringing you up by hand! It's a sad picter, to reflect that she's no longer equal to fully understanding the honour. May——"

I saw he was about to come at me again, and I stopped him.

"We'll drink her health," said I.

"Ah!" cried Mr. Pumblechook, leaning back in his chair, quite flaccid with admiration, "that's the way you know 'em, sir!" (I don't know who Sir was, but he certainly was not I, and there was no third person present); "that's the way you know the noble-minded, sir! Ever forgiving and ever affable. It might," said the servile Pumblechook, putting down his untasted glass in a hurry and getting up again, "to a common person, have the appearance of repeating— but *may I*——?"

When he had done it, he resumed his seat and drank to my sister. "Let us never be blind," said Mr. Pumblechook, "to her faults of temper, but it is to be hoped she meant well."

At about this time, I began to observe that he was getting flushed in the face; as to myself, I felt all face, steeped in wine and smarting.

I mentioned to Mr. Pumblechook that I wished to have my new clothes sent to his house, and he was ecstatic on my so distinguishing him. I mentioned my reason for desiring to avoid observation in the village, and he lauded it to the skies. There was nobody but himself, he intimated, worthy of my confidence, and—in short, might he? Then he asked me tenderly if I remembered our boyish games at sums, and how we had gone together to have me bound apprentice, and, in effect, how he had ever been my favourite fancy and my chosen friend? If I had taken ten times as many glasses of wine as I had, I should have known that he never had stood in that relation towards me, and should in my heart of hearts have repudiated the idea. Yet for all that, I remember feeling convinced that I had been much mistaken in him, and that he was a sensible practical good-hearted prime fellow.

By degrees he fell to reposing such great confidence in me, as to ask my advice in reference to his own affairs. He mentioned that there was an opportunity for a great amalgamation and monopoly of the corn and seed trade on those premises, if enlarged, such as had never occurred before in that, or any other neighbourhood. What alone was wanting to the realisation of a vast fortune, he considered to be More Capital. Those were the two little words, more capital. Now it appeared to him (Pumblechook) that if that capital were got into the business, through a sleeping partner, sir—which sleeping partner would have nothing to do but walk in, by self or deputy, whenever he pleased, and examine the books—and walk in twice a year and take his profits away in his pocket, to the tune of fifty per cent.—it appeared to him that that might be an opening for a young gentleman of spirit combined with property, which would be worthy of his attention. But what did I think? He had great confidence in my opinion, and what did I think? I gave it as my opinion, "Wait a bit!" The united vastness and distinctness of this view so struck him, that he no longer asked

me if he might shake hands with me, but said he really must
—and did.

We drank all the wine, and Mr. Pumblechook pledged
himself over and over again to keep Joseph up to the mark
(I don't know what mark), and to render me efficient and
constant service (I don't know what service). He also made
known to me for the first time in my life, and certainly after
having kept his secret wonderfully well, that he had always
said of me, "That boy is no common boy, and mark me, his
fortun' will be no common fortun'." He said with a tearful
smile that it was a singular thing to think of now, and
I said so too. Finally, I went out into the air, with a dim
perception that there was something unwonted in the conduct
of the sunshine, and found that I had slumberously got to the
turnpike without having taken any account of the road.

There, I was roused by Mr. Pumblechook's hailing me.
He was a long way down the sunny street, and was making
expressive gestures for me to stop. I stopped, and he came
up breathless.

"No, my dear friend," said he, when he had recovered wind
for speech. "Not if I can help it. This occasion shall not
entirely pass without that affability on your part.—May I, as
an old friend and well-wisher? *May* I?"

We shook hands for the hundredth time at least, and he
ordered a young carter out of my way with the greatest
indignation. Then, he blessed me, and stood waving his
hand to me until I had passed the crook in the road; and
then I turned into a field and had a long nap under a hedge
before I pursued my way home.

I had scant luggage to take with me to London, for little
of the little I possessed was adapted to my new station. But
I began packing that same afternoon, and wildly packed up
things that I knew I should want next morning, in a fiction
that there was not a moment to be lost.

So, Tuesday, Wednesday, and Thursday passed; and on
Friday morning I went to Mr. Pumblechook's, to put
on my new clothes and pay my visit to Miss Havisham.
Mr. Pumblechook's own room was given up to me to dress
in, and was decorated with clean towels expressly for the
event. My clothes were rather a disappointment, of course.
Probably every new and eagerly expected garment ever put
on since clothes came in, fell a trifle short of the wearer's
expectation. But after I had had my new suit on, some half

an hour, and had gone through an immensity of posturing with Mr. Pumblechook's very limited dressing-glass, in the futile endeavour to see my legs, it seemed to fit me better. It being market morning at a neighbouring town some ten miles off, Mr. Pumblechook was not at home. I had not told him exactly when I meant to leave, and was not likely to shake hands with him again before departing. This was all as it should be, and I went out in my new array: fearfully ashamed of having to pass the shopman, and suspicious after all that I was at a personal disadvantage, something like Joe in his Sunday suit.

I went circuitously to Miss Havisham's by all the back ways, and rang at the bell constrainedly, on account of the stiff long fingers of my gloves. Sarah Pocket came to the gate, and positively reeled back when she saw me so changed; her walnut-shell countenance likewise turned from brown to green and yellow.

"You?" said she. "You? Good gracious! What do you want?"

"I am going to London, Miss Pocket," said I, "and want to say good-bye to Miss Havisham."

I was not expected, for she left me locked in the yard, while she went to ask if I were to be admitted. After a very short delay, she returned and took me up, staring at me all the way.

Miss Havisham was taking exercise in the room with the long spread table, leaning on her crutch stick. The room was lighted as of yore, and at the sound of her entrance she stopped and turned. She was then just abreast of the rotted bride-cake.

"Don't go, Sarah," she said. "Well, Pip?"

"I start for London, Miss Havisham, to-morrow," I was exceedingly careful what I said, "and I thought you would kindly not mind my taking leave of you."

"This is a gay figure, Pip," said she, making her crutch stick play round me, as if she, the fairy godmother who had changed me, were bestowing the finishing gift.

"I have come into such good fortune since I saw you last, Miss Havisham," I murmured. "And I am so grateful for it, Miss Havisham!"

"Ay, ay!" said she, looking at the discomfited and envious Sarah, with delight. "I have seen Mr. Jaggers. I have heard about it, Pip. So you go to-morrow?"

"Yes, Miss Havisham."

"And you are adopted by a rich person?"

"Yes, Miss Havisham."

"Not named?"

"No, Miss Havisham."

"And Mr. Jaggers is made your guardian?"

"Yes, Miss Havisham."

She quite gloated on these questions and answers, so keen was her enjoyment of Sarah Pocket's jealous dismay. "Well!" she went on; "you have a promising career before you. Be good—deserve it—and abide by Mr. Jaggers's instructions." She looked at me, and looked at Sarah, and Sarah's countenance wrung out of her watchful face a cruel smile. "Good-bye, Pip!—you will always keep the name of Pip, you know."

"Yes, Miss Havisham."

"Good-bye, Pip!"

She stretched out her hand, and I went down on my knee and put it to my lips. I had not considered how I should take leave of her; it came naturally to me at the moment, to do this. She looked at Sarah Pocket with triumph in her weird eyes, and so I left my fairy godmother, with both her hands on her crutch stick, standing in the midst of the dimly lighted room beside the rotten bride-cake that was hidden in cobwebs.

Sarah Pocket conducted me down, as if I were a ghost who must be seen out. She could not get over my appearance, and was in the last degree confounded. I said "Good-bye, Miss Pocket;" but she merely stared, and did not seem collected enough to know that I had spoken. Clear of the house, I made the best of my way back to Pumblechook's, took off my new clothes, made them into a bundle, and went back home in my older dress, carrying it—to speak the truth —much more at my ease too, though I had the bundle to carry.

And now, those six days which were to have run out so slowly, had run out fast and were gone, and to-morrow looked me in the face more steadily than I could look at it. As the six evenings had dwindled away to five, to four, to three, to two, I had become more and more appreciative of the society of Joe and Biddy. On this last evening, I dressed myself out in my new clothes, for their delight, and sat in my splendour until bedtime. We had a hot supper on the occasion, graced by the inevitable roast fowl, and we had some flip to finish with. We were all very low, and none the higher for pretending to be in spirits.

I was to leave our village at five in the morning, carrying my little hand-portmanteau, and I had told Joe that I wished to walk away all alone. I am afraid—sore afraid—that this purpose originated in my sense of the contrast there would be between me and Joe, if we went to the coach together. I had pretended with myself that there was nothing of this taint in the arrangement; but when I went up to my little room on this last night, I felt compelled to admit that it might be done so, and had an impulse upon me to go down again and entreat Joe to walk with me in the morning. I did not.

All night there were coaches in my broken sleep, going to wrong places instead of to London, and having in the traces, now dogs, now cats, now pigs, now men—never horses. Fantastic failures of journeys occupied me until the day dawned and the birds were singing. Then, I got up and partly dressed, and sat at the window to take a last look out, and in taking it fell asleep.

Biddy was astir so early to get my breakfast, that, although I did not sleep at the window an hour, I smelt the smoke of the kitchen fire when I started up with a terrible idea that it must be late in the afternoon. But long after that, and long after I heard the clinking of the teacups and was quite ready, I wanted the resolution to go down-stairs. After all, I remained up there, repeatedly unlocking and unstrapping my small portmanteau and locking and strapping it up again, until Biddy called to me that I was late.

It was a hurried breakfast with no taste in it. I got up from the meal, saying with a sort of briskness, as if it had only just occurred to me, "Well! I suppose I must be off!" and then I kissed my sister, who was laughing and nodding and shaking in her usual chair, and kissed Biddy, and threw my arms around Joe's neck. Then I took up my little portmanteau and walked out. The last I saw of them was, when I presently heard a scuffle behind me, and looking back, saw Joe throwing an old shoe after me and Biddy throwing another old shoe. I stopped then, to wave my hat, and dear old Joe waved his strong right arm above his head, crying huskily, "Hooroar!" and Biddy put her apron to her face.

I walked away at a good pace, thinking it was easier to go than I had supposed it would be, and reflecting that it would never have done to have an old shoe thrown after the coach, in sight of all the High-street. I whistled and made nothing of going. But the village was very peaceful and quiet, and the light mists were solemnly rising, as if to show me the world, and I had been so innocent and little there, and all beyond was so unknown and great, that in a moment with a strong heave and sob I broke into tears. It was by the finger-post at the end of the village, and I laid my hand upon it, and said, "Good-bye, O my dear, dear friend!"

Heaven knows we need never be ashamed of our tears, for they are rain upon the blinding dust of earth, overlying our hard hearts. I was better after I had cried, than before—more sorry, more aware of my own ingratitude, more gentle. If I had cried before, I should have had Joe with me then.

So subdued I was by those tears, and by their breaking out again in the course of the quiet walk, that when I was on the coach, and it was clear of the town, I deliberated with an aching heart whether I would not get down when we changed horses and walk back, and have another evening at home, and a better parting. We changed, and I had not made up my mind, and still reflected for my comfort that it would be quite practicable to get down and walk back, when we changed again. And while I was occupied with those deliberations, I would fancy an exact resemblance to Joe in some man coming along the road towards us, and my heart would beat high.—As if he could possibly be there!

We changed again, and yet again, and it was now too late and too far to go back, and I went on. And the mists had all solemnly risen now, and the world lay spread before me.

THIS IS THE END OF THE FIRST STAGE OF
PIP'S EXPECTATIONS

CHAPTER XX

THE journey from our town to the metropolis was a journey of about five hours. It was a little past mid-day when the four-horse stage-coach by which I was a passenger, got into the ravel of traffic frayed out about the Cross Keys, Wood-street, Cheapside, London.

We Britons had at that time particularly settled that it was treasonable to doubt our having and our being the best of everything : otherwise, while I was scared by the immensity of London, I think I might have had some faint doubts whether it was not rather ugly, crooked, narrow, and dirty.

Mr. Jaggers had duly sent me his address ; it was Little Britain, and he had written after it on his card, "just out of Smithfield, and close by the coach-office." Nevertheless, a hackney-coachman, who seemed to have as many capes to his greasy great-coat as he was years old, packed me up in his coach and hemmed me in with a folding and jingling barrier of steps, as if he were going to take me fifty miles. His getting on his box, which I remember to have been decorated with an old weather-stained pea-green hammer-cloth, moth-eaten into rags, was quite a work of time. It was a wonderful equipage, with six great coronets outside, and ragged things behind for I don't know how many foot-men to hold on by, and a harrow below them, to prevent amateur footmen from yielding to the temptation.

I had scarcely had time to enjoy the coach and to think how like a straw-yard it was, and yet how like a rag-shop, and to wonder why the horses' nose-bags were kept inside, when I observed the coachman beginning to get down, as if we were going to stop presently. And stop we presently did, in a gloomy street, at certain offices with an open door, whereon was painted MR. JAGGERS.

"How much ?" I asked the coachman.

The coachman answered, "A shilling—unless you wish to make it more."

I naturally said I had no wish to make it more.

"Then it must be a shilling," observed the coachman. "I don't want to get into trouble. I know *him!*" He darkly closed an eye at Mr. Jaggers's name, and shook his head.

When he had got his shilling, and had in course of time completed the ascent to his box, and had got away (which appeared to relieve his mind), I went into the front office with my little portmanteau in my hand, and asked, was Mr. Jaggers at home?

"He is not," returned the clerk. "He is in Court at present. Am I addressing Mr. Pip?"

I signified that he was addressing Mr. Pip.

"Mr. Jaggers left word would you wait in his room? He couldn't say how long he might be, having a case on. But it stands to reason, his time being valuable, that he won't be longer than he can help."

With those words, the clerk opened a door, and ushered me into an inner chamber at the back. Here we found a gentleman with one eye, in a velveteen suit and knee-breeches, who wiped his nose with his sleeve on being interrupted in the perusal of the newspaper.

"Go and wait outside, Mike," said the clerk.

I began to say that I hoped I was not interrupting—— when the clerk shoved this gentleman out with as little ceremony as I ever saw used, and tossing his fur cap out after him, left me alone.

Mr. Jaggers's room was lighted by a skylight only, and was a most dismal place; the skylight, eccentrically patched like a broken head, and the distorted adjoining houses looking as if they had twisted themselves to peep down at me through it. There were not so many papers about, as I should have expected to see; and there were some odd objects about, that I should not have expected to see—such as an old rusty pistol, a sword in a scabbard, several strange-looking boxes and packages, and two dreadful casts on a shelf, of faces peculiarly swollen, and twitchy about the nose. Mr. Jaggers's own high-backed chair was of deadly black horse-hair, with rows of brass nails round it, like a coffin; and I fancied I could see how he leaned back in it, and bit his forefinger at the clients. The room was but small, and the clients seemed to have had a habit of backing up against the wall: the wall, especially opposite to Mr. Jaggers's chair, being greasy with shoulders. I recalled, too, that the one-eyed gentleman had shuffled forth against the wall when I was the innocent cause of his being turned out.

I sat down in the cliental chair placed over against Mr. Jaggers's chair, and became fascinated by the dismal atmosphere of the place. I called to mind that the clerk had the same air of knowing something to everybody else's disadvantage, as his master had. I wondered how many other clerks there were up-stairs, and whether they all claimed to have the same detrimental mastery of their fellow-creatures. I wondered what was the history of all the odd litter about the room, and how it came there. I wondered whether the two swollen faces were of Mr. Jaggers's family, and, if he were so unfortunate as to have had a pair of such ill-looking relations, why he stuck them on that dusty perch for the blacks and flies to settle on, instead of giving them a place at home. Of course I had no experience of a London summer day, and my spirits may have been oppressed by the hot exhausted air, and by the dust and grit that lay thick on everything. But I sat wondering and waiting in Mr. Jaggers's close room, until I really could not bear the two casts on the shelf above Mr. Jaggers's chair, and got up and went out.

When I told the clerk that I would take a turn in the air while I waited, he advised me to go round the corner and I should come into Smithfield. So, I came into Smithfield; and the shameful place, being all asmear with filth and fat and blood and foam, seemed to stick to me. So I rubbed it off with all possible speed by turning into a street where I saw the great black dome of Saint Paul's bulging at me from behind a grim stone building which a bystander said was Newgate Prison. Following the wall of the jail, I found the roadway covered with straw to deaden the noise of passing vehicles; and from this, and from the quantity of people standing about, smelling strongly of spirits and beer, I inferred that the trials were on.

While I looked about me here, an exceedingly dirty and partially drunk minister of justice asked me if I would like to step in and hear a trial or so: informing me that he could give me a front place for half-a-crown, whence I should command a full view of the Lord Chief Justice in his wig and robes—mentioning that awful personage like waxwork, and presently offering him at the reduced price of eighteenpence. As I declined the proposal on the plea of an appointment, he was so good as to take me into a yard and show me where the gallows was kept, and also where people were publicly whipped, and then he showed me the Debtors' Door, out of which culprits came to be hanged; heightening the interest of that dreadful portal by giving me to understand that "four on 'em" would come out at that door the day after to-morrow at eight in the morning to be killed in a row. This was horrible, and gave me a sickening idea of London: the more so as the Lord Chief Justice's proprietor wore (from his hat down to his boots and up again to his pocket-handkerchief inclusive) mildewed clothes, which had evidently not belonged to him originally, and which, I took it into my head, he had bought cheap of the executioner. Under these circumstances I thought myself well rid of him for a shilling.

I dropped into the office to ask if Mr. Jaggers had come in yet, and I found he had not, and I strolled out again. This time, I made the tour of Little Britain, and turned into Bartholomew Close; and now I became aware that other people were waiting about for Mr. Jaggers, as well as I. There were two men of secret appearance lounging in Bartholomew Close, and thoughtfully fitting their feet into the cracks of the pavement as they talked together, one of whom said to the other when they first passed me, that "Jaggers would do it if it was to be done." There was a knot of three men and two women standing at a corner, and one of the women was crying on her dirty shawl, and the other comforted her by saying, as she pulled her own shawl over her shoulders, "Jaggers is for him, 'Melia, and what more *could* you have?" There was a red-eyed little Jew who came into the Close while I was loitering there, in company with a second little Jew whom he sent upon an errand; and while the messenger was gone, I remarked this Jew, who was of a highly excitable temperament, performing a jig of anxiety under a lamp-post, and accompanying himself, in a kind of frenzy, with the words, "Oh Jaggerth, Jaggerth, Jaggerth! all otherth ith Cag-Maggerth, give me Jaggerth!" These testimonies to the popularity of my guardian made a deep impression on me, and I admired and wondered more than ever.

At length, as I was looking out at the iron gate of Bartholomew Close into Little Britain, I saw Mr. Jaggers coming across the road towards me. All the others who were waiting, saw him at the same time, and there was quite a rush at him. Mr. Jaggers, putting a hand on my shoulder and walking me on at his side without saying anything to me, addressed himself to his followers.

First, he took the two secret men.

"Now, I have nothing to say to *you*," said Mr. Jaggers, throwing his finger at them. "I want to know no more than I know. As to the result, it's a toss-up. I told you from the first it was a toss-up. Have you paid Wemmick?"

"We made the money up this morning, sir," said one of the men, submissively, while the other perused Mr. Jaggers's face.

"I don't ask you when you made it up, or where, or whether you made it up at all. Has Wemmick got it?"

"Yes, sir," said both the men together.

"Very well; then you may go. Now, I won't have it!" said Mr. Jaggers, waving his hand at them to put them behind him. "If you say a word to me, I'll throw up the case."

"We thought, Mr. Jaggers——" one of the men began, pulling off his hat.

"That's what I told you not to do," said Mr. Jaggers. "*You* thought! I think for you; that's enough for you. If I want you, I know where to find you; I don't want you to find me. Now I won't have it. I won't hear a word."

The two men looked at one another as Mr. Jaggers waved them behind again, and humbly fell back and were heard no more.

"And now *you!*" said Mr. Jaggers, suddenly stopping, and turning on the two women with the shawls, from whom the three men had meekly separated—"Oh! Amelia, is it?"

"Yes, Mr. Jaggers."

"And do you remember," retorted Mr. Jaggers, "that but for me you wouldn't be here and couldn't be here?"

"Oh yes, sir!" exclaimed both women together. "Lord bless you, sir, well we knows that!"

"Then why," said Mr. Jaggers, "do you come here?"

"My Bill, sir?" the crying woman pleaded.

"Now, I tell you what!" said Mr. Jaggers. "Once for all. If you don't know that your Bill's in good hands, I know it. And if you come here, bothering about your Bill, I'll make an example of both your Bill and you, and let him slip through my fingers. Have you paid Wemmick?"

"Oh yes, sir! Every farden."

"Very well. Then you have done all you have got to do. Say another word—one single word—and Wemmick shall give you your money back."

This terrible threat caused the two women to fall off immediately. No one remained now but the excitable Jew, who had already raised the skirts of Mr. Jaggers's coat to his lips several times.

"I don't know this man?" said Mr. Jaggers, in the most devastating strain. "What does this fellow want?"

"Ma thear Mithter Jaggerth. Hown brother to Habraham Latharuth!"

"Who's he?" said Mr. Jaggers. "Let go of my coat."

The suitor, kissing the hem of the garment again before relinquishing it, replied, "Habraham Latharuth, on thuthpithion of plate."

"You're too late," said Mr. Jaggers. "I am over the way."

"Holy father, Mithter Jaggerth!" cried my excitable acquaintance, turning white, "don't thay you're again Habraham Latharuth!"

"I am," said Mr. Jaggers, "and there's an end of it. Get out of the way."

"Mithter Jaggerth! Half a moment! My hown cuthen'th gone to Mithter Wemmick at thith prethenth minute to hoffer him hany termth. Mithter Jaggerth! Half a quarter of a moment! If you'd have the condethenthun to be bought off from the t'other thide—at any thuperior prithe!—money no object!—Mithter Jaggerth—Mithter——!"

My guardian threw his supplicant off with supreme indifference, and left him dancing on the pavement as if it were red-hot. Without further interruption, we reached the front office, where we found the clerk and the man in velveteen with the fur cap.

"Here's Mike," said the clerk, getting down from his stool, and approaching Mr. Jaggers confidentially.

"Oh!" said Mr. Jaggers, turning to the man who was pulling a lock of hair in the middle of his forehead, like the *Bull in Cock Robin* pulling at the bell-rope; "your man comes on this afternoon. Well?"

"Well, Mas'r Jaggers," returned Mike, in the voice of a sufferer from a constitutional cold; "arter a deal o' trouble, I've found one, sir, as might do."

"What is he prepared to swear?"

"Well, Mas'r Jaggers," said Mike, wiping his nose on his fur cap this time ; " in a general way, anythink."

Mr. Jaggers suddenly became most irate. " Now, I warned you before," said he, throwing his forefinger at the terrified client, " that if ever you presumed to talk in that way here, I'd make an example of you. You infernal scoundrel, how dare you tell ME that ? "

The client looked scared, but bewildered too, as if he were unconscious what he had done.

"Spooney ! " said the clerk, in a low voice, giving him a stir with his elbow. "Soft Head ! Need you say it face to face ? "

" Now, I ask you, you blundering booby," said my guardian, very sternly, " once more and for the last time, what the man you have brought here is prepared to swear ? "

Mike looked hard at my guardian, as if he were trying to learn a lesson from his face, and slowly replied, " Ayther to character, or to having been in his company and never left him all the night in question."

" Now, be careful. In what station of life is this man ? "

Mike looked at his cap, and looked at the floor, and looked at the ceiling, and looked at the clerk, and even looked at me, before beginning to reply in a nervous manner, "We've dressed him up like―――" when my guardian blustered out :

" What ? You WILL, will you ? "

(" Spooney ! " added the clerk again, with another stir.)

After some helpless casting about, Mike brightened and began again :

" He is dressed like a 'spectable pieman. A sort of a pastry-cook."

" Is he here ? " asked my guardian.

" I left him," said Mike, " a setting on some doorsteps round the corner."

" Take him past that window, and let me see him."

The window indicated was the office window. We all three went to it, behind the wire blind, and presently saw the client go by in an accidental manner, with a murderous-looking tall individual, in a short suit of white linen and a paper cap. This guileless confectioner was not by any means sober, and had a black eye in the green stage of recovery, which was painted over.

" Tell him to take his witness away directly," said my

guardian to the clerk, in extreme disgust, "and ask him what he means by bringing such a fellow as that."

My guardian then took me into his own room, and while he lunched, standing, from a sandwich-box and a pocket flask of sherry (he seemed to bully his very sandwich as he ate it), informed me what arrangements he had made for me. I was to go to "Barnard's Inn," to young Mr. Pocket's rooms, where a bed had been sent in for my accommodation; I was to remain with young Mr. Pocket until Monday; on Monday I was to go with him to his father's house on a visit, that I might try how I liked it. Also, I was told what my allowance was to be—it was a very liberal one—and had handed to me from one of my guardian's drawers, the cards of certain tradesmen with whom I was to deal for all kinds of clothes, and such other things as I could in reason want. "You will find your credit good, Mr. Pip," said my guardian, whose flask of sherry smelt like a whole cask-full, as he hastily refreshed himself, "but I shall by this means be able to check your bills, and to pull you up if I find you outrunning the constable. Of course you'll go wrong somehow, but that's no fault of mine."

After I had pondered a little over this encouraging sentiment, I asked Mr. Jaggers if I could send for a coach? He said it was not worth while, I was so near my destination; Wemmick should walk round with me, if I pleased.

I then found that Wemmick was the clerk in the next room. Another clerk was rung down from up-stairs to take his place while he was out, and I accompanied him into the street, after shaking hands with my guardian. We found a new set of people lingering outside, but Wemmick made a way among them by saying coolly yet decisively, "I tell you it's no use; he won't have a word to say to one of you;" and we soon got clear of them, and went on side by side.

into which those houses were divided, were in every stage of dilapidated blind and curtain, crippled flower-pot, cracked glass, dusty decay, and miserable makeshift; while To Let To Let To Let, glared at me from empty rooms, as if no new wretches ever came there, and the vengeance of the soul of Barnard were being slowly appeased by the gradual suicide of the present occupants and their unholy interment under the gravel. A frouzy mourning of soot and smoke attired this forlorn creation of Barnard, and it had strewed ashes on its head, and was undergoing penance and humiliation as a mere dust-hole. Thus far my sense of sight; while dry rot and wet rot and all the silent rots that rot in neglected roof and cellar—rot of rat and mouse and bug and coaching-stables near at hand besides—addressed themselves faintly to my sense of smell, and moaned, "Try Barnard's Mixture."

So imperfect was this realisation of the first of my great expectations, that I looked in dismay at Mr. Wemmick. "Ah!" said he, mistaking me; "the retirement reminds you of the country. So it does me."

He led me into a corner and conducted me up a flight of stairs—which appeared to me to be slowly collapsing into sawdust, so that one of those days the upper lodgers would look out at their doors and find themselves without the means of coming down—to a set of chambers on the top floor. Mr. Pocket, Jun., was painted on the door, and there was a label on the letter-box, "Return shortly."

"He hardly thought you'd come so soon," Mr. Wemmick explained. "You don't want me any more?"

"No, thank you," said I.

"As I keep the cash," Mr. Wemmick observed, "we shall most likely meet pretty often. Good day."

"Good day."

I put out my hand, and Mr. Wemmick at first looked at it as if he thought I wanted something. Then he looked at me, and said, correcting himself,

"To be sure! Yes. You're in the habit of shaking hands?"

I was rather confused, thinking it must be out of the London fashion, but said yes.

"I have got so out of it!" said Mr. Wemmick—"except at last. Very glad, I'm sure, to make your acquaintance. Good day!"

When we had shaken hands and he was gone, I opened the staircase window and had nearly beheaded myself, for the lines had rotted away, and it came down like the guillotine. Happily it was so quick that I had not put my head out. After this escape, I was content to take a foggy view of the Inn through the window's encrusting dirt, and to stand dolefully looking out, saying to myself that London was decidedly overrated.

Mr. Pocket, Junior's, idea of Shortly was not mine, for I had nearly maddened myself with looking out for half an hour, and had written my name with my finger several times in the dirt of every pane in the window, before I heard footsteps on the stairs. Gradually there arose before me the hat, head, neckcloth, waistcoat, trousers, boots, of a member of society of about my own standing. He had a paper-bag under each arm and a pottle of strawberries in one hand, and was out of breath.

"Mr. Pip?" said he.

"Mr. Pocket?" said I.

"Dear me!" he exclaimed. "I am extremely sorry; but I knew there was a coach from your part of the country at midday, and I thought you would come by that one. The fact is, I have been out on your account—not that that is any excuse—for I thought, coming from the country, you might like a little fruit after dinner, and I went to Covent Garden Market to get it good."

For a reason that I had, I felt as if my eyes would start out of my head. I acknowledged his attention incoherently, and began to think this was a dream.

"Dear me!" said Mr. Pocket, Junior. "This door sticks so!"

As he was fast making jam of his fruit by wrestling with the door while the paper-bags were under his arms, I begged him to allow me to hold them. He relinquished them with an agreeable smile, and combated with the door as if it were a wild beast. It yielded so suddenly at last, that he staggered back upon me, and I staggered back upon the opposite door, and we both laughed. But still I felt as if my eyes must start out of my head, and as if this must be a dream.

"Pray come in," said Mr. Pocket, Junior. "Allow me to lead the way. I am rather bare here, but I hope you'll be able to make out tolerably well till Monday. My father thought you would get on more agreeably through to-morrow with me than with him, and might like to take a walk about London. I am sure I shall be very happy to show London to you. As to our table, you won't find that bad, I hope, for it will be supplied from our coffee-house here, and (it is only right I should add) at your expense, such being Mr. Jaggers's directions. As to our lodging, it's not by any means splendid, because I have my own bread to earn, and my father hasn't anything to give me, and I shouldn't be willing to take it, if he had. This is our sitting-room—just such chairs and tables and carpet and so forth, you see, as they could spare from home. You mustn't give me credit for the tablecloth and spoons and castors, because they come for you from the coffee-house. This is my little bed-room; rather musty, but Barnard's *is* musty. This is your bedroom; the furniture's hired for the occasion, but I trust it will answer the purpose; if you should want anything, I'll go and fetch it. The chambers are retired, and we shall be alone together, but we shan't fight, I dare say. But, dear me, I beg your pardon, you're holding the fruit all this time. Pray let me take these bags from you. I am quite ashamed."

As I stood opposite to Mr. Pocket, Junior, delivering him the bags, One, Two, I saw the starting appearance come into his own eyes that I knew to be in mine, and he said, falling back:

"Lord bless me, you're the prowling boy!"

"And you," said I, "are the pale young gentleman!"

CHAPTER XXII

The pale young gentleman and I stood contemplating one another in Barnard's Inn, until we both burst out laughing. "The idea of its being you!" said he. "The idea of its being *you!*" said I. And then we contemplated one another afresh, and laughed again. "Well!" said the pale young gentleman, reaching out his hand good-humouredly, "it's all over now, I hope, and it will be magnanimous in you if you'll forgive me for having knocked you about so."

I derived from this speech that Mr. Herbert Pocket (for Herbert was the pale young gentleman's name) still rather confounded his intention with his execution. But I made a modest reply, and we shook hands warmly.

"You hadn't come into your good fortune at that time?" said Herbert Pocket.

"No," said I.

"No," he acquiesced: "I heard it had happened very lately. *I* was rather on the look-out for good-fortune then."

"Indeed?"

"Yes. Miss Havisham had sent for me, to see if she could take a fancy to me. But she couldn't—at all events, she didn't."

I thought it polite to remark that I was surprised to hear that.

"Bad taste," said Herbert, laughing, "but a fact. Yes, she had sent for me on a trial visit, and if I had come out of it successfully, I suppose I should have been provided for; perhaps I should have been what-you-may-called it to Estella."

"What's that?" I asked, with sudden gravity.

He was arranging his fruit in plates while we talked, which divided his attention, and was the cause of his having made this lapse of a word. "Affianced," he explained, still busy with the fruit. "Betrothed. Engaged. What's-his-named. Any word of that sort."

"How did you bear your disappointment?" I asked.

"Pooh!" said he, "I didn't care much for it. *She's* a Tartar."

"Miss Havisham?"

"I don't say no to that, but I meant Estella. That girl's hard and haughty and capricious to the last degree, and has been brought up by Miss Havisham to wreak revenge on all the male sex."

"What relation is she to Miss Havisham?"

"None," said he. "Only adopted."

"Why should she wreak revenge on all the male sex? What revenge?"

"Lord, Mr. Pip!" said he. "Don't you know?"

"No," said I.

"Dear me! It's quite a story, and shall be saved till dinner-time. And now let me take the liberty of asking you a question. How did you come there, that day?"

I told him, and he was attentive until I had finished, and then burst out laughing again, and asked me if I was sore afterwards? I didn't ask him if *he* was, for my conviction on that point was perfectly established.

"Mr. Jaggers is your guardian, I understand?" he went on.

"Yes."

"You know he is Miss Havisham's man of business and solicitor, and has her confidence when nobody else has?"

This was bringing me (I felt) towards dangerous ground. I answered with a constraint I made no attempt to disguise, that I had seen Mr. Jaggers in Miss Havisham's house on the very day of our combat, but never at any other time, and that I believed he had no recollection of having ever seen me there.

"He was so obliging as to suggest my father for your tutor, and he called on my father to propose it. Of course he knew about my father from his connexion with Miss Havisham. My father is Miss Havisham's cousin; not that that implies familiar intercourse between them, for he is a bad courtier and will not propitiate her."

Herbert Pocket had a frank and easy way with him that was very taking. I had never seen any one then, and I have never seen any one since, who more strongly expressed to me, in every look and tone, a natural incapacity to do anything secret and mean. There was something wonderfully hopeful about his general air, and something that at the same time whispered to me he would never be successful or rich. I don't know how this was. I became imbued with the notion on that first occasion before we sat down to dinner, but I cannot define by what means.

He was still a pale young gentleman, and had a certain conquered languor about him in the midst of his spirits and briskness, that did not seem indicative of natural strength. He had not a handsome face, but it was better than handsome : being extremely amiable and cheerful. His figure was a little ungainly, as in the days when my knuckles had taken such liberties with it, but it looked as if it would always be light and young. Whether Mr. Trabb's local work would have sat more gracefully on him than on me, may be a question ; but I am conscious that he carried off his rather old clothes, much better than I carried off my new suit.

As he was so communicative, I felt that reserve on my part would be a bad return unsuited to our years. I therefore told him my small story, and laid stress on my being forbidden to inquire who my benefactor was. I further mentioned that as I had been brought up a blacksmith in a country place, and knew very little of the ways of politeness, I would take it as a great kindness in him if he would give me a hint whenever he saw me at a loss or going wrong.

"With pleasure," said he, "though I venture to prophesy that you'll want very few hints. I dare say we shall be often together, and I should like to banish any needless restraint between us. Will you do me the favour to begin at once to call me by my christian name, Herbert?"

I thanked him, and said I would. I informed him in exchange that my christian name was Philip.

"I don't take to Philip," said he, smiling, "for it sounds like a moral boy out of the spelling-book, who was so lazy that he fell into a pond, or so fat that he couldn't see out of his eyes, or so avaricious that he locked up his cake till the mice ate it, or so determined to go a bird's-nesting that he got himself eaten by bears who lived handy in the neighbourhood. I tell you what I should like. We are so harmonious, and you have been a blacksmith—would you mind it?"

"I shouldn't mind anything that you propose," I answered, "but I don't understand you."

"Would you mind Handel for a familiar name? There's a charming piece of music, by Handel, called the Harmonious Blacksmith."

"I should like it very much."

"Then, my dear Handel," said he, turning round as the door opened, "here is the dinner, and I must beg of you to take the top of the table, because the dinner is of your providing."

This I would not hear of, so he took the top, and I faced him. It was a nice little dinner—seemed to me then, a very Lord Mayor's Feast—and it acquired additional relish from being eaten under those independent circumstances, with no old people by, and with London all around us. This again was heightened by a certain gipsy character that set the banquet off; for, while the table was, as Mr. Pumblechook might have said, the lap of luxury—being entirely furnished forth from the coffee-house—the circumjacent region of sitting-room was of a comparatively pastureless and shifty character: imposing on the waiter the wandering habits of putting the covers on the floor (where he fell over them), the melted butter in the armchair, the bread on the book-shelves, the cheese in the coal-scuttle, and the boiled fowl into my bed in the next room—where I found much of its parsley and butter in a state of congelation when I retired for the night. All this made the feast delightful, and when the waiter was not there to watch me, my pleasure was without alloy.

We had made some progress in the dinner, when I re-minded Herbert of his promise to tell me about Miss Havisham.

"True," he replied. "I'll redeem it at once. Let me introduce the topic, Handel, by mentioning that in London it is not the custom to put the knife in the mouth—for fear of accidents—and that while the fork is reserved for that use, it is not put further in than necessary. It is scarcely worth mentioning, only it's as well to do as other people do. Also, the spoon is not generally used over-hand, but under. This has two advantages. You get at your mouth better (which after all is the object), and you save a good deal of the attitude of opening oysters, on the part of the right elbow."

He offered these friendly suggestions in such a lively way, that we both laughed and I scarcely blushed.

" Now," he pursued, " concerning Miss Havisham. Miss Havisham, you must know, was a spoilt child. Her mother died when she was a baby, and her father denied her nothing. Her father was a country gentleman down in your part of the world, and was a brewer. I don't know why it should be a crack thing to be a brewer; but it is indisputable that while you cannot possibly be genteel and bake, you may be as genteel as never was and brew. You see it every day."

" Yet a gentleman may not keep a public-house; may he ? " said I.

" Not on any account," returned Herbert; " but a public-house may keep a gentleman. Well ! Mr. Havisham was very rich and very proud. So was his daughter."

" Miss Havisham was an only child ? " I hazarded.

" Stop a moment, I am coming to that. No, she was not an only child ; she had a half-brother. Her father privately married again—his cook, I rather think."

" I thought he was proud," said I.

" My good Handel, so he was. He married his second wife privately, because he was proud, and in course of time *she* died. When she was dead, I apprehend he first told his daughter what he had done, and then the son became a part of the family, residing in the house you are acquainted with. As the son grew a young man, he turned out riotous, extravagant, undutiful—altogether bad. At last his father disinherited him ; but he softened when he was dying, and left him well off, though not nearly so well off as Miss Havisham.—Take another glass of wine, and excuse my mentioning that society as a body does not expect one to be so strictly conscientious in emptying one's glass, as to turn it bottom upwards with the rim on one's nose."

I had been doing this, in an excess of attention to his recital. I thanked him, and apologised. He said, " Not at all," and resumed.

" Miss Havisham was now an heiress, and you may suppose was looked after as a great match. Her half-brother had now ample means again, but what with debts and what with new madness wasted them most fearfully again. There were stronger differences between him and her, than there had been between him and his father, and it is suspected that he cherished a deep and mortal grudge against her as having influenced the father's anger. Now, I come to the cruel part of the story—merely breaking off, my dear Handel, to remark that a dinner-napkin will not go into a tumbler."

Why I was trying to pack mine into my tumbler, I am wholly unable to say. I only know that I found myself, with a perseverance worthy of a much better cause, making the most strenuous exertions to compress it within those limits. Again I thanked him and apologised, and again he said in the cheerfullest manner, "Not at all, I am sure!" and resumed.

"There appeared upon the scene—say at the races, or the public balls, or anywhere else you like—a certain man, who made love to Miss Havisham. I never saw him (for this happened five-and-twenty years ago, before you and I were, Handel), but I have heard my father mention that he was a showy man, and the kind of man for the purpose. But that he was not to be, without ignorance or prejudice, mistaken for a gentleman, my father most strongly asseverates; because it is a principle of his that no man who was not a true gentleman at heart, ever was, since the world began, a true gentleman in manner. He says, no varnish can hide the grain of the wood; and that the more varnish you put on, the more the grain will express itself. Well! This man pursued Miss Havisham closely, and professed to be devoted to her. I believe she had not shown much susceptibility up to that time; but all the susceptibility she possessed, certainly came out then, and she passionately loved him. There is no doubt that she perfectly idolized him. He practised on her affection in that systematic way, that he got great sums of money from her, and he induced her to buy her brother out of a share in the brewery (which had been weakly left him by his father) at an immense price, on the plea that when he was her husband he must hold and manage it all. Your guardian was not at that time in Miss Havisham's councils, and she was too haughty and too much in love, to be advised by any one. Her relations were poor and scheming, with the exception of my father; he was poor enough, but not time-serving or jealous. The only independent one among them, he warned her that she was doing too much for this man, and was placing herself too unreservedly in his power. She took the first opportunity of angrily ordering my father out of the house, in his presence, and my father has never seen her since."

V.   G

I thought of her having said, "Matthew will come and see me at last when I am laid dead upon that table;" and I asked Herbert whether his father was so inveterate against her?

"It's not that," said he, "but she charged him, in the presence of her intended husband, with being disappointed in the hope of fawning upon her for his own advancement, and, if he were to go to her now, it would look true—even to him—and even to her. To return to the man and make an end of him. The marriage day was fixed, the wedding dresses were bought, the wedding tour was planned out, the wedding guests were invited. The day came, but not the bridegroom. He wrote a letter——"

"Which she received," I struck in, "when she was dressing for her marriage? At twenty minutes to nine?"

"At the hour and minute," said Herbert, nodding, "at which she afterwards stopped all the clocks. What was in it, further than that it most heartlessly broke the marriage off, I can't tell you, because I don't know. When she recovered from a bad illness that she had, she laid the whole place waste, as you have seen it, and she has never since looked upon the light of day."

"Is that all the story?" I asked, after considering it.

"All I know of it; and indeed I only know so much, through piecing it out for myself; for my father always avoids it, and, even when Miss Havisham invited me to go there, told me no more of it than it was absolutely requisite I should understand. But I have forgotten one thing. It has been supposed that the man to whom she gave her misplaced confidence acted throughout in concert with her half-brother; that it was a conspiracy between them; and that they shared the profits."

"I wonder he didn't marry her and get all the property," said I.

"He may have been married already, and her cruel mortification may have been a part of her half-brother's scheme," said Herbert. "Mind! I don't know that."

"What became of the two men?" I asked, after again considering the subject.

"They fell into deeper shame and degradation—if there can be deeper—and ruin."

"Are they alive now?"

"I don't know."

" You said just now that Estella was not related to Miss Havisham, but adopted. When adopted?"

Herbert shrugged his shoulders. " There has always been an Estella, since I have heard of a Miss Havisham. I know no more. And now, Handel," said he, finally throwing off the story as it were, " there is a perfectly open understanding between us. All I know about Miss Havisham, you know."

" And all I know," I retorted, " you know."

" I fully believe it. So there can be no competition or perplexity between you and me. And as to the condition on which you hold your advancement in life—namely, that you are not to inquire or discuss to whom you owe it—you may be very sure that it will never be encroached upon, or even approached, by me, or by any one belonging to me."

In truth, he said this with so much delicacy, that I felt the subject done with, even though I should be under his father's roof for years and years to come. Yet he said it with so much meaning, too, that I felt he as perfectly understood Miss Havisham to be my benefactress, as I understood the fact myself.

It had not occurred to me before, that he had led up to the theme for the purpose of clearing it out of our way; but we were so much the lighter and easier for having broached it, that I now perceived this to be the case. We were very gay and sociable, and I asked him, in the course of conversation, what he was? He replied, " A capitalist—an Insurer of Ships." I suppose he saw me glancing about the room in search of some tokens of Shipping, or capital, for he added, " In the City."

I had grand ideas of the wealth and importance of Insurers of Ships in the City, and I began to think with awe, of having laid a young Insurer on his back, blackened his enterprising eye, and cut his responsible head open. But, again, there came upon me, for my relief, that odd impression that Herbert Pocket would never be very successful or rich.

" I shall not rest satisfied with merely employing my capital in insuring ships. I shall buy up some good Life Assurance shares, and cut into the Direction. I shall also do a little in the mining way. None of these things will interfere with my chartering a few thousand tons on my own account. I think I shall trade," said he, leaning back in his chair, "to the East Indies, for silks, shawls, spices, dyes, drugs, and precious woods. It's an interesting trade."

"And the profits are large?" said I.

"Tremendous!" said he.

I wavered again, and began to think here were greater expectations than my own.

"I think I shall trade, also," said he, putting his thumbs in his waistcoat pockets, "to the West Indies, for sugar, tobacco, and rum. Also to Ceylon, especially for elephants' tusks."

"You will want a good many ships," said I.

"A perfect fleet," said he.

Quite overpowered by the magnificence of these transactions, I asked him where the ships he insured mostly traded to at present?

"I haven't begun insuring yet," he replied. "I am looking about me."

Somehow, that pursuit seemed more in keeping with Barnard's Inn. I said (in a tone of conviction), "Ah-h!"

"Yes. I am in a counting-house, and looking about me."

"Is a counting-house profitable?" I asked.

"To——do you mean to the young fellow who's in it?" he asked, in reply.

"Yes; to you."

"Why, n-no; not to me." He said this with the air of one carefully reckoning up and striking a balance. "Not directly profitable. That is, it doesn't pay me anything, and I have to——keep myself."

This certainly had not a profitable appearance, and I shook my head as if I would imply that it would be difficult to lay by much accumulative capital from such a source of income.

"But the thing is," said Herbert Pocket, "that you look about you. *That's* the grand thing. You are in a counting-house, you know, and you look about you."

It struck me as a singular implication that you couldn't be out of a counting-house, you know, and look about you; but I silently deferred to his experience.

"Then the time comes," said Herbert, "when you see your opening. And you go in, and you swoop upon it, and you make your capital, and then there you are! When you have once made your capital, you have nothing to do but employ it."

This was very like his way of conducting that encounter in the garden ; very like. His manner of bearing his poverty, too, exactly corresponded to his manner of bearing that defeat. It seemed to me that he took all blows and buffets now, with just the same air as he had taken mine then. It was evident that he had nothing around him but the simplest necessaries, for everything that I remarked upon turned out to have been sent in on my account from the coffee-house or somewhere else.

Yet, having already made his fortune in his own mind, he was so unassuming with it that I felt quite grateful to him for not being puffed up. It was a pleasant addition to his naturally pleasant ways, and we got on famously. In the evening we went out for a walk in the streets, and went half-price to the Theatre ; and next day we went to church at Westminster Abbey, and in the afternoon we walked in the Parks ; and I wondered who shod all the horses there, and wished Joe did.

On a moderate computation, it was many months, that Sunday, since I had left Joe and Biddy. The space interposed between myself and them, partook of that expansion, and our marshes were any distance off. That I could have been at our old church in my old church-going clothes, on the very last Sunday that ever was, seemed a combination of impossibilities, geographical and social, solar and lunar. Yet in the London streets, so crowded with people and so brilliantly lighted in the dusk of evening, there were depressing hints of reproaches for that I had put the poor old kitchen at home so far away ; and in the dead of night, the footsteps of some incapable impostor of a porter mooning about Barnard's Inn, under pretence of watching it, fell hollow on my heart.

On the Monday morning at a quarter before nine, Herbert went to the counting-house to report himself—to look about him, too, I suppose—and I bore him company. He was to come away in an hour or two to attend me to Hammersmith, and I was to wait about for him. It appeared to me that the eggs from which young Insurers were hatched, were incubated in dust and heat, like the eggs of ostriches, judging from the places to which those incipient giants repaired on a Monday morning. Nor did the counting-house where Herbert assisted, show in my eyes as at all a good Observatory ; being a back second floor up a yard, of a grimy presence in all particulars, and with a look into another back second floor, rather than a look out.

I waited about until it was noon, and I went upon 'Change, and I saw fluey men sitting there under the bills about shipping, whom I took to be great merchants, though I couldn't understand why they should all be out of spirits. When Herbert came, we went and had lunch at a celebrated house which I then quite venerated, but now believe to have been the most abject superstition in Europe, and where I could not help noticing, even then, that there was much more gravy on the table-cloths and knives and waiters' clothes, than in the steaks. This collation disposed of at a moderate price (considering the grease, which was not charged for), we went back to Barnard's Inn and got my little portmanteau, and then took coach for Hammersmith. We arrived there at two or three o'clock in the afternoon, and had very little way to walk to Mr. Pocket's house. Lifting the latch of a gate, we passed direct into a little garden overlooking the river, where Mr. Pocket's children were playing about. And, unless I deceive myself on a point where my interests or prepossessions are certainly not concerned, I saw that Mr. and Mrs. Pocket's children were not growing up or being brought up, but were tumbling up.

Mrs. Pocket was sitting on a garden chair under a tree, reading, with her legs upon another garden chair; and Mrs. Pocket's two nursemaids were looking about them while the children played. "Mamma," said Herbert, "this is young Mr. Pip." Upon which Mrs. Pocket received me with an appearance of amiable dignity.

"Master Alick and Miss Jane," cried one of the nurses to two of the children, "if you go a-bouncing up against them bushes you'll fall over into the river and be drownded, and what'll your pa say then?"

At the same time this nurse picked up Mrs. Pocket's handkerchief, and said, "If that don't make six times you've dropped it, Mum!" Upon which Mrs. Pocket laughed and said, "Thank you, Flopson," and settling herself in one chair only, resumed her book. Her countenance immediately assumed a knitted and intent expression as if she had been reading for a week, but before she could have read half a dozen lines, she fixed her eyes upon me, and said, "I hope your mamma is quite well?" This unexpected inquiry put me into such a difficulty that I began saying in the ab-

surdest way that if there had been any such person I had no
doubt she would have been quite well and would have been
very much obliged and would have sent her compliments,
when the nurse came to my rescue.

"Well!" she cried, picking up the pocket handkerchief,
"if that don't make seven times! What ARE you a-doing
of this afternoon, Mum!" Mrs. Pocket received her property, at first with a look of unutterable surprise as if she
had never seen it before, and then with a laugh of recognition, and said, "Thank you, Flopson," and forgot me, and
went on reading.

I found, now I had leisure to count them, that there were
no fewer than six little Pockets present, in various stages
of tumbling up. I had scarcely arrived at the total when a
seventh was heard, as in the region of air, wailing dolefully.

"If there ain't Baby!" said Flopson, appearing to think
it most surprising. "Make haste up, Millers!"

Millers, who was the other nurse, retired into the house,
and by degrees the child's wailing was hushed and stopped,
as if it were a young ventriloquist with something in its
mouth. Mrs. Pocket read all the time, and I was curious to
know what the book could be.

We were waiting, I suppose, for Mr. Pocket to come out
to us; at any rate we waited there, and so I had an opportunity of observing the remarkable family phenomenon
that whenever any of the children strayed near Mrs. Pocket
in their play, they always tripped themselves up and
tumbled over her—always very much to her momentary
astonishment, and their own more enduring lamentation.
I was at a loss to account for this surprising circumstance,
and could not help giving my mind to speculations about it,
until by-and-by Millers came down with the baby, which
baby was handed to Flopson, which Flopson was handing
it to Mrs. Pocket, when she too went fairly head foremost
over Mrs. Pocket, baby and all, and was caught by Herbert
and myself.

"Gracious me, Flopson!" said Mrs. Pocket, looking off
her book for a moment, "everybody's tumbling!"

"Gracious you, indeed, Mum!" returned Flopson, very
red in the face; "what have you got there?"

"I got here, Flopson?" asked Mrs. Pocket.

"Why, if it ain't your footstool!" cried Flopson. "And
if you keep it under your skirts like that, who's to help

tumbling? Here! Take the baby, Mum, and give me your book."

Mrs. Pocket acted on the advice, and inexpertly danced the infant a little in her lap, while the other children played about it. This had lasted but a very short time, when Mrs. Pocket issued summary orders that they were all to be taken into the house for a nap. Thus I made the second discovery on that first occasion, that the nurture of the little Pockets consisted of alternately tumbling up and lying down.

Under these circumstances, when Flopson and Millers had got the children into the house, like a little flock of sheep, and Mr. Pocket came out of it to make my acquaintance, I was not much surprised to find that Mr. Pocket was a gentleman with a rather perplexed expression of face, and with his very grey hair disordered on his head, as if he didn't quite see his way to putting anything straight.

CHAPTER XXIII

Mr. Pocket said he was glad to see me, and he hoped I was not sorry to see him. "For I really am not," he added, with his son's smile, "an alarming personage." He was a young-looking man, in spite of his perplexities and his very grey hair, and his manner seemed quite natural. I use the word natural, in the sense of its being unaffected; there was something comic in his distraught way, as though it would have been downright ludicrous but for his own perception that it was very near being so. When he had talked with me a little, he said to Mrs. Pocket, with a rather anxious contraction of his eyebrows, which were black and handsome, "Belinda, I hope you have welcomed Mr. Pip?" And she looked up from her book, and said, "Yes." She then smiled upon me in an absent state of mind, and asked me if I liked the taste of orange-flower water? As the question had no bearing, near or remote, on any foregone or subsequent transactions, I considered it to have been thrown out, like her previous approaches, in general conversational condescension.

I found out within a few hours, and may mention at once, that Mrs. Pocket was the only daughter of a certain quite accidental deceased Knight, who had invented for himself a conviction that his deceased father would have been made a Baronet but for somebody's determined opposition arising out of entirely personal motives—I forget whose, if I ever knew—the Sovereign's, the Prime Minister's, the Lord Chancellor's, the Archbishop of Canterbury's, anybody's—and had tacked himself on to the nobles of the earth in right of this quite supposititious fact. I believe he had been knighted himself for storming the English grammar at the point of the pen, in a desperate address engrossed on vellum, on the occasion of the laying of the first stone of some building or other, and for handing some Royal Personage either the trowel or the mortar. Be that as it may, he had directed Mrs. Pocket to be brought up from her cradle as one who in the nature of things must marry a title, and who was to be guarded from the acquisition of plebeian domestic knowledge.

So successful a watch and ward had been established over the young lady by this judicious parent, that she had grown up highly ornamental, but perfectly helpless and useless. With her character thus happily formed, in the first bloom of her youth she had encountered Mr. Pocket: who was also in the first bloom of youth, and not quite decided whether to mount to the Woolsack, or to roof himself in with a mitre. As his doing the one or the other was a mere question of time, he and Mrs. Pocket had taken Time by the forelock (when, to judge from its length, it would seem to have wanted cutting), and had married without the knowledge of the judicious parent. The judicious parent, having nothing to bestow or withhold but his blessing, had handsomely settled that dower upon them after a short struggle, and had informed Mr. Pocket that his wife was "a treasure for a Prince." Mr. Pocket had invested the Prince's treasure in the ways of the world ever since, and it was supposed to have brought him in but indifferent interest. Still, Mrs. Pocket was in general the object of a queer sort of respectful pity, because she had not married a title; while Mr. Pocket was the object of a queer sort of forgiving reproach, because he had never got one.

Mr. Pocket took me into the house and showed me my room; which was a pleasant one, and so furnished as that I could use it with comfort for my own private sitting-room. He then knocked at the doors of two other similar rooms and introduced me to their occupants, by name Drummle and Startop. Drummle, an old-looking young man of a heavy order of architecture, was whistling. Startop, younger in years and appearance, was reading and holding his head, as if he thought himself in danger of exploding it with too strong a charge of knowledge.

Both Mr. and Mrs. Pocket had such a noticeable air of being in somebody else's hands, that I wondered who really was in possession of the house and let them live there, until I found this unknown power to be the servants. It was a smooth way of going on, perhaps, in respect of saving trouble; but it had the appearance of being expensive, for the servants felt it a duty they owed to themselves to be nice in their eating and drinking, and to keep a deal of company down-stairs. They allowed a very liberal table to Mr. and

Mrs. Pocket, yet it always appeared to me that by far the best part of the house to have boarded in, would have been the kitchen—always supposing the boarder capable of self-defence, for, before I had been there a week, a neighbouring lady with whom the family were personally unacquainted, wrote in to say that she had seen Millers slapping the baby. This greatly distressed Mrs. Pocket, who burst into tears on receiving the note, and said that it was an extraordinary thing that the neighbours couldn't mind their own business.

By degrees I learnt, and chiefly from Herbert, that Mr. Pocket had been educated at Harrow and at Cambridge, where he had distinguished himself; but that when he had had the happiness of marrying Mrs. Pocket very early in life, he had impaired his prospects and taken up the calling of a Grinder. After grinding a number of dull blades—of whom it was remarkable that their fathers, when influential, were always going to help him to preferment, but always forgot to do it when the blades had left the Grindstone—he had wearied of that poor work and had come to London. Here, after gradually failing in loftier hopes, he had "read" with divers who had lacked opportunities or neglected them, and had refurbished divers others for special occasions, and had turned his acquirements to the account of literary compilation and correction, and on such means, added to some very moderate private resources, still maintained the house I saw.

Mr. and Mrs. Pocket had a toady neighbour; a widow lady of that highly sympathetic nature that she agreed with everybody, blessed everybody, and shed smiles and tears on everybody, according to circumstances. This lady's name was Mrs. Coiler, and I had the honour of taking her down to dinner on the day of my installation. She gave me to understand on the stairs, that it was a blow to dear Mrs. Pocket that dear Mr. Pocket should be under the necessity of receiving gentlemen to read with him. That did not extend to me, she told me in a gush of love and confidence (at that time, I had known her something less than five minutes); if they were all like Me, it would be quite another thing.

"But dear Mrs. Pocket," said Mrs. Coiler, "after her early disappointment (not that dear Mr. Pocket was to blame in that), requires so much luxury and elegance——"

"Yes, ma'am," I said, to stop her, for I was afraid she was going to cry.

"And she is of so aristocratic a disposition——"

"Yes, ma'am," I said again, with the same object as before.

"—that it *is* hard," said Mrs. Coiler, "to have dear Mr. Pocket's time and attention diverted from dear Mrs. Pocket."

I could not help thinking that it might be harder if the butcher's time and attention were diverted from dear Mrs. Pocket; but I said nothing, and indeed had enough to do in keeping a bashful watch upon my company-manners.

It came to my knowledge, through what passed between Mrs. Pocket and Drummle, while I was attentive to my knife and fork, spoon, glasses, and other instruments of self-destruction, that Drummle, whose christian name was Bentley, was actually the next heir but one to a baronetcy. It further appeared that the book I had seen Mrs. Pocket reading in the garden, was all about titles, and that she knew the exact date at which her grandpapa would have come into the book, if he ever had come at all. Drummle didn't say much, but in his limited way (he struck me as a sulky kind of fellow) he spoke as one of the elect, and recognised Mrs. Pocket as a woman and a sister. No one but themselves and Mrs. Coiler the toady neighbour showed any interest in this part of the conversation, and it appeared to me that it was painful to Herbert; but it promised to last a long time, when the page came in with the announcement of a domestic affliction. It was, in effect, that the cook had mislaid the beef. To my unutterable amazement, I now, for the first time, saw Mr. Pocket relieve his mind by going through a performance that struck me as very extraordinary, but which made no impression on anybody else, and with which I soon became as familiar as the rest. He laid down the carving-knife and fork—being engaged in carving at the moment—put his two hands into his disturbed hair, and appeared to make an extraordinary effort to lift himself up by it. When he had done this, and had not lifted himself up at all, he quietly went on with what he was about.

Mrs. Coiler then changed the subject and began to flatter me. I liked it for a few moments, but she flattered me so very grossly that the pleasure was soon over. She had a serpentine way of coming close at me when she pretended to be vitally interested in the friends and localities I had left, which was altogether snaky and fork-tongued ; and when she made an occasional bounce upon Startop (who said very little to her), or upon Drummle (who said less), I rather envied them for being on the opposite side of the table.

After dinner the children were introduced, and Mrs. Coiler made admiring comments on their eyes, noses, and legs—a sagacious way of improving their minds.   There were four little girls, and two little boys, besides the baby who might have been either, and the baby's next successor who was as yet neither.   They were brought in by Flopson and Millers, much as though those two non-commissioned officers had been recruiting somewhere for children and had enlisted these : while Mrs. Pocket looked at the young Nobles that ought to have been, as if she rather thought she had had the pleasure of inspecting them before, but didn't quite know what to make of them.

"Here!   Give me your fork, Mum, and take the baby," said Flopson.   "Don't take it that way, or you'll get its head under the table."

Thus advised, Mrs. Pocket took it the other way, and got its head upon the table ; which was announced to all present by a prodigious concussion.

"Dear, dear ! give it me back, Mum," said Flopson ; "and, Miss Jane, come and dance the baby, do ! "

One of the little girls, a mere mite who seemed to have prematurely taken upon herself some charge of the others, stepped out of her place by me, and danced to and from the baby until it left off crying, and laughed.   Then all the children laughed, and Mr. Pocket (who in the meantime had twice endeavoured to lift himself up by the hair) laughed, and we all laughed and were glad.

Flopson, by dint of doubling the baby at the joints like a Dutch doll, then got it safely into Mrs. Pocket's lap, and gave it the nutcrackers to play with : at the same time recommending Mrs. Pocket to take notice that the handles of that instrument were not likely to agree with its eyes, and sharply charging Miss Jane to look after the same.   Then, the two nurses left the room, and had a lively scuffle on the staircase with a dissipated page who had waited at dinner, and who had clearly lost half his buttons at the gaming-table.

I was made very uneasy in my mind by Mrs. Pocket's falling into a discussion with Drummle respecting two baronetcies while she ate a sliced orange steeped in sugar and wine, and forgetting all about the baby on her lap: who did most appalling things with the nutcrackers. At length little Jane perceived its young brains to be imperilled, softly left her place, and with many small artifices coaxed the dangerous weapon away. Mrs. Pocket finishing her orange at about the same time, and not approving of this, said to Jane:

"You naughty child, how dare you? Go and sit down this instant!"

"Mamma, dear," lisped the little girl, "baby ood have put hith eyeth out."

"How dare you tell me so!" retorted Mrs. Pocket. "Go and sit down in your chair this moment!"

Mrs. Pocket's dignity was so crushing, that I felt quite abashed: as if I myself had done something to rouse it.

"Belinda," remonstrated Mr. Pocket, from the other end of the table, "how can you be so unreasonable? Jane only interfered for the protection of baby."

"I will not allow anybody to interfere," said Mrs. Pocket. "I am surprised, Matthew, that you should expose me to the affront of interference."

"Good God!" cried Mr. Pocket, in an outbreak of desolate desperation. "Are infants to be nutcrackered into their tombs, and is nobody to save them?"

"I will not be interfered with by Jane," said Mrs. Pocket, with a majestic glance at that innocent little offender. "I hope I know my poor grandpapa's position. Jane indeed!"

Mr. Pocket got his hands in his hair again, and this time really did lift himself some inches out of his chair. "Hear this!" he helplessly exclaimed to the elements. "Babies are to be nutcrackered dead, for people's poor grandpapa's positions!" Then he let himself down again, and became silent.

We all looked awkwardly at the table-cloth while this was going on. A pause succeeded, during which the honest and irrepressible baby made a series of leaps and crows at little Jane, who appeared to me to be the only member of the family (irrespective of the servants) with whom it had any decided acquaintance.

"Mr. Drummle," said Mrs. Pocket, "will you ring for

Flopson? Jane, you undutiful little thing, go and lie down. Now, baby darling, come with ma!"

The baby was the soul of honour, and protested with all its might. It doubled itself up the wrong way over Mrs. Pocket's arm, exhibited a pair of knitted shoes and dimpled ankles to the company in lieu of its soft face, and was carried out in the highest state of mutiny. And it gained its point after all, for I saw it through the window within a few minutes, being nursed by little Jane.

It happened that the other five children were left behind at the dinner-table, through Flopson's having some private engagement, and their not being anybody else's business. I thus became aware of the mutual relations between them and Mr. Pocket, which were exemplified in the following manner. Mr. Pocket, with the normal perplexity of his face heightened, and his hair rumpled, looked at them for some minutes, as if he couldn't make out how they came to be boarding and lodging in that establishment, and why they hadn't been billeted by Nature on somebody else. Then, in a distant, Missionary way he asked them certain questions—as why little Joe had that hole in his frill: who said, Pa, Flopson was going to mend it when she had time—and how little Fanny came by that whitlow: who said, Pa, Millers was going to poultice it when she didn't forget. Then he melted into parental tenderness, and gave them a shilling apiece and told them to go and play; and then as they went out, with one very strong effort to lift himself up by the hair, he dismissed the hopeless subject.

In the evening there was rowing on the river. As Drummle and Startop had each a boat, I resolved to set up mine, and to cut them both out. I was pretty good at most exercises in which country-boys are adepts, but, as I was conscious of wanting elegance of style for the Thames—not to say for other waters—I at once engaged to place myself under the tuition of the winner of a prize-wherry who plied at our stairs, and to whom I was introduced by my new allies. This practical authority confused me very much, by saying I had the arm of a blacksmith. If he could have known how nearly the compliment had lost him his pupil, I doubt if he would have paid it.

There was a supper-tray after we got home at night, and I think we should all have enjoyed ourselves, but for a rather disagreeable domestic occurrence. Mr. Pocket was in good spirits, when a housemaid came in, and said, "If you please, sir, I should wish to speak to you."

"Speak to your master?" said Mrs. Pocket, whose dignity was roused again. "How can you think of such a thing? Go and speak to Flopson. Or speak to me—at some other time."

"Begging your pardon, ma'am," returned the housemaid, "I should wish to speak at once, and to speak to master."

Hereupon Mr. Pocket went out of the room, and we made the best of ourselves until he came back.

"This is a pretty thing, Belinda!" said Mr. Pocket, returning with a countenance expressive of grief and despair. "Here's the cook lying insensibly drunk on the kitchen floor, with a large bundle of fresh butter made up in the cupboard ready to sell for grease!"

Mrs. Pocket instantly showed much amiable emotion, and said, "This is that odious Sophia's doing!"

"What do you mean, Belinda?" demanded Mr. Pocket.

"Sophia has told you," said Mrs. Pocket. "Did I not see her, with my own eyes, and hear her with my own ears, come into the room just now and ask to speak to you?"

"But has she not taken me down-stairs, Belinda," returned Mr. Pocket, "and shown me the woman, and the bundle too?"

"And do you defend her, Matthew," said Mrs. Pocket. "for making mischief?"

Mr. Pocket uttered a dismal groan.

"Am I, grandpapa's granddaughter, to be nothing in the house?" said Mrs. Pocket. "Besides, the cook has always been a very nice respectful woman, and said in the most natural manner when she came to look after the situation, that she felt I was born to be a Duchess."

There was a sofa where Mr. Pocket stood, and he dropped upon it in the attitude of a Dying Gladiator. Still in that attitude he said, with a hollow voice, "Good night, Mr. Pip," when I deemed it advisable to go to bed and leave him.

CHAPTER XXIV

AFTER two or three days, when I had established myself in my room and had gone backwards and forwards to London several times, and had ordered all I wanted of my tradesmen, Mr. Pocket and I had a long talk together. He knew more of my intended career than I knew myself, for he referred to his having been told by Mr. Jaggers that I was not designed for any profession, and that I should be well enough educated for my destiny if I could "hold my own" with the average of young men in prosperous circumstances. I acquiesced, of course, knowing nothing to the contrary.

He advised my attending certain places in London, for the acquisition of such mere rudiments as I wanted, and my investing him with the functions of explainer and director of all my studies. He hoped that with intelligent assistance I should meet with little to discourage me, and should soon be able to dispense with any aid but his. Through his way of saying this, and much more to similar purpose, he placed himself on confidential terms with me in an admirable manner: and I may state at once that he was always so zealous and honourable in fulfilling his compact with me, that he made me zealous and honourable in fulfilling mine with him. If he had shown indifference as a master, I have no doubt I should have returned the compliment as a pupil; he gave me no such excuse, and each of us did the other justice. Nor did I ever regard him as having anything ludicrous about him—or anything but what was serious, honest, and good—in his tutor communication with me.

When these points were settled, and so far carried out as that I had begun to work in earnest, it occurred to me that if I could retain my bedroom in Barnard's Inn, my life would be agreeably varied, while my manners would be none the worse for Herbert's society. Mr. Pocket did not object to this arrangement, but urged that before any step could possibly be taken in it, it must be submitted to my guardian.

I felt that his delicacy arose out of the consideration that the plan would save Herbert some expense, so I went off to Little Britain and imparted my wish to Mr. Jaggers.

"If I could buy the furniture now hired for me," said I, "and one or two other little things, I should be quite at home there."

"Go it!" said Mr. Jaggers, with a short laugh. "I told you you'd get on. Well! How much do you want?"

I said I didn't know how much.

"Come!" retorted Mr. Jaggers. "How much? Fifty pounds?"

"Oh, not nearly so much."

"Five pounds?" said Mr. Jaggers.

This was such a great fall, that I said in discomfiture, "Oh! more than that."

"More than that, eh!" retorted Mr. Jaggers, lying in wait for me, with his hands in his pockets, his head on one side, and his eyes on the wall behind me; "how much more?"

"It is so difficult to fix a sum," said I, hesitating.

"Come!" said Mr. Jaggers. "Let's get at it. Twice five; will that do? Three times five; will that do? Four times five; will that do?"

I said I thought that would do handsomely.

"Four times five will do handsomely, will it?" said Mr. Jaggers, knitting his brows. "Now, what do you make of four times five?"

"What do I make of it!"

"Ah!" said Mr. Jaggers; "how much?"

"I suppose you make it twenty pounds," said I, smiling.

"Never mind what *I* make it, my friend," observed Mr. Jaggers, with a knowing and contradictory toss of the head. "I want to know what *you* make it?"

"Twenty pounds, of course."

"Wemmick!" said Mr. Jaggers, opening his office door. "Take Mr. Pip's written order, and pay him twenty pounds."

This strongly marked way of doing business made a strongly marked impression on me, and that not of an agreeable kind. Mr. Jaggers never laughed; but he wore great bright creaking boots; and, in poising himself on those boots, with his large head bent down and his eyebrows joined together, awaiting an answer, he sometimes caused the boots to creak, as if *they* laughed in a dry and suspicious way. As he happened to go out now, and as Wemmick was brisk and talkative, I said to Wemmick that I hardly knew what to make of Mr. Jaggers's manner.

"Tell him that, and he'll take it as a compliment," answered Wemmick; "he don't mean that you *should* know what to make of it.—Oh!" for I looked surprised, "it's not personal; it's professional: only professional."

Wemmick was at his desk, lunching—and crunching—on a dry hard biscuit; pieces of which he threw from time to time into his slit of a mouth, as if he were posting them.

"Always seems to me," said Wemmick, "as if he had set a man-trap and was watching it. Suddenly—click—you're caught!"

Without remarking that man-traps were not among the amenities of life, I said I supposed he was very skilful?

"Deep," said Wemmick, "as Australia." Pointing with his pen at the office floor, to express that Australia was understood, for the purposes of the figure, to be symmetrically on the opposite spot of the globe. "If there was anything deeper," added Wemmick, bringing his pen to paper, "he'd be it."

Then, I said I supposed he had a fine business, and Wemmick said, "Ca-pi-tal!" Then I asked if there were many clerks? to which he replied:

"We don't run much into clerks, because there's only one Jaggers, and people won't have him at second hand. There are only four of us. Would you like to see 'em? You are one of us, as I may say."

I accepted the offer. When Mr. Wemmick had put all the biscuit into the post, and had paid me my money from a cash-box in a safe, the key of which safe he kept somewhere down his back, and produced from his coat-collar like an iron pigtail, we went up-stairs. The house was dark and shabby, and the greasy shoulders that had left their mark in Mr. Jaggers's room seemed to have been shuffling up and down the staircase for years. In the front first floor, a clerk who looked something between a publican and a rat-catcher—a large pale puffed swollen man—was attentively engaged with three or four people of shabby appearance, whom he treated as unceremoniously as everybody seemed to be treated who contributed to Mr. Jaggers's coffers. "Getting evidence together," said Mr. Wemmick, as we came out, "for the Bailey." In the room over that, a little flabby terrier of a clerk with dangling hair (his cropping seemed to have been forgotten when he was a puppy) was similarly engaged with a man with weak eyes, whom Mr. Wemmick presented to me as a smelter who kept his pot always boiling, and who would melt me anything I pleased —and who was in an excessive white-perspiration, as if he had been trying his art on himself. In a back room, a high-shouldered man with a face-ache tied up in dirty flannel, who was dressed in old black clothes that bore the appearance of having been waxed, was stooping over his work of making fair copies of the notes of the other two gentlemen, for Mr. Jaggers's own use.

This was all the establishment. When we went downstairs again, Wemmick led me into my guardian's room, and said, "This you've seen already."

"Pray, said I, as the two odious casts with the twitchy leer upon them caught my sight again, "whose likenesses are those?"

"These?" said Wemmick, getting upon a chair, and blowing the dust off the horrible heads before bringing them down. "These are two celebrated ones. Famous clients of ours that got us a world of credit. This chap (why you must have come down in the night and been peeping into the inkstand, to get this blot upon your eyebrow, you old rascal!) murdered his master, and, considering that he wasn't brought up to evidence, didn't plan it badly."

"Is it like him?" I asked, recoiling from the brute, as Wemmick spat upon his eyebrow, and gave it a rub with his sleeve.

"Like him? It's himself, you know. The cast was made in Newgate, directly after he was taken down. You had a particular fancy for me, hadn't you, Old Artful?" said Wemmick. He then explained this affectionate apostrophe, by touching his brooch representing the lady and the weeping willow at the tomb with the urn upon it, and said, "Had it made for me express!"

"Is the lady anybody?" said I.

"No," returned Wemmick. "Only his game. (You liked your bit of game, didn't you?) No; deuce a bit of a lady in the case, Mr. Pip, except one—and she wasn't of this slender ladylike sort, and you wouldn't have caught *her* looking after this urn—unless there was something to drink in it." Wemmick's attention being thus directed to his brooch, he put down the cast, and polished the brooch with his pocket-handkerchief.

"Did that other creature come to the same end?" I asked. "He has the same look."

"You're right," said Wemmick; "it's the genuine look. Much as if one nostril was caught up with a horsehair and a little fish-hook. Yes, he came to the same end; quite the natural end here, I assure you. He forged wills, this blade did, if he didn't also put the supposed testators to sleep too. You were a gentlemanly Cove, though" (Mr. Wemmick was again apostrophising), "and you said you could write Greek. Yah, Bounceable! What a liar you were! I never met such a liar as you!" Before putting his late friend on his shelf again, Wemmick touched the largest of his mourning rings, and said, "Sent out to buy it for me, only the day before."

While he was putting up the other cast and coming down from the chair, the thought crossed my mind that all his personal jewellery was derived from like sources. As he had shown no diffidence on the subject, I ventured on the liberty of asking him the question, when he stood before me, dusting his hands.

"Oh yes," he returned, "these are all gifts of that kind. One brings another, you see; that's the way of it. I always take 'em. They're curiosities. And they're property. They may not be worth much, but, after all, they're property and portable. It don't signify to you with your brilliant look-out, but as to myself, my guiding-star always is, Get hold of portable property."

When I had rendered homage to this light, he went on to say in a friendly manner:

"If at any odd time when you have nothing better to do, you wouldn't mind coming over to see me at Walworth, I could offer you a bed, and I should consider it an honour. I have not much to show you; but such two or three curiosities as I have got, you might like to look over; and I am fond of a bit of garden and a summer-house."

I said I should be delighted to accept his hospitality.

"Thankee," said he: "then we'll consider that it's to come off, when convenient to you. Have you dined with Mr. Jaggers yet?"

"Not yet."

"Well," said Wemmick, "he'll give you wine, and good

wine. I'll give you punch, and not bad punch. And now I'll tell you something. When you go to dine with Mr. Jaggers, look at his housekeeper."

"Shall I see something very uncommon?"

"Well," said Wemmick, "you'll see a wild beast tamed. Not so very uncommon, you'll tell me. I reply, that depends on the original wildness of the beast, and the amount of taming. It won't lower your opinion of Mr. Jaggers's powers. Keep your eye on it."

I told him I would do so, with all the interest and curiosity that his preparation awakened. As I was taking my departure, he asked me if I would like to devote five minutes to seeing Mr. Jaggers "at it?"

For several reasons, and not least because I didn't clearly know what Mr. Jaggers would be found to be "at," I replied in the affirmative. We dived into the City, and came up in a crowded police-court, where a blood-relation (in the murderous sense) of the deceased with the fanciful taste in brooches, was standing at the bar, uncomfortably chewing something; while my guardian had a woman under examination or cross-examination—I don't know which—and was striking her, and the bench, and everybody with awe. If anybody, of whatsoever degree, said a word that he didn't approve of, he instantly required to have it "taken down." If anybody wouldn't make an admission, he said, "I'll have it out of you!" and if anybody made an admission, he said, "Now I have got you!" The magistrates shivered under a single bite of his finger. Thieves and thief-takers hung in dread rapture on his words, and shrank when a hair of his eyebrows turned in their direction. Which side he was on I couldn't make out, for he seemed to me to be grinding the whole place in a mill; I only know that when I stole out on tiptoe he was not on the side of the bench; for he was making the legs of the old gentleman who presided quite convulsive under the table, by his denunciations of his conduct as the representative of British law and justice in that chair that day.

CHAPTER XXV

BENTLEY DRUMMLE, who was so sulky a fellow that he even took up a book as if its writer had done him an injury, did not take up an acquaintance in a more agreeable spirit. Heavy in figure, movement, and comprehension—in the sluggish complexion of his face, and in the large awkward tongue that seemed to loll about in his mouth as he himself lolled about in a room—he was idle, proud, niggardly, reserved, and suspicious. He came of rich people down in Somersetshire, who had nursed this combination of qualities until they made the discovery that it was just of age and a blockhead. Thus, Bentley Drummle had come to Mr. Pocket when he was a head taller than that gentleman, and half a dozen heads thicker than most gentlemen.

Startop had been spoiled by a weak mother, and kept at home when he ought to have been at school, but he was devotedly attached to her, and admired her beyond measure. He had a woman's delicacy of feature, and was—"as you may see, though you never saw her," said Herbert to me—"exactly like his mother." It was but natural that I should take to him much more kindly than to Drummle, and that, even in the earliest evenings of our boating, he and I should pull homeward abreast of one another, conversing from boat to boat, while Bentley Drummle came up in our wake alone, under the overhanging banks and among the rushes. He would always creep in-shore like some uncomfortable amphibious creature, even when the tide would have sent him fast upon his way; and I always think of him as coming after us in the dark or by the back-water, when our own two boats were breaking the sunset or the moonlight in mid-stream.

Herbert was my intimate companion and friend. I presented him with a half-share in my boat, which was the occasion of his often coming down to Hammersmith; and my possession of a half-share in his chambers often took me up to London. We used to walk between the two places at all

hours. I have an affection for the road yet (though it is
not so pleasant a road as it was then), formed in the im-
pressibility of untried youth and hope.

When I had been in Mr. Pocket's family a month or two,
Mr. and Mrs. Camilla turned up. Camilla was Mr. Pocket's
sister. Georgiana, whom I had seen at Miss Havisham's on the
same occasion, also turned up. She was a cousin—an indi-
gestive single woman, who called her rigidity religion, and her
liver love. These people hated me with the hatred of cupidity
and disappointment. As a matter of course, they fawned
upon me in my prosperity with the basest meanness.
Towards Mr. Pocket, as a grown-up infant with no notion
of his own interests, they showed the complacent forbearance
I had heard them express. Mrs. Pocket they held in contempt ; but they allowed the poor soul to have been heavily
disappointed in life, because that shed a feeble reflected
light upon themselves.

These were the surroundings among which I settled down,
and applied myself to my education. I soon contracted
expensive habits, and began to spend an amount of money
that within a few short months I should have thought almost
fabulous ; but through good and evil I stuck to my books.
There was no other merit in this, than my having sense
enough to feel my deficiencies. Between Mr. Pocket and
Herbert I got on fast ; and, with one or the other always
at my elbow to give me the start I wanted, and clear
obstructions out of my road, I must have been as great a
dolt as Drummle if I had done less.

I had not seen Mr. Wemmick for some weeks, when I
thought I would write him a note and propose to go home
with him on a certain evening. He replied that it would
give him much pleasure, and that he would expect me at
the office at six o'clock. Thither I went, and there I found
him, putting the key of his safe down his back as the clock
struck.

"Did you think of walking down to Walworth ?" said he.

"Certainly," said I, "if you approve."

"Very much," was Wemmick's reply, "for I have had my
legs under the desk all day, and shall be glad to stretch
them. Now I'll tell you what I've got for supper, Mr. Pip.
I have got a stewed steak—which is of home preparation—
and a cold roast fowl—which is from the cook's-shop. I
think it's tender, because the master of the shop was a Jury-

man in some cases of ours the other day, and we let him down easy. I reminded him of it when I bought the fowl, and I said, 'Pick us out a good one, old Briton, because if we had chosen to keep you in the box another day or two, we could have done it.' He said to that, 'Let me make you a present of the best fowl in the shop.' I let him, of course. As far as it goes, it's property and portable. You don't object to an aged parent, I hope?"

I really thought he was still speaking of the fowl, until he added, "Because I have got an aged parent at my place." I then said what politeness required.

"So you haven't dined with Mr. Jaggers yet?" he pursued, as we walked along.

"Not yet."

"He told me so this afternoon when he heard you were coming. I expect you'll have an invitation to-morrow. He's going to ask your pals, too. Three of 'em; ain't there?"

Although I was not in the habit of counting Drummle as one of my intimate associates, I answered, "Yes."

"Well, he's going to ask the whole gang;" I hardly felt complimented by the word; "and whatever he gives you, he'll give you good. Don't look forward to variety, but you'll have excellence. And there's another rum thing in his house," proceeded Wemmick after a moment's pause, as if the remark followed on the housekeeper understood; "he never lets a door or window be fastened at night."

"Is he never robbed?"

"That's it!" returned Wemmick. "He says, and gives it out publicly, 'I want to see the man who'll rob me.' Lord bless you, I have heard him, a hundred times if I have heard once, say to regular cracksmen in our front office, 'You know where I live; now no bolt is ever drawn there; why don't you do a stroke of business with me? Come; can't I tempt you?' Not a man of them, sir, would be bold enough to try it on, for love or money."

"They dread him so much?" said I.

"Dread him!" said Wemmick. "I believe you, they dread him. Not but what he's artful, even in his defiance of them. No silver, sir. Britannia metal, every spoon."

"So they wouldn't have much," I observed, "even if they——"

"Ah! But he would have much," said Wemmick, cutting

me short, "and they know it. He'd have their lives, and the lives of scores of 'em. He'd have all he could get. And its impossible to say what he couldn't get, if he gave his mind to it."

I was falling into meditation on my guardian's greatness, when Wemmick remarked:

"As to the absence of plate, that's only his natural depth, you know. A river's its natural depth, and he's his natural depth. Look at his watch-chain. That's real enough."

"It's very massive," said I.

"Massive?" repeated Wemmick. "I think so. And his watch is a gold repeater, and worth a hundred pound if it's worth a penny. Mr. Pip, there are about seven hundred thieves in this town who know all about that watch; there's not a man, a woman, or a child, among them, who wouldn't identify the smallest link in that chain, and drop it as if it was red-hot, if inveigled into touching it."

At first with such discourse, and afterwards with conversation of a more general nature, did Mr. Wemmick and I beguile the time and the road, until he gave me to understand that we had arrived in the district of Walworth.

It appeared to be a collection of black lanes, ditches, and little gardens, and to present the aspect of a rather dull retirement. Wemmick's house was a little wooden cottage in the midst of plots of garden, and the top of it was cut out and painted like a battery mounted with guns.

"My own doing," said Wemmick. "Looks pretty; don't it?"

I highly commended it. I think it was the smallest house I ever saw; with the queerest gothic windows (by far the greater part of them sham), and a gothic door, almost too small to get in at.

"That's a real flagstaff, you see," said Wemmick, "and on Sundays I run up a real flag. Then look here. After I have crossed this bridge, I hoist it up—so—and cut off the communication."

The bridge was a plank, and it crossed a chasm about four feet wide and two deep. But it was very pleasant to see the pride with which he hoisted it up, and made it fast; smiling as he did so, with a relish, and not merely mechanically.

"At nine o'clock every night, Greenwich time," said Wemmick, "the gun fires. There he is, you see! And when you hear him go, I think you'll say he's a Stinger."

The piece of ordnance referred to was mounted in a separate fortress, constructed of lattice-work. It was protected from the weather by an ingenious little tarpaulin contrivance in the nature of an umbrella.

"Then, at the back," said Wemmick, "out of sight, so as not to impede the idea of fortifications—for it's a principle with me, if you have an idea, carry it out and keep it up—I don't know whether that's your opinion——"

I said, decidedly.

"—At the back, there's a pig, and there are fowls and rabbits; then I knock together my own little frame, you see, and grow cucumbers; and you'll judge at supper what sort of a salad I can raise. So, sir," said Wemmick, smiling again, but seriously, too, as he shook his head, "if you can suppose the little place besieged, it would hold out a devil of a time in point of provisions."

Then, he conducted me to a bower about a dozen yards off, but which was approached by such ingenious twists of path that it took quite a long time to get at; and in this retreat our glasses were already set forth. Our punch was cooling in an ornamental lake, on whose margin the bower was raised. This piece of water (with an island in the middle which might have been the salad for supper) was of a circular form, and he had constructed a fountain in it, which, when you set a little mill going and took a cork out of a pipe, played to that powerful extent that it made the back of your hand quite wet.

"I am my own engineer, and my own carpenter, and my own plumber, and my own gardener, and my own Jack of all Trades," said Wemmick, in acknowledging my compliments. "Well, it's a good thing, you know. It brushes the Newgate cobwebs away, and pleases the Aged. You wouldn't mind being at once introduced to the Aged, would you? It wouldn't put you out?"

I expressed the readiness I felt, and we went into the castle. There, we found, sitting by a fire, a very old man in a flannel coat: clean, cheerful, comfortable, and well cared for, but intensely deaf.

"Well, aged parent," said Wemmick, shaking hands with him in a cordial and jocose way, "how am you?"

"All right, John; all right!" replied the old man.

"Here's Mr. Pip, aged parent," said Wemmick, "and I wish you could hear his name. Nod away at him, Mr.

Pip ; that's what he likes. Nod away at him, if you please,
like winking ! "

"This is a fine place of my son's, sir," cried the old man,
while I nodded as hard as I possibly could. "This is a pretty
pleasure-ground, sir. This spot and these beautiful works
upon it ought to be kept together by the Nation, after my
son's time, for the people's enjoyment."

"You're as proud of it as Punch ; ain't you, Aged ? " said
Wemmick, contemplating the old man, with his hard face
really softened ; "*there's* a nod for you ; " giving him a tremendous one : "*there's* another for you ; " giving him a still
more tremendous one ; "you like that, don't you ? If you're
not tired, Mr. Pip—though I know it's tiring to strangers—
will you tip him one more ? You can't think how it pleases
him."

I tipped him several more, and he was in great spirits.
We left him bestirring himself to feed the fowls, and we sat
down to our punch in the arbour ; where Wemmick told me
as he smoked a pipe, that it had taken him a good many
years to bring the property up to its present pitch of
perfection.

"Is it your own, Mr. Wemmick ? "

"O yes," said Wemmick. "I have got hold of it, a bit at
a time. It's a freehold, by George ! "

"Is it, indeed ? I hope Mr. Jaggers admires it ? "

"Never seen it," said Wemmick. "Never heard of it.
Never seen the Aged. Never heard of him. No ; the office
is one thing, and private life is another. When I go into
the office, I leave the Castle behind me, and when I come
into the Castle, I leave the office behind me. If it's not in
any way disagreeable to you, you'll oblige me by doing the
same. I don't wish it professionally spoken about."

Of course I felt my good faith involved in the observance
of his request. The punch being very nice, we sat there
drinking it and talking, until it was almost nine o'clock.
"Getting near gun-fire," said Wemmick then, as he laid
down his pipe ; "it's the Aged's treat."

Proceeding into the Castle again, we found the Aged heating the poker, with expectant eyes, as a preliminary to the
performance of this great nightly ceremony. Wemmick
stood with his watch in his hand until the moment was come
for him to take the red-hot poker from the Aged, and repair
to the battery. He took it, and went out, and presently

CHAPTER XXVI

It fell out as Wemmick had told me it would, that I had an early opportunity of comparing my guardian's establishment with that of his cashier and clerk. My guardian was in his room, washing his hands with his scented soap, when I went into the office from Walworth; and he called me to him, and gave me the invitation for myself and friends which Wemmick had prepared me to receive. "No ceremony," he stipulated, "and no dinner dress, and say to-morrow." I asked him where we should come to (for I had no idea where he lived), and I believe it was in his general objection to make anything like an admission, that he replied, "Come here, and I'll take you home with me." I embrace this opportunity of remarking that he washed his clients off, as if it were a surgeon or a dentist. He had a closet in his room, fitted up for the purpose, which smelt of the scented soap like a perfumer's shop. It had an unusually large jack-towel on a roller inside the door, and he would wash his hands, and wipe them and dry them all over this towel, whenever he came in from a police-court or dismissed a client from his room. When I and my friends repaired to him at six o'clock next day, he seemed to have been engaged on a case of a darker complexion than usual, for we found him with his head butted into this closet, not only washing his hands, but laving his face and gargling his throat. And even when he had done all that, and had gone all round the jack-towel, he took out his penknife and scraped the case out of his nails before he put his coat on.

There were some people slinking about as usual when we passed out into the street, who were evidently anxious to speak with him; but there was something so conclusive in the halo of scented soap which encircled his presence, that they gave it up for that day. As we walked along westward, he was recognised ever and again by some face in the crowd of the streets, and whenever that happened he talked louder to me; but he never otherwise recognised anybody, or took notice that anybody recognised him.

He conducted us to Gerrard-street, Soho, to a house on the south side of that street, rather a stately house of its kind, but dolefully in want of painting, and with dirty windows. He took out his key and opened the door, and we all went into a stone hall, bare, gloomy, and little used. So, up a dark-brown staircase into a series of three dark brown rooms on the first floor. There were carved garlands on the panelled walls, and as he stood among them giving us welcome, I know what kind of loops I thought they looked like.

Dinner was laid in the best of these rooms; the second was his dressing-room; the third, his bedroom. He told us that he held the whole house, but rarely used more of it than we saw. The table was comfortably laid—no silver in the service, of course—and at the side of his chair was a capacious dumb-waiter, with a variety of bottles and decanters on it, and four dishes of fruit for dessert. I noticed throughout, that he kept everything under his own hand, and distributed everything himself.

There was a bookcase in the room; I saw from the backs of the books, that they were about evidence, criminal law, criminal biography, trials, acts of parliament, and such things. The furniture was all very solid and good, like his watch-chain. It had an official look, however, and there was nothing merely ornamental to be seen. In a corner was a little table of papers with a shaded lamp; so that he seemed to bring the office home with him in that respect too, and to wheel it out of an evening and fall to work.

As he had scarcely seen my three companions until now—for he and I had walked together—he stood on the hearth-rug, after ringing the bell, and took a searching look at them. To my surprise, he seemed at once to be principally, if not solely, interested in Drummle.

"Pip," said he, putting his large hand on my shoulder and moving me to the window, "I don't know one from the other. Who's the Spider?"

"The spider?" said I.

"The blotchy, sprawly, sulky fellow."

"That's Bentley Drummle," I replied; "the one with the delicate face is Startop."

Not making the least account of "the one with the delicate

face," he returned, "Bentley Drummle is his name, is it? I like the look of that fellow."

He immediately began to talk to Drummle: not at all deterred by his replying in his heavy reticent way, but apparently led on by it to screw discourse out of him. I was looking at the two, when there came between me and them, the housekeeper, with the first dish for the table.

She was a woman of about forty, I supposed—but I may have thought her younger than she was. Rather tall, of a lithe nimble figure, extremely pale, with large faded eyes, and a quantity of streaming hair. I cannot say whether any diseased affection of the heart caused her lips to be parted as if she were panting, and her face to bear a curious expression of suddenness and flutter; but I know that I had been to see Macbeth at the theatre, a night or two before, and that her face looked to me as if it were all disturbed by fiery air, like the faces I had seen rise out of the Witches' caldron.

She set the dish on, touched my guardian quietly on the arm with a finger to notify that dinner was ready, and vanished. We took our seats at the round table, and my guardian kept Drummle on one side of him, while Startop sat on the other. It was a noble dish of fish that the housekeeper had put on table, and we had a joint of equally choice mutton afterwards, and then an equally choice bird. Sauces, wines, all the accessories we wanted, and all of the best, were given out by our host from his dumb-waiter; and when they had made the circuit of the table, he always put them back again. Similarly, he dealt us clean plates and knives and forks, for each course, and dropped those just disused into two baskets on the ground by his chair. No other attendant than the housekeeper appeared. She set on every dish; and I always saw in her face, a face rising out of the caldron. Years afterwards, I made a dreadful likeness of that woman, by causing a face that had no other natural resemblance to it than it derived from flowing hair, to pass behind a bowl of flaming spirits in a dark room.

Induced to take particular notice of the housekeeper, both by her own striking appearance and by Wemmick's preparation, I observed that whenever she was in the room, she kept her eyes attentively on my guardian, and that she would remove her hands from any dish she put before him, hesitatingly, as if she dreaded his calling her back, and wanted

him to speak when she was nigh, if he had anything to say. I fancied that I could detect in his manner a consciousness of this, and a purpose of always holding her in suspense.

Dinner went off gaily, and, although my guardian seemed to follow rather than originate subjects, I knew that he wrenched the weakest part of our dispositions out of us. For myself, I found that I was expressing my tendency to lavish expenditure, and to patronise Herbert, and to boast of my great prospects, before I quite knew that I had opened my lips. It was so with all of us, but with no one more than Drummle: the development of whose inclination to gird in a grudging and suspicious way at the rest, was screwed out of him before the fish was taken off.

It was not then, but when we had got to the cheese, that our conversation turned upon our rowing feats, and that Drummle was rallied for coming up behind of a night in that slow amphibious way of his. Drummle upon this, informed our host that he much preferred our room to our company, and that as to skill he was more than our master, and that as to strength he could scatter us like chaff. By some invisible agency, my guardian wound him up to a pitch little short of ferocity about this trifle; and he fell to baring and spanning his arm to show how muscular it was, and we all fell to baring and spanning our arms in a ridiculous manner.

Now, the housekeeper was at that time clearing the table; my guardian, taking no heed of her, but with the side of his face turned from her, was leaning back in his chair biting the side of his forefinger and showing an interest in Drummle, that, to me, was quite inexplicable. Suddenly, he clapped his large hand on the housekeeper's, like a trap, as she stretched it across the table. So suddenly and smartly did he do this, that we all stopped in our foolish contention.

"If you talk of strength," said Mr. Jaggers, "*I*'ll show you a wrist. Molly, let them see your wrist."

Her entrapped hand was on the table, but she had already put her other hand behind her waist. "Master," she said, in a low voice, with her eyes attentively and entreatingly fixed upon him, "Don't."

"*I*'ll show you a wrist," repeated Mr. Jaggers, with an immovable determination to show it. "Molly, let them see your wrist."

"Master," she again murmured. "Please!"

"Molly," said Mr. Jaggers, not looking at her, but obstinately looking at the opposite side of the room, "let them see *both* your wrists. Show them. Come!"

He took his hand from hers, and turned that wrist up on the table. She brought her other hand from behind her, and held the two out side by side. The last wrist was much disfigured—deeply scarred and scarred across and across. When she held her hands out, she took her eyes from Mr. Jaggers, and turned them watchfully on every one of the rest of us in succession.

"There's power here," said Mr. Jaggers, coolly tracing out the sinews with his forefinger. "Very few men have the power of wrist that this woman has. It's remarkable what mere force of grip there is in these hands. I have had occasion to notice many hands; but I never saw stronger in that respect, man's or woman's, than these."

While he said these words in a leisurely critical style, she continued to look at every one of us in regular succession as we sat. The moment he ceased, she looked at him again. "That'll do, Molly," said Mr. Jaggers, giving her a slight nod; "you have been admired, and can go." She withdrew her hands and went out of the room, and Mr. Jaggers, putting the decanters on from his dumb-waiter, filled his glass and passed round the wine.

"At half-past nine, gentlemen," said he, "we must break up. Pray make the best use of your time. I am glad to see you all. Mr. Drummle, I drink to you."

If his object in singling out Drummle were to bring him out still more, it perfectly succeeded. In a sulky triumph, Drummle showed his morose depreciation of the rest of us, in a more and more offensive degree, until he became downright intolerable. Through all his stages, Mr. Jaggers followed him with the same strange interest. He actually seemed to serve as a zest to Mr. Jaggers's wine.

In our boyish want of discretion I dare say we took too much to drink, and I know we talked too much. We became particularly hot upon some boorish sneer of Drummle's, to the effect that we were too free with our money. It led to my remarking, with more zeal than discretion, that it came with a bad grace from him, to whom Startop had lent money in my presence but a week or so before.

"Well," retorted Drummle, "he'll be paid."

"I don't mean to imply that he won't," said I, "but it

might make you hold your tongue about us and our money, I should think."

"*You* should think!" retorted Drummle. "Oh Lord!"

"I dare say," I went on, meaning to be very severe, "that you wouldn't lend money to any of us if we wanted it."

"You are right," said Drummle. "I wouldn't lend one of you a sixpence. I wouldn't lend anybody a sixpence."

"Rather mean to borrow under those circumstances, I should say."

"*You* should say," repeated Drummle. "Oh Lord!"

This was so very aggravating—the more especially as I found myself making no way against his surly obtuseness—that I said, disregarding Herbert's efforts to check me:

"Come, Mr. Drummle, since we are on the subject, I'll tell you what passed between Herbert here and me, when you borrowed that money."

"*I* don't want to know what passed between Herbert there and you," growled Drummle. And I think he added in a lower growl, that we might both go to the devil and shake ourselves.

"I'll tell you, however," said I, "whether you want to know or not. We said that as you put it into your pocket very glad to get it, you seemed to be immensely amused at his being so weak as to lend it."

Drummle laughed outright, and sat laughing in our faces, with his hands in his pockets and his round shoulders raised; plainly signifying that it was quite true, and that he despised us as asses all.

Hereupon Startop took him in hand, though with a much better grace than I had shown, and exhorted him to be a little more agreeable. Startop, being a lively bright young fellow, and Drummle being the exact opposite, the latter was always disposed to resent him as a direct personal affront. He now retorted in a coarse lumpish way, and Startop tried to turn the discussion aside with some small pleasantry that made us all laugh. Resenting this little success more than anything, Drummle, without any threat or warning, pulled his hands out of his pockets, dropped his round shoulders, swore, took up a large glass, and would have flung it at his adversary's head, but for our entertainer's dexterously seizing it at the instant when it was raised for that purpose.

"Gentlemen," said Mr. Jaggers, deliberately putting down the glass, and hauling out his gold repeater by its massive chain, "I am exceedingly sorry to announce that it's half-past nine."

On this hint we all rose to depart. Before we got to the street door, Startop was cheerily calling Drummle "old boy," as if nothing had happened. But the old boy was so far from responding, that he would not even walk to Hammersmith on the same side of the way ; so, Herbert and I, who remained in town, saw them going down the street on opposite sides ; Startop leading, and Drummle lagging behind in the shadow of the houses, much as he was wont to follow in his boat.

As the door was not yet shut, I thought I would leave Herbert there for a moment, and run up-stairs again to say a word to my guardian. I found him in his dressing-room surrounded by his stock of boots, already hard at it, washing his hands of us.

I told him I had come up again to say how sorry I was that anything disagreeable should have occurred, and that I hoped he would not blame me much.

"Pooh!" said he, sluicing his face, and speaking through the water-drops ; "it's nothing, Pip. I like that Spider though."

He had turned towards me now, and was shaking his head, and blowing, and towelling himself.

"I am glad you like him, sir," said I—"but I don't."

"No, no," my guardian assented ; "don't have too much to do with him. Keep as clear of him as you can. But I like the fellow, Pip ; he is one of the true sort. Why, if I was a fortune-teller——"

Looking out of the towel, he caught my eye.

"But I am not a fortune-teller," he said, letting his head drop into a festoon of towel, and towelling away at his two ears. "You know what I am, don't you ? Good night, Pip."

"Good night, sir."

In about a month after that, the Spider's time with Mr. Pocket was up for good, and, to the great relief of all the house but Mrs. Pocket, he went home to the family hole.

CHAPTER XXVII

"My Dear Mr. Pip,

"I write this by request of Mr. Gargery, for to let you know that he is going to London in company with Mr. Wopsle and would be glad if agreeable to be allowed to see you. He would call at Barnard's Hotel Tuesday morning at nine o'clock, when if not agreeable please leave word. Your poor sister is much the same as when you left. We talk of you in the kitchen every night, and wonder what you are saying and doing. If now considered in the light of a liberty, excuse it for the love of poor old days. No more, dear Mr. Pip, from

"Your ever obliged, and affectionate servant,
"Biddy.

"P.S. He wishes me most particular to write _what larks_. He says you will understand. I hope and do not doubt it will be agreeable to see him even though a gentleman, for you had ever a good heart, and he is a _worthy worthy_ man. I have read him all excepting only the last little sentence, and he wishes me most particular to write again _what larks_."

I received this letter by post on Monday morning, and therefore its appointment was for next day. Let me confess exactly, with what feelings I looked forward to Joe's coming.

Not with pleasure, though I was bound to him by so many ties ; no ; with considerable disturbance, some mortification, and a keen sense of incongruity. If I could have kept him away by paying money, I certainly would have paid money. My greatest reassurance was, that he was coming to Barnard's Inn, not to Hammersmith, and consequently would not fall in Bentley Drummle's way. I had little objection to his being seen by Herbert or his father, for both of whom I had a respect ; but I had the sharpest sensitiveness as to his being seen by Drummle, whom I held in contempt. So, throughout life, our worst weaknesses and meannesses are usually committed for the sake of the people whom we most despise.

I had begun to be always decorating the chambers in some quite unnecessary and inappropriate way or other, and very expensive those wrestles with Barnard proved to be. By this time, the rooms were vastly different from what

I had found them, and I enjoyed the honour of occupying a few prominent pages in the books of a neighbouring upholsterer. I had got on so fast of late, that I had even started a boy in boots—top boots—in bondage and slavery to whom I might be said to pass my days. For, after I had made this monster (out of the refuse of my washerwoman's family) and had clothed him with a blue coat, canary waistcoat, white cravat, creamy breeches, and the boots already mentioned, I had to find him a little to do and a great deal to eat; and with both of these horrible requirements he haunted my existence.

This avenging phantom was ordered to be on duty at eight on Tuesday morning in the hall (it was two feet square, as charged for floorcloth), and Herbert suggested certain things for breakfast that he thought Joe would like. While I felt sincerely obliged to him for being so interested and considerate, I had an odd half-provoked sense of suspicion upon me, that if Joe had been coming to see *him*, he wouldn't have been quite so brisk about it.

However, I came into town on the Monday night to be ready for Joe, and I got up early in the morning, and caused the sitting-room and breakfast-table to assume their most splendid appearance. Unfortunately the morning was drizzly, and an angel could not have concealed the fact that Barnard was shedding sooty tears outside the window, like some weak giant of a Sweep.

As the time approached I should have liked to run away, but the Avenger pursuant to orders was in the hall, and presently I heard Joe, on the staircase. I knew it was Joe, by his clumsy manner of coming up-stairs—his state boots being always too big for him—and by the time it took him to read the names on the other floors in the course of his ascent. When at last he stopped outside our door, I could hear his finger tracing over the painted letters of my name, and I afterwards distinctly heard him breathing in at the keyhole. Finally he gave a faint single rap, and Pepper—such was the compromising name of the avenging boy—announced "Mr. Gargery!" I thought he never would have done wiping his feet, and that I must have gone out to lift him off the mat, but at last he came in.

"Joe, how are you, Joe?"

"Pip, how AIR you, Pip?"

With his good honest face all glowing and shining, and

his hat put down on the floor between us, he caught both my hands and worked them straight up and down, as if I had been the last-patented Pump.

"I am glad to see you, Joe. Give me your hat."

But Joe, taking it up carefully with both hands, like a bird's-nest with eggs in it, wouldn't hear of parting with that piece of property, and persisted in standing talking over it in a most uncomfortable way.

"Which you have that growed," said Joe, "and that swelled, and that gentle-folked;" Joe considered a little before he discovered this word; "as, to besure, you are a honour to your king and country."

"And you, Joe, look wonderfully well."

"Thank God," said Joe, "I'm ekerval to most. And your sister, she's no worse than she were. And Biddy, she's ever right and ready. And all friends is no backerder, if not no forarder. 'Ceptin' Wopsle: he's had a drop."

All this time (still with both hands taking great care of the bird's-nest), Joe was rolling his eyes round and round the room, and round and round the flowered pattern of my dressing-gown.

"Had a drop, Joe?"

"Why, yes," said Joe, lowering his voice, "he's left the Church and went into the playacting. Which the playacting have likewise brought him to London along with me. And his wish were," said Joe, getting the bird's-nest under his left arm for the moment, and groping in it for an egg with his right; "if no offence, as I would 'and you that."

I took what Joe gave me, and found it to be the crumpled playbill of a small metropolitan theatre, announcing the first appearance, in that very week, of "the celebrated Provincial Amateur of Roscian renown, whose unique performance in the highest tragic walk of our National Bard has lately occasioned so great a sensation in local dramatic circles."

"Were you at his performance, Joe?" I inquired.

"I _were_," said Joe, with emphasis and solemnity.

"Was there a great sensation?"

"Why," said Joe, "yes, there certainly were a peck of orange-peel. Partickler when he see the ghost. Though I put it to yourself, sir, whether it were calc'lated to keep a man up to his work with a good hart, to be continiwally cutting in betwixt him and the Ghost with 'Amen!' A man may have had a misfortun' and been in the Church," said

Joe, lowering his voice to an argumentative and feeling tone, "but that is no reason why you should put him out at such a time. Which I meantersay, if the ghost of a man's own father cannot be allowed to claim his attention, what can, Sir? Still more, when his mourning 'at is unfortunately made so small as that the weight of the black feathers brings it off, try to keep it on how you may."

A ghost-seeing effect in Joe's own countenance informed me that Herbert had entered the room. So I presented Joe to Herbert, who held out his hand; but Joe backed from it, and held on by the bird's-nest.

"Your servant, Sir," said Joe, "which I hope as you and Pip"—here his eye fell on the Avenger, who was putting some toast on table, and so plainly denoted an intention to make that young gentleman one of the family, that I frowned it down and confused him more—"I meantersay, you two gentlemen—which I hope as you gets your elths in this close spot? For the present may be a wery good inn, according to London opinions," said Joe, confidentially, "and I believe it's character do stand i; but I wouldn't keep a pig in it myself—not in the case that I wished him to fatten wholesome and to eat with a meller flavour on him."

Having borne this flattering testimony to the merits of our dwelling-place, and having incidentally shown this tendency to call me "sir," Joe, being invited to sit down to table, looked all round the room for a suitable spot on which to deposit his hat—as if it were only on some few very rare substances in nature that it could find a resting-place—and ultimately stood it on an extreme corner of the chimneypiece, from which it ever afterwards fell off at intervals.

"Do you take tea, or coffee, Mr. Gargery?" asked Herbert, who always presided of a morning.

"Thankee, Sir," said Joe, stiff from head to foot, "I'll take whichever is most agreeable to yourself."

"What do you say to coffee?"

"Thankee, Sir," returned Joe, evidently dispirited by the proposal, "since you *are* so kind as make chice of coffee, I will not run contrairy to your own opinions. But don't you never find it a little 'eating?"

"Say tea, then," said Herbert, pouring it out.

Here Joe's hat tumbled off the mantel-piece, and he started out of his chair and picked it up, and fitted it to the same exact spot. As if it were an absolute point of good breeding that it should tumble off again soon.

"When did you come to town, Mr. Gargery?"

"Were it yesterday afternoon?" said Joe, after coughing behind his hand as if he had had time to catch the whooping-cough since he came. "No it were not. Yes it were. Yes. It were yesterday afternoon" (with an appearance of mingled wisdom, relief, and strict impartiality).

"Have you seen anything of London, yet?"

"Why, yes, Sir," said Joe, "me and Wopsle went off straight to look at the Blacking Ware'us. But we didn't find that it come up to its likeness in the red bills at the shop doors: which I meantersay," added Joe, in an explanatory manner, "as it is there drawd too architectooralooral."

I really believe Joe would have prolonged this word (mightily expressive to my mind of some architecture that I know) into a perfect Chorus, but for his attention being providentially attracted by his hat, which was toppling. Indeed, it demanded from him a constant attention, and a quickness of eye and hand, very like that exacted by wicket-keeping. He made extraordinary play with it, and showed the greatest skill; now, rushing at it and catching it neatly as it dropped; now, merely stopping it midway, beating it up, and humouring it in various parts of the room and against a good deal of the pattern of the paper on the wall, before he felt it safe to close with it; finally splashing it into the slop-basin, where I took the liberty of laying hands upon it.

As to his shirt-collar, and his coat-collar, they were perplexing to reflect upon—insoluble mysteries both. Why should a man scrape himself to that extent, before he could consider himself full dressed? Why should he suppose it necessary to be purified by suffering for his holiday clothes? Then he fell into such unaccountable fits of meditation, with his fork midway between his plate and his mouth; had his eyes attracted in such strange directions; was afflicted with such remarkable coughs; sat so far from the table, and dropped so much more than he ate, and pretended that he hadn't dropped it; that I was heartily glad when Herbert left us for the city.

I had neither the good sense nor the good feeling to know that this was all my fault, and that if I had been easier with Joe, Joe would have been easier with me. I felt impatient

of him and out of temper with him ; in which condition he
heaped coals of fire on my head.

"Us two being now alone, Sir"—began Joe.

"Joe," I interrupted, pettishly, "how can you call me
Sir ?"

Joe looked at me for a single instant with something
faintly like reproach. Utterly preposterous as his cravat
was, and as his collars were, I was conscious of a sort of
dignity in the look.

"Us two being now alone," resumed Joe, "and me having
the intentions and abilities to stay not many minutes more,
I will now conclude—leastways begin—to mention what
have led to my having had the present honour. For was it
not," said Joe, with his old air of lucid exposition, "that my
only wish were to be useful to you, I should not have had
the honour of breaking wittles in the company and abode of
gentlemen."

I was so unwilling to see the look again, that I made no
remonstrance against this tone.

"Well, Sir," pursued Joe, "this is how it were. I were
at the Bargemen t'other night, Pip ; " whenever he subsided
into affection, he called me Pip, and whenever he relapsed
into politeness he called me Sir ; "when there come up in
his shay-cart Pumblechook. Which that same identical,"
said Joe, going down a new track, "do comb my 'air the
wrong way sometimes, awful, by giving out up and down
town as it were him which ever had your infant companiona-
tion and were looked upon as a playfellow by yourself."

"Nonsense. It was you, Joe."

"Which I fully believed it were, Pip," said Joe, slightly
tossing his head, "though it signify little now, Sir. Well,
Pip ; this same identical, which his manners is given to
blusterous, come to me at the Bargemen (wot a pipe and
a pint of beer do give refreshment to the working-man, Sir,
and do not over stimulate), and his word were, ʻJoseph,
Miss Havisham she wish to speak to you.ʼ"

"Miss Havisham, Joe ?"

"ʻShe wished,ʼ were Pumblechook's word, ʻto speak to
you.ʼ" Joe sat and rolled his eyes at the ceiling.

"Yes, Joe ? Go on, please."

"Next day, Sir," said Joe, looking at me as if I were a
long way off, "having cleaned myself, I go and I see Miss A."

"Miss A., Joe ? Miss Havisham ?"

"Which I say, Sir," replied Joe, with an air of legal formality, as if he were making his will, "Miss A., or otherways Havisham. Her expression air then as follering: 'Mr. Gargery. You air in correspondence with Mr. Pip?' Having had a letter from you, I were able to say 'I am.' (When I married your sister, Sir, I said, 'I will;' and when I answered your friend, Pip, I said, 'I am.') 'Would you tell him, then,' said she, 'that which Estella has come home, and would be glad to see him.'"

I felt my face fire up as I looked at Joe. I hope one remote cause of its firing, may have been my consciousness that if I had known his errand, I should have given him more encouragement.

"Biddy," pursued Joe, "when I got home and asked her fur to write the message to you, a little hung back. Biddy says, 'I know he will be very glad to have it by word of mouth, it is holiday-time, you want to see him, go!' I have now concluded, Sir," said Joe, rising from his chair, "and, Pip, I wish you ever well and ever prospering to a greater and greater height."

"But you are not going now, Joe?"

"Yes I am," said Joe.

"But you are coming back to dinner, Joe?"

"No I am not," said Joe.

Our eyes met, and all the "Sir" melted out of that manly heart as he gave me his hand.

"Pip, dear old chap, life is made of ever so many partings welded together, as I may say, and one man's a blacksmith, and one's a whitesmith, and one's a goldsmith, and one's a coppersmith. Diwisions among such must come, and must be met as they come. If there's been any fault at all to-day, it's mine. You and me is not two figures to be together in London; nor yet anywheres else but what is private, and beknown, and understood among friends. It ain't that I am proud, but that I want to be right, as you shall never see me no more in these clothes. I'm wrong in these clothes. I'm wrong out of the forge, the kitchen, or off th' meshes. You won't find half so much fault in me if you think of me in my forge dress, with my hammer in my hand, or even my pipe. You won't find half so much fault in me if, supposing as you should ever wish to see me, you come and put your head in at the forge window and see Joe the blacksmith, there, at the old anvil, in the old burnt apron, sticking to the old work. I'm awful dull, but I hope I've beat out something nigh the rights of this at last. And so God bless you, dear old Pip, old chap, God bless you!"

I had not been mistaken in my fancy that there was a simple dignity in him. The fashion of his dress could no more come in its way when he spoke these words, than it could come in its way in Heaven. He touched me gently on the forehead, and went out. As soon as I could recover myself sufficiently, I hurried out after him and looked for him in the neighbouring streets; but he was gone.

CHAPTER XXVIII

It was clear that I must repair to our town next day, and in the first flow of my repentance it was equally clear that I must stay at Joe's. But, when I had secured my box-place by to-morrow's coach, and had been down to Mr. Pocket's and back, I was not by any means convinced on the last point, and began to invent reasons and make excuses for putting up at the Blue Boar. I should be an inconvenience at Joe's; I was not expected, and my bed would not be ready; I should be too far from Miss Havisham's, and she was exacting and mightn't like it. All other swindlers upon earth are nothing to the self-swindlers, and with such pretences did I cheat myself. Surely a curious thing. That I should innocently take a bad half-crown of somebody else's manufacture, is reasonable enough; but that I should knowingly reckon the spurious coin of my own make, as good money! An obliging stranger, under pretence of compactly folding up my bank-notes for security's sake, abstracts the notes and gives me nutshells; but what is his sleight of hand to mine, when I fold up my own nutshells and pass them on myself as notes!

Having settled that I must go to the Blue Boar, my mind was much disturbed by indecision whether or no to take the Avenger. It was tempting to think of that expensive Mercenary publicly airing his boots in the archway of the Blue Boar's posting-yard: it was almost solemn to imagine him casually produced in the tailor's shop and confounding the disrespectful senses of Trabb's boy. On the other hand, Trabb's boy might worm himself into his intimacy and tell him things; or, reckless and desperate wretch as I knew he could be, might hoot him in the High-street. My patroness, too, might hear of him, and not approve. On the whole, I resolved to leave the Avenger behind.

It was the afternoon coach by which I had taken my place, and, as winter had now come round, I should not arrive at my destination until two or three hours after dark. Our time of starting from the Cross Keys was two o'clock.

I arrived on the ground with a quarter of an hour to spare, attended by the Avenger—if I may connect that expression with one who never attended on me if he could possibly help it.

At that time it was customary to carry Convicts down to the dockyards by stage-coach. As I had often heard of them in the capacity of outside passengers, and had more than once seen them on the high road dangling their ironed legs over the coach roof, I had no cause to be surprised when Herbert, meeting me in the yard, came up and told me there were two convicts going down with me. But I had a reason that was an old reason now, for constitutionally faltering whenever I heard the word convict.

" You don't mind them, Handel ? " said Herbert.

" Oh no ! "

" I thought you seemed as if you didn't like them ? "

" I can't pretend that I do like them, and I suppose you don't particularly. But I don't mind them."

" See ! There they are," said Herbert, " coming out of the Tap. What a degraded and vile sight it is ! "

They had been treating their guard, I suppose, for they had a gaoler with them, and all three came out wiping their mouths on their hands. The two convicts were handcuffed together, and had irons on their legs—iron of a pattern that I knew well. They wore the dress that I likewise knew well. Their keeper had a brace of pistols, and carried a thick-knobbed bludgeon under his arm ; but he was on terms of good understanding with them, and stood, with them beside him, looking on at the putting-to of the horses, rather with an air as if the convicts were an interesting Exhibition not formally open at the moment, and he the Curator. One was a taller and stouter man than the other, and appeared as a matter of course, according to the mysterious ways of the world both convict and free, to have had allotted to him the smaller suit of clothes. His arms and legs were like great pincushions of those shapes, and his attire disguised him absurdly ; but I knew his half-closed eye at one glance. There stood the man whom I had seen on the settle at the Three Jolly Bargemen on a Saturday night, and who had brought me down with his invisible gun !

It was easy to make sure that as yet he knew me no more than if he had never seen me in his life. He looked across at me, and his eye appraised my watch-chain, and then he incidentally spat and said something to the other convict, and they laughed and slued themselves round with a clink of their coupling manacle, and looked at something else. The great numbers on their backs, as if they were street doors ; their coarse mangy ungainly outer surface, as if they were lower animals ; their ironed legs, apologetically garlanded with pocket-handkerchiefs ; and the way in which all present looked at them and kept from them ; made them (as Herbert had said) a most disagreeable and degraded spectacle.

But this was not the worst of it. It came out that the whole of the back of the coach had been taken by a family removing from London, and that there were no places for the two prisoners but on the seat in front, behind the coachman. Hereupon, a choleric gentleman, who had taken the fourth place on that seat, flew into a most violent passion, and said that it was a breach of contract to mix him up with such villainous company, and that it was poisonous and pernicious and infamous and shameful, and I don't know what else. At this time the coach was ready and the coachman impatient, and we were all preparing to get up, and the prisoners had come over with their keeper—bringing with them that curious flavour of bread-poultice, baize, rope-yarn, and hearthstone, which attends the convict presence.

" Don't take it so much amiss, sir," pleaded the keeper to the angry passenger ; " I'll sit next you myself. I'll put 'em on the outside of the row. They won't interfere with you, sir. You needn't know they're there."

"And don't blame *me*," growled the convict I had recognised. "*I* don't want to go. *I* am quite ready to stay behind. As fur as I am concerned any one's welcome to *my* place."

"Or mine," said the other, gruffly. "*I* wouldn't have incommoded none of you, if I'd a had *my* way." Then, they both laughed, and began cracking nuts, and spitting the shells about.—As I really think I should have liked to do myself, if I had been in their place and so despised.

At length, it was voted that there was no help for the angry gentleman, and that he must either go in his chance company or remain behind. So he got into his place, still making complaints, and the keeper got into the place next him, and the convicts hauled themselves up as well as they could, and the convict I had recognised sat behind me with his breath on the hair of my head.

"Good-bye, Handel!" Herbert called out as we started. I thought what a blessed fortune it was, that he had found another name for me than Pip.

It is impossible to express with what acuteness I felt the convict's breathing, not only on the back of my head, but all along my spine. The sensation was like being touched in the marrow with some pungent and searching acid, and it set my very teeth on edge. He seemed to have more breathing business to do than another man, and to make more noise in doing it; and I was conscious of growing high-shouldered on one side, in my shrinking endeavours to fend him off.

The weather was miserably raw, and the two cursed the cold. It made us all lethargic before we had gone far, and when we had left the Half-way House behind, we habitually dozed and shivered and were silent. I dozed off, myself, in considering the question whether I ought to restore a couple of pounds sterling to this creature before losing sight of him, and how it could best be done. In the act of dipping forward as if I were going to bathe among the horses, I woke in a fright and took the question up again.

But I must have lost it longer than I had thought, since, although I could recognise nothing in the darkness and the fitful lights and shadows of our lamps, I traced marsh country in the cold damp wind that blew at us. Cowering forward for warmth and to make me a screen against the wind, the convicts were closer to me than before. The very first words I heard them interchange as I became conscious, were the words of my own thought, "Two One-Pound notes."

"How did he get 'em?" said the convict I had never seen.

"How should I know?" returned the other. "He had 'em stowed away somehows. Giv him by friends, I expect."

"I wish," said the other, with a bitter curse upon the cold, "that I had 'em here."

"Two one-pound notes, or friends?"

"Two one-pound notes. I'd sell all the friends I ever had, for one, and think it a blessed good bargain. Well? So he says——?"

"So he says," resumed the convict I had recognised——"it

was all said and done in half a minute, behind a pile of
timber in the Dockyard—'You're a going to be discharged!'
Yes, I was. Would I find out that boy that had fed him and
kep his secret, and give him them two one-pound notes?
Yes, I would. And I did."

"More fool you," growled the other. "I'd have spent 'em
on a Man, in wittles and drink. He must have been a green
one. Mean to say he knowed nothing of you?"

"Not a ha'porth. Different gangs and different ships.
He was tried again for prison-breaking, and got made a
Lifer."

"And was that—Honour!—the only time you worked out,
in this part of the country?"

"The only time."

"What might have been your opinion of the place?"

"A most beastly place. Mudbank, mist, swamp, and
work: work, swamp, mist, and mudbank."

They both execrated the place in very strong language,
and gradually growled themselves out, and had nothing left
to say.

After overhearing this dialogue, I should assuredly have
got down and been left in the solitude and darkness of the
highway, but for feeling certain that the man had no suspicion of my identity. Indeed, I was not only so changed
in the course of nature, but so differently dressed and so
differently circumstanced, that it was not at all likely he
could have known me without accidental help. Still, the
coincidence of our being together on the coach, was sufficiently strange to fill me with a dread that some other coincidence might at any moment connect me, in his hearing,
with my name. For this reason, I resolved to alight as
soon as we touched the town, and put myself out of his
hearing. This device I executed successfully. My little
portmanteau was in the boot under my feet; I had but to
turn a hinge to get it out; I threw it down before me, got
down after it, and was left at the first lamp on the first
stones of the town pavement. As to the convicts, they went
their way with the coach, and I knew at what point they
would be spirited off to the river. In my fancy, I saw the
boat with its convict crew waiting for them at the slime-
washed stairs,—again heard the gruff "Give way, you!"
like an order to dogs—again saw the wicked Noah's Ark
lying out on the black water.

I could not have said what I was afraid of, for my fear was altogether undefined and vague, but there was great fear upon me. As I walked on to the hotel, I felt that a dread, much exceeding the mere apprehension of a painful or disagreeable recognition, made me tremble. I am confident that it took no distinctness of shape, and that it was the revival for a few minutes of the terror of childhood.

The coffee-room at the Blue Boar was empty, and I had not only ordered my dinner there, but had sat down to it, before the waiter knew me. As soon as he had apologised for the remissness of his memory, he asked me if he should send Boots for Mr. Pumblechook?

"No," said I, "certainly not."

The waiter (it was he who had brought up the Great Remonstrance from the Commercials on the day when I was bound) appeared surprised, and took the earliest opportunity of putting a dirty old copy of a local newspaper so directly in my way, that I took it up and read this paragraph :

"Our readers will learn, not altogether without interest, in reference to the recent romantic rise in fortune of a young artificer in iron of this neighbourhood (what a theme, by the way, for the magic pen of our as yet not universally acknowledged townsman Tooby, the poet of our columns!) that the youth's earliest patron, companion, and friend, was a highly-respected individual not entirely unconnected with the corn and seed trade, and whose eminently convenient and commodious business premises are situate within a hundred miles of the High-street. It is not wholly irrespective of our personal feelings that we record Him as the Mentor of our young Telemachus, for it is good to know that our town produced the founder of the latter's fortunes. Does the thought-contracted brow of the local Sage or the lustrous eye of local Beauty inquire whose fortunes? We believe that Quintin Matsys was the Blacksmith of Antwerp. Verb. Sap."

I entertain a conviction, based upon large experience, that if in the days of my prosperity I had gone to the North Pole, I should have met somebody there, wandering Esquimaux or civilised man, who would have told me that Pumblechook was my earliest patron and the founder of my fortunes.

CHAPTER XXIX

BETIMES in the morning I was up and out. It was too early yet to go to Miss Havisham's, so I loitered into the country on Miss Havisham's side of town—which was not Joe's side; I could go there to-morrow—thinking about my patroness, and painting brilliant pictures of her plans for me.

She had adopted Estella, she had as good as adopted me, and it could not fail to be her intention to bring us together. She reserved it for me to restore the desolate house, admit the sunshine into the dark rooms, set the clocks a going and the cold hearths a blazing, tear down the cobwebs, destroy the vermin—in short, do all the shining deeds of the young Knight of romance, and marry the Princess. I had stopped to look at the house as I passed; and its seared red brick walls, blocked windows, and strong green ivy clasping even the stacks of chimneys with its twigs and tendons, as if with sinewy old arms, had made up a rich attractive mystery, of which I was the hero. Estella was the inspiration of it, and the heart of it, of course. But, though she had taken such strong possession of me, though my fancy and my hope were so set upon her, though her influence on my boyish life and character had been all-powerful, I did not, even that romantic morning, invest her with any attributes save those she possessed. I mention this in this place, of a fixed purpose, because it is the clue by which I am to be followed into my poor labyrinth. According to my experience, the conventional notion of a lover cannot be always true. The unqualified truth is, that when I loved Estella with the love of a man, I loved her simply because I found her irresistible. Once for all; I knew to my sorrow, often and often, if not always, that I loved her against reason, against promise, against peace, against hope, against happiness, against all discouragement that could be. Once for all; I loved her none the less because I knew it, and it had no more influence in restraining me, than if I had devoutly believed her to be human perfection.

I so shaped out my walk as to arrive at the gate at my old time. When I had rung at the bell with an unsteady hand, I turned my back upon the gate, while I tried to get my breath and keep the beating of my heart moderately quiet. I heard the side door open, and steps come across the court-yard ; but I pretended not to hear, even when the gate swung on its rusty hinges.

Being at last touched on the shoulder, I started and turned. I started much more naturally then, to find myself confronted by a man in a sober grey dress. The last man I should have expected to see in that place of porter at Miss Havisham's door.

"Orlick !"

"Ah, young master, there's more changes than yours. But come in, come in. It's opposed to my orders to hold the gate open."

I entered and he swung it, and locked it, and took the key out. "Yes !" said he, facing round, after doggedly preceding me a few steps towards the house. "Here I am !"

"How did you come here ?"

"I come here," he retorted, "on my legs. I had my box brought alongside me in a barrow."

"Are you here for good ?"

"I ain't here for harm, young master, I suppose."

I was not so sure of that. I had leisure to entertain the retort in my mind, while he slowly lifted his heavy glance from the pavement, up my legs and arms, to my face.

"Then you have left the forge ?" I said.

"Do this look like a forge ?" replied Orlick, sending his glance all round him with an air of injury. "Now, do it look like it ?"

I asked him how long he had left Gargery's forge ?

"One day is so like another here," he replied, "that I don't know without casting it up. However, I come here some time since you left."

"I could have told you that, Orlick."

"Ah !" said he, drily. "But then you've got to be a scholar."

By this time we had come to the house, where I found his room to be one just within the side door, with a little window in it looking on the court-yard. In its small proportions, it was not unlike the kind of place usually assigned to a gate-porter in Paris. Certain keys were hanging on the wall, to which he now added the gate-key; and his patchwork-covered bed was in a little inner division or recess. The whole had a slovenly, confined and sleepy look, like a cage for a human dormouse: while he, looming dark and heavy in the shadow of a corner by the window, looked like the human dormouse for whom it was fitted up —as indeed he was.

"I never saw this room before," I remarked; "but there used to be no Porter here."

"No," said he; "not till it got about that there was no protection on the premises, and it come to be considered dangerous, with convicts and Tag and Rag and Bobtail going up and down. And then I was recommended to the place as a man who could give another man as good as he brought, and I took it. It's easier than bellowsing and hammering.—That's loaded, that is."

My eye had been caught by a gun with a brass-bound stock over the chimney-piece, and his eye had followed mine.

"Well," said I, not desirous of more conversation, "shall I go up to Miss Havisham?"

"Burn me, if I know!" he retorted, first stretching himself and then shaking himself; "my orders ends here, young master. I give this here bell a rap with this here hammer, and you go on along the passage till you meet somebody."

"I am expected, I believe?"

"Burn me twice over, if I can say!" said he.

Upon that I turned down the long passage which I had first trodden in my thick boots, and he made his bell sound. At the end of the passage, while the bell was still reverberating, I found Sarah Pocket: who appeared to have now become constitutionally green and yellow by reason of me.

"Oh!" said she. "You, is it, Mr. Pip?"

"It is, Miss Pocket. I am glad to tell you that Mr. Pocket and family are all well."

"Are they any wiser?" said Sarah, with a dismal shake of the head; "they had better be wiser than well. Ah, Matthew, Matthew! You know your way, sir?"

"I must have been a singular little creature to hide and see that fight that day : but I did, and I enjoyed it very much."

"You rewarded me very much."

"Did I?" she replied, in an incidental and forgetful way. "I remember I entertained a great objection to your adversary, because I took it ill that he should be brought here to pester me with his company."

"He and I are great friends now."

"Are you? I think I recollect though, that you read with his father?"

"Yes."

I made the admission with reluctance, for it seemed to have a boyish look, and she already treated me more than enough like a boy.

"Since your change of fortune and prospects, you have changed your companions," said Estella.

"Naturally," said I.

"And necessarily," she added, in a haughty tone ; "what was fit company for you once, would be quite unfit company for you now."

In my conscience, I doubt very much whether I had any lingering intention left of going to see Joe ; but if I had, this observation put it to flight.

"You had no idea of your impending good fortune, in those times?" said Estella, with a slight wave of her hand, signifying the fighting times.

"Not the least."

The air of completeness and superiority with which she walked at my side, and the air of youthfulness and submission with which I walked at hers, made a contrast that I strongly felt. It would have rankled in me more than it did, if I had not regarded myself as eliciting it by being so set apart for her and assigned to her.

The garden was too overgrown and rank for walking in with ease, and after we had made the round of it twice or thrice, we came out again into the brewery yard. I showed her to a nicety where I had seen her walking on the casks, that first old day, and she said with a cold and careless look in that direction, "Did I?" I reminded her where she had come out of the house and given me my meat and drink, and she said, "I don't remember." "Not remember that you made me cry?" said I. "No," said she, and

shook her head and looked about her. I verily believe
that her not remembering and not minding in the least,
made me cry again, inwardly—and that is the sharpest
crying of all.

"You must know," said Estella, condescending to me as
a brilliant and beautiful woman might, "that I have no
heart—if that has anything to do with my memory."

I got through some jargon to the effect that I took the
liberty of doubting that. That I knew better. That there
could be no such beauty without it.

"Oh! I have a heart to be stabbed in or shot in, I have
no doubt," said Estella, "and, of course, if it ceased to beat
I should cease to be. But you know what I mean. I have
no softness there, no—sympathy—sentiment—nonsense."

What *was* it that was borne in upon my mind when she
stood still and looked attentively at me? Anything that
I had seen in Miss Havisham? No. In some of her looks
and gestures there was that tinge of resemblance to Miss
Havisham which may often be noticed to have been acquired
by children, from grown persons with whom they have
been much associated and secluded, and which, when childhood is passed, will produce a remarkable occasional likeness
of expression between faces that are otherwise quite different.
And yet I could not trace this to Miss Havisham. I looked
again, and though she was still looking at me, the suggestion
was gone.

What *was* it?

"I am serious," said Estella, not so much with a frown
(for her brow was smooth) as with a darkening of her face;
"if we are to be thrown much together, you had better
believe it at once. No!" imperiously stopping me as
I opened my lips. "I have not bestowed my tenderness
anywhere. I have never had any such thing."

In another moment we were in the brewery so long
disused, and she pointed to the high gallery where I had
seen her going out on that same first day, and told me she
remembered to have been up there, and to have seen me
standing scared below. As my eyes followed her white
hand, again the same dim suggestion that I could not
possibly grasp, crossed me. My involuntary start occasioned
her to lay her hand upon my arm. Instantly the ghost
passed once more and was gone.

What *was* it?

LIGHTLY TOUCHED MY SHOULDER AS WE WALKED

"What is the matter?" asked Estella. "Are you scared again?"

"I should be if I believed what you said just now," replied, to turn it off.

"Then you don't? Very well. It is said, at any rate. Miss Havisham will soon be expecting you at your old post, though I think that might be laid aside now, with other old belongings. Let us make one more round of the garden, and then go in. Come! You shall not shed tears for my cruelty to-day; you shall be my Page, and give me your shoulder."

Her handsome dress had trailed upon the ground. She held it in one hand now, and with the other lightly touched my shoulder as we walked. We walked round the ruined garden twice or thrice more, and it was all in bloom for me. If the green and yellow growth of weed in the chinks of the old wall had been the most precious flowers that ever blew, it could not have been more cherished in my remembrance.

There was no discrepancy of years between us, to remove her far from me; we were of nearly the same age, though of course the age told for more in her case than in mine; but the air of inaccessibility which her beauty and her manner gave her, tormented me in the midst of my delight, and at the height of the assurance I felt that our patroness had chosen us for one another. Wretched boy!

At last we went back into the house, and there I heard, with surprise, that my guardian had come down to see Miss Havisham on business, and would come back to dinner. The old wintry branches of chandeliers in the room where the mouldering table was spread, had been lighted while we were out, and Miss Havisham was in her chair and waiting for me.

It was like pushing the chair itself back into the past, when we began the old slow circuit round about the ashes of the bridal feast. But, in the funereal room, with that figure of the grave fallen back in the chair fixing its eyes upon her, Estella looked more bright and beautiful than before, and I was under stronger enchantment.

The time so melted away, that our early dinner-hour drew close at hand, and Estella left us to prepare herself. We had stopped near the centre of the long table, and Miss Havisham, with one of her withered arms stretched out of the chair, rested that clenched hand upon the yellow cloth.

As Estella looked back over her shoulder before going out at the door, Miss Havisham kissed that hand to her, with a ravenous intensity that was of its kind quite dreadful.

Then, Estella being gone and we two left alone, she turned to me and said in a whisper:

"Is she beautiful, graceful, well-grown? Do you admire her?"

"Everybody must who sees her, Miss Havisham."

She drew an arm round my neck, and drew my head close down to hers as she sat in the chair. "Love her, love her, love her! How does she use you?"

Before I could answer (if I could have answered so difficult a question at all), she repeated, "Love her, love her, love her! If she favours you, love her. If she wounds you, love her. If she tears your heart to pieces—and as it gets older and stronger it will tear deeper—love her, love her, love her!"

Never had I seen such passionate eagerness as was joined to her utterance of these words. I could feel the muscles of the thin arm round my neck, swell with the vehemence that possessed her.

"Hear me, Pip! I adopted her to be loved. I bred her and educated her, to be loved. I developed her into what she is, that she might be loved. Love her!"

She said the word often enough, and there could be no doubt that she meant to say it; but if the often repeated word had been hate instead of love—despair—revenge—dire death—it could not have sounded from her lips more like a curse.

"I'll tell you," said she, in the same hurried passionate whisper, "what real love is. It is blind devotion, unquestioning self-humiliation, utter submission, trust and belief against yourself and against the whole world, giving up your whole heart and soul to the smiter—as I did!"

When she came to that, and to a wild cry that followed that, I caught her round the waist. For she rose up in the chair, in her shroud of a dress, and struck at the air as if she would as soon have struck herself against the wall and fallen dead.

All this passed in a few seconds. As I drew her down into her chair, I was conscious of a scent that I knew, and turning, saw my guardian in the room.

He always carried (I have not yet mentioned it, I think)

a pocket-handkerchief of rich silk and of imposing proportions, which was of great value to him in his profession. I have seen him so terrify a client or a witness by ceremoniously unfolding this pocket-handkerchief as if he were immediately going to blow his nose, and then pausing, as if he knew he should not have time to do it, before such client or witness committed himself, that the self-committal has followed directly, quite as a matter of course. When I saw him in the room he had this expressive pocket-handkerchief in both hands, and was looking at us. On meeting my eye, he said plainly, by a momentary and silent pause in that attitude, "Indeed? Singular!" and then put the handkerchief to its right use with wonderful effect.

Miss Havisham had seen him as soon as I, and was (like everybody else) afraid of him. She made a strong attempt to compose herself, and stammered that he was as punctual as ever.

"As punctual as ever," he repeated, coming up to us. "(How do you do, Pip? Shall I give you a ride, Miss Havisham? Once round?) And so you are here, Pip?"

I told him when I had arrived, and how Miss Havisham wished me to come and see Estella. To which he replied, "Ah! Very fine young lady!" Then he pushed Miss Havisham in her chair before him, with one of his large hands, and put the other in his trousers-pocket as if the pocket were full of secrets.

"Well, Pip! How often have you seen Miss Estella before?" said he, when he came to a stop.

"How often?"

"Ah! How many times? Ten thousand times?"

"Oh! Certainly not so many."

"Twice?"

"Jaggers," interposed Miss Havisham, much to my relief; "leave my Pip alone, and go with him to your dinner."

He complied, and we groped our way down the dark stairs together. While we were still on our way to those detached apartments across the paved yard at the back, he asked me how often I had seen Miss Havisham eat and drink; offering me a breadth of choice, as usual, between a hundred times and once.

I considered, and said, "Never."

"And never will, Pip," he retorted, with a frowning smile. "She has never allowed herself to be seen doing

either, since she lived this present life of hers. She wanders
about in the night, and then lays hands on such food as she
takes."

"Pray, sir," said I, "may I ask you a question?"

"You may," said he, "and I may decline to answer it.
Put your question."

"Estella's name, is it Havisham or——?" I had nothing
to add.

"Or what?" said he.

"Is it Havisham?"

"It is Havisham."

This brought us to the dinner-table, where she and Sarah
Pocket awaited us. Mr. Jaggers presided, Estella sat opposite
to him, I faced my green and yellow friend. We dined very
well, and were waited on by a maid-servant whom I had
never seen in all my comings and goings, but who, for anything I know, had been in that mysterious house the whole
time. After dinner a bottle of choice old port was placed
before my guardian (he was evidently well acquainted with
the vintage), and the two ladies left us.

Anything to equal the determined reticence of Mr. Jaggers
under that roof I never saw elsewhere, even in him. He
kept his very looks to himself, and scarcely directed his eyes
to Estella's face once during dinner. When she spoke to
him, he listened, and in due course, answered, but never
looked at her that I could see. On the other hand, she
often looked at him, with interest and curiosity, if not distrust, but his face never showed the least consciousness.
Throughout dinner he took a dry delight in making Sarah
Pocket greener and yellower, by often referring in conversation with me to my expectations: but here, again, he showed
no consciousness, and even made it appear that he extorted
—and even did extort, though I don't know how—those
references out of my innocent self.

And when he and I were left alone together, he sat with
an air upon him of general lying by in consequence of
information he possessed, that really was too much for me.
He cross-examined his very wine when he had nothing else
in hand. He held it between himself and the candle, tasted
the port, rolled it in his mouth, swallowed it, looked at his
glass again, smelt the port, tried it, drank it, filled again,
and cross-examined the glass again, until I was as nervous
as if I had known the wine to be telling him something to

my disadvantage. Three or four times I feebly thought
I would start conversation; but whenever he saw me going
to ask him anything, he looked at me with his glass in his
hand, and rolling his wine about in his mouth, as if requesting me to take notice that it was of no use, for he couldn't
answer.

I think Miss Pocket was conscious that the sight of me
involved her in the danger of being goaded to madness, and
perhaps tearing off her cap—which was a very hideous one,
in the nature of a muslin mop—and strewing the ground
with her hair—which assuredly had never grown on *her*
head. She did not appear when we afterwards went up to
Miss Havisham's room, and we four played at whist. In the
interval, Miss Havisham, in a fantastic way, had put some
of the most beautiful jewels from her dressing-table into
Estella's hair, and about her bosom and arms; and I saw
even my guardian look at her from under his thick eyebrows,
and raise them a little when her loveliness was before him,
with those rich flushes of glitter and colour in it.

Of the manner and extent to which he took our trumps
into custody, and came out with mean little cards at the ends
of hands, before which the glory of our Kings and Queens
was utterly abased, I say nothing; nor, of the feeling that
I had, respecting his looking upon us personally in the light
of three very obvious and poor riddles that he had found out
long ago. What I suffered from, was the incompatibility
between his cold presence and my feelings towards Estella.
It was not that I knew I could never bear to speak to him
about her, that I knew I could never bear to hear him creak
his boots at her, that I knew I could never bear to see him
wash his hands of her; it was, that my admiration should be
within a foot or two of him—it was, that my feelings should
be in the same place with him—*that*, was the agonising
circumstance.

We played until nine o'clock, and then it was arranged
that when Estella came to London I should be forewarned
of her coming and should meet her at the coach; and then
I took leave of her, and touched her and left her.

My guardian lay at the Boar in the next room to mine.
Far into the night, Miss Havisham's words, "Love her, love
her, love her!" sounded in my ears. I adapted them for my
own repetition, and said to my pillow, "I love her, I love
her, I love her!" hundreds of times. Then, a burst of

gratitude came upon me, that she should be destined for me,
once the blacksmith's boy.   Then, I thought if she were, as
I feared, by no means rapturously grateful for that destiny
yet, when would she begin to be interested in me?   When
should I awaken the heart within her, that was mute and
sleeping now?

Ah me!   I thought those were high and great emotions.
But I never thought there was anything low and small in
my keeping away from Joe, because I knew she would be
contemptuous of him.   It was but a day gone, and Joe had
brought the tears into my eyes; they had soon dried, God
forgive me!   soon dried.

CHAPTER XXX

AFTER well considering the matter while I was dressing at the Blue Boar in the morning, I resolved to tell my guardian that I doubted Orlick's being the right sort of man to fill a post of trust at Miss Havisham's. "Why, of course he is not the right sort of man, Pip," said my guardian, comfortably satisfied beforehand on the general head, "because the man who fills the post of trust never is the right sort of man." It seemed quite to put him in spirits, to find that this particular post was not exceptionally held by the right sort of man, and he listened in a satisfied manner while I told him what knowledge I had of Orlick. "Very good, Pip," he observed, when I had concluded, "I'll go round presently, and pay our friend off." Rather alarmed by this summary action, I was for a little delay, and even hinted that our friend himself might be difficult to deal with. "Oh no, he won't," said my guardian, making his pocket-handkerchief-point, with perfect confidence; "I should like to see him argue the question with *me*."

As we were going back together to London by the mid-day coach, and as I breakfasted under such terrors of Pumblechook that I could scarcely hold my cup, this gave me an opportunity of saying that I wanted a walk, and that I would go on along the London-road while Mr. Jaggers was occupied, if he would let the coachman know that I would get into my place when overtaken. I was thus enabled to fly from the Blue Boar immediately after breakfast. By then making a loop of about a couple of miles into the open country at the back of Pumblechook's premises, I got round into the High-street again, a little beyond that pitfall, and felt myself in comparative security.

It was interesting to be in the quiet old town once more, and it was not disagreeable to be here and there suddenly recognised and stared after. One or two of the tradespeople even darted out of their shops, and went a little way down the street before me, that they might turn, as if they had

forgotten something, and pass me face to face—on which
occasions I don't know whether they or I made the worse
pretence ; they of not doing it, or I of not seeing it. Still
my position was a distinguished one, and I was not at all
dissatisfied with it, until Fate threw me in the way of that
unlimited miscreant, Trabb's boy.

Casting my eyes along the street at a certain point of my
progress, I beheld Trabb's boy approaching, lashing himself
with an empty blue bag. Deeming that a serene and unconscious contemplation of him would best beseem me, and
would be most likely to quell his evil mind, I advanced
with that expression of countenance, and was rather congratulating myself on my success, when suddenly the knees
of Trabb's boy smote together, his hair uprose, his cap fell
off, he trembled violently in every limb, staggered out into
the road, and crying to the populace, "Hold me ! I'm so
frightened !" feigned to be in a paroxysm of terror and
contrition, occasioned by the dignity of my appearance.
As I passed him, his teeth loudly chattered in his head,
and with every mark of extreme humiliation, he prostrated
himself in the dust.

This was a hard thing to bear, but this was nothing.
I had not advanced another two hundred yards, when, to
my inexpressible terror, amazement, and indignation, I again
beheld Trabb's boy approaching. He was coming round a
narrow corner. His blue bag was slung over his shoulder,
honest industry beamed in his eyes, a determination to
proceed to Trabb's with cheerful briskness was indicated in
his gait. With a shock he became aware of me, and was
severely visited as before ; but this time his motion was
rotatory, and he staggered round and round me with knees
more afflicted, and with uplifted hands as if beseeching for
mercy. His sufferings were hailed with the greatest joy by
a knot of spectators, and I felt utterly confounded.

I had not got as much further down the street as the
post-office, when I again beheld Trabb's boy shooting round
by a back way. This time, he was entirely changed. He
wore the blue bag in the manner of my great-coat, and was
strutting along the pavement towards me on the opposite
side of the street, attended by a company of delighted young
friends to whom he from time to time exclaimed, with
a wave of his hand, "Don't know yah !" Words cannot
state the amount of aggravation and injury wreaked upon

ne by Trabb's boy, when, passing abreast of me, he pulled up his shirt-collar, twined his side-hair, stuck an arm akimbo, and smirked extravagantly by, wriggling his elbows and body, and drawling to his attendants, "Don't know yah, don't know yah, pon my soul don't know yah!" The disgrace attendant on his immediately afterwards taking to crowing and pursuing me across the bridge with crows, as from an exceedingly dejected fowl who had known me when I was a blacksmith, culminated the disgrace with which I left the town, and was, so to speak, ejected by it into the open country.

But unless I had taken the life of Trabb's boy on that occasion, I really do not even now see what I could have done save endure. To have struggled with him in the street, or to have exacted any lower recompense from him than his heart's best blood, would have been futile and degrading. Moreover, he was a boy whom no man could hurt; an invulnerable and dodging serpent who, when chased into a corner, flew out again between his captor's legs, scornfully yelping. I wrote, however, to Mr. Trabb by next day's post, to say that Mr. Pip must decline to deal further with one who could so far forget what he owed to the best interests of society, as to employ a boy who excited Loathing in every respectable mind.

The coach, with Mr. Jaggers inside, came up in due time, and I took my box-seat again, and arrived in London safe— but not sound, for my heart was gone. As soon as I arrived, I sent a penitential codfish and barrel of oysters to Joe (as reparation for not having gone myself), and then went on to Barnard's Inn.

I found Herbert dining on cold meat, and delighted to welcome me back. Having despatched the Avenger to the coffee-house for an addition to the dinner, I felt that I must open my breast that very evening to my friend and chum. As confidence was out of the question with the Avenger in the hall, which could merely be regarded in the light of an ante-chamber to the keyhole, I sent him to the Play. A better proof of the severity of my bondage to that task-master could scarcely be afforded, than the degrading shifts to which I was constantly driven to find him employment. So mean is extremity, that I sometimes sent him to Hyde Park Corner to see what o'clock it was.

Dinner done and we sitting with our feet upon the fender,

I said to Herbert, "My dear Herbert, I have something very particular to tell you."

"My dear Handel," he returned, "I shall esteem and respect your confidence."

"It concerns myself, Herbert," said I, "and one other person."

Herbert crossed his feet, looked at the fire with his head on one side, and having looked at it in vain for some time, looked at me because I didn't go on.

"Herbert," said I, laying my hand upon his knee, "I love—I adore—Estella."

Instead of being transfixed, Herbert replied in an easy matter-of-course way, "Exactly. Well?"

"Well, Herbert. Is that all you say? Well?"

"What next, I mean?" said Herbert. "Of course I know *that*."

"How do you know it?" said I.

"How do I know it, Handel? Why, from you."

"I never told you."

"Told me! You have never told me when you have got your hair cut, but I have had senses to perceive it. You have always adored her, ever since I have known you. You brought your adoration and your portmanteau here, together. Told me! Why, you have always told me all day long. When you told me your own story, you told me plainly that you began adoring her the first time you saw her, when you were very young indeed."

"Very well, then," said I, to whom this was a new and not unwelcome light, "I have never left off adoring her. And she has come back, a most beautiful and most elegant creature. And I saw her yesterday. And if I adored her before, I now doubly adore her."

"Lucky for you then, Handel," said Herbert, "that you are picked out for her and allotted to her. Without encroaching on forbidden ground, we may venture to say, that there can be no doubt between ourselves of that fact. Have you any idea yet, of Estella's views on the adoration question?"

I shook my head gloomily. "Oh! She is thousands of miles away, from me," said I.

"Patience, my dear Handel: time enough, time enough. But you have something more to say?"

"I am ashamed to say it," I returned, "and yet it's no

worse to say it than to think it. You call me a lucky fellow. Of course, I am. I was a blacksmith's boy but yesterday; I am—what shall I say I am—to-day?"

"Say, a good fellow, if you want a phrase," returned Herbert, smiling, and clapping his hands on the back of mine: "a good fellow, with impetuosity and hesitation, boldness and diffidence, action and dreaming, curiously mixed in him."

I stopped for a moment to consider whether there really was this mixture in my character. On the whole, I by no means recognised the analysis, but thought it not worth disputing.

"When I ask what I am to call myself to-day, Herbert," I went on, "I suggest what I have in my thoughts. You say I am lucky. I know I have done nothing to raise myself in life, and that Fortune alone has raised me; that is being very lucky. And yet, when I think of Estella——"

("And when don't you, you know!" Herbert threw in, with his eyes on the fire; which I thought kind and sympathetic of him.)

"—Then, my dear Herbert, I cannot tell you how dependent and uncertain I feel, and how exposed to hundreds of chances. Avoiding forbidden ground, as you did just now, I may still say that on the constancy of one person (naming no person) all my expectations depend. And at the best, how indefinite and unsatisfactory, only to know so vaguely what they are!" In saying this, I relieved my mind of what had always been there, more or less, though no doubt most since yesterday.

"Now, Handel," Herbert replied, in his gay hopeful way, "it seems to me that in the despondency of the tender passion, we are looking into our gift-horse's mouth with a magnifying-glass. Likewise, it seems to me that, concentrating our attention on the examination, we altogether overlook one of the best points of the animal. Didn't you tell me that your guardian, Mr. Jaggers, told you in the beginning, that you were not endowed with expectations only? And even if he had not told you so—though that is a very large If, I grant—could you believe that of all men in London, Mr. Jaggers is the man to hold his present relations towards you unless he were sure of his ground?"

I said I could not deny that this was a strong point.

I said it (people often do so in such cases) like a rather reluctant concession to truth and justice;—as if I wanted to deny it!

"I should think it *was* a strong point," said Herbert, "and I should think you would be puzzled to imagine a stronger; as to the rest, you must bide your guardian's time, and he must bide his client's time. You'll be one-and-twenty before you know where you are, and then perhaps you'll get some further enlightenment. At all events, you'll be nearer getting it, for it must come at last."

"What a hopeful disposition you have!" said I, gratefully admiring his cheery ways.

"I ought to have," said Herbert, "for I have not much else. I must acknowledge, by-the-bye, that the good sense of what I have just said is not my own, but my father's. The only remark I ever heard him make on your story was the final one: 'The thing is settled and done, or Mr. Jaggers would not be in it.' And now, before I say anything more about my father, or my father's son, and repay confidence with confidence, I want to make myself seriously disagreeable to you for a moment—positively repulsive."

"You won't succeed," said I.

"Oh yes, I shall!" said he. "One, two, three, and now I am in for it. Handel, my good fellow:" though he spoke in this light tone, he was very much in earnest: "I have been thinking since we have been talking with our feet on this fender, that Estella cannot surely be a condition of your inheritance, if she was never referred to by your guardian. Am I right in so understanding what you have told me, as that he never referred to her, directly or indirectly, in any way? Never even hinted, for instance, that your patron might have views as to your marriage ultimately?"

"Never."

"Now, Handel, I am quite free from the flavour of sour grapes, upon my soul and honour! Not being bound to her, can you not detach yourself from her?—I told you I should be disagreeable."

I turned my head aside, for, with a rush and a sweep, like the old marsh winds coming up from the sea, a feeling like that which had subdued me on the morning when I left the forge, when the mists were solemnly rising, and when

realise Capital, it was his intention to marry this young lady. He added as a self-evident proposition, engendering low spirits, "But you *can't* marry, you know, while you're looking about you."

As we contemplated the fire, and as I thought what a difficult vision to realise this same Capital sometimes was, I put my hands in my pockets. A folded piece of paper in one of them attracting my attention, I opened it and found it to be the playbill I had received from Joe, relative to the celebrated provincial amateur of Roscian renown. "And bless my heart," I involuntarily added aloud, "it's to-night!"

This changed the subject in an instant, and made us hurriedly resolve to go to the play. So, when I had pledged myself to comfort and abet Herbert in the affair of his heart by all practicable and impracticable means, and when Herbert had told me that his affianced already knew me by reputation, and that I should be presented to her, and when we had warmly shaken hands upon our mutual confidence, we blew out our candles, made up our fire, locked our door, and issued forth in quest of Mr. Wopsle and Denmark.

CHAPTER XXXI

On our arrival in Denmark, we found the king and queen of that country elevated in two arm-chairs on a kitchen-table, holding a Court. The whole of the Danish nobility were in attendance; consisting of a noble boy in the wash-leather boots of a gigantic ancestor, a venerable Peer with a dirty face, who seemed to have risen from the people late in life, and the Danish chivalry with a comb in its hair and a pair of white silk legs, and presenting on the whole a feminine appearance. My gifted townsman stood gloomily apart, with folded arms, and I could have wished that his curls and forehead had been more probable.

Several curious little circumstances transpired as the action proceeded. The late king of the country not only appeared to have been troubled with a cough at the time of his decease, but to have taken it with him to the tomb, and to have brought it back. The royal phantom also carried a ghostly manuscript round its truncheon, to which it had the appearance of occasionally referring, and that, too, with an air of anxiety and a tendency to lose the place of reference which were suggestive of a state of mortality. It was this, I conceive, which led to the Shade's being advised by the gallery to "turn over!"—a recommendation which it took extremely ill. It was likewise to be noted of this majestic spirit that whereas it always appeared with an air of having been out a long time and walked an immense distance, it perceptibly came from a closely-contiguous wall. This occasioned its terrors to be received derisively. The Queen of Denmark, a very buxom lady, though no doubt historically brazen, was considered by the public to have too much brass about her; her chin being attached to her diadem by a broad band of that metal (as if she had a gorgeous toothache), her waist being encircled by another, and each of her arms by another, so that she was openly mentioned as "the kettle-drum." The noble boy in the ancestral boots, was inconsistent; representing himself, as it were in one breath, as an able seaman, a strolling actor, a gravedigger, a clergyman, and a person of the utmost importance at a Court fencing-match, on the authority of whose practised eye and nice discrimination the finest strokes were judged. This gradually led to a want of toleration for him, and even—on his being detected in holy orders, and declining to perform the funeral service—to the general indignation taking the form of nuts. Lastly, Ophelia was a prey to such slow musical madness, that when, in course of time, she had taken off her white muslin scarf, folded it up, and buried it, a sulky man who had been long cooling his impatient nose against an iron bar in the front row of the gallery, growled, "Now the baby's put to bed, let's have supper!" Which, to say the least of it, was out of keeping.

Upon my unfortunate townsman all these incidents accumulated with playful effect. Whenever that undecided Prince had to ask a question or state a doubt, the public helped him out with it. As for example; on the question whether 'twas nobler in the mind to suffer, some roared yes, and some no, and some inclining to both opinions said "toss up for it;" and quite a Debating Society arose. When he asked what should such fellows as he do crawling between earth and heaven, he was encouraged with loud cries of "Hear, hear!" When he appeared with his stocking disordered (its disorder expressed, according to usage, by one very neat fold in the top, which I suppose to be always got up with a flat iron), a conversation took place in the gallery respecting the paleness of his leg, and whether it was occasioned by the turn the ghost had given him. On his taking the recorders—very like a little black flute that had just been played in the orchestra and handed out at the door—he was called upon unanimously for Rule Britannia. When he recommended the player not to saw the air thus, the sulky man said, "And don't *you* do it, neither; you're a deal worse than *him!*" And I grieve to add that peals of laughter greeted Mr. Wopsle on every one of these occasions.

But his greatest trials were in the churchyard: which had the appearance of a primeval forest, with a kind of small ecclesiastical wash-house on one side, and a turnpike gate on the other. Mr. Wopsle, in a comprehensive black cloak, being descried entering at the turnpike, the gravedigger was admonished in a friendly way, "Look out! Here's the undertaker a coming, to see how you're getting on with your work!" I believe it is well known in a constitutional country that Mr. Wopsle could not possibly have returned the skull, after moralising over it, without dusting his fingers on a white napkin taken from his breast; but even that innocent and indispensable action did not pass without the comment "Wai-ter!" The arrival of the body for interment (in an empty black box with the lid tumbling open), was the signal for a general joy which was much enhanced by the discovery, among the bearers, of an individual obnoxious to identification. The joy attended Mr. Wopsle through his struggle with Laertes on the brink of the orchestra and the grave, and slackened no more until he had tumbled the king off the kitchen-table, and had died by inches from the ankles upward.

We had made some pale efforts in the beginning to applaud Mr. Wopsle; but they were too hopeless to be persisted in. Therefore we had sat, feeling keenly for him, but laughing, nevertheless, from ear to ear. I laughed in spite of myself all the time, the whole thing was so droll; and yet I had a latent impression that there was something decidedly fine in Mr. Wopsle's elocution—not for old associations' sake, I am afraid, but because it was very slow, very dreary, very up-hill and down-hill, and very unlike any way in which any man in any natural circumstances of life or death ever expressed himself about anything. When the tragedy was over, and he had been called for and hooted, I said to Herbert, "Let us go at once, or perhaps we shall meet him."

We made all the haste we could down-stairs, but we were not quick enough either. Standing at the door was a Jewish man with an unnatural heavy smear of eyebrow, who caught my eyes as we advanced, and said, when we came up with him:

"Mr. Pip and friend?"

Identity of Mr. Pip and friend confessed.

"Mr. Waldengarver," said the man, "would be glad to have the honour."

"Waldengarver?" I repeated—when Herbert murmured in my ear, "Probably Wopsle."

"Oh!" said I. "Yes. Shall we follow you?"

"A few steps, please." When we were in a side alley,

he turned and asked, "How do you think he looked?—
I dressed him."

I don't know what he had looked like, except a funeral;
with the addition of a large Danish sun or star hanging
round his neck by a blue ribbon, that had given him the
appearance of being insured in some extraordinary Fire
Office. But I said he had looked very nice.

"When he come to the grave," said our conductor, "he
showed his cloak beautiful. But, judging from the wing, it
looked to me that when he see the ghost in the queen's
apartment, he might have made more of his stockings."

I modestly assented, and we all fell through a little dirty
swing door, into a sort of hot packing-case immediately
behind it. Here Mr. Wopsle was divesting himself of his
Danish garments, and here there was just room for us to
look at him over one another's shoulders, by keeping the
packing-case door, or lid, wide open.

"Gentlemen," said Mr. Wopsle, "I am proud to see you.
I hope, Mr. Pip, you will excuse my sending round. I had
the happiness to know you in former times, and the Drama
has ever had a claim which has ever been acknowledged, on
the noble and the affluent."

Meanwhile, Mr. Waldengarver, in a frightful perspiration,
was trying to get himself out of his princely sables.

"Skin the stockings off, Mr. Waldengarver," said the
owner of that property, "or you'll bust 'em. Bust 'em, and
you'll bust five-and-thirty shillings. Shakspeare never was
complimented with a finer pair. Keep quiet in your chair
now, and leave 'em to me."

With that, he went upon his knees, and began to flay his
victim; who, on the first stocking coming off, would
certainly have fallen over backward with his chair, but for
there being no room to fall anyhow.

I had been afraid until then to say a word about the play.
But then, Mr. Waldengarver looked up at us complacently,
and said:

"Gentlemen, how did it seem to you to go, in front?"

Herbert said from behind (at the same time poking me),
"capitally." So I said "capitally."

"How did you like my reading of the character, gentlemen?" said Mr. Waldengarver, almost, if not quite, with
patronage.

Herbert said from behind (again poking me), "massive

and concrete." So I said boldly, as if I had originated it, and must beg to insist upon it, "massive and concrete."

"I am glad to have your approbation, gentlemen," said Mr. Waldengarver, with an air of dignity, in spite of his being ground against the wall at the time, and holding on by the seat of the chair.

"But I'll tell you one thing, Mr. Waldengarver," said the man who was on his knees, "in which you're out in your reading. Now mind! I don't care who says contrary; I tell you so. You're out in your reading of Hamlet when you get your legs in profile. The last Hamlet as I dressed, made the same mistakes in his reading at rehearsal, till I got him to put a large red wafer on each of his shins, and then at that rehearsal (which was the last) I went in front, sir, to the back of the pit, and whenever his reading brought him into profile, I called out, 'I don't see no wafers!' And at night his reading was lovely."

Mr. Waldengarver smiled at me, as much as to say "a faithful dependent—I overlook his folly;" and then said aloud, "My view is a little too classic and thoughtful for them here; but they will improve, they will improve."

Herbert and I said together, Oh, no doubt they would improve.

"Did you observe, gentlemen," said Mr. Waldengarver, "that there was a man in the gallery who endeavoured to cast derision on the service—I mean, the representation?"

We basely replied that we rather thought we had noticed such a man. I added, "He was drunk, no doubt."

"Oh dear no, sir," said Mr. Wopsle, "not drunk. His employer would see to that, sir. His employer would not allow him to be drunk."

"You know his employer?" said I.

Mr. Wopsle shut his eyes, and opened them again; performing both ceremonies very slowly. "You must have observed, gentlemen," said he, "an ignorant and a blatant ass, with a rasping throat and a countenance expressive of low malignity, who went through—I will not say sustained —the rôle (if I may use a French expression) of Claudius King of Denmark. That is his employer, gentlemen. Such is the profession!"

Without distinctly knowing whether I should have been more sorry for Mr. Wopsle if he had been in despair, I was so sorry for him as it was, that I took the opportunity of his turning round to have his braces put on—which jostled us out at the doorway—to ask Herbert what he thought of having him home to supper? Herbert said he thought it would be kind to do so; therefore I invited him, and he went to Barnard's with us, wrapped up to the eyes, and we did our best for him, and he sat until two o'clock in the morning, reviewing his success and developing his plans. I forget in detail what they were, but I have a general recollection that he was to begin with reviving the Drama, and to end with crushing it; inasmuch as his decease would leave it utterly bereft and without a chance or hope.

Miserably I went to bed after all, and miserably thought of Estella, and miserably dreamed that my expectations were all cancelled, and that I had to give my hand in marriage to Herbert's Clara, or play Hamlet to Miss Havisham's Ghost, before twenty thousand people, without knowing twenty words of it.

CHAPTER XXXII

ONE day when I was busy with my books and Mr. Pocket, I received a note by the post, the mere outside of which threw me into a great flutter; for, though I had never seen the handwriting in which it was addressed, I divined whose hand it was. It had no set beginning, as Dear Mr. Pip, or Dear Pip, or Dear Sir, or Dear Anything, but ran thus:

" I am to come to London the day after to-morrow by the mid-day coach. I believe it was settled you should meet me? At all events Miss Havisham has that impression, and I write in obedience to it. She sends you her regard.—Yours, ESTELLA."

If there had been time, I should probably have ordered several suits of clothes for this occasion; but as there was not, I was fain to be content with those I had. My appetite vanished instantly, and I knew no peace or rest until the day arrived. Not that its arrival brought me either; for, then I was worse than ever, and began haunting the coach-office in Wood-street, Cheapside, before the coach had left the Blue Boar in our town. For all that I knew this perfectly well, I still felt as if it were not safe to let the coach-office be out of my sight longer than five minutes at a time; and in this condition of unreason I had performed the first half-hour of a watch of four or five hours, when Wemmick ran against me.

"Halloa, Mr. Pip," said he, "how do you do? I should hardly have thought this was *your* beat."

I explained that I was waiting to meet somebody who was coming up by coach, and I inquired after the Castle and the Aged.

"Both flourishing, thankye," said Wemmick, "and particularly the Aged. He's in wonderful feather. He'll be eighty-two next birthday. I have a notion of firing eighty-two times, if the neighbourhood shouldn't complain, and that cannon of mine should prove equal to the pressure.

However, this is not London talk. Where do you think I am going to?"

"To the office," said I, for he was tending in that direction.

"Next thing to it," returned Wemmick, "I am going to Newgate. We are in a banker's-parcel case just at present, and I have been down the road taking a squint at the scene of action, and thereupon must have a word or two with our client."

"Did your client commit the robbery?" I asked.

"Bless your soul and body, no," answered Wemmick, very drily. "But he is accused of it. So might you or I be. Either of us might be accused of it, you know."

"Only neither of us is," I remarked.

"Yah!" said Wemmick, touching me on the breast with his forefinger; "you're a deep one, Mr. Pip! Would you like to have a look at Newgate? Have you time to spare?"

I had so much time to spare that the proposal came as a relief, notwithstanding its irreconcilability with my latent desire to keep my eye on the coach-office. Muttering that I would make the inquiry whether I had time to walk with him, I went into the office, and ascertained from the clerk with the nicest precision and much to the trying of his temper, the earliest moment at which the coach could be expected—which I knew beforehand, quite as well as he. I then rejoined Mr. Wemmick, and affecting to consult my watch and to be surprised by the information I had received, accepted his offer.

We were at Newgate in a few minutes, and we passed through the lodge where some fetters were hanging up on the bare walls among the prison rules, into the interior of the jail. At that time, jails were much neglected, and the period of exaggerated reaction consequent on all public wrong-doing—and which is always its heaviest and longest punishment—was still far off. So, felons were not lodged and fed better than soldiers (to say nothing of paupers), and seldom set fire to their prisons with the excusable object of improving the flavour of their soup. It was visiting time when Wemmick took me in; and a potman was going his rounds with beer; and the prisoners, behind bars in yards, were buying beer, and talking to friends; and a frouzy, ugly, disorderly, depressing scene it was.

It struck me that Wemmick walked among the prisoners,

much as a gardener might walk among his plants. This was first put into my head by his seeing a shoot that had come up in the night, and saying, "What, Captain Tom? Are *you* there? Ah, indeed?" and also, "Is that Black Bill behind the cistern? Why I didn't look for you these two months; how do you find yourself?" Equally in his stopping at the bars and attending to anxious whisperers—always singly—Wemmick, with his post-office in an immovable state, looked at them while in conference, as if he were taking particular notice of the advance they had made, since last observed, towards coming out in full blow at their trial.

He was highly popular, and I found that he took the familiar department of Mr. Jaggers's business: though something of the state of Mr. Jaggers hung about him too, forbidding approach beyond certain limits. His personal recognition of each successive client was comprised in a nod, and in his settling his hat a little easier on his head with both hands, and then tightening the post-office, and putting his hands in his pockets. In one or two instances, there was a difficulty respecting the raising of fees, and then Mr. Wemmick, backing as far as possible from the insufficient money produced, said, "It's no use, my boy. I am only a subordinate. I can't take it. Don't go on in that way with a subordinate. If you are unable to make up your quantum, my boy, you had better address yourself to a principal; there are plenty of principals in the profession, you know, and what is not worth the while of one, may be worth the while of another; that's my recommendation to you, speaking as a subordinate. Don't try on useless measures. Why should you? Now who's next?"

Thus, we walked through Wemmick's greenhouse, until he turned to me and said, "Notice the man I shall shake hands with." I should have done so, without the preparation, as he had shaken hands with no one yet.

Almost as soon as he had spoken, a portly upright man (whom I can see now, as I write) in a well-worn olive-coloured frock-coat, with a peculiar pallor overspreading the red in his complexion, and eyes that went wandering about when he tried to fix them, came up to a corner of the bars, and put his hand to his hat—which had a greasy and fatty surface like cold broth—with a half-serious and half-jocose military salute.

"Colonel, to you!" said Wemmick; "how are you, Colonel?"

"All right, Mr. Wemmick."

"Everything was done that could be done, but the evidence was too strong for us, Colonel."

"Yes, it was too strong, sir—but *I* don't care."

"No, no," said Wemmick, coolly, "*you* don't care." Then, turning to me, "Served His Majesty, this man. Was a soldier in the line and bought his discharge."

I said, "Indeed?" and the man's eyes looked at me, and then looked over my head, and then looked all round me, and then he drew his hand across his lips and laughed.

"I think I shall be out of this on Monday, sir," he said to Wemmick.

"Perhaps," returned my friend, "but there's no knowing."

"I am glad to have the chance of bidding you good-bye, Mr. Wemmick," said the man, stretching out his hand between two bars.

"Thankye," said Wemmick, shaking hands with him. "Same to you, Colonel."

"If what I had upon me when taken, had been real, Mr. Wemmick," said the man, unwilling to let his hand go, "I should have asked the favour of your wearing another ring—in acknowledgment of your attentions."

"I'll accept the will for the deed," said Wemmick. "By-the-bye; you were quite a pigeon-fancier." The man looked up at the sky. "I am told you had a remarkable breed of tumblers. *Could* you commission any friend of yours to bring me a pair, if you've no further use for 'em?"

"It shall be done, sir."

"All right," said Wemmick, "they shall be taken care of. Good afternoon, Colonel. Good-bye!" They shook hands again, and as we walked away Wemmick said to me, "A Coiner, a very good workman. The Recorder's report is made to-day, and he is sure to be executed on Monday. Still you see, as far as it goes, a pair of pigeons are portable property, all the same." With that he looked back, and nodded at his dead plant, and then cast his eyes about him in walking out of the yard, as if he were considering what other pot would go best in its place.

As we came out of the prison through the lodge, I found that the great importance of my guardian was appreciated by the turnkeys, no less than by those whom they held in

charge. "Well, Mr. Wemmick," said the turnkey, who kept
us between the two studded and spiked lodge gates, and who
carefully locked one before he unlocked the other, "what's
Mr. Jaggers going to do with that Waterside murder? Is
he going to make it manslaughter, or what is he going to
make of it?"

"Why don't you ask him?" returned Wemmick.

"Oh, yes, I dare say!" said the turnkey.

"Now, that's the way with them here, Mr. Pip," remarked
Wemmick, turning to me with his post-office elongated.
"They don't mind what they ask of me, the subordinate;
but you'll never catch 'em asking any questions of my
principal."

"Is this young gentleman one of the 'prentices or articled
ones of your office?" asked the turnkey, with a grin at
Mr. Wemmick's humour.

"There he goes again, you see!" cried Wemmick, "I told
you so! Asks another question of the subordinate before
the first is dry! Well, supposing Mr. Pip is one of them?"

"Why then," said the turnkey, grinning again, "he knows
what Mr. Jaggers is."

"Yah!" cried Wemmick, suddenly hitting out at the
turnkey in a facetious way, "you're as dumb as one of your
own keys when you have to do with my principal, you know
you are. Let us out, you old fox, or I'll get him to bring
an action against you for false imprisonment."

The turnkey laughed, and gave us good day, and stood
laughing at us over the spikes of the wicket when we
descended the steps into the street.

"Mind you, Mr. Pip," said Wemmick, gravely in my ear,
as he took my arm to be more confidential; "I don't know
that Mr. Jaggers does a better thing than the way in which
he keeps himself so high. He's always so high. His
constant height is of a piece with his immense abilities.
That Colonel durst no more take leave of *him*, than that
turnkey durst ask him his intentions respecting a case.
Then, between his height and them, he slips in his subordinate—don't you see?—and so he has 'em, soul and
body."

I was very much impressed, and not for the first time, by
my guardian's subtlety. To confess the truth, I very heartily
wished, and not for the first time, that I had had some other
guardian of minor abilities.

Mr. Wemmick and I parted at the office in Little Britain, where suppliants for Mr. Jaggers's notice were lingering about as usual, and I returned to my watch in the street of the coach-office, with some three hours on hand. I consumed the whole time in thinking how strange it was that I should be encompassed by all this taint of prison and crime; that, in my childhood out on our lonely marshes on a winter evening I should have first encountered it; that, it should have reappeared on two occasions, starting out like a stain that was faded but not gone; that, it should in this new way pervade my fortune and advancement. While my mind was thus engaged, I thought of the beautiful young Estella, proud and refined, coming towards me, and I thought with absolute abhorrence of the contrast between the jail and her. I wished that Wemmick had not met me, or that I had not yielded to him and gone with him, so that, of all days in the year on this day, I might not have had Newgate in my breath and on my clothes. I beat the prison dust off my feet as I sauntered to and fro, and I shook it out of my dress, and I exhaled its air from my lungs. So contaminated did I feel, remembering who was coming, that the coach came quickly after all, and I was not yet free from the soiling consciousness of Mr. Wemmick's conservatory, when I saw her face at the coach window and her hand waving to me.

What *was* the nameless shadow which again in that one instant had passed?

CHAPTER XXXIII

IN her furred travelling-dress, Estella seemed more delicately beautiful than she had ever seemed yet, even in my eyes. Her manner was more winning than she had cared to let it be to me before, and I thought I saw Miss Havisham's influence in the change.

We stood in the Inn Yard while she pointed out her luggage to me, and when it was all collected I remembered —having forgotten everything but herself in the meanwhile—that I knew nothing of her destination.

"I am going to Richmond," she told me. "Our lesson is, that there are two Richmonds, one in Surrey and one in Yorkshire, and that mine is the Surrey Richmond. The distance is ten miles. I am to have a carriage, and you are to take me. This is my purse, and you are to pay my charges out of it. Oh, you must take the purse! We have no choice, you and I, but to obey our instructions. We are not free to follow our own devices, you and I."

As she looked at me in giving me the purse, I hoped there was an inner meaning in her words. She said them slightingly, but not with displeasure.

"A carriage will have to be sent for, Estella. Will you rest here a little?"

"Yes, I am to rest here a little, and I am to drink some tea, and you are to take care of me the while."

She drew her arm through mine, as if it must be done, and I requested a waiter who had been staring at the coach like a man who had never seen such a thing in his life, to show us a private sitting-room. Upon that, he pulled out a napkin, as if it were a magic clue without which he couldn't find the way up-stairs, and led us to the black hole of the establishment: fitted up with a diminishing mirror (quite a superfluous article considering the hole's proportions), an anchovy sauce-cruet, and somebody's pattens. On my objecting to this retreat, he took us into another room with a dinner-table for thirty, and in the grate a scorched

WE STOOD IN THE INN YARD

leaf of a copy-book under a bushel of coal-dust. Having looked at this extinct conflagration and shaken his head, he took my order: which, proving to be merely "Some tea for the lady," sent him out of the room in a very low state of mind.

I was, and I am, sensible that the air of this chamber, in its strong combination of stable with soup-stock, might have led one to infer that the coaching department was not doing well, and that the enterprising proprietor was boiling down the horses for the refreshment department. Yet the room was all in all to me, Estella being in it. I thought that with her I could have been happy there for life. (I was not at all happy there at the time, observe, and I knew it well.)

"Where are you going to, at Richmond?" I asked Estella.

"I am going to live," said she, "at a great expense, with a lady there, who has the power—or says she has—of taking me about, and introducing me, and showing people to me and showing me to people."

"I suppose you will be glad of variety and admiration?"

"Yes, I suppose so."

She answered so carelessly, that I said, "You speak of yourself as if you were some one else."

"Where did you learn how I speak of others? Come, come," said Estella, smiling delightfully, "you must not expect me to go to school to *you*; I must talk in my own way. How do you thrive with Mr. Pocket?"

"I live quite pleasantly there; at least——" It appeared to me that I was losing a chance.

"At least?" repeated Estella.

"As pleasantly as I could anywhere, away from you."

"You silly boy," said Estella, quite composedly, "how can you talk such nonsense? Your friend Mr. Matthew, I believe, is superior to the rest of his family?"

"Very superior indeed. He is nobody's enemy——"

"—Don't add but his own," interposed Estella, "for I hate that class of man. But he really is disinterested, and above small jealousy and spite, I have heard?"

"I am sure I have every reason to say so."

"You have not every reason to say so of the rest of his people," said Estella, nodding at me with an expression of face that was at once grave and rallying, "for they beset

Miss Havisham with reports and insinuations to your disadvantage. They watch you, misrepresent you, write letters about you (anonymous sometimes), and you are the torment and occupation of their lives. You can scarcely realise to yourself the hatred those people feel for you."

"They do me no harm, I hope?"

Instead of answering, Estella burst out laughing. This was very singular to me, and I looked at her in considerable perplexity. When she left off—and she had not laughed languidly, but with real enjoyment—I said, in my diffident way with her:

"I hope I may suppose that you would not be amused if they did me any harm?"

"No, no, you may be sure of that," said Estella. "You may be certain that I laugh because they fail. Oh, those people with Miss Havisham, and the tortures they undergo!" She laughed again, and even now, when she had told me why, her laughter was very singular to me, for I could not doubt its being genuine, and yet it seemed too much for the occasion. I thought there must really be something more here than I knew; she saw the thought in my mind and answered it.

"It is not easy for even you," said Estella, "to know what satisfaction it gives me to see those people thwarted, or what an enjoyable sense of the ridiculous I have when they are made ridiculous. For you were not brought up in that strange house from a mere baby.—I was. You had not your little wits sharpened by their intriguing against you, suppressed and defenceless, under the mask of sympathy and pity and what not, that is soft and soothing.—I had. You did not gradually open your round childish eyes wider and wider to the discovery of that impostor of a woman who calculates her stores of peace of mind for when she wakes up in the night.—I did."

It was no laughing matter with Estella now, nor was she summoning these remembrances from any shallow place. I would not have been the cause of that look of hers, for all my expectations in a heap.

"Two things I can tell you," said Estella. "First, notwithstanding the proverb, that constant dropping will wear away a stone, you may set your mind at rest that these people never will—never would in a hundred years—impair your ground with Miss Havisham, in any particular, great or small. Second, I am beholden to you as the cause of their being so busy and so mean in vain, and there is my hand upon it."

As she gave it me playfully—for her darker mood had been but momentary—I held it and put it to my lips. "You ridiculous boy," said Estella, "will you never take warning? Or do you kiss my hand in the same spirit in which I once let you kiss my cheek?"

"What spirit was that?" said I.

"I must think a moment. A spirit of contempt for the fawners and plotters."

"If I say yes, may I kiss the cheek again?"

"You should have asked before you touched the hand. But, yes, if you like."

I leaned down, and her calm face was like a statue's. "Now," said Estella, gliding away the instant I touched her cheek, "you are to take care that I have some tea, and you are to take me to Richmond."

Her reverting to this tone, as if our association were forced upon us and we were mere puppets, gave me pain; but everything in our intercourse did give me pain. Whatever her tone with me happened to be, I could put no trust in it, and build no hope on it; and yet I went on against trust and against hope. Why repeat it a thousand times? So it always was.

I rang for the tea, and the waiter, reappearing with his magic clue, brought in by degrees some fifty adjuncts to that refreshment, but of tea not a glimpse. A teaboard, cups and saucers, plates, knives and forks (including carvers), spoons (various), salt-cellars, a meek little muffin confined with the utmost precaution under a strong iron cover, Moses in the bulrushes typified by a soft bit of butter in a quantity of parsley, a pale loaf with a powdered head, two proof impressions of the bars of the kitchen fireplace on triangular bits of bread, and ultimately a fat family urn: which the waiter staggered in with, expressing in his countenance burden and suffering. After a prolonged absence at this stage of the entertainment, he at length came back with a casket of precious appearance containing twigs. These I steeped in hot water, and so from the whole of these appliances extracted one cup of I don't know what, for Estella.

The bill paid, and the waiter remembered, and the ostler

not forgotten, and the chambermaid taken into consideration
—in a word, the whole house bribed into a state of contempt
and animosity, and Estella's purse much lightened—we got
into our post-coach and drove away. Turning into Cheapside
and rattling up Newgate-street, we were soon under the
walls of which I was so ashamed.

"What place is that?" Estella asked me.

I made a foolish pretence of not at first recognising it, and
then told her. As she looked at it, and drew in her head
again, murmuring "Wretches!" I would not have confessed
to my visit for any consideration.

"Mr. Jaggers," said I, by way of putting it neatly on
somebody else, "has the reputation of being more in the
secrets of that dismal place than any man in London."

"He is more in the secrets of every place, I think," said
Estella, in a low voice.

"You have been accustomed to see him often, I suppose?"

"I have been accustomed to see him at uncertain intervals,
ever since I can remember. But I know him no better now,
than I did before I could speak plainly. What is your own
experience of him? Do you advance with him?"

"Once habituated to his distrustful manner," said I, "I
have done very well."

"Are you intimate?"

"I have dined with him at his private house."

"I fancy," said Estella, shrinking, "that must be a curious
place."

"It is a curious place."

I should have been chary of discussing my guardian too
freely even with her; but I should have gone on with the
subject so far as to describe the dinner in Gerrard-street, if
we had not then come into a sudden glare of gas. It
seemed, while it lasted, to be all alight and alive with that
inexplicable feeling I had had before; and when we were
out of it, I was as much dazed for a few moments as if
I had been in Lightning.

So, we fell into other talk, and it was principally about
the way by which we were travelling, and about what parts
of London lay on this side of it, and what on that. The
great city was almost new to her, she told me, for she had
never left Miss Havisham's neighbourhood until she had
gone to France, and she had merely passed through London
then in going and returning. I asked her if my guardian

had any charge of her while she remained here? To that she emphatically said, "God forbid!" and no more.

It was impossible for me to avoid seeing that she cared to attract me; that she made herself winning; and would have won me even if the task had needed pains. Yet this made me none the happier, for, even if she had not taken that tone of our being disposed of by others, I should have felt that she held my heart in her hand because she wilfully chose to do it, and not because it would have wrung any tenderness in her, to crush it and throw it away.

When we passed through Hammersmith, I showed her where Mr. Matthew Pocket lived, and said it was no great way from Richmond, and that I hoped I should see her sometimes.

"Oh yes, you are to see me; you are to come when you think proper; you are to be mentioned to the family; indeed you are already mentioned."

I inquired was it a large household she was going to be a member of?

"No; there are only two; mother and daughter. The mother is a lady of some station, though not averse to increasing her income."

"I wonder Miss Havisham could part with you again so soon."

"It is a part of Miss Havisham's plans for me, Pip," said Estella, with a sigh, as if she were tired; "I am to write to her constantly and see her regularly, and report how I go on—I and the jewels—for they are nearly all mine now."

It was the first time she had ever called me by my name. Of course she did so purposely, and knew that I should treasure it up.

We came to Richmond all too soon, and our destination there was a house by the Green: a staid old house, where hoops and powder and patches, embroidered coats, rolled stockings, ruffles, and swords, had had their court days many a time. Some ancient trees before the house were still cut into fashions as formal and unnatural as the hoops and wigs and stiff skirts; but their own allotted places in the great procession of the dead were not far off, and they would soon drop into them and go the silent way of the rest.

A bell with an old voice—which I dare say in its time had often said to the house, Here is the green farthingale, Here is the diamond-hilted sword, Here are the shoes with red

heels and the blue solitaire,—sounded gravely in the moonlight, and two cherry-coloured maids came fluttering out to
receive Estella. The doorway soon absorbed her boxes, and
she gave me her hand and a smile, and said good night, and
was absorbed likewise. And still I stood looking at the
house, thinking how happy I should be if I lived there with
her, and knowing that I never was happy with her, but
always miserable.

I got into the carriage to be taken back to Hammersmith,
and I got in with a bad heart-ache, and I got out with
a worse heart-ache. At our own door I found little Jane
Pocket coming home from a little party, escorted by her
little lover; and I envied her little lover, in spite of his
being subject to Flopson.

Mr. Pocket was out lecturing; for he was a most delightful
lecturer on domestic economy, and his treatises on the
management of children and servants were considered the
very best text-books on those themes. But Mrs. Pocket was
at home, and was in a little difficulty, on account of the
baby's having been accommodated with a needle-case to keep
him quiet during the unaccountable absence (with a relative
in the Foot Guards) of Millers. And more needles were
missing than it could be regarded as quite wholesome for
a patient of such tender years either to apply externally or to
take as a tonic.

Mr. Pocket being justly celebrated for giving most excellent
practical advice, and for having a clear and sound perception
of things and a highly judicious mind, I had some notion in
my heart-ache of begging him to accept my confidence. But
happening to look up at Mrs. Pocket as she sat reading her
book of dignities after prescribing Bed as a sovereign remedy
for baby, I thought—Well—No, I wouldn't.

CHAPTER XXXIV

As I had grown accustomed to my expectations, I had insensibly begun to notice their effect upon myself and those around me. Their influence on my own character I disguised from my recognition as much as possible, but I knew very well that it was not all good. I lived in a state of chronic uneasiness respecting my behaviour to Joe. My conscience was not by any means comfortable about Biddy. When I woke up in the night—like Camilla—I used to think, with a weariness on my spirits, that I should have been happier and better if I had never seen Miss Havisham's face, and had risen to manhood content to be partners with Joe in the honest old forge. Many a time of an evening, when I sat alone looking at the fire, I thought, after all, there was no fire like the forge fire and the kitchen fire at home.

Yet Estella was so inseparable from all my restlessness and disquiet of mind, that I really fell into confusion as to the limits of my own part in its production. That is to say, supposing I had had no expectations, and yet had had Estella to think of, I could not make out to my satisfaction that I should have done much better. Now, concerning the influence of my position on others, I was in no such difficulty, and so I perceived—though dimly enough perhaps—that it was not beneficial to anybody, and, above all, that it was not beneficial to Herbert. My lavish habits led his easy nature into expenses that he could not afford, corrupted the simplicity of his life, and disturbed his peace with anxieties and regrets. I was not at all remorseful for having unwittingly set those other branches of the Pocket family to the poor arts they practised : because such littlenesses were their natural bent, and would have been evoked by anybody else, if I had left them slumbering. But Herbert's was a very different case, and it often caused me a twinge to think that I had done him evil service in crowding his sparely-furnished chambers with incongruous upholstery work, and placing the canary-breasted Avenger at his disposal.

So now, as an infallible way of making little ease great
ease, I began to contract a quantity of debt.   I could hardly
begin but Herbert must begin too, so he soon followed.   At
Startop's suggestion, we put ourselves down for election into
a club called the Finches of the Grove : the object of which
institution I have never divined, if it were not that the
members should dine expensively once a fortnight, to quarrel
among themselves as much as possible after dinner, and to
cause six waiters to get drunk on the stairs.   I know that
these gratifying social ends were so invariably accomplished,
that Herbert and I understood nothing else to be referred to
in the first standing toast of the society : which ran, " Gentlemen, may the present promotion of good feeling ever reign
predominant among the Finches of the Grove."

The Finches spent their money foolishly (the Hotel we
dined at was in Covent Garden), and the first Finch I saw
when I had the honour of joining the Grove was Bentley
Drummle : at that time floundering about town in a cab of
his own, and doing a great deal of damage to the posts at
the street corners.   Occasionally, he shot himself out of his
equipage head-foremost over the apron ; and I saw him on
one occasion deliver himself at the door of the Grove in this
unintentional way—like coals.   But here I anticipate a little,
for I was not a Finch, and could not be, according to the
sacred laws of the society, until I came of age.

In my confidence in my own resources, I would willingly
have taken Herbert's expenses on myself ; but Herbert was
proud, and I could make no such proposal to him.   So, he
got into difficulties in every direction, and continued to look
about him.   When we gradually fell into keeping late hours
and late company, I noticed that he looked about him with
a desponding eye at breakfast-time ; that he began to look
about him more hopefully about mid-day ; that he drooped
when he came into dinner ; that he seemed to descry Capital
in the distance, rather clearly, after dinner ; that he all but
realised Capital towards midnight ; and that about two
o'clock in the morning, he became so deeply despondent
again as to talk of buying a rifle and going to America,
with a general purpose of compelling buffaloes to make his
fortune.

I was usually at Hammersmith about half the week, and
when I was at Hammersmith I haunted Richmond : whereof
separately by-and-by.   Herbert would often come to Hammer-

smith when I was there, and I think at those seasons his father would occasionally have some passing perception that the opening he was looking for had not appeared yet. But in the general tumbling up of the family, his tumbling out in life somewhere was a thing to transact itself somehow. In the meantime Mr. Pocket grew greyer, and tried oftener to lift himself out of his perplexities by the hair. While Mrs. Pocket tripped up the family with her footstool, read her book of dignities, lost her pocket-handkerchief, told us about her grandpapa, and taught the young idea how to shoot, by shooting it into bed whenever it attracted her notice.

As I am now generalising a period of my life with the object of clearing my way before me, I can scarcely do so better than by at once completing the description of our usual manners and customs at Barnard's Inn.

We spent as much money as we could, and got as little for it as people could make up their minds to give us. We were always more or less miserable, and most of our acquaintance were in the same condition. There was a gay fiction among us that we were constantly enjoying ourselves, and a skeleton truth that we never did. To the best of my belief, our case was in the last aspect a rather common one.

Every morning, with an air ever new, Herbert went into the City to look about him. I often paid him a visit in the dark back-room in which he consorted with an ink-jar, a hat-peg, a coal-box, a string-box, an almanack, a desk and stool, and a ruler; and I do not remember that I ever saw him do anything else but look about him. If we all did what we undertake to do, as faithfully as Herbert did, we might live in a Republic of the Virtues. He had nothing else to do, poor fellow, except at a certain hour of every afternoon to "go to Lloyd's"—in observance of a ceremony of seeing his principal, I think. He never did anything else in connexion with Lloyd's that I could find out, except come back again. When he felt his case unusually serious, and that he positively must find an opening, he would go on 'Change at a busy time, and walk in and out, in a kind of gloomy country dance figure, among the assembled magnates. "For," says Herbert to me, coming home to dinner on one of those special occasions, "I find the truth to be, Handel, that an opening won't come to one, but one must go to it——so I have been."

If we had been less attached to one another, I think we must have hated one another regularly every morning. I detested the chambers beyond expression at that period of repentance, and could not endure the sight of the Avenger's livery: which had a more expensive and a less remunerative appearance then, than at any other time in the four-and-twenty hours. As we got more and more into debt, breakfast became a hollower and hollower form, and being on one occasion at breakfast-time threatened (by letter) with legal proceedings, "not unwholly unconnected," as my local paper might put it, "with jewellery," I went so far as to seize the Avenger by his blue collar and shake him off his feet—so that he was actually in the air, like a booted Cupid—for presuming to suppose that we wanted a roll.

At certain times—meaning at uncertain times, for they depended on our humour—I would say to Herbert, as if it were a remarkable discovery:

"My dear Herbert, we are getting on badly."

"My dear Handel," Herbert would say to me, in all sincerity, "if you will believe me, those very words were on my lips, by a strange coincidence."

"Then, Herbert," I would respond, "let us look into our affairs."

We always derived profound satisfaction from making an appointment for this purpose. I always thought this was business, this was the way to confront the thing, this was the way to take the foe by the throat. And I know Herbert thought so too.

We ordered something rather special for dinner, with a bottle of something similarly out of the common way, in order that our minds might be fortified for the occasion, and we might come well up to the mark. Dinner over, we produced a bundle of pens, a copious supply of ink, and a goodly show of writing and blotting paper. For there was something very comfortable in having plenty of stationery.

I would then take a sheet of paper, and write across the top of it, in a neat hand, the heading, "Memorandum of Pip's debts;" with Barnard's Inn and the date very carefully added. Herbert would also take a sheet of paper, and write across it with similar formalities, "Memorandum of Herbert's debts."

Each of us would then refer to a confused heap of papers

at his side, which had been thrown into drawers, worn into holes in pockets, half-burnt in lighting candles, stuck for weeks into the looking-glass, and otherwise damaged. The sound of our pens going refreshed us exceedingly, insomuch that I sometimes found it difficult to distinguish between this edifying business proceeding and actually paying the money. In point of meritorious character, the two things seemed about equal.

When we had written a little while, I would ask Herbert how he got on? Herbert probably would have been scratching his head in a most rueful manner at the sight of his accumulating figures.

"They are mounting up, Handel," Herbert would say; "upon my life they are mounting up."

"Be firm, Herbert," I would retort, plying my own pen with great assiduity. "Look the thing in the face. Look into your affairs. Stare them out of countenance."

"So I would, Handel, only they are staring *me* out of countenance."

However, my determined manner would have its effect, and Herbert would fall to work again. After a time he would give up once more, on the plea that he had not got Cobbs's bill, or Lobbs's, or Nobbs's, as the case might be.

"Then, Herbert, estimate; estimate it in round numbers, and put it down."

"What a fellow of resource you are!" my friend would reply, with admiration. "Really your business powers are very remarkable."

I thought so too. I established with myself, on these occasions, the reputation of a first-rate man of business— prompt, decisive, energetic, clear, cool-headed. When I had got all my responsibilities down upon my list, I compared each with the bill, and ticked it off. My self-approval when I ticked an entry was quite a luxurious sensation. When I had no more ticks to make, I folded all my bills up uniformly, docketed each on the back, and tied the whole into a symmetrical bundle. Then I did the same for Herbert (who modestly said he had not my administrative genius), and felt that I had brought his affairs into a focus for him.

My business habits had one other bright feature, which I called "leaving a Margin." For example: supposing Herbert's debts to be one hundred and sixty-four pounds

four-and-twopence, I would say, "Leave a margin, and put
them down at two hundred." Or, supposing my own to be
four times as much, I would leave a margin, and put them
down at seven hundred. I had the highest opinion of the
wisdom of this same Margin, but I am bound to acknowledge
that, on looking back, I deem it to have been an expensive
device. For we always ran into new debt immediately, to
the full extent of the margin, and sometimes, in the sense
of freedom and solvency it imparted, got pretty far on into
another margin.

But there was a calm, a rest, a virtuous hush, consequent
on these examinations of our affairs, that gave me, for the
time, an admirable opinion of myself. Soothed by my exertions, my method, and Herbert's compliments, I would sit
with his symmetrical bundle and my own on the table before
me among the stationery, and feel like a Bank of some sort,
rather than a private individual.

We shut our outer door on these solemn occasions in
order that we might not be interrupted. I had fallen into
my serene state one evening, when we heard a letter dropped
through the slit in the said door, and fall on the ground.
"It's for you, Handel," said Herbert, going out and coming
back with it, "and I hope there is nothing the matter."
This was in allusion to its heavy black seal and border.

The letter was signed Trabb & Co., and its contents were
simply, that I was an honoured sir, and that they begged to
inform me that Mrs. J. Gargery had departed this life on
Monday last at twenty minutes past six in the evening, and
that my attendance was requested at the interment on
Monday next at three o'clock in the afternoon.

CHAPTER XXXV

IT was the first time that a grave had opened in my road of life, and the gap it made in the smooth ground was wonderful. The figure of my sister in her chair by the kitchen fire haunted me night and day. That the place could possibly be, without her, was something my mind seemed unable to compass ; and whereas she had seldom or never been in my thoughts of late, I had now the strangest idea that she was coming towards me in the street, or that she would presently knock at the door. In my rooms too, with which she had never been at all associated, there was at once the blankness of death and a perpetual suggestion of the sound of her voice or the turn of her face or figure, as if she were still alive and had been often there.

Whatever my fortunes might have been, I could scarcely have recalled my sister with much tenderness. But I suppose there is a shock of regret which may exist without much tenderness. Under its influence (and perhaps to make up for the want of the softer feeling) I was seized with a violent indignation against the assailant from whom she had suffered so much ; and I felt that on sufficient proof I could have revengefully pursued Orlick, or any one else, to the last extremity.

Having written to Joe, to offer him consolation, and to assure him that I would come to the funeral, I passed the intermediate days in the curious state of mind I have glanced at. I went down early in the morning, and alighted at the Blue Boar, in good time to walk over to the forge.

It was fine summer weather again, and, as I walked along, the times when I was a little helpless creature, and my sister did not spare me, vividly returned. But they returned with a gentle tone upon them, that softened even the edge of Tickler. For now, the very breath of the beans and clover whispered to my heart that the day must come when it would be well for my memory that others walking in the sunshine should be softened as they thought of me.

At last I came within sight of the house, and saw that

Trabb and Co. had put in a funereal execution and taken possession. Two dismally absurd persons, each ostentatiously exhibiting a crutch done up in a black bandage—as if that instrument could possibly communicate any comfort to anybody—were posted at the front door; and in one of them I recognised a postboy discharged from the Boar for turning a young couple into a sawpit on their bridal morning, in consequence of intoxication rendering it necessary for him to ride his horse clasped round the neck with both arms. All the children of the village, and most of the women, were admiring these sable warders and the closed windows of the house and forge; and as I came up, one of the two warders (the postboy) knocked at the door—implying that I was far too much exhausted by grief, to have strength remaining to knock for myself.

Another sable warder (a carpenter, who had once eaten two geese for a wager) opened the door, and showed me into the best parlour. Here, Mr. Trabb had taken unto himself the best table, and had got all the leaves up, and was holding a kind of black Bazaar, with the aid of a quantity of black pins. At the moment of my arrival, he had just finished putting somebody's hat into black long-clothes, like an African baby; so he held out his hand for mine. But I, misled by the action, and confused by the occasion, shook hands with him with every testimony of warm affection.

Poor dear Joe, entangled in a little black cloak tied in a large bow under his chin, was seated apart at the upper end of the room; where, as chief mourner, he had evidently been stationed by Trabb. When I bent down and said to him, "Dear Joe, how are you?" he said, "Pip, old chap, you know'd her when she were a fine figure of a——" and clasped my hand and said no more.

Biddy, looking very neat and modest in her black dress, went quietly here and there, and was very helpful. When I had spoken to Biddy, as I thought it not a time for talking, I went and sat down near Joe, and there began to wonder in what part of the house it—she—my sister—was. The air of the parlour being faint with the smell of sweet cake, I looked about for the table of refreshments; it was scarcely visible until one had got accustomed to the gloom, but there was a cut-up plum-cake upon it, and there were cut-up oranges, and sandwiches, and biscuits, and two decanters that I knew very well as ornaments, but had never seen used in all my life: one full of port, and one of sherry. Standing at this table, I became conscious of the servile Pumblechook in a black cloak and several yards of hatband, who was alternately stuffing himself, and making obsequious movements to catch my attention. The moment he succeeded, he came over to me (breathing sherry and crumbs), and said in a subdued voice, "May I, dear sir?" and did. I then descried Mr. and Mrs. Hubble; the last-named in a decent speechless paroxysm in a corner. We were all going to "follow," and were all in course of being tied up separately (by Trabb) into ridiculous bundles.

"Which I meantersay, Pip," Joe whispered me, as we were being what Mr. Trabb called "formed" in the parlour, two and two—and it was dreadfully like a preparation for some grim kind of dance; "which I meantersay, sir, as I would in preference have carried her to the church myself, along with three or four friendly ones wot come to it with willing harts and arms, but it were considered wot the neighbours would look down on such and would be of opinions as it were wanting in respect."

"Pocket-handkerchiefs out, all!" cried Mr. Trabb at this point, in a depressed business-like voice—"Pocket-handkerchiefs out! We are ready!"

So, we all put our pocket-handkerchiefs to our faces, as if our noses were bleeding, and filed out two and two; Joe and I; Biddy and Pumblechook; Mr. and Mrs. Hubble. The remains of my poor sister had been brought round by the kitchen door, and, it being a point of Undertaking ceremony that the six bearers must be stifled and blinded under a horrible black velvet housing with a white border, the whole looked like a blind monster with twelve human legs, shuffling and blundering along under the guidance of two keepers—the postboy and his comrade.

The neighbourhood, however, highly approved of these arrangements, and we were much admired as we went through the village; the more youthful and vigorous part of the community making dashes now and then to cut us off, and lying in wait to intercept us at points of vantage. At such times the more exuberant among them called out in an excited manner on our emergence round some corner of expectancy, "*Here* they come!" "*Here* they are!" and we were all but cheered. In this progress I was much annoyed by the abject Pumblechook, who, being behind me, persisted all the way, as a delicate attention, in arranging my streaming hatband, and smoothing my cloak. My thoughts were further distracted by the excessive pride of Mr. and Mrs. Hubble, who were surpassingly conceited and vainglorious in being members of so distinguished a procession.

And now the range of marshes lay clear before us, with the sails of the ships on the river growing out of it; and we went into the churchyard, close to the graves of my unknown parents, Philip Pirrip, late of this parish, and Also Georgiana, Wife of the Above. And there, my sister was laid quietly in the earth while the larks sang high above it, and the light wind strewed it with beautiful shadows of clouds and trees.

Of the conduct of the worldly-minded Pumblechook while this was doing, I desire to say no more than it was all addressed to me; and that even when those noble passages were read which reminded humanity how it brought nothing into the world and can take nothing out, and how it fleeth like a shadow and never continueth long in one stay, I heard him cough a reservation of the case of a young gentleman who came unexpectedly into a large property. When we got back, he had the hardihood to tell me that he wished my sister could have known I had done her so much honour, and to hint that she would have considered it reasonably purchased at the price of her death. After that, he drank all the rest of the sherry, and Mr. Hubble drank the port, and the two talked (which I have since observed to be customary in such cases) as if they were of quite another race from the deceased, and were notoriously immortal. Finally, he went away with Mr. and Mrs. Hubble—to make an evening of it, I felt sure, and to tell the Jolly Bargemen that he was the founder of my fortunes and my earliest benefactor.

When they were all gone, and when Trabb and his men —but not his boy: I looked for him—had crammed their mummery into bags, and were gone too, the house felt wholesomer. Soon afterwards, Biddy, Joe, and I, had a cold dinner together; but we dined in the best parlour, not in the old kitchen, and Joe was so exceedingly particular what he did with his knife and fork and the salt-cellar and what not, that there was great restraint upon us. But after dinner, when I made him take his pipe, and when I had loitered with him about the forge, and when we sat down together on the great block of stone outside it, we got on better. I noticed that after the funeral Joe changed his clothes so far, as to make a compromise between his Sunday dress and working dress: in which the dear fellow looked natural, and like the Man he was.

He was very much pleased by my asking if I might sleep in my own little room, and I was pleased too; for I felt that I had done rather a great thing in making the request. When the shadows of evening were closing in, I took an opportunity of getting into the garden with Biddy for a little talk.

"Biddy," said I, "I think you might have written to me about these sad matters."

"Do you, Mr. Pip?" said Biddy. "I should have written if I had thought that."

"Don't suppose that I mean to be unkind, Biddy, when I say I consider that you ought to have thought that."

"Do you, Mr. Pip?"

She was so quiet, and had such an orderly, good, and pretty way with her, that I did not like the thought of making her cry again. After looking a little at her downcast eyes as she walked beside me, I gave up that point.

"I suppose it will be difficult for you to remain here now, Biddy, dear?"

"Oh! I can't do so, Mr. Pip," said Biddy, in a tone of regret, but still of quiet conviction. "I have been speaking to Mrs. Hubble, and I am going to her to-morrow. I hope we shall be able to take some care of Mr. Gargery, together, until he settles down."

"How are you going to live, Biddy? If you want any mo——"

"How am I going to live?" repeated Biddy, striking in, with a momentary flush upon her face. "I'll tell you, Mr. Pip. I am going to try to get the place of mistress in the new school nearly finished here. I can be well recommended by all the neighbours, and I hope I can be industrious and patient, and teach myself while I teach others. You know, Mr. Pip," pursued Biddy, with a smile, as she raised her eyes to my face, "the new schools are not like the old, but I learnt a good deal from you after that time, and have had time since then to improve."

"I think you would always improve, Biddy, under any circumstances."

"Ah! Except in my bad side of human nature." murmured Biddy.

It was not so much a reproach, as an irresistible thinking aloud. Well! I thought I would give up that point too. So, I walked a little further with Biddy, looking silently at her downcast eyes.

"I have not heard the particulars of my sister's death. Biddy."

"They are very slight, poor thing. She had been in one of her bad states—though they had got better of late, rather than worse—for four days, when she came out of it in the evening, just at tea-time, and said quite plainly, 'Joe.' As she had never said any word for a long while, I ran and fetched in Mr. Gargery from the forge. She made signs to me that she wanted him to sit down close to her, and wanted me to put her arms round his neck. So I put them round his neck, and she laid her head down on his shoulder quite content and satisfied. And so she presently said 'Joe' again, and once 'Pardon,' and once 'Pip.' And so she never lifted her head up any more, and it was just an hour later when we laid it down on her own bed, because we found she was gone."

Biddy cried; the darkening garden, and the lane, and the stars that were coming out, were blurred in my own sight.

"Nothing was ever discovered, Biddy?"

"Nothing."

"Do you know what is become of Orlick?"

'I should think from the colour of his clothes that he is working in the quarries."

"Of course you have seen him then?—Why are you looking at that dark tree in the lane?"

"I saw him there, on the night she died."

"That was not the last time either, Biddy?"

"No; I have seen him there since we have been walking here.—It is of no use," said Biddy, laying her hand upon my arm, as I was for running out, "you know I would not deceive you; he was not there a minute, and he is gone."

It revived my utmost indignation to find that she was still pursued by this fellow, and I felt inveterate against him. I told her so, and told her that I would spend any money or take any pains to drive him out of that country. By degrees she led me into more temperate talk, and she told me how Joe loved me, and how Joe never complained of anything—she didn't say, of me; she had no need; I knew what she meant—but ever did his duty in his way of life, with a strong hand, a quiet tongue, and a gentle heart.

"Indeed, it would be hard to say too much for him," said I; "and, Biddy, we must often speak of these things, for of course I shall be often down here now. I am not going to leave poor Joe alone."

Biddy said never a single word.

"Biddy, don't you hear me?"

"Yes, Mr. Pip."

"Not to mention your calling me Mr. Pip—which appears to me to be in bad taste, Biddy—what do you mean?"

"What do I mean?" asked Biddy, timidly.

"Biddy," said I, in a virtuously self-asserting manner, "I must request to know what you mean by this?"

"By this?" said Biddy.

"No, don't echo," I retorted. "You used not to echo, Biddy."

"Used not!" said Biddy. "O Mr. Pip! Used!"

Well! I rather thought I would give up that point too. After another silent turn in the garden, I fell back on the main position.

"Biddy," said I, "I made a remark respecting my coming down here often, to see Joe, which you received with a marked silence. Have the goodness, Biddy, to tell me why."

"Are you quite sure, then, that you WILL come to see him often?" asked Biddy, stopping in the narrow garden walk, and looking at me under the stars, with a clear and honest eye.

"Oh dear me!" said I, as I found myself compelled to give up Biddy in despair. "This really is a very bad side of human nature! Don't say any more, if you please, Biddy. This shocks me very much."

For which cogent reason I kept Biddy at a distance during supper, and when I went up to my own old little room, took as stately a leave of her as I could, in my murmuring soul, deem reconcilable with the churchyard and the event of the day. As often as I was restless in the night, and that was every quarter of an hour, I reflected what an unkindness, what an injury, what an injustice, Biddy had done me.

Early in the morning, I was to go. Early in the morning,

I was out, and looking in, unseen, at one of the wooden windows of the forge. There I stood, for minutes, looking at Joe, already at work with a glow of health and strength upon his face that made it show as if the bright sun of the life in store for him were shining on it.

"Good-bye, dear Joe!—No, don't wipe it off—for God's sake, give me your blackened hand!—I shall be down soon and often."

"Never too soon, sir," said Joe, "and never too often, Pip!"

Biddy was waiting for me at the kitchen door, with a mug of new milk and a crust of bread. "Biddy," said I, when I gave her my hand at parting, "I am not angry, but I am hurt."

"No, don't be hurt," she pleaded quite pathetically; "let only me be hurt, if I have been ungenerous."

Once more, the mists were rising as I walked away. If they disclosed to me as I suspect they did, that I should *not* come back, and that Biddy was quite right, all I can say is —they were quite right too.

CHAPTER XXXVI

HERBERT and I went on from bad to worse, in the way of increasing our debts, looking into our affairs, leaving Margins, and the like exemplary transactions; and Time went on, whether or no, as he has a way of doing; and I came of age—in fulfilment of Herbert's prediction, that I should do so before I knew where I was.

Herbert himself had come of age, eight months before me. As he had nothing else than his majority to come into, the event did not make a profound sensation in Barnard's Inn. But we had looked forward to my one-and-twentieth birthday, with a crowd of speculations and anticipations, for we had both considered that my guardian could hardly help saying something definite on that occasion.

I had taken care to have it well understood in Little Britain when my birthday was. On the day before it, I received an official note from Wemmick, informing me that Mr. Jaggers would be glad if I would call upon him at five in the afternoon of the auspicious day. This convinced us that something great was to happen, and threw me into an unusual flutter when I repaired to my guardian's office, a model of punctuality.

In the outer office Wemmick offered me his congratulations, and incidentally rubbed the side of his nose with a folded piece of tissue-paper that I liked the look of. But he said nothing respecting it, and motioned me with a nod into my guardian's room. It was November, and my guardian was standing before his fire leaning his back against the chimney-piece, with his hands under his coat-tails.

"Well, Pip," said he, "I must call you Mr. Pip to-day. Congratulations, Mr. Pip."

We shook hands—he was always a remarkably short shaker—and I thanked him.

"Take a chair, Mr. Pip," said my guardian.

As I sat down, and he preserved his attitude and bent his brows at his boots, I felt at a disadvantage, which reminded me of that old time when I had been put upon a tombstone. The two ghastly casts on the shelf were not far from him, and their expression was as if they were making a stupid apoplectic attempt to attend to the conversation.

"Now, my young friend," my guardian began, as if I were a witness in the box, "I am going to have a word or two with you."

"If you please, sir."

"What do you suppose," said Mr. Jaggers, bending forward to look at the ground, and then throwing his head back to look at the ceiling, "what do you suppose you are living at the rate of?"

"At the rate of, sir?"

"At," repeated Mr. Jaggers, still looking at the ceiling, "the—rate—of?" And then looked all round the room, and paused with his pocket-handkerchief in his hand, half-way to his nose.

I had looked into my affairs so often, that I had thoroughly destroyed any slight notion I might ever have had of their bearings. Reluctantly, I confessed myself quite unable to answer the question. This reply seemed agreeable to Mr. Jaggers, who said, "I thought so!" and blew his nose with an air of satisfaction.

"Now, I have asked *you* a question, my friend," said Mr. Jaggers. "Have you anything to ask *me*?"

"Of course it would be a great relief to me to ask you several questions, sir; but I remember your prohibition."

"Ask one," said Mr. Jaggers.

"Is my benefactor to be made known to me to-day?"

"No. Ask another."

"Is that confidence to be imparted to me soon?"

"Waive that, a moment," said Mr. Jaggers, "and ask another."

I looked about me, but there appeared to be now no possible escape from the inquiry, "Have—I—anything to receive, sir?" On that, Mr. Jaggers said, triumphantly, "I thought we should come to it!" and called to Wemmick to give him that piece of paper. Wemmick appeared, handed it in, and disappeared.

"Now, Mr. Pip," said Mr. Jaggers, "attend if you please. You have been drawing pretty freely here; your name occurs

"NOW, MY YOUNG FRIEND," MY GUARDIAN BEGAN

pretty often in Wemmick's cash-book : but you are in debt, of course ? "

" I am afraid I must say yes, sir."

" You know you must say yes; don't you ? " said Mr. Jaggers.

" Yes, sir."

" I don't ask you what you owe, because you don't know ; and if you did know, you wouldn't tell me ; you would say less. Yes, yes, my friend," cried Mr. Jaggers, waving his forefinger to stop me, as I made a show of protesting : " it's likely enough that you think you wouldn't, but you would. You'll excuse me, but I know better than you. Now, take this piece of paper in your hand. You have got it ? Very good. Now, unfold it and tell me what it is."

" This is a bank-note," said I, " for five hundred pounds."

" That is a bank-note," repeated Mr. Jaggers, " for five hundred pounds. And a very handsome sum of money too, I think. You consider it so ? "

" How could I do otherwise ! "

" Ah ! But answer the question," said Mr. Jaggers.

" Undoubtedly."

" You consider it, undoubtedly, a handsome sum of money. Now, that handsome sum of money, Pip, is your own. It is a present to you on this day, in earnest of your expectations. And at the rate of that handsome sum of money per annum, and at no higher rate, you are to live until the donor of the whole appears. That is to say, you will now take your money affairs entirely into your own hands, and you will draw from Wemmick one hundred and twenty-five pounds per quarter, until you are in communication with the fountain-head, and no longer with the mere agent. As I have told you before, I am the mere agent. I execute my instructions, and I am paid for doing so. I think them injudicious, but I am not paid for giving any opinion on their merits."

I was beginning to express my gratitude to my benefactor for the great liberality with which I was treated, when Mr. Jaggers stopped me. " I am not paid, Pip," said he, coolly, " to carry your words to any one ; " and then gathered up his coat-tails, as he had gathered up the subject, and stood frowning at his boots as if he suspected them of designs against him.

After a pause, I hinted :

"There was a question just now, Mr. Jaggers, which you desired me to waive for a moment. I hope I am doing nothing wrong in asking it again?"

"What is it?" said he.

I might have known that he would never help me out; but it took me aback to have to shape the question afresh, as if it were quite new. "Is it likely," I said, after hesitating, "that my patron, the fountain-head you have spoken of, Mr. Jaggers, will soon —— " there I delicately stopped.

"Will soon what?" asked Mr. Jaggers. "That's no question as it stands, you know."

"Will soon come to London," said I, after casting about for a precise form of words, "or summon me anywhere else?"

"Now here," replied Mr. Jaggers, fixing me for the first time with his dark deep-set eyes, "we must revert to the evening when we first encountered one another in your village. What did I tell you then, Pip?"

"You told me, Mr. Jaggers, that it might be years hence when that person appeared."

"Just so," said Mr. Jaggers; "that's my answer."

As we looked full at one another, I felt my breath come quicker in my strong desire to get something out of him. And as I felt that it came quicker, and as I felt that he saw that it came quicker, I felt that I had less chance than ever of getting anything out of him.

"Do you suppose it will still be years hence, Mr. Jaggers?"

Mr. Jaggers shook his head—not in negativing the question, but in altogether negativing the notion that he could anyhow be got to answer it—and the two horrible casts of the twitched faces looked, when my eyes strayed up to them, as if they had come to a crisis in their suspended attention, and were going to sneeze.

"Come!" said Mr. Jaggers, warming the backs of his legs with the backs of his warmed hands, "I'll be plain with you, my friend Pip. That's a question I must not be asked. You'll understand that, better, when I tell you it's a question that might compromise *me*. Come! I'll go a little further with you; I'll say something more."

He bent down so low to frown at his boots, that he was able to rub the calves of his legs in the pause he made.

"When that person discloses," said Mr. Jaggers, straightening himself, "you and that person will settle your own affairs. When that person discloses, my part in this business will cease and determine. When that person discloses, it will not be necessary for me to know anything about it. And that's all I have got to say."

We looked at one another until I withdrew my eyes, and looked thoughtfully at the floor. From this last speech I derived the notion that Miss Havisham, for some reason or no reason, had not taken him into her confidence as to her designing me for Estella; that he resented this, and felt a jealousy about it; or that he really did object to that scheme, and would have nothing to do with it. When I raised my eyes again, I found that he had been shrewdly looking at me all the time, and was doing so still.

"If that is all you have to say, sir," I remarked, "there can be nothing left for me to say."

He nodded assent, and pulled out his thief-dreaded watch, and asked me where I was going to dine? I replied at my own chambers, with Herbert. As a necessary sequence, I asked him if he would favour us with his company, and he promptly accepted the invitation. But he insisted on walking home with me, in order that I might make no extra preparation for him, and first he had a letter or two to write, and (of course) had his hands to wash. So I said I would go into the outer office and talk to Wemmick.

The fact was, that when the five hundred pounds had come into my pocket, a thought had come into my head which had been often there before; and it appeared to me that Wemmick was a good person to advise with, concerning such thought.

He had already locked up his safe, and made preparations for going home. He had left his desk, brought out his two greasy office candlesticks and stood them in line with the snuffers on a slab near the door, ready to be extinguished; he had raked his fire low, put his hat and great-coat ready, and was beating himself all over the chest with his safe-key as an athletic exercise after business.

"Mr. Wemmick," said I, "I want to ask your opinion. I am very desirous to serve a friend."

Wemmick tightened his post-office and shook his head, as if his opinion were dead against any fatal weakness of that sort.

"This friend," I pursued, "is trying to get on in com-

personal capacities, and that he would be glad if I could come and see him again upon it. So I went out to Walworth again, and yet again, and yet again, and I saw him by appointment in the City several times, but never held any communication with him on the subject in or near Little Britain. The upshot was, that we found a worthy young merchant or shipping-broker, not long established in business, who wanted intelligent help, and who wanted capital, and who in due course of time and receipt would want a partner. Between him and me, secret articles were signed of which Herbert was the subject, and I paid him half of my five hundred pounds down, and engaged for sundry other payments : some, to fall due at certain dates out of my income : some contingent on my coming into my property. Miss Skiffins's brother conducted the negotiation. Wemmick pervaded it throughout, but never appeared in it.

The whole business was so cleverly managed, that Herbert had not the least suspicion of my hand being in it. I never shall forget the radiant face with which he came home one afternoon, and told me as a mighty piece of news, of his having fallen in with one Clarriker (the young merchant's name), and of Clarriker's having shown an extraordinary inclination towards him, and of his belief that the opening had come at last. Day by day as his hopes grew stronger and his face brighter, he must have thought me a more and more affectionate friend, for I had the greatest difficulty in restraining my tears of triumph when I saw him so happy.

At length, the thing being done, and he having that day entered Clarriker's House, and he having talked to me for a whole evening in a flush of pleasure and success, I did really cry in good earnest when I went to bed, to think that my expectations had done some good to somebody.

A great event in my life, the turning-point of my life, now opens on my view. But, before I proceed to narrate it, and before I pass on to all the changes it involved, I must give one chapter to Estella. It is not much to give to the theme that so long filled my heart.

CHAPTER XXXVIII

IF that staid old house near the Green at Richmond should ever come to be haunted when I am dead, it will be haunted, surely, by my ghost. O the many, many nights and days through which the unquiet spirit within me haunted that house when Estella lived there! Let my body be where it would, my spirit was always wandering, wandering, wandering about that house.

The lady with whom Estella was placed, Mrs. Brandley by name, was a widow, with one daughter several years older than Estella. The mother looked young and the daughter looked old; the mother's complexion was pink, and the daughter's was yellow; the mother set up for frivolity, and the daughter for theology. They were in what is called a good position, and visited, and were visited by, numbers of people. Little, if any, community of feeling subsisted between them and Estella, but the understanding was established that they were necessary to her, and that she was necessary to them. Mrs. Brandley had been a friend of Miss Havisham's before the time of her seclusion.

In Mrs. Brandley's house and out of Mrs. Brandley's house, I suffered every kind and degree of torture that Estella could cause me. The nature of my relations with her, which placed me on terms of familiarity without placing me on terms of favour, conduced to my distraction. She made use of me to tease other admirers, and she turned the very familiarity between herself and me, to the account of putting a constant slight on my devotion to her. If I had been her secretary, steward, half-brother, poor relation—if I had been a younger brother of her appointed husband—I could not have seemed to myself further from my hopes when I was nearest to her. The privilege of calling her by her name and hearing her call me by mine, became under the circumstances an aggravation of my trials; and while I think it likely that it almost maddened her other lovers, I knew too certainly that it almost maddened me.

She had admirers without end. No doubt my jealousy made an admirer of every one who went near her; but there were more than enough of them without that.

I saw her often at Richmond, I heard of her often in town, and I used often to take her and the Brandleys on the water; there were pic-nics, fête days, plays, operas, concerts, parties, all sorts of pleasures, through which I pursued her—and they were all miseries to me. I never had one hour's happiness in her society, and yet my mind all round the four-and-twenty hours was harping on the happiness of having her with me unto death.

Throughout this part of our intercourse—and it lasted, as will presently be seen, for what I then thought a long time —she habitually reverted to that tone which expressed that our association was forced upon us. There were other times when she would come to a sudden check in this tone and in all her many tones, and would seem to pity me.

"Pip, Pip," she said one evening, coming to such a check, when we sat apart at a darkening window of the house in Richmond; "will you never take warning?"

"Of what?"

"Of me."

"Warning not to be attracted by you, do you mean, Estella?"

"Do I mean! If you don't know what I mean, you are blind."

I should have replied that Love was commonly reputed blind, but for the reason that I always was restrained—and this was not the least of my miseries—by a feeling that it was ungenerous to press myself upon her, when she knew that she could not choose but obey Miss Havisham. My dread always was, that this knowledge on her part laid me under a heavy disadvantage with her pride, and made me the subject of a rebellious struggle in her bosom.

"At any rate," said I, "I have no warning given me just now, for you wrote to me to come to you, this time."

"That's true," said Estella, with a cold careless smile that always chilled me.

After looking at the twilight without, for a little while, she went on to say:

"The time has come round when Miss Havisham wishes to have me for a day at Satis. You are to take me there, and bring me back, if you will. She would rather I did not travel alone, and objects to receiving my maid, for she has a sensitive horror of being talked of by such people. Can you take me?"

"Can I take you, Estella!"

"You can then? The day after to-morrow, if you please. You are to pay all charges out of my purse. You hear the condition of your going?"

"And must obey," said I.

This was all the preparation I received for that visit, or for others like it: Miss Havisham never wrote to me, nor had I ever so much as seen her handwriting. We went down on the next day but one, and we found her in the room where I had first beheld her, and it is needless to add that there was no change in Satis House.

She was even more dreadfully fond of Estella than she had been when I last saw them together; I repeat the word advisedly, for there was something positively dreadful in the energy of her looks and embraces. She hung upon Estella's beauty, hung upon her words, hung upon her gestures, and sat mumbling her own trembling fingers while she looked at her, as though she were devouring the beautiful creature she had reared.

From Estella she looked at me, with a searching glance that seemed to pry into my heart and probe its wounds. "How does she use you, Pip, how does she use you?" she asked me again, with her witch-like eagerness, even in Estella's hearing. But when we sat by her flickering fire at night, she was most weird; for then, keeping Estella's hand drawn through her arm and clutched in her own hand, she extorted from her by dint of referring back to what Estella had told her in her regular letters, the names and conditions of the men whom she had fascinated; and as Miss Havisham dwelt upon this roll, with the intensity of a mind mortally hurt and diseased, she sat with her other hand on her crutch stick, and her chin on that, and her wan bright eyes glaring at me, a very spectre.

I saw in this, wretched though it made me, and bitter the sense of dependence, even of degradation, that it awakened— I saw in this, that Estella was set to wreak Miss Havisham's revenge on men, and that she was not to be given to me until she had gratified it for a term. I saw in this, a reason for her being beforehand assigned to me. Sending her out to attract and torment and do mischief, Miss Havisham

sent her with the malicious assurance that she was beyond
the reach of all admirers, and that all who staked upon
that cast were secured to lose. I saw in this, that I, too,
was tormented by a perversion of ingenuity, even while the
prize was reserved for me. I saw in this, the reason for
my being staved off so long, and the reason for my late
guardian's declining to commit himself to the formal knowledge of such a scheme. In a word, I saw in this, Miss
Havisham as I had her then and there before my eyes, and
always had had her before my eyes; and I saw in this,
the distinct shadow of the darkened and unhealthy house
in which her life was hidden from the sun.

The candles that lighted that room of hers were placed
in sconces on the wall. They were high from the ground,
and they burnt with the steady dulness of artificial light in
air that is seldom renewed. As I looked round at them,
and at the pale gloom they made, and at the stopped clock,
and at the withered articles of bridal dress upon the table
and the ground, and at her own awful figure with its
ghostly reflection thrown large by the fire upon the ceiling
and the wall, I saw in everything the construction that my
mind had come to, repeated and thrown back to me. My
thoughts passed into the great room across the landing
where the table was spread, and I saw it written, as it were,
in the falls of the cobwebs from the centre-piece, in the
crawlings of the spiders on the cloth, in the tracks of the
mice as they betook their little quickened hearts behind the
panels, and in the gropings and pausings of the beetles on
the floor.

It happened on the occasion of this visit that some sharp
words arose between Estella and Miss Havisham. It was
the first time I had ever seen them opposed.

We were seated by the fire, as just now described, and
Miss Havisham still had Estella's arm drawn through her
own, and still clutched Estella's hand in hers, when Estella
gradually began to detach herself. She had shown a proud
impatience more than once before, and had rather endured
that fierce affection than accepted or returned it.

"What!" said Miss Havisham, flashing her eyes upon
her, "are you tired of me?"

"Only a little tired of myself," replied Estella, disengag-
ing her arm, and moving to the great chimney-piece, where
she stood looking down at the fire.

"Speak the truth, you ingrate!" cried Miss Havisham, passionately striking her stick upon the floor; "you are tired of me."

Estella looked at her with perfect composure, and again looked down at the fire. Her graceful figure and her beautiful face expressed a self-possessed indifference to the wild heat of the other, that was almost cruel.

"You stock and stone!" exclaimed Miss Havisham. "You cold, cold heart!"

"What!" said Estella, preserving her attitude of indifference as she leaned against the great chimney-piece and only moving her eyes; "do you reproach me for being cold? You?"

"Are you not?" was the fierce retort.

"You should know," said Estella. "I am what you have made me. Take all the praise, take all the blame; take all the success, take all the failure; in short, take me."

"O, look at her, look at her!" cried Miss Havisham, bitterly. "Look at her, so hard and thankless, on the hearth where she was reared! Where I took her into this wretched breast when it was first bleeding from its stabs, and where I have lavished years of tenderness upon her!"

"At least I was no party to the compact," said Estella, "for if I could walk and speak, when it was made, it was as much as I could do. But what would you have? You have been very good to me, and I owe everything to you. What would you have?"

"Love," replied the other.

"You have it."

"I have not," said Miss Havisham.

"Mother by adoption," retorted Estella, never departing from the easy grace of her attitude, never raising her voice as the other did, never yielding either to anger or tenderness, "Mother by adoption, I have said that I owe everything to you. All I possess is freely yours. All that you have given me is at your command to have again. Beyond that, I have nothing. And if you ask me to give you what you never gave me, my gratitude and duty cannot do impossibilities."

"Did I never give her love!" cried Miss Havisham, turning wildly to me. "Did I never give her a burning love, inseparable from jealousy at all times, and from sharp

pain, while she speaks thus to me! Let her call me mad,
let her call me mad!"

"Why should I call you mad," returned Estella, "I, of all
people? Does any one live, who knows what set purposes
you have, half as well as I do? Does any one live, who
knows what a steady memory you have, half as well as I do?
I who have sat on this same hearth on the little stool that
is even now beside you there, learning your lessons and
looking up into your face, when your face was strange and
frightened me!"

"Soon forgotten!" moaned Miss Havisham. "Times
soon forgotten!"

"No, not forgotten," retorted Estella. "Not forgotten,
but treasured up in my memory. When have you found
me false to your teaching? When have you found me
unmindful of your lessons? When have you found me giving
admission here," she touched her bosom with her hand, "to
anything that you excluded? Be just to me."

"So proud, so proud!" moaned Miss Havisham, pushing
away her grey hair with both her hands.

"Who taught me to be proud?" returned Estella. "Who
praised me when I learnt my lesson?"

"So hard, so hard!" moaned Miss Havisham, with her
former action.

"Who taught me to be hard?" returned Estella. "Who
praised me when I learnt my lesson?"

"But to be proud and hard to *me*!" Miss Havisham quite
shrieked, as she stretched out her arms. "Estella, Estella,
Estella, to be proud and hard to *me*!"

Estella looked at her for a moment with a kind of calm
wonder, but was not otherwise disturbed; when the moment
was passed, she looked down at the fire again.

"I cannot think," said Estella, raising her eyes after a
silence, "why you should be so unreasonable when I come
to see you after a separation. I have never forgotten your
wrongs and their causes. I have never been unfaithful to
you or your schooling. I have never shown any weakness
that I can charge myself with."

"Would it be weakness to return my love?" exclaimed
Miss Havisham. "But yes, yes, she would call it so!"

"I begin to think," said Estella, in a musing way, after
another moment of calm wonder, "that I almost understand
how this comes about. If you had brought up your adopted

daughter wholly in the dark confinement of these rooms, and had never let her know that there was such a thing as the daylight by which she has never once seen your face—if you had done that, and then, for a purpose, had wanted her to understand the daylight and know all about it, you would have been disappointed and angry?"

Miss Havisham, with her head in her hands, sat making a low moaning, and swaying herself on her chair, but gave no answer.

"Or," said Estella, "—which is a nearer case—if you had taught her, from the dawn of her intelligence, with your utmost energy and might, that there was such a thing as daylight, but that it was made to be her enemy and destroyer, and she must always turn against it, for it had blighted you and would else blight her ;—if you had done this, and then, for a purpose, had wanted her to take naturally to the daylight and she could not do it, you would have been disappointed and angry?"

Miss Havisham sat listening (or it seemed so, for I could not see her face), but still made no answer.

"So," said Estella, "I must be taken as I have been made. The success is not mine, the failure is not mine, but the two together make me."

Miss Havisham had settled down, I hardly knew how, upon the floor, among the faded bridal relics with which it was strewn. I took advantage of the moment—I had sought one from the first—to leave the room, after beseeching Estella's attention to her with a movement of my hand. When I left, Estella was yet standing by the great chimney-piece, just as she had stood throughout. Miss Havisham's grey hair was all adrift upon the ground, among the other bridal wrecks, and was a miserable sight to see.

It was with a depressed heart that I walked in the starlight for an hour and more, about the court-yard, and about the brewery, and about the ruined garden. When I at last took courage to return to the room, I found Estella sitting at Miss Havisham's knee, taking up some stitches in one of those old articles of dress that were dropping to pieces, and of which I have often been reminded since by the faded tatters of old banners that I have seen hanging up in cathedrals. Afterwards, Estella and I played at cards, as of yore—only we were skilful now, and played French games—and so the evening wore away, and I went to bed.

I lay in that separate building across the court-yard. It was the first time I had ever lain down to rest in Satis House, and sleep refused to come near me. A thousand Miss Havishams haunted me. She was on this side of my pillow, on that, at the head of the bed, at the foot, behind the half-opened door of the dressing-room, in the dressing-room, in the room overhead, in the room beneath—everywhere. At last, when the night was slow to creep on towards two o'clock, I felt that I absolutely could no longer bear the place as a place to lie down in, and that I must get up. I therefore got up and put on my clothes, and went out across the yard into the long stone passage, designing to gain the outer court-yard and walk there for the relief of my mind. But I was no sooner in the passage than I extinguished my candle; for I saw Miss Havisham going along it in a ghostly manner, making a low cry. I followed her at a distance, and saw her go up the staircase. She carried a bare candle in her hand, which she had probably taken from one of the sconces in her own room, and was a most unearthly object by its light. Standing at the bottom of the staircase, I felt the mildewed air of the feast-chamber, without seeing her open the door, and I heard her walking there, and so across into her own room, and so across again into that, never ceasing the low cry. After a time, I tried in the dark both to get out and to go back, but I could do neither until some streaks of day strayed in and showed me where to lay my hands. During the whole interval, whenever I went to the bottom of the staircase, I heard her footstep, saw her candle pass above, and heard her ceaseless low cry.

Before we left next day, there was no revival of the difference between her and Estella, nor was it ever revived on any similar occasion; and there were four similar occasions, to the best of my remembrance. Nor did Miss Havisham's manner towards Estella in anywise change, except that I believed it to have something like fear infused among its former characteristics.

It is impossible to turn this leaf of my life without putting Bentley Drummle's name upon it; or I would, very gladly.

On a certain occasion when the Finches were assembled in force, and when good feeling was being promoted in the usual manner by nobody's agreeing with anybody else, the presiding Finch called the Grove to order, forasmuch as

Mr. Drummle had not yet toasted a lady; which, according to the solemn constitution of the society, it was the brute's turn to do that day. I thought I saw him leer in an ugly way at me while the decanters were going round, but as there was no love lost between us, that might easily be. What was my indignant surprise when he called upon the company to pledge him to "Estella!"

"Estella who?" said I.

"Never you mind," retorted Drummle.

"Estella of where?" said I. "You are bound to say of where." Which he was, as a Finch.

"Of Richmond, gentlemen," said Drummle, putting me out of the question, "and a peerless beauty."

Much he knew about peerless beauties, a mean miserable idiot! I whispered Herbert.

"I know that lady," said Herbert, across the table, when the toast had been honoured.

"*Do* you?" said Drummle.

"And so do I," I added with a scarlet face.

"*Do* you?" said Drummle. "*Oh*, Lord!"

This was the only retort—except glass or crockery—that the heavy creature was capable of making; but, I became as highly incensed by it as if it had been barbed with wit, and I immediately rose in my place and said that I could not but regard it as being like the honourable Finch's impudence to come down to that Grove—we always talked about coming down to that Grove, as a neat Parliamentary turn of expression—down to that Grove, proposing a lady of whom he knew nothing. Mr. Drummle upon this, starting up, demanded what I meant by that? Whereupon I made him the extreme reply that I believed he knew where I was to be found.

Whether it was possible in a Christian country to get on without blood, after this, was a question on which the Finches were divided. The debate upon it grew so lively, indeed, that at least six more honourable members told six more, during the discussion, that they believed *they* knew where *they* were to be found. However, it was decided at last (the Grove being a Court of Honour) that if Mr. Drummle would bring never so slight a certificate from the lady, importing that he had the honour of her acquaintance, Mr. Pip must express his regret, as a gentleman and a Finch, for "having been betrayed into a warmth which."

Next day was appointed for the production (lest our honour should take cold from delay), and next day Drummle appeared with a polite little avowal in Estella's hand, that she had had the honour of dancing with him several times. This left me no course but to regret that I had been "betrayed into a warmth which," and on the whole to repudiate, as untenable, the idea that I was to be found anywhere. Drummle and I then sat snorting at one another for an hour, while the Grove engaged in indiscriminate contradiction, and finally the promotion of good feeling was declared to have gone ahead at an amazing rate.

I tell this lightly, but it was no light thing to me. For I cannot adequately express what pain it gave me to think that Estella should show any favour to a contemptible, clumsy, sulky booby, so very far below the average. To the present moment, I believe it to have been referable to some pure fire of generosity and disinterestedness in my love for her, that I could not endure the thought of her stooping to that hound. No doubt I should have been miserable whomsoever she had favoured; but a worthier object would have caused me a different kind and degree of distress.

It was easy for me to find out, and I did soon find out, that Drummle had begun to follow her closely, and that she allowed him to do it. A little while, and he was always in pursuit of her, and he and I crossed one another every day. He held on, in a dull persistent way, and Estella held him on; now with encouragement, now with discouragement, now almost flattering him, now openly despising him, now knowing him very well, now scarcely remembering who he was.

The Spider, as Mr. Jaggers had called him, was used to lying in wait, however, and had the patience of his tribe. Added to that, he had a blockhead confidence in his money and in his family greatness, which sometimes did him good service—almost taking the place of concentration and determined purpose. So, the Spider, doggedly watching Estella, outwatched many brighter insects, and would often uncoil himself and drop at the right nick of time.

At a certain Assembly Ball at Richmond (there used to be Assembly Balls at most places then), where Estella had outshone all other beauties, this blundering Drummle so hung about her, and with so much toleration on her part, that I resolved to speak to her concerning him. I took the next opportunity: which was when she was waiting for Mrs. Brandley to take her home, and was sitting apart among some flowers, ready to go. I was with her, for I almost always accompanied them to and from such places.

"Are you tired, Estella?"

"Rather, Pip."

"You should be."

"Say, rather, I should not be; for I have my letter to Satis House to write, before I go to sleep."

"Recounting to-night's triumph?" said I. "Surely a very poor one, Estella."

"What do you mean? I didn't know there had been any."

"Estella," said I, "do look at that fellow in the corner yonder, who is looking over here at us."

"Why should I look at him?" returned Estella, with her eyes on me instead. "What is there in that fellow in the corner yonder—to use your words—that I need look at?"

"Indeed, that is the very question I want to ask you," said I. "For he has been hovering about you all night."

"Moths, and all sorts of ugly creatures," replied Estella, with a glance towards him, "hover about a lighted candle. Can the candle help it?"

"No," I returned: "but cannot the Estella help it?"

"Well!" said she, laughing after a moment, "perhaps. Yes. Anything you like."

"But, Estella, do hear me speak. It makes me wretched that you should encourage a man so generally despised as Drummle. You know he is despised."

"Well?" said she.

"You know he is as ungainly within as without. A deficient, ill-tempered, lowering, stupid fellow."

"Well?" said she.

"You know he has nothing to recommend him but money, and a ridiculous roll of addle-headed predecessors; now, don't you?"

"Well?" said she again; and each time she said it, she opened her lovely eyes the wider.

To overcome the difficulty of getting past that mono-syllable, I took it from her, and said, repeating it with emphasis, "Well! Then, that is why it makes me wretched."

Now, if I could have believed that she favoured Drummle

with any idea of making me—me—wretched, I should have been in better heart about it; but in that habitual way of hers, she put me so entirely out of the question, that I could believe nothing of the kind.

"Pip," said Estella, casting her glance over the room, "don't be foolish about its effect on you. It may have its effect on others, and may be meant to have. It's not worth discussing."

"Yes it is," said I, "because I cannot bear that people should say, 'she throws away her graces and attractions on a mere boor, the lowest in the crowd.'"

"I can bear it," said Estella.

"Oh! don't be so proud, Estella, and so inflexible."

"Calls me proud and inflexible in this breath!" said Estella, opening her hands. "And in his last breath reproached me for stooping to a boor!"

"There is no doubt you do," said I, something hurriedly, "for I have seen you give him looks and smiles this very night, such as you never give to—me."

"Do you want me then," said Estella, turning suddenly with a fixed and serious, if not angry look, "to deceive and entrap you?"

"Do you deceive and entrap him, Estella?"

"Yes, and many others—all of them but you. Here is Mrs. Brandley. I'll say no more."

And now that I have given the one chapter to the theme that so filled my heart, and so often made it ache and ache again, I pass on, unhindered, to the event that had impended over me longer yet; the event that had begun to be prepared for, before I knew that the world held Estella, and in the days when her baby intelligence was receiving its first distortions from Miss Havisham's wasting hands.

In the Eastern story, the heavy slab that was to fall on the bed of state in the flush of conquest was slowly wrought out of the quarry, the tunnel for the rope to hold it in its place was slowly carried through the leagues of rock, the slab was slowly raised and fitted in the roof, the rope was rove to it and slowly taken through the miles of hollow to the great iron ring. All being made ready with much labour, and the hour come, the sultan was aroused in the dead of the night, and the sharpened axe that was to sever the rope from the great iron ring was put into his hand, and he struck with it, and the rope parted and rushed away, and the ceiling fell. So in my case; all the work, near and afar, that tended to the end, had been accomplished; and in an instant the blow was struck, and the roof of my stronghold dropped upon me.

CHAPTER XXXIX

I was three-and-twenty years of age. Not another word had I heard to enlighten me on the subject of my expectations, and my twenty-third birthday was a week gone. We had left Barnard's Inn more than a year, and lived in the Temple. Our chambers were in Garden-court, down by the river.

Mr. Pocket and I had for some time parted company as to our original relations, though we continued on the best terms. Notwithstanding my inability to settle to anything—which I hope arose out of the restless and incomplete tenure on which I held my means—I had a taste for reading, and read regularly so many hours a day. That matter of Herbert's was still progressing, and everything with me was as I have brought it down to the close of the last preceding chapter.

Business had taken Herbert on a journey to Marseilles. I was alone, and had a dull sense of being alone. Dispirited and anxious, long hoping that to-morrow or next week would clear my way, and long disappointed, I sadly missed the cheerful face and ready response of my friend.

It was wretched weather; stormy and wet, stormy and wet; mud, mud, mud, deep in all the streets. Day after day, a vast heavy veil had been driving over London from the East, and it drove still, as if in the East there were an eternity of cloud and wind. So furious had been the gusts, that high buildings in town had had the lead stripped off their roofs; and in the country, trees had been torn up, and sails of windmills carried away; and gloomy accounts had come in from the coast, of shipwreck and death. Violent blasts of rain had accompanied these rages of wind, and the day just closed as I sat down to read had been the worst of all.

Alterations have been made in that part of the Temple since that time, and it has not now so lonely a character as it had then, nor is it so exposed to the river. We lived at the top of the last house, and the wind rushing up the river shook the house that night, like discharges of cannon, or breakings of a sea. When the rain came with it and dashed against the windows, I thought, raising my eyes to them as they rocked, that I might have fancied myself in a storm-beaten light-house. Occasionally, the smoke came rolling down the chimney as though it could not bear to go out into such a night; and when I set the doors open and looked down the staircase, the staircase lamps were blown out; and when I shaded my face with my hands and looked through the black windows (opening them, ever so little, was out of the question in the teeth of such wind and rain) I saw that the lamps in the court were blown out, and that the lamps on the bridges and the shore were shuddering, and that the coal fires in barges on the river were being carried away before the wind like red-hot splashes in the rain.

I read with my watch upon the table, purposing to close my book at eleven o'clock. As I shut it, Saint Paul's, and all the many church-clocks in the City—some leading, some accompanying, some following—struck that hour. The sound was curiously flawed by the wind; and I was listening, and thinking how the wind assailed and tore it, when I heard a footstep on the stair.

What nervous folly made me start, and awfully connect it with the footstep of my dead sister, matters not. It was past in a moment, and I listened again, and heard the footstep stumble in coming on. Remembering then that the staircase lights were blown out, I took up my reading-lamp and went out to the stair-head. Whoever was below had stopped on seeing my lamp, for all was quiet.

"There is some one down there, is there not?" I called out, looking down.

"Yes," said a voice from the darkness beneath.

"What floor do you want?"

"The top. Mr. Pip."

"That is my name.—There is nothing the matter?"

"Nothing the matter," returned the voice. And the man came on.

I stood with my lamp held out over the stair-rail, and he came slowly within its light. It was a shaded lamp, to shine upon a book, and its circle of light was very contracted; so that he was in it for a mere instant, and then out of it. In the instant I had seen a face that was strange to me, looking up with an incomprehensible air of being touched and pleased by the sight of me.

Moving the lamp as the man moved, I made out that he was substantially dressed, but roughly; like a voyager by sea. That he had long iron-grey hair. That his age was about sixty. That he was a muscular man, strong on his legs, and that he was browned and hardened by exposure to weather. As he ascended the last stair or two, and the light of my lamp included us both, I saw, with a stupid kind of amazement, that he was holding out both his hands to me.

"Pray what is your business?" I asked him.

"My business?" he repeated, pausing. "Ah! Yes. I will explain my business, by your leave."

"Do you wish to come in?"

"Yes," he replied; "I wish to come in, Master."

I had asked him the question inhospitably enough, for I resented the sort of bright and gratified recognition that still shone in his face. I resented it, because it seemed to imply that he expected me to respond to it. But I took him into the room I had just left, and, having set the lamp on the table, asked him as civilly as I could to explain himself.

He looked about him with the strangest air—an air of wondering pleasure, as if he had some part in the things he admired—and he pulled off a rough outer coat, and his hat. Then I saw that his head was furrowed and bald, and that the long iron-grey hair grew only on its sides. But I saw nothing that in the least explained him. On the contrary, I saw him next moment once more holding out both his hands to me.

"What do you mean?" said I, half suspecting him to be mad.

He stopped in his looking at me, and slowly rubbed his right hand over his head. "It's disappointing to a man," he said, in a coarse broken voice, "arter having looked for'ard so distant, and come so fur; but you're not to blame for that—neither on us is to blame for that. I'll speak in half a minute. Give me half a minute, please."

He sat down on a chair that stood before the fire, and covered his forehead with his large brown veinous hands. I looked at him attentively then, and recoiled a little from him; but I did not know him.

"There's no one nigh," said he, looking over his shoulder; "is there?"

"Why do you, a stranger coming into my rooms at this time of the night, ask that question?" said I.

"You're a game one," he returned, shaking his head at me with a deliberate affection, at once most unintelligible and most exasperating; "I'm glad you've grow'd up a game one! But don't catch hold of me. You'd be sorry arterwards to have done it."

I relinquished the intention he had detected, for I knew him! Even yet I could not recall a single feature, but I knew him! If the wind and the rain had driven away the intervening years, had scattered all the intervening objects, had swept us to the churchyard where we first stood face to face on such different levels, I could not have known my convict more distinctly than I knew him now, as he sat in the chair before the fire. No need to take a file from his pocket and show it to me; no need to take the handkerchief from his neck and twist it round his head; no need to hug himself with both his arms, and take a shivering turn across the room, looking back at me for recognition. I knew him before he gave me one of those aids, though, a moment before, I had not been conscious of remotely suspecting his identity.

He came back to where I stood, and again held out both his hands. Not knowing what to do—for, in my astonishment I had lost my self-possession—I reluctantly gave him my hands. He grasped them heartily, raised them to his lips, kissed them, and still held them.

"You acted nobly, my boy," said he. "Noble Pip! And I have never forgot it!"

At a change in his manner as if he were even going to embrace me, I laid a hand upon his breast and put him away.

"Stay!" said I. "Keep off! If you are grateful to me for what I did when I was a little child, I hope you have shown your gratitude by mending your way of life. If you have come here to thank me, it was not necessary. Still, however, you have found me out, there must be something good in the feeling that has brought you here, and I will not repulse you; but surely you must understand—I——"

My attention was so attracted by the singularity of his fixed look at me, that the words died away on my tongue.

"You was a saying," he observed, when we had confronted one another in silence, "that surely I must understand. What, surely must I understand?"

"That I cannot wish to renew that chance intercourse with you of long ago, under these different circumstances. I am glad to believe you have repented and recovered yourself. I am glad to tell you so. I am glad that, thinking I deserve to be thanked, you have come to thank me. But our ways are different ways, none the less. You are wet, and you look weary. Will you drink something before you go?"

He had replaced his neckerchief loosely, and had stood, keenly observant of me, biting a long end of it. "I think," he answered, still with the end at his mouth and still observant of me, "that I *will* drink (I thank you) afore I go."

There was a tray ready on a side-table. I brought it to the table near the fire, and asked him what he would have? He touched one of the bottles without looking at it or speaking, and I made him some hot rum-and-water. I tried to keep my hand steady while I did so, but his look at me as he leaned back in his chair with the long draggled end of his neckerchief between his teeth—evidently forgotten— made my hand very difficult to master. When at last I put the glass to him, I saw with amazement that his eyes were full of tears.

Up to this time I had remained standing, not to disguise that I wished him gone. But I was softened by the softened aspect of the man, and felt a touch of reproach. "I hope," said I, hurriedly putting something into a glass for myself, and drawing a chair to the table, "that you will not think I spoke harshly to you just now. I had no intention of doing it, and I am sorry for it if I did. I wish you well, and happy!"

As I put my glass to my lips, he glanced with surprise at the end of his neckerchief, dropping from his mouth when he opened it, and stretched out his hand. I gave him mine, and then he drank, and drew his sleeve across his eyes and forehead.

"How are you living?" I asked him.

"I've been a sheep-farmer, stock-breeder, other trades besides, away in the new world," said he: "many a thousand mile of stormy water off from this."

"I hope you have done well?"

"I've done wonderful well. There's others went out

I MADE HIM SOME HOT RUM-AND-WATER

alonger me as has done well too, but no man has done nigh as well as me. I'm famous for it."

"I am glad to hear it."

"I hope to hear you say so, my dear boy."

Without stopping to try to understand those words or the tone in which they were spoken, I turned off to a point that had just come into my mind.

"Have you ever seen a messenger you once sent to me," I inquired, "since he undertook that trust?"

"Never set eyes upon him. I warn't likely to it."

"He came faithfully, and he brought me the two one-pound notes. I was a poor boy then, as you know, and to a poor boy they were a little fortune. But, like you, I have done well since, and you must let me pay them back. You can put them to some other poor boy's use." I took out my purse.

He watched me as I laid my purse upon the table and opened it, and he watched me as I separated two one-pound notes from its contents. They were clean and new, and I spread them out and handed them over to him. Still watching me, he laid them one upon the other, folded them longwise, gave them a twist, set fire to them at the lamp, and dropped the ashes into the tray.

"May I make so bold," he said then, with a smile that was like a frown, and with a frown that was like a smile, "as ask you *how* you have done well, since you and me was out on them lone shivering marshes?"

"How?"

"Ah!"

He emptied his glass, got up, and stood at the side of the fire, with his heavy brown hand on the mantelshelf. He put a foot up to the bars, to dry and warm it, and the wet boot began to steam; but, he neither looked at it, nor at the fire, but steadily looked at me. It was only now that I began to tremble.

When my lips had parted, and had shaped some words that were without sound, I forced myself to tell him (though I could not do it distinctly), that I had been chosen to succeed to some property.

"Might a mere warmint ask what property?" said he.

I faltered, "I don't know."

"Might a mere warmint ask whose property?" said he.

I faltered again, "I don't know."

"Could I make a guess, I wonder," said the Convict, "at your income since you come of age! As to the first figure, now. Five?"

With my heart beating like a heavy hammer of disordered action, I rose out of my chair, and stood with my hand upon the back of it, looking wildly at him.

"Concerning a guardian," he went on. "There ought to have been some guardian or such-like, whiles you was a minor. Some lawyer, maybe. As to the first letter of that lawyer's name, now. Would it be J?"

All the truth of my position came flashing on me; and its disappointments, dangers, disgraces, consequences of all kinds, rushed in in such a multitude that I was borne down by them and had to struggle for every breath I drew. "Put it," he resumed, "as the employer of that lawyer whose name begun with a J, and might be Jaggers—put it as he had come over sea to Portsmouth, and had landed there, and had wanted to come on to you. 'However, you have found me out,' you says just now. Well! however did I find you out? Why, I wrote from Portsmouth to a person in London, for particulars of your address. That person's name? Why, Wemmick."

I could not have spoken one word, though it had been to save my life. I stood, with a hand on the chair-back and a hand on my breast, where I seemed to be suffocating— I stood so, looking wildly at him, until I grasped at the chair, when the room began to surge and turn. He caught me, drew me to the sofa, put me up against the cushions, and bent on one knee before me: bringing the face that I now well remembered, and that I shuddered at, very near to mine.

"Yes, Pip, dear boy, I've made a gentleman on you! It's me wot has done it! I swore that time, sure as ever I earned a guinea, that guinea should go to you. I swore arterwards, sure as ever I spec'lated and got rich, you should get rich. I lived rough, that you should live smooth; I worked hard that you should be above work. What odds, dear boy? Do I tell it fur you to feel a obliga-tion? Not a bit. I tell it, fur you to know as that there hunted dunghill dog wot you kep life in, got his head so high that he could make a gentleman—and, Pip, you're him!"

The abhorrence in which I held the man, the dread I had

of him, the repugnance with which I shrank from him, could not have been exceeded if he had been some terrible beast.

"Look'ee here, Pip. I'm your second father. You're my son—more to me nor any son. I've put away money, only for you to spend. When I was a hired-out shepherd in a solitary hut, not seeing no faces but faces of sheep till I half forgot wot men's and women's faces wos like, I see yourn. I drops my knife many a time in that hut when I was a eating my dinner or my supper, and I says, 'Here's the boy again, a looking at me whiles I eats and drinks!' I see you there a many times as plain as ever I see you on them misty marshes. 'Lord strike me dead!' I says each time—and I goes out in the open air to say it under the open heavens—'but wot, if I gets liberty and money, I'll make that boy a gentleman!' And I done it. Why, look at you, dear boy! Look at these here lodgings of yourn, fit for a lord! A lord? Ah! You shall show money with lords for wagers, and beat 'em!"

In his heat and triumph, and in his knowledge that I had been nearly fainting, he did not remark on my reception of all this. It was the one grain of relief I had.

"Look'ee here!" he went on, taking my watch out of my pocket, and turning towards him a ring on my finger, while I recoiled from his touch as if he had been a snake, "a gold 'un and a beauty: *that's* a gentleman's, I hope! A diamond all set round with rubies; *that's* a gentleman's, I hope! Look at your linen; fine and beautiful! Look at your clothes; better ain't to be got! And your books too," turning his eyes round the room, "mounting up, on their shelves, by hundreds! And you read 'em; don't you? I see you'd been a reading of 'em when I come in. Ha, ha, ha! You shall read 'em to me, dear boy! And if they're in foreign languages wot I don't understand, I shall be just as proud as if I did."

Again he took both my hands and put them to his lips, while my blood ran cold within me.

"Don't you mind talking, Pip," said he, after again drawing his sleeve over his eyes and forehead, as the click came in his throat which I well remembered—and he was all the more horrible to me that he was so much in earnest; "you can't do better nor keep quiet, dear boy. You ain't looked slowly forward to this as I have; you wasn't prepared for this, as I wos. But didn't you never think it might be me?"

"O no, no, no," I returned. "Never, never!"

"Well, you see it *wos* me, and single-handed. Never a soul in it but my own self and Mr. Jaggers."

"Was there no one else?" I asked.

"No," said he, with a glance of surprise: "who else should there be? And, dear boy, how good-looking you have growed! There's bright eyes somewheres—eh? Isn't there bright eyes somewheres, wot you love the thoughts on?"

O Estella, Estella!

"They shall be yourn, dear boy, if money can buy 'em. Not that a gentleman like you, so well set up as you, can't win 'em off of his own game; but money shall back you! Let me finish wot I was a telling you, dear boy. From that there hut and that there hiring-out, I got money left me by my master (which died, and had been the same as me), and got my liberty and went for myself. In every single thing I went for, I went for you. 'Lord strike a blight upon it,' I says, wotever it was I went for, 'if it ain't for him!' It all prospered wonderful. As I giv' you to understand just now, I'm famous for it. It was the money left me, and the gains of the first few year, wot I sent home to Mr. Jaggers—all for you—when he first come arter you, agreeable to my letter."

O, that he had never come! That he had left me at the forge—far from contented, yet, by comparison, happy!

"And then, dear boy, it was a recompense to me, look'ee here, to know in secret that I was making a gentleman. The blood horses of them colonists might fling up the dust over me as I was walking; what do I say? I says to myself, 'I'm making a better gentleman nor ever *you*'ll be!' When one of 'em says to one another, 'He was a convict, a few years ago, and is a ignorant common fellow now, for all he's lucky,' what do I say? I says to myself, 'If I ain't a gentleman, nor yet ain't got no learning, I'm the owner of such. All on you owns stock and land; which on you owns a brought-up London gentleman?' This way I kep myself a going. And this way I held steady afore my mind that I would for certain come one day and see my boy, and make myself known to him, on his own ground."

He laid his hand on my shoulder. I shuddered at the

thought that for anything I knew, his hand might be stained with blood.

"It warn't easy, Pip, for me to leave them parts, nor yet it warn't safe. But I held to it, and the harder it was, the stronger I held, for I was determined, and my mind firm made up. At last I done it. Dear boy, I done it!"

I tried to collect my thoughts, but I was stunned. Throughout, I had seemed to myself to attend more to the wind and the rain than to him; even now, I could not separate his voice from those voices, though those were loud and his was silent.

"Where will you put me?" he asked, presently. "I must be put somewheres, dear boy."

"To sleep?" said I.

"Yes. And to sleep long and sound," he answered; "for I've been sea-tossed and sea-washed, months and months."

"My friend and companion," said I, rising from the sofa, "is absent; you must have his room."

"He won't come back to-morrow; will he?"

"No," said I, answering almost mechanically, in spite of my utmost efforts; "not to-morrow."

"Because, look'ee here, dear boy," he said, dropping his voice, and laying a long finger on my breast in an impressive manner, "caution is necessary."

"How do you mean? Caution?"

"By G—, it's Death!"

"What's death?"

"I was sent for life. It's death to come back. There's been overmuch coming back of late years, and I should of a certainty be hanged if took."

Nothing was needed but this; the wretched man, after loading me with his wretched gold and silver chains for years, had risked his life to come to me, and I held it there in my keeping! If I had loved him instead of abhorring him; if I had been attracted to him by the strongest admiration and affection, instead of shrinking from him with the strongest repugnance; it could have been no worse. On the contrary, it would have been better, for his preservation would then have naturally and tenderly addressed my heart.

My first care was to close the shutters, so that no light might be seen from without, and then to close and make fast the doors. While I did so, he stood at the table drinking rum and eating biscuit; and when I saw him thus engaged, I saw my convict on the marshes at his meal again. It almost seemed to me as if he must stoop down presently, to file at his leg.

When I had gone into Herbert's room, and had shut off any other communication between it and the staircase than through the room in which our conversation had been held, I asked him if he would go to bed? He said yes, but asked me for some of my "gentleman's linen" to put on in the morning. I brought it out, and laid it ready for him, and my blood again ran cold when he again took me by both hands to give me good night.

I got away from him, without knowing how I did it, and mended the fire in the room where we had been together, and sat down by it, afraid to go to bed. For an hour or more, I remained too stunned to think; and it was not until I began to think, that I began fully to know how wrecked I was, and how the ship in which I had sailed was gone to pieces.

Miss Havisham's intentions towards me, all a mere dream; Estella not designed for me; I only suffered in Satis House as a convenience, a sting for the greedy relations, a model with a mechanical heart to practise on when no other practice was at hand; those were the first smarts I had. But, sharpest and deepest pain of all—it was for the convict, guilty of I knew not what crimes, and liable to be taken out of those rooms where I sat thinking, and hanged at the Old Bailey door, that I had deserted Joe.

I would not have gone back to Joe now, I would not have gone back to Biddy now, for any consideration: simply, I suppose, because my sense of my own worthless conduct to them was greater than every consideration. No wisdom on earth could have given me the comfort that I should have derived from their simplicity and fidelity; but I could never, never, never, undo what I had done.

In every rage of wind and rush of rain, I heard pursuers. Twice, I could have sworn there was a knocking and whispering at the outer door. With these fears upon me, I began either to imagine or recall that I had had mysterious warnings of this man's approach. That, for weeks gone by, I had passed faces in the streets which I had thought like his. That, these likenesses had grown more numerous, as he, coming over the sea, had drawn nearer. That, his wicked spirit had somehow sent these messengers to mine, and that now on this stormy night he was as good as his word, and with me.

Crowding up with these reflections came the reflection that I had seen him with my childish eyes to be a desperately violent man; that I had heard that other convict reiterate that he had tried to murder him; that I had seen him down in the ditch, tearing and fighting like a wild beast. Out of such remembrances I brought into the light of the fire, a half-formed terror that it might not be safe to be shut up there with him in the dead of the wild solitary night. This dilated until it filled the room, and impelled me to take a candle and go in and look at my dreadful burden.

He had rolled a handkerchief round his head, and his face was set and lowering in his sleep. But he was asleep, and quietly too, though he had a pistol lying on the pillow. Assured of this, I softly removed the key to the outside of his door, and turned it on him before I again sat down by the fire. Gradually I slipped from the chair and lay on the floor. When I awoke without having parted in my sleep with the perception of my wretchedness, the clocks of the Eastward churches were striking five, the candles were wasted out, the fire was dead, and the wind and rain intensified the thick black darkness.

THIS IS THE END OF THE SECOND STAGE OF PIP'S EXPECTATIONS

CHAPTER XL

IT was fortunate for me that I had to take precautions to insure (so far as I could) the safety of my dreaded visitor; for, this thought pressing on me when I awoke, held other thoughts in a confused concourse at a distance.

The impossibility of keeping him concealed in the chambers was self-evident. It could not be done, and the attempt to do it would inevitably engender suspicion. True, I had no Avenger in my service now, but I was looked after by an inflammatory old female, assisted by an animated rag-bag whom she called her niece; and to keep a room secret from them would be to invite curiosity and exaggeration. They both had weak eyes, which I had long attributed to their chronically looking in at keyholes, and they were always at hand when not wanted; indeed that was their only reliable quality besides larceny. Not to get up a mystery with these people, I resolved to announce in the morning that my uncle had unexpectedly come from the country.

This course I decided on while I was yet groping about in the darkness for the means of getting a light. Not stumbling on the means after all, I was fain to go out to the adjacent Lodge and get the watchman there to come with his lantern. Now, in groping my way down the black staircase I fell over something, and that something was a man crouching in a corner.

As the man made no answer when I asked him what he did there, but eluded my touch in silence, I ran to the Lodge and urged the watchman to come quickly: telling him of the incident on the way back. The wind being as fierce as ever, we did not care to endanger the light in the lantern by rekindling the extinguished lamps on the staircase, but we examined the staircase from the bottom to the top and found no one there. It then occurred to me as possible that the man might have slipped into my rooms; so, lighting my candle at the watchman's, and leaving him standing at the door, I examined them carefully, including the room in which my dreaded guest lay asleep. All was quiet, and assuredly no other man was in those chambers.

It troubled me that there should have been a lurker on the stairs, on that night of all nights in the year, and I asked the watchman, on the chance of eliciting some hopeful explanation as I handed him a dram at the door, whether he had admitted at his gate any gentleman who had perceptibly been dining out? Yes, he said; at different times of the night, three. One lived in Fountain Court, and the other two lived in the Lane, and he had seen them all go home. Again, the only other man who dwelt in the house of which my chambers formed a part, had been in the country for some weeks; and he certainly had not returned in the night, because we had seen his door with his seal on it as we came up-stairs.

"The night being so bad, sir," said the watchman, as he gave me back my glass, "uncommon few have come in at my gate. Besides them three gentlemen that I have named, I don't call to mind another since about eleven o'clock, when a stranger asked for you."

"My uncle," I muttered. "Yes."

"You saw him, sir?"

"Yes. Oh yes."

"Likewise the person with him?"

"Person with him!" I repeated.

"I judged the person to be with him," returned the watchman. "The person stopped, when he stopped to make inquiry of me, and the person took this way when he took this way."

"What sort of person?"

The watchman had not particularly noticed; he should say a working person; to the best of his belief, he had a dust-coloured kind of clothes on, under a dark coat. The watchman made more light of the matter than I did, and naturally; not having my reason for attaching weight to it.

When I had got rid of him, which I thought it well to do without prolonging explanations, my mind was much troubled by these two circumstances taken together. Whereas they were easy of innocent solution apart—as, for instance, some diner-out or diner-at-home, who had not gone near this watchman's gate, might have strayed to my staircase and dropped asleep there—and my nameless

visitor might have brought some one with him to show
him the way—still, joined, they had an ugly look to one
as prone to distrust and fear as the changes of a few hours
had made me.

I lighted my fire, which burnt with a raw pale flare at
that time of the morning, and fell into a doze before it.
I seemed to have been dozing a whole night when the clocks
struck six. As there was full an hour and a half between
me and daylight, I dozed again; now, waking up uneasily,
with prolix conversations about nothing, in my ears; now,
making thunder of the wind in the chimney; at length,
falling off into a profound sleep from which the daylight
woke me with a start.

All this time I had never been able to consider my own
situation, nor could I do so yet. I had not the power to
attend to it. I was greatly dejected and distressed, but in
an incoherent wholesale sort of way. As to forming any
plan for the future, I could as soon have formed an elephant.
When I opened the shutters and looked out at the wet wild
morning, all of a leaden hue; when I walked from room to
room; when I sat down again shivering, before the fire,
waiting for my laundress to appear; I thought how miserable I was, but hardly knew why, or how long I had been so,
or on what day of the week I made the reflection, or even
who I was that made it.

At last the old woman and the niece came in—the latter
with a head not easily distinguishable from her dusty broom
—and testified surprise at sight of me and the fire. To
whom I imparted how my uncle had come in the night
and was then asleep, and how the breakfast preparations
were to be modified accordingly. Then, I washed and
dressed while they knocked the furniture about and made
a dust; and so, in a sort of dream or sleep-walking, I found
myself sitting by the fire again, waiting for—Him—to come
to breakfast.

By-and-by, his door opened and he came out. I could not
bring myself to bear the sight of him, and I thought he had
a worse look by daylight.

"I do not even know," said I, speaking low as he took his
seat at the table, "by what name to call you. I have given
out that you are my uncle."

"That's it, dear boy! Call me uncle."

"You assumed some name, I suppose, on board ship?"

"Yes, dear boy. I took the name of Provis."

"Do you mean to keep that name?"

"Why, yes, dear boy, it's as good as another—unless you'd like another."

"What is your real name?" I asked him in a whisper.

"Magwitch," he answered, in the same tone; "chrisen'd Abel."

"What were you brought up to be?"

"A warmint, dear boy."

He answered quite seriously, and used the word as if it denoted some profession.

"When you came into the Temple last night——" said I, pausing to wonder whether that could really have been last night, which seemed so long ago.

"Yes, dear boy?"

"When you came in at the gate and asked the watchman the way here, had you any one with you?"

"With me? No, dear boy."

"But there was some one there?"

"I didn't take particular notice," he said, dubiously, "not knowing the ways of the place. But I think there *was* a person, too, come in alonger me."

"Are you known in London?"

"I hope not!" said he, giving his neck a jerk with his forefinger that made me turn hot and sick.

"Were you known in London, once?"

"Not over and above, dear boy. I was in the provinces mostly."

"Were you—tried—in London?"

"Which time?" said he, with a sharp look.

"The last time."

He nodded. "First knowed Mr. Jaggers that way. Jaggers was for me."

It was on my lips to ask him what he was tried for, but he took up a knife, gave it a flourish, and with the words, "And what I done is worked out and paid for!" fell to at his breakfast.

He ate in a ravenous way that was very disagreeable, and all his actions were uncouth, noisy, and greedy. Some of his teeth had failed him since I saw him eat on the marshes, and as he turned his food in his mouth, and turned his head sideways to bring his strongest fangs to bear upon it, he looked terribly like a hungry old dog.

If I had begun with any appetite, he would have taken it away, and I should have sat much as I did—repelled from him by an insurmountable aversion, and gloomily looking at the cloth.

"I'm a heavy grubber, dear boy," he said, as a polite kind of apology when he had made an end of his meal, "but I always was. If it had been in my constitution to be a lighter grubber, I might ha' got into lighter trouble. Similarly, I must have my smoke. When I was first hired out as shepherd t'other side the world, it's my belief I should ha' turned into a molloncolly-mad sheep myself, if I hadn't a had my smoke."

As he said so he got up from table, and putting his hand into the breast of the pea-coat he wore, brought out a short black pipe, and a handful of loose tobacco of the kind that is called negro-head. Having filled his pipe, he put the surplus tobacco back again, as if his pocket were a drawer. Then, he took a live coal from the fire with the tongs, and lighted his pipe at it, and then turned round on the hearth-rug with his back to the fire, and went through his favourite action of holding out both his hands for mine.

"And this," said he, dandling my hands up and down in his, as he puffed at his pipe; "and this is the gentleman what I made! The real genuine One! It does me good fur to look at you, Pip. All I stip'late is, to stand by and look at you, dear boy!"

I released my hands as soon as I could, and found that I was beginning slowly to settle down to the contemplation of my condition. What I was chained to, and how heavily, became intelligible to me, as I heard his hoarse voice, and sat looking up at his furrowed bald head with its iron-grey hair at the sides.

"I mustn't see my gentleman a footing it in the mire of the streets; there mustn't be no mud on *his* boots. My gentleman must have horses, Pip! Horses to ride, and horses to drive, and horses for his servant to ride and drive as well. Shall colonists have their horses (and blood-'uns, if you please, good Lord!) and not my London gentleman? No, no. We'll show 'em another pair of shoes than that, Pip; won't us?"

He took out of his pocket a great thick pocket-book, bursting with papers, and tossed it on the table.

"There's something worth spending in that there book,

dear boy. It's yourn. All I've got ain't mine; it's yourn. Don't you be afeerd on it. There's more where that come from. I've come to the old country fur to see my gentleman spend his money *like* a gentleman. That'll be *my* pleasure. *My* pleasure 'ull be fur to see him do it. And blast you all!" he wound up, looking round the room and snapping his fingers once with a loud snap, "blast you every one, from the judge in his wig, to the colonist a stirring up the dust, I'll show a better gentleman than the whole kit on you put together!"

"Stop!" said I, almost in a frenzy of fear and dislike, "I want to speak to you. I want to know what is to be done. I want to know how you are to be kept out of danger, how long you are going to stay, what projects you have."

"Look'ee here, Pip," said he, laying his hand on my arm in a suddenly altered and subdued manner; "first of all, look'ee here. I forgot myself half a minute ago. What I said was low; that's what it was; low. Look'ee here, Pip. Look over it. I ain't a going to be low."

"First," I resumed, half-groaning, "what precautions can be taken against your being recognised and seized?"

"No, dear boy," he said, in the same tone as before, "that don't go first. Lowness goes first. I ain't took so many year to make a gentleman, not without knowing what's due to him. Look'ee here, Pip. I was low; that's what I was; low. Look over it, dear boy."

Some sense of the grimly-ludicrous moved me to a fretful laugh, as I replied, "I *have* looked over it. In Heaven's name, don't harp upon it!"

"Yes, but look'ee here," he persisted. "Dear boy, I ain't come so fur, not fur to be low. Now, go on, dear boy. You was a saying——"

"How are you to be guarded from the danger you have incurred?"

"Well, dear boy, the danger ain't so great. Without I was informed agen, the danger ain't so much to signify. There's Jaggers, and there's Wemmick, and there's you. Who else is there to inform?"

"Is there no chance person who might identify you in the street?" said I.

"Well," he returned, "there ain't many. Nor yet I don't intend to advertise myself in the newspapers by the name of

A. M. come back from Botany Bay; and years have rolled away, and who's to gain by it? Still, look'ee here, Pip. If the danger had been fifty times as great, I should ha' come to see you, mind you, just the same."

"And how long do you remain?"

"How long?" said he, taking his black pipe from his mouth, and dropping his jaw as he stared at me. "I'm not a going back. I've come for good."

"Where are you to live?" said I. "What is to be done with you? Where will you be safe?"

"Dear boy," he returned, "there's disguising wigs can be bought for money, and there's hair powder, and spectacles, and black clothes—shorts and what not. Others has done it safe afore, and what others has done afore, others can do agen. As to the where and how of living, dear boy, give me your own opinions on it."

"You take it smoothly now," said I, "but you were very serious last night, when you swore it was Death."

"And so I swear it is Death," said he, putting his pipe back in his mouth, "and Death by the rope, in the open street not fur from this, and it's serious that you should fully understand it to be so. What then, when that's once done? Here I am. To go back now, 'ud be as bad as to stand ground—worse. Besides, Pip, I'm here, because I've meant it by you, years and years. As to what I dare, I'm a old bird now, as has dared all manner of traps since first he was fledged, and I'm not afeerd to perch upon a scarecrow. If there's Death hid inside of it, there is, and let him come out, and I'll face him, and then I'll believe in him and not afore. And now let me have a look at my gentleman agen."

Once more he took me by both hands and surveyed me with an air of admiring proprietorship, smoking with great complacency all the while.

It appeared to me that I could do no better than secure him some quiet lodging hard by, of which he might take possession when Herbert returned: whom I expected in two or three days. That the secret must be confided to Herbert as a matter of unavoidable necessity, even if I could have put the immense relief I should derive from sharing it with him out of the question, was plain to me. But it was by no means so plain to Mr. Provis (I resolved to call him by that name), who reserved his consent to Herbert's participation until he should have seen him and formed a favourable judgment of his physiognomy. "And even then, dear boy," said he, pulling a greasy little clasped black Testament out of his pocket, "we'll have him on his oath."

To state that my terrible patron carried this little black book about the world solely to swear people on in cases of emergency, would be to state what I never quite established —but this I can say, that I never knew him put it to any other use. The book itself had the appearance of having been stolen from some court of justice, and perhaps his knowledge of its antecedents, combined with his own experience in that wise, gave him a reliance on its powers as a sort of legal spell or charm. On this first occasion of his producing it, I recalled how he had made me swear fidelity in the churchyard long ago, and how he had described himself last night as always swearing to his resolutions in his solitude.

As he was at present dressed in a seafaring slop suit, in which he looked as if he had some parrots and cigars to dispose of, I next discussed with him what dress he should wear. He cherished an extraordinary belief in the virtues of "shorts" as a disguise, and had in his own mind sketched a dress for himself that would have made him something between a dean and a dentist. It was with considerable difficulty that I won him over to the assumption of a dress more like a prosperous farmer's; and we arranged that he should cut his hair close, and wear a little powder. Lastly, as he had not yet been seen by the laundress or her niece, he was to keep himself out of their view until his change of dress was made.

It would seem a simple matter to decide on these precautions; but in my dazed, not to say distracted, state, it took so long, that I did not get out to further them until two or three in the afternoon. He was to remain shut up in the chambers while I was gone, and was on no account to open the door.

There being to my knowledge a respectable lodging-house in Essex-street, the back of which looked into the Temple, and was almost within hail of my windows, I first of all repaired to that house, and was so fortunate as to secure the second floor for my uncle, Mr. Provis. I then went from shop to shop, making such purchases as were necessary to the change in his appearance. This business transacted, I turned my face, on my own account, to Little Britain. Mr. Jaggers was at his desk, but, seeing me enter, got up immediately and stood before his fire.

"Now, Pip," said he, "be careful."

"I will, sir," I returned. For, coming along I had thought well of what I was going to say.

"Don't commit yourself," said Mr. Jaggers, "and don't commit any one. You understand—any one. Don't tell me anything: I don't want to know anything: I am not curious."

Of course I saw that he knew the man was come.

"I merely want, Mr. Jaggers," said I, "to assure myself what I have been told is true. I have no hope of its being untrue, but at least I may verify it."

Mr. Jaggers nodded. "But did you say 'told' or 'informed'?" he asked me, with his head on one side, and not looking at me, but looking in a listening way at the floor. "Told would seem to imply verbal communication. You can't have verbal communication with a man in New South Wales, you know."

"I will say, informed, Mr. Jaggers."

"Good."

"I have been informed by a person named Abel Magwitch, that he is the benefactor so long unknown to me."

"That is the man," said Mr. Jaggers, "—in New South Wales."

"And only he?" said I.

"And only he," said Mr. Jaggers.

"I am not so unreasonable, sir, as to think you at all responsible for my mistakes and wrong conclusions; but I always supposed it was Miss Havisham."

"As you say, Pip," returned Mr. Jaggers, turning his eyes upon me coolly, and taking a bite at his forefinger, "I am not at all responsible for that."

"And yet it looked so like it, sir," I pleaded with a downcast heart.

"Not a particle of evidence, Pip," said Mr. Jaggers, shaking his head and gathering up his skirts. "Take nothing on its looks; take everything on evidence. There's no better rule."

"I have no more to say," said I, with a sigh, after standing silent for a little while. "I have verified my information, and there's an end."

"And Magwitch—in New South Wales—having at last disclosed himself," said Mr. Jaggers, "you will comprehend, Pip, how rigidly throughout my communication with you I have always adhered to the strict line of fact. There has never been the least departure from the strict line of fact. You are quite aware of that?"

"Quite, sir."

"I communicated to Magwitch—in New South Wales—when he first wrote to me—from New South Wales—the caution that he must not expect me ever to deviate from the strict line of fact. I also communicated to him another caution. He appeared to me to have obscurely hinted in his letter at some distant idea of seeing you in England here. I cautioned him that I must hear no more of that; that he was not at all likely to obtain a pardon; that he was expatriated for the term of his natural life; and that his presenting him in this country would be an act of felony, rendering him liable to the extreme penalty of the law. I gave Magwitch that caution," said Mr. Jaggers, looking hard at me; "I wrote it to New South Wales. He guided himself by it, no doubt."

"No doubt," said I.

"I have been informed by Wemmick," pursued Mr. Jaggers, still looking hard at me, "that he has received a letter, under date Portsmouth, from a colonist of the name of Purvis, or——"

"Or Provis," I suggested.

"Or Provis—thank you, Pip. Perhaps it *is* Provis? Perhaps you know it's Provis?"

"Yes," said I.

"You know it's Provis. A letter, under date Portsmouth, from a colonist of the name of Provis, asking for the particulars of your address, on behalf of Magwitch. Wemmick sent him the particulars, I understand, by return of post. Probably it is through Provis that you have received the explanation of Magwitch—in New South Wales?"

"It came through Provis," I replied.

"Good day, Pip," said Mr. Jaggers, offering his hand; "glad to have seen you. In writing by post to Magwitch—in New South Wales—or in communicating with him through Provis, have the goodness to mention that the particulars and vouchers of our long account shall be sent to you, together with the balance ; for there is still a balance remaining. Good day, Pip ! "

We shook hands, and he looked hard at me as long as he could see me. I turned at the door, and he was still looking hard at me, while the two vile casts on the shelf seemed to be trying to get their eyelids open, and to force out of their swollen throats, " O, what a man he is ! "

Wemmick was out, and though he had been at his desk he could have done nothing for me. I went straight back to the Temple, where I found the terrible Provis drinking rum-and-water and smoking negro-head, in safety.

Next day the clothes I had ordered all came home, and he put them on. Whatever he put on, became him less (it dismally seemed to me) than what he had worn before. To my thinking there was something in him that made it hopeless to attempt to disguise him. The more I dressed him, and the better I dressed him, the more he looked like the slouching fugitive on the marshes. This effect on my anxious fancy was partly referable, no doubt, to his old face and manner growing more familiar to me : but I believed too that he dragged one of his legs as if there were still a weight of iron on it, and that from head to foot there was Convict in the very grain of the man.

The influences of his solitary hut-life were upon him besides, and gave him a savage air that no dress could tame ; added to these were the influences of his subsequent branded life among men, and, crowning all, his consciousness that he was dodging and hiding now. In all his ways of sitting and standing, and eating and drinking—of brooding about, in a high-shouldered reluctant style—of taking out his great horn-handled jack-knife and wiping it on his legs and cutting his food—of lifting light glasses and cups to his lips, as if they were clumsy pannikins—of chopping a wedge off his bread, and soaking up with it the last fragments of gravy round and round his plate, as if to make the most of an allowance, and then drying his fingers on it, and then swallowing it—in these ways and a thousand other small nameless instances arising every minute in the day, there was Prisoner, Felon, Bondsman, plain as plain could be.

It had been his own idea to wear that touch of powder, and I conceded the powder after overcoming the shorts. But I can compare the effect of it, when on, to nothing but the probable effect of rouge upon the dead ; so awful was the manner in which everything in him, that it was most desirable to repress, started through that thin layer of pretence, and seemed to come blazing out at the crown of his head. It was abandoned as soon as tried, and he wore his grizzled hair cut short.

Words cannot tell what a sense I had, at the same time, of the dreadful mystery that he was to me. When he fell asleep of an evening, with his knotted hands clenching the sides of the easy-chair, and his bald head tattooed with deep wrinkles falling forward on his breast, I would sit and look at him, wondering what he had done, and loading him with all the crimes in the Calendar, until the impulse was powerful on me to start up and fly from him. Every hour so increased my abhorrence of him, that I even think I might have yielded to this impulse in the first agonies of being so haunted, notwithstanding all he had done for me and the risk he ran, but for the knowledge that Herbert must soon come back. Once, I actually did start out of bed in the night, and begin to dress myself in my worst clothes, hurriedly intending to leave him there with everything else I possessed, and enlist for India as a private soldier.

I doubt if a ghost could have been more terrible to me, up in those lonely rooms in the long evenings and long nights, with the wind and the rain always rushing by. A ghost could not have been taken and hanged on my account, and the consideration that he could be, and the dread that he would be, were no small addition to my horrors. When he was not asleep, or playing a complicated kind of Patience with a ragged pack of cards of his own—a game that I never saw before or since, and in which he recorded his winnings by sticking his jack-knife into the table—when he was not engaged in either of these pursuits, he would ask me to read to him—" Foreign language, dear boy ! " While I complied, he, not comprehending a single word, would stand before the fire surveying me with the air of an Exhibitor, and I would see him, between the fingers of the hand with which I shaded my face, appealing in dumb show to the furniture to take notice of my proficiency. The imaginary student pursued by the misshapen creature he had impiously made, was not more wretched than I, pursued by the creature who had made me, and recoiling from him with a stronger repulsion, the more he admired me and the fonder he was of me.

This is written of, I am sensible, as if it had lasted a year. It lasted about five days. Expecting Herbert all the time, I dared not go out, except when I took Provis for an airing after dark. At length, one evening when dinner was over and I had dropped into a slumber quite worn out—for my nights had been agitated and my rest broken by fearful dreams—I was roused by the welcome footstep on the staircase. Provis, who had been asleep too, staggered up at the noise I made, and in an instant I saw his jack-knife shining in his hand.

"Quiet! It's Herbert!" I said; and Herbert came bursting in, with the airy freshness of six hundred miles of France upon him.

"Handel, my dear fellow, how are you, and again how are you, and again how are you? I seem to have been gone a twelvemonth! Why, so I must have been, for you have grown quite thin and pale! Handel, my——Halloa! I beg your pardon."

He was stopped in his running on and in his shaking hands with me, by seeing Provis. Provis, regarding him with a fixed attention, was slowly putting up his jack-knife, and groping in another pocket for something else.

"Herbert, my dear friend," said I, shutting the double doors, while Herbert stood staring and wondering, "something very strange has happened. This is—a visitor of mine."

"It's all right, dear boy!" said Provis, coming forward, with his little clasped black book, and then addressing himself to Herbert. "Take it in your right hand. Lord strike you dead on the spot, if ever you split in any way sumever. Kiss it!"

"Do so, as he wishes it," I said to Herbert. So Herbert, looking at me with a friendly uneasiness and amazement, complied, and Provis immediately shaking hands with him, said, "Now, you're on your oath, you know. And never believe me on mine, if Pip shan't make a gentleman on you!"

CHAPTER XLI

In vain should I attempt to describe the astonishment and disquiet of Herbert, when he and I and Provis sat down before the fire, and I recounted the whole of the secret. Enough that I saw my own feelings reflected in Herbert's face, and, not least among them, my repugnance towards the man who had done so much for me.

What would alone have set a division between that man and us, if there had been no other dividing circumstance, was his triumph in my story. Saving his troublesome sense of having been "low" on one occasion since his return—on which point he began to hold forth to Herbert, the moment my revelation was finished—he had no perception of the possibility of my finding any fault with my good fortune. His boast that he had made me a gentleman, and that he had come to see me support the character on his ample resources, was made for me quite as much as for himself. And that it was a highly agreeable boast to both of us, and that we must both be very proud of it, was a conclusion quite established in his own mind.

"Though, look'ee here, Pip's comrade," he said to Herbert, after having discoursed for some time, "I know very well that once since I come back—for half a minute—I've been low. I said to Pip, I knowed as I had been low. But don't you fret yourself on that score. I ain't made Pip a gentleman, and Pip ain't a-goin' to make you a gentleman, not fur me not to know what's due to ye both. Dear boy, and Pip's comrade, you two may count upon me always having a genteel muzzle on. Muzzled I have been since that half a minute when I was betrayed into lowness, muzzled I am at the present time, muzzled I ever will be."

Herbert said, "Certainly," but looked as if there were no specific consolation in this, and remained perplexed and dismayed. We were anxious for the time when he would go to his lodging, and leave us together, but he was evidently jealous of leaving us together, and sat late. It was midnight before I took him round to Essex-street, and saw him safely in at his own dark door. When it closed upon him, I experienced the first moment of relief I had known since the night of his arrival.

Never quite free from an uneasy remembrance of the man on the stairs, I had always looked about me in taking my guest out after dark, and in bringing him back; and I looked about me now. Difficult as it is in a large city to avoid the suspicion of being watched when the mind is conscious of danger in that regard, I could not persuade myself that any of the people within sight cared about my movements. The few who were passing, passed on their several ways, and the street was empty when I turned back into the Temple. Nobody had come out at the gate with us, nobody went in at the gate with me. As I crossed by the fountain, I saw his lighted back windows looking bright and quiet, and, when I stood for a few moments in the doorway of the building where I lived, before going up the stairs, Garden-court was as still and lifeless as the staircase was when I ascended it.

Herbert received me with open arms, and I had never felt before so blessedly what it is to have a friend. When he had spoken some sound words of sympathy and encouragement, we sat down to consider the question, What was to be done?

The chair that Provis had occupied still remaining where it had stood—for he had a barrack way with him of hanging about one spot, in one unsettled manner, and going through one round of observances with his pipe and his negro-head and his jack-knife and his pack of cards, and what not, as if it were all put down for him on a slate—I say, his chair remaining where it had stood, Herbert unconsciously took it, but next moment started out of it, pushed it away, and took another. He had no occasion to say, after that, that he had conceived an aversion for my patron, neither had I occasion to confess my own. We interchanged that confidence without shaping a syllable.

"What," said I to Herbert, when he was safe in another chair, "what is to be done?"

"My poor dear Handel," he replied, holding his head, "I am too stunned to think."

"So was I, Herbert, when the blow first fell. Still, something must be done. He is intent upon various new expenses—horses, and carriages, and lavish appearances of all kinds. He must be stopped somehow."

"You mean that you can't accept—— "

"How can I?" I interposed, as Herbert paused. "Think of him! Look at him!"

An involuntary shudder passed over both of us.

"Yet I am afraid the dreadful truth is, Herbert, that he is attached to me, strongly attached to me. Was there ever such a fate!"

"My poor dear Handel," Herbert repeated.

"Then," said I, "after all, stopping short here, never taking another penny from him, think what I owe him already! Then again: I am heavily in debt—very heavily for me, who have now no expectations—and I have been bred to no calling, and I am fit for nothing."

"Well, well, well!" Herbert remonstrated. "Don't say fit for nothing."

"What am I fit for? I know only one thing that I am fit for, and that is, to go for a soldier. And I might have gone, my dear Herbert, but for the prospect of taking counsel with your friendship and affection."

Of course I broke down there; and of course Herbert, beyond seizing a warm grip of my hand, pretended not to know it.

"Anyhow, my dear Handel," said he presently, "soldiering won't do. If you were to renounce this patronage and these favours, I suppose you would do so with some faint hope of one day repaying what you have already had. Not very strong, that hope, if you went soldiering. Besides, it's absurd. You would be infinitely better in Clarriker's house, small as it is. I am working up towards a partnership, you know."

Poor fellow! He little suspected with whose money.

"But there is another question," said Herbert. "This is an ignorant determined man, who has long had one fixed idea. More than that, he seems to me (I may misjudge him) to be a man of a desperate and fierce character."

"I know he is," I returned. "Let me tell you what evidence I have seen of it." And I told him what I had not mentioned in my narrative; of that encounter with the other convict.

"See, then," said Herbert; "think of this! He comes here at the peril of his life, for the realisation of his fixed idea. In the moment of realisation, after all his toil and waiting, you cut the ground from under his feet, destroy his idea, and make his gains worthless to him. Do you see nothing that he might do under the disappointment?"

"I have seen it, Herbert, and dreamed of it ever since the fatal night of his arrival. Nothing has been in my thoughts so distinctly as his putting himself in the way of being taken."

"Then you may rely upon it," said Herbert, "that there would be great danger of his doing it. That is his power over you as long as he remains in England, and that would be his reckless course if you forsook him."

I was so struck by the horror of this idea, which had weighed upon me from the first, and the working out of which would make me regard myself, in some sort, as his murderer, that I could not rest in my chair, but began pacing to and fro. I said to Herbert, meanwhile, that even if Provis were recognised and taken, in spite of himself, I should be wretched as the cause, however innocently. Yes; even though I was so wretched in having him at large and near me, and even though I would far rather have worked at the forge all the days of my life than I would ever have come to this!

But there was no raving off the question, What was to be done?

"The first and the main thing to be done," said Herbert, "is to get him out of England. You will have to go with him, and then he may be induced to go."

"But get him where I will, could I prevent his coming back?"

"My good Handel, is it not obvious that with Newgate in the next street, there must be far greater hazard in your breaking your mind to him and making him reckless, here, than elsewhere? If a pretext to get him away could be made out of that other convict, or out of anything else in his life, now."

"There again!" said I, stopping before Herbert, with my open hands held out, as if they contained the desperation of the case. "I know nothing of his life. It has almost made me mad to sit here of a night and see him before me, so bound up with my fortunes and misfortunes, and yet so unknown to me, except as the miserable wretch who terrified me two days in my childhood!"

Herbert got up, and linked his arm in mine, and we slowly walked to and fro together, studying the carpet.

"Handel," said Herbert, stopping, "you feel convinced that you can take no further benefits from him; do you?"

"Fully. Surely you would, too, if you were in my place?"

"And you feel convinced that you must break with him?"

"Herbert, can you ask me?"

"And you have, and are bound to have, that tenderness for the life he has risked on your account, that you must save him, if possible, from throwing it away. Then you must get him out of England before you stir a finger to extricate yourself. That done, extricate yourself, in Heaven's name, and we'll see it out together, dear old boy."

It was a comfort to shake hands upon it, and walk up and down again, with only that done.

"Now, Herbert," said I, "with reference to gaining some knowledge of his history. There is but one way that I know of. I must ask him point-blank."

"Yes. Ask him," said Herbert, "when we sit at breakfast in the morning." For, he had said, on taking leave of Herbert, that he would come to breakfast with us.

With this project formed, we went to bed. I had the wildest dreams concerning him, and woke unrefreshed; I woke, too, to recover the fear which I had lost in the night, of his being found out as a returned transport. Waking, I never lost that fear.

He came round at the appointed time, took out his jack-knife, and sat down to his meal. He was full of plans "for his gentleman's coming out strong, and like a gentleman," and urged me to begin speedily upon the pocket-book, which he had left in my possession. He considered the chambers and his own lodging as temporary residences, and advised me to look out at once for a "fashionable crib" near Hyde Park, in which he could have "a shake-down." When he had made an end of his breakfast, and was wiping his knife on his leg, I said to him, without a word of preface:

"After you were gone last night, I told my friend of the struggle that the soldiers found you engaged in on the marshes, when we came up. You remember?"

"Remember!" said he. "I think so!"

"We want to know something about that man—and about you. It is strange to know no more about either, and particularly you, than I was able to tell last night. Is not this as good a time as another for our knowing more?"

"Well!" he said, after consideration. "You're on your oath, you know, Pip's comrade?"

"Assuredly," replied Herbert.

"As to anything I say, you know," he insisted. "The oath applies to all."

"I understand it to do so."

"And look'ee here! Wotever I done, is worked out and paid for," he insisted again.

"So be it."

He took out his black pipe and was going to fill it with negro-head, when, looking at the tangle of tobacco in his hand, he seemed to think it might perplex the thread of his narrative. He put it back again, stuck his pipe in a button-hole of his coat, spread a hand on each knee, and, after turning an angry eye on the fire for a few silent moments, looked around at us and said what follows.

CHAPTER XLII

"Dear boy and Pip's comrade. I am not a going fur to tell you my life, like a song or a story-book. But to give it you short and handy, I'll put it at once into a mouthful of English. In jail and out of jail, in jail and out of jail, in jail and out of jail. There, you've got it. That's *my* life pretty much, down to such times as I got shipped off, arter Pip stood my friend.

"I've been done everything to, pretty well—except hanged. I've been locked up, as much as a silver tea-kittle. I've been carted here and carted there, and put out of this town and put out of that town, and stuck in the stocks, and whipped and worried and drove. I've no more notion where I was born than you have—if so much. I first become aware of myself, down in Essex, a thieving turnips for my living. Summun had run away from me—a man—a tinker—and he'd took the fire with him, and left me wery cold.

"I know'd my name to be Magwitch, chrisen'd Abel. How did I know it? Much as I know'd the birds' names in the hedges to be chaffinch, sparrer, thrush. I might have thought it was all lies together, only as the birds' names come out true, I supposed mine did.

"So fur as I could find, there warn't a soul that see young Abel Magwitch, with as little on him as in him, but wot caught fright at him, and either drove him off, or took him up. I was took up, took up, took up, to that extent that I reg'larly grow'd up took up.

"This is the way it was, that when I was a ragged little creetur as much to be pitied as ever I see (not that I looked in the glass, for there warn't many insides of furnished houses known to me), I got the name of being hardened. 'This is a terrible hardened one,' they says to prison wisitors, picking out me. 'May be said to live in jails, this boy.' Then they looked at me, and I looked at them, and they measured my head, some on 'em—they had better a measured my stomach—and others on 'em giv me tracts what I couldn't read, and made me speeches what I couldn't unnerstand. They always went on agen me about the Devil. But what the devil was I to do? I must put something into my stomach, mustn't I?—Howsomever, I'm a getting low, and I know what's due. Dear boy and Pip's comrade, don't you be afeerd of me being low.

"Tramping, begging, thieving, working sometimes when I could—though that warn't as often as you may think, till you put the question whether you would ha' been over-ready to give me work yourselves—a bit of a poacher, a bit of a labourer, a bit of a waggoner, a bit of a haymaker, a bit of a hawker, a bit of most things that don't pay and lead to trouble, I got to be a man. A deserting soldier in a Traveller's Rest, what lay hid up to the chin under a lot of taturs, learnt me to read; and a travelling Giant what signed his name at a penny a time learnt me to write. I warn't locked up as often now as formerly, but I wore out my good share of key-metal still.

"At Epsom races, a matter of over twenty year ago, I got acquainted wi' a man whose skull I'd crack wi' this poker, like the claw of a lobster, if I'd got it on this hob. His right name was Compeyson; and that's the man, dear boy, what you see me a pounding in the ditch, according to what you truly told your comrade arter I was gone last night.

"He set up fur a gentleman, this Compeyson, and he'd been to a public boarding-school and had learning. He was a smooth one to talk, and was a dab at the ways of gentle-folks. He was good-looking too. It was the night afore the great race, when I found him on the heath, in a booth that I know'd on. Him and some more was a sitting among the tables when I went in, and the landlord (which had a knowledge of me, and was a sporting one) called him out, and said, 'I think this is a man that might suit you'—meaning I was.

"Compeyson, he looks at me very noticing, and I look at him. He has a watch and a chain and a ring and a breast-pin and a handsome suit of clothes.

"'To judge from appearances, you're out of luck,' says Compeyson to me.

"'Yes, master, and I've never been in it much.' (I had come out of Kingston Jail last on a vagrancy committal. Not but what it might have been for something else; but it warn't.)

"'Luck changes,' says Compeyson; 'perhaps yours is going to change.'

"I says, 'I hope it may be so. There's room.'

"'What can you do?' says Compeyson.

"'Eat and drink,' I says; 'if you'll find the materials.'

"Compeyson laughed, looked at me again very noticing, giv me five shillings, and appointed me for next night. Same place.

"I went to Compeyson next night, same place, and Compeyson took me on to be his man and pardner. And what was Compeyson's business in which we was to go pardners? Compeyson's business was the swindling, hand-writing forging, stolen bank-note passing, and such-like. All sorts of traps as Compeyson could set with his head, and keep his own legs out of and get the profits from and let another man in for, was Compeyson's business. He'd no more heart than a iron file, he was as cold as death, and he had the head of the Devil afore mentioned.

"There was another in with Compeyson, as was called Arthur—not as being so chrisen'd, but as a surname. He was in a Decline, and was a shadow to look at. Him and Compeyson had been in a bad thing with a rich lady some years afore, and they'd made a pot of money by it; but Compeyson betted and gamed, and he'd have run through the king's taxes. So, Arthur was a dying and a dying poor and with the horrors on him, and Compeyson's wife (which Compeyson kicked mostly) was a having pity on him when she could, and Compeyson was a having pity on nothing and nobody.

"I might a took warning by Arthur, but I didn't; and I won't pretend I was partick'ler—for where 'ud be the good on it, dear boy and comrade? So I begun wi' Compeyson, and a poor tool I was in his hands. Arthur lived at the top of Compeyson's house (over nigh Brentford it was), and Compeyson kept a careful account agen him for board and lodging, in case he should ever get better to work it out. But Arthur soon settled the account. The second or third time as ever I see him, he come a tearing down into Compeyson's parlour late at night, in only a flannel gown, with his hair all in a sweat, and he says to Compeyson's wife, 'Sally, she really is up-stairs alonger me, now, and I can't get rid of her. She's all in white,' he says, 'wi' white flowers in her hair, and she's awful mad, and she's got a shroud hanging over her arm, and she says she'll put it on me at five in the morning.'

"Says Compeyson: 'Why, you fool, don't you know she's got a living body? And how should she be up there, without coming through the door, or in at the window, and up the stairs?'

"'I don't know how she's there,' says Arthur, shivering dreadful with the horrors, 'but she's standing in the corner at the foot of the bed, awful mad. And over where her heart's broke—_you_ broke it!—there's drops of blood.'

"Compeyson spoke hardy, but he was always a coward. 'Go up alonger this drivelling sick man,' he says to his wife, 'and, Magwitch, lend her a hand, will you?' But he never come nigh himself.

"Compeyson's wife and me took him up to bed agen, and he raved most dreadful. 'Why look at her!' he cries out. 'She's a shaking the shroud at me! Don't you see her? Look at her eyes! Ain't it awful to see her so mad?' Next, he cries, 'She'll put it on me, and then I'm done for! Take it away from her, take it away!' And then he catched hold of us, and kep on a talking to her, and answering of her, till I half believed I see her myself.

"Compeyson's wife, being used to him, give him some liquor to get the horrors off, and by-and-by he quieted. 'Oh, she's gone! Has her keeper been for her?' he says. 'Yes,' says Compeyson's wife. 'Did you tell him to lock and bar her in?' 'Yes.' 'And to take that ugly thing away from her?' 'Yes, yes, all right.' 'You're a good creetur,' he says, 'don't leave me, whatever you do, and thank you!'

"He rested pretty quiet till it might want a few minutes of five, and then he starts up with a scream, and screams out, 'Here she is! She's got the shroud again. She's unfolding it. She's coming out of the corner. She's coming to the bed. Hold me, both on you—one of each side—don't let her touch me with it. Hah! She missed me that time. Don't let her throw it over my shoulders. Don't let her lift me up to get it round me. She's lifting me up. Keep me down!' Then he lifted himself up hard, and was dead.

"Compeyson took it easy as a good riddance for both sides. Him and me was soon busy, and first he swore me (being ever artful) on my own book—this here little black book, dear boy, what I swore your comrade on.

"Not to go into the things that Compeyson planned, and I done—which 'ud take a week—I'll simply say to you, dear boy, and Pip's comrade, that that man got me into such nets as made me his black slave. I was always in debt to him, always under his thumb, always a working, always a getting into danger. He was younger than me, but he'd got craft, and he'd got learning, and he overmatched me five hundred times told and no mercy. My Missis as I had the hard time wi'——Stop though! I ain't brought *her* in——"

He looked about him in a confused way, as if he had lost his place in the book of his remembrance; and he turned his face to the fire, and spread his hands broader on his knees, and lifted them off and put them on again.

"There ain't no need to go into it," he said, looking round once more. "The time wi' Compeyson was a'most as hard a time as ever I had; that said, all's said. Did I tell you as I was tried, alone, for misdemeanour, while with Compeyson?"

I answered, No.

"Well!" he said, "I *was*, and got convicted. As to took up on suspicion, that was twice or three times in the four or five year that it lasted; but evidence was wanting. At last, me and Compeyson was both committed for felony—on a charge of putting stolen notes in circulation—and there was other charges behind. Compeyson says to me, 'Separate defences, no communication,' and that was all. And I was so miserable poor, that I sold all the clothes I had, except what hung on my back, afore I could get Jaggers.

"When we was put in the dock, I noticed first of all what a gentleman Compeyson looked, wi' his curly hair and his black clothes and his white pocket-handkercher, and what a common sort of a wretch I looked. When the prosecution opened and the evidence was put short, afore-hand, I noticed how heavy it all bore on me, and how light on him. When the evidence was giv in the box, I noticed how it was always me that had come for'ard, and could be swore to, how it was always me that the money had been paid to, how it was always me that had seemed to work the thing and get the profit. But, when the defence come on, then I see the plan plainer; for, says the counsellor for Compeyson, 'My lord and gentlemen, here you has afore you, side by side, two persons as your eyes can separate wide; one, the younger, well brought up, who will be spoke to as such; one, the elder, ill brought up, who will be spoke to as such; one, the younger, seldom if ever seen in these here transactions, and only suspected; t'other, the elder, always seen in 'em and always wi' his guilt brought home. Can you doubt, if there is but one in it, which is the one, and if there is two in it, which is much the worst one?' And such-like. And when it come to character, warn't it Compeyson as had been to school, and warn't it his schoolfellows as was in this position and in that, and warn't it him as had been know'd by witnesses in such clubs and societies, and nowt to his disadvantage? And warn't it me as had been tried afore, and as had been know'd up hill and down dale in Bridewells and Lock-Ups? And when it come to speech-making, warn't it Compeyson as could speak to 'em wi' his face dropping every now and then into his white pocket-handkercher—ah! and wi' verses in his speech, too—and warn't it me as could only say, 'Gentlemen, this man at my side is a most precious rascal'? And when the verdict come, warn't it Compeyson as was recommended to mercy on account of good character and bad company, and giving up all the information he could agen me, and warn't it me as got never a word but Guilty? And when I says to Compeyson, 'Once out of this court, I'll smash that face of yourn!' ain't it Compeyson as prays the Judge to be protected, and gets two turnkeys stood betwixt us? And when we're sentenced, ain't it him as gets seven year, and me fourteen, and ain't it him as the Judge is sorry for, because he might a done so well, and ain't it me as the Judge perceives to be a old offender of wiolent passion, likely to come to worse?"

He had worked himself into a state of great excitement, but he checked it, took two or three short breaths, swallowed as often, and stretching out his hand towards me, said, in a reassuring manner, "I ain't a going to be low, dear boy!"

He had so heated himself that he took out his handkerchief and wiped his face and head and neck and hands, before he could go on.

"I had said to Compeyson that I'd smash that face of his, and I swore Lord smash mine! to do it. We was in the same prison-ship, but I couldn't get at him for long, though I tried. At last I come behind him and hit him on the cheek to turn him round and get a smashing one at him, when I was seen and seized. The black-hole of that ship warn't a strong one, to a judge of black-holes that could swim and dive. I escaped to the shore, and I was a hiding among the graves there, envying them as was in 'em and all over, when I first see my boy!"

He regarded me with a look of affection that made him almost abhorrent to me again, though I had felt great pity for him.

"By my boy, I was giv to understand as Compeyson was out on them marshes too. Upon my soul, I half believe he escaped in his terror, to get quit of me, not knowing it was me as had got ashore. I hunted him down. I smashed his face. 'And now,' says I, 'as the worst thing I can do, caring nothing for myself, I'll drag you back.' And I'd have swum off, towing him by the hair, if it had come to that, and I'd a got him aboard without the soldiers.

"Of course he'd much the best of it to the last—his character was so good. He had escaped when he was made half-wild by me and my murderous intentions; and his punishment was light. I was put in irons, brought to trial again, and sent for life. I didn't stop for life, dear boy and Pip's comrade, being here."

He wiped himself again, as he had done before, and then slowly took his tangle of tobacco from his pocket, and plucked his pipe from his button-hole, and slowly filled it, and began to smoke.

"Is he dead?" I asked after a silence.

"Is who dead, dear boy?"

"Compeyson."

"He hopes *I* am, if he's alive, you may be sure," with a fierce look. "I never heard no more of him."

Herbert had been writing with his pencil in the cover of a book. He softly pushed the book over to me, as Provis stood smoking with his eyes on the fire, and I read in it:

"Young Havisham's name was Arthur. Compeyson is the man who professed to be Miss Havisham's lover."

I shut the book and nodded slightly to Herbert, and put the book by; but we neither of us said anything, and both looked at Provis as he stood smoking by the fire.

CHAPTER XLIII

WHY should I pause to ask how much of my shrinking from Provis might be traced to Estella? Why should I loiter on my road, to compare the state of mind in which I had tried to rid myself of the stain of the prison before meeting her at the coach-office, with the state of mind in which I now reflected on the abyss between Estella in her pride and beauty, and the returned transport whom I harboured? The road would be none the smoother for it, the end would be none the better for it; he would not be helped, nor I extenuated.

A new fear had been engendered in my mind by his narrative; or rather, his narrative had given form and purpose to the fear that was already there. If Compeyson were alive and should discover his return, I could hardly doubt the consequence. That Compeyson stood in mortal fear of him, neither of the two could know much better than I; and that any such man as that man had been described to be, would hesitate to release himself for good from a dreaded enemy by the safe means of becoming an informer, was scarcely to be imagined.

Never had I breathed, and never would I breathe—or so I resolved—a word of Estella to Provis. But, I said to Herbert that before I could go abroad, I must see both Estella and Miss Havisham. This was when we were left alone on the night of the day when Provis told us his story. I resolved to go out to Richmond next day, and I went.

On my presenting myself at Mrs. Brandley's, Estella's maid was called to tell me that Estella had gone into the country. Where? To Satis House, as usual. Not as usual, I said, for she had never yet gone there without me; when was she coming back? There was an air of reservation in the answer which increased my perplexity, and the answer was that her maid believed she was only coming back at all for a little while. I could make nothing of this, except that it was meant that I should make nothing of it, and I went home again in complete discomfiture.

Another night-consultation with Herbert after Provis was gone home (I always took him home, and always looked well about me), led us to the conclusion that nothing should be said about going abroad until I came back from Miss Havisham's. In the meantime Herbert and I were to consider separately what it would be best to say; whether we should devise any pretence of being afraid that he was under suspicious observation; or whether I, who had never yet been abroad, should propose an expedition. We both knew that I had but to propose anything, and he would consent. We agreed that his remaining many days in his present hazard was not to be thought of.

Next day, I had the meanness to feign that I was under a binding promise to go down to Joe; but I was capable of almost any meanness towards Joe or his name. Provis was to be strictly careful while I was gone, and Herbert was to take the charge of him that I had taken. I was to be absent only one night, and, on my return, the gratification of his impatience for my starting as a gentleman on a greater scale was to be begun. It occurred to me then, and as I afterwards found to Herbert also, that he might be best got away across the water, on that pretence—as, to make purchases, or the like.

Having thus cleared the way for my expedition to Miss Havisham's, I set off by the early morning coach before it was yet light, and was out in the open country-road when the day came creeping on, halting and whimpering and shivering, and wrapped in patches of cloud and rags of mist, like a beggar. When we drove up to the Blue Boar after a drizzly ride, whom should I see come out under the gateway, toothpick in hand, to look at the coach, but Bentley Drummle!

As he pretended not to see me, I pretended not to see him. It was a very lame pretence on both sides; the lamer, because we both went into the coffee-room, where he had just finished his breakfast, and where I had ordered mine. It was poisonous to me to see him in the town, for I very well knew why he had come there.

Pretending to read a smeary newspaper long out of date, which had nothing half so legible in its local news, as the foreign matter of coffee, pickles, fish-sauces, gravy, melted butter, and wine, with which it was sprinkled all over, as if it had taken the measles in a highly irregular form, I sat at my table while he stood before the fire. By degrees it became an enormous injury to me that he stood before the fire. And I got up, determined to have my share of it. I had to put my hands behind his legs for the poker when I went up to the fireplace to stir the fire, but still pretended not to know him.

"Is this a cut?" said Mr. Drummle.

"Oh?" said I, poker in hand; "it's you, is it? How do you do? I was wondering who it was, who kept the fire off."

With that I poked tremendously, and having done so, planted myself side by side with Mr. Drummle, my shoulders squared, and my back to the fire.

"You have just come down?" said Mr. Drummle, edging me a little away with his shoulder.

"Yes," said I, edging *him* a little away with *my* shoulder.

"Beastly place," said Drummle—"Your part of the country, I think?"

"Yes," I assented. "I am told it's very like your Shropshire."

"Not in the least like it," said Drummle.

Here Mr. Drummle looked at his boots and I looked at mine, and then Mr. Drummle looked at my boots and I looked at his.

"Have you been here long?" I asked, determined not to yield an inch of the fire.

"Long enough to be tired of it," returned Drummle, pretending to yawn, but equally determined.

"Do you stay here long?"

"Can't say," answered Mr. Drummle. "Do you?"

"Can't say," said I.

I felt here, through a tingling in my blood, that if Mr. Drummle's shoulder had claimed another hair's breadth of room, I should have jerked him into the window; equally, that if my shoulder had urged a similar claim, Mr. Drummle would have jerked me into the nearest box. He whistled a little. So did I.

"Large tract of marshes about here, I believe?" said Drummle.

"Yes. What of that?" said I.

this man, whose back was towards me, reminded me of Orlick.

Too heavily out of sorts to care much at the time whether it were he or no, or after all to touch the breakfast, I washed the weather and the journey from my face and hands, and went out to the memorable old house that it would have been so much the better for me never to have entered, never to have seen.

CHAPTER XLIV

In the room where the dressing-table stood, and where the wax candles burnt on the wall, I found Miss Havisham and Estella; Miss Havisham seated on a settee near the fire, and Estella on a cushion at her feet. Estella was knitting, and Miss Havisham was looking on. They both raised their eyes as I went in, and both saw an alteration in me. I derived that from the look they interchanged.

"And what wind," said Miss Havisham, "blows you here, Pip?"

Though she looked steadily at me, I saw that she was rather confused. Estella, pausing a moment in her knitting with her eyes upon me, and then going on, I fancied that I read in the action of her fingers, as plainly as if she had told me in the dumb alphabet, that she perceived I had discovered my real benefactor.

"Miss Havisham," said I, "I went to Richmond yesterday, to speak to Estella; and finding that some wind had blown *her* here, I followed."

Miss Havisham motioning to me for the third or fourth time to sit down, I took the chair by the dressing-table, which I had often seen her occupy. With all that ruin at my feet and about me, it seemed a natural place for me, that day.

"What I had to say to Estella, Miss Havisham, I will say before you, presently—in a few moments. It will not surprise you, it will not displease you. I am as unhappy as you can ever have meant me to be."

Miss Havisham continued to look steadily at me. I could see in the action of Estella's fingers as they worked, that she attended to what I said: but she did not look up.

"I have found out who my patron is. It is not a fortunate discovery, and is not likely ever to enrich me in reputation, station, fortune, anything. There are reasons why I must say no more of that. It is not my secret, but another's."

As I was silent for a while, looking at Estella and con-

sidering how to go on, Miss Havisham repeated, "It is not your secret, but another's. Well?"

"When you first caused me to be brought here, Miss Havisham; when I belonged to the village over yonder, that I wish I had never left; I suppose I did really come here, as any other chance boy might have come—as a kind of servant, to gratify a want or a whim, and to be paid for it?"

"Ay, Pip," replied Miss Havisham, steadily nodding her head; "you did."

"And that Mr. Jaggers——"

"Mr. Jaggers," said Miss Havisham, taking me up in a firm tone, "had nothing to do with it, and knew nothing of it. His being my lawyer, and his being the lawyer of your patron, is a coincidence. He holds the same relation towards numbers of people, and it might easily arise. Be that as it may, it did arise, and was not brought about by any one."

Any one might have seen in her haggard face that there was no suppression or evasion so far.

"But when I fell into the mistake I have so long remained in, at least you led me on?" said I.

"Yes," she returned, again nodding steadily, "I let you go on."

"Was that kind?"

"Who am I," cried Miss Havisham, striking her stick upon the floor and flashing into wrath so suddenly that Estella glanced up at her in surprise, "who am I, for God's sake, that I should be kind?"

It was a weak complaint to have made, and I had not meant to make it. I told her so, as she sat brooding over this outburst.

"Well, well, well!" she said. "What else?"

"I was liberally paid for my old attendance here," I said, to soothe her, "in being apprenticed, and I have asked these questions only for my own information. What follows has another (and I hope more disinterested) purpose. In humouring my mistake, Miss Havisham, you punished—practised on—perhaps you will supply whatever term expresses your intention, without offence—your self-seeking relations?"

"I did. Why, they would have it so! So would you. What has been my history, that I should be at the pains of entreating either them or you not to have it so! You made your own snares. I never made them."

Waiting until she was quiet again—for this, too, flashed out of her in a wild and sudden way—I went on.

"I have been thrown among one family of your relations, Miss Havisham, and have been constantly among them since I went to London. I know them to have been as honestly under my delusion as I myself. And I should be false and base if I did not tell you, whether it is acceptable to you or no, and whether you are inclined to give credence to it or no, that you deeply wrong both Mr. Matthew Pocket and his son Herbert, if you suppose them to be otherwise than generous, upright, open, and incapable of anything designing or mean."

"They are your friends," said Miss Havisham.

"They made themselves my friends," said I, "when they supposed me to have superseded them; and when Sarah Pocket, Miss Georgiana, and Mistress Camilla were not my friends, I think."

This contrasting of them with the rest seemed, I was glad to see, to do them good with her. She looked at me keenly for a little while, and then said quietly:

"What do you want for them?"

"Only," said I, "that you would not confound them with the others. They may be of the same blood, but, believe me, they are not of the same nature."

Still looking at me keenly, Miss Havisham repeated:

"What do you want for them?"

"I am not so cunning, you see," I said in answer, conscious that I reddened a little, "as that I could hide from you, even if I desired, that I do want something. Miss Havisham, if you could spare the money to do my friend Herbert a lasting service in life, but which from the nature of the case must be done without his knowledge, I could show you how."

"Why must it be done without his knowledge?" she asked, settling her hands upon her stick, that she might regard me the more attentively.

"Because," said I, "I began the service myself, more than two years ago, without his knowledge, and I don't want to be betrayed. Why I fail in my ability to finish it, I cannot explain. It is a part of the secret which is another person's and not mine."

She gradually withdrew her eyes from me, and turned them on the fire. After watching it for what appeared in

the silence and by the light of the slowly wasting candles to be a long time, she was roused by the collapse of some of the red coals, and looked towards me again—at first, vacantly—then, with a gradually concentrating attention. All this time, Estella knitted on. When Miss Havisham had fixed her attention on me, she said, speaking as if there had been no lapse in our dialogue:

"What else?"

"Estella," said I, turning to her now, and trying to command my trembling voice, "you know I love you. You know that I have loved you long and dearly."

She raised her eyes to my face, on being thus addressed, and her fingers plied their work, and she looked at me with an unmoved countenance. I saw that Miss Havisham glanced from me to her, and from her to me.

"I should have said this sooner, but for my long mistake. It induced me to hope that Miss Havisham meant us for one another. While I thought you could not help yourself, as it were, I refrained from saying it. But I must say it now."

Preserving her unmoved countenance, and with her fingers still going, Estella shook her head.

"I know," said I, in answer to that action; "I know. I have no hope that I shall ever call you mine, Estella. I am ignorant what may become of me very soon, how poor I may be, or where I may go. Still, I love you. I have loved you ever since I first saw you in this house."

Looking at me perfectly unmoved and with her fingers busy, she shook her head again.

"It would have been cruel in Miss Havisham, horribly cruel, to practise on the susceptibility of a poor boy, and to torture me through all these years with a vain hope and an idle pursuit, if she had reflected on the gravity of what she did. But I think she did not. I think that in the endurance of her own trial, she forgot mine, Estella."

I saw Miss Havisham put her hand to her heart and hold it there, as she sat looking by turns at Estella and at me.

"It seems," said Estella, very calmly, "that there are sentiments, fancies—I don't know how to call them—which I am not able to comprehend. When you say you love me, I know what you mean, as a form of words; but nothing more. You address nothing in my breast, you touch nothing there. I don't care for what you say at all. I have tried to warn you of this; now, have I not?"

I said in a miserable manner, "Yes."

"Yes. But you would not be warned, for you thought I did not mean it. Now, did you not think so?"

"I thought and hoped you could not mean it. You, so young, untried, and beautiful, Estella! Surely it is not in Nature."

"It is in *my* nature," she returned. And then she added, with a stress upon the words, "It is in the nature formed within me. I make a great difference between you and all other people when I say so much. I can do no more."

"Is it not true," said I, "that Bentley Drummle is in town here, and pursuing you?"

"It is quite true," she replied, referring to him with the indifference of utter contempt.

"That you encourage him, and ride out with him, and that he dines with you this very day?"

She seemed a little surprised that I should know it, but again replied, "Quite true."

"You cannot love him, Estella?"

Her fingers stopped for the first time, as she retorted rather angrily, "What have I told you? Do you still think, in spite of it, that I do not mean what I say?"

"You would never marry him, Estella?"

She looked towards Miss Havisham, and considered for a moment with her work in her hands. Then she said, "Why not tell you the truth? I am going to be married to him."

I dropped my face into my hands, but was able to control myself better than I could have expected, considering what agony it gave me to hear her say those words. When I raised my face again, there was such a ghastly look upon Miss Havisham's that it impressed me, even in my passionate hurry and grief.

"Estella, dearest, dearest Estella, do not let Miss Havisham lead you into this fatal step. Put me aside for ever— you have done so, I well know—but bestow yourself on some worthier person than Drummle. Miss Havisham gives you to him, as the greatest slight and injury that could be done to the many far better men who admire you, and to the few who truly love you. Among those few, there may be one who loves you even as dearly, though he has not loved you as long, as I. Take him, and I can bear it better for your sake!"

My earnestness awoke a wonder in her that seemed
as if it would have been touched with compassion, if she
could have rendered me at all intelligible to her own
mind.

"I am going," she said again, in a gentler voice, "to be
married to him. The preparations for my marriage are
making, and I shall be married soon. Why do you in-
juriously introduce the name of my mother by adoption?
It is my own act."

"Your own act, Estella, to fling yourself away upon a
brute?"

"On whom should I fling myself away?" she retorted,
with a smile. "Should I fling myself away upon the man
who would the soonest feel (if people do feel such things)
that I took nothing to him? There! It is done. I shall
do well enough, and so will my husband. As to leading me
into what you call this fatal step, Miss Havisham would have
had me wait, and not marry yet; but I am tired of the life
I have led, which has very few charms for me, and I am
willing enough to change it. Say no more. We shall never
understand each other."

"Such a mean brute, such a stupid brute!" I urged in
despair.

"Don't be afraid of my being a blessing to him," said
Estella; "I shall not be that. Come! Here is my hand.
Do we part on this, you visionary boy—— or man?"

"O Estella!" I answered, as my bitter tears fell fast on
her hand, do what I would to restrain them; "even if I
remained in England and could hold my head up with the
rest, how could I see you Drummle's wife?"

"Nonsense," she returned, "nonsense. This will pass in
no time."

"Never, Estella!"

"You will get me out of your thoughts in a week."

"Out of my thoughts! You are part of my existence, part
of myself. You have been in every line I have ever read,
since I first came here, the rough common boy whose poor
heart you wounded even then. You have been in every
prospect I have ever seen since—on the river, on the sails
of the ships, on the marshes, in the clouds, in the light, in
the darkness, in the wind, in the woods, in the sea, in the
streets. You have been the embodiment of every graceful
fancy that my mind has ever become acquainted with. The

stones of which the strongest London buildings are made, are not more real, or more impossible to be displaced by your hands, than your presence and influence have been to me, there and everywhere, and will be. Estella, to the last hour of my life, you cannot choose but remain part of my character, part of the little good in me, part of the evil. But, in this separation I associate you only with the good, and I will faithfully hold you to that always, for you must have done me far more good than harm, let me feel now what sharp distress I may. O God bless you, God forgive you!"

In what ecstasy of unhappiness I got these broken words out of myself, I don't know. The rhapsody welled up within me, like blood from an inward wound, and gushed out. I held her hand to my lips some lingering moments, and so I left her. But ever afterwards, I remembered—and soon afterwards with stronger reason—that while Estella looked at me merely with incredulous wonder, the spectral figure of Miss Havisham, her hand still covering her heart, seemed all resolved into a ghastly stare of pity and remorse.

All done, all gone! So much was done and gone, that when I went out at the gate, the light of day seemed of a darker colour than when I went in. For a while, I hid myself among some lanes and by-paths, and then struck off to walk all the way to London. For, I had by that time come to myself so far, as to consider that I could not go back to the inn and see Drummle there; that I could not bear to sit upon the coach and be spoken to; that I could do nothing half so good for myself as tire myself out.

It was past midnight when I crossed London Bridge. Pursuing the narrow intricacies of the streets which at that time tended westward near the Middlesex shore of the river, my readiest access to the Temple was close by the river-side, through Whitefriars. I was not expected till to-morrow, but I had my keys, and, if Herbert were gone to bed, could get to bed myself without disturbing him.

As it seldom happened that I came in at that Whitefriars gate after the Temple was closed, and as I was very muddy and weary, I did not take it ill that the night-porter examined me with much attention as he held the gate a little way open for me to pass in. To help his memory I mentioned my name.

"I was not quite sure, sir, but I thought so. Here's a

note, sir. The messenger that brought it said, would you be so good as read it by my lantern?"

Much surprised by the request, I took the note. It was directed to Philip Pip, Esquire, and on the top of the superscription were the words, "PLEASE READ THIS HERE." I opened it, the watchman holding up his light, and read inside, in Wemmick's writing:

"DON'T GO HOME."

CHAPTER XLV

TURNING from the Temple gate as soon as I had read the warning, I made the best of my way to Fleet-street, and there got a late hackney chariot and drove to the Hummums in Covent Garden. In those times a bed was always to be got there at any hour of the night, and the chamberlain, letting me in at his ready wicket, lighted the candle next in order on his shelf, and showed me straight into the bedroom next in order on his list. It was a sort of vault on the ground floor at the back, with a despotic monster of a four-post bedstead in it, straddling over the whole place, putting one of his arbitrary legs into the fireplace, and another into the doorway, and squeezing the wretched little washing-stand in quite a Divinely Righteous manner.

As I had asked for a night-light, the chamberlain had brought me in, before he left me, the good old constitutional rush-light of those virtuous days—an object like the ghost of a walking-cane, which instantly broke its back if it were touched, which nothing could ever be lighted at, and which was placed in solitary confinement at the bottom of a high tin tower, perforated with round holes that made a staringly wide-awake pattern on the walls. When I had got into bed, and lay there, footsore, weary, and wretched, I found that I could no more close my own eyes than I could close the eyes of this foolish Argus. And thus, in the gloom and death of the night, we stared at one another.

What a doleful night ! How anxious, how dismal, how long ! There was an inhospitable smell in the room, of cold soot and hot dust ; and, as I looked up into the corners of the tester over my head, I thought what a number of blue-bottle flies from the butcher's, and earwigs from the market, and grubs from the country, must be holding on up there, lying by for next summer. This led me to speculate whether any of them ever tumbled down, and then I fancied that I felt light falls on my face—a disagreeable turn of thought, suggesting other and more objectionable approaches up my back. When I had lain awake a little while, those extraordinary voices with which silence teems, began to make themselves audible. The closet whispered, the fireplace sighed, the little washing-stand ticked, and one guitar-string played occasionally in the chest of drawers. At about the same time, the eyes on the wall acquired a new expression, and in every one of those staring rounds I saw written, DON'T GO HOME.

Whatever night-fancies and night-noises crowded on me, they never warded off this DON'T GO HOME. It plaited itself into whatever I thought of, as a bodily pain would have done. Not long before, I had read in the newspapers how a gentleman unknown had come to the Hummums in the night, and had gone to bed, and had destroyed himself, and had been found in the morning weltering in blood. It came into my head that he must have occupied this very vault of mine, and I got out of bed to assure myself that there were no red marks about; then opened the door to look out into the passages, and cheer myself with the companionship of a distant light, near which I knew the chamberlain to be dozing. But all this time, why I was not to go home, and what had happened at home, and when I should go home, and whether Provis was safe at home, were questions occupying my mind so busily, that one might have supposed there could be no more room in it for any other theme. Even when I thought of Estella, and how we had parted that day for ever, and when I recalled all the circumstances of our parting, and all her looks and tones, and the action of her fingers while she knitted—even then I was pursuing, here and there and everywhere, the caution Don't go home. When at last I dozed, in sheer exhaustion of mind and body, it became a vast shadowy verb which I had to conjugate, Imperative mood, present tense: Do not thou go home, let him not go home, let us not go home, do not ye or you go home, let not them go home. Then, potentially: I may not and I cannot go home; and I might not, could not, would not, and should not go home ; until I felt that I was going distracted, and rolled over on the pillow, and looked at the staring rounds upon the wall again.

I had left directions that I was to be called at seven ; for it was plain that I must see Wemmick before seeing any one else, and equally plain that this was a case in which his Walworth sentiments, only, could be taken. It was a relief to get out of the room where the night had been so miserable, and I needed no second knocking at the door to startle me from my uneasy bed.

The Castle battlements arose upon my view at eight o'clock. The little servant happening to be entering the fortress with two hot rolls, I passed through the postern and crossed the drawbridge, in her company, and so came without announcement into the presence of Wemmick as he was making tea for himself and the Aged. An open door afforded a perspective view of the Aged in bed.

"Halloa, Mr. Pip!" said Wemmick. "You did come home, then?"

"Yes," I returned; "but I didn't go home."

"That's all right," said he, rubbing his hands. "I left a note for you at each of the Temple gates, on the chance. Which gate did you come to?"

I told him.

"I'll go round to the others in the course of the day and destroy the notes," said Wemmick; "it's a good rule never to leave documentary evidence if you can help it, because you don't know when it may be put in. I'm going to take a liberty with you—*Would* you mind toasting this sausage for the Aged P. ?"

I said I should be delighted to do it.

"Then you can go about your work, Mary Anne," said Wemmick to the little servant; "which leaves us to ourselves, don't you see, Mr. Pip?" he added, winking, as she disappeared.

I thanked him for his friendship and caution, and our discourse proceeded in a low tone, while I toasted the Aged's sausage and he buttered the crumb of the Aged's roll.

"Now, Mr. Pip, you know," said Wemmick, "you and I understand one another. We are in our private and personal capacities, and we have been engaged in a confidential transaction before to-day. Official sentiments are one thing. We are extra-official."

I cordially assented. I was so very nervous, that I had already lighted the Aged's sausage like a torch, and been obliged to blow it out.

"I accidentally heard, yesterday morning," said Wemmick, "being in a certain place where I once took you— even between you and me, it's as well not to mention names when avoidable——"

"Much better not," said I.   "I understand you."

"I heard there by chance, yesterday morning," said Wemmick, "that a certain person not altogether of un-colonial pursuits, and not unpossessed of portable property—I don't know who it may really be—we won't name this person——"

"Not necessary," said I.

"—had made some little stir in a certain part of the world where a good many people go, not always in gratifica-tion of their own inclinations, and not quite irrespective of the government expense——"

In watching his face, I made quite a firework of the Aged's sausage, and greatly discomposed both my own attention and Wemmick's; for which I apologised.

"—by disappearing from such place, and being no more heard of thereabouts.   From which," said Wemmick, "con-jectures had been raised and theories formed.   I also heard that you at your chambers in Garden-court, Temple, had been watched, and might be watched again."

"By whom?" said I.

"I wouldn't go into that," said Wemmick, evasively, "it might clash with official responsibilities.   I heard it, as I have in my time heard other curious things in the same place.   I don't tell it you on information received.   I heard it."

He took the toasting-fork and sausage from me as he spoke, and set forth the Aged's breakfast neatly on a little tray.   Previous to placing it before him, he went into the Aged's room with a clean white cloth, and tied the same under the old gentleman's chin, and propped him up, and put his night-cap on one side, and gave him quite a rakish air.   Then, he placed his breakfast before him with great care, and said, "All right, ain't you, Aged P.?"   To which the cheerful Aged replied, "All right, John, my boy, all right!"   As there seemed to be a tacit understanding that the Aged was not in a presentable state, and was there-fore to be considered invisible, I made a pretence of being in complete ignorance of these proceedings.

"This watching of me at my chambers (which I have once had reason to suspect)," I said to Wemmick when he came back, "is inseparable from the person to whom you have adverted; is it?"

Wemmick looked very serious.   "I couldn't undertake to

say that, of my own knowledge. I mean, I couldn't undertake to say it was at first. But it either is, or it will be, or
it's in great danger of being."

As I saw that he was restrained by fealty to Little Britain
from saying as much as he could, and as I knew with thankfulness to him how far out of his way he went to say what
he did, I could not press him. But I told him, after a little
meditation over the fire, that I would like to ask him a
question, subject to his answering or not answering, as he
deemed right, and sure that his course would be right. He
paused in his breakfast, and crossing his arms, and pinching
his shirt-sleeves (his notion of indoor comfort was to sit
without any coat), he nodded to me once, to put my
question.

"You have heard of a man of bad character, whose true
name is Compeyson?"

He answered with one other nod.

"Is he living?"

One other nod.

"Is he in London?"

He gave me one other nod, compressed the post-office
exceedingly, gave me one last nod, and went on with his
breakfast.

"Now," said Wemmick, "questioning being over;" which
he emphasised and repeated for my guidance; "I come to
what I did, after hearing what I heard. I went to Garden-
court to find you; not finding you, I went to Clarriker's to
find Mr. Herbert."

"And him you found?" said I, with great anxiety.

"And him I found. Without mentioning any names or
going into any details, I gave him to understand that if he
was aware of anybody—Tom, Jack, or Richard—being about
the chambers, or about the immediate neighbourhood, he had
better get Tom, Jack, or Richard, out of the way while you
were out of the way."

"He would be greatly puzzled what to do?"

"He *was* puzzled what to do; not the less, because I gave
him my opinion that it was not safe to try to get Tom, Jack,
or Richard, too far out of the way at present. Mr. Pip, I'll
tell you something. Under existing circumstances there is
no place like a great city when you are once in it. Don't
break cover too soon. Lie close. Wait till things slacken,
before you try the open, even for foreign air."

I thanked him for his valuable advice, and asked him what Herbert had done?

"Mr. Herbert," said Wemmick, "after being all of a heap for half an hour, struck out a plan. He mentioned to me as a secret that he is courting a young lady who has, as no doubt you are aware, a bedridden Pa. Which Pa, having been in the Purser line of life, lies a-bed in a bow-window where he can see the ships sail up and down the river. You are acquainted with the young lady, most probably?"

"Not personally," said I.

The truth was, that she had objected to me as an expensive companion who did Herbert no good, and that, when Herbert had first proposed to present me to her, she had received the proposal with such very moderate warmth, that Herbert had felt himself obliged to confide the state of the case to me, with a view to the lapse of a little time before I made her acquaintance. When I had begun to advance Herbert's prospects by stealth, I had been able to bear this with cheerful philosophy; he and his affianced, for their part, had naturally not been very anxious to introduce a third person into their interviews; and thus, although I was assured that I had risen in Clara's esteem, and although the young lady and I had long regularly interchanged messages and remembrances by Herbert, I had never seen her. However, I did not trouble Wemmick with those particulars.

"The house with the bow-window," said Wemmick, "being by the river-side, down the Pool there between Limehouse and Greenwich, and being kept, it seems, by a very respectable widow, who has a furnished upper floor to let, Mr. Herbert put it to me, what did I think of that as a temporary tenement for Tom, Jack, or Richard? Now, I thought very well of it, for three reasons I'll give you. That is to say. Firstly. It's altogether out of all your beats, and is well away from the usual heap of streets great and small. Secondly. Without going near it yourself, you could always hear of the safety of Tom, Jack, or Richard, through Mr. Herbert. Thirdly. After a while and when it might be prudent, if you should want to slip Tom, Jack, or Richard, on board a foreign packet-boat, there he is—ready."

Much comforted by these considerations, I thanked Wemmick again and again, and begged him to proceed.

"Well, sir! Mr. Herbert threw himself into the business with a will, and by nine o'clock last night he housed Tom, Jack, or Richard—whichever it may be—you and I don't want to know—quite successfully. At the old lodgings it was understood that he was summoned to Dover, and in fact he was taken down the Dover road and cornered out of it. Now, another great advantage of all this is, that it was done without you, and when, if any one was concerning himself about your movements, you must be known to be ever so many miles off, and quite otherwise engaged. This diverts suspicion and confuses it; and for the same reason I recommended that even if you came back last night, you should not go home. It brings in more confusion, and you want confusion."

Wemmick, having finished his breakfast, here looked at his watch, and began to get his coat on.

"And now, Mr. Pip," said he, with his hands still in the sleeves, "I have probably done the most I can do; but if I can ever do more—from a Walworth point of view, and in a strictly private and personal capacity—I shall be glad to do it. Here's the address. There can be no harm in your going here to-night and seeing for yourself that all is well with Tom, Jack, or Richard, before you go home—which is another reason for your not going home last night. But after you have gone home, don't go back here. You are very welcome, I am sure, Mr. Pip;" his hands were now out of his sleeves, and I was shaking them; "and let me finally impress one important point upon you." He laid his hands upon my shoulders, and added in a solemn whisper: "Avail yourself of this evening to lay hold of his portable property. You don't know what may happen to him. Don't let anything happen to the portable property."

Quite despairing of making my mind clear to Wemmick on this point, I forbore to try.

"Time's up," said Wemmick, "and I must be off. If you had nothing more pressing to do than to keep here till dark, that's what I should advise. You look very much worried, and it would do you good to have a perfectly quiet day with the Aged—he'll be up presently—and a little bit of——you remember the pig?"

"Of course," said I.

"Well; and a little bit of *him*. That sausage you toasted was his, and he was in all respects a first-rater. Do try him, if it is only for old acquaintance sake. Good-bye, Aged Parent!" in a cheery shout.

"All right, John; all right, my boy!" piped the old man from within.

I soon fell asleep before Wemmick's fire, and the Aged and I enjoyed one another's society by falling asleep before it more or less all day. We had loin of pork for dinner, and greens grown on the estate, and I nodded at the Aged with a good intention whenever I failed to do it drowsily. When it was quite dark, I left the Aged preparing the fire for toast; and I inferred from the number of tea-cups, as well as from his glances at the two little doors in the wall, that Miss Skiffins was expected.

CHAPTER XLVI

EIGHT o'clock had struck before I got into the air that was scented, not disagreeably, by the chips and shavings of the long-shore boat-builders, and mast, oar, and block makers. All that water-side region of the upper and lower Pool below Bridge, was unknown ground to me, and when I struck down by the river, I found that the spot I wanted was not where I had supposed it to be, and was anything but easy to find. It was called Mill Pond Bank, Chinks's Basin; and I had no other guide to Chinks's Basin than the Old Green Copper Rope-Walk.

It matters not what stranded ships repairing in dry docks I lost myself among, what old hulls of ships in course of being knocked to pieces, what ooze and slime and other dregs of tide, what yards of ship-builders and ship-breakers, what rusty anchors blindly biting into the ground though for years off duty, what mountainous country of accumulated casks and timber, how many rope-walks that were not the Old Green Copper. After several times falling short of my destination and as often over-shooting it, I came unexpectedly round a corner, upon Mill Pond Bank. It was a fresh kind of place, all circumstances considered, where the wind from the river had room to turn itself round; and there were two or three trees in it, and there was the stump of a ruined windmill, and there was the Old Green Copper Rope-Walk—whose long and narrow vista I could trace in the moonlight, along a series of wooden frames set in the ground, that looked like superannuated haymaking-rakes which had grown old and lost most of their teeth.

Selecting from the few queer houses upon Mill Pond Bank, a house with a wooden front and three stories of bow-window (not bay-window, which is another thing), I looked at the plate upon the door, and read there Mrs. Whimple. That being the name I wanted, I knocked, and an elderly woman of a pleasant and thriving appearance responded. She was immediately deposed, however, by Herbert, who silently led me into the parlour and shut the door. It was an odd sensation to see his very familiar face established quite at home in that very unfamiliar room and region; and I found myself looking at him, much as I looked at the corner cupboard with the glass and china, the shells upon the chimney-piece, and the coloured engravings on the wall, representing the death of Captain Cook, a ship-launch, and his Majesty King George the Third in a state coachman's wig, leather breeches, and top-boots, on the terrace at Windsor.

"All is well, Handel," said Herbert, "and he is quite satisfied, though eager to see you. My dear girl is with her father; and if you'll wait till she comes down, I'll make you known to her, and then we'll go up-stairs.——*That's* her father."

I had become aware of an alarming growling overhead, and had probably expressed the fact in my countenance.

"I am afraid he is a sad old rascal," said Herbert, smiling, "but I have never seen him. Don't you smell rum? He is always at it."

"At rum?" said I.

"Yes," returned Herbert, "and you may suppose how mild it makes his gout. He persists, too, in keeping all the provisions up-stairs in his room, and serving them out. He keeps them on shelves over his head, and *will* weigh them all. His room must be like a chandler's shop."

While he thus spoke, the growling noise became a prolonged roar, and then died away.

"What else can be the consequence," said Herbert, in explanation, "if he *will* cut the cheese? A man with the gout in his right hand—and everywhere else—can't expect to get through a Double Gloucester without hurting himself."

He seemed to have hurt himself very much, for he gave another furious roar.

"To have Provis for an upper lodger is quite a godsend to Mrs. Whimple," said Herbert, "for of course people in general won't stand that noise. A curious place, Handel; isn't it?"

It was a curious place, indeed; but remarkably well kept and clean.

"Mrs. Whimple," said Herbert, when I told him so, "is the best of housewives, and I really do not know what my Clara would do without her motherly help. For Clara has no mother of her own, Handel, and no relation in the world but old Gruffandgrim."

"Surely that's not his name, Herbert?"

"No, no," said Herbert, "that's my name for him. His name is Mr. Barley. But what a blessing it is for the son of my father and mother to love a girl who has no relations, and who can never bother herself, or anybody else, about her family!"

Herbert had told me on former occasions, and now reminded me, that he first knew Miss Clara Barley when she was completing her education at an establishment at Hammersmith, and that on her being recalled home to nurse her father, he and she had confided their affection to the motherly Mrs. Whimple, by whom it had been fostered and regulated with equal kindness and discretion ever since. It was understood that nothing of a tender nature could possibly be confided to Old Barley, by reason of his being totally unequal to the consideration of any subject more psychological than Gout, Rum, and Purser's stores.

As we were thus conversing in a low tone while Old Barley's sustained growl vibrated in the beam that crossed the ceiling, the room door opened, and a very pretty, slight, dark-eyed girl of twenty or so, came in with a basket in her hand: whom Herbert tenderly relieved of the basket, and presented blushing, as "Clara." She really was a most charming girl, and might have passed for a captive fairy, whom that truculent Ogre, Old Barley, had pressed into his service.

"Look here," said Herbert, showing me the basket, with a compassionate and tender smile after we had talked a little; "here's poor Clara's supper, served out every night. Here's her allowance of bread, and here's her slice of cheese, and here's her rum—which I drink. This is Mr. Barley's breakfast for to-morrow, served out to be cooked. Two mutton chops, three potatoes, some split peas, a little flour, two ounces of butter, a pinch of salt, and all this black pepper. It's stewed up together, and taken hot, and it's a nice thing for the gout, I should think!"

There was something so natural and winning in Clara's resigned way of looking at these stores in detail, as Herbert pointed them out,—and something so confiding, loving and innocent, in her modest manner of yielding herself to Herbert's embracing arm—and something so gentle in her, so much needing protection on Mill Pond Bank, by Chinks's Basin, and the Old Green Copper Rope-Walk, with Old Barley growling in the beam—that I would not have undone the engagement between her and Herbert for all the money in the pocket-book I had never opened.

I was looking at her with pleasure and admiration, when suddenly the growl swelled into a roar again, and a frightful bumping noise was heard above, as if a giant with a wooden leg were trying to bore it through the ceiling to come at us. Upon this Clara said to Herbert, "Papa wants me, darling!" and ran away.

"There is an unconscionable old shark for you!" said Herbert. "What do you suppose he wants now, Handel?"

"I don't know," said I. "Something to drink?"

"That's it!" cried Herbert, as if I had made a guess of extraordinary merit. "He keeps his grog ready-mixed in a little tub on the table. Wait a moment, and you'll hear Clara lift him up to take some.—There he goes!" Another roar, with a prolonged shake at the end. "Now," said Herbert, as it was succeeded by silence, "he's drinking. Now," said Herbert, as the growl resounded in the beam once more, "he's down again on his back!"

Clara returned soon afterwards, and Herbert accompanied me up-stairs to see our charge. As we passed Mr. Barley's door, he was heard hoarsely muttering within, in a strain that rose and fell like wind, the following Refrain; in which I substitute good wishes for something quite the reverse.

"Ahoy! Bless your eyes, here's old Bill Barley. Here's old Bill Barley, bless your eyes. Here's old Bill Barley on the flat of his back, by the Lord. Lying on the flat of his back, like a drifting old dead flounder, here's your old Bill Barley, bless your eyes. Ahoy! Bless you."

In this strain of consolation, Herbert informed me the invisible Barley would commune with himself by the day and night together; often while it was light, having, at the same time, one eye at a telescope which was fitted on his bed for the convenience of sweeping the river.

In his two cabin rooms at the top of the house, which were fresh and airy, and in which Mr. Barley was less audible than below, I found Provis comfortably settled. He expressed no alarm, and seemed to feel none that was worth mentioning; but it struck me that he was softened—indefinably, for I could not have said how, and could never afterwards recall how when I tried ; but certainly.

The opportunity that the day's rest had given me for reflection had resulted in my fully determining to say nothing to him respecting Compeyson. For anything I knew, his animosity towards the man might otherwise lead to his seeking him out and rushing on his own destruction. Therefore, when Herbert and I sat down with him by his fire, I asked him first of all whether he relied on Wemmick's judgment and sources of information ?

"Ay, ay, dear boy !" he answered, with a grave nod, "Jaggers knows."

"Then, I have talked with Wemmick," said I, "and have come to tell you what caution he gave me and what advice."

This I did accurately, with the reservation just mentioned ; and I told him how Wemmick had heard, in Newgate prison (whether from officers or prisoners I could not say), that he was under some suspicion, and that my chambers had been watched ; how Wemmick had recommended his keeping close for a time, and my keeping away from him ; and what Wemmick had said about getting him abroad. I added, that of course, when the time came, I should go with him, or should follow close upon him, as might be safest in Wemmick's judgment. What was to follow that, I did not touch upon ; neither indeed was I at all clear or comfortable about it in my own mind, now that I saw him in that softer condition, and in declared peril for my sake. As to altering my way of living, by enlarging my expenses, I put it to him whether in our present unsettled and difficult circumstances, it would not be simply ridiculous, if it were no worse ?

He could not deny this, and indeed was very reasonable throughout. His coming back was a venture, he said, and he had always known it to be a venture. He would do nothing to make it a desperate venture, and he had very little fear of his safety with such good help.

Herbert, who had been looking at the fire and pondering, here said that something had come into his thoughts arising out of Wemmick's suggestion, which it might be worth while to pursue. "We are both good watermen, Handel, and could take him down the river ourselves when the right time comes. No boat would then be hired for the purpose, and no boatmen; that would save at least a chance of suspicion, and any chance is worth saving. Never mind the season; don't you think it might be a good thing if you began at once to keep a boat at the Temple stairs, and were in the habit of rowing up and down the river? You fall into that habit, and then who notices or minds? Do it twenty or fifty times, and there is nothing special in your doing it the twenty-first or fifty-first."

I liked this scheme, and Provis was quite elated by it. We agreed that it should be carried into execution, and that Provis should never recognise us if we came below Bridge and rowed past Mill Pond Bank. But, we further agreed that he should pull down the blind in that part of his window which gave upon the east, whenever he saw us, and all was right.

Our conference being now ended, and everything arranged, I rose to go; remarking to Herbert that he and I had better not go home together, and that I would take half an hour's start of him. "I don't like to leave you here," I said to Provis, "though I cannot doubt your being safer here than near me. Good-bye!"

"Dear boy," he answered, clasping my hands, "I don't know when we may meet again, and I don't like Good-bye. Say Good night!"

"Good night! Herbert will go regularly between us, and when the time comes you may be certain I shall be ready. Good night, Good night!"

We thought it best that he should stay in his own rooms, and we left him on the landing outside his door, holding a light over the stair-rail to light us down-stairs. Looking back at him, I thought of the first night of his return when our positions were reversed, and when I little supposed my heart could ever be as heavy and anxious at parting from him as it was now.

Old Barley was growling and swearing when we repassed his door, with no appearance of having ceased or of meaning to cease. When we got to the foot of the stairs, I asked Herbert whether he had preserved the name of Provis? He replied, certainly not, and that the lodger was Mr. Campbell. He also explained that the utmost known of Mr. Campbell there, was that he (Herbert) had Mr. Campbell consigned to him, and felt a strong personal interest in his being well cared for and living a secluded life. So, when we went into the parlour where Mrs. Whimple and Clara were seated at work, I said nothing of my own interest in Mr. Campbell, but kept it to myself.

When I had taken leave of the pretty gentle dark-eyed girl, and of the motherly woman who had not outlived her honest sympathy with a little affair of true love, I felt as if the Old Green Copper Rope-Walk had grown quite a different place. Old Barley might be as old as the hills, and might swear like a whole field of troopers, but there were redeeming youth and trust and hope enough in Chinks's Basin to fill it to overflowing. And then I thought of Estella, and of our parting, and went home very sadly.

All things were as quiet in the Temple as ever I had seen them. The windows of the rooms of that side, lately occupied by Provis, were dark and still, and there was no lounger in Garden-court. I walked past the fountain twice or thrice before I descended the steps that were between me and my rooms, but I was quite alone. Herbert coming to my bedside when he came in—for I went straight to bed, dispirited and fatigued—made the same report. Opening one of the windows after that, he looked out into the moonlight, and told me that the pavement was as solemnly empty as the pavement of any Cathedral at that same hour.

Next day, I set myself to get the boat. It was soon done, and the boat was brought round to the Temple stairs, and lay where I could reach her within a minute or two. Then, I began to go out as for training and practice: sometimes alone, sometimes with Herbert. I was often out in cold, rain, and sleet, but nobody took much note of me after I had been out a few times. At first, I kept above Blackfriars Bridge; but as the hours of the tide changed, I took towards London Bridge. It was Old London Bridge in those days, and at certain states of the tide there was a race and a fall of water there which gave it a bad reputation. But I knew well enough how to "shoot" the bridge after seeing it done, and so began to row about among the shipping in the Pool, and down to Erith. The first time I passed Mill Pond Bank, Herbert and I were pulling a pair of oars; and, both in going and returning, we saw the blind towards the east come down. Herbert was rarely there less frequently than three times in a week, and he never brought me a single word of intelligence that was at all alarming. Still, I knew that there was cause for alarm, and I could not get rid of the notion of being watched. Once received, it is a haunting idea; how many undesigning persons I suspected of watching me, it would be hard to calculate.

In short, I was always full of fears for the rash man who was in hiding. Herbert had sometimes said to me that he found it pleasant to stand at one of our windows after dark, when the tide was running down, and to think that it was flowing, with everything it bore, towards Clara. But I thought with dread that it was flowing towards Magwitch, and that any black mark on its surface might be his pursuers, going swiftly, silently and surely, to take him.

CHAPTER XLVII

SOME weeks passed without bringing any change. We waited for Wemmick, and he made no sign. If I had never known him out of Little Britain, and had never enjoyed the privilege of being on a familiar footing at the Castle, I might have doubted him; not so for a moment, knowing him as I did.

My worldly affairs began to wear a gloomy appearance, and I was pressed for money by more than one creditor. Even I myself began to know the want of money (I mean of ready money in my own pocket), and to relieve it by converting some easily spared articles of jewellery into cash. But I had quite determined that it would be a heartless fraud to take more money from my patron in the existing state of my uncertain thoughts and plans. Therefore, I had sent him the unopened pocket-book by Herbert, to hold in his own keeping, and I felt a kind of satisfaction—whether it was a false kind or a true, I hardly know—in not having profited by his generosity since his revelation of himself.

As the time wore on, an impression settled heavily upon me that Estella was married. Fearful of having it confirmed, though it was all but a conviction, I avoided the newspapers, and begged Herbert (to whom I had confided the circumstances of our last interview) never to speak of her to me. Why I hoarded up this last wretched little rag of the robe of hope that was rent and given to the winds, how do I know! Why did you who read this, commit that not dissimilar inconsistency of your own, last year, last month, last week?

It was an unhappy life that I lived, and its one dominant anxiety, towering over all its other anxieties like a high mountain above a range of mountains, never disappeared from my view. Still, no new cause for fear arose. Let me start from my bed as I would, with the terror fresh upon me that he was discovered; let me sit listening as I would, with dread for Herbert's returning step at night, lest it should be leeter than ordinary, and winged with evil news; for all hat, and much more to like purpose, the round of things vent on. Condemned to inaction and a state of constant estlessness and suspense, I rowed about in my boat, and vaited, waited, waited, as I best could.

There were states of the tide when, having been down the river, I could not get back through the eddy-chafed arches and starlings of Old London Bridge; then, I left my boat at a wharf near the Custom House, to be brought up afterwards o the Temple stairs. I was not averse to doing this, as it served to make me and my boat a commoner incident among he water-side people there. From this slight occasion sprang two meetings that I have now to tell of.

One afternoon, late in the month of February, I came ashore at the wharf at dusk. I had pulled down as far as Greenwich with the ebb tide, and had turned with the tide. It had been a fine bright day, but had become foggy as the sun dropped, and I had had to feel my way back among the shipping pretty carefully. Both in going and returning, I had seen the signal in his window, All well.

As it was a raw evening and I was cold, I thought I would comfort myself with dinner at once; and as I had hours of dejection and solitude before me if I went home to the Temple, I thought I would afterwards go to the play. The theatre where Mr. Wopsle had achieved his questionable triumph was in that water-side neighbourhood (it is nowhere now), and to that theatre I resolved to go. I was aware that Mr. Wopsle had not succeeded in reviving the Drama, but, on the contrary, had rather partaken of its decline. He had been ominously heard of, through the playbills, as a faithful Black, in connexion with a little girl of noble birth, and a monkey. And Herbert had seen him as a predatory Tartar of comic propensities, with a face like a red brick, and an outrageous hat all over bells.

I dined at what Herbert and I used to call a Geographical chop-house—where there were maps of the world in porter-pot rims on every half-yard of the table-cloths, and charts of gravy on every one of the knives—to this day there is scarcely a single chop-house within the Lord Mayor's dominions which is not Geographical—and wore out the time in dozing over crumbs, staring at gas, and baking in a hot blast of dinners. By-and-by, I roused myself and went to the play. There, I found a virtuous boatswain in his Majesty's ser-

vice—a most excellent man, though I could have wished h
trousers not quite so tight in some places and not quite s
loose in others—who knocked all the little men's hats ove
their eyes, though he was very generous and brave, and wh
wouldn't hear of anybody's paying taxes, though he wa
very patriotic. He had a bag of money in his pocket, lik
a pudding in the cloth, and on that property married
young person in bed-furniture, with great rejoicings; th
whole population of Portsmouth (nine in number at the la
Census) turning out on the beach, to rub their own hand
and shake everybody else's, and sing, "Fill, fill!" A certai
dark-complexioned Swab, however, who wouldn't fill, or d
anything else that was proposed to him, and whose heart wa
openly stated (by the boatswain) to be as black as his figur
head, proposed to two other Swabs to get all mankind int
difficulties; which was so effectually done (the Swab famil
having considerable political influence) that it took half th
evening to set things right, and then it was only brough
about through an honest little grocer with a white hat, blac
gaiters, and red nose, getting into a clock, with a gridiro
and listening, and coming out, and knocking everybody dow
from behind with the gridiron whom he couldn't confut
with what he had overheard. This led to Mr. Wopsle's (wh
had never been heard of before) coming in with a star an
garter on, as a plenipotentiary of great power direct fror
the Admiralty, to say that the Swabs were all to go to priso
on the spot, and that he had brought the boatswain dow
the Union Jack, as a slight acknowledgment of his publi
services. The boatswain, unmanned for the first time
respectfully dried his eyes on the Jack, and then cheerin
up and addressing Mr. Wopsle as Your Honour, solicite
permission to take him by the fin. Mr. Wopsle concedin
his fin with a gracious dignity, was immediately shoved int
a dusty corner while everybody danced a hornpipe; and fron
that corner, surveying the public with a discontented eye
became aware of me.

The second piece was the last new grand comic Christma
pantomime, in the first scene of which it pained me t
suspect that I detected Mr. Wopsle, with red worsted leg
under a highly magnified phosphoric countenance and
shock of red curtain-fringe for his hair, engaged in th
manufacture of thunderbolts in a mine, and displaying grea
cowardice when his gigantic master came home (very hoarse

o dinner. But he presently presented himself under worthier circumstances; for, the Genius of Youthful Love being in want of assistance—on account of the parental brutality of an ignorant farmer who opposed the choice of his daughter's heart, by purposely falling upon the object in a flour sack out of the first-floor window—summoned a sententious Enchanter; and he, coming up from the antipodes rather unsteadily, after an apparently violent journey, proved to be Mr. Wopsle in a high-crowned hat, with a necromantic work in one volume under his arm. The business of this enchanter on earth, being principally to be talked at, sung at, butted at, danced at, and flashed at with fires of various colours, he had a good deal of time on his hands. And I observed, with great surprise, that he devoted it to staring in my direction as if he were lost in amazement.

There was something so remarkable in the increasing glare of Mr. Wopsle's eye, and he seemed to be turning so many things over in his mind and to grow so confused, that I could not make it out. I sat thinking of it, long after he had ascended to the clouds in a large watch-case, and still I could not make it out. I was still thinking of it when I came out of the theatre an hour afterwards, and found him waiting for me near the door.

"How do you do?" said I, shaking hands with him as we turned down the street together. "I saw that you saw me."

"Saw you, Mr. Pip!" he returned. "Yes, of course I saw you. But who else was there?"

"Who else?"

"It is the strangest thing," said Mr. Wopsle, drifting into his lost look again; "and yet I could swear to him."

Becoming alarmed, I entreated Mr. Wopsle to explain his meaning.

"Whether I should have noticed him at first but for your being there," said Mr. Wopsle, going on in the same lost way, "I can't be positive; yet I think I should."

Involuntarily I looked round me, as I was accustomed to look round me when I went home; for these mysterious words gave me a chill.

"Oh! He can't be in sight," said Mr. Wopsle. "He went out, before I went off; I saw him go."

Having the reason that I had for being suspicious, I even suspected this poor actor. I mistrusted a design to entrap

me into some admission. Therefore, I glanced at him as we
walked on together, but said nothing.

"I had a ridiculous fancy that he must be with you,
Mr. Pip, till I saw that you were quite unconscious of him,
sitting behind you there like a ghost."

My former chill crept over me again, but I was resolved
not to speak yet, for it was quite consistent with his words
that he might be set on to induce me to connect these
references with Provis. Of course, I was perfectly sure and
safe that Provis had not been there.

"I dare say you wonder at me, Mr. Pip; indeed, I see you
do. But it is so very strange! You'll hardly believe what
I am going to tell you. I could hardly believe it myself,
if you told me."

"Indeed?" said I.

"No, indeed. Mr. Pip, you remember in old times a
certain Christmas Day, when you were quite a child, and
I dined at Gargery's, and some soldiers came to the door to
get a pair of handcuffs mended?"

"I remember it very well."

"And you remember that there was a chase after two
convicts, and that we joined in it, and that Gargery took
you on his back, and that I took the lead and you kept up
with me as well as you could?"

"I remember it all very well." Better than he thought—
except the last clause.

"And you remember that we came up with the two in
a ditch, and that there was a scuffle between them, and that
one of them had been severely handled and much mauled
about the face by the other?"

"I see it all before me."

"And that the soldiers lighted torches, and put the two
in the centre, and that we went on to see the last of them,
over the black marshes, with the torchlight shining on their
faces—I am particular about that; with the torchlight
shining on their faces, when there was an outer ring of dark
night all about us?"

"Yes," said I. "I remember all that."

"Then, Mr. Pip, one of those two prisoners sat behind
you to-night. I saw him over your shoulder."

"Steady!" I thought. I asked him then, "Which of the
two do you suppose you saw?"

"The one who had been mauled," he answered readily,

" and I'll swear I saw him! The more I think of him, the more certain I am of him."

"This is very curious!" said I, with the best assumption I could put on, of its being nothing more to me. "Very curious indeed!"

I cannot exaggerate the enhanced disquiet into which this conversation threw me, or the special and peculiar terror I felt at Compeyson's having been behind me "like a ghost." For if he had ever been out of my thoughts for a few moments together since the hiding had begun, it was in those very moments when he was closest to me; and to think that I should be so unconscious and off my guard after all my care, was as if I had shut an avenue of a hundred doors to keep him out, and then had found him at my elbow. I could not doubt either that he was there, because I was there, and that however slight an appearance of danger there might be about us, danger was always near and active.

I put such questions to Mr. Wopsle as, When did the man come in? He could not tell me that; he saw me, and over my shoulder he saw the man. It was not until he had seen him for some time that he began to identify him; but he had from the first vaguely associated him with me, and known him as somehow belonging to me in the old village time. How was he dressed? Prosperously, but not noticeably otherwise; he thought, in black. Was his face at all disfigured? No, he believed not. I believed not, too, for although in my brooding state I had taken no especial notice of the people behind me, I thought it likely that a face at all disfigured would have attracted my attention.

When Mr. Wopsle had imparted to me all that he could recall or I extract, and when I had treated him to a little appropriate refreshment after the fatigues of the evening, we parted. It was between twelve and one o'clock when I reached the Temple, and the gates were shut. No one was near me when I went in and went home.

Herbert had come in, and we held a very serious council by the fire. But there was nothing to be done, saving to communicate to Wemmick what I had that night found out, and to remind him that we waited for his hint. As I thought that I might compromise him if I went too often to the Castle, I made this communication by letter. I wrote it before I went to bed and went out and posted it; and again no one was near me. Herbert and I agreed that we could do nothing else but be very cautious. And we were very cautious indeed—more cautious than before, if that were possible—and I for my part never went near Chinks's Basin, except when I rowed by, and then I only looked at Mill Pond Bank as I looked at anything else.

CHAPTER XLVIII

THE second of the two meetings referred to in the last chapter occurred about a week after the first. I had again left my boat at the wharf below Bridge; the time was an hour earlier in the afternoon; and, undecided where to dine, I had strolled up into Cheapside, and was strolling along it, surely the most unsettled person in all the busy concourse, when a large hand was laid upon my shoulder by some one overtaking me. It was Mr. Jaggers's hand, and he passed it through my arm.

"As we are going in the same direction, Pip, we may walk together. Where are you bound for?"

"For the Temple, I think," said I.

"Don't you know?" said Mr. Jaggers.

"Well," I returned, glad for once to get the better of him in cross-examination, "I do *not* know, for I have not made up my mind."

"You are going to dine?" said Mr. Jaggers. "You don't mind admitting that, I suppose?"

"No," I returned, "I don't mind admitting that."

"And are not engaged?"

"I don't mind admitting, also, that I am not engaged."

"Then," said Mr. Jaggers, "come and dine with me."

I was going to excuse myself, when he added, "Wemmick's coming." So I changed my excuse into an acceptance —the few words I had uttered serving for the beginning of either—and we went along Cheapside and slanted off to Little Britain, while the lights were springing up brilliantly in the shop windows, and the street lamp-lighters, scarcely finding ground enough to plant their ladders on in the midst of the afternoon's bustle, were skipping up and down and running in and out, opening more red eyes in the gathering fog than my rushlight tower at the Hummums had opened white eyes in the ghostly wall.

At the office in Little Britain there was the usual letter-writing, hand-washing, candle-snuffing, and safe-locking, that closed the business of the day. As I stood idle by Mr. Jaggers's fire, its rising and falling flame made the two casts on the shelf look as if they were playing a diabolical game at bo-peep with me; while the pair of coarse fat office-candles that dimly lighted Mr. Jaggers as he wrote in a corner, were decorated with dirty winding-sheets, as if in remembrance of a host of hanged clients.

We went to Gerrard-street, all three together, in a hackney-coach: and as soon as we got there, dinner was served. Although I should not have thought of making, in that place, the most distant reference by so much as a look to Wemmick's Walworth sentiments, yet I should have had no objection to catching his eye now and then in a friendly way. But it was not to be done. He turned his eyes on Mr. Jaggers whenever he raised them from the table, and was as dry and distant to me as if there were twin Wemmicks and this was the wrong one.

"Did you send that note of Miss Havisham's to Mr. Pip, Wemmick?" Mr. Jaggers asked, soon after we began dinner.

"No, sir," returned Wemmick; "it was going by post, when you brought Mr. Pip into the office. Here it is." He handed it to his principal, instead of to me.

"It's a note of two lines, Pip," said Mr. Jaggers, handing it on, "sent up to me by Miss Havisham, on account of her not being sure of your address. She tells me that she wants to see you on a little matter of business you mentioned to her. You'll go down?"

"Yes," said I, casting my eyes over the note, which was exactly in those terms.

"When do you think of going down?"

"I have an impending engagement," said I, glancing at Wemmick, who was putting fish into the post-office, "that renders me rather uncertain of my time. At once, I think."

"If Mr. Pip has the intention of going at once," said Wemmick to Mr. Jaggers, "he needn't write an answer, you know."

Receiving this as an intimation that it was best not to delay, I settled that I would go to-morrow, and said so. Wemmick drank a glass of wine and looked with a grimly satisfied air at Mr. Jaggers, but not at me.

"So, Pip! Our friend the Spider," said Mr. Jaggers, "has played his cards. He has won the pool."

It was as much as I could do to assent.

"Hah! He is a promising fellow—in his way—but he may not have it all his own way. The stronger will win in the end, but the stronger has to be found out first. If he should turn to and beat her——"

"Surely," I interrupted, with a burning face and heart, "you do not seriously think that he is scoundrel enough for that, Mr. Jaggers?"

"I didn't say so, Pip. I am putting a case. If he should turn to and beat her, he may possibly get the strength on his side; if it should be a question of intellect, he certainly will not. It would be chance work to give an opinion how a fellow of that sort will turn out in such circumstances, because it's a toss-up between two results."

"May I ask what they are?"

"A fellow like our friend the Spider," answered Mr. Jaggers, "either beats or cringes. He may cringe and growl, or cringe and not growl; but he either beats or cringes. Ask Wemmick *his* opinion."

"Either beats or cringes," said Wemmick, not at all addressing himself to me.

"So, here's to Mrs. Bentley Drummle," said Mr. Jaggers, taking a decanter of choicer wine from his dumb-waiter, and filling for each of us and for himself, "and may the question of supremacy be settled to the lady's satisfaction! To the satisfaction of the lady *and* the gentleman, it never will be. Now, Molly, Molly, Molly, Molly, how slow you are to-day!"

She was at his elbow when he addressed her, putting a dish upon the table. As she withdrew her hands from it, she fell back a step or two, nervously muttering some excuse. And a certain action of her fingers as she spoke arrested my attention.

"What's the matter?" said Mr. Jaggers.

"Nothing. Only the subject we were speaking of," said I, "was rather painful to me."

The action of her fingers was like the action of knitting. She stood looking at her master, not understanding whether she was free to go, or whether he had more to say to her and would call her back if she did go. Her look was very intent. Surely, I had seen exactly such eyes and such hands, on a memorable occasion very lately!

He dismissed her, and she glided out of the room. But she remained before me, as plainly as if she were still there.

I looked at those hands, I looked at those eyes, I looked at that flowing hair; and I compared them with other hands, other eyes, other hair, that I knew of, and with what those might be after twenty years of a brutal husband and a stormy life. I looked again at those hands and eyes of the housekeeper, and thought of the inexplicable feeling that had come over me when I last walked—not alone—in the ruined garden, and through the deserted brewery. I thought how the same feeling had come back when I saw a face looking at me, and a hand waving to me, from a stage-coach window; and how it had come back again and had flashed about me like lightning, when I had passed in a carriage —not alone—through a sudden glare of light in a dark street. I thought how one link of association had helped that identification in the theatre, and how such a link, wanting before, had been riveted for me now, when I had passed by a chance swift from Estella's name to the fingers with their knitting action, and the attentive eyes. And I felt absolutely certain that this woman was Estella's mother.

Mr. Jaggers had seen me with Estella, and was not likely to have missed the sentiments I had been at no pains to conceal. He nodded when I said the subject was painful to me, clapped me on the back, put round the wine again, and went on with his dinner.

Only twice more did the housekeeper reappear, and then her stay in the room was very short, and Mr. Jaggers was sharp with her. But her hands were Estella's hands, and her eyes were Estella's eyes, and if she had reappeared a hundred times I could have been neither more sure nor less sure that my conviction was the truth.

It was a dull evening, for Wemmick drew his wine when it came round, quite as a matter of business—just as he might have drawn his salary when that came round—and with his eyes on his chief, sat in a state of perpetual readiness for cross-examination. As to the quantity of wine, his post-office was as indifferent and ready as any other post-office for its quantity of letters. From my point of view, he was the wrong twin all the time, and only externally like the Wemmick of Walworth.

We took our leave early, and left together. Even when we were groping among Mr. Jaggers's stock of boots for our hats, I felt that the right twin was on his way back; and we had not gone half a dozen yards down Gerrard-street in

the Walworth direction before I found that I was walking
arm-in-arm with the right twin, and that the wrong twin
had evaporated into the evening air.

"Well!" said Wemmick, "that's over! He's a wonderful
man, without his living likeness; but I feel that I have to
screw myself up when I dine with him—and I dine more
comfortably unscrewed."

I felt that this was a good statement of the case, and told
him so.

"Wouldn't say it to anybody but yourself," he answered.
"I know that what is said between you and me goes no
further."

I asked him if he had ever seen Miss Havisham's adopted
daughter, Mrs. Bentley Drummle? He said no. To avoid
being too abrupt, I then spoke of the Aged, and of Miss
Skiffins. He looked rather sly when I mentioned Miss
Skiffins, and stopped in the street to blow his nose, with
a roll of the head and a flourish not quite free from latent
boastfulness.

"Wemmick," said I, "do you remember telling me, before
I first went to Mr. Jaggers's private house, to notice that
housekeeper?"

"Did I?" he replied. "Ah, I dare say I did. Deuce
take me," he added sullenly, "I know I did. I find I am
not quite unscrewed yet."

"A wild beast tamed, you called her?"

"And what did *you* call her?"

"The same. How did Mr. Jaggers tame her, Wemmick?"

"That's his secret. She has been with him many a long
year."

"I wish you would tell me her story. I feel a particular
interest in being acquainted with it. You know that what
is said between you and me goes no further."

"Well!" Wemmick replied, "I don't know her story—
that is, I don't know all of it. But what I do know, I'll
tell you. We are in our private and personal capacities, of
course."

"Of course."

"A score or so of years ago, that woman was tried at the
Old Bailey for murder and was acquitted. She was a very
handsome young woman, and I believe had some gipsy
blood in her. Anyhow, it was hot enough when it was up,
as you may suppose."

"But she was acquitted."

"Mr. Jaggers was for her," pursued Wemmick, with a look full of meaning, "and worked the case in a way quite astonishing. It was a desperate case, and it was comparatively early days with him then, and he worked it to general admiration; in fact, it may almost be said to have made him. He worked it himself at the police-office, day after day for many days, contending against even a committal; and at the trial where he couldn't work it himself, sat under counsel, and—every one knew—put in all the salt and pepper. The murdered person was a woman; a woman, a good ten years older, very much larger, and very much stronger. It was a case of jealousy. They both led tramping lives, and this woman in Gerrard-street here had been married very young, over the broomstick (as we say), to a tramping man, and was a perfect fury in point of jealousy. The murdered woman—more a match for the man, certainly, in point of years—was found dead in a barn near Hounslow Heath. There had been a violent struggle, perhaps a fight. She was bruised and scratched and torn, and had been held by the throat at last and choked. Now, there was no reasonable evidence to implicate any person but this woman, and, on the improbabilities of her having been able to do it, Mr. Jaggers principally rested his case. You may be sure," said Wemmick, touching me on the sleeve, "that he never dwelt upon the strength of her hands then, though he sometimes does now."

I had told Wemmick of his showing us her wrists, that day of the dinner party.

"Well, sir!" Wemmick went on; "it happened—happened, don't you see?—that this woman was so very artfully dressed from the time of her apprehension, that she looked much slighter than she really was; in particular, her sleeves are always remembered to have been so skilfully contrived that her arms had quite a delicate look. She had only a bruise or two about her—nothing for a tramp—but the backs of her hands were lacerated, and the question was, was it with finger-nails? Now, Mr. Jaggers showed that she had struggled through a great lot of brambles which were not as high as her face; but which she could not have got through and kept her hands out of; and bits of those brambles were actually found in her skin and put in evidence, as well as the fact that the brambles in question were found on examination to have been broken through, and to have little shreds of her dress and little spots of blood upon them here and there. But the boldest point he made was this. It was attempted to be set up in proof of her jealousy, that she was under strong suspicion of having, at about the time of the murder, frantically destroyed her child by this man—some three years old—to revenge herself upon him. Mr. Jaggers worked that in this way. 'We say these are not marks of finger-nails, but marks of brambles, and we show you the brambles. You say they are marks of finger-nails, and you set up the hypothesis that she destroyed her child. You must accept all consequences of that hypothesis. For anything we know, she may have destroyed her child, and the child in clinging to her may have scratched her hands. What then? You are not trying her for the murder of her child; why don't you? As to this case, if you *will* have scratches, we say that, for anything we know, you may have accounted for them, assuming for the sake of argument that you have not invented them?' To sum up, sir," said Wemmick, "Mr. Jaggers was altogether too many for the Jury, and they gave in."

"Has she been in his service ever since?"

"Yes; but not only that," said Wemmick, "she went into his service immediately after her acquittal, tamed as she is now. She has since been taught one thing and another in the way of her duties, but she was tamed from the beginning."

"Do you remember the sex of the child?"

"Said to have been a girl."

"You have nothing more to say to me to-night?"

"Nothing. I got your letter and destroyed it. Nothing."

We exchanged a cordial Good Night, and I went home, with new matter for my thoughts, though with no relief from the old.

CHAPTER XLIX

PUTTING Miss Havisham's note in my pocket, that it might
serve as my credentials for so soon reappearing at Satis
House, in case her waywardness should lead her to express
any surprise at seeing me, I went down again by the coach
next day. But I alighted at the Half-way House, and breakfasted there, and walked the rest of the distance ; for I
sought to get into the town quietly by the unfrequented
ways, and to leave it in the same manner.

The best light of the day was gone when I passed along
the quiet echoing courts behind the High-street. The nooks
of ruin where the old monks had once had their refectories
and gardens, and where the strong walls were now pressed
into the service of humble sheds and stables, were almost
as silent as the old monks in their graves. The cathedral
chimes had at once a sadder and a more remote sound
to me, as I hurried on avoiding observation, than they
had ever had before ; so, the swell of the old organ was
borne to my ears like funeral music ; and the rooks, as
they hovered about the grey tower and swung in the bare
high trees of the priory garden, seemed to call to me that
the place was changed, and that Estella was gone out of it
for ever.

An elderly woman, whom I had seen before as one of the
servants who lived in the supplementary house across the
back court-yard, opened the gate. The lighted candle stood
in the dark passage within, as of old, and I took it up and
ascended the staircase alone. Miss Havisham was not in her
own room, but was in the larger room across the landing.
Looking in at the door, after knocking in vain, I saw her
sitting on the hearth in a ragged chair, close before, and lost
in the contemplation of, the ashy fire.

Doing as I had often done, I went in and stood, touching
the old chimney-piece, where she could see me when she
raised her eyes. There was an air of utter loneliness upon her,
that would have moved me to pity though she had wilfully

done me a deeper injury than I could charge her with. As I stood compassionating her, and thinking how in the progress of time I too had come to be a part of the wrecked fortunes of that house, her eyes rested on me. She stared, and said in a low voice, " Is it real ? "

" It is I, Pip. Mr. Jaggers gave me your note yesterday, and I have lost no time."

"Thank you. Thank you."

As I brought another of the ragged chairs to the hearth and sat down, I remarked a new expression on her face, as if she were afraid of me.

" I want," she said, " to pursue that subject you mentioned to me when you were last here, and to show you that I am not all stone. But perhaps you can never believe, now, that there is anything human in my heart ? "

When I said some reassuring words, she stretched out her tremulous right hand, as though she was going to touch me ; but she recalled it again before I understood the action, or knew how to receive it.

" You said, speaking for your friend, that you could tell me how to do something useful and good. Something that you would like done, is it not ? "

" Something that I would like done very very much."

" What is it ? "

I began explaining to her that secret history of the partnership. I had not got far into it, when I judged from her looks that she was thinking in a discursive way of me, rather than of what I said. It seemed to be so, for, when I stopped speaking, many moments passed before she showed that she was conscious of the fact.

" Do you break off," she asked then, with her former air of being afraid of me, " because you hate me too much to bear to speak to me ? "

" No, no," I answered, " how can you think so, Miss Havisham ! I stopped because I thought you were not following what I said."

" Perhaps I was not," she answered, putting a hand to her head. " Begin again, and let me look at something else. Stay ! Now tell me."

She set her hand upon her stick, in the resolute way that sometimes was habitual to her, and looked at the fire with a strong expression of forcing herself to attend. I went on with my explanation, and told her how I had hoped to complete the transaction out of my means, but how in this I was disappointed. That part of the subject (I reminded her) involved matters which could form no part of my explanation, for they were the weighty secrets of another.

"So!" said she, assenting with her head, but not looking at me. "And how much money is wanting to complete the purchase?"

I was rather afraid of stating it, for it sounded a large sum. "Nine hundred pounds."

"If I give you the money for this purpose, will you keep my secret as you have kept your own?"

"Quite as faithfully."

"And your mind will be more at rest?"

"Much more at rest."

"Are you very unhappy now?"

She asked this question, still without looking at me, but in an unwonted tone of sympathy. I could not reply at the moment, for my voice failed me. She put her left arm across the head of her stick, and softly laid her forehead on it.

"I am far from happy, Miss Havisham; but I have other causes of disquiet than any you know of. They are the secrets I have mentioned."

After a little while she raised her head, and looked at the fire again.

"'Tis noble in you to tell me that you have other causes of unhappiness. Is it true?"

"Too true."

"Can I only serve you, Pip, by serving your friend? Regarding that as done, is there nothing I can do for you yourself?"

"Nothing. I thank you for the question. I thank you even more for the tone of the question. But, there is nothing."

She presently rose from her seat, and looked about the blighted room for the means of writing. There were none there, and she took from her pocket a yellow set of ivory tablets, mounted in tarnished gold, and wrote upon them with a pencil in a case of tarnished gold that hung from her neck.

"You are still on friendly terms with Mr. Jaggers?"

"Quite. I dined with him yesterday."

"This is an authority to him to pay you that money, to

lay out at your irresponsible discretion for your friend. I keep no money here; but if you would rather Mr. Jaggers knew nothing of the matter, I will send it to you."

"Thank you, Miss Havisham; I have not the least objection to receiving it from him."

She read me what she had written, and it was direct and clear, and evidently intended to absolve me from any suspicion of profiting by the receipt of the money. I took the tablets from her hand, and it trembled again, and it trembled more as she took off the chain to which the pencil was attached, and put it in mine. All this she did without looking at me.

"My name is on the first leaf. If you can ever write under my name, 'I forgive her,' though ever so long after my broken heart is dust—pray do it!"

"O Miss Havisham," said I, "I can do it now. There have been sore mistakes; and my life has been a blind and thankless one; and I want forgiveness and direction far too much, to be bitter with you."

She turned her face to me for the first time since she had averted it, and to my amazement, I may even add to my terror, dropped on her knees at my feet; with her folded hands raised to me in the manner in which, when her poor heart was young and fresh and whole, they must often have been raised to Heaven from her mother's side.

To see her with her white hair and her worn face, kneeling at my feet, gave me a shock through all my frame. I entreated her to rise, and got my arms about her to help her up; but she only pressed that hand of mine which was nearest to her grasp, and hung her head over it and wept. I had never seen her shed a tear before, and in the hope that the relief might do her good, I bent over her without speaking. She was not kneeling now, but was down upon the ground.

"O!" she cried, despairingly. "What have I done! What have I done!"

"If you mean, Miss Havisham, what have you done to injure me, let me answer. Very little. I should have loved her under any circumstances.—Is she married?"

"Yes!"

It was a needless question, for a new desolation in the desolate house had told me so.

"What have I done! What have I done!" She wrung

her hands, and crushed her white hair, and returned to this cry over and over again. "What have I done!"

I knew not how to answer or how to comfort her. That she had done a grievous thing in taking an impressionable child to mould into the form that her wild resentment, spurned affection, and wounded pride found vengeance in, I knew full well. But that, in shutting out the light of day, she had shut out infinitely more; that, in seclusion, she had secluded herself from a thousand natural and healing influences; that her mind, brooding solitary, had grown diseased, as all minds do and must and will that reverse the appointed order of their Maker, I knew equally well. And could I look upon her without compassion, seeing her punishment in the ruin she was, in her profound unfitness for this earth on which she was placed, in the vanity of sorrow which had become a master mania, like the vanity of penitence, the vanity of remorse, the vanity of unworthiness, and other monstrous vanities that have been curses in this world?

"Until you spoke to her the other day, and until I saw in you a looking-glass that showed me what I once felt myself, I did not know what I had done. What have I done! What have I done!" And so again, twenty, fifty times over, What had she done!

"Miss Havisham," I said, when her cry had died away, "you may dismiss me from your mind and conscience. But Estella is a different case, and if you can ever undo any scrap of what you have done amiss in keeping a part of her right nature away from her, it will be better to do that, than to bemoan the past through a hundred years."

"Yes, yes, I know it. But, Pip—my Dear!" There was an earnest womanly compassion for me in her new affection. "My dear! Believe this: when she first came to me, I meant to save her from misery like my own. At first I meant no more."

"Well, well!" said I. "I hope so."

"But as she grew, and promised to be very beautiful, I gradually did worse, and with my praises, and with my jewels, and with my teachings, and with this figure of myself always before her, a warning to back and point my lessons, I stole her heart away and put ice in its place."

"Better," I could not help saying, "to have left her a natural heart, even to be bruised or broken."

With that, Miss Havisham looked distractedly at me for a while, and then burst out again, What had she done!

"If you knew all my story," she pleaded, "you would have some compassion for me and a better understanding of me."

"Miss Havisham," I answered, as delicately as I could, "I believe I may say that I do know your story, and have known it ever since I first left this neighbourhood. It has inspired me with great commiseration, and I hope I understand it and its influences. Does what has passed between us give me any excuse for asking you a question relative to Estella? Not as she is, but as she was when she first came here?"

She was seated on the ground, with her arms on the ragged chair, and her head leaning on them. She looked full at me when I said this, and replied, "Go on."

"Whose child was Estella!"

She shook her head.

"You don't know?"

She shook her head again.

"But Mr. Jaggers brought her here, or sent her here?'

"Brought her here."

"Will you tell me how that came about?"

She answered in a low whisper and with caution: "I had been shut up in these rooms a long time (I don't know how long; you know what time the clocks keep here), when I told him that I wanted a little girl to rear and love, and save from my fate. I had first seen him when I sent for him to lay this place waste for me; having read of him in the newspapers before I and the world parted. He told me that he would look about him for such an orphan child. One night he brought her here asleep, and I called her Estella."

"Might I ask her age then?"

"Two or three. She herself knows nothing, but that she was left an orphan and I adopted her."

So convinced I was of that woman's being her mother, that I wanted no evidence to establish the fact in my mind. But to any mind, I thought, the connection here was clear and straight.

What more could I hope to do by prolonging the interview? I had succeeded on behalf of Herbert, Miss Havisham had told me all she knew of Estella, I had said and done what I could to ease her mind. No matter with what other words we parted ; we parted.

Twilight was closing in when I went down-stairs into the natural air. I called to the woman who had opened the gate when I entered, that I would not trouble her just yet, but would walk round the place before leaving. For, I had a presentiment that I should never be there again, and I felt that the dying light was suited to my last view of it.

By the wilderness of casks that I had walked on long ago, and on which the rain of years had fallen since, rotting them in many places, and leaving miniature swamps and pools of water upon those that stood on end, I made my way to the ruined garden. I went all round it ; round by the corner where Herbert and I had fought our battle ; round by the paths where Estella and I had walked. So cold, so lonely, so dreary all !

Taking the brewery on my way back, I raised the rusty latch of a little door at the garden end of it, and walked through. I was going out at the opposite door—not easy to open now, for the damp wood had started and swelled, and the hinges were yielding, and the threshold was encumbered with a growth of fungus—when I turned my head to look back. A childish association revived with wonderful force in the moment of the slight action, and I fancied that I saw Miss Havisham hanging to the beam. So strong was the impression, that I stood under the beam shuddering from head to foot before I knew it was a fancy—though to be sure I was there in an instant.

The mournfulness of the place and time, and the great terror of this illusion, though it was but momentary, caused me to feel an indescribable awe as I came out between the open wooden gates where I had once wrung my hair after Estella had wrung my heart. Passing on into the front court-yard, I hesitated whether to call the woman to let me out at the locked gate, of which she had the key, or first to go up-stairs and assure myself that Miss Havisham was as safe and well as I had left her. I took the latter course and went up.

I looked into the room where I had left her, and I saw her seated in the ragged chair upon the hearth close to the fire, with her back towards me. In the moment when I was withdrawing my head to go quietly away, I saw a great flaming light spring up. In the same moment I saw her running at me, shrieking, with a whirl of fire blazing all about her, and soaring at least as many feet above her head as she was high.

I had a double-caped great-coat on, and over my arm another thick coat. That I got them off, closed with her, threw her down, and got them over her; that I dragged the great cloth from the table for the same purpose, and with it dragged down the heap of rottenness in the midst, and all the ugly things that sheltered there; that we were on the ground struggling like desperate enemies, and that the closer I covered her, the more wildly she shrieked and tried to free herself; that this occurred I knew through the result, but not through anything I felt, or thought, or knew I did. I knew nothing until I knew that we were on the floor by the great table, and that patches of tinder yet alight were floating in the smoky air, which a moment ago had been her faded bridal dress.

Then, I looked round and saw the disturbed beetles and spiders running away over the floor, and the servants coming in with breathless cries at the door. I still held her forcibly down with all my strength, like a prisoner who might escape; and I doubt if I even knew who she was, or why we had struggled, or that she had been in flames, or that the flames were out, until I saw the patches of tinder that had been her garments, no longer alight, but falling in a black shower around us.

She was insensible, and I was afraid to have her moved, or even touched. Assistance was sent for, and I held her until it came, as if I unreasonably fancied (I think I did) that if I let her go, the fire would break out again and consume her. When I got up, on the surgeon's coming to her with other aid, I was astonished to see that both my hands were burnt; for I had no knowledge of it through the sense of feeling.

On examination it was pronounced that she had received serious hurts, but that they of themselves were far from hopeless; the danger lay mainly in the nervous shock. By the surgeon's directions, her bed was carried into that room and laid upon the great table, which happened to be well suited to the dressing of her injuries. When I saw her again, an hour afterwards, she lay indeed where I had seen her strike her stick, and had heard her say she would lie one day.

Though every vestige of her dress was burnt, as they told me, she still had something of her old ghastly bridal appearance; for, they had covered her to the throat with white-cotton wool, and as she lay with a white sheet loosely overlying that, the phantom air of something that had been and was changed was still upon her.

I found, on questioning the servants, that Estella was in Paris, and I got a promise from the surgeon that he would write by the next post. Miss Havisham's family I took upon myself; intending to communicate with Matthew Pocket only, and leave him to do as he liked about informing the rest. This I did next day, through Herbert, as soon as I returned to town.

There was a stage, that evening, when she spoke collectedly of what had happened, though with a certain terrible vivacity. Towards midnight she began to wander in her speech, and after that it gradually set in that she said innumerable times in a low solemn voice, "What have I done!" And then, "When she first came, I meant to save her from misery like mine." And then, "Take the pencil and write under my name, 'I forgive her!'" She never changed the order of these three sentences, but she sometimes left out a word in one or other of them; never putting in another word, but always leaving a blank and going on to the next word.

As I could do no service there, and as I had, nearer home, that pressing reason for anxiety and fear which even her wanderings could not drive out of my mind, I decided in the course of the night that I would return by the early morning coach: walking on a mile or so, and being taken up clear of the town. At about six o'clock of the morning, therefore, I leaned over her and touched her lips with mine, just as they said, not stopping for being touched, "Take the pencil and write under my name, 'I forgive her.'"

CHAPTER L

My hands had been dressed twice or thrice in the night, and again in the morning. My left arm was a good deal burned to the elbow, and, less severely, as high as the shoulder; it was very painful, but the flames had set in that direction, and I felt thankful it was no worse. My right hand was not so badly burnt but that I could move the fingers. It was bandaged, of course, but much less inconveniently than my left hand and arm; those I carried in a sling; and I could only wear my coat like a cloak, loose over my shoulders and fastened at the neck. My hair had been caught by the fire, but not my head or face.

When Herbert had been down to Hammersmith and had seen his father, he came back to me at our chambers, and devoted the day to attending on me. He was the kindest of nurses, and at stated times took off the bandages, and steeped them in the cooling liquid that was kept ready, and put them on again, with a patient tenderness that I was deeply grateful for.

At first, as I lay quiet on the sofa, I found it painfully difficult, I might say impossible, to get rid of the impression of the glare of the flames, their hurry and noise, and the fierce burning smell. If I dozed for a minute, I was awakened by Miss Havisham's cries, and by her running at me with all that height of fire above her head. This pain of the mind was much harder to strive against than any bodily pain I suffered; and Herbert, seeing that, did his utmost to hold my attention engaged.

Neither of us spoke of the boat, but we both thought of it. That was made apparent by our avoidance of the subject, and by our agreeing—without agreement—to make my recovery of the use of my hands a question of so many hours, not of so many weeks.

My first question when I saw Herbert had been, of course, whether all was well down the river? As he replied in the affirmative, with perfect confidence and cheerfulness, we did not resume the subject until the day was wearing away.

But then, as Herbert changed the bandages, more by the light of the fire than by the outer light, he went back to it spontaneously.

"I sat with Provis last night, Handel, two good hours."

"Where was Clara?"

"Dear little thing!" said Herbert. "She was up and down with Gruffandgrim all the evening. He was perpetually pegging at the floor, the moment she left his sight. I doubt if he can hold out long though. What with rum and pepper—and pepper and rum—I should think his pegging must be nearly over."

"And then you will be married, Herbert?"

"How can I take care of the dear child otherwise?—Lay your arm out upon the back of the sofa, my dear boy, and I'll sit down here, and get the bandage off so gradually that you shall not know when it comes. I was speaking of Provis. Do you know, Handel, he improves?"

"I said to you I thought he was softened when I last saw him."

"So you did. And so he is. He was very communicative last night, and told me more of his life. You remember his breaking off here about some woman that he had had great trouble with.—Did I hurt you?"

I had started, but not under his touch. His words had given me a start.

"I had forgotten that, Herbert, but I remember it now you speak of it."

"Well! He went into that part of his life, and a dark wild part it is. Shall I tell you? Or would it worry you just now?"

"Tell me by all means. Every word."

Herbert bent forward to look at me more nearly, as if my reply had been rather more hurried or more eager than he could quite account for. "Your head is cool?" he said, touching it.

"Quite," said I. "Tell me what Provis said, my dear Herbert."

"It seems," said Herbert, "—there's a bandage off most charmingly, and now comes the cool one—makes you shrink at first, my poor dear fellow, don't it? but it will be comfortable presently—it seems that the woman was a young woman, and a jealous woman, and a revengeful woman; revengeful, Handel, to the last degree."

"To what last degree?"

"Murder.—Does it strike too cold on that sensitive place?"

"I don't feel it. How did she murder? Whom did she murder?"

"Why, the deed may not have merited quite so terrible a name," said Herbert, "but she was tried for it, and Mr. Jaggers defended her, and the reputation of that defence first made his name known to Provis. It was another and a stronger woman who was the victim, and there had been a struggle—in a barn. Who began it, or how fair it was, or how unfair, may be doubtful; but how it ended is certainly not doubtful, for the victim was found throttled."

"Was the woman brought in guilty?"

"No; she was acquitted.—My poor Handel, I hurt you!"

"It is impossible to be gentler, Herbert. Yes? What else?"

"This acquitted young woman and Provis had a little child: a little child of whom Provis was exceedingly fond. On the evening of the very night when the object of her jealousy was strangled as I tell you, the young woman presented herself before Provis for one moment, and swore that she would destroy the child (which was in her possession), and he should never see it again; then, she vanished.—There's the worst arm comfortably in the sling once more, and now there remains but the right hand, which is a far easier job. I can do it better by this light than by a stronger, for my hand is steadiest when I don't see the poor blistered patches too distinctly.—You don't think your breathing is affected, my dear boy? You seem to breathe quickly."

"Perhaps I do, Herbert. Did the woman keep her oath?"

"There comes the darkest part of Provis's life. She did."

"That is, he says she did."

"Why, of course, my dear boy," returned Herbert, in a tone of surprise, and again bending forward to get a nearer look at me. "He says it all. I have no other information."

"No, to be sure."

"Now, whether," pursued Herbert, "he had used the child's mother ill, or whether he had used the child's mother well, Provis doesn't say; but, she had shared some four or five years of the wretched life he described to us at this fireside, and he seems to have felt pity for her, and forbearance towards her. Therefore, fearing he should be called upon to depose about this destroyed child, and so be the cause of her death, he hid himself (much as he grieved for the child), kept himself dark, as he says, out of the way and out of the trial, and was only vaguely talked of as a certain man called Abel, out of whom the jealousy arose. After the acquittal she disappeared, and thus he lost the child and the child's mother."

"I want to ask——"

"A moment, my dear boy, and I have done. That evil genius, Compeyson, the worst of scoundrels among many scoundrels, knowing of his keeping out of the way at that time, and of his reasons for doing so, of course afterwards held the knowledge over his head as a means of keeping him poorer, and working him harder. It was clear last night that this barbed the point of Provis's animosity."

"I want to know," said I, "and particularly, Herbert, whether he told you when this happened?"

"Particularly? Let me remember, then, what he said as to that. His expression was, 'a round score o' year ago, and a'most directly after I took up wi' Compeyson.' How old were you when you came upon him in the little churchyard?"

"I think in my seventh year."

"Ay. It had happened some three or four years then, he said, and you brought into his mind the little girl so tragically lost, who would have been about your age."

"Herbert," said I, after a short silence, in a hurried way, "can you see me best by the light of the window, or the light of the fire?"

"By the firelight," answered Herbert, coming close again.

"Look at me."

"I do look at you, my dear boy."

"Touch me."

"I do touch you, my dear boy."

"You are not afraid that I am in any fever, or that my head is much disordered by the accident of last night?"

"N-no, my dear boy," said Herbert, after taking time to examine me. "You are rather excited, but you are quite yourself."

"I know I am quite myself. And the man we have in hiding down the river is Estella's Father."

CHAPTER LI

WHAT purpose I had in view when I was hot on tracing out and proving Estella's parentage, I cannot say. It will presently be seen that the question was not before me in a distinct shape, until it was put before me by a wiser head than my own.

But, when Herbert and I had held our momentous conversation, I was seized with a feverish conviction that I ought to hunt the matter down—that I ought not to let it rest, but that I ought to see Mr. Jaggers, and come at the bare truth. I really do not know whether I felt that I did this for Estella's sake, or whether I was glad to transfer to the man, in whose preservation I was so much concerned, some rays of the romantic interest that had so long surrounded me. Perhaps the latter possibility may be the nearer to the truth.

Any way, I could scarcely be withheld from going out to Gerrard-street that night. Herbert's representations that if I did I should probably be laid up and stricken useless, when our fugitive's safety would depend upon me, alone restrained my impatience. On the understanding, again and again reiterated that come what would I was to go to Mr. Jaggers to-morrow, I at length submitted to keep quiet, and to have my hurts looked after, and to stay at home. Early next morning we went out together, and at the corner of Giltspur-street by Smithfield, I left Herbert to go his way into the City, and took my way to Little Britain.

There were periodical occasions when Mr. Jaggers and Mr. Wemmick went over the office accounts, and checked off the vouchers, and put all things straight. On these occasions Wemmick took his books and papers into Mr. Jaggers's room, and one of the up-stairs clerks came down into the outer office. Finding such clerk on Wemmick's post that morning, I knew what was going on; but I was not sorry to have Mr. Jaggers and Wemmick together, as Wemmick would then hear for himself that I said nothing to compromise him.

My appearance, with my arm bandaged and my coat loose over my shoulders, favoured my object. Although I had sent Mr. Jaggers a brief account of the accident as soon as I had arrived in town, yet I had to give him all the details now; and the specialty of the occasion caused our talk to be less dry and hard, and less strictly regulated by the rules of evidence, than it had been before. While I described the disaster, Mr. Jaggers stood, according to his wont, before the fire. Wemmick leaned back in his chair, staring at me, with his hands in the pockets of his trousers, and his pen put horizontally into the post. The two brutal casts, always inseparable in my mind from the official proceedings, seemed to be congestively considering whether they didn't smell fire at the present moment.

My narrative finished, and their questions exhausted, I then produced Miss Havisham's authority to receive the nine hundred pounds for Herbert. Mr. Jaggers's eyes retired a little deeper into his head when I handed him the tablets, but he presently handed them over to Wemmick, with instructions to draw the cheque for his signature. While that was in course of being done, I looked on at Wemmick as he wrote, and Mr. Jaggers, poising and swaying himself on his well-polished boots, looked on at me. "I am sorry, Pip," said he, as I put the cheque in my pocket, when he had signed it, "that we do nothing for *you*."

"Miss Havisham was good enough to ask me," I returned, "whether she could do nothing for me, and I told her No."

"Everybody should know his own business," said Mr. Jaggers. And I saw Wemmick's lips form the words "portable property."

"I should *not* have told her No, if I had been you," said Mr. Jaggers; "but every man ought to know his own business best."

"Every man's business," said Wemmick, rather reproachfully towards me, "is 'portable property.'"

As I thought the time was now come for pursuing the theme I had at heart, I said, turning on Mr. Jaggers:

"I did ask something of Miss Havisham, however, sir. I asked her to give me some information relative to her adopted daughter, and she gave me all she possessed."

"Did she?" said Mr. Jaggers, bending forward to look at his boots and then straightening himself. "Hah! I don't think I should have done so, if I had been Miss Havisham. But *she* ought to know her own business best."

"I know more of the history of Miss Havisham's adopted child than Miss Havisham herself does, sir. I know her mother."

Mr. Jaggers looked at me inquiringly, and repeated 'Mother?'

"I have seen her mother within these three days."

"Yes?" said Mr. Jaggers.

"And so have you, sir. And you have seen her still more recently."

"Yes?" said Mr. Jaggers.

"Perhaps I know more of Estella's history than even you do," said I. "I know her father, too."

A certain stop that Mr. Jaggers came to in his manner— he was too self-possessed to change his manner, but he could not help its being brought to an indefinably attentive stop— assured me that he did not know who her father was. This I had strongly suspected from Provis's account (as Herbert had repeated it) of his having kept himself dark; which I pieced on to the fact that he himself was not Mr. Jaggers's client until some four years later, and when he could have no reason for claiming his identity. But, I could not be sure of this unconsciousness on Mr. Jaggers's part before, though I was quite sure of it now.

"So! You know the young lady's father, Pip?" said Mr. Jaggers.

"Yes," I replied, "and his name is Provis—from New South Wales."

Even Mr. Jaggers started when I said those words. It was the slightest start that could escape a man, the most carefully repressed and the sooner checked, but he did start, though he made it a part of the action of taking out his pocket-handkerchief. How Wemmick received the announcement I am unable to say, for I was afraid to look at him just then, lest Mr. Jaggers's sharpness should detect that there had been some communication unknown to him between us.

"And on what evidence, Pip," asked Mr. Jaggers, very coolly, as he paused with his handkerchief half-way to his nose, "does Provis make this claim?"

"He does not make it," said I, "and has never made it, and has no knowledge or belief that his daughter is in existence."

For once, the powerful pocket-handkerchief failed. My reply was so unexpected that Mr. Jaggers put the handkerchief back into his pocket without completing the usual performance, folded his arms, and looked with stern attention at me, though with an immovable face.

Then I told him all I knew, and how I knew it; with the one reservation that I left him to infer that I knew from Miss Havisham what I in fact knew from Wemmick. I was very careful indeed as to that. Nor did I look towards Wemmick until I had finished all I had to tell, and had been for some time silently meeting Mr. Jaggers's look. When I did at last turn my eyes in Wemmick's direction, I found that he had unposted his pen, and was intent upon the table before him.

"Hah!" said Mr. Jaggers at last, as he moved towards the papers on the table. "—What item was it you were at, Wemmick, when Mr. Pip came in?"

But I could not submit to be thrown off in that way, and I made a passionate, almost an indignant appeal to him to be more frank and manly with me. I reminded him of the false hopes into which I had lapsed, the length of time they had lasted, and the discovery I had made: and I hinted at the danger that weighed upon my spirits. I represented myself as being surely worthy of some little confidence from him, in return for the confidence I had just now imparted. I said that I did not blame him, or suspect him, or mistrust him, but I wanted assurance of the truth from him. And if he asked me why I wanted it and why I thought I had any right to it, I would tell him, little as he cared for such poor dreams, that I had loved Estella dearly and long, and that, although I had lost her and must live a bereaved life, whatever concerned her was still nearer and dearer to me than anything else in the world. And seeing that Mr. Jaggers stood quite still and silent, and apparently quite obdurate, under this appeal, I turned to Wemmick, and said, "Wemmick, I know you to be a man with a gentle heart. I have seen your pleasant home, and your old father, and all the innocent cheerful playful ways with which you refresh your business life. And I entreat you to say a word for me to Mr. Jaggers, and to represent to him that, all circumstances considered, he ought to be more open with me!"

I have never seen two men look more oddly at one another than Mr. Jaggers and Wemmick did after this apostrophe.

At first, a misgiving crossed me that Wemmick would be instantly dismissed from his employment; but, it melted as I saw Mr. Jaggers relax into something like a smile, and Wemmick become bolder.

"What's all this?" said Mr. Jaggers. "You with an old father, and you with pleasant and playful ways?"

"Well!" returned Wemmick. "If I don't bring 'em here, what does it matter?"

"Pip," said Mr. Jaggers, laying his hand upon my arm, and smiling openly, "this man must be the most cunning impostor in all London."

"Not a bit of it," returned Wemmick, growing bolder and bolder. "I think you're another."

Again they exchanged their former odd looks, each apparently still distrustful that the other was taking him in.

"*You* with a pleasant home?" said Mr. Jaggers.

"Since it don't interfere with business," returned Wemmick, "let it be so. Now, I look at you, sir, I shouldn't wonder if *you* might be planning and contriving to have a pleasant home of your own, one of these days, when you're tired of all this work."

Mr. Jaggers nodded his head retrospectively two or three times, and actually drew a sigh. "Pip," said he, "we won't talk about 'poor dreams;' you know more about such things than I, having much fresher experience of that kind. But now, about this other matter. I'll put a case to you. Mind! I admit nothing."

He waited for me to declare that I quite understood that he expressly said that he admitted nothing.

"Now, Pip," said Mr. Jaggers, "put this case. Put the case that a woman, under such circumstances as you have mentioned, held her child concealed, and was obliged to communicate the fact to her legal adviser, on his representing to her that he must know, with an eye to the latitude of his defence, how the fact stood about that child. Put the case that at the same time he held a trust to find a child for an eccentric rich lady to adopt and bring up."

"I follow you, sir."

"Put the case that he lived in an atmosphere of evil, and that all he saw of children was, their being generated in great numbers for certain destruction. Put the case that he often saw children solemnly tried at a criminal bar, where they were held up to be seen; put the case that he habitually knew of their being imprisoned, whipped, transported, neglected, cast out, qualified in all ways for the hangman, and growing up to be hanged. Put the case that pretty nigh all the children he saw in his daily business life, he had reason to look upon as so much spawn, to develop into the fish that were to come to his net—to be prosecuted, defended, forsworn, made orphans, bedevilled somehow."

"I follow you, sir."

"Put the case, Pip, that here was one pretty little child out of the heap who could be saved; whom the father believed dead, and dared make no stir about; as to whom, over the mother, the legal adviser had this power: 'I know what you did, and how you did it. You came so and so, you did such and such things to divert suspicion. I have tracked you through it all, and I tell it you all. Part with the child, unless it should be necessary to produce it to clear you, and then it shall be produced. Give the child into my hands, and I will do my best to bring you off. If you are saved, your child will be saved too; if you are lost, your child is still saved.' Put the case that this was done, and that the woman was cleared."

"I understand you perfectly."

"But that I make no admissions?"

"That you make no admissions." And Wemmick repeated, "No admissions."

"Put the case, Pip, that passion and the terror of death had a little shaken the woman's intellects, and that when she was set at liberty, she was scared out of the ways of the world and went to him to be sheltered. Put the case that he took her in, and that he kept down the old wild violent nature, whenever he saw an inkling of its breaking out, by asserting his power over her in the old way. Do you comprehend the imaginary case?"

"Quite."

"Put the case that the child grew up, and was married for money. That the mother was still living. That the father was still living. That the mother and father, unknown to one another, were dwelling within so many miles, furlongs, yards if you like, of one another. That the secret was still a secret, except that you had got wind of it. Put that last case to yourself very carefully."

"I do."

"I ask Wemmick to put it to *himself* very carefully."

And Wemmick said, "I do."

"For whose sake would you reveal the secret? For the father's? I think he would not be much the better for the mother. For the mother's? I think if she had done such a deed she would be safer where she was. For the daughter's? I think it would hardly serve her, to establish her parentage for the information of her husband, and to drag her back to disgrace, after an escape of twenty years, pretty secure to last for life. But, add the case that you had loved her, Pip, and had made her the subject of those 'poor dreams' which have, at one time or another, been in the heads of more men than you think likely, then I tell you that you had better—and would much sooner when you had thought well of it—chop off that bandaged left hand of yours with your bandaged right hand, and then pass the chopper on to Wemmick there, to cut *that* off too."

I looked at Wemmick, whose face was very grave. He gravely touched his lips with his forefinger. I did the same. Mr. Jaggers did the same. "Now, Wemmick," said the latter then, resuming his usual manner, "what item was it you were at, when Mr. Pip came in?"

Standing by for a little, while they were at work, I observed that the odd looks they had cast at one another were repeated several times: with this difference now, that each of them seemed suspicious, not to say conscious, of having shown himself in a weak and unprofessional light to the other. For this reason, I suppose, they were now inflexible with one another; Mr. Jaggers being highly dictatorial, and Wemmick obstinately justifying himself whenever there was the smallest point in abeyance for a moment. I had never seen them on such ill terms; for generally they got on very well indeed together.

But, they were both happily relieved by the opportune appearance of Mike, the client with the fur cap, and the habit of wiping his nose on his sleeve, whom I had seen on the very first day of my appearance within those walls. This individual, who, either in his own person or in that of some member of his family, seemed to be always in trouble (which in that place meant Newgate), called to announce that his eldest daughter was taken up on suspicion of shop-lifting. As he imparted this melancholy circumstance to Wemmick, Mr. Jaggers standing magisterially before the fire and taking no share in the proceedings, Mike's eye happened to twinkle with a tear.

"What are you about?" demanded Wemmick, with the utmost indignation. "What do you come snivelling here for?"

"I didn't go to do it, Mr. Wemmick."

"You did," said Wemmick. "How dare you? You're not in a fit state to come here, if you can't come here without spluttering like a bad pen. What do you mean by it?"

"A man can't help his feelings, Mr. Wemmick," pleaded Mike.

"His what?" demanded Wemmick. quite savagely. "Say that again!"

"Now look here, my man," said Mr. Jaggers, advancing a step, and pointing to the door. "Get out of this office. I'll have no feelings here. Get out."

"It serves you right," said Wemmick. "Get out."

So the unfortunate Mike very humbly withdrew, and Mr. Jaggers and Wemmick appeared to have re-established their good understanding, and went to work again with an air of refreshment upon them as if they had just had lunch.

CHAPTER LII

From Little Britain I went, with my cheque in my pocket, to Miss Skiffins's brother, the accountant; and Miss Skiffins's brother, the accountant, going straight to Clarriker's and bringing Clarriker to me, I had the great satisfaction of concluding that arrangement. It was the only good thing I had done, and the only completed thing I had done, since I was first apprised of my great expectations.

Clarriker informing me on that occasion that the affairs of the House were steadily progressing, that he would now be able to establish a small branch-house in the East which was much wanted for the extension of the business, and that Herbert in his new partnership capacity would go out and take charge of it, I found that I must have prepared for a separation from my friend, even though my own affairs had been more settled. And now indeed I felt as if my last anchor were loosening its hold, and I should soon be driving with the winds and waves.

But there was recompense in the joy with which Herbert would come home of a night and tell me of these changes, little imagining that he told me no news, and would sketch airy pictures of himself conducting Clara Barley to the land of the Arabian Nights, and of me going out to join them (with a caravan of camels, I believe), and of our all going up the Nile and seeing wonders. Without being sanguine as to my own part in those bright plans, I felt that Herbert's way was clearing fast, and that old Bill Barley had but to stick to his pepper and rum, and his daughter would soon be happily provided for.

We had now got into the month of March. My left arm, though it presented no bad symptoms, took in the natural course so long to heal that I was still unable to get a coat on. My right arm was tolerably restored;—disfigured, but fairly serviceable.

On a Monday morning, when Herbert and I were at

breakfast, I received the following letter from Wemmick by the post.

"Walworth. Burn this as soon as read. Early in the week, or say Wednesday, you might do what you know of, if you felt disposed to try it. Now burn."

When I had shown this to Herbert and had put it in the fire—but not before we had both got it by heart—we considered what to do. For, of course, my being disabled could now be no longer kept out of view.

"I have thought it over, again and again," said Herbert, "and I think I know a better course than taking a Thames waterman. Take Startop. A good fellow, a skilled hand, fond of us, and enthusiastic and honourable."

I had thought of him more than once.

"But how much would you tell him, Herbert?"

"It is necessary to tell him very little. Let him suppose it a mere freak, but a secret one, until the morning comes: then let him know that there is urgent reason for your getting Provis aboard and away. You go with him?"

"No doubt."

"Where?"

It had seemed to me, in the many anxious considerations I had given the point, almost indifferent what port we made for—Hamburg, Rotterdam, Antwerp—the place signified little, so that he was out of England. Any foreign steamer that fell in our way and would take us up would do. I had always proposed to myself to get him well down the river in the boat; certainly well beyond Gravesend, which was a critical place for search or inquiry if suspicion were afoot. As foreign steamers would leave London at about the time of high-water, our plan would be to get down the river by a previous ebb-tide, and lie by in some quiet spot until we could pull off to one. The time when one would be due where we lay, wherever that might be, could be calculated pretty nearly, if we made inquiries beforehand.

Herbert assented to all this, and we went out immediately after breakfast to pursue our investigations. We found that a steamer for Hamburg was likely to suit our purpose best, and we directed our thoughts chiefly to that vessel. But we noted down what other foreign steamers would leave London with the same tide, and we satisfied ourselves that we knew the build and colour of each. We then separated for a few hours; I to get at once such passports as were necessary; Herbert, to see Startop at his lodgings. We both did what we had to do without any hindrance, and when we met again at one o'clock reported it done. I, for my part, was prepared with passports; Herbert had seen Startop, and he was more than ready to join.

Those two would pull a pair of oars, we settled, and I would steer: our charge would be sitter, and keep quiet; as speed was not our object, we should make way enough. We arranged that Herbert should not come home to dinner before going to Mill Pond Bank that evening; that he should not go there at all to-morrow evening, Tuesday; that he should prepare Provis to come down to some Stairs hard by the house, on Wednesday, when he saw us approach, and not sooner; that all the arrangements with him should be concluded that Monday night; and that he should be communicated with no more in any way, until we took him on board.

These precautions well understood by both of us, I went home.

On opening the outer door of our chambers with my key, I found a letter in the box, directed to me; a very dirty letter, though not ill-written. It had been delivered by hand (of course since I left home), and its contents were these:

"If you are not afraid to come to the old marshes to-night or to-morrow night at Nine, and to come to the little sluice-house by the limekiln, you had better come. If you want information regarding *your uncle Provis*, you had much better come and tell no one and lose no time. *You must come alone.* Bring this with you."

I had had load enough upon my mind before the receipt of this strange letter. What to do now, I could not tell. And the worst was, that I must decide quickly, or I should miss the afternoon coach, which would take me down in time for to-night. To-morrow night I could not think of going, for it would be too close upon the time of flight. And again, for anything I knew, the proffered information might have some important bearing on the flight itself.

If I had had ample time for consideration, I believe I should still have gone. Having hardly any time for consideration—my watch showing me that the coach started within half an hour—I resolved to go. I should certainly not have gone, but for the reference to my Uncle Provis.

That, coming on Wemmick's letter and the morning's busy preparation, turned the scale.

It is so difficult to become clearly possessed of the contents of almost any letter, in a violent hurry, that I had to read this mysterious epistle again, twice, before its injunction to me to be secret got mechanically into my mind. Yielding to it in the same mechanical kind of way, I left a note in pencil for Herbert, telling him that as I should be so soon going away, I knew not for how long, I had decided to hurry down and back, to ascertain for myself how Miss Havisham was faring. I had then barely time to get my great-coat, lock up the chambers, and make for the coach-office by the short by-ways. If I had taken a hackney-chariot and gone by the streets, I should have missed my aim; going as I did, I caught the coach just as it came out of the yard. I was the only inside passenger, jolting away knee-deep in straw, when I came to myself.

For I really had not been myself since the receipt of the letter; it had so bewildered me, ensuing on the hurry of the morning. The morning hurry and flutter had been great, for, long and anxiously as I had waited for Wemmick, his hint had come like a surprise at last. And now, I began to wonder at myself for being in the coach, and to doubt whether I had sufficient reason for being there, and to consider whether I should get out presently and go back, and to argue against ever heeding an anonymous communication, and, in short, to pass through all those phases of contradiction and indecision to which I suppose very few hurried people are strangers. Still, the reference to Provis by name mastered everything. I reasoned as I had reasoned already without knowing it—if that be reasoning—in case any harm should befall him through my not going, how could I ever forgive myself!

It was dark before we got down, and the journey seemed long and dreary to me who could see little of it inside, and who could not go outside in my disabled state. Avoiding the Blue Boar, I put up at an inn of minor reputation down the town, and ordered some dinner. While it was preparing, I went to Satis House and inquired for Miss Havisham; she was still very ill, though considered something better.

My inn had once been a part of an ancient ecclesiastical house, and I dined in a little octagonal common-room, like

a font. As I was not able to cut my dinner, the old landlord with a shining bald head did it for me. This bringing
us into conversation, he was so good as to entertain me with
my own story—of course with the popular feature that
Pumblechook was my earliest benefactor and the founder of
my fortunes.

"Do you know the young man?" said I.

"Know him?" repeated the landlord. "Ever since he
was—no height at all."

"Does he ever come back to this neighbourhood?"

"Ay, he comes back," said the landlord, "to his great
friends, now and again, and gives the cold shoulder to the
man that made him."

"What man is that?"

"Him that I speak of," said the landlord. "Mr. Pumblechook."

"Is he ungrateful to no one else?"

"No doubt he would be, if he could," returned the landlord, "but he can't. And why? Because Pumblechook
done everything for him."

"Does Pumblechook say so?"

"Say so!" replied the landlord. "He han't no call to
say so."

"But does he say so?"

"It would turn a man's blood to white wine winegar, to
hear him tell of it, sir," said the landlord.

I thought, "Yet Joe, dear Joe, *you* never tell of it. Long-
suffering and loving Joe, *you* never complain. Nor you,
sweet-tempered Biddy!"

"Your appetite's been touched like, by your accident,"
said the landlord, glancing at the bandaged arm under my
coat. "Try a tenderer bit."

"No thank you," I replied, turning from the table to
brood over the fire. "I can eat no more. Please take it
away."

I had never been struck at so keenly, for my thanklessness
to Joe, as through the brazen impostor Pumblechook. The
falser he, the truer Joe; the meaner he, the nobler Joe.

My heart was deeply and most deservedly humbled as
I mused over the fire for an hour or more. The striking of
the clock aroused me, but not from my dejection or remorse,
and I got up and had my coat fastened round my neck, and
went out. I had previously sought in my pockets for the

letter, that I might refer to it again, but I could not find it, and was uneasy to think that it must have been dropped in the straw of the coach. I knew very well, however, that the appointed place was the little sluice-house by the lime-kiln on the marshes, and the hour nine. Towards the marshes I now went straight, having no time to spare.

CHAPTER LIII

It was a dark night, though the full moon rose as I left the enclosed lands, and passed out upon the marshes. Beyond their dark line there was a ribbon of clear sky, hardly broad enough to hold the red large moon. In a few minutes she had ascended out of that clear field, in among the piled mountains of cloud.

There was a melancholy wind, and the marshes were very dismal. A stranger would have found them insupportable, and even to me they were so oppressive that I hesitated, half inclined to go back. But I knew them, and could have found my way on a far darker night, and had no excuse for returning, being there. So, having come there against my inclination, I went on against it.

The direction that I took was not that in which my old home lay, nor that in which we had pursued the convicts. My back was turned towards the distant Hulks as I walked on, and, though I could see the old lights away on the spits of sand, I saw them over my shoulder. I knew the limekiln as well as I knew the old Battery, but they were miles apart; so that if a light had been burning at each point that night, there would have been a long strip of the blank horizon between the two bright specks.

At first I had to shut some gates after me, and now and then to stand still while the cattle that were lying in the banked-up pathway arose and blundered down among the grass and reeds. But after a little while, I seemed to have the whole flats to myself.

It was another half-hour before I drew near to the kiln. The lime was burning with a sluggish stifling smell, but the fires were made up and left, and no workmen were visible. Hard by was a small stone quarry. It lay directly in my way, and had been worked that day, as I saw by the tools and barrows that were lying about.

Coming up again to the marsh level out of this excavation

—for the rude path lay through it—I saw a light in the old sluice-house. I quickened my pace, and knocked at the door with my hand. Waiting for some reply, I looked about me, noticing how the sluice was abandoned and broken, and how the house—of wood with a tiled roof— would not be proof against the weather much longer, if it were so even now, and how the mud and ooze were coated with lime, and how the choking vapour of the kiln crept in a ghostly way towards me. Still there was no answer, and I knocked again. No answer still, and I tried the latch.

It rose under my hand, and the door yielded. Looking in, I saw a lighted candle on a table, a bench, and a mattress on a truckle bedstead. As there was a loft above, I called, "Is there any one here?" but no voice answered. Then, I looked at my watch, and, finding that it was past nine, called again, "Is there any one here?" There being still no answer, I went out at the door, irresolute what to do.

It was beginning to rain fast. Seeing nothing save what I had seen already, I turned back into the house, and stood just within the shelter of the doorway, looking out into the night. While I was considering that some one must have been there lately and must soon be coming back, or the candle would not be burning, it came into my head to look if the wick were long. I turned round to do so, and had taken up the candle in my hand, when it was extinguished by some violent shock, and the next thing I comprehended was, that I had been caught in a strong running noose, thrown over my head from behind.

"Now," said a suppressed voice with an oath, "I've got you!"

"What is this?" I cried, struggling. "Who is it? Help, help, help!"

Not only were my arms pulled close to my sides, but the pressure on my bad arm caused me exquisite pain. Sometimes a strong man's hand, sometimes a strong man's breast, was set against my mouth to deaden my cries, and with a hot breath always close to me, I struggled ineffectually in the dark, while I was fastened tight to the wall. "And now," said the suppressed voice with another oath, "call out again, and I'll make short work of you!"

Faint and sick with the pain of my injured arm, bewildered by the surprise, and yet conscious how easily this

threat could be put in execution, I desisted, and tried to ease
my arm were it ever so little. But it was bound too tight
for that. I felt as if, having been burnt before, it were now
being boiled.

The sudden exclusion of the night and the substitution of
black darkness in its place warned me that the man had
closed a shutter. After groping about for a little, he found
the flint and steel he wanted, and began to strike a light.
I strained my sight upon the sparks that fell among the
tinder, and upon which he breathed and breathed, match in
hand, but I could only see his lips, and the blue point of
the match ; even those but fitfully. The tinder was damp
—no wonder there—and one after another the sparks died
out.

The man was in no hurry, and struck again with the flint
and steel. As the sparks fell thick and bright about him,
I could see his hands and touches of his face, and could
make out that he was seated and bending over the table ;
but nothing more. Presently I saw his blue lips again,
breathing on the tinder, and then a flare of light flashed up,
and showed me Orlick.

Whom I had looked for, I don't know. I had not looked
for him. Seeing him, I felt that I was in a dangerous strait
indeed, and I kept my eyes upon him.

He lighted the candle from the flaring match with great
deliberation, and dropped the match, and trod it out. Then,
he put the candle away from him on the table, so that he
could see me, and sat with his arms folded on the table and
looked at me. I made out that I was fastened to a stout
perpendicular ladder a few inches from the wall—a fixture
there—the means of ascent to the loft above.

"Now," said he, when we had surveyed one another for
some time, "I've got you."

"Unbind me. Let me go!"

"Ah!" he returned, "*I'll* let you go. I'll let you go to
the moon, I'll let you go to the stars. All in good time."

"Why have you lured me here?"

"Don't you know?" said he, with a deadly look.

"Why have you set upon me in the dark?"

"Because I mean to do it all myself. One keeps a secret
better than two. Oh you enemy, you enemy!"

His enjoyment of the spectacle I furnished, as he sat with
his arms folded on the table, shaking his head at me and

hugging himself, had a malignity in it that made me tremble. As I watched him in silence, he put his hand into the corner at his side, and took up a gun with a brass-bound stock.

"Do you know this?" said he, making as if he would take aim at me. "Do you know where you saw it afore? Speak, wolf!"

"Yes," I answered.

"You cost me that place. You did. Speak!"

"What else could I do?"

"You did that, and that would be enough, without more. How dared you come betwixt me and a young woman I liked?"

"When did I?"

"When didn't you? It was you as always give Old Orlick a bad name to her."

"You gave it to yourself; you gained it for yourself. I could have done you no harm, if you had done yourself none."

"You're a liar. And you'll take any pains, and spend any money, to drive me out of this country, will you?" said he, repeating my words to Biddy, in the last interview I had with her. "Now, I'll tell you a piece of information. It was never so worth your while to get me out of this country, as it is to-night. Ah! If it was all your money twenty times told, to the last brass farden!" As he shook his heavy hand at me, with his mouth snarling like a tiger's, I felt that it was true.

"What are you going to do to me?"

"I'm a going," said he, bringing his fist down upon the table with a heavy blow, and rising as the blow fell, to give it greater force, "I'm a going to have your life!"

He leaned forward staring at me, slowly unclenched his hand and drew it across his mouth as if his mouth watered for me, and sat down again.

"You was always in Old Orlick's way since ever you was a child. You goes out of his way this present night. He'll have no more on you. You're dead."

I felt that I had come to the brink of my grave. For a moment I looked wildly round my trap for any chance of escape; but there was none.

"More than that," said he, folding his arms on the table again, "I won't have a rag of you, I won't have a bone of

"DO YOU KNOW THIS?" SAID HE

you, left on earth. I'll put your body in the kiln—I'd carry two such to it, on my shoulders—and, let people suppose what they may of you, they shall never know nothing."

My mind, with inconceivable rapidity, followed out all the consequences of such a death. Estella's father would believe I had deserted him, would be taken, would die accusing me; even Herbert would doubt me, when he compared the letter I had left for him with the fact that I had called at Miss Havisham's gate for only a moment; Joe and Biddy would never know how sorry I had been that night, none would ever know what I had suffered, how true I had meant to be, what an agony I had passed through. The death close before me was terrible, but far more terrible than death was the dread of being misremembered after death. And so quick were my thoughts, that I saw myself despised by unborn generations—Estella's children, and their children—while the wretch's words were yet on his lips.

"Now, wolf," said he, "afore I kill you like any other beast—which is wot I mean to do and wot I have tied you up for—I'll have a good look at you and a good goad at you. Oh, you enemy!"

It had passed through my thoughts to cry out for help again; though few could know better than I, the solitary nature of the spot, and the hopelessness of aid. But as he sat gloating over me, I was supported by a scornful detestation of him that sealed my lips. Above all things, I resolved that I would not entreat him, and that I would die making some last poor resistance to him. Softened as my thoughts of all the rest of men were in that dire extremity; humbly beseeching pardon, as I did, of Heaven; melted at heart, as I was, by the thought that I had taken no farewell, and never now could take farewell, of those who were dear to me, or could explain myself to them, or ask for their compassion on my miserable errors; still, if I could have killed him, even in dying, I would have done it.

He had been drinking, and his eyes were red and bloodshot. Around his neck was slung a tin bottle, as I had often seen his meat and drink slung about him in other days. He brought the bottle to his lips, and took a fiery drink from it; and I smelt the strong spirits that I saw flash into his face.

"Wolf!" said he, folding his arms again, "Old Orlick's

a going to tell you somethink. It was you as did for your shrew sister."

Again my mind, with its former inconceivable rapidity, had exhausted the whole subject of the attack upon my sister, her illness, and her death, before his slow and hesitating speech had formed those words.

"It was you, villain," said I.

"I tell you it was your doing—I tell you it was done through you," he retorted, catching up the gun, and making a blow with the stock at the vacant air between us. "I come upon her from behind, as I come upon you to-night. I giv' it her! I left her for dead, and, if there had been a lime-kiln as nigh her as there is now nigh you, she shouldn't have come to life again. But it warn't Old Orlick as did it; it was you. You was favoured, and he was bullied and beat. Old Orlick bullied and beat, eh? Now you pays for it. You done it; now you pays for it."

He drank again, and became more ferocious. I saw by his tilting of the bottle that there was no great quantity left in it. I distinctly understood that he was working himself up with its contents, to make an end of me. I knew that every drop it held was a drop of my life. I knew that when I was changed into a part of the vapour that had crept towards me but a little while before, like my own warning ghost, he would do as he had done in my sister's case—make all haste to the town, and be seen slouching about there, drinking at the ale-houses. My rapid mind pursued him to the town, made a picture of the street with him in it, and contrasted its lights and life with the lonely marsh and the white vapour creeping over it, into which I should have dissolved.

It was not only that I could have summed up years and years and years while he said a dozen words, but that what he did say presented pictures to me, and not mere words. In the excited and exalted state of my brain, I could not think of a place without seeing it, or of persons without seeing them. It is impossible to over-state the vividness of these images, and yet I was so intent, all the time, upon him himself—who would not be intent on the tiger crouching to spring!—that I knew of the slightest action of his fingers.

When he had drunk this second time, he rose from the bench on which he sat, and pushed the table aside. Then, he took up the candle, and shading it with his murderous hand so as to throw its light on me, stood before me, looking at me and enjoying the sight.

"Wolf, I'll tell you something more. It was Old Orlick as you tumbled over on your stairs that night."

I saw the staircase with its extinguished lamps. I saw the shadows of the heavy stair-rails, thrown by the watchman's lantern on the wall. I saw the rooms that I was never to see again; here, a door half open; there, a door closed; all the articles of furniture around.

"And why was Old Orlick there? I'll tell you something more, wolf. You and her *have* pretty well hunted me out of this country, so far as getting a easy living in it goes, and I've took up with new companions and new masters. Some of 'em writes my letters when I wants 'em wrote—do you mind?—writes my letters, wolf! They writes fifty hands; they're not like sneaking you, as writes but one. I've had a firm mind and a firm will to have your life, since you was down here at your sister's burying. I han't seen a way to get you safe, and I've looked arter you to know your ins and outs. For, says Old Orlick to himself, 'Somehow or another I'll have him!' What! When I looks for you, I finds your uncle Provis, eh?"

Mill Pond Bank, and Chinks's Basin, and the Old Green Copper Rope-Walk, all so clear and plain! Provis in his rooms, the signal whose use was over, pretty Clara, the good motherly woman, old Billy Barley on his back, all drifting by, as on the swift stream of my life fast running out to sea!

"*You* with a uncle too! Why, I knowed you at Gargery's when you was so small a wolf that I could have took your weazen betwixt this finger and thumb and chucked you away dead (as I'd thought o' doing, odd times, when I saw you a loitering among the pollards on a Sunday), and you hadn't found no uncles then. No, not you! But when Old Orlick come for to hear that your uncle Provis had mostlike wore the leg-iron wot Old Orlick had picked up, filed asunder, on these meshes ever so many year ago, and wot he kep by him till he dropped your sister with it, like a bullock, as he means to drop you—hey?—when he come for to hear that—hey?——"

In his savage taunting, he flared the candle so close at me, that I turned my face aside to save it from the flame.

"Ah!" he cried, laughing, after doing it again, "the burnt child dreads the fire! Old Orlick knowed you was burnt, Old Orlick knowed you was a smuggling your uncle Provis away, Old Orlick's a match for you and know'd you'd come to-night! Now I'll tell you something more, wolf, and this ends it. There's them that's as good a match for your uncle Provis as Old Orlick has been for you. Let him 'ware them when he's lost his nevvy. Let him 'ware them when no man can't find a rag of his dear relation's clothes, nor yet a bone of his body. There's them that can't and that won't have Magwitch—yes, *I* know the name!—alive in the same land with them, and that's had such sure information of him when he was alive in another land, as that he couldn't and shouldn't leave it unbeknown and put them in danger. P'raps it's them that writes fifty hands, and that's not like sneaking you as writes but one. 'Ware Compeyson, Magwitch, and the gallows!"

He flared the candle at me again, smoking my face and hair, and for an instant blinding me, and turned his powerful back as he replaced the light on the table. I had thought a prayer, and had been with Joe and Biddy and Herbert, before he turned towards me again.

There was a clear space of a few feet between the table and the opposite wall. Within this space, he now slouched backwards and forwards. His great strength seemed to sit stronger upon him than ever before, as he did this with his hands hanging loose and heavy at his sides, and with his eyes scowling at me. I had no grain of hope left. Wild as my inward hurry was, and wonderful the force of the pictures that rushed by me instead of thoughts, I could yet clearly understand that unless he had resolved that I was within a few moments of surely perishing out of all human knowledge, he would never have told me what he had told.

Of a sudden, he stopped, took the cork out of his bottle, and tossed it away. Light as it was, I heard it fall like a plummet. He swallowed slowly, tilting up the bottle by little and little, and now he looked at me no more. The last few drops of liquor he poured into the palm of his hand, and licked up. Then with a sudden hurry of violence and swearing horribly, he threw the bottle from him, and stooped ; and I saw in his hand a stone-hammer with a long heavy handle.

The resolution I had made did not desert me, for, without uttering one vain word of appeal to him, I shouted out with all my might, and struggled with all my might. It was only my head and my legs that I could move, but to that extent I struggled with all the force, until then unknown, that was within me. In the same instant I heard responsive shouts, saw figures and a gleam of light dash in at the door, heard voices and tumult, and saw Orlick emerge from a struggle of men, as if it were tumbling water, clear the table at a leap, and fly out into the night!

After a blank, I found that I was lying unbound, on the floor, in the same place, with my head on some one's knee. My eyes were fixed on the ladder against the wall, when I came to myself—had opened on it before my mind saw it—and thus as I recovered consciousness, I knew that I was in the place where I had lost it.

Too indifferent at first, even to look round and ascertain who supported me, I was lying looking at the ladder, when there came between me and it, a face. The face of Trabb's boy!

"I think he's all right!" said Trabb's boy, in a sober voice; "but ain't he just pale though!"

At these words, the face of him who supported me looked over into mine, and I saw my supporter to be——

"Herbert! Great Heaven!"

"Softly," said Herbert. "Gently, Handel. Don't be too eager."

"And our old comrade, Startop!" I cried, as he too bent over me.

"Remember what he is going to assist us in," said Herbert, "and be calm."

The allusion made me spring up; though I dropped again from the pain in my arm. "The time has not gone by, Herbert, has it? What night is to-night? How long have I been here?" For I had a strange and strong misgiving that I had been lying there a long time—a day and a night—two days and nights—more.

"The time has not gone by. It is still Monday night."

"Thank God!"

"And you have all to-morrow, Tuesday, to rest in," said Herbert. "But you can't help groaning, my dear Handel. What hurt have you got? Can you stand?"

"Yes, yes," said I, "I can walk. I have no hurt but in this throbbing arm."

They laid it bare, and did what they could. It was violently swollen and inflamed, and I could scarcely endure to have it touched. But they tore up their handkerchiefs to make fresh bandages, and carefully replaced it in the sling, until we could get to the town and obtain some cooling lotion to put upon it. In a little while we had shut the door of the dark and empty sluice-house, and were passing through the quarry on our way back. Trabb's boy— Trabb's overgrown young man now—went before us with a lantern, which was the light I had seen come in at the door. But the moon was a good two hours higher than when I had last seen the sky, and the night though rainy was much lighter. The white vapour of the kiln was passing from us as we went by, and, as I had thought a prayer before, I thought a thanksgiving now.

Entreating Herbert to tell me how he had come to my rescue—which at first he had flatly refused to do, but had insisted on my remaining quiet—I learnt that I had in my hurry dropped the letter, open, in our chambers, where he, coming home to bring with him Startop, whom he had met in the street on his way to me, found it, very soon after I was gone. Its tone made him uneasy, and the more so because of the inconsistency between it and the hasty letter I had left for him. His uneasiness increasing instead of subsiding after a quarter of an hour's consideration, he set off for the coach-office, with Startop, who volunteered his company, to make inquiry when the next coach went down. Finding that the afternoon coach was gone, and finding that his uneasiness grew into positive alarm, as obstacles came in his way, he resolved to follow in a post-chaise. So, he and Startop arrived at the Blue Boar, fully expecting there to find me, or tidings of me; but, finding neither, went on to Miss Havisham's, where they lost me. Hereupon they went back to the hotel (doubtless at about the time when I was hearing the popular local version of my own story) to refresh themselves, and to get some one to guide them out upon the marshes. Among the loungers under the Boar's archway happened to be Trabb's boy—true to his ancient habit of happening to be everywhere where he had no business—and Trabb's boy had seen me passing from Miss Havisham's, in the direction of my dining-place. Thus Trabb's boy became their guide, and with him they went out to the sluice-house: though by the town way to the marshes, which I had avoided. Now, as they went along, Herbert reflected that I might, after all, have been brought there on some genuine and serviceable errand tending to Provis's safety, and bethinking himself that in that case interruption might be mischievous, left his guide and Startop on the edge of the quarry, and went on by himself, and stole round the house two or three times, endeavouring to ascertain whether all was right within. As he could hear nothing but indistinct sounds of one deep rough voice (this was while my mind was so busy), he even at last began to doubt whether I was there, when suddenly I cried out loudly, and he answered the cries, and rushed in, closely followed by the other two.

When I told Herbert what had passed within the house, he was for our immediately going before a magistrate in the town, late at night as it was, and getting out a warrant. But I had already considered that such a course, by detaining us there, or binding us to come back, might be fatal to Provis. There was no gainsaying this difficulty, and we relinquished all thoughts of pursuing Orlick at that time. For the present, under the circumstances, we deemed it prudent to make rather light of the matter to Trabb's boy; who I am convinced would have been much affected by disappointment, if he had known that his intervention saved me from the limekiln. Not that Trabb's boy was of a malignant nature, but that he had too much spare vivacity, and that it was in his constitution to want variety and excitement at anybody's expense. When we parted, I presented him with two guineas (which seemed to meet his views), and told him that I was sorry ever to have had an ill opinion of him (which made no impression on him at all).

Wednesday being so close upon us, we determined to go back to London that night, three in the post-chaise; the rather, as we should then be clear away, before the night's adventure began to be talked of. Herbert got a large bottle of stuff for my arm, and by dint of having this stuff dropped over it all the night through, I was just able to bear its pain on the journey. It was daylight when we reached the Temple, and I went at once to bed, and lay in bed all day.

My terror, as I lay there, of falling ill and being unfitted for to-morrow, was so besetting, that I wonder it did not disable me of itself. It would have done so, pretty surely, in conjunction with the mental wear and tear I had suffered, but for the unnatural strain upon me that to-morrow was. So anxiously looked forward to, charged with such consequences, its results so impenetrably hidden though so near.

No precaution could have been more obvious than our refraining from communication with him that day; yet this again increased my restlessness. I started at every footstep and every sound, believing that he was discovered and taken, and this was the messenger to tell me so. I persuaded myself that I knew he was taken; that there was something more upon my mind than a fear or a presentiment; that the fact had occurred, and I had a mysterious knowledge of it. As the day wore on and no ill news came, as the day closed in and darkness fell, my overshadowing dread of being disabled by illness before to-morrow morning, altogether mastered me. My burning arm throbbed, and my burning head throbbed, and I fancied I was beginning to wander. I counted up to high numbers, to make sure of myself, and repeated passages that I knew in prose and verse. It happened sometimes that in the mere escape of a fatigued mind, I dozed for some moments or forgot; then I would say to myself with a start, "Now it has come, and I am turning delirious!"

They kept me very quiet all day, and kept my arm constantly dressed, and gave me cooling drinks. Whenever I fell asleep, I awoke with the notion I had had in the sluice-house, that a long time had elapsed and the opportunity to save him was gone. About midnight I got out of bed and went to Herbert, with the conviction that I had been asleep for four-and-twenty hours, and that Wednesday was past. It was the last self-exhausting effort of my fretfulness, for after that I slept soundly.

Wednesday morning was dawning when I looked out of window. The winking lights upon the bridges were already pale, the coming sun was like a marsh of fire on the horizon. The river, still dark and mysterious, was spanned by bridges that were turning coldly grey, with here and there at top a warm touch from the burning in the sky. As I looked along the clustered roofs, with church towers and spires shooting into the unusually clear air, the sun rose up, and a veil seemed to be drawn from the river, and millions of sparkles burst out upon its waters. From me, too, a veil seemed to be drawn, and I felt strong and well.

Herbert lay asleep in his bed, and our old fellow-student lay asleep on the sofa. I could not dress myself without help, but I made up the fire which was still burning, and got some coffee ready for them. In good time they too started up strong and well, and we admitted the sharp morning air at the windows, and looked at the tide that was still flowing towards us.

"When it turns at nine o'clock," said Herbert, cheerfully, "look out for us, and stand ready, you over there at Mill Pond Bank!"

CHAPTER LIV

It was one of those March days when the sun shines hot and the wind blows cold: when it is summer in the light, and winter in the shade. We had our pea-coats with us, and I took a bag. Of all my worldly possessions I took no more than the few necessaries that filled the bag. Where I might go, what I might do, or when I might return, were questions utterly unknown to me ; nor did I vex my mind with them, for it was wholly set on Provis's safety. I only wondered for the passing moment, as I stopped at the door and looked back, under what altered circumstances I should next see those rooms, if ever.

We loitered down to the Temple stairs, and stood loitering there, as if we were not quite decided to go upon the water at all. Of course I had taken care that the boat should be ready, and everything in order. After a little show of indecision, which there were none to see but the two or three amphibious creatures belonging to our Temple stairs, we went on board and cast off ; Herbert in the bow, I steering. It was then about high-water—half-past eight.

Our plan was this. The tide, beginning to run down at nine, and being with us until three, we intended still to creep on after it had turned, and row against it until dark. We should then be well in those long reaches below Graves-end, between Kent and Essex, where the river is broad and solitary, where the water-side inhabitants are very few, and where lone public-houses are scattered here and there, of which we could choose one for a resting-place. There, we meant to lie by, all night. The steamer for Hamburg, and the steamer for Rotterdam, would start from London at about nine on Thursday morning. We should know at what time to expect them, according to where we were, and would hail the first ; so that if by any accident we were not taken aboard, we should have another chance. We knew the distinguishing marks of each vessel.

The relief of being at last engaged in the execution of the purpose, was so great to me that I felt it difficult to realise the condition in which I had been in a few hours before. The crisp air, the sunlight, the movement on the river, and the moving river itself—the road that ran with us, seeming to sympathise with us, animate us, and encourage us on—freshened me with new hope. I felt mortified to be of so little use in the boat; but there were few better oarsmen than my two friends, and they rowed with a steady stroke that was to last all day.

At that time, the steam-traffic on the Thames was far below its present extent, and watermen's boats were far more numerous. Of barges, sailing colliers, and coasting traders, there were perhaps as many as now; but of steam-ships, great and small, not a tithe or a twentieth part so many. Early as it was, there were plenty of scullers going here and there that morning, and plenty of barges dropping down with the tide; the navigation of the river between bridges, in an open boat, was a much easier and commoner matter in those days than it is in these; and we went ahead among many skiffs and wherries, briskly.

Old London Bridge was soon passed, and old Billingsgate market with its oyster-boats and Dutchmen, and the White Tower and Traitor's Gate, and we were in among the tiers of shipping. Here, were the Leith, Aberdeen, and Glasgow steamers, loading and unloading goods, and looking immensely high out of the water as we passed alongside; here, were colliers by the score and score, with the coal-whippers plunging off stages on deck, as counterweights to measures of coal swinging up, which were then rattled over the side into barges; here, at her moorings, was to-morrow's steamer for Rotterdam, of which we took good notice; and here to-morrow's for Hamburg, under whose bowsprit we crossed. And now I, sitting in the stern, could see with a faster beating heart, Mill Pond Bank and Mill Pond stairs.

"Is he there?" said Herbert.

"Not yet."

"Right! He was not to come down till he saw us. Can you see his signal?"

"Not well from here; but I think I see it.—Now I see him! Pull both. Easy, Herbert. Oars!"

We touched the stairs lightly for a single moment, and

he was on board and we were off again. He had a boat-cloak with him, and a black canvas bag, and he looked as like a river-pilot as my heart could have wished.

"Dear boy!" he said, putting his arm on my shoulder, as he took his seat. "Faithful dear boy, well done. Thankye, thankye!"

Again among the tiers of shipping, in and out, avoiding rusty chain-cables, frayed hempen hawsers, and bobbing buoys, sinking for the moment floating broken baskets, scattering floating chips of wood and shaving, cleaving floating scum of coal, in and out, under the figure-head of the John of Sunderland making a speech to the winds (as is done by many Johns), and the Betsy of Yarmouth with a firm formality of bosom and her knobby eyes starting two inches out of her head; in and out, hammers going in ship-builders' yards, saws going at timber, clashing engines going at things unknown, pumps going in leaky ships, capstans going, ships going out to sea, and unintelligible sea-creatures roaring curses over the bulwarks at respondent lightermen; in and out—out at last upon the clearer river, where the ships' boys might take their fenders in, no longer fishing in troubled waters with them over the side, and where the festooned sails might fly out to the wind.

At the Stairs where we had taken him aboard, and ever since, I had looked warily for any token of our being suspected. I had seen none. We certainly had not been, and at that time as certainly we were not, either attended or followed by any boat. If we had been waited on by any boat, I should have run in to shore, and have obliged her to go on, or to make her purpose evident. But we held our own, without any appearance of molestation.

He had his boat-cloak on him, and looked, as I have said, a natural part of the scene. It was remarkable (but perhaps the wretched life he had led accounted for it), that he was the least anxious of any of us. He was not indifferent, for he told me that he hoped to live to see his gentleman one of the best of gentlemen in a foreign country; he was not disposed to be passive or resigned, as I understood it; but he had no notion of meeting danger half-way. When it came upon him, he confronted it, but it must come before he troubled himself.

"If you knowed, dear boy," he said to me, "what it is to sit here alonger my dear boy and have my smoke, arter having been day by day betwixt four walls, you'd envy me. But you don't know what it is."

"I think I know the delights of freedom," I answered.

"Ah," said he, shaking his head gravely. "But you don't know it equal to me. You must have been under lock and key, dear boy, to know it equal to me—but I ain't a going to be low."

It occurred to me as inconsistent, that for any mastering idea he should have endangered his freedom and even his life. But I reflected that perhaps freedom without danger was too much apart from all the habit of his existence to be to him what it would be to another man. I was not far out, since he said, after smoking a little :

"You see, dear boy, when I was over yonder, t'other side the world, I was always a looking to this side; and it come flat to be there, for all I was a growing rich. Everybody knowed Magwitch, and Magwitch could come, and Magwitch could go, and nobody's head would be troubled about him. They ain't so easy concerning me here, dear boy—wouldn't be, leastwise, if they knowed where I was."

"If all goes well," said I, "you will be perfectly free and safe again, within a few hours."

"Well," he returned, drawing a long breath, "I hope so."

"And think so ?"

He dipped his hand in the water over the boat's gunwale, and said, smiling with that softened air upon him which was not new to me :

"Ay, I s'pose I think so, dear boy. We'd be puzzled to be more quiet and easy-going than we are at present. But—it's a flowing so soft and pleasant through the water, p'raps, as makes me think it—I was a thinking through my smoke just then, that we can no more see to the bottom of the next few hours, than we can see to the bottom of this river what I catches hold of. Nor yet we can't no more hold their tide than I can hold this. And it's run through my fingers and gone, you see !" holding up his dripping hand.

"But for your face, I should think you were a little despondent," said I.

"Not a bit on it, dear boy ! It comes of flowing on so quiet, and of that there rippling at the boat's head making a sort of a Sunday tune. Maybe I'm a growing a trifle old besides."

He put his pipe back in his mouth with an undisturbed expression of face, and sat as composed and contented as if we were already out of England.   Yet he was as submissive to a word of advice as if he had been in constant terror, for when we ran ashore to get some bottles of beer into the boat, and he was stepping out, I hinted that I thought he would be safest where he was, and he said, "Do you, dear boy?" and quietly sat down again.

The air felt cold upon the river, but it was a bright day, and the sunshine was very cheering.   The tide ran strong, I took care to lose none of it, and our steady stroke carried us on thoroughly well.   By imperceptible degrees, as the tide ran out, we lost more and more of the nearer woods and hills, and dropped lower and lower between the muddy banks, but the tide was yet with us when we were off Gravesend.   As our charge was wrapped in his cloak, I purposely passed within a boat or two's length of the floating Custom House, and so out to catch the stream, alongside of two emigrant ships, and under the bows of a large transport with troops on the forecastle looking down at us.   And soon the tide began to slacken, and the craft lying at anchor to swing, and presently they had all swung round, and the ships that were taking advantage of the new tide to get up to the Pool, began to crowd upon us in a fleet, and we kept under the shore, as much out of the strength of the tide now as we could, standing carefully off from low shallows and mud-banks.

Our oarsmen were so fresh, by dint of having occasionally let her drive with the tide for a minute or two, that a quarter of an hour's rest proved full as much as they wanted.   We got ashore among some slippery stones while we ate and drank what we had with us, and looked about.   It was like my own marsh country, flat and monotonous, and with a dim horizon; while the winding river turned and turned, and the great floating buoys upon it turned and turned, and everything else seemed stranded and still.   For now the last of the fleet of ships was round the last low point we had headed; and the last green barge, straw-laden, with a brown sail, had followed; and some ballast-lighters, shaped like a child's first rude imitation of a boat, lay low in the mud; and a little squat shoal-lighthouse on open piles, stood crippled in the mud on stilts and crutches; and slimy stakes stuck out of the mud, and slimy stones stuck out of the mud, and red landmarks and tidemarks stuck out of the mud, and an old landing-stage and an old roofless building slipped into the mud, and all about us was stagnation and mud.

We pushed off again, and made what way we could. It was much harder work now, but Herbert and Startop persevered, and rowed, and rowed, and rowed, until the sun went down. By that time the river had lifted us a little, so that we could see above the bank. There was the red sun, on the low level of the shore, in a purple haze, fast deepening into black; and there was the solitary flat marsh; and far away there were the rising grounds, between which and us there seemed to be no life, save here and there in the foreground a melancholy gull.

As the night was fast falling, and as the moon, being past the full, would not rise early, we held a little council: a short one, for clearly our course was to lie by at the first lonely tavern we could find. So they plied their oars once more, and I looked out for anything like a house. Thus we held on, speaking little, for four or five dull miles. It was very cold, and a collier coming by us, with her galley-fire smoking and flaring, looked like a comfortable home. The night was dark by this time as it would be until morning; what light we had, seemed to come more from the river than the sky, as the oars in their dipping struck at a few reflected stars.

At this dismal time we were evidently all possessed by the idea that we were followed. As the tide made, it flapped heavily at irregular intervals against the shore; and whenever such a sound came, one or other of us was sure to start and look in that direction. Here and there, the set of the current had worn down the bank into a little creek, and we were all suspicious of such places, and eyed them nervously. Sometimes, "What was that ripple?" one of us would say in a low voice. Or another, "Is that a boat yonder?" And afterwards, we would fall into a dead silence, and I would sit impatiently thinking with what an unusual amount of noise the oars worked in the thowels.

At length we descried a light and a roof, and presently afterwards ran alongside a little causeway made of stones that had been picked up hard by. Leaving the rest in the boat, I stepped ashore, and found the light to be in the window of a public-house. It was a dirty place enough, and I dare say not unknown to smuggling adventurers;

but there was a good fire in the kitchen, and there were eggs and bacon to eat, and various liquors to drink. Also, there were two double-bedded rooms—"such as they were," the landlord said. No other company was in the house than the landlord, his wife, and a grizzled male creature, the "Jack" of the little causeway, who was as slimy and smeary as if he had been low water-mark too.

With this assistant, I went down to the boat again, and we all came ashore, and brought out the oars, and rudder, and boat-hook, and all else, and hauled her up for the night. We made a very good meal by the kitchen fire, and then apportioned the bedrooms: Herbert and Startop were to occupy one; I and our charge the other. We found the air as carefully excluded from both as if air were fatal to life; and there were more dirty clothes and bandboxes under the beds, than I should have thought the family possessed. But we considered ourselves well off, notwithstanding, for a more solitary place we could not have found.

While we were comforting ourselves by the fire after our meal, the Jack—who was sitting in a corner, and who had a bloated pair of shoes on, which he had exhibited while we were eating our eggs and bacon, as interesting relics that he had taken a few days ago from the feet of a drowned seaman washed ashore—asked me if we had seen a four-oared galley going up with the tide? When I told him No, he said she must have gone down then, and yet she "took up too," when she left there.

"They must ha' thought better on't for some reason or another," said the Jack, "and gone down."

"A four-oared galley, did you say?" said I.

"A four," said the Jack, "and two sitters."

"Did they come ashore here?"

"They put in with a stone two-gallon jar, for some beer. I'd ha' been glad to pison the beer myself," said the Jack, "or put some rattling physic in it."

"Why?"

"*I* know why," said the Jack. He spoke in a slushy voice, as if much mud had washed into his throat.

"He thinks," said the landlord: a weakly meditative man with a pale eye, who seemed to rely greatly on his Jack: "he thinks they was, what they wasn't."

"*I* knows what I thinks," observed the Jack.

"*You* thinks Custom 'Us, Jack?" said the landlord.

"I do," said the Jack.

"Then you're wrong, Jack."

"Am I!"

In the infinite meaning of his reply and his boundless confidence in his views, the Jack took one of his bloated shoes off, looked into it, knocked a few stones out of it on the kitchen floor, and put it on again. He did this with the air of a Jack who was so right that he could afford to do anything.

"Why, what do you make out that they done with their buttons, then, Jack?" asked the landlord, vacillating weakly.

"Done with their buttons?" returned the Jack. "Chucked 'em overboard. Swallered 'em. Sowed 'em, to come up small salad. Done with their buttons!"

"Don't be cheeky, Jack," remonstrated the landlord, in a melancholy and pathetic way.

"A Custom 'Us officer knows what to do with his Buttons," said the Jack, repeating the obnoxious word with the greatest contempt, "when they comes betwixt him and his own light. A Four and two sitters don't go hanging and hovering, up with one tide and down with another, and both with and against another, without there being Custom 'Us at the bottom of it." Saying which he went out in disdain; and the landlord, having no one to rely upon, found it impracticable to pursue the subject.

This dialogue made us all uneasy, and me very uneasy. The dismal wind was muttering round the house, the tide was flapping at the shore, and I had a feeling that we were caged and threatened. A four-oared galley hovering about in so unusual a way as to attract this notice, was an ugly circumstance that I could not get rid of. When I had induced Provis to go up to bed, I went outside with my two companions (Startop by this time knew the state of the case), and held another council. Whether we should remain at the house until near the steamer's time, which would be about one in the afternoon; or whether we should put off early in the morning; was the question we discussed. On the whole we deemed it the better course to lie where we were, until within an hour or so of the steamer's time, and then to get out in her track, and drift easily with the tide. Having settled to do this, we returned into the house and went to bed.

I lay down with the greater part of my clothes on, and

slept well for a few hours. When I awoke, the wind had risen, and the sign of the house (the Ship) was creaking and banging about, with noises that startled me. Rising softly, for my charge lay fast asleep, I looked out of the window. It commanded the causeway where we had hauled up our boat, and, as my eyes adapted themselves to the light of the clouded moon, I saw two men looking into her. They passed by under the window, looking at nothing else, and they did not go down to the landing-place which I could discern to be empty, but struck across the marsh in the direction of the Nore.

My first impulse was to call up Herbert, and show him the two men going away. But, reflecting before I got into his room, which was at the back of the house and adjoined mine, that he and Startop had had a harder day than I, and were fatigued, I forbore. Going back to my window I could see the two men moving over the marsh. In that light, however, I soon lost them, and feeling very cold, lay down to think of the matter, and fell asleep again.

We were up early. As we walked to and fro, all four together, before breakfast, I deemed it right to recount what I had seen. Again our charge was the least anxious of the party. It was very likely that the men belonged to the Custom House, he said quietly, and that they had no thought of us. I tried to persuade myself that it was so—as, indeed, it might easily be. However, I proposed that he and I should walk away together to a distant point we could see, and that the boat should take us aboard there, or as near there as might prove feasible, at about noon. This being considered a good precaution, soon after breakfast he and I set forth, without saying anything at the tavern.

He smoked his pipe as we went along, and sometimes stopped to clap me on the shoulder. One would have supposed that it was I who was in danger, not he, and that he was reassuring me. We spoke very little. As we approached the point, I begged him to remain in a sheltered place, while I went on to reconnoitre ; for it was towards it that the men had passed in the night. He complied, and I went on alone. There was no boat off the point, nor any boat drawn up anywhere near it, nor were there any signs of the men having embarked there. But, to be sure, the tide was high, and there might have been some footprints under water.

When he looked out from his shelter in the distance, and

saw that I waved my hat to him to come up, he rejoined me, and there we waited; sometimes lying on the bank wrapped in our coats, and sometimes moving about to warm ourselves: until we saw our boat coming round. We got aboard easily, and rowed out into the track of the steamer. By that time it wanted but ten minutes of one o'clock, and we began to look out for her smoke.

But it was half-past one before we saw her smoke, and soon after we saw behind it the smoke of another steamer. As they were coming on at full speed, we got the two bags ready, and took that opportunity of saying good-bye to Herbert and Startop. We had all shaken hands cordially, and neither Herbert's eyes nor mine were quite dry, when I saw a four-oared galley shoot out from under the bank but a little way ahead of us, and row out into the same track.

A stretch of shore had been as yet between us and the steamer's smoke, by reason of the bend and wind of the river; but now she was visible coming head on. I called to Herbert and Startop to keep before the tide, that she might see us lying by for her, and adjured Provis to sit quite still, wrapped in his cloak. He answered cheerily, "Trust to me, dear boy," and sat like a statue. Meanwhile the galley, which was skilfully handled, had crossed us, let us come up with her, and fallen alongside. Leaving just room enough for the play of the oars, she kept alongside, drifting when we drifted, and pulling a stroke or two when we pulled. Of the two sitters, one held the rudder lines, and looked at us attentively—as did all the rowers; the other sitter was wrapped up, much as Provis was, and seemed to shrink, and whisper some instruction to the steerer as he looked at us. Not a word was spoken in either boat.

Startop could make out, after a few minutes, which steamer was first, and gave me the word "Hamburg," in a low voice as we sat face to face. She was nearing us very fast, and the beating of her paddles grew louder and louder. I felt as if her shadow were absolutely upon us, when the galley hailed us. I answered.

"You have a returned transport there," said the man who held the lines. "That's the man, wrapped in the cloak. His name is Abel Magwitch, otherwise Provis. I apprehend that man, and call upon him to surrender, and you to assist."

At the same moment, without giving any audible direction to his crew, he ran the galley aboard of us. They had pulled one sudden stroke ahead, had got their oars in, had run athwart us, and were holding on to our gunwale, before we knew what they were doing. This caused great confusion on board of the steamer, and I heard them calling to us, and heard the order given to stop the paddles, and heard them stop, but felt her driving down upon us irresistibly. In the same moment, I saw the steersman of the galley lay his hand on his prisoner's shoulder, and saw that both boats were swinging round with the force of the tide, and saw that all hands on board the steamer were running forward quite frantically. Still in the same moment, I saw the prisoner start up, lean across his captor, and pull the cloak from the neck of the shrinking sitter in the galley. Still in the same moment, I saw that the face disclosed was the face of the other convict of long ago. Still in the same moment, I saw the face tilt backward with a white terror on it that I shall never forget, and heard a great cry on board the steamer and a loud splash in the water, and felt the boat sink from under me.

It was but for an instant that I seemed to struggle with a thousand mill-weirs and a thousand flashes of light; that instant past, I was taken on board the galley. Herbert was there, and Startop was there; but our boat was gone, and the two convicts were gone.

What with the cries aboard the steamer, and the furious blowing off of her steam, and her driving on, and our driving on, I could not at first distinguish sky from water or shore from shore; but the crew of the galley righted her with great speed, and, pulling certain swift strong strokes ahead, lay upon their oars, every man looking silently and eagerly at the water astern. Presently a dark object was seen in it, bearing towards us on the tide. No man spoke, but the steersman held up his hand, and all softly backed water, and kept the boat straight and true before it. As it came nearer, I saw it to be Magwitch, swimming, but not swimming freely. He was taken on board, and instantly manacled at the wrists and ankles.

The galley was kept steady, and the silent eager look-out at the water was resumed. But the Rotterdam steamer now came up, and apparently not understanding what had happened, came on at speed. By the time she had been

hailed and stopped, both steamers were drifting away from us, and we were rising and falling in a troubled wake of water. The look-out was kept, long after all was still again and the two steamers were gone ; but everybody knew that it was hopeless now.

At length we gave it up, and pulled under the shore towards the tavern we had lately left, where we were received with no little surprise. Here I was able to get some comforts for Magwitch—Provis no longer—who had received some very severe injury in the chest and a deep cut in the head.

He told me that he believed himself to have gone under the keel of the steamer, and to have been struck on the head in rising. The injury to his chest (which rendered his breathing extremely painful) he thought he had received against the side of the galley. He added that he did not pretend to say what he might or might not have done to Compeyson, but that in the moment of his laying his hand on his cloak to identify him, that villain had staggered up and staggered back, and they had both gone overboard together ; when the sudden wrenching of him (Magwitch) out of our boat, and the endeavour of his captor to keep him in it, had capsized us. He told me in a whisper that they had gone down, fiercely locked in each other's arms, and that there had been a struggle under water, and that he had disengaged himself, struck out, and swam away.

I never had any reason to doubt the exact truth of what he had told me. The officer who steered the galley gave the same account of their going overboard.

When I asked this officer's permission to change the prisoner's wet clothes by purchasing any spare garments I could get at the public-house, he gave it readily : merely observing that he must take charge of everything his prisoner had about him. So the pocket-book which had once been in my hands, passed into the officer's. He further gave me leave to accompany the prisoner to London ; but declined to accord that grace to my two friends.

The Jack at the Ship was instructed where the drowned man had gone down, and undertook to search for the body in the places where it was likeliest to come ashore. His interest in its recovery seemed to me to be much heightened when he heard that it had stockings on. Probably it took about a dozen drowned men to fit him out completely ; and

that may have been the reason why the different articles of his dress were in various stages of decay.

We remained at the public-house until the tide turned, and then Magwitch was carried down to the galley and put on board. Herbert and Startop were to get to London by land, as soon as they could. We had a doleful parting, and when I took my place by Magwitch's side, I felt that that was my place henceforth while he lived.

For now my repugnance to him had all melted away, and in the hunted wounded shackled creature who held my hand in his, I only saw a man who had meant to be my benefactor, and who had felt affectionately, gratefully, and generously, towards me with great constancy through a series of years. I only saw in him a much better man than I had been to Joe.

His breathing became more difficult and painful as the night drew on, and often he could not repress a groan. I tried to rest him on the arm I could use, in any easy position ; but it was dreadful to think that I could not be sorry at heart for his being badly hurt, since it was un-questionably best that he should die. That there were, still living, people enough who were able and willing to identify him, I could not doubt. That he would be leniently treated, I could not hope. He who had been presented in the worst light at his trial, who had since broken prison and been tried again, who had returned from transportation under a life sentence, and who had occasioned the death of the man who was the cause of his arrest.

As we returned towards the setting sun we had yesterday left behind us, and as the stream of our hopes seemed all running back, I told him how grieved I was to think he had come home for my sake.

"Dear boy," he answered, "I'm quite content to take my chance. I've seen my boy, and he can be a gentleman without me."

No. I had thought about that while we had been there side by side. No. Apart from any inclinations of my own, I understand Wemmick's hint now. I foresaw that, being convicted, his possessions would be forfeited to the Crown.

"Lookee here, dear boy," said he. "It's best as a gentle-man should not be knowed to belong to me now. Only come to see me as if you come by chance alonger Wemmick.

Sit where I can see you when I am swore to, for the last o' many times, and I don't ask no more."

"I will never stir from your side," said I, "when I am suffered to be near you. Please God, I will be as true to you as you have been to me!"

I felt his hand tremble as it held mine, and he turned his face away as he lay in the bottom of the boat, and I heard that old sound in his throat—softened now, like all the rest of him. It was a good thing that he had touched this point, for it put into my mind what I might not otherwise have thought of until too late: that he need never know how his hopes of enriching me had perished.

CHAPTER LV

HE was taken to the Police Court next day, and would have been immediately committed for trial, but that it was necessary to send down for an old officer of the prison-ship from which he had once escaped, to speak to his identity. Nobody doubted it; but Compeyson, who had meant to depose to it, was tumbling on the tides, dead, and it happened that there was not at that time any prison officer in London who could give the required evidence. I had gone direct to Mr. Jaggers at his private house, on my arrival over-night, to retain his assistance, and Mr. Jaggers on the prisoner's behalf would admit nothing. It was the sole resource, for he told me that the case must be over in five minutes when the witness was there, and that no power on earth could prevent its going against us.

I imparted to Mr. Jaggers my design of keeping him in ignorance of the fate of his wealth. Mr. Jaggers was querulous and angry with me for having "let it slip through my fingers," and said we must memorialise by-and-by, and try at all events for some of it. But he did not conceal from me that although there might be many cases in which forfeiture would not be exacted, there were no circumstances in this case to make it one of them. I understood that very well. I was not related to the outlaw, or connected with him by any recognisable tie; he had put his hand to no writing or settlement in my favour before his apprehension, and to do so now would be idle. I had no claim, and I finally resolved, and ever afterwards abided by the resolution, that my heart should never be sickened with the hopeless task of attempting to establish one.

There appeared to be reason for supposing that the drowned informer had hoped for a reward out of this forfeiture, and had obtained some accurate knowledge of Magwitch's affairs. When his body was found, many miles from the scene of his death, and so horribly disfigured that he was only recognisable by the contents of his pockets, notes were still legible, folded in a case he carried. Among these were the name of a banking-house in New South Wales where a sum of money was, and the designation of certain lands of considerable value. Both those heads of information were in a list that Magwitch, while in prison, gave to Mr. Jaggers, of the possessions he supposed I should inherit. His ignorance, poor fellow, at last served him; he never mistrusted but that my inheritance was quite safe, with Mr. Jaggers's aid.

After three days' delay, during which the crown prosecution stood over for the production of the witness from the prison-ship, the witness came, and completed the easy case. He was committed to take his trial at the next Session, which would come on in a month.

It was at this dark time of my life that Herbert returned home one evening, a good deal cast down, and said:

"My dear Handel, I fear I shall soon have to leave you."

His partner having prepared me for that, I was less surprised than he thought.

"We shall lose a fine opportunity if I put off going to Cairo, and I am very much afraid I must go, Handel, when you most need me."

"Herbert, I shall always need you, because I shall always love you; but my need is no greater now, than at another time."

"You will be so lonely."

"I have not leisure to think of that," said I. "You know that I am always with him to the full extent of the time allowed, and that I should be with him all day long, if I could. And when I come away from him, you know that my thoughts are with him."

The dreadful condition to which he was brought, was so appalling to both of us, that we could not refer to it in plainer words.

"My dear fellow," said Herbert, "let the near prospect of our separation—for it is very near—be my justification for troubling you about yourself. Have you thought of your future?"

"No, for I have been afraid to think of any future."

"But yours cannot be dismissed; indeed, my dear, dear Handel, it must not be dismissed. I wish you would enter on it now, as far as a few friendly words go, with me."

"I will," said I.

"In this branch house of ours, Handel, we must have a——"

I saw that his delicacy was avoiding the right word, so I said, "A clerk."

"A clerk. And I hope it is not at all unlikely that he may expand (as a clerk of your acquaintance has expanded) into a partner. Now, Handel——in short, my dear boy, will you come to me?"

There was something charmingly cordial and engaging in the manner in which after saying, "Now, Handel," as if it were the grave beginning of a portentous business exordium, he had suddenly given up that tone, stretched out his honest hand, and spoken like a schoolboy.

"Clara and I have talked about it again and again," Herbert pursued, "and the dear little thing begged me only this evening, with tears in her eyes, to say to you that if you will live with us when we come together, she will do her best to make you happy, and to convince her husband's friend that he is her friend too. We should get on so well, Handel!"

I thanked her heartily, and I thanked him heartily, but said I could not yet make sure of joining him as he so kindly offered. Firstly, my mind was too preoccupied to be able to take in the subject clearly. Secondly——Yes! Secondly, there was a vague something lingering in my thoughts that will come out very near the end of this slight narrative.

"But if you thought, Herbert, that you could, without doing any injury to your business, leave the question open for a little while——"

"For any while," cried Herbert. "Six months, a year!"

"Not so long as that," said I. "Two or three months at most."

Herbert was highly delighted when we shook hands on this arrangement, and said he could now take courage to tell me that he believed he must go away at the end of the week.

"And Clara?" said I.

"The dear little thing," returned Herbert, "holds dutifully to her father as long as he lasts; but he won't last long. Mrs. Whimple confides to me that he is certainly going."

perspective of his bedroom, I observed that his bed was empty.

When we had fortified ourselves with the rum-and-milk and biscuits, and were going out for the walk with that training preparation on us, I was considerably surprised to see Wemmick take up a fishing-rod, and put it over his shoulder. "Why, we are not going fishing!" said I. "No," returned Wemmick, "but I like to walk with one."

I thought this odd; however, I said nothing, and we set off. We went towards Camberwell Green, and when we were thereabouts, Wemmick said suddenly:

"Halloa! Here's a church!"

There was nothing very surprising in that; but again, I was rather surprised, when he said, as if he were animated by a brilliant idea:

"Let's go in!"

We went in, Wemmick leaving his fishing-rod in the porch, and looked all round. In the mean time, Wemmick was diving into his coat-pockets, and getting something out of paper there.

"Halloa!" said he. "Here's a couple of pair of gloves! Let's put 'em on!"

As the gloves were white kid gloves, and as the post-office was widened to its utmost extent, I now began to have my strong suspicions. They were strengthened into certainty when I beheld the Aged enter at a side door, escorting a lady.

"Halloa!" said Wemmick. "Here's Miss Skiffins! Let's have a wedding."

That discreet damsel was attired as usual, except that she was now engaged in substituting for her green kid gloves, a pair of white. The Aged was likewise occupied in preparing a similar sacrifice for the altar of Hymen. The old gentleman, however, experienced so much difficulty in getting his gloves on, that Wemmick found it necessary to put him with his back against a pillar, and then to get behind the pillar himself and pull away at them, while I for my part held the old gentleman round the waist, that he might present an equal and safe resistance. By dint of this ingenious scheme, his gloves were got on to perfection.

The clerk and clergyman then appearing, we were ranged in order at those fatal rails. True to his notion of seeming to do it all without preparation, I heard Wemmick say to himself as he took something out of his waistcoat-pocket before the service began, "Halloa! Here's a ring!"

I acted in the capacity of backer, or best-man, to the bridegroom; while a little limp pew-opener in a soft bonnet like a baby's, made a feint of being the bosom friend of Miss Skiffins. The responsibility of giving the lady away, devolved upon the Aged, which led to the clergyman's being unintentionally scandalised, and it happened thus. When he said, "Who giveth this woman to be married to this man?" the old gentleman, not in the least knowing what point of the ceremony we had arrived at, stood most amiably beaming at the ten commandments. Upon which, the clergyman said again, "WHO giveth this woman to be married to this man?" The old gentleman being still in a state of most estimable unconsciousness, the bridegroom cried out in his accustomed voice, "Now, Aged P., you know; who giveth?" To which the Aged replied with great briskness, before saying that *he* gave, "All right, John, all right, my boy!" And the clergyman came to so gloomy a pause upon it, that I had doubts for the moment whether we should get completely married that day.

It was completely done, however, and when we were going out of church, Wemmick took the cover off the font, and put his white gloves in it, and put the cover on again. Mrs. Wemmick, more heedful of the future, put her white gloves in her pocket and assumed her green. "*Now*, Mr. Pip," said Wemmick, triumphantly shouldering the fishing-rod as we came out, "let me ask you whether anybody would suppose this to be a wedding-party!"

Breakfast had been ordered at a pleasant little tavern, a mile or so away upon the rising ground beyond the green; and there was a bagatelle board in the room, in case we should desire to unbend our minds after the solemnity. It was pleasant to observe that Mrs. Wemmick no longer un-wound Wemmick's arm when it adapted itself to her figure, but sat in a high-backed chair against the wall, like a violon-cello in its case, and submitted to be embraced as that melo-dious instrument might have done.

We had an excellent breakfast, and when any one declined anything on table, Wemmick said, "Provided by contract, you know; don't be afraid of it!" I drank to the new couple, drank to the Aged, drank to the Castle, saluted the bride at parting, and made myself as agreeable as I could.

Wemmick came down to the door with me, and I again shook hands with him, and wished him joy.

"Thankee!" said Wemmick, rubbing his hands. "She's such a manager of fowls, you have no idea. You shall have some eggs and judge for yourself. I say, Mr. Pip!" calling me back and speaking low. "This is altogether a Walworth sentiment, please."

"I understand. Not to be mentioned in Little Britain," said I.

Wemmick nodded. "After what you let out the other day, Mr. Jaggers may as well not know of it. He might think my brain was softening, or something of the kind."

CHAPTER LVI

He lay in prison very ill, during the whole interval between his committal for trial, and the coming round of the Sessions. He had broken two ribs, they had wounded one of his lungs, and he breathed with great pain and difficulty, which increased daily. It was a consequence of his hurt that he spoke so low as to be scarcely audible; therefore he spoke very little. But he was ever ready to listen to me, and it became the first duty of my life to say to him, and read to him, what I knew he ought to hear.

Being far too ill to remain in the common prison, he was removed, after the first day or so, into the infirmary. This gave me opportunities of being with him that I could not otherwise have had. And but for his illness he would have been put in irons, for he was regarded as a determined prison-breaker, and I know not what else.

Although I saw him every day, it was for only a short time; hence the regularly recurring spaces of our separation were long enough to record on his face any slight changes that occurred in his physical state. I do not recollect that I once saw any change in it for the better; he wasted, and became slowly weaker and worse, day by day from the day when the prison door closed upon him.

The kind of submission or resignation that he showed, was that of a man who was tired out. I sometimes derived an impression, from his manner or from a whispered word or two which escaped him, that he pondered over the question whether he might have been a better man under better circumstances. But he never justified himself by a hint tending that way, or tried to bend the past out of its eternal shape.

It happened on two or three occasions in my presence, that his desperate reputation was alluded to by one or other of the people in attendance on him. A smile crossed his face then, and he turned his eyes on me with a trustful look, as if he were confident that I had seen some small redeeming touch in him, even so long ago as when I was a little child. As to all the rest, he was humble and contrite, and I never knew him complain.

When the Sessions came round, Mr. Jaggers caused an application to be made for the postponement of his trial until the following Sessions. It was obviously made with the assurance that he could not live so long, and was refused. The trial came on at once, and when he was put to the bar, he was seated in a chair. No objection was made to my getting close to the dock, on the outside of it, and holding the hand that he stretched forth to me.

The trial was very short and very clear. Such things as could be said for him, were said—how he had taken to industrious habits, and had thriven lawfully and reputably. But nothing could unsay the fact that he had returned, and was there in presence of the Judge and Jury. It was impossible to try him for that, and do otherwise than find him guilty.

At that time it was the custom (as I learnt from my terrible experience of that Sessions) to devote a concluding day to the passing of Sentences, and to make a finishing effect with the Sentence of Death. But for the indelible picture that my remembrance now holds before me, I could scarcely believe, even as I write these words, that I saw two-and-thirty men and women put before the Judge to receive that sentence together. Foremost among the two-and-thirty was he; seated, that he might get breath enough to keep life in him.

The whole scene starts out again in the vivid colours of the moment, down to the drops of April rain on the windows of the court, glittering in the rays of April sun. Penned in the dock, as I again stood outside it at the corner with his hand in mine, were the two-and-thirty men and women; some defiant, some stricken with terror, some sobbing and weeping, some covering their faces, some staring gloomily about. There had been shrieks from among the women convicts, but they had been stilled, and a hush had succeeded. The sheriffs with their great chains and nosegays, other civic gewgaws and monsters, criers, ushers, a great gallery full of people—a large theatrical audience—looked on, as the two-and-thirty and the Judge were solemnly confronted. Then the Judge addressed them. Among the wretched creatures before him whom he must single out for special address,

was one who almost from his infancy had been an offender
against the laws; who, after repeated imprisonments and
punishments, had been at length sentenced to exile for
a term of years; and who, under circumstances of great
violence and daring, had made his escape and been re-
sentenced to exile for life.   That miserable man would
seem for a time to have become convinced of his errors,
when far removed from the scenes of his old offences, and
to have lived a peaceable and honest life.   But in a fatal
moment, yielding to those propensities and passions, the
indulgence of which had so long rendered him a scourge
to society, he had quitted his haven of rest and repentance,
and had come back to the country where he was proscribed.
Being here presently denounced, he had for a time succeeded
in evading the officers of Justice, but being at length seized
while in the act of flight, he had resisted them, and had—
he best knew whether by express design, or in the blindness
of his hardihood—caused the death of his denouncer, to
whom his whole career was known.   The appointed punishment for his return to the land that had cast him out being
Death, and his case being this aggravated case, he must
prepare himself to Die.

The sun was striking in at the great windows of the court,
through the glittering drops of rain upon the glass, and it
made a broad shaft of light between the two-and-thirty and
the Judge, linking both together, and perhaps reminding
some among the audience, how both were passing on, with
absolute equality, to the greater Judgment that knoweth all
things and cannot err.   Rising for a moment, a distinct
speck of face in this way of light, the prisoner said, "My
Lord, I have received my sentence of Death from the
Almighty, but I bow to yours," and sat down again.   There
was some hushing, and the Judge went on with what he had
to say to the rest.   Then, they were all formally doomed,
and some of them were supported out, and some of them
sauntered out with a haggard look of bravery, and a few
nodded to the gallery, and two or three shook hands, and
others went out chewing the fragments of herb they had
taken from the sweet herbs lying about.   He went last of
all, because of having to be helped from his chair and to go
very slowly; and he held my hand while all the others were
removed, and while the audience got up (putting their dresses
right, as they might at church or elsewhere) and pointed

down at this criminal or at that, and most of all at him and me.

I earnestly hoped and prayed that he might die before the Recorder's Report was made, but, in the dread of his lingering on, I began that night to write out a petition to the Home Secretary of State, setting forth my knowledge of him, and how it was that he had come back for my sake. I wrote it as fervently and pathetically as I could, and when I had finished it and sent it in, I wrote out other petitions to such men in authority as I hoped were the most merciful, and drew up one to the Crown itself. For several days and nights after he was sentenced I took no rest, except when I fell asleep in my chair, but was wholly absorbed in these appeals. And after I had sent them in, I could not keep away from the places where they were, but felt as if they were more hopeful and less desperate when I was near them. In this unreasonable restlessness and pain of mind, I would roam the streets of an evening, wandering by those offices and houses where I had left the petitions. To the present hour, the weary western streets of London on a cold dusty spring night, with their ranges of stern shut-up mansions and their long rows of lamps, are melancholy to me from this association.

The daily visits I could make him were shortened now, and he was more strictly kept. Seeing, or fancying, that I was suspected of an intention of carrying poison to him, I asked to be searched before I sat down at his bedside, and told the officer who was always there, that I was willing to do anything that would assure him of the singleness of my designs. Nobody was hard with him or with me. There was duty to be done, and it was done, but not harshly. The officer always gave me the assurance that he was worse, and some other sick prisoners in the room, and some other prisoners who attended on them as sick nurses (malefactors, but not incapable of kindness, GOD be thanked!), always joined in the same report.

As the days went on, I noticed more and more that he would lie placidly looking at the white ceiling, with an absence of light in his face, until some word of mine brightened it for an instant, and then it would subside again. Sometimes he was almost, or quite, unable to speak ; then, he would answer me with slight pressures on my hand, and I grew to understand his meaning very well.

The number of the days had risen to ten, when I saw a greater change in him than I had seen yet. His eyes were turned towards the door, and lighted up as I entered.

"Dear boy," he said, as I sat down by his bed: "I thought you was late. But I knowed you couldn't be that."

"It is just the time," said I. "I waited for it at the gate."

"You always waits at the gate; don't you, dear boy?"

"Yes. Not to lose a moment of the time."

"Thank'ee, dear boy, thank'ee. God bless you! You've never deserted me, dear boy."

I pressed his hand in silence, for I could not forget that I had once meant to desert him.

"And what's the best of all," he said, "you've been more comfortable alonger me, since I was under a dark cloud, than when the sun shone. That's best of all."

He lay on his back, breathing with great difficulty. Do what he would, and love me though he did, the light left his face ever and again, and a film came over the placid look at the white ceiling.

"Are you in much pain to-day?"

"I don't complain of none, dear boy."

"You never do complain."

He had spoken his last words. He smiled, and I understood his touch to mean that he wished to lift my hand, and lay it on his breast. I laid it there, and he smiled again, and put both his hands upon it.

The allotted time ran out, while we were thus; but, looking round, I found the governor of the prison standing near me, and he whispered, "You needn't go yet." I thanked him gratefully, and asked, "Might I speak to him, if he can hear me?"

The governor stepped aside, and beckoned the officer away. The change, though it was made without noise, drew back the film from the placid look at the white ceiling, and he looked most affectionately at me.

"Dear Magwitch, I must tell you, now at last. You understand what I say?"

A gentle pressure on my hand.

"You had a child once, whom you loved and lost."

A stronger pressure on my hand.

"She lived and found powerful friends. She is living now. She is a lady and very beautiful. And I love her!"

With a last faint effort, which would have been powerless but for my yielding to it, and assisting it, he raised my hand to his lips. Then he gently let it sink upon his breast again, with his own hands lying on it. The placid look at the white ceiling came back, and passed away, and his head dropped quietly on his breast.

Mindful, then, of what we had read together, I thought of the two men who went up into the Temple to pray, and I knew there were no better words that I could say beside his bed, than " O Lord, be merciful to him a sinner ! "

CHAPTER LVII

Now that I was left wholly to myself I gave notice of my intention to quit the chambers in the Temple as soon as my tenancy could legally determine, and in the meanwhile to underlet them. At once I put bills up in the windows; for I was in debt, and had scarcely any money, and began to be seriously alarmed by the state of my affairs. I ought rather to write that I should have been alarmed if I had had energy and concentration enough to help me to the clear perception of any truth beyond the fact that I was falling very ill. The late stress upon me had enabled me to put off illness, but not to put it away; I knew that it was coming on me now, and I knew very little else, and was even careless as to that.

For a day or two, I lay on the sofa, or on the floor—anywhere, according as I happened to sink down—with a heavy head and aching limbs, and no purpose, and no power. Then there came one night which appeared of great duration, and which teemed with anxiety and horror; and when in the morning I tried to sit up in my bed and think of it, I found I could not do so.

Whether I really had been down in Garden-court in the dead of the night, groping about for the boat that I supposed to be there; whether I had two or three times come to myself on the staircase with great terror, not knowing how I had got out of bed; whether I had found myself lighting the lamp, possessed by the idea that he was coming up the stairs, and that the lights were blown out; whether I had been inexpressibly harassed by the distracted talking, laughing, and groaning, of some one, and had half suspected those sounds to be of my own making; whether there had been a closed iron furnace in a dark corner of the room, and a voice had called out over and over again that Miss Havisham was consuming within it; these were things that I tried to settle with myself and get into some order, as I lay that morning on my bed. But the vapour of a limekiln would come between me and them, disordering them all, and it was through the vapour at last that I saw two men looking at me.

"What do you want?" I asked, starting; "I don't know you."

"Well, sir," returned one of them, bending down and touching me on the shoulder, "this is a matter that you'll soon arrange, I dare say, but you're arrested."

"What is the debt?"

"Hundred and twenty-three pound, fifteen, six. Jeweller's account, I think."

"What is to be done?"

"You had better come to my house," said the man. "I keep a very nice house."

I made some attempt to get up and dress myself. When I next attended to them, they were standing a little off from the bed, looking at me. I still lay there.

"You see my state," said I. "I would come with you if I could; but indeed I am quite unable. If you take me from here, I think I shall die by the way."

Perhaps they replied, or argued the point, or tried to encourage me to believe that I was better than I thought. Forasmuch as they hang in my memory by only this one slender thread, I don't know what they did, except that they forbore to remove me.

That I had a fever and was avoided, that I suffered greatly, that I often lost my reason, that the time seemed interminable, that I confounded impossible existences with my own identity; that I was a brick in the house wall, and yet entreating to be released from the giddy place where the builders had set me; that I was a steel beam of a vast engine, clashing and whirling over a gulf, and yet that I implored in my own person to have the engine stopped, and my part in it hammered off; that I passed through these phases of disease, I know of my own remembrance, and did in some sort know at the time. That I sometimes struggled with real people, in the belief that they were murderers, and that I would all at once comprehend that they meant to do me good, and would then sink exhausted in their arms, and suffer them to lay me down, I also knew at the time. But, above all, I knew that there was a constant tendency in all these people—who, when I was very ill, would present all kinds of extraordinary transformations of the human face, and would be much dilated in size—above all, I say, I knew that there was an extraordinary tendency in all these people, sooner or later, to settle down into the likeness of Joe.

After I had turned the worst point of my illness, I began to notice that while all its other features changed, this one consistent feature did not change. Whoever came about me, still settled down into Joe. I opened my eyes in the night, and I saw in the great chair at the bedside, Joe. I opened my eyes in the day, and, sitting on the window-seat, smoking his pipe in the shaded open window, still I saw Joe. I asked for cooling drink, and the dear hand that gave it me was Joe's. I sank back on my pillow after drinking, and the face that looked so hopefully and tenderly upon me was the face of Joe.

At last, one day, I took courage, and said, "*Is* it Joe?"

And the dear old home-voice answered, "Which it air, old chap."

"O Joe, you break my heart! Look angry at me, Joe. Strike me, Joe. Tell me of my ingratitude. Don't be so good to me!"

For Joe had actually laid his head down on the pillow at my side, and put his arm round my neck, in his joy that I knew him.

"Which dear old Pip, old chap," said Joe, "you and me was ever friends. And when you're well enough to go out for a ride—what larks!"

After which, Joe withdrew to the window, and stood with his back towards me, wiping his eyes. And as my extreme weakness prevented me from getting up and going to him, I lay there, penitently whispering, "O God bless him! O God bless this gentle Christian man!"

Joe's eyes were red when I next found him beside me; but I was holding his hand and we both felt happy.

"How long, dear Joe?"

"Which you meantersay, Pip, how long have your illness lasted, dear old chap?"

"Yes, Joe."

"It's the end of May, Pip. To-morrow is the first of June."

"And have you been here all the time, dear Joe?"

"Pretty nigh, old chap. For, as I says to Biddy when the news of your being ill were brought by letter, which it were brought by the post, and being formerly single he is now married though underpaid for a deal of walking and shoe-leather, but wealth were not a object on his part, and marriage were the great wish of his hart—— "

"It is so delightful to hear you, Joe! But I interrupt you in what you said to Biddy."

"Which it were," said Joe, "that how you might be amongst strangers, and that how you and me having been ever friends, a wisit at such a moment might not prove unacceptabobble. And Biddy, her word were, 'Go to him, without loss of time.' That," said Joe, summing up with his judicial air, "were the word of Biddy. 'Go to him,' Biddy say, 'without loss of time.' In short, I shouldn't greatly deceive you," Joe added, after a little grave reflection, " if I represented to you that the word of that young woman were, 'without a minute's loss of time.'"

There Joe cut himself short, and informed me that I was to be talked to in great moderation, and that I was to take a little nourishment at stated frequent times, whether I felt inclined for it or not, and that I was to submit myself to all his orders. So, I kissed his hand, and lay quiet, while he proceeded to indite a note to Biddy, with my love in it.

Evidently Biddy had taught Joe to write. As I lay in bed looking at him, it made me, in my weak state, cry again with pleasure to see the pride with which he set about his letter. My bedstead, divested of its curtains, had been removed, with me upon it, into the sitting-room, as the airiest and largest, and the carpet had been taken away, and the room kept always fresh and wholesome night and day. At my own writing-table, pushed into a corner and cumbered with little bottles, Joe now sat down to his great work, first choosing a pen from the pen-tray as if it were a chest of large tools, and tucking up his sleeves as if he were going to wield a crowbar or sledge-hammer. It was necessary for Joe to hold on heavily to the table with his left elbow, and to get his right leg well out behind him, before he could begin, and when he did begin he made every down-stroke so slowly that it might have been six feet long, while at every up-stroke I could hear his pen spluttering extensively. He had a curious idea that the inkstand was on the side of him where it was not, and constantly dipped his pen into space, and seemed quite satisfied with the result. Occasionally, he was tripped up by some orthographical stumbling-block, but

on the whole he got on very well indeed, and when he had
signed his name, and had removed a finishing blot from the
paper to the crown of his head with his two forefingers, he
got up and hovered about the table, trying the effect of his
performance from various points of view as it lay there, with
unbounded satisfaction.

Not to make Joe uneasy by talking too much, even if
I had been able to talk much, I deferred asking him about
Miss Havisham until next day. He shook his head when
I then asked him if she had recovered?

"Is she dead, Joe?"

"Why, you see, old chap," said Joe, in a tone of remonstrance, and by way of getting at it by degrees, "I wouldn't
go so far as to say that, for that's a deal to say; but she
ain't——"

"Living, Joe?"

"That's nigher where it is," said Joe; "she ain't living."

"Did she linger long, Joe?"

"Arter you was took ill, pretty much about what you
might call (if you was put to it) a week," said Joe; still
determined, on my account, to come at everything by
degrees.

"Dear Joe, have you heard what becomes of her property?"

"Well, old chap," said Joe, "it do appear that she had
settled the most of it, which I meantersay tied it up, on Miss
Estella. But she had wrote out a little coddleshell in her
own hand a day or two afore the accident, leaving a cool
four thousand to Mr. Matthew Pocket. And why, do you
suppose, above all things, Pip, she left that cool four thousand
unto him? 'Because of Pip's account of him the said
Matthew.' I am told by Biddy, that air the writing," said
Joe, repeating the legal turn as if it did him infinite good,
"'account of him the said Matthew.' And a cool four
thousand, Pip!"

I never discovered from whom Joe derived the conventional
temperature of the four thousand pounds, but it appeared to
make the sum of money more to him, and he had a manifest
relish in insisting on its being cool.

This account gave me great joy, as it perfected the only
good thing I had done. I asked Joe whether he had heard
if any of the other relations had any legacies?

"Miss Sarah," said Joe, "she have twenty-five pound per-
annium fur to buy pills, on account of being bilious. Miss

Georgiana, she have twenty pound down. Mrs. —— what's the name of them wild beasts with humps, old chap?"

"Camels?" said I, wondering why he could possibly want to know.

Joe nodded. "Mrs. Camels," by which I presently understood he meant Camilla, "she have five pound fur to buy rushlights to put her in spirits when she wake up in the night."

The accuracy of these recitals was sufficiently obvious to me, to give me great confidence in Joe's information. "And now," said Joe, "you ain't that strong yet, old chap, that you can take in more nor one additional shovel-full to-day. Old Orlick he's been a bustin' open a dwelling-ouse."

"Whose?" said I.

"Not, I grant you, but what his manners is given to blusterous," said Joe, apologetically; "still, a Englishman's ouse is his Castle, and castles must not be busted 'cept when done in war time. And wotsume'er the failings on his part, he were a corn and seedsman in his hart."

"Is it Pumblechook's house that has been broken into, then?"

"That's it, Pip," said Joe; "and they took his till, and they took his cash-box, and they drinked his wine, and they partook of his wittles, and they slapped his face, and they pulled his nose, and they tied him up to his bedpust, and they giv' him a dozen, and they stuffed his mouth full of flowering annuals to perwent his crying out. But he knowed Orlick, and Orlick's in the county jail."

By these approaches we arrived at unrestricted conversation. I was slow to gain strength, but I did slowly and surely become less weak, and Joe stayed with me, and I fancied I was little Pip again.

For the tenderness of Joe was so beautifully proportioned to my need, that I was like a child in his hands. He would sit and talk to me in the old confidence, and with the old simplicity, and in the old unassertive protecting way, so that I would half believe that all my life since the days of the old kitchen was one of the mental troubles of the fever that was gone. He did everything for me except the household work, for which he had engaged a very decent woman, after paying off the laundress on his first arrival. "Which I do assure you, Pip," he would often say, in explanation of that liberty; "I found her a tapping the spare bed, like a cask of beer, and drawing off the feathers in a bucket, for sale. Which she would have tapped yourn next, and draw'd it off with you a laying on it, and was then a carrying away the coals gradiwally in the soup-tureen and wegetable dishes, and the wine and spirits in your Wellington boots."

We looked forward to the day when I should go out for a ride, as we had once looked forward to the day of my apprenticeship. And when the day came, and an open carriage was got into the Lane, Joe wrapped me up, took me in his arms, carried me down to it, and put me in, as if I were still the small helpless creature to whom he had so abundantly given of the wealth of his great nature.

And Joe got in beside me, and we drove away together into the country, where the rich summer growth was already on the trees and on the grass, and sweet summer scents filled all the air. The day happened to be Sunday, and when I looked on the loveliness around me, and thought how it had grown and changed, and how the little wild flowers had been forming, and the voices of the birds had been strengthening, by day and by night, under the sun and under the stars, while poor I lay burning and tossing on my bed, the mere remembrance of having burned and tossed there, came like a check upon my peace. But, when I heard the Sunday bells, and looked around a little more upon the outspread beauty, I felt that I was not nearly thankful enough—that I was too weak yet, to be even that—and I laid my head on Joe's shoulder, as I had laid it long ago when he had taken me to the Fair or where not, and it was too much for my young senses.

More composure came to me after a while, and we talked as we used to talk, lying on the grass at the old Battery. There was no change whatever in Joe. Exactly what he had been in my eyes then, he was in my eyes still; just as simply faithful, just as simply right.

When we got back again and he lifted me out, and carried me—so easily!—across the court and up the stairs, I thought of that eventful Christmas Day when he had carried me over the marshes. We had not yet made any allusion to my change of fortune, nor did I know how much of my late history he was acquainted with. I was so doubtful of myself now, and put so much trust in him, that I could not satisfy myself whether I ought to refer to it when he did not.

"Have you heard, Joe," I asked him that evening, upon further consideration, as he smoked his pipe at the window, "who my patron was?"

"I heerd," returned Joe, "as it were not Miss Havisham, old chap."

"Did you hear who it was, Joe?"

"Well! I heerd as it were a person what sent the person what giv' you the bank-notes at the Jolly Bargemen, Pip."

"So it was."

"Astonishing!" said Joe, in the placidest way.

"Did you hear that he was dead, Joe?" I presently asked, with increasing diffidence.

"Which? Him as sent the bank-notes, Pip?"

"Yes."

"I think," said Joe, after meditating a long time, and looking rather evasively at the window-seat, "as I *did* hear tell that how he were something or another in a general way in that direction."

"Did you hear anything of his circumstances, Joe?"

"Not partickler, Pip."

"If you would like to hear, Joe——" I was beginning, when Joe got up and came to my sofa.

"Lookee here, old chap," said Joe, bending over me. "Ever the best of friends; ain't us, Pip?"

I was ashamed to answer him.

"Werry good, then," said Joe, as if I *had* answered; "that's all right; that's agreed upon. Then why go into subjects, old chap, which as betwixt two sech must be for ever onnecessary? There's subjects enough as betwixt two sech, without onnecessary ones. Lord! To think of your poor sister and her Rampages! And don't you remember Tickler?"

"I do indeed, Joe."

"Lookee here, old chap," said Joe. "I done what I could to keep you and Tickler in sunders, but my power were not always fully equal to my inclinations. For when your poor sister had a mind to drop into you, it were not so much," said Joe, in his favourite argumentative way, "that she dropped into me too, if I put myself in opposition to her, but that she dropped into you always heavier for it. I noticed that. It ain't a grab at a man's whisker, nor yet a shake or two of a man (to which your sister was quite welcome),

that 'ud put a man off from getting a little child out of
punishment.   But when that little child is dropped into,
heavier, for that grab of whisker or shaking, then that man
naterally up and says to himself, 'Where is the good as you
are a doing?   I grant you I see the 'arm,' says the man,
'but I don't see the good.   I call upon you, sir, therefore, to
pint out the good.'"

"The man says?" I observed, as Joe waited for me to
speak.

"The man says," Joe assented.   "Is he right, that man?"

"Dear Joe, he is always right."

"Well, old chap," said Joe, "then abide by your words.
If he's always right (which in general he's more likely wrong),
he's right when he says this:—Supposing ever you kep any
little matter to yourself, when you was a little child, you kep
it mostly because you know'd as J. Gargery's power to part
you and Tickler in sunders, were not fully equal to his
inclinations.   Theerfore, think no more of it as betwixt two
sech, and do not let us pass remarks upon onnecessary
subjects.   Biddy giv' herself a deal o' trouble with me afore
I left (for I am most awful dull), as I should view it in this
light, and, viewing it in this light, as I should ser put it.
Both of which," said Joe, quite charmed with his logical
arrangement, "being done, now this to you a true friend, say.
Namely.   You mustn't go a over-doing on it, but you must
have your supper and your wine-and-water, and you must be
put betwixt the sheets."

The delicacy with which Joe dismissed this theme, and the
sweet tact and kindness with which Biddy—who with her
woman's wit had found me out so soon—had prepared him
for it, made a deep impression on my mind.   But whether
Joe knew how poor I was. and how my great expectations
had all dissolved, like our own marsh mists before the sun,
I could not understand.

Another thing in Joe that I could not understand when it
first began to develop itself, but which I soon arrived at
a sorrowful comprehension of, was this: As I became stronger
and better, Joe became a little less easy with me.   In my
weakness and entire dependence on him, the dear fellow
had fallen into the old tone, and called me by the old
names, the dear "old Pip, old chap," that now were music
in my ears.   I too had fallen into the old ways, only happy
and thankful that he let me.   But, imperceptibly, though

I held by them fast, Joe's hold upon them began to slacken; and whereas I wondered at this, at first, I soon began to understand that the cause of it was in me, and that the fault of it was all mine.

Ah! Had I given Joe no reason to doubt my constancy, and to think that in prosperity I should grow cold to him and cast him off? Had I given Joe's innocent heart no cause to feel instinctively that as I got stronger, his hold upon me would be weaker, and that he had better loosen it in time and let me go, before I plucked myself away?

It was on the third or fourth occasion of my going out walking in the Temple Gardens, leaning on Joe's arm, that I saw this change in him very plainly. We had been sitting in the bright warm sunlight, looking at the river, and I chanced to say as we got up:

"See, Joe! I can walk quite strongly. Now, you shall see me walk back by myself."

"Which do not over-do it, Pip," said Joe; "but I shall be happy fur to see you able, sir."

The last word grated on me; but how could I remonstrate! I walked no further than the gate of the gardens, and then pretended to be weaker than I was, and asked Joe for his arm. Joe gave it me, but was thoughtful.

I, for my part, was thoughtful too; for how best to check this growing change in Joe was a great perplexity to my remorseful thoughts. That I was ashamed to tell him exactly how I was placed, and what I had come down to, I do not seek to conceal; but I hope my reluctance was not quite an unworthy one. He would want to help me out of his little savings, I knew, and I knew that he ought not to help me, and that I must not suffer him to do it.

It was a thoughtful evening with both of us. But, before we went to bed, I had resolved that I would wait over to-morrow, to-morrow being Sunday, and would begin my new course with the new week. On Monday morning I would speak to Joe about this change, I would lay aside this last vestige of reserve, I would tell him what I had in my thoughts (that Secondly, not yet arrived at), and why I had not decided to go out to Herbert, and then the change would be conquered for ever. As I cleared, Joe cleared, and it seemed as though he had sympathetically arrived at a resolution too.

We had a quiet day on the Sunday, and we rode out into the country, and then walked in the fields.

"I feel thankful that I have been ill, Joe," I said.

"Dear old Pip, old chap, you're a'most come round, sir."

"It has been a memorable time for me, Joe."

"Likeways for myself, sir," Joe returned.

"We have had a time together, Joe, that I can never forget. There were days once, I know, that I did for a while forget; but I never shall forget these."

"Pip," said Joe, appearing a little hurried and troubled, "there has been larks. And, dear sir, what have been betwixt us—have been."

At night, when I had gone to bed, Joe came into my room, as he had done all through my recovery. He asked me if I felt sure that I was as well as in the morning?

"Yes, dear Joe, quite."

"And are always a getting stronger, old chap?"

"Yes, dear Joe, steadily."

Joe patted the coverlet on my shoulder with his great good hand, and said, in what I thought a husky voice, "Good night!"

When I got up in the morning, refreshed and stronger yet, I was full of my resolution to tell Joe all, without delay. I would tell him before breakfast. I would dress at once and go to his room and surprise him; for it was the first day I had been up early. I went to his room, and he was not there. Not only was he not there, but his box was gone.

I hurried then to the breakfast-table, and on it found a letter. These were its brief contents.

"Not wishful to intrude I have departured fur you are well again dear Pip and will do better without   "Jo.

"P.S. Ever the best of friends."

Enclosed in the letter was a receipt for the debt and costs on which I had been arrested. Down to that moment I had vainly supposed that my creditor had withdrawn or suspended proceedings until I should be quite recovered. I had never dreamed of Joe's having paid the money; but Joe had paid it, and the receipt was in his name.

What remained for me now, but to follow him to the dear old forge, and there to have out my disclosure to him, and my penitent remonstrance with him, and there to relieve

my mind and heart of that reserved Secondly, which had begun as a vague something lingering in my thoughts, and had formed into a settled purpose?

The purpose was, that I would go to Biddy, that I would show her how humbled and repentant I came back, that I would tell her how I had lost all I once hoped for, that I would remind her of our old confidences in my first unhappy time. Then I would say to her, "Biddy, I think you once liked me very well, when my errant heart, even while it strayed away from you, was quieter and better with you than it ever has been since. If you can like me only half as well once more, if you can take me with all my faults and disappointments on my head, if you can receive me like a forgiven child (and indeed I am as sorry, Biddy, and have as much need of a hushing voice and a soothing hand), I hope I am a little worthier of you than I was—not much, but a little. And, Biddy, it shall rest with you to say whether I shall work at the forge with Joe, or whether I shall try for any different occupation down in this country, or whether we shall go away to a distant place where an opportunity awaits me which I set aside when it was offered, until I knew your answer. And now, dear Biddy, if you can tell me that you will go through the world with me, you will surely make it a better world for me, and me a better man for it, and I will try hard to make it a better world for you."

Such was my purpose. After three days more of recovery, I went down to the old place, to put it in execution. And how I sped in it, is all I have left to tell.

CHAPTER LVIII

THE tidings of my high fortunes having had a heavy fall, had got down to my native place and its neighbourhood, before I got there. I found the Blue Boar in possession of the intelligence, and I found that it made a great change in the Boar's demeanour. Whereas the Boar had cultivated my good opinion with warm assiduity when I was coming into property, the Boar was exceedingly cool on the subject now that I was going out of property.

It was evening when I arrived, much fatigued by the journey I had so often made so easily. The Boar could not put me into my usual bedroom, which was engaged (probably by some one who had expectations), and could only assign me a very indifferent chamber among the pigeons and post-chaises up the yard. But I had as sound a sleep in that lodging as in the most superior accommodation the Boar could have given me, and the quality of my dreams was about the same as in the best bedroom.

Early in the morning while my breakfast was getting ready, I strolled round by Satis House. There were printed bills on the gate and on bits of carpet hanging out of the windows, announcing a sale by auction of the Household Furniture and Effects, next week. The House itself was to be sold as old building materials, and pulled down. LOT 1 was marked in whitewashed knock-knee letters on the brew-house; LOT 2 on that part of the main building which had been so long shut up. Other lots were marked off on other parts of the structure, and the ivy had been torn down to make room for the inscriptions, and much of it trailed low in the dust and was withered already. Stepping in for a moment at the open gate and looking around me with the uncomfortable air of a stranger who had no business there, I saw the auctioneer's clerk walking on the casks and telling them off for the information of a catalogue compiler, pen in hand, who made a temporary desk of the wheeled chair I had so often pushed along to the tune of Old Clem.

When I got back to my breakfast in the Boar's coffee-room, I found Mr. Pumblechook conversing with the landlord. Mr. Pumblechook (not improved in appearance by his late nocturnal adventure) was waiting for me, and addressed me in the following terms.

"Young man, I am sorry to see you brought low. But what else could be expected! what else could be expected!"

As he extended his hand with a magnificently forgiving air, and as I was broken by illness and unfit to quarrel, I took it.

"William," said Mr. Pumblechook to the waiter, "put a muffin on table. And has it come to this! Has it come to this!"

I frowningly sat down to my breakfast. Mr. Pumblechook stood over me and poured out my tea—before I could touch the teapot—with the air of a benefactor who was resolved to be true to the last.

"William," said Mr. Pumblechook, mournfully, "put the salt on. In happier times," addressing me, "I think you took sugar? And did you take milk? You did. Sugar and milk. William, bring a watercress."

"Thank you," said I, shortly, "but I don't eat watercresses."

"You don't eat 'em," returned Mr. Pumblechook, sighing and nodding his head several times, as if he might have expected that, and as if abstinence from watercresses were consistent with my downfall. "True. The simple fruits of the earth. No. You needn't bring any, William."

I went on with my breakfast, and Mr. Pumblechook continued to stand over me, staring fishily and breathing noisily, as he always did.

"Little more than skin and bone!" mused Mr. Pumblechook, aloud. "And yet when he went away from here (I may say with my blessing), and I spread afore him my humble store, like the Bee, he was as plump as a Peach!"

This reminded me of the wonderful difference between the servile manner in which he had offered his hand in my new prosperity, saying, "May I?" and the ostentatious clemency with which he had just now exhibited the same fat five fingers.

"Hah!" he went on, handing me the bread-and-butter. "And air you a going to Joseph?"

"In Heaven's name," said I, firing in spite of myself,

"what does it matter to you where I am going? Leave that teapot alone."

It was the worst course I could have taken, because it gave Pumblechook the opportunity he wanted.

"Yes, young man," said he, releasing the handle of the article in question, retiring a step or two from my table, and speaking for the behoof of the landlord and waiter at the door, "I *will* leave that teapot alone. You are right, young man. For once, you are right. I forgit myself when I take such an interest in your breakfast, as to wish your frame, exhausted by the debilitating effects of prodigygality, to be stimilated by the 'olesome nourishment of your forefathers. And yet," said Pumblechook, turning to the landlord and waiter, and pointing me out at arm's length, "this is him as I ever sported with in his days of happy infancy! Tell me not it cannot be; I tell you this is him!"

A low murmur from the two replied. The waiter appeared to be particularly affected.

"This is him," said Pumblechook, "as I have rode in my shay-cart. This is him as I have seen brought up by hand. This is him untoe the sister of which I was uncle by marriage, as her name was Georgiana M'ria from her own mother, let him deny it if he can!"

The waiter seemed convinced that I could not deny it, and that it gave the case a black look.

"Young man," said Pumblechook, screwing his head at me in the old fashion, "you air a going to Joseph. What does it matter to me, you ask me, where you air a going? I say to you, Sir, you air a going to Joseph."

The waiter coughed, as if he modestly invited me to get over that.

"Now," said Pumblechook, and all this with a most exasperating air of saying in the cause of virtue what was perfectly convincing and conclusive, "I will tell you what to say to Joseph. Here is Squires of the Boar present, known and respected in this town, and here is William, which his father's name was Potkins if I do not deceive myself."

"You do not, sir," said William.

"In their presence," pursued Pumblechook, "I will tell you, young man, what to say to Joseph. Says you, 'Joseph, I have this day seen my earliest benefactor and the founder of my fortun's. I will name no names, Joseph, but so they are pleased to call him up-town, and I have seen that man.'"

"I swear I don't see him here," said I.

"Say that likewise," retorted Pumblechook. "Say you said that, and even Joseph will probably betray surprise."

"There you quite mistake him," said I. "I know better."

"Says you," Pumblechook went on, "'Joseph, I have seen that man, and that man bears you no malice and bears me no malice. He knows your character, Joseph, and is well acquainted with your pig-headedness and ignorance; and he knows my character, Joseph, and he knows my want of gratitoode. Yes, Joseph,' says you," here Pumblechook shook his head and hand at me, "''he knows my total deficiency of common human gratitoode. *He* knows it, Joseph, as none can. *You* do not know it, Joseph, having no call to know it, but that man do.'"

Windy donkey as he was, it really amazed me that he could have the face to talk thus to mine.

"Says you, 'Joseph, he gave me a little message, which I will now repeat. It was, that in my being brought low, he saw the finger of Providence. He knowed that finger when he saw it, Joseph, and he saw it plain. It pinted out this writing, Joseph. *Reward of ingratitoode to earliest bene-factor, and founder of fortun's.* But that man said that he did not repent of what he had done, Joseph. Not at all. It was right to do it, it was kind to do it, it was benevolent to do it, and he would do it again.'"

"It's a pity," said I, scornfully, as I finished my inter-rupted breakfast, "that the man did not say what he had done and would do again."

"Squires of the Boar!" Pumblechook was now addressing the landlord, "and William! I have no objections to your mentioning, either up-town or down-town, if such should be your wishes, that it was right to do it, kind to do it, benevolent to do it, and that I would do it again."

With those words the Impostor shook them both by the hand, with an air, and left the house; leaving me much more astonished than delighted by the virtues of that same indefinite "it." I was not long after him in leaving the house too, and when I went down the High-street I saw him holding forth (no doubt to the same effect) at his shop door to a select group, who honoured me with very unfavourable glances as I passed on the opposite side of the way.

But it was only the pleasanter to turn to Biddy and to Joe, whose great forbearance shone more brightly than before, if that could be, contrasted with this brazen pretender. I went towards them slowly, for my limbs were weak, but with a sense of increasing relief as I drew nearer to them, and a sense of leaving arrogance and untruthfulness further and further behind.

The June weather was delicious. The sky was blue, the larks were soaring high over the green corn, I thought all that country-side more beautiful and peaceful by far than I had ever known it to be yet. Many pleasant pictures of the life that I would lead there, and of the change for the better that would come over my character when I had a guiding spirit at my side whose simple faith and clear home-wisdom I had proved, beguiled my way. They awakened a tender emotion in me; for my heart was softened by my return, and such a change had come to pass, that I felt like one who was toiling home barefoot from distant travel, and whose wanderings had lasted many years.

The schoolhouse where Biddy was mistress, I had never seen; but the little roundabout lane, by which I entered the village for quietness' sake, took me past it. I was disappointed to find that the day was a holiday; no children were there, and Biddy's house was closed. Some hopeful notion of seeing her, busily engaged in her daily duties, before she saw me, had been in my mind and was defeated.

But the forge was a very short distance off, and I went towards it under the sweet green limes, listening for the clink of Joe's hammer. Long after I ought to have heard it, and long after I had fancied I heard it and found it but a fancy, all was still. The limes were there, and the white thorns were there, and the chestnut-trees were there, and their leaves rustled harmoniously when I stopped to listen; but the clink of Joe's hammer was not in the midsummer wind.

Almost fearing, without knowing why, to come in view of the forge, I saw it at last, and saw that it was closed. No gleam of fire, no glittering shower of sparks, no roar of bellows; all shut up, and still.

But the house was not deserted, and the best parlour seemed to be in use, for there were white curtains fluttering in its window, and the window was open and gay with flowers. I went softly towards it, meaning to peep over the flowers, when Joe and Biddy stood before me, arm in arm.

At first Biddy gave a cry, as if she thought it was my apparition, but in another moment she was in my embrace. I wept to see her, and she wept to see me; I, because she looked so fresh and pleasant; she, because I looked so worn and white.

"But, dear Biddy, how smart you are!"

"Yes, dear Pip."

"And Joe, how smart *you* are!"

"Yes, dear old Pip, old chap."

I looked at both of them, from one to the other, and then——

"It's my wedding-day," cried Biddy, in a burst of happiness, "and I am married to Joe!"

*   *   *   *   *   *   *

They had taken me into the kitchen, and I had laid my head down on the old deal table. Biddy held one of my hands to her lips, and Joe's restoring touch was on my shoulder. "Which he warn't strong enough, my dear, fur to be surprised," said Joe. And Biddy said, "I ought to have thought of it, dear Joe, but I was too happy." They were both so overjoyed to see me, so proud to see me, so touched by my coming to them, so delighted that I should have come by accident to make their day complete!

My first thought was one of great thankfulness that I had never breathed this last baffled hope to Joe. How often, while he was with me in my illness, had it risen to my lips. How irrevocable would have been his knowledge of it, if he had remained with me but another hour!

"Dear Biddy," said I, "you have the best husband in the whole world, and if you could have seen him by my bed you would have——But no, you couldn't love him better than you do."

"No, I couldn't indeed," said Biddy.

"And, dear Joe, you have the best wife in the whole world, and she will make you as happy as even you deserve to be, you dear, good, noble Joe!"

Joe looked at me with a quivering lip, and fairly put his sleeve before his eyes.

"And Joe and Biddy both, as you have been to church to-day and are in charity and love with all mankind, receive my humble thanks for all you have done for me, and all

I have so ill repaid! And when I say that I am going away within the hour, for I am soon going abroad, and that I shall never rest until I have worked for the money with which you have kept me out of prison, and have sent it to you, don't think, dear Joe and Biddy, that if I could repay it a thousand times over, I suppose I could cancel a farthing of the debt I owe you, or that I would do so if I could!"

They were both melted by these words, and both entreated me to say no more.

"But I must say more. Dear Joe, I hope you will have children to love, and that some little fellow will sit in this chimney corner of a winter night, who may remind you of another little fellow gone out of it for ever. Don't tell him, Joe, that I was thankless; don't tell him, Biddy, that I was ungenerous and unjust; only tell him that I honoured you both, because you were both so good and true, and that, as your child, I said it would be natural to him to grow up a much better man than I did."

"I ain't a going," said Joe, from behind his sleeve, "to tell him nothink o' that natur, Pip. Nor Biddy ain't. Nor yet no one ain't."

And now, though I know you have already done it in your own kind hearts, pray tell me, both, that you forgive me! Pray let me hear you say the words, that I may carry the sound of them away with me, and then I shall be able to believe that you can trust me, and think better of me, in the time to come!"

"O dear old Pip, old chap," said Joe. "God knows as I forgive you, if I have anythink to forgive!"

"Amen! And God knows I do!" echoed Biddy.

"Now let me go up and look at my old little room, and rest there a few minutes by myself. And then when I have eaten and drunk with you, go with me as far as the finger-post, dear Joe and Biddy, before we say good-bye!"

I sold all I had, and put aside as much as I could, for a composition with my creditors—who gave me ample time to pay them in full—and I went out and joined Herbert. Within a month I had quitted England, and within two months I was clerk to Clarriker and Co., and within four months I assumed my first undivided responsibility. For the beam across the parlour ceiling at Mill Pond Bank had then ceased to tremble under old Bill Barley's growls and was at peace, and Herbert had gone away to marry Clara, and I was left in sole charge of the Eastern Branch until he brought her back.

Many a year went round before I was a partner in the House; but I lived happily with Herbert and his wife, and lived frugally, and paid my debts, and maintained a constant correspondence with Biddy and Joe. It was not until I became third in the Firm, that Clarriker betrayed me to Herbert; but he then declared that the secret of Herbert's partnership had been long enough upon his conscience, and he must tell it. So he told it, and Herbert was as much moved as amazed, and the dear fellow and I were not the worse friends for the long concealment. I must not leave it to be supposed that we were ever a great House, or that we made mints of money. We were not in a grand way of business, but we had a good name, and worked for our profits, and did very well. We owed so much to Herbert's ever cheerful industry and readiness, that I often wondered how I had conceived that old idea of his inaptitude, until I was one day enlightened by the reflection, that perhaps the inaptitude had never been in him at all, but had been in me.

CHAPTER LIX

For eleven years I had not seen Joe nor Biddy with my bodily eyes—though they had both been often before my fancy in the East—when, upon an evening in December, an hour or two after dark, I laid my hand softly on the latch of the old kitchen door. I touched it so softly that I was not heard, and I looked in unseen. There, smoking his pipe in the old place by the kitchen firelight, as hale and as strong as ever, though a little grey, sat Joe; and there, fenced into the corner with Joe's leg, and sitting on my own little stool looking at the fire, was——I again!

"We giv' him the name of Pip for your sake, dear old chap," said Joe, delighted when I took another stool by the child's side (but I did *not* rumple his hair), "and we hoped he might grow a little bit like you, and we think he do."

I thought so too, and I took him out for a walk next morning, and we talked immensely, understanding one another to perfection. And I took him down to the church-yard, and set him on a certain tombstone there, and he showed me from that elevation which stone was sacred to the memory of Philip Pirrip, late of this Parish, and Also Georgiana, Wife of the Above.

"Biddy," said I, when I talked with her after dinner, as her little girl lay sleeping in her lap, "you must give Pip to me, one of these days; or lend him, at all events."

"No, no," said Biddy, gently. "You must marry."

"So Herbert and Clara say, but I don't think I shall, Biddy. I have so settled down in their home, that it's not at all likely. I am already quite an old bachelor."

Biddy looked down at her child, and put its little hand to her lips, and then put the good matronly hand with which she had touched it, into mine. There was something in the action and in the light pressure of Biddy's wedding-ring, that had a very pretty eloquence in it.

"Dear Pip," said Biddy, "you are sure you don't fret for her?"

"O no—I think not, Biddy."

"Tell me as an old friend. Have you quite forgotten her?"

"My dear Biddy, I have forgotten nothing in my life that ever had a foremost place there, and little that ever had any place there. But that poor dream, as I once used to call it, has all gone by, Biddy, all gone by!"

Nevertheless, I knew while I said those words, that I secretly intended to revisit the site of the old house that evening, alone, for her sake. Yes, even so. For Estella's sake.

I had heard of her as leading a most unhappy life, and as being separated from her husband, who had used her with great cruelty, and who had become quite renowned as a compound of pride, avarice, brutality, and meanness. And I had heard of the death of her husband, from an accident consequent on his ill-treatment of a horse. This release had befallen her some two years before; for anything I knew, she was married again.

The early dinner-hour at Joe's left me abundance of time, without hurrying my talk with Biddy, to walk over to the old spot before dark. But, what with loitering on the way, to look at old objects and to think of old times, the day had quite declined when I came to the place.

There was no house now, no brewery, no building whatever left, but the wall of the old garden. The cleared space had been enclosed with a rough fence, and looking over it, I saw that some of the old ivy had struck root anew, and was growing green on low quiet mounds of ruin. A gate in the fence standing ajar, I pushed it open and went in.

A cold silvery mist had veiled the afternoon, and the moon was not yet up to scatter it. But the stars were shining beyond the mist, and the moon was coming, and the evening was not dark. I could trace out where every part of the old house had been, and where the brewery had been, and where the gates, and where the casks. I had done so, and was looking along the desolate garden-walk, when I beheld a solitary figure in it.

The figure showed itself aware of me as I advanced. It had been moving towards me, but it stood still. As I drew nearer, I saw it to be the figure of a woman. As I drew nearer yet, it was about to turn away, when it stopped, and let me come up with it. Then, it faltered as if much surprised, and uttered my name, and I cried out:

"Estella!"

"I am greatly changed. I wonder you know me."

The freshness of her beauty was indeed gone, but its indescribable majesty and its indescribable charm remained. Those attractions in it I had seen before; what I had never seen before was the saddened softened light of the once proud eyes; what I had never felt before was the friendly touch of the once insensible hand.

We sat down on a bench that was near, and I said, "After so many years, it is strange that we should thus meet again, Estella, here where our first meeting was! Do you often come back?"

"I have never been here since."

"Nor I."

The moon began to rise, and I thought of the placid look at the white ceiling, which had passed away. The moon began to rise, and I thought of the pressure on my hand when I had spoken the last words he had heard on earth.

Estella was the next to break the silence that ensued between us.

"I have very often hoped and intended to come back, but have been prevented by many circumstances. Poor, poor old place!"

The silvery mist was touched with the first rays of the moonlight, and the same rays touched the tears that dropped from her eyes. Not knowing that I saw them, and setting herself to get the better of them, she said quietly:

"Were you wondering, as you walked along, how it came to be left in this condition?"

"Yes, Estella."

"The ground belongs to me. It is the only possession I have not relinquished. Everything else has gone from me, little by little, but I have kept this. It was the subject of the only determined resistance I made in all the wretched years."

"Is it to be built on?"

"At last it is. I came here to take leave of it before its change. And you," she said, in a voice of touching interest to a wanderer, "you live abroad still."

"Still."

"And do well, I am sure?"

"I work pretty hard for a sufficient living, and therefore —Yes, I do well!"

"I have often thought of you," said Estella.

"Have you?"

"Of late, very often. There was a long hard time when I kept far from me the remembrance of what I had thrown away when I was quite ignorant of its worth. But, since my duty has not been incompatible with the admission of that remembrance, I have given it a place in my heart."

"You have always held your place in *my* heart," I answered.

And we were silent again until she spoke.

"I little thought," said Estella, "that I should take leave of you in taking leave of this spot. I am very glad to do so."

"Glad to part again, Estella? To me parting is a painful thing. To me, the remembrance of our last parting has been ever mournful and painful."

"But you said to me," returned Estella, very earnestly, "'God bless you, God forgive you!' And if you could say that to me then, you will not hesitate to say that to me now—now, when suffering has been stronger than all other teaching, and has taught me to understand what your heart used to be. I have been bent and broken, but—I hope—into a better shape. Be as considerate and good to me as you were, and tell me we are friends."

"We are friends," said I, rising and bending over her, as she rose from the bench.

"And will continue friends apart," said Estella.

I took her hand in mine, and we went out of the ruined place; and, as the morning mists had risen long ago when I first left the forge, so, the evening mists were rising now, and in all the broad expanse of tranquil light they showed to me, I saw no shadow of another parting from her.

THE END

The Oxford India Paper Dickens, Complete Edition
With Illustrations by Cruikshank, 'Phiz,' &c.
In Seventeen Volumes

Reprinted Pieces

Also

The Lamplighter
To be Read at Dusk
&
Sunday under Three Heads

This Edition of the

COMPLETE WORKS OF CHARLES DICKENS

Is issued in Seventeen Volumes.

— ✦ —

THE LONG VOYAGE

Reprinted Pieces

Also

The Lamplighter
To be Read at Dusk
&
Sunday under Three Heads

By

Charles Dickens

With Three Illustrations

By F. Walker

London

Chapman & Hall, Limited ; and

Humphrey Milford

New York : Oxford University Press American Branch
35 West 32nd Street

Printed by HORACE HART
University Press, Oxford

CONTENTS

REPRINTED PIECES

LIST OF ILLUSTRATIONS

CHARACTERS

THE LONG VOYAGE

CAPTAIN BLIGH, master of the *Bounty*.
MR. BRIMER, fifth mate of the *Halsewell*.
FLETCHER CHRISTIAN, an officer of the *Bounty*; a mutineer.
MR. MACMANUS, a midshipman on the *Halsewell*.
MISS MANSEL, a passenger in the *Halsewell*.
MR. HENRY MERITON, second mate of the *Halsewell*.
CAPTAIN PIERCE, master of the *Halsewell*.
MR. ROGERS, third mate of the *Halsewell*.

"BIRTHS. MRS. MEEK, OF A SON"

MRS. BIGBY, mother of Mrs. Meek.
AUGUSTUS GEORGE MEEK, infant son of Mr. George Meek.
MR. GEORGE MEEK, a quiet man, of small stature and weak voice.
MRS. MEEK, his wife.
MRS. PRODGIT, nurse to Mrs. Meek.

A POOR MAN'S TALE OF A PATENT

WILLIAM BUTCHER, a Chartist.
JOHN, a working smith, who endeavours to patent an invention.
THOMAS JOY, a carpenter with whom John lodges.

A FLIGHT

THE COMPACT ENCHANTRESS, a French actress.
DON DIEGO, inventor of the last new flying-machine.
LAMIEL, a tall, grave, melancholy Frenchman.

THE DETECTIVE POLICE; AND THREE "DETECTIVE" ANECDOTES

MR. CLARKSON, counsel for Shepherdson and other thieves.
SERGEANT DORNTON, a detective police-officer.
DR. DUNDEY, a man who robs an Irish bank.
SERGEANT FENDALL, a detective police-officer.
FIKEY, a man accused of forgery.

ELIZA GRIMWOOD, a handsome young woman, called "The Countess."
AARON MESHECK, a fraudulent Jewish bill-broker.
SERGEANT MITH, a detective police-officer.
MR. PHIBBS, a haberdasher.
THOMAS PIGEON (*alias* TALLY-HO THOMPSON), a famous horse-stealer.
SHEPHERDSON, a thief.
INSPECTOR STALKER }
SERGEANT STRAW   } detective police-officers.
MR. TATT, an amateur detective.
MR. TRINKLE, a young man suspected of murder.
INSPECTOR WIELD   }
SERGEANT WITCHEM   } detective police-officers.

ON DUTY WITH INSPECTOR FIELD

BULLY BARK, a lodging-house keeper and receiver of stolen goods.
BLACKEY, a beggar with a painted skin to represent disease.
MR. CLICK, a rogue.
INSPECTOR FIELD, a detective officer.
BOB MILES, a rogue and jail-bird.
THE EARL OF WARWICK, a thief, so styled.

PRINCE BULL. A FAIRY TALE

PRINCE BEAR [Russia], an enemy of Prince Bull.
PRINCE BULL [the English Government], a powerful but corpulent and rather sleepy Prince.
TAPE, a tyrannical old godmother to Prince Bull.

OUR SCHOOL

MR. BLINKINS, the Latin master.
MASTER DUMBLEDON, a goggle-eyed parlour-boarder.
MISS FROST, a schoolgirl.
MASTER MAWLS, a schoolboy of uncouth manners.
MASTER MAXBY, a schoolboy, favoured by the usher.
PHIL, a serving-man.

OUR VESTRY

CAPTAIN BANGER, a vestryman, and opponent of Mr. Tiddypot.
MR. CHIB, the Father of the Vestry.
MR. DOGGINSON, a vestryman regarded as "a regular John Bull."
MR. MAGG, one of the first orators of the Vestry.
MR. TIDDYPOT, a vestryman, opposed to Captain Banger.
MR. WIGSBY, a debater of great eminence.

REPRINTED PIECES

THE LONG VOYAGE

WHEN the wind is blowing and the sleet or rain is driving against the dark windows, I love to sit by the fire, thinking of what I have read in books of voyage and travel. Such books have had a strong fascination for my mind from my earliest childhood; and I wonder it should have come to pass that I never have been round the world, never have been shipwrecked, ice-environed, tomahawked, or eaten.

Sitting on my ruddy hearth in the twilight of New Year's Eve, I find incidents of travel rise around me from all the latitudes and longitudes of the globe. They observe no order or sequence, but appear and vanish as they will— "come like shadows, so depart." Columbus, alone upon the sea with his disaffected crew, looks over the waste of waters from his high station on the poop of his ship, and sees the first uncertain glimmer of the light, "rising and falling with the waves, like a torch in the bark of some fisherman," which is the shining star of a new world. Bruce is caged in Abyssinia, surrounded by the gory horrors which shall often startle him out of his sleep at home when years have passed away. Franklin, come to the end of his unhappy overland journey—would that it had been his last!—lies perishing of hunger with his brave companions: each emaciated figure stretched upon its miserable bed without the power to rise: all, dividing the weary days between their prayers, their remembrances of the dear ones at home, and conversation on the pleasures of eating; the last-named topic being ever present to them, likewise, in their dreams. All the African travellers, wayworn, solitary and sad, submit themselves again to drunken, murderous, man-selling despots, of the

lowest order of humanity ; and Mungo Park, fainting under
a tree and succoured by a woman, gratefully remembers how
his Good Samaritan has always come to him in woman's
shape, the wide world over.

A shadow on the wall, in which my mind's eye can discern some traces of a rocky sea-coast, recalls to me a fearful
story of travel derived from that unpromising narrator of
such stories, a parliamentary blue-book. A convict is its
chief figure, and this man escapes with other prisoners from
a penal settlement. It is an island, and they seize a boat,
and get to the main land. Their way is by a rugged and
precipitous sea-shore, and they have no earthly hope of
ultimate escape, for the party of soldiers despatched by an
easier course to cut them off, must inevitably arrive at their
distant bourne long before them, and retake them if by any
hazard they survive the horrors of the way. Famine, as
they all must have foreseen, besets them early in their
course. Some of the party die and are eaten ; some are
murdered by the rest and eaten. This one awful creature
eats his fill, and sustains his strength, and lives on to be
recaptured and taken back. The unrelateable experiences
through which he has passed have been so tremendous, that
he is not hanged as he might be, but goes back to his old
chained-gang work. A little time, and he tempts one other
prisoner away, seizes another boat, and flies once more—
necessarily in the old hopeless direction, for he can take no
other. He is soon cut off, and met by the pursuing party
face to face, upon the beach. He is alone. In his former
journey he acquired an inappeasable relish for his dreadful
food. He urged the new man away, expressly to kill him
and eat him. In the pockets on one side of his coarse
convict-dress, are portions of the man's body, on which he
is regaling ; in the pockets on the other side is an untouched
store of salted pork (stolen before he left the island) for
which he has no appetite. He is taken back, and he is
hanged. But I shall never see that sea-beach on the wall or
in the fire, without him, solitary monster, eating as he
prowls along, while the sea rages and rises at him.

Captain Bligh (a worse man to be entrusted with arbitrary
power there could scarcely be) is handed over the side of the
Bounty, and turned adrift on the wide ocean in an open
boat, by order of Fletcher Christian, one of his officers, at
this very minute. Another flash of my fire, and "Thursday

October Christian," five-and-twenty years of age, son of the dead and gone Fletcher by a savage mother, leaps aboard His Majesty's ship Briton, hove-to off Pitcairn's Island; says his simple grace before eating, in good English; and knows that a pretty little animal on board is called a dog, because in his childhood he had heard of such strange creatures from his father and the other mutineers, grown grey under the shade of the bread-fruit trees, speaking of their lost country far away.

See the Halsewell, East Indiaman outward bound, driving madly on a January night towards the rocks near Seacombe, on the island of Purbeck! The captain's two dear daughters are aboard, and five other ladies. The ship has been driving many hours, has seven feet of water in her hold, and her mainmast has been cut away. The description of her loss, familiar to me from my early boyhood, seems to be read aloud as she rushes to her destiny.

" About two in the morning of Friday the sixth of January, the ship still driving, and approaching very fast to the shore, Mr. Henry Meriton, the second mate, went again into the cuddy, where the captain then was. Another conversation taking place, Captain Pierce expressed extreme anxiety for the preservation of his beloved daughters, and earnestly asked the officer if he could devise any method of saving them. On his answering with great concern, that he feared it would be impossible, but that their only chance would be to wait for morning, the captain lifted up his hands in silent and distressful ejaculation.

" At this dreadful moment the ship struck, with such violence as to dash the heads of those standing in the cuddy against the deck above them, and the shock was accompanied by a shriek of horror that burst at one instant from every quarter of the ship.

" Many of the seamen, who had been remarkably inattentive and remiss in their duty during great part of the storm, now poured upon deck, where no exertions of the officers could keep them, while their assistance might have been useful. They had actually skulked in their hammocks, leaving the working of the pumps and other necessary labours to the officers of the ship and the soldiers, who had made uncommon exertions. Roused by a sense of their danger, the same seamen, at this moment, in frantic exclamations, demanded of heaven and their fellow-sufferers that succour which their own efforts, timely made, might possibly have procured.

"The ship continued to beat on the rocks; and soon bilging, fell with her broadside towards the shore. When she struck, a number of the men climbed up the ensign-staff, under an apprehension of her immediately going to pieces.

"Mr. Meriton, at this crisis, offered to these unhappy beings the best advice which could be given; he recommended that all should come to the side of the ship lying lowest on the rocks, and singly to take the opportunities which might then offer, of escaping to the shore.

"Having thus provided, to the utmost of his power, for the safety of the desponding crew, he returned to the round-house, where, by this time, all the passengers and most of the officers had assembled. The latter were employed in offering consolation to the unfortunate ladies; and, with unparalleled magnanimity, suffering their compassion for the fair and amiable companions of their misfortunes to prevail over the sense of their own danger.

"In this charitable work of comfort Mr. Meriton now joined, by assurances of his opinion, that the ship would hold together till the morning, when all would be safe. Captain Pierce, observing one of the young gentlemen loud in his exclamations of terror, and frequently cry that the ship was parting, cheerfully bid him be quiet, remarking that though the ship should go to pieces, he would not, but would be safe enough.

"It is difficult to convey a correct idea of the scene of this deplorable catastrophe, without describing the place where it happened. The Halsewell struck on the rocks at a part of the shore where the cliff is of vast height, and rises almost perpendicular from its base. But at this particular spot, the foot of the cliff is excavated into a cavern of ten or twelve yards in depth, and of breadth equal to the length of a large ship. The sides of the cavern are so nearly upright, as to be of extremely difficult access; and the bottom is strewed with sharp and uneven rocks, which seem, by some convulsion of the earth, to have been detached from its roof.

"The ship lay with her broadside opposite to the mouth of this cavern, with her whole length stretched almost from side to side of it. But when she struck, it was too dark for the unfortunate persons on board to discover the real magnitude of the danger, and the extreme horror of such a situation.

"In addition to the company already in the round-house, they had admitted three black women and two soldiers' wives; who, with the husband of one of them, had been allowed to come in, though the seamen, who had tumultuously demanded entrance to get the lights, had been opposed and kept out by Mr. Rogers and Mr. Brimer, the third and fifth mates. The numbers there were, therefore, now increased to near fifty. Captain Pierce sat on a chair, a cot, or some other moveable, with a daughter on each side, whom he alternately pressed to his affectionate breast. The rest of the melancholy assembly were seated on the deck, which was strewed with musical instruments, and the wreck of furniture and other articles.

"Here also Mr. Meriton, after having cut several wax-candles in pieces, and stuck them up in various parts of the round-house, and lighted up all the glass lanthorns he could find, took his seat, intending to wait the approach of dawn, and then assist the partners of his dangers to escape. But, observing that the poor ladies appeared parched and exhausted, he brought a basket of oranges and prevailed on some of them to refresh themselves by sucking a little of the juice. At this time they were all tolerably composed, except Miss Mansel, who was in hysteric fits on the floor of the deck of the round-house.

"But on Mr. Meriton's return to the company, he perceived a considerable alteration in the appearance of the ship; the sides were visibly giving way; the deck seemed to be lifting, and he discovered other strong indications that she could not hold much longer together. On this account, he attempted to go forward to look out, but immediately saw that the ship had separated in the middle, and that the forepart having changed its position, lay rather further out towards the sea. In such an emergency, when the next moment might plunge him into eternity, he determined to seize the present opportunity, and follow the example of the crew and the soldiers, who were now quitting the ship in numbers, and making their way to the shore, though quite ignorant of its nature and description.

"Among other expedients, the ensign-staff had been unshipped, and attempted to be laid between the ship's side and some of the rocks, but without success, for it snapped asunder before it reached them. However, by the light of a lanthorn, which a seaman handed through the skylight of the round-house to the deck, Mr. Meriton discovered a spar which appeared to be laid from the ship's side to the rocks, and on this spar he resolved to attempt his escape.

"Accordingly, lying down upon it, he thrust himself forward; however, he soon found that it had no communication with the rock; he reached the end of it, and then slipped off, receiving a very violent bruise in his fall, and before he could recover his legs, he was washed off by the surge. He now supported himself by swimming, until a returning wave dashed him against the back part of the cavern. Here he laid hold of a small projection in the rock, but was so much benumbed that he was on the point of quitting it, when a seaman, who had already gained a footing, extended his hand, and assisted him until he could secure himself a little on the rock; from which he clambered on a shelf still higher, and out of the reach of the surf.

"Mr. Rogers, the third mate, remained with the captain and the unfortunate ladies and their companions nearly twenty minutes after Mr. Meriton had quitted the ship. Soon after the latter left the round-house, the captain asked what was become of him, to which Mr. Rogers replied, that he was gone on deck to see what could be done. After this, a heavy sea breaking over the ship, the ladies exclaimed, 'Oh poor Meriton! he is drowned; had he stayed with us he would have been safe!' and they all, particularly Miss Mary Pierce, expressed great concern at the apprehension of his loss.

"The sea was now breaking in at the fore part of the ship, and reached as far as the mainmast. Captain Pierce gave Mr. Rogers a nod, and they took a lamp and went together into the stern-gallery, where, after viewing the rocks for some time, Captain Pierce asked Mr. Rogers if he thought there was any possibility of saving the girls; to which he replied, he feared there was none; for they could only discover the black face of the perpendicular rock, and not the cavern which afforded shelter to those who escaped. They then returned to the round-house, where Mr. Rogers hung up the lamp, and Captain Pierce sat down between his two daughters.

"The sea continuing to break in very fast, Mr. Macmanus, a midshipman, and Mr. Schutz, a passenger, asked Mr. Rogers what they could do to escape. 'Follow me,' he replied, and they all went into the stern-gallery, and from thence to the upper-quarter-gallery on the poop. While there, a very heavy sea fell on board, and the round-house gave way; Mr. Rogers heard the ladies shriek at intervals, as if the water reached them; the noise of the sea at other times drowning their voices.

"Mr. Brimer had followed him to the poop, where they remained together about five minutes, when on the breaking of this heavy sea, they jointly seized a hen-coop. The same wave which proved fatal to some of those below, carried him and his companion to the rock, on which they were violently dashed and miserably bruised.

"Here on the rock were twenty-seven men; but it now being low water, and as they were convinced that on the flowing of the tide all must be washed off, many attempted to get to the back or the sides of the cavern, beyond the reach of the returning sea. Scarcely more than six, besides Mr. Rogers and Mr. Brimer, succeeded.

"Mr. Rogers, on gaining this station, was so nearly exhausted, that had his exertions been protracted only a few minutes longer, he must have sunk under them. He was now prevented from joining Mr. Meriton, by at least twenty men between them, none of whom could move, without the imminent peril of his life.

"They found that a very considerable number of the crew, seamen and soldiers, and some petty officers, were in the same situation as themselves, though many who had reached the rocks below perished in attempting to ascend. They could yet discern some part of the ship, and in their dreary station solaced themselves with the hopes of its remaining entire until day-break; for, in the midst of their own distress, the sufferings of the females on board affected them with the most poignant anguish; and every sea that broke inspired them with terror for their safety.

"But, alas, their apprehensions were too soon realised! Within a very few minutes of the time that Mr. Rogers gained the rock, an universal shriek, which long vibrated in their ears, in which the voice of female distress was lamentably distinguished, announced the dreadful catastrophe. In a few moments all was hushed, except the roaring of the winds and the dashing of the waves ; the wreck was buried in the deep, and not an atom of it was ever afterwards seen."

The most beautiful and affecting incident I know, associated with a shipwreck, succeeds this dismal story for a winter night. The Grosvenor, East Indiaman, homeward bound, goes ashore on the coast of Caffraria. It is resolved that the officers, passengers, and crew, in number one hundred and thirty-five souls, shall endeavour to penetrate on foot, across trackless deserts, infested by wild beasts and cruel savages, to the Dutch settlements at the Cape of Good Hope. With this forlorn object before them, they finally separate into two parties—never more to meet on earth.

There is a solitary child among the passengers—a little boy of seven years old who has no relation there ; and when the first party is moving away he cries after some member of it who has been kind to him. The crying of a child might be supposed to be a little thing to men in such great extremity; but it touches them, and he is immediately taken into that detachment.

From which time forth, this child is sublimely made a sacred charge. He is pushed, on a little raft, across broad rivers by the swimming sailors ; they carry him by turns through the deep sand and long grass (he patiently walking at all other times) ; they share with him such putrid fish as they find to eat ; they lie down and wait for him when the rough carpenter, who becomes his especial friend, lags behind. Beset by lions and tigers, by savages, by thirst, by hunger, by death in a crowd of ghastly shapes, they never— O Father of all mankind, thy name be blessed for it !—forget this child. The captain stops exhausted, and his faithful coxswain goes back and is seen to sit down by his side, and neither of the two shall be any more beheld until the great last day ; but, as the rest go on for their lives, they take the child with them. The carpenter dies of poisonous berries eaten in starvation ; and the steward, succeeding to the command of the party, succeeds to the sacred guardianship of the child.

God knows all he does for the poor baby ; how he cheerfully carries him in his arms when he himself is weak and ill ; how he feeds him when he himself is griped with want ; how he folds his ragged jacket round him, lays his little

worn face with a woman's tenderness upon his sunburnt breast, soothes him in his sufferings, sings to him as he limps along, unmindful of his own parched and bleeding feet. Divided for a few days from the rest, they dig a grave in the sand and bury their good friend the cooper—these two companions alone in the wilderness—and then the time comes when they both are ill, and beg their wretched partners in despair, reduced and few in number now, to wait by them one day. They wait by them one day, they wait by them two days. On the morning of the third, they move very softly about, in making their preparations for the resumption of their journey; for the child is sleeping by the fire, and it is agreed with one consent that he shall not be disturbed until the last moment. The moment comes, the fire is dying—and the child is dead.

His faithful friend, the steward, lingers but a little while behind him. His grief is great, he staggers on for a few days, lies down in the desert, and dies. But he shall be re-united in his immortal spirit—who can doubt it!—with the child, where he and the poor carpenter shall be raised up with the words, "Inasmuch as ye have done it unto the least of these, ye have done it unto Me."

As I recall the dispersal and disappearance of nearly all the participators in this once famous shipwreck (a mere handful being recovered at last), and the legends that were long afterwards revived from time to time among the English officers at the Cape, of a white woman with an infant, said to have been seen weeping outside a savage hut far in the interior, who was whisperingly associated with the remembrance of the missing ladies saved from the wrecked vessel, and who was often sought but never found, thoughts of another kind of travel came into my mind.

Thoughts of a voyager unexpectedly summoned from home, who travelled a vast distance, and could never return. Thoughts of this unhappy wayfarer in the depths of his sorrow, in the bitterness of his anguish, in the helplessness of his self-reproach, in the desperation of his desire to set right what he had left wrong, and do what he had left undone.

For there were many many things he had neglected. Little matters while he was at home and surrounded by them, but things of mighty moment when he was at an immeasurable distance. There were many many blessings

that he had inadequately felt, there were many trivial injuries that he had not forgiven, there was love that he had but poorly returned, there was friendship that he had too lightly prized : there were a million kind words that he might have spoken, a million kind looks that he might have given, uncountable slight easy deeds in which he might have been most truly great and good. O for a day (he would exclaim), for but one day to make amends ! But the sun never shone upon that happy day, and out of his remote captivity he never came.

Why does this traveller's fate obscure, on New Year's Eve, the other histories of travellers with which my mind was filled but now, and cast a solemn shadow over me ! Must I one day make his journey ? Even so. Who shall say, that I may not then be tortured by such late regrets : that I may not then look from my exile on my empty place and undone work ? I stand upon a sea-shore, where the waves are years. They break and fall, and I may little heed them ; but with every wave the sea is rising, and I know that it will float me on this traveller's voyage at last.

THE BEGGING-LETTER WRITER

THE amount of money he annually diverts from wholesome and useful purposes in the United Kingdom, would be a set-off against the Window Tax. He is one of the most shameless frauds and impositions of this time. In his idleness, his mendacity, and the immeasurable harm he does to the deserving,—dirtying the stream of true benevolence, and muddling the brains of foolish justices, with inability to distinguish between the base coin of distress, and the true currency we have always among us,—he is more worthy of Norfolk Island than three-fourths of the worst characters who are sent there. Under any rational system, he would have been sent there long ago.

I, the writer of this paper, have been, for some time, a chosen receiver of Begging Letters. For fourteen years, my house has been made as regular a Receiving House for such communications as any one of the great branch Post-Offices is for general correspondence. I ought to know something of the Begging-Letter Writer. He has besieged my door at all hours of the day and night; he has fought my servant; he has lain in ambush for me, going out and coming in; he has followed me out of town into the country; he has appeared at provincial hotels, where I have been staying for only a few hours; he has written to me from immense distances, when I have been out of England. He has fallen sick; he has died and been buried; he has come to life again, and again departed from this transitory scene: he has been his own son, his own mother, his own baby, his idiot brother, his uncle, his aunt, his aged grandfather. He has wanted a greatcoat, to go to India in; a pound to set him up in life for ever; a pair of boots to take him to the coast of China; a hat to get him into a permanent situation under Government. He has frequently been exactly seven-and-sixpence short of independence. He has had such openings at Liverpool—posts of great trust and confidence in merchants' houses, which nothing but seven-and-sixpence was wanting to him to secure—that I wonder he is not Mayor of that flourishing town at the present moment.

The natural phenomena of which he has been the victim, are of a most astounding nature.   He has had two children who have never grown up; who have never had anything to cover them at night; who have been continually driving him mad, by asking in vain for food; who have never come out of fevers and measles (which, I suppose, has accounted for his fuming his letters with tobacco smoke, as a dis-infectant); who have never changed in the least degree through fourteen long revolving years.   As to his wife, what that suffering woman has undergone, nobody knows.   She has always been in an interesting situation through the same long period, and has never been confined yet.   His devotion to her has been unceasing.   He has never cared for himself; *he* could have perished—he would rather, in short—but was it not his Christian duty as a man, a husband, and a father, to write begging letters when he looked at her?   (He has usually remarked that he would call in the evening for an answer to this question.)

He has been the sport of the strangest misfortunes.   What his brother has done to him would have broken anybody else's heart.   His brother went into business with him, and ran away with the money; his brother got him to be security for an immense sum and left him to pay it; his brother would have given him employment to the tune of hundreds a-year, if he would have consented to write letters on a Sunday; his brother enunciated principles incompatible with his religious views, and he could not (in consequence) permit his brother to provide for him.   His landlord has never shown a spark of human feeling.   When he put in that execution I don't know, but he has never taken it out.   The broker's man has grown grey in possession.   They will have to bury him some day.

He has been attached to every conceivable pursuit.   He has been in the army, in the navy, in the church, in the law; connected with the press, the fine arts, public institu-tions, every description and grade of business.   He has been brought up as a gentleman; he has been at every college in Oxford and Cambridge; he can quote Latin in his letters (but generally mis-spells some minor English word); he can tell you what Shakespeare says about begging, better than you know it. It is to be observed, that in the midst of his afflictions he always reads the newspapers; and rounds off his appeal with some allusion, that may be supposed to be in my way, to the popular subject of the hour.

His life presents a series of inconsistencies. Sometimes he has never written such a letter before. He blushes with shame. That is the first time; that shall be the last. Don't answer it, and let it be understood that, then, he will kill himself quietly. Sometimes (and more frequently) he *has* written a few such letters. Then he encloses the answers, with an intimation that they are of inestimable value to him, and a request that they may be carefully returned. He is fond of enclosing something—verses, letters, pawn-brokers' duplicates, anything to necessitate an answer. He is very severe upon "the pampered minion of fortune," who refused him the half-sovereign referred to in the enclosure number two—but he knows me better.

He writes in a variety of styles; sometimes in low spirits; sometimes quite jocosely. When he is in low spirits he writes down-hill and repeats words—these little indications being expressive of the perturbation of his mind. When he is more vivacious, he is frank with me; he is quite the agreeable rattle. I know what human nature is,—who better? Well! He had a little money once, and he ran through it—as many men have done before him. He finds his old friends turn away from him now—many men have done that before him too! Shall he tell me why he writes to me? Because he has no kind of claim upon me. He puts it on that ground plainly; and begs to ask for the loan (as I know human nature) of two sovereigns, to be repaid next Tuesday six weeks, before twelve at noon.

Sometimes, when he is sure that I have found him out, and that there is no chance of money, he writes to inform me that I have got rid of him at last. He has enlisted into the Company's service, and is off directly—but he wants a cheese. He is informed by the serjeant that it is essential to his prospects in the regiment that he should take out a single Gloucester cheese, weighing from twelve to fifteen pounds. Eight or nine shillings would buy it. He does not ask for money, after what has passed; but if he calls at nine to-morrow morning may he hope to find a cheese? And is there anything he can do to show his gratitude in Bengal?

Once he wrote me rather a special letter, proposing relief in kind. He had got into a little trouble by leaving parcels of mud done up in brown paper, at people's houses, on pretence of being a Railway-Porter, in which character he received carriage money. This sportive fancy he expiated in the House of Correction. Not long after his release, and on a Sunday morning, he called with a letter (having first dusted himself all over), in which he gave me to understand that, being resolved to earn an honest livelihood, he had been travelling about the country with a cart of crockery. That he had been doing pretty well until the day before, when his horse had dropped down dead near Chatham, in Kent. That this had reduced him to the unpleasant necessity of getting into the shafts himself, and drawing the cart of crockery to London—a somewhat exhausting pull of thirty miles. That he did not venture to ask again for money; but that if I would have the goodness to leave him out a donkey, he would call for the animal before breakfast!

At another time my friend (I am describing actual experiences) introduced himself as a literary gentleman in the last extremity of distress. He had had a play accepted at a certain Theatre—which was really open; its representation was delayed by the indisposition of a leading actor—who was really ill; and he and his were in a state of absolute starvation. If he made his necessities known to the Manager of the Theatre, he put it to me to say what kind of treatment he might expect? Well! we got over that difficulty to our mutual satisfaction. A little while afterwards he was in some other strait. I think Mrs. Southcote, his wife, was in extremity—and we adjusted that point too. A little while afterwards he had taken a new house, and was going headlong to ruin for want of a water-butt. I had my misgivings about the water-butt, and did not reply to that epistle. But a little while afterwards, I had reason to feel penitent for my neglect. He wrote me a few broken-hearted lines, informing me that the dear partner of his sorrows died in his arms last night at nine o'clock!

I despatched a trusty messenger to comfort the bereaved mourner and his poor children; but the messenger went so soon, that the play was not ready to be played out; my friend was not at home, and his wife was in a most delightful state of health. He was taken up by the Mendicity Society (informally it afterwards appeared), and I presented myself at a London Police-Office with my testimony against him. The Magistrate was wonderfully struck by his educational acquirements, deeply impressed by the excellence of his letters, exceedingly sorry to see a man of his attainments there, complimented him highly on his powers of composition, and was quite charmed to have the agreeable duty of discharging him. A collection was made for the "poor fellow," as he was called in the reports, and I left the court with a comfortable sense of being universally regarded as a sort of monster. Next day comes to me a friend of mine, the governor of a large prison. "Why did you ever go to the Police-Office against that man," says he, "without coming to me first? I know all about him and his frauds. He lodged in the house of one of my warders, at the very time when he first wrote to you; and then he was eating spring-lamb at eighteen-pence a pound, and early asparagus at I don't know how much a bundle!" On that very same day, and in that very same hour, my injured gentleman wrote a solemn address to me, demanding to know what compensation I proposed to make him for his having passed the night in a "loathsome dungeon." And next morning an Irish gentleman, a member of the same fraternity, who had read the case, and was very well persuaded I should be chary of going to that Police-Office again, positively refused to leave my door for less than a sovereign, and resolved to besiege me into compliance, literally "sat down" before it for ten mortal hours. The garrison being well provisioned, I remained within the walls; and he raised the siege at midnight with a prodigious alarum on the bell.

The Begging-Letter Writer often has an extensive circle of acquaintance. Whole pages of the "Court Guide" are ready to be references for him. Noblemen and gentlemen write to say there never was such a man for probity and virtue. They have known him time out of mind, and there is nothing they wouldn't do for him. Somehow, they don't give him that one pound ten he stands in need of; but perhaps it is not enough—they want to do more, and his modesty will not allow it. It is to be remarked of his trade that it is a very fascinating one. He never leaves it; and those who are near to him become smitten with a love of it, too, and sooner or later set up for themselves. He employs a messenger—man, woman, or child. That messenger is certain ultimately to become an independent Begging-Letter

Writer. His sons and daughters succeed to his calling, and
write begging-letters when he is no more. He throws off
the infection of begging-letter writing, like the contagion
of disease. What Sydney Smith so happily called "the
dangerous luxury of dishonesty" is more tempting, and
more catching, it would seem, in this instance than in any
other.

He always belongs to a Corresponding-Society of Begging-
Letter Writers. Any one who will, may ascertain this fact.
Give money to-day in recognition of a begging-letter,—no
matter how unlike a common begging-letter,—and for the
next fortnight you will have a rush of such communications.
Steadily refuse to give ; and the begging-letters become
Angels' visits, until the Society is from some cause or other
in a dull way of business, and may as well try you as anybody else. It is of little use inquiring into the Begging-
Letter Writer's circumstances. He may be sometimes
accidentally found out, as in the case already mentioned
(though that was not the first inquiry made) ; but apparent
misery is always a part of his trade, and real misery very
often is, in the intervals of spring-lamb and early asparagus.
It is naturally an incident of his dissipated and dishonest
life.

That the calling is a successful one, and that large sums
of money are gained by it, must be evident to anybody who
reads the Police Reports of such cases. But prosecutions
are of rare occurrence, relatively to the extent to which the
trade is carried on. The cause of this is to be found (as no
one knows better than the Begging-Letter Writer, for it is a
part of his speculation) in the aversion people feel to exhibit
themselves as having been imposed upon, or as having weakly
gratified their consciences with a lazy, flimsy substitute for
the noblest of all virtues. There is a man at large, at the
moment when this paper is preparing for the press (on the
29th of April, 1850), and never once taken up yet, who,
within these twelve months, has been probably the most
audacious and the most successful swindler that even this
trade has ever known. There has been something singularly
base in this fellow's proceedings ; it has been his business to
write to all sorts and conditions of people, in the names of
persons of high reputation and unblemished honour, profess-
ing to be in distress—the general admiration and respect for
whom has ensured a ready and generous reply.

Now, in the hope that the results of the real experience of a real person may do something more to induce reflection on this subject than any abstract treatise—and with a personal knowledge of the extent to which the Begging-Letter Trade has been carried on for some time, and has been for some time constantly increasing—the writer of this paper entreats the attention of his readers to a few concluding words. His experience is a type of the experience of many ; some on a smaller, some on an infinitely larger scale. All may judge of the soundness or unsoundness of his conclusions from it.

Long doubtful of the efficacy of such assistance in any case whatever, and able to recall but one, within his whole individual knowledge, in which he had the least after-reason to suppose that any good was done by it, he was led, last autumn, into some serious considerations. The begging-letters flying about by every post made it perfectly manifest that a set of lazy vagabonds were interposed between the general desire to do something to relieve the sickness and misery under which the poor were suffering, and the suffering poor themselves. That many who sought to do some little to repair the social wrongs, inflicted in the way of preventible sickness and death upon the poor, were strengthening those wrongs, however innocently, by wasting money on pestilent knaves cumbering society. That imagination,—soberly following one of these knaves into his life of punishment in jail, and comparing it with the life of one of these poor in a cholera-stricken alley, or one of the children of one of these poor, soothed in its dying hour by the late lamented Mr. Drouet,—contemplated a grim farce, impossible to be presented very much longer before God or man. That the crowning miracle of all the miracles summed up in the New Testament, after the miracle of the blind seeing, and the lame walking, and the restoration of the dead to life, was the miracle that the poor had the Gospel preached to them. That while the poor were unnaturally and unnecessarily cut off by the thousand, in the prematurity of their age, or in the rottenness of their youth—for of flower or blossom such youth has none—the Gospel was NOT preached to them, saving in hollow and unmeaning voices. That of all wrongs, this was the first mighty wrong the Pestilence warned us to set right. And that no Post-Office Order to any amount, given to a Begging-Letter Writer for the quieting of an uneasy

breast, would be presentable on the Last Great Day as anything towards it.

The poor never write these letters. Nothing could be
more unlike their habits. The writers are public robbers;
and we who support them are parties to their depredations.
They trade upon every circumstance within their knowledge
that affects us, public or private, joyful or sorrowful; they
pervert the lessons of our lives; they change what ought to
be our strength and virtue into weakness and encouragement
of vice. There is a plain remedy, and it is in our own
hands. We must resolve, at any sacrifice of feeling, to be
deaf to such appeals, and crush the trade.

There are degrees in murder. Life must be held sacred
among us in more ways than one—sacred, not merely from
the murderous weapon, or the subtle poison, or the cruel
blow, but sacred from preventible diseases, distortions, and
pains. That is the first great end we have to set against
this miserable imposition. Physical life respected, moral life
comes next. What will not content a Begging-Letter Writer
for a week, would educate a score of children for a year.
Let us give all we can; let us give more than ever. Let us
do all we can; let us do more than ever. But let us give,
and do, with a high purpose; not to endow the scum of the
earth, to its own greater corruption, with the offals of our
duty.

and while he was so little that he never yet had spoken word, he stretched his tiny form out on his bed, and died.

Again the child dreamed of the open star, and of the company of angels, and the train of people, and the rows of angels with their beaming eyes all turned upon those people's faces.

Said his sister's angel to the leader:

"Is my brother come?"

And he said, "Not that one, but another."

As the child beheld his brother's angel in her arms, he cried, "O, sister, I am here! Take me!" And she turned and smiled upon him, and the star was shining.

He grew to be a young man, and was busy at his books when an old servant came to him and said:

"Thy mother is no more. I bring her blessing on her darling son!"

Again at night he saw the star, and all that former company. Said his sister's angel to the leader:

"Is my brother come?"

And he said, "Thy mother!"

A mighty cry of joy went forth through all the star, because the mother was re-united to her two children. And he stretched out his arms and cried, "O, mother, sister, and brother, I am here! Take me!" And they answered him, "Not yet," and the star was shining.

He grew to be a man, whose hair was turning grey, and he was sitting in his chair by the fireside, heavy with grief, and with his face bedewed with tears, when the star opened once again.

Said his sister's angel to the leader: "Is my brother come?"

And he said, "Nay, but his maiden daughter."

And the man who had been the child saw his daughter, newly lost to him, a celestial creature among those three, and he said, "My daughter's head is on my sister's bosom, and her arm is around my mother's neck, and at her feet there is the baby of old time, and I can bear the parting from her, God be praised!"

And the star was shining.

Thus the child came to be an old man, and his once smooth face was wrinkled, and his steps were slow and feeble, and his back was bent. And one night as he lay upon his bed, his children standing round, he cried, as he had cried so long ago :

"I see the star !"

They whispered one another, "He is dying."

And he said, "I am. My age is falling from me like a garment, and I move towards the star as a child. And O, my Father, now I thank thee that it has so often opened, to receive those dear ones who await me !"

And the star was shining ; and it shines upon his grave.

OUR ENGLISH WATERING-PLACE

In the Autumn-time of the year, when the great metropolis is so much hotter, so much noisier, so much more dusty or so much more water-carted, so much more crowded, so much more disturbing and distracting in all respects, than it usually is, a quiet sea-beach becomes indeed a blessed spot. Half awake and half asleep, this idle morning in our sunny window on the edge of a chalk-cliff in the old-fashioned watering-place to which we are a faithful resorter, we feel a lazy inclination to sketch its picture.

The place seems to respond. Sky, sea, beach, and village, lie as still before us as if they were sitting for the picture. It is dead low-water. A ripple plays among the ripening corn upon the cliff, as if it were faintly trying from recollection to imitate the sea ; and the world of butterflies hovering over the crop of radish-seed are as restless in their little way as the gulls are in their larger manner when the wind blows. But the ocean lies winking in the sunlight like a drowsy lion—its glassy waters scarcely curve upon the shore—the fishing-boats in the tiny harbour are all stranded in the mud —our two colliers (our watering-place has a maritime trade employing that amount of shipping) have not an inch of water within a quarter of a mile of them, and turn, exhausted, on their sides, like faint fish of an antediluvian species. Rusty cables and chains, ropes and rings, undermost parts of posts and piles and confused timber-defences against the waves, lie strewn about, in a brown litter of tangled sea-weed and fallen cliff which looks as if a family of giants had been making tea here for ages, and had observed an untidy custom of throwing their tea-leaves on the shore.

In truth, our watering-place itself has been left somewhat high and dry by the tide of years. Concerned as we are for its honour, we must reluctantly admit that the time when this pretty little semi-circular sweep of houses tapering off at the end of the wooden pier into a point in the sea, was a gay place, and when the lighthouse overlooking it shone at daybreak on company dispersing from public balls, is but dimly traditional now. There is a bleak chamber in our watering-place which is yet called the Assembly "Rooms," and understood to be available on hire for balls or concerts ; and, some few seasons since, an ancient little gentleman came down and stayed at the hotel, who said that he had danced there, in bygone ages, with the Honourable Miss Peepy, well known to have been the Beauty of her day and the cruel occasion of innumerable duels. But he was so old and shrivelled, and so very rheumatic in the legs, that it demanded more imagination than our watering-place can usually muster, to believe him ; therefore, except the Master of the "Rooms" (who to this hour wears knee-breeches, and who confirmed the statement with tears in his eyes), nobody did believe in the little lame old gentleman, or even in the Honourable Miss Peepy, long deceased.

As to subscription balls in the Assembly Rooms of our watering-place now red-hot cannon balls are less improbable. Sometimes, a misguided wanderer of a Ventriloquist, or an Infant Phenomenon, or a Juggler, or somebody with an Orrery that is several stars behind the time, takes the place for a night, and issues bills with the name of his last town lined out, and the name of ours ignominiously written in, but you may be sure this never happens twice to the same unfortunate person. On such occasions the discoloured old Billiard Table that is seldom played at (unless the ghost of the Honourable Miss Peepy plays at pool with other ghosts) is pushed into a corner, and benches are solemnly constituted into front seats, back seats, and reserved seats—which are much the same after you have paid—and a few dull candles are lighted—wind permitting—and the performer and the scanty audience play out a short match which shall make the other most low-spirited—which is usually a drawn game. After that the performer instantly departs with maledictory expressions, and is never heard of more.

But the most wonderful feature of our Assembly Rooms, is, that an annual sale of "Fancy and other China," is announced here with mysterious constancy and perseverance. Where the china comes from, where it goes to, why it is annually put up to auction when nobody ever thinks of bidding for it, how it comes to pass that it is always the same china, whether it would not have been cheaper, with the sea at hand, to have thrown it away, say in eighteen hundred and thirty, are standing enigmas. Every year the bills come out, every year the Master of the Rooms gets into a little pulpit on a table, and offers it for sale, every year nobody buys it, every year it is put away somewhere till next year, when it appears again as if the whole thing were a new idea. We have a faint remembrance of an unearthly collection of clocks, purporting to be the work of Parisian and Genevese artists—chiefly bilious-faced clocks, supported on sickly white crutches, with their pendulums dangling like lame legs—to which a similar course of events occurred for several years, until they seemed to lapse away, of mere imbecility.

Attached to our Assembly Rooms is a library. There is a wheel of fortune in it, but it is rusty and dusty, and never turns. A large doll, with moveable eyes, was put up to be raffled for, by five-and-twenty members at two shillings, seven years ago this autumn, and the list is not full yet. We are rather sanguine, now, that the raffle will come off next year. We think so, because we only want nine members, and should only want eight, but for number two having grown up since her name was entered, and withdrawn it when she was married. Down the street, there is a toy-ship of considerable burden, in the same condition. Two of the boys who were entered for that raffle have gone to India in real ships, since; and one was shot, and died in the arms of his sister's lover, by whom he sent his last words home.

This is the library for the Minerva Press. If you want that kind of reading, come to our watering-place. The leaves of the romances, reduced to a condition very like curl-paper, are thickly studded with notes in pencil: sometimes complimentary, sometimes jocose. Some of these commentators, like commentators in a more extensive way, quarrel with one another. One young gentleman who sarcastically writes "Oh ! ! !" after every sentimental passage, is pursued through his literary career by another, who writes "Insulting Beast!" Miss Julia Mills has read the whole collection of these books. She has left marginal notes on the pages, as "Is not this truly touching ? J. M." "How thrilling ! J. M." "Entranced here by the Magician's potent spell. J. M." She has also italicised her favourite traits in the description of the hero, as "his hair, which was *dark* and *wavy*, clustered in *rich profusion* around a *marble brow*, whose lofty paleness bespoke the intellect within." It reminds her of another hero. She adds, "How like B. L. Can this be mere coincidence? J. M."

You would hardly guess which is the main street of our watering-place, but you may know it by its being always stopped up with donkey-chaises. Whenever you come here, and see harnessed donkeys eating clover out of barrows drawn completely across a narrow thoroughfare, you may be quite sure you are in our High Street. Our Police you may know by his uniform, likewise by his never on any account interfering with anybody—especially the tramps and vagabonds. In our fancy shops we have a capital collection of damaged goods, among which the flies of countless summers "have been roaming." We are great in obsolete seals, and in faded pin-cushions, and in rickety camp-stools, and in exploded cutlery, and in miniature vessels, and in stunted little telescopes, and in objects made of shells that pretend not to be shells. Diminutive spades, barrows, and baskets, are our principal articles of commerce; but even they don't look quite new somehow. They always seem to have been offered and refused somewhere else, before they came down to our watering-place.

Yet it must not be supposed that our watering-place is an empty place, deserted by all visitors except a few staunch persons of approved fidelity. On the contrary, the chances are that if you came down here in August or September, you wouldn't find a house to lay your head in. As to finding either house or lodging of which you could reduce the terms, you could scarcely engage in a more hopeless pursuit. For all this, you are to observe that every season is the worst season ever known, and that the householding population of our watering-place are ruined regularly every autumn. They are like the farmers, in regard that it is surprising how much ruin they will bear. We have an excellent hotel—capital baths, warm, cold, and shower—firstrate bathing-machines—and as good butchers, bakers, and grocers, as heart could desire. They all do business, it is to be presumed, from motives of philanthropy—but it is quite certain that they are all being ruined. Their interest in strangers, and their politeness under ruin, bespeak their amiable nature. You would say so, if you only saw the baker helping a new comer to find suitable apartments.

So far from being at a discount as to company, we are in fact what would be popularly called rather a nobby place.

Some tip-top " Nobbs " come down occasionally—even Dukes and Duchesses. We have known such carriages to blaze among the donkey-chaises, as made beholders wink. Attendant on these equipages come resplendent creatures in plush and powder, who are sure to be stricken disgusted with the indifferent accommodation of our watering-place, and who, of an evening (particularly when it rains), may be seen very much out of drawing, in rooms far too small for their fine figures, looking discontentedly out of little back windows into bye-streets. The lords and ladies get on well enough and quite good-humouredly: but if you want to see the gorgeous phenomena who wait upon them at a perfect nonplus, you should come and look at the resplendent creatures with little back parlours for servants' halls, and turn-up bedsteads to sleep in, at our watering-place. You have no idea how they take it to heart.

We have a pier—a queer old wooden pier, fortunately without the slightest pretensions to architecture, and very picturesque in consequence. Boats are hauled up upon it, ropes are coiled all over it; lobster-pots, nets, masts, oars, spars, sails, ballast, and rickety capstans, make a perfect labyrinth of it. For ever hovering about this pier, with their hands in their pockets, or leaning over the rough bulwark it opposes to the sea, gazing through telescopes which they carry about in the same profound receptacles, are the Boatmen of our watering-place. Looking at them, you would say that surely these must be the laziest boatmen in the world. They lounge about, in obstinate and inflexible pantaloons that are apparently made of wood, the whole season through. Whether talking together about the shipping in the Channel, or gruffly unbending over mugs of beer at the public-house, you would consider them the slowest of men. The chances are a thousand to one that you might stay here for ten seasons, and never see a boatman in a hurry. A certain expression about his loose hands, when they are not in his pockets, as if he were carrying a considerable lump of iron in each, without any inconvenience, suggests strength, but he never seems to use it. He has the appearance of perpetually strolling—running is too inappropriate a word to be thought of—to seed. The only subject on which he seems to feel any approach to enthusiasm, is pitch. He pitches everything he can lay hold of,—the pier, the palings, his boat, his house,—when there is

nothing else left he turns to and even pitches his hat, or
his rough-weather clothing. Do not judge him by deceitful
appearances. These are among the bravest and most skilful
mariners that exist. Let a gale arise and swell into a storm,
let a sea run that might appal the stoutest heart that ever
beat, let the Light-boat on these dangerous sands throw up
a rocket in the night, or let them hear through the angry
roar the signal-guns of a ship in distress, and these men
spring up into activity so dauntless, so valiant, and heroic,
that the world cannot surpass it. Cavillers may object that
they chiefly live upon the salvage of valuable cargoes. So
they do, and God knows it is no great living that they get
out of the deadly risks they run. But put that hope of gain
aside. Let these rough fellows be asked, in any storm, who
volunteers for the life-boat to save some perishing souls, as
poor and empty-handed as themselves, whose lives the
perfection of human reason does not rate at the value of
a farthing each; and that boat will be manned, as surely
and as cheerfully, as if a thousand pounds were told down
on the weather-beaten pier. For this, and for the recollection
of their comrades whom we have known, whom the raging
sea has engulfed before their children's eyes in such brave
efforts, whom the secret sand has buried, we hold the
boatmen of our watering-place in our love and honour, and
are tender of the fame they well deserve.

So many children are brought down to our watering-place
that, when they are not out of doors, as they usually are in
fine weather, it is wonderful where they are put: the whole
village seeming much too small to hold them under cover.
In the afternoons, you see no end of salt and sandy little
boots drying on upper window-sills. At bathing-time in
the morning, the little bay re-echoes with every shrill variety
of shriek and splash—after which, if the weather be at all
fresh, the sands teem with small blue mottled legs. The
sands are the children's great resort. They cluster there,
like ants: so busy burying their particular friends, and
making castles with infinite labour which the next tide
overthrows, that it is curious to consider how their play,
to the music of the sea, foreshadows the realities of their
after lives.

It is curious, too, to observe a natural ease of approach
that there seems to be between the children and the boatmen. They mutually make acquaintance, and take indi-

vidual likings, without any help. You will come upon one of those slow heavy fellows sitting down patiently mending a little ship for a mite of a boy, whom he could crush to death by throwing his lightest pair of trousers on him. You will be sensible of the oddest contrast between the smooth little creature, and the rough man who seems to be carved out of hard-grained wood—between the delicate hand expectantly held out, and the immense thumb and finger that can hardly feel the rigging of thread they mend—between the small voice and the gruff growl—and yet there is a natural propriety in the companionship : always to be noted in confidence between a child and a person who has any merit of reality and genuineness : which is admirably pleasant.

We have a preventive station at our watering-place, and much the same thing may be observed—in a lesser degree, because of their official character—of the coast blockade ; a steady, trusty, well-conditioned, well-conducted set of men, with no misgiving about looking you full in the face, and with a quiet thorough-going way of passing along to their duty at night, carrying huge sou'-wester clothing in reserve, that is fraught with all good prepossession. They are handy fellows—neat about their houses—industrious at gardening —would get on with their wives, one thinks, in a desert island—and people it, too, soon.

As to the naval officer of the station, with his hearty fresh face, and his blue eye that has pierced all kinds of weather, it warms our hearts when he comes into church on a Sunday, with that bright mixture of blue coat, buff waistcoat, black neckerchief, and gold epaulette, that is associated in the minds of all Englishmen with brave, unpretending, cordial, national service. We like to look at him in his Sunday state ; and if we were First Lord (really possessing the indispensable qualification for the office of knowing nothing whatever about the sea), we would give him a ship to-morrow.

We have a church, by-the-by, of course—a hideous temple of flint, like a great petrified haystack. Our chief clerical dignitary, who, to his honour, has done much for education both in time and money, and has established excellent schools, is a sound, shrewd, healthy gentleman, who has got into little occasional difficulties with the neighbouring farmers, but has had a pestilent trick of being right. Under

a new regulation, he has yielded the church of our watering-place to another clergyman. Upon the whole we get on in church well. We are a little bilious sometimes, about these days of fraternisation, and about nations arriving at a new and more unprejudiced knowledge of each other (which our Christianity don't quite approve), but it soon goes off, and then we get on very well.

There are two dissenting chapels, besides, in our small watering-place; being in about the proportion of a hundred and twenty guns to a yacht. But the dissension that has torn us lately, has not been a religious one. It has arisen on the novel question of Gas. Our watering-place has been convulsed by the agitation, Gas or No Gas. It was never reasoned why No Gas, but there was a great No Gas party. Broadsides were printed and stuck about—a startling circumstance in our watering-place. The No Gas party rested content with chalking "No Gas!" and "Down with Gas!" and other such angry war-whoops, on the few back gates and scraps of wall which the limits of our watering-place afford; but the Gas party printed and posted bills, wherein they took the high ground of proclaiming against the No Gas party, that it was said Let there be light and there was light; and that not to have light (that is gas-light) in our watering-place, was to contravene the great decree. Whether by these thunderbolts or not, the No Gas party were defeated; and in this present season we have had our handful of shops illuminated for the first time. Such of the No Gas party, however, as have got shops, remain in opposition and burn tallow—exhibiting in their windows the very picture of the sulkiness that punishes itself, and a new illustration of the old adage about cutting off your nose to be revenged on your face, in cutting off their gas to be revenged on their business.

Other population than we have indicated, our watering-place has none. There are a few old used-up boatmen who creep about in the sunlight with the help of sticks, and there is a poor imbecile shoemaker who wanders his lonely life away among the rocks, as if he were looking for his reason—which he will never find. Sojourners in neighbouring watering-places come occasionally in flys to stare at us, and drive away again as if they thought us very dull; Italian boys come, Punch comes, the Fantoccini come, the Tumblers come, the Ethiopians come; Glee-singers come at

night, and hum and vibrate (not always melodiously) under our windows. But they all go soon, and leave us to ourselves again. We once had a travelling Circus and Wombwell's Menagerie at the same time. They both know better than ever to try it again; and the Menagerie had nearly razed us from the face of the earth in getting the elephant away—his caravan was so large, and the watering-place so small. We have a fine sea, wholesome for all people; profitable for the body, profitable for the mind. The poet's words are sometimes on its awful lips:

> And the stately ships go on
>   To their haven under the hill;
> But O for the touch of a vanish'd hand,
>   And the sound of a voice that is still!

> Break, break, break,
>   At the foot of thy crags, O sea!
> But the tender grace of a day that is dead
>   Will never come back to me.

Yet it is not always so, for the speech of the sea is various, and wants not abundant resource of cheerfulness, hope, and lusty encouragement. And since I have been idling at the window here, the tide has risen. The boats are dancing on the bubbling water; the colliers are afloat again; the white-bordered waves rush in; the children

> Do chase the ebbing Neptune, and do fly him
> When he comes back;

the radiant sails are gliding past the shore, and shining on the far horizon; all the sea is sparkling, heaving, swelling up with life and beauty, this bright morning.

OUR FRENCH WATERING-PLACE

HAVING earned by many years of fidelity, the right to be
sometimes inconstant to our English watering-place, we have
dallied for two or three seasons with a French watering-place:
once solely known to us as a town with a very long street,
beginning with an abattoir and ending with a steam-boat,
which it seemed our fate to behold only at daybreak on
winter mornings, when (in the days before continental railroads), just sufficiently awake to know that we were most
uncomfortably asleep, it was our destiny always to clatter
through it, in the coupé of the diligence from Paris, with a
sea of mud behind us, and a sea of tumbling waves before.
In relation to which latter monster, our mind's eye now
recalls a worthy Frenchman in a seal-skin cap with a braided
hood over it, once our travelling companion in the coupé
aforesaid, who, waking up with a pale and crumpled visage,
and looking ruefully out at the grim row of breakers enjoying themselves fanatically on an instrument of torture called
"the Bar," inquired of us whether we were ever sick at sea?
Both to prepare his mind for the abject creature we were
presently to become, and also to afford him consolation, we
replied, "Sir, your servant is always sick when it is possible
to be so." He returned, altogether uncheered by the bright
example, "Ah, Heaven, but I am always sick, even when it
is impossible to be so."

The means of communication between the French capital
and our French watering-place are wholly changed since
those days; but the Channel remains unbridged as yet, and
the old floundering and knocking about go on there. It
must be confessed that saving in reasonable (and therefore
rare) sea-weather, the act of arrival at our French watering-
place from England is difficult to be achieved with dignity.
Several little circumstances combine to render the visitor
an object of humiliation. In the first place, the steamer no
sooner touches the port, than all the passengers fall into
captivity: being boarded by an overpowering force of
Custom-house officers, and marched into a gloomy dungeon.

floor window, might conceive himself another Jack, alighting on enchanted ground from another bean-stalk. It is a place wonderfully populous in children ; English children, with governesses reading novels as they walk down the shady lanes of trees, or nursemaids interchanging gossip on the seats ; French children with their smiling bonnes in snow-white caps, and themselves—if little boys—in straw head-gear like beehives, work-baskets and church hassocks. Three years ago, there were three weazen old men, one bearing a frayed red ribbon in his threadbare button-hole, always to be found walking together among these children, before dinner-time. If they walked for an appetite, they doubtless lived en pension—were contracted for—otherwise their poverty would have made it a rash action. They were stooping, blear-eyed, dull old men, slip-shod and shabby, in long-skirted short-waisted coats and meagre trousers, and yet with a ghost of gentility hovering in their company. They spoke little to each other, and looked as if they might have been politically discontented if they had had vitality enough. Once, we overheard red-ribbon feebly complain to the other two that somebody, or something, was "a Robber;" and then they all three set their mouths so that they would have ground their teeth if they had had any. The ensuing winter gathered red-ribbon unto the great company of faded ribbons, and next year the remaining two were there—getting themselves entangled with hoops and dolls—familiar mysteries to the children—probably in the eyes of most of them, harmless creatures who had never been like children, and whom children could never be like. Another winter came, and another old man went, and so, this present year, the last of the triumvirate left off walking —it was no good, now—and sat by himself on a little soli-tary bench, with the hoops and the dolls as lively as ever all about him.

In the Place d'Armes of this town, a little decayed market is held, which seems to slip through the old gateway, like water, and go rippling down the hill, to mingle with the murmuring market in the lower town, and get lost in its movement and bustle. It is very agreeable on an idle summer morning to pursue this market-stream from the hill-top. It begins, dozingly and dully, with a few sacks of corn ; starts into a surprising collection of boots and shoes ; goes brawling down the hill in a diversified channel of old cordage, old iron, old crockery, old clothes, civil and military, old rags, new cotton goods, flaming prints of saints, little looking-glasses, and incalculable lengths of tape; dives into a backway, keeping out of sight for a little while, as streams will, or only sparkling for a moment in the shape of a market drinking-shop; and suddenly reappears behind the great church, shooting itself into a bright confusion of white-capped women and blue-bloused men, poultry, vegetables, fruits, flowers, pots, pans, praying-chairs, soldiers, country butter, umbrellas and other sun-shades, girl-porters waiting to be hired with baskets at their backs, and one weazen little old man in a cocked hat, wearing a cuirass of drinking-glasses and carrying on his shoulder a crimson temple fluttering with flags, like a glorified pavior's rammer without the handle, who rings a little bell in all parts of the scene, and cries his cooling drink Hola, Hola, Ho-o-o! in a shrill cracked voice that somehow makes itself heard, above all the chaffering and vending hum. Early in the afternoon, the whole course of the stream is dry. The praying-chairs are put back in the church, the umbrellas are folded up, the unsold goods are carried away, the stalls and stands disappear, the square is swept, the hackney coaches lounge there to be hired, and on all the country roads (if you walk about, as much as we do) you will see the peasant women, always neatly and comfortably dressed, riding home, with the pleasantest saddle-furniture of clean milk-pails, bright butter-kegs, and the like, on the jolliest little donkeys in the world.

We have another market in our French watering-place—that is to say, a few wooden hutches in the open street, down by the Port—devoted to fish. Our fishing-boats are famous everywhere; and our fishing people, though they love lively colours and taste is neutral (see Bilkins), are among the most picturesque people we ever encountered. They have not only a quarter of their own in the town itself, but they occupy whole villages of their own on the neighbouring cliffs. Their churches and chapels are their own; they consort with one another, they intermarry among themselves, their customs are their own, and their costume is their own and never changes. As soon as one of their boys can walk, he is provided with a long bright red nightcap; and one of their men would as soon think of going afloat without his head, as without that indispensable appendage to it. Then, they wear the noblest boots, with the hugest tops—flapping and bulging over anyhow; above which, they encase themselves in such wonderful overalls and petticoat trousers, made to all appearance of tarry old sails, so additionally stiffened with pitch and salt, that the wearers have a walk of their own, and go straddling and swinging about among the boats and barrels and nets and rigging, a sight to see. Then, their younger women, by dint of going down to the sea barefoot, to fling their baskets into the boats as they come in with the tide, and bespeak the first fruits of the haul with propitiatory promises to love and marry that dear fisherman who shall fill that basket like an Angel, have the finest legs ever carved by Nature in the brightest mahogany, and they walk like Juno. Their eyes, too, are so lustrous that their long gold ear-rings turn dull beside those brilliant neighbours; and when they are dressed, what with these beauties, and their fine fresh faces, and their many petticoats—striped petticoats, red petticoats, blue petticoats, always clean and smart, and never too long —and their home-made stockings, mulberry-coloured, blue, brown, purple, lilac—which the older women, taking care of the Dutch-looking children, sit in all sorts of places knitting, knitting, knitting from morning to night—and what with their little saucy bright blue jackets, knitted too, and fitting close to their handsome figures; and what with the natural grace with which they wear the commonest cap, or fold the commonest handkerchief round their luxuriant hair—we say, in a word and out of breath, that taking all these premises into our consideration, it has never been a matter of the least surprise to us that we have never once met, in the cornfields, on the dusty roads, by the breezy windmills, on the plots of short sweet grass overhanging the sea—anywhere—a young fisherman and fisherwoman of our French watering-place together, but the arm of that fisherman has invariably been, as a matter of course and without any absurd attempt to disguise so plain a necessity, round the neck or waist of that fisherwoman. And we have had no doubt whatever, standing looking at their uphill streets, house rising above house, and terrace above terrace, and bright garments here and there lying sunning on rough stone parapets, that the pleasant mist on all such objects, caused by their being seen through the brown nets hung across on poles to dry, is, in the eyes of every true young fisherman, a mist of love and beauty, setting off the goddess of his heart.

Moreover it is to be observed that these are an industrious people, and a domestic people, and an honest people. And though we are aware that at the bidding of Bilkins it is our duty to fall down and worship the Neapolitans, we make bold very much to prefer the fishing people of our French watering-place—especially since our last visit to Naples within these twelve months, when we found only four conditions of men remaining in the whole city: to wit, lazzaroni, priests, spies, and soldiers, and all of them beggars; the paternal government having banished all its subjects except the rascals.

But we can never henceforth separate our French watering-place from our own landlord of two summers, M. Loyal Devasseur, citizen and town-councillor. Permit us to have the pleasure of presenting M. Loyal Devasseur.

His own family name is simply Loyal; but as he is married, and as in that part of France a husband always adds to his own name the family name of his wife, he writes himself Loyal Devasseur. He owns a compact little estate of some twenty or thirty acres on a lofty hill-side, and on it he has built two country houses, which he lets furnished. They are by many degrees the best houses that are so let near our French watering-place; we have had the honour of living in both, and can testify. The entrance-hall of the first we inhabited was ornamented with a plan of the estate, representing it as about twice the size of Ireland; insomuch that when we were yet new to the property (M. Loyal always speaks of it as " La propriété ") we went three miles straight on end in search of the bridge of Austerlitz—which we afterwards found to be immediately outside the window. The Château of the Old Guard, in another part of the grounds, and, according to the plan, about two leagues from the little dining-room, we sought in vain for a week, until, happening one evening to sit upon a bench in the forest (forest in the plan), a few yards from the house-door, we observed at our feet, in the ignominious circumstances of being upside down and greenly rotten, the Old Guard himself: that is to say, the painted effigy of a member of that distinguished corps, seven feet high, and in the act of carrying arms, who had had the misfortune to be blown down in the previous winter. It will be perceived that M. Loyal is a staunch admirer of the great Napoleon. He is an old soldier himself—captain of the National Guard, with a handsome gold vase on his chimney-piece, presented to him by his company—and his respect for the memory of the illustrious general is enthusiastic. Medallions of him, portraits of him, busts of him, pictures of him, are thickly sprinkled all over the property. During the first month of our occupation, it was our affliction to be constantly knocking down Napoleon: if we touched a shelf in a dark corner, he toppled over with a crash ; and every door we opened, shook him to the soul. Yet M. Loyal is not a man of mere castles in the air, or, as he would say, in Spain. He has a specially practical, contriving, clever, skilful eye and hand. His houses are delightful. He unites French elegance and English comfort, in a happy manner quite his own. He has an extraordinary genius for making tasteful little bedrooms in angles of his roofs, which an Englishman would as soon think of turning to any account as he would think of cultivating the Desert. We have ourself reposed deliciously in an elegant chamber of M. Loyal's construction, with our head as nearly in the kitchen chimney-pot as we can conceive it likely for the head of any gentleman, not by profession a Sweep, to be. And into whatsoever strange nook M. Loyal's genius penetrates, it, in that nook, infallibly constructs a cupboard and a row of pegs. In either of our houses, we could have put away the knapsacks and hung up the hats of the whole regiment of Guides.

Aforetime, M. Loyal was a tradesman in the town. You can transact business with no present tradesman in the town, and give your card " chez M. Loyal," but a brighter face shines upon you directly. We doubt if there is, ever was, or ever will be, a man so universally pleasant in the minds of people as M. Loyal is in the minds of the citizens of our French watering-place. They rub their hands and laugh when they speak of him. Ah, but he is such a good child, such a brave boy, such a generous spirit, that Monsieur Loyal ! It is the honest truth. M. Loyal's nature is the nature of a gentleman. He cultivates his ground with his own hands (assisted by one little labourer, who falls into a fit now and then); and he digs and delves from morn to eve in prodigious perspirations—" works always," as he says—but, cover him with dust, mud, weeds, water, any stains you will, you never can cover the gentleman in M. Loyal. A portly, upright, broad-shouldered, brown faced man, whose soldierly bearing gives him the appearance of being taller than he is, look into the bright eye of M. Loyal, standing before you in his working-blouse and cap, not particularly well shaved, and, it may be, very earthy, and you shall discern in M. Loyal a gentleman whose true politeness is in grain, and confirmation of whose word by his bond you would blush to think of. Not without reason is M. Loyal when he tells that story, in his own vivacious way, of his travelling to Fulham, near London, to buy all these hundreds and hundreds of trees you now see upon the Property, then a bare, bleak hill; and of his sojourning in Fulham three months; and of his jovial evenings with the market-gardeners; and of the crowning banquet before his departure, when the market-gardeners rose as one man, clinked their glasses all together (as the custom at Fulham is), and cried, "Vive Loyal!"

M. Loyal has an agreeable wife, but no family; and he loves to drill the children of his tenants, or run races with them, or do anything with them, or for them, that is good-natured. He is of a highly convivial temperament, and his hospitality is unbounded. Billet a soldier on him, and he is delighted. Five-and-thirty soldiers had M. Loyal billeted on him this present summer, and they all got fat and red-faced in two days. It became a legend among the troops that whosoever got billeted on M. Loyal rolled in clover; and so it fell out that the fortunate man who drew the billet "M. Loyal Devasseur" always leaped into the air, though in heavy marching order. M. Loyal cannot bear to admit anything that might seem by any implication to disparage the military profession. We hinted to him once, that we were conscious of a remote doubt arising in our mind, whether a sou a day for pocket-money, tobacco, stockings, drink, washing, and social pleasures in general, left a very large margin for a soldier's enjoyment. Pardon! said Monsieur Loyal, rather wincing. It was not a fortune, but—à la bonne heure—it was better than it used to be! What, we asked him on another occasion, were all those neighbouring peasants, each living with his family in one room, and each having a soldier (perhaps two) billeted on him every other night, required to provide for those soldiers? "Faith!" said M. Loyal, reluctantly; "a bed, monsieur, and fire to cook with, and a candle. And they share their supper with those soldiers. It is not possible that they could eat alone."—"And what allowance do they get for this?" said we. Monsieur Loyal drew himself up taller, took a step back, laid his hand upon his breast, and said, with majesty, as speaking for himself and all France, "Monsieur, it is a contribution to the State!"

It is never going to rain, according to M. Loyal. When it is impossible to deny that it is now raining in torrents, he says it will be fine—charming—magnificent—to-morrow. It is never hot on the Property, he contends. Likewise it is never cold. The flowers, he says, come out, delighting to grow there; it is like Paradise this morning; it is like the Garden of Eden. He is a little fanciful in his language: smilingly observing of Madame Loyal, when she is absent at vespers, that she is "gone to her salvation"—allée à son salut. He has a great enjoyment of tobacco, but nothing would induce him to continue smoking face to face with a lady. His short black pipe immediately goes into his breast pocket, scorches his blouse, and nearly sets him on fire. In the Town Council and on occasions of ceremony, he appears in a full suit of black, with a waistcoat of magnificent breadth across the chest, and a shirt-collar of fabulous proportions. Good M. Loyal! Under blouse or waistcoat, he carries one of the gentlest hearts that beat in a nation teeming with gentle people. He has had losses, and has been at his best under them. Not only the loss of his way by night in the Fulham times—when a bad subject of an Englishman, under pretence of seeing him home, took him into all the night public-houses, drank "arfanarf" in every one at his expense, and finally fled, leaving him shipwrecked at Cleefeeway, which we apprehend to be Ratcliffe Highway—but heavier losses than that. Long ago a family of children and a mother were left in one of his houses without money, a whole year. M. Loyal—anything but as rich as we wish he had been—had not the heart to say "you must go;" so they stayed on and stayed on, and paying-tenants who would have come in couldn't come in, and at last they managed to get helped home across the water; and M. Loyal kissed the whole group, and said, "Adieu, my poor infants!" and sat down in their deserted salon and smoked his pipe of peace.—"The rent, M. Loyal?" "Eh! well! The rent!" M. Loyal shakes his head. "Le bon Dieu," says M. Loyal presently, "will recompense me," and he laughs and smokes his pipe of peace. May he smoke it on the Property, and not be recompensed, these fifty years!

There are public amusements in our French watering-place, or it would not be French. They are very popular, and very cheap. The sea-bathing—which may rank as the most favoured daylight entertainment, inasmuch as the French visitors bathe all day long, and seldom appear to think of remaining less than an hour at a time in the water—is astoundingly cheap. Omnibuses convey you, if you please, from a convenient part of the town to the beach and back again ; you have a clean and comfortable bathing-machine, dress, linen, and all appliances ; and the charge for the whole is half-a-franc, or fivepence. On the pier, there is usually a guitar, which seems presumptuously enough to set its tinkling against the deep hoarseness of the sea, and there is always some boy or woman who sings, without any voice, little songs without any tune : the strain we have most frequently heard being an appeal to "the sportsman" not to bag that choicest of game, the swallow. For bathing purposes, we have also a subscription establishment with an esplanade, where people lounge about with telescopes, and seem to get a good deal of weariness for their money ; and we have also an association of individual machine proprietors combined against this formidable rival. M. Féroce, our own particular friend in the bathing line, is one of these. How he ever came by his name we cannot imagine. He is as gentle and polite a man as M. Loyal Devasseur himself ; immensely stout withal, and of a beaming aspect. M. Féroce has saved so many people from drowning, and has been decorated with so many medals in consequence, that his stoutness seems a special dispensation of Providence to enable him to wear them ; if his girth were the girth of an ordinary man, he could never hang them on, all at once. It is only on very great occasions that M. Féroce displays his shining honours. At other times they lie by, with rolls of manuscript testifying to the causes of their presentation, in a huge glass case in the red-sofa'd salon of his private residence on the beach, where M. Féroce also keeps his family pictures, his portraits of himself as he appears both in bathing life and in private life, his little boats that rock by clockwork, and his other ornamental possessions.

Then, we have a commodious and gay Theatre—or had, for it is burned down now—where the opera was always preceded by a vaudeville, in which (as usual) everybody, down to the little old man with the large hat and the little cane by-the-by, as involving a good deal of noise, appears to me to be occasionally confounded with the Drummer.

The foregoing reflections presented themselves to my mind, the other day, as I contemplated (being newly come to London from the East Riding of Yorkshire, on a house-hunting expedition for next May) an old warehouse which rotting paste and rotting paper had brought down to the condition of an old cheese. It would have been impossible to say, on the most conscientious survey, how much of its front was brick and mortar, and how much decaying and decayed plaster. It was so thickly encrusted with fragments of bills, that no ship's keel after a long voyage could be half so foul. All traces of the broken windows were billed out, the doors were billed across, the water-spout was billed over. The building was shored up to prevent its tumbling into the street ; and the very beams erected against it were less wood than paste and paper, they had been so continually posted and reposted. The forlorn dregs of old posters so encumbered this wreck, that there was no hold for new posters, and the stickers had abandoned the place in despair, except one enterprising man who had hoisted the last masquerade to a clear spot near the level of the stack of chimneys, where it waved and drooped like a shattered flag. Below the rusty cellar-grating, crumpled remnants of old bills torn down rotted away in wasting heaps of fallen leaves. Here and there, some of the thick rind of the house had peeled off in strips, and fluttered heavily down, littering the street ; but still, below these rents and gashes, layers of decomposing posters showed themselves, as if they were interminable. I thought the building could never even be pulled down, but in one adhesive heap of rottenness and poster. As to getting in—I don't believe that if the Sleeping Beauty and her Court had been so billed up, the young Prince could have done it.

Knowing all the posters that were yet legible, intimately, and pondering on their ubiquitous nature, I was led into the reflections with which I began this paper, by considering what an awful thing it would be, ever to have wronged— say M. JULLIEN for example—and to have his avenging name in characters of fire incessantly before my eyes. Or to have injured MADAME TUSSAUD, and undergo a similar retribution. Has any man a self-reproachful thought associated with pills, or ointment ? What an avenging spirit to

BILL-STICKING

IF I had an enemy whom I hated—which Heaven forbid!
—and if I knew of something which sat heavy on his conscience, I think I would introduce that something into
a Posting-Bill, and place a large impression in the hands of
an active sticker. I can scarcely imagine a more terrible
revenge. I should haunt him, by this means, night and
day. I do not mean to say that I would publish his secret,
in red letters two feet high, for all the town to read: I would
darkly refer to it. It should be between him, and me, and
the Posting-Bill. Say, for example, that, at a certain period
of his life, my enemy had surreptitiously possessed himself
of a key. I would then embark my capital in the lock
business, and conduct that business on the advertising principle. In all my placards and advertisements, I would
throw up the line SECRET KEYS. Thus, if my enemy passed
an uninhabited house, he would see his conscience glaring
down on him from the parapets, and peeping up at him
from the cellars. If he took a dead wall in his walk, it
would be alive with reproaches. If he sought refuge in an
omnibus, the panels thereof would become Belshazzar's
palace to him. If he took boat, in a wild endeavour to
escape, he would see the fatal words lurking under the
arches of the bridges over the Thames. If he walked the
streets with downcast eyes, he would recoil from the very
stones of the pavement, made eloquent by lamp-black litho-
graph. If he drove or rode, his way would be blocked up
by enormous vans, each proclaiming the same words over
and over again from its whole extent of surface. Until,
having gradually grown thinner and paler, and having at
last totally rejected food, he would miserably perish, and
I should be revenged. This conclusion I should, no doubt,
celebrate by laughing a hoarse laugh in three syllables, and
folding my arms tight upon my chest agreeably to most of
the examples of glutted animosity that I have had an opportunity of observing in connexion with the Drama—which,

that man is PROFESSOR HOLLOWAY! Have I sinned in oil? CABBURN pursues me. Have I a dark remembrance associated with any gentlemanly garments, bespoke or ready made? MOSES AND SON are on my track. Did I ever aim a blow at a defenceless fellow-creature's head? That head eternally being measured for a wig, or that worse head which was bald before it used the balsam, and hirsute afterwards—enforcing the benevolent moral, "Better to be bald as a Dutch cheese than come to this,"—undoes me. Have I no sore places in my mind which MECHI touches— which NICOLL probes—which no registered article whatever lacerates? Does no discordant note within me thrill responsive to mysterious watchwords, as "Revalenta Arabica," or "Number One St. Paul's Churchyard"? Then may I enjoy life, and be happy.

Lifting up my eyes, as I was musing to this effect, I beheld advancing towards me (I was then on Cornhill, near to the Royal Exchange) a solemn procession of three advertising vans, of first-class dimensions, each drawn by a very little horse. As the cavalcade approached, I was at a loss to reconcile the careless deportment of the drivers of these vehicles with the terrific announcements they conducted through the city, which being a summary of the contents of a Sunday newspaper, were of the most thrilling kind. Robbery, fire, murder, and the ruin of the United Kingdom —each discharged in a line by itself, like a separate broadside of red-hot shot—were among the least of the warnings addressed to an unthinking people. Yet the Ministers of Fate, who drove the awful cars, leaned forward with their arms upon their knees in a state of extreme lassitude, for want of any subject of interest. The first man, whose hair I might naturally have expected to see standing on end, scratched his head—one of the smoothest I ever beheld— with profound indifference. The second whistled. The third yawned.

Pausing to dwell upon this apathy, it appeared to me, as the fatal cars came by me, that I descried in the second car, through the portal in which the charioteer was seated, a figure stretched upon the floor. At the same time, I thought I smelt tobacco. The latter impression passed quickly from me; the former remained. Curious to know whether this prostrate figure was the one impressible man of the whole capital who had been stricken insensible by the terrors revealed to him, and whose form had been placed in the car by the charioteer, from motives of humanity, I followed the procession. It turned into Leadenhall-market, and halted at a public-house. Each driver dismounted. I then distinctly heard, proceeding from the second car, where I had dimly seen the prostrate form, the words:

"And a pipe!"

The driver entering the public-house with his fellows, apparently for purposes of refreshment, I could not refrain from mounting on the shaft of the second vehicle, and looking in at the portal. I then beheld, reclining on his back upon the floor, on a kind of mattress or divan, a little man in a shooting-coat. The exclamation "Dear me," which irresistibly escaped my lips, caused him to sit upright and survey me. I found him to be a good-looking little man of about fifty, with a shining face, a tight head, a bright eye, a moist wink, a quick speech, and a ready air. He had something of a sporting way with him.

He looked at me, and I looked at him, until the driver displaced me by handing in a pint of beer, a pipe, and what I understand is called "a screw" of tobacco—an object which has the appearance of a curl-paper taken off the barmaid's head, with the curl in it.

"I beg your pardon," said I, when the removed person of the driver again admitted of my presenting my face at the portal. "But—excuse my curiosity, which I inherit from my mother—do you live here?"

"That's good, too!" returned the little man, composedly laying aside a pipe he had smoked out, and filling the pipe just brought to him.

"Oh, you *don't* live here then?" said I.

He shook his head, as he calmly lighted his pipe by means of a German tinder-box, and replied, "This is my carriage. When things are flat, I take a ride sometimes, and enjoy myself. I am the inventor of these wans."

His pipe was now alight. He drank his beer all at once, and he smoked and he smiled at me.

"It was a great idea!" said I.

"Not so bad," returned the little man, with the modesty of merit.

"Might I be permitted to inscribe your name upon the tablets of my memory?" I asked.

"There's not much odds in the name," returned the little

man, "—no name particular—I am the King of the Bill-Stickers."

"Good gracious!" said I.

The monarch informed me, with a smile, that he had never been crowned or installed with any public ceremonies, but that he was peaceably acknowledged as King of the Bill-Stickers in right of being the oldest and most respected member of "the old school of bill-sticking." He likewise gave me to understand that there was a Lord Mayor of the Bill-Stickers, whose genius was chiefly exercised within the limits of the city. He made some allusion, also, to an inferior potentate, called "Turkey-legs;" but I did not understand that this gentleman was invested with much power. I rather inferred that he derived his title from some peculiarity of gait, and that it was of an honorary character.

"My father," pursued the King of the Bill-Stickers, "was Engineer, Beadle, and Bill-Sticker to the parish of St. Andrew's, Holborn, in the year one thousand seven hundred and eighty. My father stuck bills at the time of the riots of London."

"You must be acquainted with the whole subject of bill-sticking, from that time to the present!" said I.

"Pretty well so," was the answer.

"Excuse me," said I; "but I am a sort of collector——"

"Not Income-tax?" cried His Majesty, hastily removing his pipe from his lips.

"No, no," said I.

"Water-rate?" said His Majesty.

"No, no," I returned.

"Gas? Assessed? Sewers?" said His Majesty.

"You misunderstand me," I replied, soothingly. "Not that sort of collector at all: a collector of facts."

"Oh, if it's only facts," cried the King of the Bill-Stickers, recovering his good-humour, and banishing the great mistrust that had suddenly fallen upon him, "come in and welcome! If it had been income, or winders, I think I should have pitched you out of the wan, upon my soul!"

Readily complying with the invitation, I squeezed myself in at the small aperture. His Majesty, graciously handing me a little three-legged stool on which I took my seat in a corner, inquired if I smoked.

"I do;—that is, I can," I answered.

"Pipe and a screw!" said His Majesty to the attendant

charioteer. "Do you prefer a dry smoke, or do you moisten it?"

As unmitigated tobacco produces most disturbing effects upon my system (indeed, if I had perfect moral courage, I doubt if I should smoke at all, under any circumstances), I advocated moisture, and begged the Sovereign of the Bill-Stickers to name his usual liquor, and to concede to me the privilege of paying for it. After some delicate reluctance on his part, we were provided, through the instrumentality of the attendant charioteer, with a can of cold rum-and-water, flavoured with sugar and lemon. We were also furnished with a tumbler, and I was provided with a pipe. His Majesty, then observing that we might combine business with conversation, gave the word for the car to proceed; and, to my great delight, we jogged away at a foot pace.

I say to my great delight, because I am very fond of novelty, and it was a new sensation to be jolting through the tumult of the city in that secluded Temple, partly open to the sky, surrounded by the roar without, and seeing nothing but the clouds. Occasionally, blows from whips fell heavily on the Temple's walls, when by stopping up the road longer than usual, we irritated carters and coachmen to madness; but they fell harmless upon us within and disturbed not the serenity of our peaceful retreat. As I looked upward, I felt, I should imagine, like the Astronomer Royal. I was enchanted by the contrast between the freezing nature of our external mission on the blood of the populace, and the perfect composure reigning within those sacred precincts: where His Majesty, reclining easily on his left arm, smoked his pipe and drank his rum-and-water from his own side of the tumbler, which stood impartially between us. As I looked down from the clouds and caught his royal eye, he understood my reflections. "I have an idea," he observed, with an upward glance, "of training scarlet runners across in the season,—making a arbour of it,—and sometimes taking tea in the same, according to the song."

I nodded approval.

"And here you repose and think?" said I.

"And think," said he, "of posters—walls—and hoardings."

We were both silent, contemplating the vastness of the subject. I remembered a surprising fancy of dear THOMAS HOOD's, and wondered whether this monarch ever sighed to repair to the great wall of China, and stick bills all over it.

"And so," said he, rousing himself, "it's facts as you collect?"

"Facts," said I.

"The facts of bill-sticking," pursued His Majesty, in a benignant manner, "as known to myself, air as following. When my father was Engineer, Beadle, and Bill-Sticker to the parish of St. Andrew's, Holborn, he employed women to post bills for him. He employed women to post bills at the time of the riots of London. He died at the age of seventy-five year, and was buried by the murdered Eliza Grimwood, over in the Waterloo Road."

As this was somewhat in the nature of a royal speech, I listened with deference and silently. His Majesty, taking a scroll from his pocket, proceeded, with great distinctness, to pour out the following flood of information :—

"'The bills being at that period mostly proclamations and declarations, and which were only a demy size, the manner of posting the bills (as they did not use brushes) was by means of a piece of wood which they called a 'dabber.' Thus things continued till such time as the State Lottery was passed, and then the printers began to print larger bills, and men were employed instead of women, as the State Lottery Commissioners then began to send men all over England to post bills, and would keep them out for six or eight months at a time, and they were called by the London bill-stickers 'trampers,' their wages at the time being ten shillings per day, besides expenses. They used sometimes to be stationed in large towns for five or six months together, distributing the schemes to all the houses in the town. And then there were more caricature wood-block engravings for posting-bills than there are at the present time, the principal printers, at that time, of posting-bills being Messrs. Evans and Ruffy, of Budge Row; Thoroughgood and Whiting, of the present day; and Messrs. Gye and Balne, Gracechurch Street, City. The largest bills printed at that period were a two-sheet double crown ; and when they commenced printing four-sheet bills, two bill-stickers would work together. They had no settled wages per week, but had a fixed price for their work, and the London bill-stickers, during a lottery week, have been known to earn, each, eight or nine pounds per week, till the day of drawing ; likewise the men who carried boards in the street used to have one pound per week, and the bill-stickers at that time would not allow any one to wilfully cover or destroy their bills, as they had a society amongst themselves, and very frequently dined together at some public-house where they used to go of an evening to have their work delivered out untoe 'em.'"

All this His Majesty delivered in a gallant manner ; posting it, as it were, before me, in a great proclamation. I took advantage of the pause he now made, to inquire what a "two-sheet double crown" might express ?

"A two-sheet double crown," replied the King, "is a bill thirty-nine inches wide by thirty inches high."

"Is it possible," said I, my mind reverting to the gigantic admonitions we were then displaying to the multitude— which were as infants to some of the posting-bills on the rotten old warehouse—"that some few years ago the largest bill was no larger than that?"

"The fact," returned the King, "is undoubtedly so." Here he instantly rushed again into the scroll.

"'Since the abolishing of the State Lottery all that good feeling has gone, and nothing but jealousy exists, through the rivalry of each other. Several bill-sticking companies have started, but have failed. The first party that started a company was twelve year ago ; but what was left of the old school and their dependants joined together and opposed them. And for some time we were quiet again, till a printer of Hatton Garden formed a company by hiring the sides of houses ; but he was not supported by the public, and he left his wooden frames fixed up for rent. The last company that started, took advantage of the New Police Act, and hired of Messrs. Grissell and Peto the hoarding of Trafalgar Square, and established a bill-sticking office in Cursitor Street, Chancery Lane, and engaged some of the new bill-stickers to do their work, and for a time got the half of all our work, and with such spirit did they carry on their opposition towards us, that they used to give us in charge before the magistrate, and get us fined ; but they found it so expensive that they could not keep it up, for they were always employing a lot of ruffians from the Seven Dials to come and fight us ; and on one occasion the old bill-stickers went to Trafalgar Square to attempt to post bills, when they were given in custody by the watchman in their employ, and fined at Queen Square five pounds, as they would not allow any of us to speak in the office ; but when they were gone, we had an interview with the magistrate, who mitigated the fine to fifteen shillings. During the time the men were waiting for the fine, this company started off to a public-house that we were in the habit of using, and waited for us coming back, where a fighting scene took place that beggars description. Shortly after this, the principal one day came and shook hands with us, and acknowledged that he had broken up the company, and that he himself had lost five hundred pound in trying to overthrow us. We then took possession of the hoarding in Trafalgar Square; but Messrs. Grissell and Peto would not allow us to post our bills on the said hoarding without paying them—and from first to last we paid upwards of two hundred pounds for that hoarding, and likewise the hoarding of the Reform Club-house, Pall Mall.'"

His Majesty, being now completely out of breath, laid down his scroll (which he appeared to have finished), puffed at his pipe, and took some rum-and-water. I embraced the opportunity of asking how many divisions the art and mystery of bill-sticking comprised? He replied, three—auctioneers' bill-sticking, theatrical bill-sticking, general bill-sticking.

"The auctioneers' porters," said the King, "who do their bill-sticking, are mostly respectable and intelligent, and generally well paid for their work, whether in town or country. The price paid by the principal auctioneers for country work is nine shillings per day; that is, seven shillings for day's work, one shilling for lodging, and one for paste. Town work is five shillings a day, including paste."

"Town work must be rather hot work," said I, "if there be many of those fighting scenes that beggar description, among the bill-stickers?"

"Well," replied the King, "I an't a stranger, I assure you, to black eyes; a bill-sticker ought to know how to handle his fists a bit. As to that row I have mentioned, that grew out of competition, conducted in an uncompromising spirit. Besides a man in a horse-and-shay continually following us about, the company had a watchman on duty, night and day, to prevent us sticking bills upon the hoarding in Trafalgar Square. We went there, early one morning, to stick bills and to black-wash their bills if we were interfered with. We *were* interfered with, and I gave the word for laying on the wash. It *was* laid on—pretty brisk—and we were all taken to Queen Square: but they couldn't fine *me*. *I* knew that," —with a bright smile—" I'd only give directions—I was only the General."

Charmed with this monarch's affability, I inquired if he had ever hired a hoarding himself.

"Hired a large one," he replied, "opposite the Lyceum Theatre, when the buildings was there. Paid thirty pound for it; let out places on it, and called it 'The External Paper-Hanging Station.' But it didn't answer. Ah!" said His Majesty thoughtfully, as he filled the glass, "Bill-stickers have a deal to contend with. The bill-sticking clause was got into the Police Act by a member of Parliament that employed me at his election. The clause is pretty stiff respecting where bills go; but *he* didn't mind where *his* bills went. It was all right enough, so long as they was *his* bills!"

Fearful that I observed a shadow of misanthropy on the King's cheerful face, I asked whose ingenious invention that was, which I greatly admired, of sticking bills under the arches of the bridges.

"Mine!" said His Majesty. "I was the first that ever stuck a bill under a bridge! Imitators soon rose up, of course.—When don't they? But they stuck 'em at low-water, and the tide came and swept the bills clean away. *I* knew that!" The King laughed.

"What may be the name of that instrument, like an immense fishing-rod," I inquired, "with which bills are posted on high places?"

"The joints," returned His Majesty. "Now, we use the joints where formerly we used ladders—as they do still in country places. Once, when Madame" (Vestris, understood) "was playing in Liverpool, another bill-sticker and me were at it together on the wall outside the Clarence Dock—me with the joints—him on a ladder. Lord! I had my bill up, right over his head, yards above him, ladder and all, while he was crawling to his work. The people going in and out of the docks stood and laughed!—It's about thirty years since the joints come in."

"Are there any bill-stickers who can't read?" I took the liberty of inquiring.

"Some," said the King. "But they know which is the right side up'ards of their work. They keep it as it's given out to 'em. I have seen a bill or so stuck wrong side up'ards. But it's very rare."

Our discourse sustained some interruption at this point, by the procession of cars occasioning a stoppage of about three-quarters of a mile in length, as nearly as I could judge. His Majesty, however, entreating me not to be discomposed by the contingent uproar, smoked with great placidity, and surveyed the firmament.

When we were again in motion, I begged to be informed what was the largest poster His Majesty had ever seen. The King replied, "A thirty-six sheet poster." I gathered, also, that there were about a hundred and fifty bill-stickers in London, and that his Majesty considered an average hand equal to the posting of one hundred bills (single sheets) in a day. The King was of opinion that, although posters had much increased in size, they had not increased in number; as the abolition of the State Lotteries had occasioned a great falling off, especially in the country. Over and above which change, I bethought myself that the custom of advertising in newspapers had greatly increased. The completion of many London improvements, as Trafalgar Square (I particularly observed the singularity of His Majesty's calling *that* an improvement), the Royal Exchange, &c., had of late years reduced the number of advantageous posting-places. Bill-Stickers at present rather confine themselves to districts, than to particular descriptions of work. One man would strike over Whitechapel, another would take round Houndsditch, Shoreditch, and the City Road; one (the King said) would stick to the Surrey side; another would make a beat of the West-end.

His Majesty remarked, with some approach to severity, on the neglect of delicacy and taste, gradually introduced into the trade by the new school: a profligate and inferior race of impostors who took jobs at almost any price, to the detriment of the old school, and the confusion of their own misguided employers. He considered that the trade was overdone with competition, and observed, speaking of his subjects, "There are too many of 'em." He believed, still, that things were a little better than they had been; adducing, as a proof, the fact that particular posting-places were now reserved, by common consent, for particular posters; those places, however, must be regularly occupied by those posters, or, they lapsed and fell into other hands. It was of no use giving a man a Drury Lane bill this week and not next. Where was it to go? He was of opinion that going to the expense of putting up your own board on which your sticker could display your own bills, was the only complete

way of posting yourself at the present time; but, even to
effect this, on payment of a shilling a week to the keepers of
steamboat piers and other such places, you must be able,
besides, to give orders for theatres and public exhibitions, or
you would be sure to be cut out by somebody. His Majesty
regarded the passion for orders, as one of the most unap-
peasable appetites of human nature. If there were a building, or if there were repairs, going on anywhere, you could
generally stand something and make it right with the fore-
man of the works; but orders would be expected from you,
and the man who could give the most orders was the man
who would come off best. There was this other objectionable point, in orders, that workmen sold them for drink,
and often sold them to persons who were likewise troubled
with the weakness of thirst: which led (His Majesty said)
to the presentation of your orders at Theatre doors, by individuals who were "too shakery" to derive intellectual profit
from the entertainments, and who brought a scandal on you.
Finally, His Majesty said that you could hardly put too
little in a poster; what you wanted was, two or three good
catch-lines for the eye to rest on—then, leave it alone—and
there you were!

These are the minutes of my conversation with His
Majesty, as I noted them down shortly afterwards. I am
not aware that I have been betrayed into any alteration or
suppression. The manner of the King was frank in the
extreme; and he seemed to me to avoid, at once, that slight
tendency to repetition which may have been observed in the
conversation of His Majesty King George the Third, and
that slight under-current of egotism which the curious observer may perhaps detect in the conversation of Napoleon
Bonaparte.

I must do the King the justice to say that it was I, and
not he, who closed the dialogue. At this juncture, I became
the subject of a remarkable optical delusion; the legs of my
stool appeared to me to double up; the car to spin round
and round with great violence; and a mist to arise between
myself and His Majesty. In addition to these sensations,
I felt extremely unwell. I refer these unpleasant effects,
either to the paste with which the posters were affixed to
the van: which may have contained some small portion of
arsenic; or to the printer's ink, which may have contained
some equally deleterious ingredient. Of this I cannot be

his unconscious face upwards, now the back of his bald head, until the unnatural feat was accomplished, and the bandage secured by a pin, which I have every reason to believe entered the body of my only child. In this tourniquet, he passes the present phase of his existence. Can I know it, and smile!

I fear I have been betrayed into expressing myself warmly, but I feel deeply. Not for myself; for Augustus George. I dare not interfere. Will any one? Will any publication? Any doctor? Any parent? Any body? I do not complain that Mrs. Prodgit (aided and abetted by Mrs. Bigby) entirely alienates Maria Jane's affections from me, and interposes an impassable barrier between us. I do not complain of being made of no account. I do not want to be of any account. But Augustus George is a production of Nature (I cannot think otherwise), and I claim that he should be treated with some remote reference to Nature. In my opinion, Mrs. Prodgit is, from first to last, a convention and a superstition. Are all the faculty afraid of Mrs. Prodgit? If not, why don't they take her in hand and improve her?

P.S. Maria Jane's Mama boasts of her own knowledge of the subject, and says she brought up seven children besides Maria Jane. But how do *I* know that she might not have brought them up much better? Maria Jane herself is far from strong, and is subject to headaches, and nervous indigestion. Besides which, I learn from the statistical tables that one child in five dies within the first year of its life; and one child in three, within the fifth. That don't look as if we could never improve in these particulars, I think!

P.P.S. Augustus George is in convulsions.

intended by Nature to have rashes brought out upon it, by the premature and incessant use of those formidable little instruments?

Is my son a Nutmeg, that he is to be grated on the stiff edges of sharp frills? Am I the parent of a Muslin boy, that his yielding surface is to be crimped and small plaited? Or is my child composed of Paper or of Linen, that impressions of the finer getting-up art, practised by the laundress, are to be printed off, all over his soft arms and legs, as I constantly observe them? The starch enters his soul; who can wonder that he cries?

Was Augustus George intended to have limbs, or to be born a Torso? I presume that limbs were the intention, as they are the usual practice. Then, why are my poor child's limbs fettered and tied up? Am I to be told that there is any analogy between Augustus George Meek and Jack Sheppard?

Analyse Castor Oil at any Institution of Chemistry that may be agreed upon, and inform me what resemblance, in taste, it bears to that natural provision which it is at once the pride and duty of Maria Jane to administer to Augustus George! Yet, I charge Mrs. Prodgit (aided and abetted by Mrs. Bigby) with systematically forcing Castor Oil on my innocent son, from the first hour of his birth. When that medicine, in its efficient action, causes internal disturbance to Augustus George, I charge Mrs. Prodgit (aided and abetted by Mrs. Bigby) with insanely and inconsistently administering opium to allay the storm she has raised! What is the meaning of this?

If the days of Egyptian Mummies are past, how dare Mrs. Prodgit require, for the use of my son, an amount of flannel and linen that would carpet my humble roof? Do I wonder that she requires it? No! This morning, within an hour, I beheld this agonising sight. I beheld my son—Augustus George—in Mrs. Prodgit's hands, and on Mrs. Prodgit's knee, being dressed. He was at the moment, comparatively speaking, in a state of nature; having nothing on but an extremely short shirt, remarkably disproportionate to the length of his usual outer garments. Trailing from Mrs. Prodgit's lap, on the floor, was a long narrow roller or bandage—I should say of several yards in extent. In this, I saw Mrs. Prodgit tightly roll the body of my unoffending infant, turning him over and over, now presenting

Sherry Wine while the deliberations were in progress; that they always ended in Maria Jane's being in wretched spirits on the sofa; and that Maria Jane's Mama always received me, when I was recalled, with a look of desolate triumph that too plainly said, "*Now*, George Meek! You see my child, Maria Jane, a ruin, and I hope you are satisfied!"

I pass, generally, over the period that intervened between the day when Mrs. Prodgit entered her protest against male parties, and the ever-memorable midnight when I brought her to my unobtrusive home in a cab, with an extremely large box on the roof, and a bundle, a bandbox, and a basket, between the driver's legs. I have no objection to Mrs. Prodgit (aided and abetted by Mrs. Bigby, who I never can forget is the parent of Maria Jane) taking entire possession of my unassuming establishment. In the recesses of my own breast, the thought may linger that a man in possession cannot be so dreadful as a woman, and that woman Mrs. Prodgit; but I ought to bear a good deal, and I hope I can, and do. Huffing and snubbing prey upon my feelings; but I can bear them without complaint. They may tell in the long run; I may be hustled about, from post to pillar, beyond my strength; nevertheless, I wish to avoid giving rise to words in the family.

The voice of Nature, however, cries aloud in behalf of Augustus George, my infant son. It is for him that I wish to utter a few plaintive household words. I am not at all angry; I am mild—but miserable.

I wish to know why, when my child, Augustus George, was expected in our circle, a provision of pins was made, as if the little stranger were a criminal who was to be put to the torture immediately on his arrival, instead of a holy babe? I wish to know why haste was made to stick those pins all over his innocent form, in every direction? I wish to be informed why light and air are excluded from Augustus George, like poisons? Why, I ask, is my unoffending infant so hedged into a basket-bedstead, with dimity and calico, with miniature sheets and blankets, that I can only hear him snuffle (and no wonder!) deep down under the pink hood of a little bathing-machine, and can never peruse even so much of his lineaments as his nose.

Was I expected to be the father of a French Roll, that the brushes of All Nations were laid in, to rasp Augustus George? Am I to be told that his sensitive skin was ever

The female in question stood in the corner behind the door, consuming Sherry Wine. From the nutty smell of that beverage pervading the apartment, I have no doubt she was consuming a second glassful. She wore a black bonnet of large dimensions, and was copious in figure. The expression of her countenance was severe and discontented. The words to which she gave utterance on seeing me, were these, "Oh git along with you, Sir, if *you* please; me and Mrs. Bigby don't want no male parties here!"

That female was Mrs. Prodgit.

I immediately withdrew, of course. I was rather hurt, but I made no remark. Whether it was that I showed a lowness of spirits after dinner, in consequence of feeling that I seemed to intrude, I cannot say. But Maria Jane's Mama said to me on her retiring for the night: in a low distinct voice, and with a look of reproach that completely subdued me: "George Meek, Mrs. Prodgit is your wife's nurse!"

I bear no ill-will towards Mrs. Prodgit. Is it likely that I, writing this with tears in my eyes, should be capable of deliberate animosity towards a female, so essential to the welfare of Maria Jane? I am willing to admit that Fate may have been to blame, and not Mrs. Prodgit; but it is undeniably true, that the latter female brought desolation and devastation into my lowly dwelling.

We were happy after her first appearance; we were sometimes exceedingly so. But whenever the parlour door was opened, and "Mrs. Prodgit!" announced (and she was very often announced), misery ensued. I could not bear Mrs. Prodgit's look. I felt that I was far from wanted, and had no business to exist in Mrs. Prodgit's presence. Between Maria Jane's Mama and Mrs. Prodgit, there was a dreadful, secret, understanding—a dark mystery and conspiracy, pointing me out as a being to be shunned. I appeared to have done something that was evil. Whenever Mrs. Prodgit called after dinner—I retired to my dressing-room—where the temperature is very low, indeed, in the wintry time of the year—and sat looking at my frosty breath as it rose before me, and at my rack of boots; a serviceable article of furniture, but never, in my opinion, an exhilarating object. The length of the councils that were held with Mrs. Prodgit, under these circumstances, I will not attempt to describe. I will merely remark, that Mrs. Prodgit always consumed

LYING AWAKE

"My uncle lay with his eyes half closed, and his nightcap drawn almost down to his nose. His fancy was already wandering, and began to mingle up the present scene with the crater of Vesuvius, the French Opera, the Coliseum at Rome, Dolly's Chop-house in London, and all the farrago of noted places with which the brain of a traveller is crammed; in a word, he was just falling asleep."

Thus, that delightful writer, WASHINGTON IRVING, in his Tales of a Traveller. But, it happened to me the other night to be lying: not with my eyes half closed, but with my eyes wide open; not with my nightcap drawn almost down to my nose, for on sanitary principles I never wear a nightcap: but with my hair pitchforked and touzled all over the pillow; not just falling asleep by any means, but glaringly, persistently, and obstinately, broad awake. Perhaps, with no scientific intention or invention, I was illustrating the theory of the Duality of the Brain; perhaps one part of my brain, being wakeful, sat up to watch the other part which was sleepy. Be that as it may, something in me was as desirous to go to sleep as it possibly could be, but something else in me *would not* go to sleep, and was as obstinate as George the Third.

Thinking of George the Third—for I devote this paper to my train of thoughts as I lay awake: most people lying awake sometimes, and having some interest in the subject—put me in mind of BENJAMIN FRANKLIN, and so Benjamin Franklin's paper on the art of procuring pleasant dreams, which would seem necessarily to include the art of going to sleep, came into my head. Now, as I often used to read that paper when I was a very small boy, and as I recollect everything I read then as perfectly as I forget everything I read now, I quoted "Get out of bed, beat up and turn your pillow, shake the bed-clothes well with at least twenty shakes, then throw the bed open and leave it to cool; in the meanwhile, continuing undrest, walk about your chamber.

When you begin to feel the cold air unpleasant, then return
to your bed, and you will soon fall asleep, and your sleep
will be sweet and pleasant." Not a bit of it! I performed
the whole ceremony, and if it were possible for me to be
more saucer-eyed than I was before, that was the only result
that came of it.

Except Niagara. The two quotations from Washington
Irving and Benjamin Franklin may have put it in my head
by an American association of ideas; but there I was, and
the Horse-shoe Fall was thundering and tumbling in my
eyes and ears, and the very rainbows that I left upon the
spray when I really did last look upon it, were beautiful
to see. The night-light being quite as plain, however, and
sleep seeming to be many thousand miles further off than
Niagara, I made up my mind to think a little about Sleep;
which I no sooner did than I whirled off in spite of myself
to Drury Lane Theatre, and there saw a great actor and
dear friend of mine (whom I had been thinking of in the
day) playing Macbeth, and heard him apostrophising "the
death of each day's life," as I have heard him many a time,
in the days that are gone.

But, Sleep. I *will* think about Sleep. I am determined
to think (this is the way I went on) about Sleep. I must
hold the word Sleep tight and fast, or I shall be off at
a tangent in half a second. I feel myself unaccountably
straying, already, into Clare Market. Sleep. It would be
curious, as illustrating the equality of sleep, to inquire how
many of its phenomena are common to all classes, to all
degrees of wealth and poverty, to every grade of education
and ignorance. Here, for example, is her Majesty Queen
Victoria in her palace, this present blessed night, and here
is Winking Charley, a sturdy vagrant, in one of her Majesty's
jails. Her Majesty has fallen, many thousands of times,
from that same Tower, which *I* claim a right to tumble off
now and then. So has Winking Charley. Her Majesty in
her sleep has opened or prorogued Parliament, or has held
a Drawing Room, attired in some very scanty dress, the
deficiencies and improprieties of which have caused her
great uneasiness. I, in my degree, have suffered unspeakable agitation of mind from taking the chair at a public
dinner at the London Tavern in my night-clothes, which
not all the courtesy of my kind friend and host MR. BATHE
could persuade me were quite adapted to the occasion.

Winking Charley has been repeatedly tried in a worse condition. Her Majesty is no stranger to a vault or firmament, of a sort of floorcloth, with an indistinct pattern distantly resembling eyes, which occasionally obtrudes itself on her repose. Neither am I. Neither is Winking Charley. It is quite common to all three of us to skim along with airy strides a little above the ground ; also to hold, with the deepest interest, dialogues with various people, all represented by ourselves ; and to be at our wit's end to know what they are going to tell us ; and to be indescribably astonished by the secrets they disclose. It is probable that we have all three committed murders and hidden bodies. It is pretty certain that we have all desperately wanted to cry out, and have had no voice ; that we have all gone to the play and not been able to get in ; that we have all dreamed much more of our youth than of our later lives ; that—I have lost it ! The thread's broken.

And up I go. I, lying here with the night-light before me, up I go, for no reason on earth that I can find out, and drawn by no links that are visible to me, up the Great Saint Bernard ! I have lived in Switzerland, and rambled among the mountains ; but why I should go there now, and why up the Great Saint Bernard in preference to any other mountain, I have no idea. As I lie here broad awake, and with every sense so sharpened that I can distinctly hear distant noises inaudible to me at another time, I make that journey, as I really did, on the same summer day, with the same happy party—ah ! two since dead, I grieve to think —and there is the same track, with the same black wooden arms to point the way, and there are the same storm-refuges here and there ; and there is the same snow falling at the top, and there are the same frosty mists, and there is the same intensely cold convent with its ménagerie smell, and the same breed of dogs fast dying out, and the same breed of jolly young monks whom I mourn to know as humbugs, and the same convent parlour with its piano and the sitting round the fire, and the same supper, and the same lone night in a cell, and the same bright fresh morning when going out into the highly rarefied air was like a plunge into an icy bath. Now, see here what comes along ; and why does this thing stalk into my mind on the top of a Swiss mountain !

It is a figure that I once saw, just after dark, chalked

upon a door in a little back lane near a country church—
my first church. How young a child I may have been at
the time I don't know, but it horrified me so intensely—in
connexion with the churchyard, I suppose, for it smokes
a pipe, and has a big hat with each of its ears sticking out
in a horizontal line under the brim, and is not in itself more
oppressive than a mouth from ear to ear, a pair of goggle
eyes, and hands like two bunches of carrots, five in each, can
make it—that it is still vaguely alarming to me to recall (as
I have often done before, lying awake) the running home,
the looking behind, the horror, of its following me ; though
whether disconnected from the door, or door and all, I can't
say, and perhaps never could. It lays a disagreeable train.
I must resolve to think of something on the voluntary
principle.

The balloon ascents of this last season. They will do to
think about, while I lie awake, as well as anything else. I
must hold them tight though, for I feel them sliding away,
and in their stead are the Mannings, husband and wife, hanging on the top of Horsemonger Lane Jail. In connexion
with which dismal spectacle, I recall this curious fantasy of
the mind. That, having beheld that execution, and having
left those two forms dangling on the top of the entrance
gateway—the man's, a limp, loose suit of clothes as if the
man had gone out of them ; the woman's, a fine shape, so
elaborately corseted and artfully dressed, that it was quite
unchanged in its trim appearance as it slowly swung from
side to side—I never could, by my uttermost efforts, for
some weeks, present the outside of that prison to myself
(which the terrible impression I had received continually
obliged me to do) without presenting it with the two figures
still hanging in the morning air. Until, strolling past the
gloomy place one night, when the street was deserted and
quiet, and actually seeing that the bodies were not there,
my fancy was persuaded, as it were, to take them down and
bury them within the precincts of the jail, where they have
lain ever since.

The balloon ascents of last season. Let me reckon them
up. There were the horse, the bull, the parachute, and the
tumbler hanging on—chiefly by his toes, I believe—below
the car. Very wrong, indeed, and decidedly to be stopped.
But, in connexion with these and similar dangerous exhibitions, it strikes me that that portion of the public whom

they entertain, is unjustly reproached. Their pleasure is in the difficulty overcome. They are a public of great faith, and are quite confident that the gentleman will not fall off the horse, or the lady off the bull or out of the parachute, and that the tumbler has a firm hold with his toes. They do not go to see the adventurer vanquished, but triumphant. There is no parallel in public combats between men and beasts, because nobody can answer for the particular beast —unless it were always the same beast, in which case it would be a mere stage-show, which the same public would go in the same state of mind to see, entirely believing in the brute being beforehand safely subdued by the man. That they are not accustomed to calculate hazards and dangers with any nicety, we may know from their rash exposure of themselves in overcrowded steamboats, and unsafe conveyances and places of all kinds. And I cannot help thinking that instead of railing, and attributing savage motives to a people naturally well disposed and humane, it is better to teach them, and lead them argumentatively and reasonably—for they are very reasonable, if you will discuss a matter with them—to more considerate and wise conclusions.

This is a disagreeable intrusion! Here is a man with his throat cut, dashing towards me as I lie awake! A recollection of an old story of a kinsman of mine, who, going home one foggy winter night to Hampstead, when London was much smaller and the road lonesome, suddenly encountered such a figure rushing past him, and presently two keepers from a madhouse in pursuit. A very unpleasant creature indeed, to come into my mind unbidden, as I lie awake.

—The balloon ascents of last season. I must return to the balloons. Why did the bleeding man start out of them? Never mind; if I inquire, he will be back again. The balloons. This particular public have inherently a great pleasure in the contemplation of physical difficulties overcome; mainly, as I take it, because the lives of a large majority of them are exceedingly monotonous and real, and further, are a struggle against continual difficulties, and further still, because anything in the form of accidental injury, or any kind of illness or disability is so very serious in their own sphere. I will explain this seeming paradox of mine. Take the case of a Christmas Pantomime. Surely nobody supposes that the young mother in the pit who falls into fits of laughter when the baby is boiled or sat upon, would be at all diverted by such an occurrence off the stage. Nor is the decent workman in the gallery, who is transported beyond the ignorant present by the delight with which he sees a stout gentleman pushed out of a two pair of stairs window, to be slandered by the suspicion that he would be in the least entertained by such a spectacle in any street in London, Paris, or New York. It always appears to me that the secret of this enjoyment lies in the temporary superiority to the common hazards and mischances of life ; in seeing casualties, attended when they really occur with bodily and mental suffering, tears, and poverty, happen through a very rough sort of poetry without the least harm being done to any one—the pretence of distress in a pantomime being so broadly humorous as to be no pretence at all. Much as in the comic fiction I can understand the mother with a very vulnerable baby at home, greatly relishing the invulnerable baby on the stage, so in the Cremorne reality I can understand the mason who is always liable to fall off a scaffold in his working jacket and to be carried to the hospital, having an infinite admiration of the radiant personage in spangles who goes into the clouds upon a bull, or upside down, and who, he takes it for granted—not reflecting upon the thing—has, by uncommon skill and dexterity, conquered such mischances as those to which he and his acquaintance are continually exposed.

I wish the Morgue in Paris would not come here as I lie awake, with its ghastly beds, and the swollen saturated clothes hanging up, and the water dripping, dripping all day long, upon that other swollen saturated something in the corner, like a heap of crushed over-ripe figs that I have seen in Italy ! And this detestable Morgue comes back again at the head of a procession of forgotten ghost stories. This will never do. I must think of something else as I lie awake ; or, like that sagacious animal in the United States who recognised the colonel who was such a dead shot, I am a gone 'Coon. What shall I think of ? The late brutal assaults. Very good subject. The late brutal assaults.

(Though whether, supposing I should see, here before me as I lie awake, the awful phantom described in one of those ghost stories, who, with a head-dress of shroud, was always seen looking in through a certain glass door at a certain dead hour—whether, in such a case it would be the least consolation to me to know on philosophical grounds that it was merely my imagination, is a question I can't help asking myself by the way.)

The late brutal assaults. I strongly question the expediency of advocating the revival of whipping for those crimes. It is a natural and generous impulse to be indignant at the perpetration of inconceivable brutality, but I doubt the whipping panacea gravely. Not in the least regard or pity for the criminal, whom I hold in far lower estimation than a mad wolf, but in consideration for the general tone and feeling, which is very much improved since the whipping times. It is bad for a people to be familiarised with such punishments. When the whip went out of Bridewell, and ceased to be flourished at the cart's tail and at the whipping-post, it began to fade out of madhouses, and workhouses, and schools and families, and to give place to a better system everywhere, than cruel driving. It would be hasty, because a few brutes may be inadequately punished, to revive, in any aspect, what, in so many aspects, society is hardly yet happily rid of. The whip is a very contagious kind of thing, and difficult to confine within one set of bounds. Utterly abolish punishment by fine—a barbarous device, quite as much out of date as wager by battle, but particularly connected in the vulgar mind with this class of offence —at least quadruple the term of imprisonment for aggravated assaults—and above all let us, in such cases, have no Pet Prisoning, vain glorifying, strong soup, and roasted meats, but hard work, and one unchanging and uncompromising dietary of bread and water, well or ill; and we shall do much better than by going down into the dark to grope for the whip among the rusty fragments of the rack, and the branding iron, and the chains and gibbet from the public roads, and the weights that pressed men to death in the cells of Newgate.

I had proceeded thus far, when I found I had been lying awake so long that the very dead began to wake too, and to crowd into my thoughts most sorrowfully. Therefore, I resolved to lie awake no more, but to get up and go out for a night walk—which resolution was an acceptable relief to me, as I dare say it may prove now to a great many more.

THE GHOST OF ART

I AM a bachelor, residing in rather a dreary set of chambers in the Temple. They are situated in a square court of high houses, which would be a complete well, but for the want of water and the absence of a bucket. I live at the top of the house, among the tiles and sparrows. Like the little man in the nursery-story, I live by myself, and all the bread and cheese I get—which is not much—I put upon a shelf. I need scarcely add, perhaps, that I am in love, and that the father of my charming Julia objects to our union.

I mention these little particulars as I might deliver a letter of introduction. The reader is now acquainted with me, and perhaps will condescend to listen to my narrative.

I am naturally of a dreamy turn of mind; and my abundant leisure—for I am called to the Bar—coupled with much lonely listening to the twittering of sparrows, and the pattering of rain, has encouraged that disposition. In my "top set" I hear the wind howl on a winter night, when the man on the ground floor believes it is perfectly still weather. The dim lamps with which our Honourable Society (supposed to be as yet unconscious of the new discovery called Gas) make the horrors of the staircase visible, deepen the gloom which generally settles on my soul when I go home at night.

I am in the Law, but not of it. I can't exactly make out what it means. I sit in Westminster Hall sometimes (in character) from ten to four; and when I go out of Court, I don't know whether I am standing on my wig or my boots.

It appears to me (I mention this in confidence) as if there were too much talk and too much law—as if some grains of truth were started overboard into a tempestuous sea of chaff.

All this may make me mystical. Still, I am confident that what I am going to describe myself as having seen and heard, I actually did see and hear.

It is necessary that I should observe that I have a great delight in pictures. I am no painter myself, but I have studied pictures and written about them. I have seen all the most famous pictures in the world; my education and reading have been sufficiently general to possess me beforehand with a knowledge of most of the subjects to which a Painter is likely to have recourse; and, although I might be in some doubt as to the rightful fashion of the scabbard of King Lear's sword, for instance, I think I should know King Lear tolerably well, if I happened to meet with him.

I go to all the Modern Exhibitions every season, and of course I revere the Royal Academy. I stand by its forty Academical articles almost as firmly as I stand by the thirty-nine Articles of the Church of England. I am convinced that in neither case could there be, by any rightful possibility, one article more or less.

It is now exactly three years—three years ago, this very month—since I went from Westminster to the Temple, one Thursday afternoon, in a cheap steamboat. The sky was black, when I imprudently walked on board. It began to thunder and lighten immediately afterwards, and the rain poured down in torrents. The deck seeming to smoke with the wet, I went below; but so many passengers were there, smoking too, that I came up again, and buttoning my pea-coat, and standing in the shadow of the paddle-box, stood as upright as I could, and made the best of it.

It was at this moment that I first beheld the terrible Being, who is the subject of my present recollections.

Standing against the funnel, apparently with the intention of drying himself by the heat as fast as he got wet, was a shabby man in threadbare black, and with his hands in his pockets, who fascinated me from the memorable instant when I caught his eye.

Where had I caught that eye before? Who was he? Why did I connect him, all at once, with the Vicar of Wakefield, Alfred the Great, Gil Blas, Charles the Second, Joseph and his Brethren, the Fairy Queen, Tom Jones, the Decameron of Boccaccio, Tam O'Shanter, the Marriage of the Doge of Venice with the Adriatic, and the Great Plague of London? Why, when he bent one leg, and placed one hand upon the back of the seat near him, did my mind associate him wildly with the words, "Number one hundred and forty-two, Portrait of a gentleman?" Could it be that I was going mad?

I looked at him again, and now I could have taken my affidavit that he belonged to the Vicar of Wakefield's family. Whether he was the Vicar, or Moses, or Mr. Burchill, or the Squire, or a conglomeration of all four, I knew not; but I was impelled to seize him by the throat, and charge him with being, in some fell way, connected with the Primrose blood. He looked up at the rain, and then—oh Heaven!— he became St. John. He folded his arms, resigning himself to the weather, and I was frantically inclined to address him as the Spectator, and firmly demand to know what he had done with Sir Roger de Coverley.

The frightful suspicion that I was becoming deranged, returned on me with redoubled force. Meantime, this awful stranger, inexplicably linked to my distress, stood drying himself at the funnel; and ever, as the steam rose from his clothes, diffusing a mist around him, I saw through the ghostly medium all the people I have mentioned, and a score more, sacred and profane.

I am conscious of a dreadful inclination that stole upon me, as it thundered and lightened, to grapple with this man, or demon, and plunge him over the side. But I constrained myself—I know not how—to speak to him, and in a pause of the storm, I crossed the deck, and said:

"What are you?"

He replied, hoarsely, "A Model."

"A what?" said I.

"A Model," he replied. "I sets to the profession for a bob a-hour." (All through this narrative I give his own words, which are indelibly imprinted on my memory.)

The relief which this disclosure gave me, the exquisite delight of the restoration of my confidence in my own sanity, I cannot describe. I should have fallen on his neck, but for the consciousness of being observed by the man at the wheel.

"You then," said I, shaking him so warmly by the hand, that I wrung the rain out of his coat-cuff, "are the gentleman whom I have so frequently contemplated, in connection with a high-backed chair with a red cushion, and a table with twisted legs."

"I am that Model," he rejoined moodily, "and I wish I was anything else."

"Say not so," I returned. "I have seen you in the society of many beautiful young women ; " as in truth I had, and always (I now remember) in the act of making the most of his legs.

"No doubt," said he. "And you've seen me along with warses of flowers, and any number of table-kivers, and antique cabinets, and warious gammon."

"Sir ? " said I.

"And warious gammon," he repeated, in a louder voice. "You might have seen me in armour, too, if you had looked sharp. Blessed if I ha'n't stood in half the suits of armour as ever came out of Pratt's shop : and sat, for weeks together, a-eating nothing, out of half the gold and silver dishes as has ever been lent for the purpose out of Storrses, and Mortimerses, or Garrardses, and Davenportseseses."

Excited, as it appeared, by a sense of injury, I thought he would never have found an end for the last word. But at length it rolled sullenly away with the thunder.

"Pardon me," said I, "you are a well-favoured, well-made man, and yet—forgive me—I find, on examining my mind, that I associate you with—that my recollection indistinctly makes you, in short—excuse me—a kind of powerful monster."

"It would be a wonder if it didn't," he said. "Do you know what my points are ? "

"No," said I.

"My throat and my legs," said he. "When I don't set for a head, I mostly sets for a throat and a pair of legs. Now, granted you was a painter, and was to work at my throat for a week together, I suppose you'd see a lot of lumps and bumps there, that would never be there at all, if you looked at me, complete, instead of only my throat. Wouldn't you ? "

"Probably," said I, surveying him.

"Why, it stands to reason," said the Model. "Work another week at my legs, and it'll be the same thing. You'll make 'em out as knotty and as knobby, at last, as if they was the trunks of two old trees. Then, take and stick my legs and throat on to another man's body, and you'll make a reg'lar monster. And that's the way the public gets their reg'lar monsters, every first Monday in May, when the Royal Academy Exhibition opens."

"You are a critic," said I, with an air of deference.

"I'm in an uncommon ill humour, if that's it," rejoined the Model, with great indignation. "As if it warn't bad enough for a bob a-hour, for a man to be mixing himself up with that there jolly old furniter that one 'ud think the public know'd the wery nails in by this time—or to be putting on greasy old 'ats and cloaks, and playing tambourines in the Bay o' Naples, with Wesuvius a smokin' according to pattern in the background, and the wines a bearing wonderful in the middle distance—or to be unpolitely kicking up his legs among a lot o' gals, with no reason whatever in his mind, but to show 'em—as if this warn't bad enough, I'm to go and be thrown out of employment too ! "

"Surely no !" said I.

"Surely yes," said the indignant Model. "BUT I'LL GROW ONE."

The gloomy and threatening manner in which he muttered the last words, can never be effaced from my remembrance. My blood ran cold.

I asked of myself, what was it that this desperate Being was resolved to grow. My breast made no response.

I ventured to implore him to explain his meaning. With a scornful laugh, he uttered this dark prophecy :

"I"LL GROW ONE. AND, MARK MY WORDS, IT SHALL HAUNT YOU ! "

We parted in the storm, after I had forced half-a-crown on his acceptance, with a trembling hand. I conclude that something supernatural happened to the steamboat, as it bore his reeking figure down the river ; but it never got into the papers.

Two years elapsed, during which I followed my profession without any vicissitudes ; never holding so much as a motion, of course. At the expiration of that period, I found myself making my way home to the Temple, one night, in precisely such another storm of thunder and lightning as that by which I had been overtaken on board the steamboat—except that this storm, bursting over the town at midnight, was rendered much more awful by the darkness and the hour.

As I turned into my court, I really thought a thunderbolt would fall, and plough the pavement up. Every brick and stone in the place seemed to have an echo of its own for the thunder. The waterspouts were overcharged, and the rain came tearing down from the house-tops as if they had been mountain-tops.

Mrs. Parkins, my laundress—wife of Parkins the porter, then newly dead of a dropsy—had particular instructions to place a bedroom candle and a match under the staircase lamp on my landing, in order that I might light my candle there, whenever I came home. Mrs. Parkins invariably disregarding all instructions, they were never there. Thus it happened that on this occasion I groped my way into my sitting-room to find the candle, and came out to light it.

What were my emotions when, underneath the staircase lamp, shining with wet as if he had never been dry since our last meeting, stood the mysterious Being whom I had encountered on the steamboat in a thunderstorm, two years before ! His prediction rushed upon my mind, and I turned faint.

"I said I'd do it," he observed, in a hollow voice, "and I have done it. May I come in ? "

"Misguided creature, what have you done ? " I returned.

"I'll let you know," was his reply, "if you'll let me in."

Could it be murder that he had done ? And had he been so successful that he wanted to do it again, at my expense ?

I hesitated.

"May I come in ? " said he.

I inclined my head, with as much presence of mind as I could command, and he followed me into my chambers. There, I saw that the lower part of his face was tied up, in what is commonly called a Belcher handkerchief. He slowly removed this bandage, and exposed to view a long dark beard, curling over his upper lip, twisting about the corners of his mouth, and hanging down upon his breast.

"What is this ? " I exclaimed involuntarily, "and what have you become ? "

"I am the Ghost of Art ! " said he.

The effect of these words, slowly uttered in the thunderstorm at midnight, was appalling in the last degree. More dead than alive, I surveyed him in silence.

"The German taste came up," said he, "and threw me out of bread. I am ready for the taste now."

He made his beard a little jagged with his hands, folded his arms, and said,

"Severity ! "

I shuddered. It was so severe.

He made his beard flowing on his breast, and, leaning both hands on the staff of a carpet-broom which Mrs. Parkins had left among my books, said:

"Benevolence."

I stood transfixed. The change of sentiment was entirely in the beard. The man might have left his face alone, or had no face. The beard did everything.

He lay down, on his back, on my table, and with that action of his head threw up his beard at the chin.

"That's death!" said he.

He got off my table and, looking up at the ceiling. cocked his beard a little awry; at the same time making it stick out before him.

"Adoration, or a vow of vengeance," he observed.

He turned his profile to me, making his upper lip very bulky with the upper part of his beard.

"Romantic character," said he.

He looked sideways out of his beard, as if it were an ivy-bush. "Jealousy," said he. He gave it an ingenious twist in the air, and informed me that he was carousing. He made it shaggy with his fingers—and it was Despair; lank—and it was avarice; tossed it all kinds of ways—and it was rage. The beard did everything.

"I am the Ghost of Art," said he. "Two bob a-day now, and more when it's longer! Hair's the true expression. There is no other. I SAID I'D GROW IT, AND I'VE GROWN IT, AND IT SHALL HAUNT YOU!"

He may have tumbled down-stairs in the dark, but he never walked down or ran down. I looked over the banisters, and I was alone with the thunder.

Need I add more of my terrific fate? IT HAS haunted me ever since. It glares upon me from the walls of the Royal Academy, (except when MACLISE subdues it to his genius,) it fills my soul with terror at the British Institution, it lures young artists on to their destruction. Go where I will, the Ghost of Art, eternally working the passions in hair, and expressing everything by beard, pursues me. The prediction is accomplished, and the victim has no rest.

OUT OF TOWN

SITTING, on a bright September morning, among my books and papers at my open window on the cliff overhanging the sea-beach, I have the sky and ocean framed before me like a beautiful picture. A beautiful picture, but with such movement in it, such changes of light upon the sails of ships and wake of steamboats, such dazzling gleams of silver far out at sea, such fresh touches on the crisp wave-tops as they break and roll towards me—a picture with such music in the billowy rush upon the shingle, the blowing of morning wind through the corn-sheaves where the farmers' waggons are busy, the singing of the larks, and the distant voices of children at play—such charms of sight and sound as all the Galleries on earth can but poorly suggest.

So dreamy is the murmur of the sea below my window, that I may have been here, for anything I know, one hundred years. Not that I have grown old, for, daily on the neighbouring downs and grassy hill-sides, I find that I can still in reason walk any distance, jump over anything, and climb up anywhere; but that the sound of the ocean seems to have become so customary to my musings, and other realities seem so to have gone aboard ship and floated away over the horizon, that, for aught I will undertake to the contrary, I am the enchanted son of the King my father, shut up in a tower on the sea-shore, for protection against an old she-goblin who insisted on being my godmother, and who foresaw at the font—wonderful creature!—that I should get into a scrape before I was twenty-one. I remember to have been in a City (my Royal parent's dominions, I suppose), and apparently not long ago either, that was in the dreariest condition. The principal inhabitants had all been changed into old newspapers, and in that form were preserving their window-blinds from dust, and wrapping all their smaller household gods in curl-papers. I walked through gloomy streets where every house was shut up and newspapered, and where my solitary footsteps echoed on the deserted pave-

ments. In the public rides there were no carriages, no
horses, no animated existence, but a few sleepy policemen,
and a few adventurous boys taking advantage of the devastation to swarm up the lamp-posts. In the Westward streets
there was no traffic ; in the Westward shops, no business.
The water-patterns which the 'Prentices had trickled out on
the pavements early in the morning, remained uneffaced by
human feet. At the corners of mews, Cochin-China fowls
stalked gaunt and savage ; nobody being left in the deserted
city (as it appeared to me), to feed them. Public Houses,
where splendid footmen swinging their legs over gorgeous
hammer-cloths beside wigged coachmen were wont to regale,
were silent, and the unused pewter pots shone, too bright
for business, on the shelves. I beheld a Punch's Show
leaning against a wall near Park Lane, as if it had fainted.
It was deserted, and there were none to heed its desolation.
In Belgrave Square I met the last man—an ostler—sitting
on a post in a ragged red waistcoat, eating straw, and mildew-
ing away.

If I recollect the name of the little town, on whose shore
this sea is murmuring—but I am not just now, as I have
premised, to be relied upon for anything—it is Pavilionstone.
Within a quarter of a century, it was a little fishing town,
and they do say, that the time was, when it was a little
smuggling town. I have heard that it was rather famous in
the hollands and brandy way, and that coevally with that
reputation the lamplighter's was considered a bad life at the
Assurance Offices. It was observed that if he were not
particular about lighting up, he lived in peace ; but that, if
he made the best of the oil-lamps in the steep and narrow
streets, he usually fell over the cliff at an early age. Now,
gas and electricity run to the very water's edge, and the
South-Eastern Railway Company screech at us in the dead
of night.

But the old little fishing and smuggling town remains,
and is so tempting a place for the latter purpose, that I
think of going out some night next week, in a fur cap and
a pair of petticoat trousers, and running an empty tub, as
a kind of archæological pursuit. Let nobody with corns come
to Pavilionstone, for there are breakneck flights of ragged
steps, connecting the principal streets by back-ways, which
will cripple that visitor in half an hour. These are the ways
by which, when I run that tub, I shall escape. I shall make

a Thermopylæ of the corner of one of them, defend it with my cutlass against the coast-guard until my brave companions have sheered off, then dive into the darkness, and regain my Susan's arms. In connection with these breakneck steps I observe some wooden cottages, with tumble-down out-houses, and back-yards three feet square, adorned with garlands of dried fish, in one of which (though the General Board of Health might object) my Susan dwells.

The South-Eastern Company have brought Pavilionstone into such vogue, with their tidal trains and splendid steam-packets, that a new Pavilionstone is rising up. I am, myself, of New Pavilionstone. We are a little mortary and limey at present, but we are getting on capitally. Indeed, we were getting on so fast, at one time, that we rather overdid it, and built a street of shops, the business of which may be expected to arrive in about ten years. We are sensibly laid out in general; and with a little care and pains (by no means wanting, so far), shall become a very pretty place. We ought to be, for our situation is delightful, our air is delicious, and our breezy hills and downs, carpeted with wild thyme, and decorated with millions of wild flowers, are, on the faith of a pedestrian, perfect. In New Pavilionstone we are a little too much addicted to small windows with more bricks in them than glass, and we are not over-fanciful in the way of decorative architecture, and we get unexpected sea-views through cracks in the street doors; on the whole, however, we are very snug and comfortable, and well accom-modated. But the Home Secretary (if there be such an officer) cannot too soon shut up the burial-ground of the old parish church. It is in the midst of us, and Pavilionstone will get no good of it, if it be too long left alone.

The lion of Pavilionstone is its Great Hotel. A dozen years ago, going over to Paris by South-Eastern Tidal Steamer, you used to be dropped upon the platform of the main line Pavilionstone Station (not a junction then), at eleven o'clock on a dark winter's night, in a roaring wind; and in the howling wilderness outside the station, was a short omnibus which brought you up by the forehead the instant you got in at the door; and nobody cared about you, and you were alone in the world. You bumped over infinite chalk, until you were turned out at a strange building which had just left off being a barn without having quite begun to be a house, where nobody expected your coming, or knew what to do with you when you were come, and where you were usually blown about, until you happened to be blown against the cold beef, and finally into bed. At five in the morning you were blown out of bed, and after a dreary breakfast, with crumpled company, in the midst of confusion, were hustled on board a steamboat and lay wretched on deck until you saw France lunging and surging at you with great vehemence over the bowsprit.

Now, you come down to Pavilionstone in a free and easy manner, an irresponsible agent, made over in trust to the South-Eastern Company, until you get out of the railway-carriage at high-water mark. If you are crossing by the boat at once, you have nothing to do but walk on board and be happy there if you can—I can't. If you are going to our Great Pavilionstone Hotel, the sprightliest porters under the sun, whose cheerful looks are a pleasant welcome, shoulder your luggage, drive it off in vans, bowl it away in trucks, and enjoy themselves in playing athletic games with it. If you are for public life at our great Pavilionstone Hotel, you walk into that establishment as if it were your club; and find ready for you, your news-room, dining-room, smoking-room, billiard-room, music-room, public breakfast, public dinner twice a-day (one plain, one gorgeous), hot baths and cold baths. If you want to be bored, there are plenty of bores always ready for you, and from Saturday to Monday in particular, you can be bored (if you like it) through and through. Should you want to be private at our Great Pavilionstone Hotel, say but the word, look at the list of charges, choose your floor, name your figure—there you are, established in your castle, by the day, week, month, or year, innocent of all comers or goers, unless you have my fancy for walking early in the morning down the groves of boots and shoes, which so regularly flourish at all the chamber-doors before breakfast, that it seems to me as if nobody ever got up or took them in. Are you going across the Alps, and would you like to air your Italian at our Great Pavilionstone Hotel? Talk to the Manager—always conversational, accomplished, and polite. Do you want to be aided, abetted, comforted, or advised, at our Great Pavilionstone Hotel? Send for the good landlord, and he is your friend. Should you, or any one belonging to you, ever be taken ill at our Great Pavilionstone Hotel, you will not soon forget him or his kind wife. And when you pay your bill at our Great Pavilionstone Hotel, you will not be put out of humour by anything you find in it.

A thoroughly good inn, in the days of coaching and posting, was a noble place. But no such inn would have been equal to the reception of four or five hundred people, all of them wet through, and half of them dead sick, every day in the year. This is where we shine, in our Pavilionstone Hotel. Again—who, coming and going, pitching and tossing, boating and training, hurrying in, and flying out, could ever have calculated the fees to be paid at an old-fashioned house? In our Pavilionstone Hotel vocabulary, there is no such word as fee. Everything is done for you; every service is provided at a fixed and reasonable charge; all the prices are hung up in all the rooms; and you can make out your own bill beforehand, as well as the book-keeper.

In the case of your being a pictorial artist, desirous of studying at small expense the physiognomies and beards of different nations, come, on receipt of this, to Pavilionstone. You shall find all the nations of the earth, and all the styles of shaving and not shaving, hair cutting and hair letting alone, for ever flowing through our hotel. Couriers you shall see by hundreds; fat leathern bags for five-franc pieces, closing with violent snaps, like discharges of fire-arms, by thousands; more luggage in a morning than, fifty years ago, all Europe saw in a week. Looking at trains, steamboats, sick travellers, and luggage, is our great Pavilionstone recreation. We are not strong in other public amusements. We have a Literary and Scientific Institution, and we have a Working Men's Institution—may it hold many gipsy holidays in summer fields, with the kettle boiling, the band of music playing, and the people dancing; and may I be on the hillside, looking on with pleasure at a wholesome sight too rare in England!—and we have two or three churches, and more chapels than I have yet added up. But public amusements are scarce with us. If a poor theatrical manager comes with his company to give us, in a loft, Mary Bax, or the Murder on the Sand Hills, we don't care much for him—starve him out, in fact. We take more kindly to wax-work, especially if it moves; in which case it keeps much clearer of the second commandment than when it is still. Cooke's Circus (Mr. Cooke is my friend, and always leaves a good name behind him) gives us only a night in passing through. Nor does the travelling menagerie think us worth a longer visit.

It gave us a look-in the other day, bringing with it the residentiary van with the stained glass windows, which Her Majesty kept ready-made at Windsor Castle, until she found a suitable opportunity of submitting it for the proprietor's acceptance. I brought away five wonderments from this exhibition. I have wondered ever since, Whether the beasts ever do get used to those small places of confinement; Whether the monkeys have that very horrible flavour in their free state; Whether wild animals have a natural ear for time and tune, and therefore every four-footed creature began to howl in despair when the band began to play; What the giraffe does with his neck when his cart is shut up; and, Whether the elephant feels ashamed of himself when he is brought out of his den to stand on his head in the presence of the whole Collection.

We are a tidal harbour at Pavilionstone, as indeed I have implied already in my mention of tidal trains. At low water, we are a heap of mud, with an empty channel in it where a couple of men in big boots always shovel and scoop: with what exact object, I am unable to say. At that time, all the stranded fishing-boats turn over on their sides, as if they were dead marine monsters; the colliers and other shipping stick disconsolate in the mud; the steamers look as if their white chimneys would never smoke more, and their red paddles never turn again; the green sea-slime and weed upon the rough stones at the entrance, seem records of obsolete high tides never more to flow; the flagstaff-halyards droop; the very little wooden lighthouse shrinks in the idle glare of the sun. And here I may observe of the very little wooden lighthouse, that when it is lighted at night,—red and green,—it looks so like a medical man's, that several distracted husbands have at various times been found, on occasions of premature domestic anxiety, going round and round it, trying to find the Night-bell.

But the moment the tide begins to make, the Pavilionstone Harbour begins to revive. It feels the breeze of the rising water before the water comes, and begins to flutter and stir. When the little shallow waves creep in, barely overlapping one another, the vanes at the mastheads wake, and become agitated. As the tide rises, the fishing-boats get into good spirits and dance, the flagstaff hoists a bright red flag, the steamboat smokes, cranes creak, horses and carriages dangle in the air, stray passengers and luggage appear. Now, the shipping is afloat, and comes up buoyantly, to look at the wharf. Now, the carts that have come down for coals, load away as hard as they can load. Now, the steamer smokes immensely, and occasionally blows at the paddle-boxes like a vaporous whale—greatly disturbing nervous loungers. Now, both the tide and the breeze have risen, and you are holding your hat on (if you want to see how the ladies hold *their* hats on, with a stay, passing over the broad brim and down the nose, come to Pavilionstone). Now, everything in the harbour splashes, dashes, and bobs. Now, the Down Tidal Train is telegraphed, and you know (without knowing how you know), that two hundred and eighty-seven people are coming. Now, the fishing-boats that have been out, sail in at the top of the tide. Now, the bell goes, and the locomotive hisses and shrieks, and the train comes gliding in, and the two hundred and eighty-seven come scuffling out. Now, there is not only a tide of water, but a tide of people, and a tide of luggage—all tumbling and flowing and bouncing about together. Now, after infinite bustle, the steamer steams out, and we (on the Pier) are all delighted when she rolls as if she would roll her funnel out, and are all disappointed when she don't. Now, the other steamer is coming in, and the Custom House prepares, and the wharf-labourers assemble, and the hawsers are made ready, and the Hotel Porters come rattling down with van and truck, eager to begin more Olympic games with more luggage. And this is the way in which we go on, down at Pavilionstone, every tide. And if you want to live a life of luggage, or to see it lived, or to breathe sweet air which will send you to sleep at a moment's notice at any period of the day or night, or to disport yourself upon or in the sea, or to scamper about Kent, or to come out of town for the enjoyment of all or any of these pleasures, come to Pavilionstone.

OUT OF THE SEASON

It fell to my lot, this last bleak Spring, to find myself in a watering-place out of the Season. A vicious north-east squall blew me into it from foreign parts, and I tarried in it alone for three days, resolved to be exceedingly busy.

On the first day, I began business by looking for two hours at the sea, and staring the Foreign Militia out of countenance. Having disposed of these important engagements, I sat down at one of the two windows of my room, intent on doing something desperate in the way of literary composition, and writing a chapter of unheard-of excellence —with which the present essay has no connexion.

It is a remarkable quality in a watering-place out of the season, that everything in it will and must be looked at. I had no previous suspicion of this fatal truth; but the moment I sat down to write, I began to perceive it. I had scarcely fallen into my most promising attitude, and dipped my pen in the ink, when I found the clock upon the pier— a red-faced clock with a white rim—importuning me in a highly vexatious manner to consult my watch, and see how I was off for Greenwich time. Having no intention of making a voyage or taking an observation, I had not the least need of Greenwich time, and could have put up with watering-place time as a sufficiently accurate article. The pier-clock, however, persisting, I felt it necessary to lay down my pen, compare my watch with him, and fall into a grave solicitude about half-seconds. I had taken up my pen again, and was about to commence that valuable chapter, when a Custom-house cutter under the window requested that I would hold a naval review of her, immediately.

It was impossible, under the circumstances, for any mental resolution, merely human, to dismiss the Custom-house cutter, because the shadow of her topmast fell upon my paper, and the vane played on the masterly blank chapter. I was therefore under the necessity of going to the other window; sitting astride of the chair there, like

Napoleon bivouacking in the print; and inspecting the cutter as she lay, all, O! that day, in the way of my chapter. She was rigged to carry a quantity of canvas, but her hull was so very small that four giants aboard of her (three men and a boy) who were vigilantly scraping at her, all together, inspired me with a terror lest they should scrape her away. A fifth giant, who appeared to consider himself "below"— as indeed he was, from the waist downwards—meditated, in such close proximity with the little gusty chimney-pipe, that he seemed to be smoking it. Several boys looked on from the wharf, and, when the gigantic attention appeared to be fully occupied, one or other of these would furtively swing himself in mid-air over the Custom-house cutter, by means of a line pendant from her rigging, like a young spirit of the storm. Presently, a sixth hand brought down two little water-casks; presently afterwards a truck came and delivered a hamper. I was now under an obligation to consider that the cutter was going on a cruise, and to wonder where she was going, and when she was going, and why she was going, and at what date she might be expected back, and who commanded her? With these pressing questions I was fully occupied when the Packet, making ready to go across, and blowing off her spare steam, roared, "Look at me!"

It became a positive duty to look at the Packet preparing to go across; aboard of which, the people newly come down by the railroad were hurrying in a great fluster. The crew had got their tarry overalls on—and one knew what *that* meant—not to mention the white basins, ranged in neat little piles of a dozen each, behind the door of the after-cabin. One lady as I looked, one resigning and far-seeing woman, took her basin from the store of crockery, as she might have taken a refreshment-ticket, laid herself down on deck with that utensil at her ear, muffled her feet in one shawl, solemnly covered her countenance after the antique manner with another, and on the completion of these preparations appeared by the strength of her volition to become insensible. The mail-bags (O that I myself had the sea-legs of a mail-bag!) were tumbled aboard; the Packet left off roaring, warped out, and made at the white line upon the bar. One dip, one roll, one break of the sea over her bows, and Moore's Almanack or the sage Raphael could not have told me more of the state of things aboard, than I knew.

The famous chapter was all but begun now, and would have been quite begun, but for the wind. It was blowing stiffly from the east, and it rumbled in the chimney and shook the house. That was not much; but, looking out into the wind's grey eye for inspiration, I laid down my pen again to make the remark to myself, how emphatically everything by the sea declares that it has a great concern in the state of the wind. The trees blown all one way; the defences of the harbour reared highest and strongest against the raging point; the shingle flung up on the beach from the same direction; the number of arrows pointed at the common enemy; the sea tumbling in and rushing towards them as if it were inflamed by the sight. This put it in my head that I really ought to go out and take a walk in the wind; so I gave up the magnificent chapter for that day, entirely persuading myself that I was under a moral obligation to have a blow.

I had a good one, and that on the high road—the very high road—on the top of the cliffs, where I met the stage-coach with all the outsides holding their hats on and themselves too, and overtook a flock of sheep with the wool about their necks blown into such great ruffs that they looked like fleecy owls. The wind played upon the light-house as if it were a great whistle, the spray was driven over the sea in a cloud of haze, the ships rolled and pitched heavily, and at intervals long slants and flaws of light made mountain-steeps of communication between the ocean and the sky. A walk of ten miles brought me to a seaside town without a cliff, which, like the town I had come from, was out of the season too. Half of the houses were shut up; half of the other half were to let; the town might have done as much business as it was doing then, if it had been at the bottom of the sea. Nobody seemed to flourish save the attorney; his clerk's pen was going in the bow-window of his wooden house; his brass door-plate alone was free from salt, and had been polished up that morning. On the beach, among the rough luggers and capstans, groups of storm-beaten boatmen, like a sort of marine monsters, watched under the lee of those objects, or stood leaning forward against the wind, looking out through battered spy-glasses. The parlour bell in the Admiral Benbow had grown so flat with being out of the season, that neither could I hear it ring when I pulled the handle for lunch, nor

could the young woman in black stockings and strong shoes, who acted as waiter out of the season, until it had been tinkled three times.

Admiral Benbow's cheese was out of the season, but his home-made bread was good, and his beer was perfect. Deluded by some earlier spring day which had been warm and sunny, the Admiral had cleared the firing out of his parlour stove, and had put some flower-pots in—which was amiable and hopeful in the Admiral, but not judicious: the room being, at that present visiting, transcendantly cold. I therefore took the liberty of peeping out across a little stone passage into the Admiral's kitchen, and, seeing a high settle with its back towards me drawn out in front of the Admiral's kitchen fire, I strolled in, bread and cheese in hand, munching and looking about. One landsman and two boatmen were seated on the settle, smoking pipes and drinking beer out of thick pint crockery mugs— mugs peculiar to such places, with parti-coloured rings round them, and ornaments between the rings like frayed-out roots. The landsman was relating his experience, as yet only three nights old, of a fearful running-down case in the Channel, and therein presented to my imagination a sound of music that it will not soon forget.

"At that identical moment of time," said he (he was a prosy man by nature, who rose with his subject), "the night being light and calm, but with a grey mist upon the water that didn't seem to spread for more than two or three mile, I was walking up and down the wooden causeway next the pier, off where it happened, along with a friend of mine, which his name is Mr. Clocker. Mr. Clocker is a grocer over yonder." (From the direction in which he pointed the bowl of his pipe, I might have judged Mr. Clocker to be a merman, established in the grocery trade in five-and-twenty fathoms of water.) "We were smoking our pipes, and walking up and down the causeway, talking of one thing and talking of another. We were quite alone there, except that a few hovellers" (the Kentish name for 'long-shore boatmen like his companions) "were hanging about their lugs, waiting while the tide made, as hovellers will." (One of the two boatmen, thoughtfully regarding me, shut up one eye ; this I understood to mean : first, that he took me into the conversation : secondly, that he confirmed the proposition : thirdly, that he announced himself as a hoveller.)

"All of a sudden Mr. Clocker and me stood rooted to the spot, by hearing a sound come through the stillness, right over the sea, *like a great sorrowful flute or Æolian harp*. We didn't in the least know what it was, and judge of our surprise when we saw the hovellers, to a man, leap into the boats and tear about to hoist sail and get off, as if they had every one of 'em gone, in a moment, raving mad! But *they* knew it was the cry of distress from the sinking emigrant ship."

When I got back to my watering-place out of the season, and had done my twenty miles in good style, I found that the celebrated Black Mesmerist intended favouring the public that evening in the Hall of the Muses, which he had engaged for the purpose. After a good dinner, seated by the fire in an easy chair, I began to waver in a design I had formed of waiting on the Black Mesmerist, and to incline towards the expediency of remaining where I was. Indeed a point of gallantry was involved in my doing so, inasmuch as I had not left France alone, but had come from the prisons of St. Pélagie with my distinguished and unfortunate friend Madame Roland (in two volumes which I bought for two francs each, at the book-stall in the Place de la Concorde, Paris, at the corner of the Rue Royale). Deciding to pass the evening tête-à-tête with Madame Roland, I derived, as I always do, great pleasure from that spiritual woman's society, and the charms of her brave soul and engaging conversation. I must confess that if she had only some more faults, only a few more passionate failings of any kind, I might love her better; but I am content to believe that the deficiency is in me, and not in her. We spent some sadly interesting hours together on this occasion, and she told me again of her cruel discharge from the Abbaye, and of her being re-arrested before her free feet had sprung lightly up half-a-dozen steps of her own staircase, and carried off to the prison which she only left for the guillotine.

Madame Roland and I took leave of one another before midnight, and I went to bed full of vast intentions for next day, in connexion with the unparalleled chapter. To hear the foreign mail-steamers coming in at dawn of day, and to know that I was not aboard or obliged to get up, was very comfortable; so I rose for the chapter in great force.

I had advanced so far as to sit down at my window again

on my second morning, and to write the first half-line of the chapter and strike it out, not liking it, when my conscience reproached me with not having surveyed the watering-place out of the season, after all, yesterday, but with having gone straight out of it at the rate of four miles and a half an hour. Obviously the best amends that I could make for this remissness was to go and look at it without another moment's delay. So—altogether as a matter of duty— I gave up the magnificent chapter for another day, and sauntered out with my hands in my pockets.

All the houses and lodgings ever let to visitors were to let that morning. It seemed to have snowed bills with To Let upon them. This put me upon thinking what the owners of all those apartments did, out of the season; how they employed their time, and occupied their minds. They could not be always going to the Methodist chapels, of which I passed one every other minute. They must have some other recreation. Whether they pretended to take one another's lodgings, and opened one another's tea-caddies in fun? Whether they cut slices off their own beef and mutton, and made believe that it belonged to somebody else? Whether they played little dramas of life, as children do, and said, "I ought to come and look at your apartments, and you ought to ask two guineas a-week too much, and then I ought to say I must have the rest of the day to think of it, and then you ought to say that another lady and gentleman with no children in family had made an offer very close to your own terms, and you had passed your word to give them a positive answer in half an hour, and indeed were just going to take the bill down when you heard the knock, and then I ought to take them you know?" Twenty such speculations engaged my thoughts. Then, after passing, still clinging to the walls, defaced rags of the bills of last year's Circus, I came to a back field near a timber-yard where the Circus itself had been, and where there was yet a sort of monkish tonsure on the grass, indicating the spot where the young lady had gone round upon her pet steed Firefly in her daring flight. Turning into the town again, I came among the shops, and they were emphatically out of the season. The chemist had no boxes of ginger-beer powders, no beautifying sea-side soaps and washes, no attractive scents; nothing but his great goggle-eyed red bottles, looking as if the winds of winter and the

drift of the salt sea had inflamed them. The grocers' hot
pickles, Harvey's Sauce, Doctor Kitchener's Zest, Anchovy
Paste, Dundee Marmalade, and the whole stock of luxurious
helps to appetite, were hybernating somewhere underground.
The china-shop had no trifles from anywhere. The Bazaar
had given in altogether, and presented a notice on the
shutters that this establishment would re-open at Whitsun-
tide, and that the proprietor in the meantime might be
heard of at Wild Lodge, East Cliff. At the Sea-bathing
Establishment, a row of neat little wooden houses seven or
eight feet high, I *saw* the proprietor in bed in the shower-
bath. As to the bathing-machines, they were (how they got
there is not for me to say) at the top of a hill at least a mile
and a half off. The library, which I had never seen otherwise than wide open, was tight shut; and two peevish bald
old gentlemen seemed to be hermetically sealed up inside,
eternally reading the paper. That wonderful mystery, the
music-shop, carried it off as usual (except that it had more
cabinet pianos in stock), as if season or no season were all
one to it. It made the same prodigious display of bright
brazen wind-instruments, horribly twisted, worth, as I should
conceive, some thousands of pounds, and which it is utterly
impossible that anybody in any season can ever play or want
to play. It had five triangles in the window, six pairs of
castanets, and three harps; likewise every polka with a
coloured frontispiece that ever was published; from the
original one where a smooth male and female Pole of high
rank are coming at the observer with their arms a-kimbo,
to the Ratcatcher's Daughter. Astonishing establishment,
amazing enigma! Three other shops were pretty much out
of the season, what they were used to be in it. First, the
shop where they sell the sailors' watches, which had still
the old collection of enormous timekeepers, apparently
designed to break a fall from the masthead: with places to
wind them up, like fire-plugs. Secondly, the shop where
they sell the sailors' clothing, which displayed the old sou'-
westers, and the old oily suits, and the old pea-jackets, and
the old one sea-chest, with its handles like a pair of rope
ear-rings. Thirdly, the unchangeable shop for the sale of
literature that has been left behind. Here, Dr. Faustus was
still going down to very red and yellow perdition, under the
superintendence of three green personages of a scaly humour,
with excrescential serpents growing out of their blade-bones.

Here, the Golden Dreamer and the Norwood Fortune Teller were still on sale at sixpence each, with instructions for making the dumb cake, and reading destinies in tea-cups, and with a picture of a young woman with a high waist lying on a sofa in an attitude so uncomfortable as almost to account for her dreaming at one and the same time of a conflagration, a shipwreck, an earthquake, a skeleton, a church-porch, lightning, funerals performed, and a young man in a bright blue coat and canary pantaloons. Here, were Little Warblers and Fairburn's Comic Songsters. Here, too, were ballads on the old ballad paper and in the old confusion of types; with an old man in a cocked hat, and an arm-chair, for the illustration to Will Watch the bold Smuggler; and the Friar of Orders Grey, represented by a little girl in a hoop, with a ship in the distance. All these as of yore, when they were infinite delights to me!

It took me so long fully to relish these many enjoyments, that I had not more than an hour before bedtime to devote to Madame Roland. We got on admirably together on the subject of her convent education, and I rose next morning with the full conviction that the day for the great chapter was at last arrived.

It had fallen calm, however, in the night, and as I sat at breakfast I blushed to remember that I had not yet been on the Downs. I a walker, and not yet on the Downs! Really, on so quiet and bright a morning this must be set right. As an essential part of the Whole Duty of Man, therefore, I left the chapter to itself—for the present—and went on the Downs. They were wonderfully green and beautiful, and gave me a good deal to do. When I had done with the free air and the view, I had to go down into the valley and look after the hops (which I know nothing about), and to be equally solicitous as to the cherry orchards. Then I took it on myself to cross-examine a tramping family in black (mother alleged, I have no doubt by herself in person, to have died last week), and to accompany eighteenpence, which produced a great effect, with moral admonitions which produced none at all. Finally, it was late in the afternoon before I got back to the unprecedented chapter, and then I determined that it was out of the season, as the place was, and put it away.

I went at night to the benefit of Mrs. B. Wedgington at the Theatre, who had placarded the town with the admonition, "Don't forget it!" I made the house, according to my calculation, four and ninepence to begin with, and it may have warmed up, in the course of the evening, to half a sovereign. There was nothing to offend any one,—the good Mr. Baines of Leeds excepted. Mrs. B. Wedgington sang to a grand piano. Mr. B. Wedgington did the like, and also took off his coat, tucked up his trousers, and danced in clogs. Master B. Wedgington, aged ten months, was nursed by a shivering young person in the boxes, and the eye of Mrs. B. Wedgington wandered that way more than once. Peace be with all the Wedgingtons from A. to Z. May they find themselves in the Season somewhere!

A POOR MAN'S TALE OF A PATENT

I AM not used to writing for print. What working-man,
that never labours less (some Mondays, and Christmas Time
and Easter Time excepted) than twelve or fourteen hours
a day, is? But I have been asked to put down, plain, what
I have got to say; and so I take pen-and-ink, and do it to
the best of my power, hoping defects will find excuse.

I was born nigh London, but have worked in a shop at
Birmingham (what you would call Manufactories, we call
Shops) almost ever since I was out of my time. I served
my apprenticeship at Deptford, nigh where I was born, and
I am a smith by trade. My name is John. I have been
called "Old John" ever since I was nineteen year of age, on
account of not having much hair. I am fifty-six year of age
at the present time, and I don't find myself with more hair,
nor yet with less, to signify, than at nineteen year of age
aforesaid.

I have been married five and thirty year, come next April.
I was married on All Fools' Day. Let them laugh that win.
I won a good wife that day, and it was as sensible a day to
me as ever I had.

We have had a matter of ten children, six whereof are
living. My eldest son is engineer in the Italian steam-
packet "Mezzo Giorno, plying between Marseilles and Naples,
and calling at Genoa, Leghorn, and Civita Vecchia." He
was a good workman. He invented a many useful little
things that brought him in—nothing. I have two sons
doing well at Sydney, New South Wales—single, when last
heard from. One of my sons (James) went wild and for
a soldier, where he was shot in India, living six weeks in
hospital with a musket-ball lodged in his shoulder-blade,
which he wrote with his own hand. He was the best
looking. One of my two daughters (Mary) is comfortable
in her circumstances, but water on the chest. The other
(Charlotte), her husband run away from her in the basest

manner, and she and her three children live with us. The youngest, six year old, has a turn for mechanics.

I am not a Chartist, and I never was. I don't mean to say but what I see a good many public points to complain of, still I don't think that's the way to set them right. If I did think so, I should be a Chartist. But I don't think so, and I am not a Chartist. I read the paper, and hear discussion, at what we call "a parlour," in Birmingham, and I know many good men and workmen who are Chartists. Note. Not Physical force.

It won't be took as boastful in me, if I make the remark (for I can't put down what I have got to say, without putting that down before going any further), that I have always been of an ingenious turn. I once got twenty pound by a screw, and it's in use now. I have been twenty year, off and on, completing an Invention and perfecting it. I perfected of it, last Christmas Eve at ten o'clock at night. Me and my wife stood and let some tears fall over the Model, when it was done and I brought her in to take a look at it.

A friend of mine, by the name of William Butcher, is a Chartist. Moderate. He is a good speaker. He is very animated. I have often heard him deliver that what is, at every turn, in the way of us working-men, is, that too many places have been made, in the course of time, to provide for people that never ought to have been provided for; and that we have to obey forms and to pay fees to support those places when we shouldn't ought. "True," (delivers William Butcher), "all the public has to do this, but it falls heaviest on the working-man, because he has least to spare; and likewise because impediments shouldn't be put in his way, when he wants redress of wrong or furtherance of right." Note. I have wrote down those words from William Butcher's own mouth. W. B. delivering them fresh for the aforesaid purpose.

Now, to my Model again. There it was, perfected, on Christmas Eve, gone nigh a year, at ten o'clock at night. All the money I could spare I had laid out upon the Model; and when times was bad, or my daughter Charlotte's children sickly, or both, it had stood still, months at a spell. I had pulled it to pieces, and made it over again with improvements, I don't know how often. There it stood, at last, a perfected Model as aforesaid.

William Butcher and me had a long talk, Christmas Day,

A POOR MAN'S TALE OF A PATENT

respecting of the Model. William is very sensible. But sometimes cranky. William said, "What will you do with it, John?" I said, "Patent it." William said, "How patent it, John?" I said, "By taking out a Patent." William then delivered that the law of Patent was a cruel wrong. William said, "John, if you make your invention public, before you get a Patent, any one may rob you of the fruits of your hard work. You are put in a cleft stick, John. Either you must drive a bargain very much against yourself, by getting a party to come forward beforehand with the great expenses of the Patent; or, you must be put about, from post to pillar, among so many parties, trying to make a better bargain for yourself, and showing your invention, that your invention will be took from you over your head." I said, "William Butcher, are you cranky? You are sometimes cranky." William said, "No, John, I tell you the truth;" which he then delivered more at length. I said to W. B. I would Patent the invention myself.

My wife's brother, George Bury of West Bromwich (his wife unfortunately took to drinking, made away with everything, and seventeen times committed to Birmingham Jail before happy release in every point of view), left my wife, his sister, when he died, a legacy of one hundred and twenty-eight pound ten, Bank of England Stocks. Me and my wife never broke into that money yet. Note. We might come to be old and past our work. We now agreed to Patent the invention. We said we would make a hole in it—I mean in the aforesaid money—and Patent the invention. William Butcher wrote me a letter to Thomas Joy, in London. T. J. is a carpenter, six foot four in height, and plays quoits well. He lives in Chelsea, London, by the church. I got leave from the shop, to be took on again when I come back. I am a good workman. Not a Teetotaller; but never drunk. When the Christmas holidays were over, I went up to London by the Parliamentary Train, and hired a lodging for a week with Thomas Joy. He is married. He has one son gone to sea.

Thomas Joy delivered (from a book he had) that the first step to be took, in Patenting the invention, was to prepare a petition unto Queen Victoria. William Butcher had delivered similar, and drawn it up. Note. William is a ready writer. A declaration before a Master in Chancery was to be added to it. That, we likewise drew up. After a deal of

trouble I found out a Master, in Southampton Buildings, Chancery Lane, nigh Temple Bar, where I made the declaration, and paid eighteen-pence. I was told to take the declaration and petition to the Home Office, in Whitehall, where I left it to be signed by the Home Secretary (after I had found the office out), and where I paid two pound, two, and sixpence. In six days he signed it, and I was told to take it to the Attorney-General's chambers, and leave it there for a report. I did so, and paid four pound, four. Note. Nobody all through, ever thankful for their money, but all uncivil.

My lodging at Thomas Joy's was now hired for another week, whereof five days were gone. The Attorney-General made what they called a Report-of-course (my invention being, as William Butcher had delivered before starting, unopposed), and I was sent back with it to the Home Office. They made a Copy of it, which was called a Warrant. For this warrant, I paid seven pound, thirteen, and six. It was sent to the Queen, to sign. The Queen sent it back, signed. The Home Secretary signed it again. The gentleman throwed it at me when I called, and said, "Now take it to the Patent Office in Lincoln's Inn." I was then in my third week at Thomas Joy's, living very sparing, on account of fees. I found myself losing heart.

At the Patent Office in Lincoln's Inn, they made "a draft of the Queen's bill," of my invention, and a "docket of the bill." I paid five pound, ten, and six, for this. They "engrossed two copies of the bill; one for the Signet Office, and one for the Privy-Seal Office." I paid one pound, seven, and six, for this. Stamp duty over and above, three pound. The Engrossing Clerk of the same office engrossed the Queen's bill for signature. I paid him one pound, one. Stamp duty, again, one pound, ten. I was next to take the Queen's bill to the Attorney-General again, and get it signed again. I took it, and paid five pound more. I fetched it away, and took it to the Home Secretary again. He sent it to the Queen again. She signed it again. I paid seven pound, thirteen, and six, more, for this. I had been over a month at Thomas Joy's. I was quite wore out, patience and pocket.

Thomas Joy delivered all this, as it went on, to William Butcher. William Butcher delivered it again to three Birmingham Parlours, from which it got to all the other

Parlours, and was took, as I have been told since, right through all the shops in the North of England. Note. William Butcher delivered, at his Parlour, in a speech, that it was a Patent way of making Chartists.

But I hadn't nigh done yet. The Queen's bill was to be took to the Signet Office in Somerset House, Strand— where the stamp shop is. The Clerk of the Signet made "a Signet bill for the Lord Keeper of the Privy Seal." I paid him four pound, seven. The Clerk of the Lord Keeper of the Privy Seal made "a Privy-Seal bill for the Lord Chancellor." I paid him four pound, two. The Privy-Seal bill was handed over to the Clerk of the Patents, who engrossed the aforesaid. I paid him five pound, seventeen, and eight ; at the same time, I paid Stamp-duty for the Patent, in one lump, thirty pound. I next paid for "boxes for the Patent," nine and sixpence. Note. Thomas Joy would have made the same at a profit for eighteen-pence. I next paid "fees to the Deputy, the Lord Chancellor's Purse-bearer," two pound, two. I next paid "fees to the Clerk of the Hanaper," seven pound, thirteen. I next paid "fees to the Deputy Clerk of the Hanaper," ten shillings. I next paid, to the Lord Chancellor again, one pound, eleven, and six. Last of all, I paid "fees to the Deputy Sealer, and Deputy Chaff-wax," ten shillings and sixpence. I had lodged at Thomas Joy's over six weeks, and the unopposed Patent for my invention, for England only, had cost me ninety-six pound, seven, and eightpence. If I had taken it out for the United Kingdom, it would have cost me more than three hundred pound.

Now, teaching had not come up but very limited when I was young. So much the worse for me, you'll say. I say the same. William Butcher is twenty year younger than me. He knows a hundred year more. If William Butcher had wanted to Patent an invention, he might have been sharper than myself when hustled backwards and forwards among all those offices, though I doubt if so patient. Note. William being sometimes cranky, and consider porters, messengers, and clerks.

Thereby I say nothing of my being tired of my life, while I was Patenting my invention. But I put this : Is it reasonable to make a man feel as if, in inventing an ingenious improvement meant to do good, he had done something wrong ? How else can a man feel, when he is met by such difficulties at every turn? All inventors taking out a Patent MUST feel so. And look at the expense. How hard on me, and how hard on the country if there's any merit in me (and my invention is took up now, I am thankful to say, and doing well), to put me to all that expense before I can move a finger! Make the addition yourself, and it'll come to ninety-six pound, seven, and eightpence. No more, and no less.

What can I say against William Butcher, about places? Look at the Home Secretary, the Attorney-General, the Patent Office, the Engrossing Clerk, the Lord Chancellor, the Privy Seal, the Clerk of the Patents, the Lord Chancellor's Purse-bearer, the Clerk of the Hanaper, the Deputy Clerk of the Hanaper, the Deputy Sealer, and the Deputy Chaff-wax. No man in England could get a Patent for an Indian-rubber band, or an iron-hoop, without feeing all of them. Some of them, over and over again. I went through thirty-five stages. I began with the Queen upon the Throne. I ended with the Deputy Chaff-wax. Note. I should like to see the Deputy Chaff-wax. Is it a man, or what is it?

What I had to tell, I have told. I have wrote it down. I hope it's plain. Not so much in the handwriting (though nothing to boast of there), as in the sense of it. I will now conclude with Thomas Joy. Thomas said to me, when we parted, "John, if the laws of this country were as honest as they ought to be, you would have come to London— registered an exact description and drawing of your invention—paid half-a-crown or so for doing of it—and therein and thereby have got your Patent."

My opinion is the same as Thomas Joy. Further. In William Butcher's delivering "that the whole gang of Hanapers and Chaff-waxes must be done away with, and that England has been chaffed and waxed sufficient." I agree.

THE NOBLE SAVAGE

To come to the point at once, I beg to say that I have not the least belief in the Noble Savage. I consider him a prodigious nuisance, and an enormous superstition. His calling rum fire-water, and me a pale face, wholly fail to reconcile me to him. I don't care what he calls me. I call him a savage, and I call a savage a something highly desirable to be civilised off the face of the earth. I think a mere gent (which I take to be the lowest form of civilisation) better than a howling, whistling, clucking, stamping, jumping, tearing savage. It is all one to me, whether he sticks a fish-bone through his visage, or bits of trees through the lobes of his ears, or bird's feathers in his head; whether he flattens his hair between two boards, or spreads his nose over the breadth of his face, or drags his lower lip down by great weights, or blackens his teeth, or knocks them out, or paints one cheek red and the other blue, or tattoos himself, or oils himself, or rubs his body with fat, or crimps it with knives. Yielding to whichsoever of these agreeable eccentricities, he is a savage—cruel, false, thievish, murderous; addicted more or less to grease, entrails, and beastly customs; a wild animal with the questionable gift of boasting; a conceited, tiresome, bloodthirsty, monotonous humbug.

Yet it is extraordinary to observe how some people will talk about him, as they talk about the good old times; how they will regret his disappearance, in the course of this world's development, from such and such lands where his absence is a blessed relief and an indispensable preparation for the sowing of the very first seeds of any influence that can exalt humanity; how, even with the evidence of himself before them, they will either be determined to believe, or will suffer themselves to be persuaded into believing, that he is something which their five senses tell them he is not.

There was Mr. Catlin, some few years ago, with his

Ojibbeway Indians. Mr. Catlin was an energetic, earnest man, who had lived among more tribes of Indians than I need reckon up here, and who had written a picturesque and glowing book about them. With his party of Indians squatting and spitting on the table before him, or dancing their miserable jigs after their own dreary manner, he called, in all good faith, upon his civilised audience to take notice of their symmetry and grace, their perfect limbs, and the exquisite expression of their pantomime; and his civilised audience, in all good faith, complied and admired. Whereas, as mere animals, they were wretched creatures, very low in the scale and very poorly formed; and as men and women possessing any power of truthful dramatic expression by means of action, they were no better than the chorus at an Italian Opera in England—and would have been worse if such a thing were possible.

Mine are no new views of the noble savage. The greatest writers on natural history found him out long ago. BUFFON knew what he was, and showed why he is the sulky tyrant that he is to his women, and how it happens (Heaven be praised!) that his race is spare in numbers. For evidence of the quality of his moral nature, pass himself for a moment and refer to his "faithful dog." Has he ever improved a dog, or attached a dog, since his nobility first ran wild in woods, and was brought down (at a very long shot) by POPE? Or does the animal that is the friend of man always degenerate in his low society?

It is not the miserable nature of the noble savage that is the new thing; it is the whimpering over him with maudlin admiration, and the affecting to regret him, and the drawing of any comparison of advantage between the blemishes of civilisation and the tenor of his swinish life. There may have been a change now and then in those diseased absurdities, but there is none in him.

Think of the Bushmen. Think of the two men and the two women who have been exhibited about England for some years. Are the majority of persons—who remember the horrid little leader of that party in his festering bundle of hides, with his filth and his antipathy to water, and his straddled legs, and his odious eyes shaded by his brutal hand, and his cry of "Qu-u-u-u-aaa!" (Bosjesman for something desperately insulting, I have no doubt)—conscious of an affectionate yearning towards that noble savage, or is it

idiosyncratic in me to abhor, detest, abominate, and abjure him? I have no reserve on this subject, and will frankly state that, setting aside that stage of the entertainment when he counterfeited the death of some creature he had shot, by laying his head on his hand and shaking his left leg—at which time I think it would have been justifiable homicide to slay him—I have never seen that group sleeping, smoking, and expectorating round their brazier, but I have sincerely desired that something might happen to the charcoal smouldering therein, which would cause the immediate suffocation of the whole of the noble strangers.

There is at present a party of Zulu Kaffirs exhibiting at the St. George's Gallery, Hyde Park Corner, London. These noble savages are represented in a most agreeable manner; they are seen in an elegant theatre, fitted with appropriate scenery of great beauty, and they are described in a very sensible and unpretending lecture, delivered with a modesty which is quite a pattern to all similar exponents. Though extremely ugly, they are much better shaped than such of their predecessors as I have referred to; and they are rather picturesque to the eye, though far from odoriferous to the nose. What a visitor left to his own interpretings and imaginings might suppose these noblemen to be about, when they give vent to that pantomimic expression which is quite settled to be the natural gift of the noble savage, I cannot possibly conceive; for it is so much too luminous for my personal civilisation that it conveys no idea to my mind beyond a general stamping, ramping, and raving, remarkable (as everything in savage life is) for its dire uniformity. But let us—with the interpreter's assistance, of which I for one stand so much in need—see what the noble savage does in Zulu Kaffirland.

The noble savage sets a king to reign over him, to whom he submits his life and limbs without a murmur or question, and whose whole life is passed chin deep in a lake of blood; but who, after killing incessantly, is in his turn killed by his relations and friends, the moment a grey hair appears on his head. All the noble savage's wars with his fellow-savages (and he takes no pleasure in anything else) are wars of extermination—which is the best thing I know of him, and the most comfortable to my mind when I look at him. He has no moral feelings of any kind, sort, or

description; and his "mission" may be summed up as simply diabolical.

The ceremonies with which he faintly diversifies his life are, of course, of a kindred nature. If he wants a wife he appears before the kennel of the gentleman whom he has selected for his father-in-law, attended by a party of male friends of a very strong flavour, who screech and whistle and stamp an offer of so many cows for the young lady's hand. The chosen father-in-law—also supported by a high-flavoured party of male friends—screeches, whistles, and yells (being seated on the ground, he can't stamp) that there never was such a daughter in the market as his daughter, and that he must have six more cows. The son-in-law and his select circle of backers screech, whistle, stamp, and yell in reply, that they will give three more cows. The father-in-law (an old deluder, overpaid at the beginning) accepts four, and rises to bind the bargain. The whole party, the young lady included, then falling into epileptic convulsions, and screeching, whistling, stamping, and yelling together—and nobody taking any notice of the young lady (whose charms are not to be thought of without a shudder)—the noble savage is considered married, and his friends make demoniacal leaps at him by way of congratulation.

When the noble savage finds himself a little unwell, and mentions the circumstance to his friends, it is immediately perceived that he is under the influence of witchcraft. A learned personage, called an Imyanger or Witch Doctor, is immediately sent for to Nooker the Umtargartie, or smell out the witch. The male inhabitants of the kraal being seated on the ground, the learned doctor, got up like a grizzly bear, appears, and administers a dance of a most terrific nature, during the exhibition of which remedy he incessantly gnashes his teeth, and howls :—" I am the original physician to Nooker the Umtargartie. Yow yow yow! No connexion with any other establishment. Till till till! All other Umtargarties are feigned Umtargarties, Boroo Boroo! but I perceive here a genuine and real Umtargartie, Hoosh Hoosh Hoosh! in whose blood I, the original Imyanger and Nookerer, Blizzerum Boo! will wash these bear's claws of mine. O yow yow yow!" All this time the learned physician is looking out among the attentive faces for some unfortunate man who owes him a cow, or who has given him any small offence, or against whom, without offence,

he has conceived a spite. Him he never fails to Nooker as the Umtargartie, and he is instantly killed. In the absence of such an individual, the usual practice is to Nooker the quietest and most gentlemanly person in company. But the nookering is invariably followed on the spot by the butchering.

Some of the noble savages in whom Mr. Catlin was so strongly interested, and the diminution of whose numbers, by rum and small-pox, greatly affected him, had a custom not unlike this, though much more appalling and disgusting in its odious details.

The women being at work in the fields, hoeing the Indian corn, and the noble savage being asleep in the shade, the chief has sometimes the condescension to come forth, and lighten the labour by looking at it. On these occasions, he seats himself in his own savage chair, and is attended by his shield-bearer: who holds over his head a shield of cowhide—in shape like an immense mussel shell—fearfully and wonderfully, after the manner of a theatrical supernumerary. But lest the great man should forget his greatness in the contemplation of the humble works of agriculture, there suddenly rushes in a poet, retained for the purpose, called a Praiser. This literary gentleman wears a leopard's head over his own, and a dress of tigers' tails; he has the appearance of having come express on his hind legs from the Zoological Gardens; and he incontinently strikes up the chief's praises, plunging and tearing all the while. There is a frantic wickedness in this brute's manner of worrying the air, and gnashing out, "O what a delightful chief he is! O what a delicious quantity of blood he sheds! O how majestically he laps it up! O how charmingly cruel he is! O how he tears the flesh of his enemies and crunches the bones! O how like the tiger and the leopard and the wolf and the bear he is! O, row row row row, how fond I am of him!" which might tempt the Society of Friends to charge at a hand-gallop into the Swartz-Kop location and exterminate the whole kraal.

When war is afoot among the noble savages—which is always—the chief holds a council to ascertain whether it is the opinion of his brothers and friends in general that the enemy shall be exterminated. On this occasion, after the performance of an Umsebeuza, or war song,—which is exactly like all the other songs,—the chief makes a speech

to his brothers and friends, arranged in single file. No particular order is observed during the delivery of this address, but every gentleman who finds himself excited by the subject, instead of crying " Hear, hear ! " as is the custom with us, darts from the rank and tramples out the life, or crushes the skull, or mashes the face, or scoops out the eyes, or breaks the limbs, or performs a whirlwind of atrocities on the body, of an imaginary enemy. Several gentlemen becoming thus excited at once, and pounding away without the least regard to the orator, that illustrious person is rather in the position of an orator in an Irish House of Commons. But several of these scenes of savage life bear a strong generic resemblance to an Irish election, and I think would be extremely well received and understood at Cork.

In all these ceremonies the noble savage holds forth to the utmost possible extent about himself; from which (to turn him to some civilised account) we may learn, I think, that as egotism is one of the most offensive and contemptible littlenesses a civilised man can exhibit, so it is really incompatible with the interchange of ideas ; inasmuch as if we all talked about ourselves we should soon have no listeners, and must be all yelling and screeching at once on our own separate accounts : making society hideous. It is my opinion that if we retained in us anything of the noble savage, we could not get rid of it too soon. But the fact is clearly otherwise. Upon the wife and dowry question, substituting coin for cows, we have assuredly nothing of the Zulu Kaffir left. The endurance of despotism is one great distinguishing mark of a savage always. The improving world has quite got the better of that too. In like manner, Paris is a civilised city, and the Théâtre Français a highly civilised theatre ; and we shall never hear, and never have heard in these later days (of course) of the Praiser *there*. No, no, civilised poets have better work to do. As to Nookering Umtargarties, there are no pretended Umtargarties in Europe, and no European powers to Nooker them ; that would be mere spydom, subordination, small malice, superstition, and false pretence. And as to private Umtargarties, are we not in the year eighteen hundred and fifty-three, with spirits rapping at our doors ?

To conclude as I began. My position is, that if we have anything to learn from the Noble Savage, it is what to avoid. His virtues are a fable ; his happiness is a delusion ;

his nobility, nonsense. We have no greater justification for being cruel to the miserable object, than for being cruel to a WILLIAM SHAKESPEARE or an ISAAC NEWTON; but he passes away before an immeasurably better and higher power than ever ran wild in any earthly woods, and the world will be all the better when his place knows him no more.

A FLIGHT

WHEN Don Diego de—I forget his name—the inventor of
the last new Flying Machines, price so many francs for
ladies, so many more for gentlemen—when Don Diego, by
permission of Deputy Chaff-wax and his noble band, shall
have taken out a Patent for the Queen's dominions, and
shall have opened a commodious Warehouse in an airy
situation ; and when all persons of any gentility will keep
at least a pair of wings, and be seen skimming about in
every direction ; I shall take a flight to Paris (as I soar
round the world) in a cheap and independent manner. At
present, my reliance is on the South-Eastern Railway
Company, in whose Express Train here I sit, at eight of
the clock on a very hot morning, under the very hot roof
of the Terminus at London Bridge, in danger of being
"forced" like a cucumber or a melon, or a pine-apple.
And talking of pine-apples, I suppose there never were so
many pine-apples in a Train as there appear to be in this
Train.

Whew ! The hot-house air is faint with pine-apples.
Every French citizen or citizeness is carrying pine-apples
home. The compact little Enchantress in the corner of my
carriage (French actress, to whom I yielded up my heart
under the auspices of that brave child, "MEAT-CHELL," at
the St. James's Theatre the night before last) has a pine-
apple in her lap. Compact Enchantress's friend, confidante,
mother, mystery, Heaven knows what, has two pine-apples
in her lap, and a bundle of them under the seat. Tobacco-
smoky Frenchman in Algerine wrapper, with peaked hood
behind, who might be Abd-el-Kader dyed rifle-green, and
who seems to be dressed entirely in dirt and braid, carries
pine-apples in a covered basket. Tall, grave, melancholy
Frenchman, with black Vandyke beard, and hair close-
cropped, with expansive chest to waistcoat, and compressive
waist to coat : saturnine as to his pantaloons, calm as to his
feminine boots, precious as to his jewellery, smooth and

white as to his linen: dark-eyed, high-foreheaded, hawk-nosed—got up, one thinks, like Lucifer or Mephistopheles, or Zamiel, transformed into a highly genteel Parisian—has the green end of a pine-apple sticking out of his neat valise.

Whew! If I were to be kept here long, under this forcing-frame, I wonder what would become of me—whether I should be forced into a giant, or should sprout or blow into some other phenomenon! Compact Enchantress is not ruffled by the heat—she is always composed, always compact. O look at her little ribbons, frills, and edges, at her shawl, at her gloves, at her hair, at her bracelets, at her bonnet, at everything about her! How is it accomplished? What does she do to be so neat? How is it that every trifle she wears belongs to her, and cannot choose but be a part of her? And even Mystery, look at *her!* A model. Mystery is not young, not pretty, though still of an average candle-light passability; but she does such miracles in her own behalf, that, one of these days, when she dies, they'll be amazed to find an old woman in her bed, distantly like her. She was an actress once, I shouldn't wonder, and had a Mystery attendant on herself. Perhaps, Compact Enchantress will live to be a Mystery, and to wait with a shawl at the side-scenes, and to sit opposite to Mademoiselle in railway carriages, and smile and talk subserviently, as Mystery does now. That's hard to believe!

Two Englishmen, and now our carriage is full. First Englishman, in the monied interest—flushed, highly respectable—Stock Exchange, perhaps—City, certainly. Faculties of second Englishman entirely absorbed in hurry. Plunges into the carriage, blind. Calls out of window concerning his luggage, deaf. Suffocates himself under pillows of great-coats, for no reason, and in a demented manner. Will receive no assurance from any porter whatsoever. Is stout and hot, and wipes his head, and makes himself hotter by breathing so hard. Is totally incredulous respecting assurance of Collected Guard, that "there's no hurry." No hurry! And a flight to Paris in eleven hours!

It is all one to me in this drowsy corner, hurry or no hurry. Until Don Diego shall send home my wings, my flight is with the South-Eastern Company. I can fly with the South-Eastern, more lazily, at all events, than in the upper air. I have but to sit here thinking as idly as I please, and be whisked away. I am not accountable to

anybody for the idleness of my thoughts in such an idle summer flight; my flight is provided for by the South-Eastern and is no business of mine.

The bell! With all my heart. It does not require *me* to do so much as even to flap my wings. Something snorts for me, something shrieks for me, something proclaims to everything else that it had better keep out of my way,—and away I go.

Ah! The fresh air is pleasant after the forcing-frame, though it does blow over these interminable streets, and scatter the smoke of this vast wilderness of chimneys. Here we are—no, I mean there we were, for it has darted far into the rear—in Bermondsey where the tanners live. Flash! The distant shipping in the Thames is gone. Whirr! The little streets of new brick and red tile, with here and there a flagstaff growing like a tall weed out of the scarlet beans, and, everywhere, plenty of open sewer and ditch for the promotion of the public health, have been fired off in a volley. Whizz! Dust-heaps, market-gardens, and waste grounds. Rattle! New Cross Station. Shock! There we were at Croydon. Bur-r-r-r! The tunnel.

I wonder why it is that when I shut my eyes in a tunnel I begin to feel as if I were going at an Express pace the other way. I am clearly going back to London now. Compact Enchantress must have forgotten something, and reversed the engine. No! After long darkness, pale fitful streaks of light appear. I am still flying on for Folkestone. The streaks grow stronger—become continuous—become the ghost of day—become the living day—became I mean—the tunnel is miles and miles away, and here I fly through sunlight, all among the harvest and the Kentish hops.

There is a dreamy pleasure in this flying. I wonder where it was, and when it was, that we exploded, blew into space somehow, a Parliamentary Train, with a crowd of heads and faces looking at us out of cages, and some hats waving. Monied Interest says it was at Reigate Station. Expounds to Mystery how Reigate Station is so many miles from London, which Mystery again develops to Compact Enchantress. There might be neither a Reigate nor a London for me, as I fly away among the Kentish hops and harvest. What do *I* care?

Bang! We have let another Station off, and fly away regardless. Everything is flying. The hop-gardens turn

gracefully towards me, presenting regular avenues of hops in rapid flight, then whirl away. So do the pools and rushes, haystacks, sheep, clover in full bloom delicious to the sight and smell, corn-sheaves, cherry-orchards, apple-orchards, reapers, gleaners, hedges, gates, fields that taper off into little angular corners, cottages, gardens, now and then a church. Bang, bang! A double-barrelled Station! Now a wood, now a bridge, now a landscape, now a cutting, now a——Bang! a single-barrelled Station—there was a cricket-match somewhere with two white tents, and then four flying cows, then turnips—now the wires of the electric telegraph are all alive, and spin, and blurr their edges, and go up and down, and make the intervals between each other most irregular: contracting and expanding in the strangest manner. Now we slacken. With a screwing, and a grinding, and a smell of water thrown on ashes, now we stop!

Demented Traveller, who has been for two or three minutes watchful, clutches his great-coats, plunges at the door, rattles it, cries "Hi!" eager to embark on board of impossible packets, far inland. Collected Guard appears. "Are you for Tunbridge, sir?" "Tunbridge? No. Paris." "Plenty of time, sir. No hurry. Five minutes here, sir, for refreshment." I am so blest (anticipating Zamiel, by half a second) as to procure a glass of water for Compact Enchantress.

Who would suppose we had been flying at such a rate, and shall take wing again directly? Refreshment-room full, platform full, porter with watering-pot deliberately cooling a hot wheel, another porter with equal deliberation helping the rest of the wheels bountifully to ice cream. Monied Interest and I re-entering the carriage first, and being there alone, he intimates to me that the French are "no go" as a Nation. I ask why? He says, that Reign of Terror of theirs was quite enough. I ventured to inquire whether he remembers anything that preceded said Reign of Terror? He says not particularly. "Because," I remark, "the harvest that is reaped, has sometimes been sown." Monied Interest repeats, as quite enough for him, that the French are revolutionary,—"and always at it."

Bell. Compact Enchantress, helped in by Zamiel (whom the stars confound!), gives us her charming little side-box look, and smites me to the core. Mystery eating sponge-cake. Pine-apple atmosphere faintly tinged with suspicions

of sherry.   Demented Traveller flits past the carriage, looking for it.   Is blind with agitation, and can't see it.   Seems
singled out by Destiny to be the only unhappy creature in
the flight, who has any cause to hurry himself.   Is nearly
left behind.   Is seized by Collected Guard after the Train is
in motion, and bundled in.   Still, has lingering suspicions
that there must be a boat in the neighbourhood, and *will*
look wildly out of window for it.

Flight   resumed.   Corn-sheaves,   hop-gardens,   reapers,
gleaners,   apple-orchards,   cherry-orchards,   Stations   single
and double-barrelled, Ashford.   Compact Enchantress (constantly talking to Mystery, in an exquisite manner) gives
a little scream ; a sound that seems to come from high up
in her precious little head ; from behind her bright little
eyebrows.   "Great Heaven, my pine-apple !   My Angel !
It is lost !"   Mystery is desolated.   A search made.   It is
not lost.   Zamiel finds it.   I curse him (flying) in the
Persian manner.   May his face be turned upside down,
and jackasses sit upon his uncle's grave !

Now fresher air, now glimpses of unenclosed Down-land
with flapping crows flying over it whom we soon outfly, now
the Sea, now Folkestone at a quarter after ten.   "Tickets
ready, gentlemen !"   Demented dashes at the door.   "For
Paris, sir ?"   No hurry.

Not the least.   We are dropped slowly down to the Port,
and sidle to and fro (the whole Train) before the insensible
Royal George Hotel, for some ten minutes.   The Royal
George takes no more heed of us than its namesake under
water at Spithead, or under earth at Windsor, does.   The
Royal George's dog lies winking and blinking at us, without
taking the trouble to sit up ; and the Royal George's
"wedding party" at the open window (who seem, I must
say, rather tired of bliss) don't bestow a solitary glance
upon us, flying thus to Paris in eleven hours.   The first
gentleman in Folkestone is evidently used up, on this
subject.

Meanwhile, Demented chafes.   Conceives that every man's
hand is against him, and exerting itself to prevent his getting to Paris.   Refuses consolation.   Rattles door.   Sees
smoke on the horizon, and "knows" it's the boat gone
without him.   Monied Interest resentfully explains that *he*
is going to Paris too.   Demented signifies that if Monied
Interest chooses to be left behind, *he* don't.

"Refreshments in the Waiting-Room, ladies and gentlemen. No hurry, ladies and gentlemen, for Paris. No hurry whatever!"

Twenty minutes' pause, by Folkestone clock, for looking at Enchantress while she eats a sandwich, and at Mystery while she eats of everything there that is eatable, from pork-pie, sausage, jam, and gooseberries, to lumps of sugar. All this time, there is a very waterfall of luggage, with a spray of dust, tumbling slantwise from the pier into the steamboat. All this time, Demented (who has no business with it) watches it with starting eyes, fiercely requiring to be shown *his* luggage. When it at last concludes the cataract, he rushes hotly to refresh—is shouted after, pursued, jostled, brought back, pitched into the departing steamer upside down, and caught by mariners disgracefully.

A lovely harvest-day, a cloudless sky, a tranquil sea. The piston-rods of the engines so regularly coming up from below, to look (as well they may) at the bright weather, and so regularly almost knocking their iron heads against the cross beam of the skylight, and never doing it! Another Parisian actress is on board, attended by another Mystery. Compact Enchantress greets her sister artist—Oh, the Compact One's pretty teeth!—and Mystery greets Mystery. *My* Mystery soon ceases to be conversational—is taken poorly, in a word, having lunched too miscellaneously—and goes below. The remaining Mystery then smiles upon the sister artists (who, I am afraid, wouldn't greatly mind stabbing each other), and is upon the whole ravished.

And now I find that all the French people on board begin to grow, and all the English people to shrink. The French are nearing home, and shaking off a disadvantage, whereas we are shaking it on. Zamiel is the same man, and Abd-el-Kader is the same man, but each seems to come into possession of an indescribable confidence that departs from us—from Monied Interest, for instance, and from me. Just what they gain, we lose. Certain British "Gents" about the steersman, intellectually nurtured at home on parody of everything and truth of nothing, become subdued, and in a manner forlorn; and when the steersman tells them (not exultingly) how he has "been upon this station now eight year, and never see the old town of Bullum yet," one of them, with an imbecile reliance on a reed, asks him what he considers to be the best hotel in Paris?

Now, I tread upon French ground, and am greeted by the three charming words, Liberty, Equality, Fraternity, painted up (in letters a little too thin for their height) on the Custom-house wall—also by the sight of large cocked hats, without which demonstrative head-gear nothing of a public nature can be done upon this soil. All the rabid Hotel population of Boulogne howl and shriek outside a distant barrier, frantic to get at us. Demented, by some unlucky means peculiar to himself, is delivered over to their fury, and is presently seen struggling in a whirl-pool of Touters—is somehow understood to be going to Paris—is, with infinite noise, rescued by two cocked hats, and brought into Custom-house bondage with the rest of us.

Here, I resign the active duties of life to an eager being, of preternatural sharpness, with a shelving forehead and a shabby snuff-coloured coat, who (from the wharf) brought me down with his eye before the boat came into port. He darts upon my luggage, on the floor where all the luggage is strewn like a wreck at the bottom of the great deep; gets it proclaimed and weighed as the property of "Monsieur a traveller unknown;" pays certain francs for it, to a certain functionary behind a Pigeon Hole, like a pay-box at a Theatre (the arrangements in general are on a wholesale scale, half military and half theatrical); and I suppose I shall find it when I come to Paris—he says I shall. I know nothing about it, except that I pay him his small fee, and pocket the ticket he gives me, and sit upon a counter, involved in the general distraction.

Railway station. "Lunch or dinner, ladies and gentlemen. Plenty of time for Paris. Plenty of time!" Large hall, long counter, long strips of dining-table, bottles of wine, plates of meat, roast chickens, little loaves of bread, basins of soup, little caraffes of brandy, cakes, and fruit. Comfortably restored from these resources, I begin to fly again.

I saw Zamiel (before I took wing) presented to Compact Enchantress and Sister Artist, by an officer in uniform, with a waist like a wasp's, and pantaloons like two balloons. They all got into the next carriage together, accompanied by the two Mysteries. They laughed. I am alone in the carriage (for I don't consider Demented anybody) and alone in the world.

Fields, windmills, low grounds, pollard-trees, windmills,

fields, fortifications, Abbeville, soldiering and drumming. I wonder where England is, and when I was there last —about two years ago, I should say. Flying in and out among these trenches and batteries, skimming the clattering drawbridges, looking down into the stagnant ditches, I become a prisoner of state, escaping. I am confined with a comrade in a fortress. Our room is in an upper story. We have tried to get up the chimney, but there's an iron grating across it, imbedded in the masonry. After months of labour, we have worked the grating loose with the poker, and can lift it up. We have also made a hook, and twisted our rugs and blankets into ropes. Our plan is, to go up the chimney, hook our ropes to the top, descend hand over hand upon the roof of the guard-house far below, shake the hook loose, watch the opportunity of the sentinel's pacing away, hook again, drop into the ditch, swim across it, creep into the shelter of the wood. The time is come—a wild and stormy night. We are up the chimney, we are on the guard-house roof, we are swimming in the murky ditch, when lo! "Qui v'là?" a bugle, the alarm, a crash! What is it? Death? No, Amiens.

More fortifications, more soldiering and drumming, more basins of soup, more little loaves of bread, more bottles of wine, more caraffes of brandy, more time for refreshment. Everything good, and everything ready. Bright, unsubstantial-looking, scenic sort of station. People waiting. Houses, uniforms, beards, moustaches, some sabots, plenty of neat women, and a few old-visaged children. Unless it be a delusion born of my giddy flight, the grown-up people and the children seem to change places in France. In general, the boys and girls are little old men and women, and the men and women lively boys and girls.

Bugle, shriek, flight resumed. Monied Interest has come into my carriage. Says the manner of refreshing is "not bad," but considers it French. Admits great dexterity and politeness in the attendants. Thinks a decimal currency may have something to do with their despatch in settling accounts, and don't know but what it's sensible and convenient. Adds, however, as a general protest, that they're a revolutionary people—and always at it.

Ramparts, canals, cathedral, river, soldiering and drumming, open country, river, earthenware manufactures, Creil. Again ten minutes. Not even Demented in a hurry. Station, a drawing-room with a verandah: like a planter's house. Monied Interest considers it a band-box, and not made to last. Little round tables in it, at one of which the Sister Artists and attendant Mysteries are established with Wasp and Zamiel, as if they were going to stay a week.

Anon, with no more trouble than before, I am flying again, and lazily wondering as I fly. What has the South-Eastern done with all the horrible little villages we used to pass through, in the *Diligence?* What have they done with all the summer dust, with all the winter mud, with all the dreary avenues of little trees, with all the ramshackle post-yards, with all the beggars (who used to turn out at night with bits of lighted candle, to look in at the coach windows), with all the long-tailed horses who were always biting one another, with all the big postillions in jack-boots—with all the mouldy cafés that we used to stop at, where a long mildewed table-cloth, set forth with jovial bottles of vinegar and oil, and with a Siamese arrangement of pepper and salt, was never wanting? Where are the grass-grown little towns, the wonderful little market-places all unconscious of markets, the shops that nobody kept, the streets that nobody trod, the churches that nobody went to, the bells that nobody rang, the tumble-down old buildings plastered with many-coloured bills that nobody read? Where are the two-and-twenty weary hours of long long day and night journey, sure to be either insupportably hot or insupportably cold? Where are the pains in my bones, where are the fidgets in my legs, where is the Frenchman with the nightcap who never *would* have the little coupé-window down, and who always fell upon me when he went to sleep, and always slept all night snoring onions?

A voice breaks in with "Paris! Here we are!"

I have overflown myself, perhaps, but I can't believe it. I feel as if I were enchanted or bewitched. It is barely eight o'clock yet—it is nothing like half-past—when I have had my luggage examined at that briskest of Custom-houses attached to the station, and am rattling over the pavement in a hackney-cabriolet.

Surely, not the pavement of Paris? Yes, I think it is, too. I don't know any other place where there are all these high houses, all these haggard-looking wine shops, all these billiard tables, all these stocking-makers with flat red or yellow legs of wood for signboard, all these fuel shops with stacks of billets painted outside, and real billets sawing in the gutter, all these dirty corners of streets, all these cabinet pictures over dark doorways representing discreet matrons nursing babies. And yet this morning—I'll think of it in a warm-bath.

Very like a small room that I remember in the Chinese baths upon the Boulevard, certainly; and, though I see it through the steam, I think that I might swear to that peculiar hot-linen basket, like a large wicker hour-glass. When can it have been that I left home? When was it that I paid "through to Paris" at London Bridge, and discharged myself of all responsibility, except the preservation of a voucher ruled into three divisions, of which the first was snipped off at Folkestone, the second aboard the boat, and the third taken at my journey's end? It seems to have been ages ago. Calculation is useless. I will go out for a walk.

The crowds in the streets, the lights in the shops and balconies, the elegance, variety, and beauty of their decorations, the number of the theatres, the brilliant cafés with their windows thrown up high and their vivacious groups at little tables on the pavement, the light and glitter of the houses turned as it were inside out, soon convince me that it is no dream; that I am in Paris, howsoever I got here. I stroll down to the sparkling Palais Royal, up the Rue de Rivoli, to the Place Vendôme. As I glance into a print-shop window, Monied Interest, my late travelling companion, comes upon me, laughing with the highest relish of disdain. "Here's a people!" he says, pointing to Napoleon in the window and Napoleon on the column. "Only one idea all over Paris! A monomania!" Humph! I THINK I have seen Napoleon's match? There WAS a statue, when I came away, at Hyde Park Corner, and another in the City, and a print or two in the shops.

I walk up to the Barrière de l'Etoile, sufficiently dazed by my flight to have a pleasant doubt of the reality of everything about me; of the lively crowd, the overhanging trees, the performing dogs, the hobby-horses, the beautiful perspectives of shining lamps: the hundred and one enclosures, where the singing is, in gleaming orchestras of azure and gold, and where a star-eyed Houri comes round with a box for voluntary offerings. So, I pass to my hotel, enchanted; sup, enchanted; go to bed, enchanted; pushing back this morning (if it really were this morning) into the remoteness of time, blessing the South-Eastern Company for realising the Arabian Nights in these prose days, murmuring, as I wing my idle flight into the land of dreams, "No hurry, ladies and gentlemen, going to Paris in eleven hours. It is so well done, that there really is no hurry!"

THE DETECTIVE POLICE

WE are not by any means devout believers in the old Bow Street Police. To say the truth, we think there was a vast amount of humbug about those worthies. Apart from many of them being men of very indifferent character, and far too much in the habit of consorting with thieves and the like, they never lost a public occasion of jobbing and trading in mystery and making the most of themselves. Continually puffed besides by incompetent magistrates anxious to conceal their own deficiencies, and hand-in-glove with the penny-a-liners of that time, they became a sort of superstition. Although as a Preventive Police they were utterly ineffective, and as a Detective Police were very loose and uncertain in their operations, they remain with some people a superstition to the present day.

On the other hand, the Detective Force organised since the establishment of the existing Police, is so well chosen and trained, proceeds so systematically and quietly, does its business in such a workmanlike manner, and is always so calmly and steadily engaged in the service of the public, that the public really do not know enough of it, to know a tithe of its usefulness. Impressed with this conviction, and interested in the men themselves, we represented to the authorities at Scotland Yard, that we should be glad, if there were no official objection, to have some talk with the Detectives. A most obliging and ready permission being given, a certain evening was appointed with a certain Inspector for a social conference between ourselves and the Detectives, at The Household Words Office in Wellington Street, Strand, London. In consequence of which appointment the party "came off," which we are about to describe. And we beg to repeat that, avoiding such topics as it might for obvious reasons be injurious to the public, or disagreeable to respectable individuals, to touch upon in print, our description is as exact as we can make it.

The reader will have the goodness to imagine the Sanctum

Sanctorum of Household Words. Anything that best suits the reader's fancy, will best represent that magnificent chamber. We merely stipulate for a round table in the middle, with some glasses and cigars arranged upon it; and the editorial sofa elegantly hemmed in between that stately piece of furniture and the wall.

It is a sultry evening at dusk. The stones of Wellington Street are hot and gritty, and the watermen and hackney-coachmen at the Theatre opposite, are much flushed and aggravated. Carriages are constantly setting down the people who have come to Fairy-Land; and there is a mighty shouting and bellowing every now and then, deafening us for the moment, through the open windows.

Just at dusk, Inspectors Wield and Stalker are announced; but we do not undertake to warrant the orthography of any of the names here mentioned. Inspector Wield presents Inspector Stalker. Inspector Wield is a middle-aged man of a portly presence, with a large, moist, knowing eye, a husky voice, and a habit of emphasising his conversation by the aid of a corpulent fore-finger, which is constantly in juxta-position with his eyes or nose. Inspector Stalker is a shrewd, hard-headed Scotchman—in appearance not at all unlike a very acute, thoroughly-trained schoolmaster, from the Normal Establishment at Glasgow. Inspector Wield one might have known, perhaps, for what he is—Inspector Stalker, never.

The ceremonies of reception over, Inspectors Wield and Stalker observe that they have brought some sergeants with them. The sergeants are presented—five in number, Sergeant Dornton, Sergeant Witchem, Sergeant Mith, Sergeant Fendall, and Sergeant Straw. We have the whole Detective Force from Scotland Yard, with one exception. They sit down in a semi-circle (the two Inspectors at the two ends) at a little distance from the round table, facing the editorial sofa. Every man of them, in a glance, immediately takes an inventory of the furniture and an accurate sketch of the editorial presence. The Editor feels that any gentleman in company could take him up, if need should be, without the smallest hesitation, twenty years hence.

The whole party are in plain clothes. Sergeant Dornton about fifty years of age, with a ruddy face and a high sun-burnt forehead, has the air of one who has been a Sergeant in the army—he might have sat to Wilkie for the Soldier in the Reading of the Will. He is famous for steadily pursuing the inductive process, and, from small beginnings, working on from clue to clue until he bags his man. Sergeant Witchem, shorter and thicker-set, and marked with the small-pox, has something of a reserved and thoughtful air, as if he were engaged in deep arithmetical calculations. He is renowned for his acquaintance with the swell mob. Sergeant Mith, a smooth-faced man with a fresh bright complexion, and a strange air of simplicity, is a dab at housebreakers. Sergeant Fendall, a light-haired, well-spoken, polite person, is a prodigious hand at pursuing private inquiries of a delicate nature. Straw, a little wiry Sergeant of meek demeanour and strong sense, would knock at a door and ask a series of questions in any mild character you choose to prescribe to him, from a charity-boy upwards, and seem as innocent as an infant. They are, one and all, respectable-looking men; of perfectly good deportment and unusual intelligence; with nothing lounging or slinking in their manners; with an air of keen observation and quick perception when addressed; and generally presenting in their faces, traces more or less marked of habitually leading lives of strong mental excitement. They have all good eyes; and they all can, and they all do, look full at whomsoever they speak to.

We light the cigars, and hand round the glasses (which are very temperately used indeed), and the conversation begins by a modest amateur reference on the Editorial part to the swell mob. Inspector Wield immediately removes his cigar from his lips, waves his right hand, and says, "Regarding the swell mob, sir, I can't do better than call upon Sergeant Witchem. Because the reason why? I'll tell you. Sergeant Witchem is better acquainted with the swell mob than any officer in London."

Our heart leaping up when we beheld this rainbow in the sky, we turn to Sergeant Witchem, who very concisely, and in well-chosen language, goes into the subject forthwith. Meantime, the whole of his brother officers are closely interested in attending to what he says, and observing its effect. Presently they begin to strike in, one or two together, when an opportunity offers, and the conversation becomes general. But these brother officers only come in to the assistance of each other—not to the contradiction—and a more amicable brotherhood there could not be. From the swell mob, we diverge to the kindred topics of cracksmen, fences, public-house dancers, area-sneaks, designing young people who go out "gonophing," and other "schools." It is observable throughout these revelations, that Inspector Stalker, the Scotchman, is always exact and statistical, and that when any question of figures arises, everybody as by one consent pauses, and looks to him.

When we have exhausted the various schools of Art—during which discussion the whole body have remained profoundly attentive, except when some unusual noise at the Theatre over the way has induced some gentleman to glance inquiringly towards the window in that direction, behind his next neighbour's back—we burrow for information on such points as the following. Whether there really are any highway robberies in London, or whether some circumstances not convenient to be mentioned by the aggrieved party, usually precede the robberies complained of, under that head, which quite change their character? Certainly the latter, almost always. Whether in the case of robberies in houses, where servants are necessarily exposed to doubt, innocence under suspicion ever becomes so like guilt in appearance, that a good officer need be cautious how he judges it? Undoubtedly. Nothing is so common or deceptive as such appearances at first. Whether in a place of public amusement, a thief knows an officer, and an officer knows a thief—supposing them, beforehand, strangers to each other—because each recognises in the other, under all disguise, an inattention to what is going on, and a purpose that is not the purpose of being entertained? Yes. That's the way exactly. Whether it is reasonable or ridiculous to trust to the alleged experiences of thieves as narrated by themselves, in prisons, or penitentiaries, or anywhere? In general, nothing more absurd. Lying is their habit and their trade; and they would rather lie—even if they hadn't an interest in it, and didn't want to make themselves agreeable—than tell the truth.

From these topics, we glide into a review of the most celebrated and horrible of the great crimes that have been committed within the last fifteen or twenty years. The men engaged in the discovery of almost all of them, and in the pursuit or apprehension of the murderers, are here, down to the very last instance. One of our guests gave chase to and boarded the emigrant ship, in which the murderess last hanged in London was supposed to have embarked. We learn from him that his errand was not announced to the passengers, who may have no idea of it to this hour. That he went below, with the captain, lamp in hand—it being dark, and the whole steerage abed and sea-sick—and engaged the Mrs. Manning who *was* on board, in a conversation about her luggage, until she was, with no small pains, induced to raise her head, and turn her face towards the light. Satisfied that she was not the object of his search, he quietly re-embarked in the Government steamer alongside, and steamed home again with the intelligence.

When we have exhausted these subjects, too, which occupy a considerable time in the discussion, two or three leave their chairs, whisper Sergeant Witchem, and resume their seats. Sergeant Witchem leaning forward a little, and placing a hand on each of his legs, then modestly speaks as follows:

"My brother-officers wish me to relate a little account of my taking Tally-ho Thompson. A man oughtn't to tell what he has done himself; but still, as nobody was with me, and, consequently, as nobody but myself can tell it, I'll do it in the best way I can, if it should meet your approval."

We assure Sergeant Witchem that he will oblige us very much, and we all compose ourselves to listen with great interest and attention.

"Tally-ho Thompson," says Sergeant Witchem, after merely wetting his lips with his brandy-and-water, "Tally-ho Thompson was a famous horse-stealer, couper, and magsman. Thompson, in conjunction with a pal that occasionally worked with him, gammoned a countryman out of a good round sum of money, under pretence of getting him a situation— the regular old dodge—and was afterwards in the 'Hue and Cry' for a horse—a horse that he stole, down in Hertfordshire. I had to look after Thompson, and I applied myself, of course, in the first instance, to discovering where he was. Now, Thompson's wife lived, along with a little daughter, at Chelsea. Knowing that Thompson was somewhere in the country, I watched the house—especially at post-time in the morning—thinking Thompson was pretty likely to write to her. Sure enough, one morning the postman comes up, and delivers a letter at Mrs. Thompson's door. Little girl opens the door, and takes it in. We're not

always sure of postmen, though the people at the post-offices
are always very obliging. A postman may help us, or he
may not,—just as it happens. However, I go across the
road, and I say to the postman, after he has left the letter,
'Good morning! how are you?' 'How are *you?*' says he.
'You've just delivered a letter for Mrs. Thompson.' 'Yes,
I have.' 'You didn't happen to remark what the post-mark
was, perhaps?' 'No,' says he, 'I didn't.' 'Come,' says I,
'I'll be plain with you. I'm in a small way of business,
and I have given Thompson credit, and I can't afford to
lose what he owes me. I know he's got money, and I know
he's in the country, and if you could tell me what the post-
mark was, I should be very much obliged to you, and you'd
do a service to a tradesman in a small way of business that
can't afford a loss.' 'Well,' he said, 'I do assure you that
I did not observe what the post-mark was; all I know is,
that there was money in the letter—I should say a sovereign.'
This was enough for me, because of course I knew that
Thompson having sent his wife money, it was probable she'd
write to Thompson, by return of post, to acknowledge the
receipt. So I said 'Thankee' to the postman, and I kept
on the watch. In the afternoon I saw the little girl come
out. Of course I followed her. She went into a stationer's
shop, and I needn't say to you that I looked in at the
window. She bought some writing-paper and envelopes,
and a pen. I think to myself, 'That'll do!'—watch her
home again—and don't go away, you may be sure, knowing
that Mrs. Thompson was writing her letter to Tally-ho,
and that the letter would be posted presently. In about
an hour or so, out came the little girl again, with the letter
in her hand. I went up, and said something to the child,
whatever it might have been; but I couldn't see the direction
of the letter, because she held it with the seal upwards.
However, I observed that on the back of the letter there
was what we call a kiss—a drop of wax by the side of the
seal—and again, you understand, that was enough for me.
I saw her post the letter, waited till she was gone, then
went into the shop, and asked to see the Master. When
he came out, I told him, 'Now, I'm an Officer in the
Detective Force; there's a letter with a kiss been posted here
just now, for a man that I'm in search of; and what I have
to ask of you, is, that you will let me look at the direction
of that letter.' He was very civil—took a lot of letters from

the box in the window—shook 'em out on the counter with
the faces downwards—and there among 'm was the identical
letter with the kiss. It was directed, Mr. Thomas Pigeon,
Post Office, B——, to be left 'till called for. Down I went
to B—— (a hundred and twenty miles or so) that night.
Early next morning I went to the Post Office; saw the
gentleman in charge of that department; told him who
I was; and that my object was to see, and track, the party
that should come for the letter for Mr. Thomas Pigeon.
He was very polite, and said, 'You shall have every assistance
we can give you; you can wait inside the office; and we'll
take care to let you know when anybody comes for the letter.'
Well, I waited there three days, and began to think that
nobody ever *would* come. At last the clerk whispered to
me, 'Here! Detective! Somebody's come for the letter!'
'Keep him a minute,' said I, and I ran round to the outside
of the office. There I saw a young chap with the appearance
of an Ostler, holding a horse by the bridle—stretching the
bridle across the pavement, while he waited at the Post
Office window for the letter. I began to pat the horse, and
that; and I said to the boy, 'Why, this is Mr. Jones's
Mare!' 'No. It an't.' 'No?' said I. 'She's very like
Mr. Jones's Mare!' 'She an't Mr. Jones's Mare, anyhow,'
says he. 'It's Mr. So and So's, of the Warwick Arms.'
And up he jumped, and off he went—letter and all. I got
a cab, followed on the box, and was so quick after him that
I came into the stable-yard of the Warwick Arms, by one
gate, just as he came in by another. I went into the bar,
where there was a young woman serving, and called for
a glass of brandy-and-water. He came in directly, and
handed her the letter. She casually looked at it, without
saying anything, and stuck it up behind the glass over the
chimney-piece. What was to be done next?

"I turned it over in my mind while I drank my brandy-
and-water (looking pretty sharp at the letter the while),
but I couldn't see my way out of it at all. I tried to get
lodgings in the house, but there had been a horse-fair, or
something of that sort, and it was full. I was obliged to
put up somewhere else, but I came backwards and forwards
to the bar for a couple of days, and there was the letter
always behind the glass. At last I thought I'd write a letter
to Mr. Pigeon myself, and see what that would do. So
I wrote one, and posted it, but I purposely addressed it,

taking 'em up. 'Those are Mr. Trinkle's gloves,' says her cousin. 'Oh!' says she, 'they are very dirty, and of no use to him, I am sure. I shall take 'em away for my girl to clean the stoves with.' And she put 'em in her pocket. The girl had used 'em to clean the stoves, and, I have no doubt, had left 'em lying on the bedroom mantelpiece, or on the drawers, or somewhere; and her mistress, looking round to see that the room was tidy, had caught 'em up and put 'em under the pillow where I found 'em.

"That's the story, sir."

II. THE ARTFUL TOUCH

"One of the most *beautiful* things that ever was done, perhaps," said Inspector Wield, emphasising the adjective, as preparing us to expect dexterity or ingenuity rather than strong interest, "was a move of Sergeant Witchem's. It was a lovely idea!

"Witchem and me were down at Epsom one Derby Day, waiting at the station for the Swell Mob. As I mentioned, when we were talking about these things before, we are ready at the station when there's races, or an Agricultural Show, or a Chancellor sworn in for an university, or Jenny Lind, or anything of that sort; and as the Swell Mob come down, we send 'em back again by the next train. But some of the Swell Mob, on the occasion of this Derby that I refer to, so far kidded us as to hire a horse and shay; start away from London by Whitechapel, and miles round; come into Epsom from the opposite direction; and go to work, right and left, on the course, while we were waiting for 'em at the Rail. That, however, ain't the point of what I'm going to tell you.

"While Witchem and me were waiting at the station, there comes up one Mr. Tatt; a gentleman formerly in the public line, quite an amateur Detective in his way, and very much respected. 'Halloa, Charley Wield,' he says. 'What are you doing here? On the look out for some of your old friends?' 'Yes, the old move, Mr. Tatt.' 'Come along,' he says, 'you and Witchem, and have a glass of sherry.' 'We can't stir from the place,' says I, 'till the next train comes in; but after that, we will with pleasure.' Mr. Tatt waits, and the train comes in, and then Witchem and me go off with him to the Hotel. Mr. Tatt he's got up quite regardless of expense, for the occasion; and in his shirt-front there's a beautiful diamond prop, cost him fifteen or twenty pound —a very handsome pin indeed. We drink our sherry at the bar, and have had our three or four glasses, when Witchem cries suddenly, 'Look out, Mr. Wield! stand fast!' and a dash is made into the place by the Swell Mob—four of 'em —that have come down as I tell you, and in a moment Mr. Tatt's prop is gone! Witchem, he cuts 'em off at the door. I lay about me as hard as I can, Mr. Tatt shows fight like a good 'un, and there we are, all down together, heads and heels, knocking about on the floor of the bar—perhaps you never see such a scene of confusion! However, we stick to our men (Mr. Tatt being as good as any officer), and we take 'em all, and carry 'em off to the station. The station's full of people, who have been took on the course; and it's a precious piece of work to get 'em secured. However, we do it at last, and we search 'em; but nothing's found upon 'em, and they're locked up; and a pretty state of heat we are in by that time, I assure you!

"I was very blank over it, myself, to think that the prop had been passed away; and I said to Witchem, when we had set 'em to rights, and were cooling ourselves along with Mr. Tatt, 'we don't take much by *this* move, anyway, for nothing's found upon 'em, and it's only the braggadocia[1], after all.' 'What do you mean, Mr. Wield?' says Witchem. 'Here's the diamond pin!' and in the palm of his hand there it was, safe and sound! 'Why, in the name of wonder,' says me and Mr. Tatt, in astonishment, 'how did you come by that?' 'I'll tell you how I come by it,' says he. 'I saw which of 'em took it; and when we were all down on the floor together, knocking about, I just gave him a little touch on the back of his hand, as I knew his pal would; and he thought it was his pal; and gave it me!' It was beautiful, beau-ti-ful!

"Even that was hardly the best of the case, for that chap was tried at the Quarter Sessions at Guildford. You know what Quarter Sessions are, sir. Well, if you'll believe me, while them slow justices were looking over the Acts of Parliament, to see what they could do to him, I'm blowed if he didn't cut out of the dock before their faces! He cut out of the dock, sir, then and there; swam across a river; and

---

[1] Three months' imprisonment as reputed thieves.

got up into a tree to dry himself. In the tree he was took
—an old woman having seen him climb up—and Witchem's
artful touch transported him!"

III.   THE SOFA

"What young men will do, sometimes, to ruin themselves
and break their friends' hearts," said Sergeant Dornton, "it's
surprising! I had a case at Saint Blank's Hospital which
was of this sort. A bad case, indeed, with a bad end!"

"The Secretary, and the House-Surgeon, and the Treasurer,
of Saint Blank's Hospital, came to Scotland Yard to give
information of numerous robberies having been committed on
the students. The students could leave nothing in the pockets
of their great-coats, while the great-coats were hanging at
the hospital, but it was almost certain to be stolen. Property
of various descriptions was constantly being lost; and the
gentlemen were naturally uneasy about it, and anxious, for
the credit of the institution, that the thief or thieves should
be discovered. The case was entrusted to me, and I went
to the hospital.

"'Now, gentlemen,' said I, after we had talked it over; 'I
understand this property is usually lost from one room.'

"Yes, they said. It was.

"'I should wish, if you please,' said I, 'to see the room.'

"It was a good-sized bare room down-stairs, with a few
tables and forms in it, and a row of pegs, all round, for hats
and coats.

"'Next, gentlemen,' said I, 'do you suspect anybody?'

"Yes, they said. They did suspect somebody. They were
sorry to say, they suspected one of the porters.

"'I should like,' said I, 'to have that man pointed out to
me, and to have a little time to look after him.'

"He was pointed out, and I looked after him, and then I
went back to the hospital, and said, 'Now, gentlemen, it's
not the porter. He's, unfortunately for himself, a little too
fond of drink, but he's nothing worse. My suspicion is, that
these robberies are committed by one of the students; and
if you'll put me a sofa into that room where the pegs are
—as there's no closet—I think I shall be able to detect the
thief. I wish the sofa, if you please, to be covered with
chintz, or something of that sort, so that I may lie on my
chest, underneath it, without being seen.'

THE SOFA

"The sofa was provided, and next day at eleven o'clock, before any of the students came, I went there, with those gentlemen, to get underneath it. It turned out to be one of those old-fashioned sofas with a great cross-beam at the bottom, that would have broken my back in no time if I could ever have got below it. We had quite a job to break all this away in the time; however, I fell to work, and they fell to work, and we broke it out, and made a clear place for me. I got under the sofa, lay down on my chest, took out my knife, and made a convenient hole in the chintz to look through. It was then settled between me and the gentlemen that when the students were all up in the wards, one of the gentlemen should come in, and hang up a great-coat on one of the pegs. And that that great-coat should have, in one of the pockets, a pocket-book containing marked money.

"After I had been there some time, the students began to drop into the room, by ones, and twos, and threes, and to talk about all sorts of things, little thinking there was anybody under the sofa—and then to go up-stairs. At last there came in one who remained until he was alone in the room by himself. A tallish, good-looking young man of one or two and twenty, with a light whisker. He went to a particular hat-peg, took off a good hat that was hanging there, tried it on, hung his own hat in its place, and hung that hat on another peg, nearly opposite to me. I then felt quite certain that he was the thief, and would come back by-and-by.

"When they were all up-stairs, the gentleman came in with the great-coat. I showed him where to hang it, so that I might have a good view of it; and he went away; and I lay under the sofa on my chest, for a couple of hours or so, waiting.

"At last, the same young man came down. He walked across the room, whistling—stopped and listened—took another walk and whistled—stopped again, and listened—then began to go regularly round the pegs, feeling in the pockets of all the coats. When he came to THE great-coat, and felt the pocket-book, he was so eager and so hurried that he broke the strap in tearing it open. As he began to put the money in his pocket, I crawled out from under the sofa, and his eyes met mine.

"My face, as you may perceive, is brown now, but it was pale at that time, my health not being good; and looked as long as a horse's. Besides which, there was a great draught of air from the door, underneath the sofa, and I had tied a handkerchief round my head; so what I looked like, altogether, I don't know. He turned blue—literally blue—when he saw me crawling out, and I couldn't feel surprised at it.

"'I am an officer of the Detective Police,' said I, 'and have been lying here, since you first came in this morning. I regret, for the sake of yourself and your friends, that you should have done what you have; but this case is complete. You have the pocket-book in your hand and the money upon you; and I must take you into custody!'

"It was impossible to make out any case in his behalf, and on his trial he pleaded guilty. How or when he got the means I don't know; but while he was awaiting his sentence, he poisoned himself in Newgate."

We inquired of this officer, on the conclusion of the foregoing anecdote, whether the time appeared long, or short, when he lay in that constrained position under the sofa?

"Why, you see, sir," he replied, "if he hadn't come in, the first time, and I had not been quite sure he was the thief, and would return, the time would have seemed long. But, as it was, I being dead certain of my man, the time seemed pretty short."

ON DUTY WITH INSPECTOR FIELD

How goes the night? Saint Giles's clock is striking nine. The weather is dull and wet, and the long lines of street lamps are blurred, as if we saw them through tears. A damp wind blows and rakes the pieman's fire out, when he opens the door of his little furnace, carrying away an eddy of sparks.

Saint Giles's clock strikes nine. We are punctual. Where is Inspector Field? Assistant Commissioner of Police is already here, enwrapped in oil-skin cloak, and standing in the shadow of Saint Giles's steeple. Detective Sergeant, weary of speaking French all day to foreigners unpacking at the Great Exhibition, is already here. Where is Inspector Field?

Inspector Field is, to-night, the guardian genius of the British Museum. He is bringing his shrewd eye to bear on every corner of its solitary galleries, before he reports "all right." Suspicious of the Elgin marbles, and not to be done by cat-faced Egyptian giants with their hands upon their knees, Inspector Field, sagacious, vigilant, lamp in hand, throwing monstrous shadows on the walls and ceilings, passes through the spacious rooms. If a mummy trembled in an atom of its dusty covering, Inspector Field would say, " Come out of that, Tom Green. I know you!" If the smallest "Gonoph" about town were crouching at the bottom of a classic bath, Inspector Field would nose him with a finer scent than the ogre's, when adventurous Jack lay trembling in his kitchen copper. But all is quiet, and Inspector Field goes warily on, making little outward show of attending to anything in particular, just recognising the Ichthyosaurus as a familiar acquaintance, and wondering, perhaps, how the detectives did it in the days before the Flood.

Will Inspector Field be long about this work? He may be half-an-hour longer. He sends his compliments by Police Constable, and proposes that we meet at St. Giles's Station

House, across the road. Good. It were as well to stand by the fire, there, as in the shadow of Saint Giles's steeple.

Anything doing here to-night? Not much. We are very quiet. A lost boy, extremely calm and small, sitting by the fire, whom we now confide to a constable to take home, for the child says that if you show him Newgate Street, he can show you where he lives—a raving drunken woman in the cells, who has screeched her voice away, and has hardly power enough left to declare, even with the passionate help of her feet and arms, that she is the daughter of a British officer, and, strike her blind and dead, but she'll write a letter to the Queen! but who is soothed with a drink of water—in another cell, a quiet woman, with a child at her breast, for begging—in another, her husband in a smock-frock, with a basket of watercresses—in another, a pickpocket —in another, a meek tremulous old pauper man who has been out for a holiday "and has took but a little drop, but it has overcome him after so many months in the house"—and that's all as yet. Presently, a sensation at the Station House door. Mr. Field, gentlemen!

Inspector Field comes in, wiping his forehead, for he is of a burly figure, and has come fast from the ores and metals of the deep mines of the earth, and from the Parrot Gods of the South Sea Islands, and from the birds and beetles of the tropics, and from the Arts of Greece and Rome, and from the Sculptures of Nineveh, and from the traces of an elder world, when these were not. Is Rogers ready? Rogers is ready, strapped and great-coated, with a flaming eye in the middle of his waist, like a deformed Cyclops. Lead on, Rogers, to Rats' Castle!

How many people may there be in London, who, if we had brought them deviously and blindfold, to this street, fifty paces from the Station House, and within call of Saint Giles's church, would know it for a not remote part of the city in which their lives are passed? How many, who amidst this compound of sickening smells, these heaps of filth, these tumbling houses, with all their vile contents, animate and inanimate, slimily overflowing into the black road, would believe that they breathe *this* air? How much Red Tape may there be, that could look round on the faces which now hem us in—for our appearance here has caused a rush from all points to a common centre—the lowering foreheads, the sallow cheeks, the brutal eyes, the matted hair, the infected, vermin-haunted heaps of rags—and say, "I have thought of this. I have not dismissed the thing. I have neither blustered it away, nor frozen it away, nor tied it up and put it away, nor smoothly said pooh, pooh! to it when it has been shown to me?"

This is not what Rogers wants to know, however. What Rogers wants to know, is, whether you *will* clear the way here, some of you, or whether you won't; because if you don't do it right on end, he'll lock you up! "What! *You* are there, are you, Bob Miles? You haven't had enough of it yet, haven't you? You want three months more, do you? Come away from that gentleman! What are you creeping round there for?"

"What am I a doing, thinn, Mr. Rogers?" says Bob Miles, appearing, villainous, at the end of a lane of light, made by the lantern.

"I'll let you know pretty quick, if you don't hook it. WILL you hook it?"

A sycophantic murmur rises from the crowd. "Hook it, Bob, when Mr. Rogers and Mr. Field tells you! Why don't you hook it, when you are told to?"

The most importunate of the voices strikes familiarly on Mr. Rogers's ear. He suddenly turns his lantern on the owner.

"What! *You* are there, are you, Mister Click? You hook it too—come!"

"What for?" says Mr. Click, discomfited.

"You hook it, will you!" says Mr. Rogers with stern emphasis.

Both Click and Miles *do* "hook it," without another word, or, in plainer English, sneak away.

"Close up there, my men!" says Inspector Field to two constables on duty who have followed. "Keep together, gentlemen; we are going down here. Heads!"

Saint Giles's church strikes half-past ten. We stoop low, and creep down a precipitous flight of steps into a dark close cellar. There is a fire. There is a long deal table. There are benches. The cellar is full of company, chiefly very young men in various conditions of dirt and raggedness. Some are eating supper. There are no girls or women present. Welcome to Rats' Castle, gentlemen, and to this company of noted thieves!

"Well, my lads! How are you, my lads? What have

you been doing to-day? Here's some company come to see you, my lads! *There's* a plate of beefsteak, sir, for the supper of a fine young man! And there's a mouth for a steak, sir! Why, I should be too proud of such a mouth as that, if I had it myself! Stand up and show it, sir! Take off your cap. There's a fine young man for a nice little party, sir! An't he?"

Inspector Field is the bustling speaker. Inspector Field's eye is the roving eye that searches every corner of the cellar as he talks. Inspector Field's hand is the well-known hand that has collared half the people here, and motioned their brothers, sisters, fathers, mothers, male and female friends, inexorably to New South Wales. Yet Inspector Field stands in this den, the Sultan of the place. Every thief here cowers before him, like a schoolboy before his schoolmaster. All watch him, all answer when addressed, all laugh at his jokes, all seek to propitiate him. This cellar company alone —to say nothing of the crowd surrounding the entrance from the street above, and making the steps shine with eyes—is strong enough to murder us all, and willing enough to do it; but let Inspector Field have a mind to pick out one thief here, and take him; let him produce that ghostly truncheon from his pocket, and say, with his business-air, "My lad, I want you!" and all Rats' Castle shall be stricken with paralysis, and not a finger move against him, as he fits the handcuffs on!

Where's the Earl of Warwick?—Here he is, Mr. Field! Here's the Earl of Warwick, Mr. Field!—O, there you are, my Lord. Come for'ard. There's a chest, sir, not to have a clean shirt on. An't it? Take your hat off, my Lord. Why, I should be ashamed if I was you—and an Earl, too— to show myself to a gentleman with my hat on!—The Earl of Warwick laughs and uncovers. All the company laugh. One pickpocket, especially, laughs with great enthusiasm. O what a jolly game it is, when Mr. Field comes down—and don't want nobody!

"So, *you* are here, too, are you, you tall, grey, soldierly-looking, grave man, standing by the fire?—Yes, sir. Good evening, Mr. Field!—Let us see. You lived servant to a nobleman once?—Yes, Mr. Field.—And what is it you do now; I forget?—Well, Mr. Field, I job about as well as I can. I left my employment on account of delicate health. The family is still kind to me. Mr. Wix of Piccadilly also very kind to me when I am hard up. Likewise Mr. Nix of Oxford Street. I get a trifle from them occasionally, and rub on as well as I can, Mr. Field. Mr. Field's eye rolls enjoyingly, for this man is a notorious begging-letter writer.—Good night, my lads!—Good night, Mr. Field, and thank'ee, sir!

Clear the street here, half a thousand of you! Cut it, Mrs. Stalker—none of that—we don't want you! Rogers of the flaming eye, lead on to the tramps' lodging-house!

A dream of baleful faces attends to the door. Now, stand back all of you! In the rear Detective Sergeant plants himself, composedly whistling, with his strong right arm across the narrow passage. Mrs. Stalker, I am something'd that need not be written here, if you won't get yourself into trouble, in about half a minute, if I see that face of yours again!

Saint Giles's church clock, striking eleven, hums through our hand from the dilapidated door of a dark outhouse as we open it, and are stricken back by the pestilent breath that issues from within. Rogers to the front with the light, and let us look!

Ten, twenty, thirty—who can count them! Men, women, children, for the most part naked, heaped upon the floor like maggots in a cheese! Ho! In that dark corner yonder! Does anybody lie there? Me sir, Irish me, a widder, with six children. And yonder? Me sir, Irish me, with me wife and eight poor babes. And to the left there? Me sir, Irish me, along with two more Irish boys as is me friends. And to the right there? Me sir and the Murphy fam'ly, numbering five blessed souls. And what's this, coiling, now, about my foot? Another Irish me, pitifully in want of shaving, whom I have awakened from sleep—and across my other foot lies his wife—and by the shoes of Inspector Field lie their three eldest—and their three youngest are at present squeezed between the open door and the wall. And why is there no one on that little mat before the sullen fire? Because O'Donovan, with his wife and daughter, is not come in from selling Lucifers! Nor on the bit of sacking in the nearest corner? Bad luck! Because that Irish family is late to-night, a-cadging in the streets!

They are all awake now, the children excepted, and most of them sit up, to stare. Wheresoever Mr. Rogers turns the flaming eye, there is a spectral figure rising, unshrouded,

from a grave of rags. Who is the landlord here?—I am,
Mr. Field! says a bundle of ribs and parchment against the
wall, scratching itself.—Will you spend this money fairly,
in the morning, to buy coffee for 'em all?—Yes, sir, I will!
—O he'll do it, sir, he'll do it fair. He's honest! cry the
spectres. And with thanks and Good Night sink into their
graves again.

Thus, we make our New Oxford Streets, and our other
new streets, never heeding, never asking, where the wretches
whom we clear out, crowd. With such scenes at our doors,
with all the plagues of Egypt tied up with bits of cobweb in
kennels so near our homes, we timorously make our Nuisance
Bills and Boards of Health, nonentities, and think to keep
away the Wolves of Crime and Filth, by our electioneering
ducking to little vestrymen and our gentlemanly handling
of Red Tape!

Intelligence of the coffee-money has got abroad. The
yard is full, and Rogers of the flaming eye is beleaguered
with entreaties to show other Lodging Houses. Mine next!
Mine! Mine! Rogers, military, obdurate, stiff-necked, immovable, replies not, but leads away; all falling back before
him. Inspector Field follows. Detective Sergeant, with
his barrier of arm across the little passage, deliberately
waits to close the procession. He sees behind him, without
any effort, and exceedingly disturbs one individual far in
the rear by coolly calling out, "It won't do, Mr. Michael!
Don't try it!"

After council holden in the street, we enter other lodging-
houses, public-houses, many lairs and holes; all noisome and
offensive; none so filthy and so crowded as where Irish are.
In one, The Ethiopian party are expected home presently
—were in Oxford Street when last heard of—shall be
fetched, for our delight, within ten minutes. In another,
one of the two or three Professors who draw Napoleon
Buonaparte and a couple of mackerel, on the pavement, and
then let the work of art out to a speculator, is refreshing
after his labours. In another, the vested interest of the profitable nuisance has been in one family for a hundred years,
and the landlord drives in comfortably from the country to
his snug little stew in town. In all, Inspector Field is
received with warmth. Coiners and smashers droop before
him; pickpockets defer to him; the gentle sex (not very
gentle here) smile upon him. Half-drunken hags check

themselves in the midst of pots of beer, or pints of gin, to drink to Mr. Field, and pressingly to ask the honour of his finishing the draught. One beldame in rusty black has such admiration for him, that she runs a whole street's length to shake him by the hand; tumbling into a heap of mud by the way, and still pressing her attentions when her very form has ceased to be distinguishable through it. Before the power of the law, the power of superior sense— for common thieves are fools beside these men—and the power of a perfect mastery of their character, the garrison of Rats' Castle and the adjacent Fortresses make but a skulking show indeed when reviewed by Inspector Field.

Saint Giles's clock says it will be midnight in half-an-hour, and Inspector Field says we must hurry to the Old Mint in the Borough. The cab-driver is low-spirited, and has a solemn sense of his responsibility. Now, what's your fare, my lad?—O *you* know, Inspector Field, what's the good of asking *me!*

Say, Parker, strapped and great-coated, and waiting in dim Borough doorway by appointment, to replace the trusty Rogers whom we left deep in Saint Giles's, are you ready? Ready, Inspector Field, and at a motion of my wrist behold my flaming eye.

This narrow street, sir, is the chief part of the Old Mint, full of low lodging-houses, as you see by the transparent canvas-lamps and blinds, announcing beds for travellers! But it is greatly changed, friend Field, from my former knowledge of it; it is infinitely quieter and more subdued than when I was here last, some seven years ago? O yes! Inspector Haynes, a first-rate man, is on this station now and plays the Devil with them!

Well, my lads! How are you to-night, my lads? Playing cards here, eh? Who wins?—Why, Mr. Field, I, the sulky gentleman with the damp flat side-curls, rubbing my bleared eye with the end of my neckerchief which is like a dirty eel-skin, am losing just at present, but I suppose I must take my pipe out of my mouth, and be submissive to *you*— I hope I see you well, Mr. Field?—Aye, all right, my lad. Deputy, who have you got up-stairs? Be pleased to show the rooms!

Why Deputy, Inspector Field can't say. He only knows that the man who takes care of the beds and lodgers is always called so. Steady, O Deputy, with the flaring candle

in the blacking-bottle, for this is a slushy back-yard, and
the wooden staircase outside the house creaks and has holes
in it.

Again, in these confined intolerable rooms, burrowed out
like the holes of rats or the nests of insect-vermin, but fuller
of intolerable smells, are crowds of sleepers, each on his foul
truckle-bed coiled up beneath a rug.   Halloa here !   Come !
Let us see you !   Show your face !   Pilot Parker goes from
bed to bed and turns their slumbering heads towards us, as
a salesman might turn sheep.   Some wake up with an
execration and a threat.—What ! who spoke ?   O !   If it's
the accursed glaring eye that fixes me, go where I will, I am
helpless.   Here !   I sit up to be looked at.   Is it me you
want ?   Not you, lie down again !   and I lie down, with
a woful growl.

Wherever the turning lane of light becomes stationary for
a moment, some sleeper appears at the end of it, submits
himself to be scrutinised, and fades away into the darkness.

There should be strange dreams here, Deputy.   They sleep
sound enough, says Deputy, taking the candle out of the
blacking-bottle, snuffing it with his fingers, throwing the
snuff into the bottle, and corking it up with the candle ;
that's all *I* know.   What is the inscription, Deputy, on all
the discoloured sheets ?   A precaution against loss of linen.
Deputy turns down the rug of an unoccupied bed and
discloses it.   STOP THIEF !

To lie at night, wrapped in the legend of my slinking life ;
to take the cry that pursues me, waking, to my breast in
sleep ; to have it staring at me, and clamouring for me, as
soon as consciousness returns ; to have it for my first-foot
on New-Year's day, my Valentine, my Birthday salute, my
Christmas greeting, my parting with the old year.   STOP
THIEF !

And to know that I *must* be stopped, come what will.
To know that I am no match for this individual energy and
keenness, or this organised and steady system !   Come across
the street, here, and, entering by a little shop, and yard,
examine these intricate passages and doors, contrived for
escape, flapping and counter-flapping, like the lids of the
conjurer's boxes.   But what avail they ?   Who gets in by a
nod, and shows their secret working to us ?   Inspector Field.

Don't forget the old Farm House, Parker !   Parker is not
the man to forget it.   We are going there, now.   It is the

old Manor-House of these parts, and stood in the country once. Then, perhaps, there was something, which was not the beastly street, to see from the shattered low fronts of the overhanging wooden houses we are passing under—shut up now, pasted over with bills about the literature and drama of the Mint, and mouldering away. This long paved yard was a paddock or a garden once, or a court in front of the Farm House. Perchance, with a dovecot in the centre, and fowls pecking about—with fair elm trees, then, where discoloured chimney-stacks and gables are now—noisy, then, with rooks which have yielded to a different sort of rookery. It's likelier than not, Inspector Field thinks, as we turn into the common kitchen, which is in the yard, and many paces from the house.

Well, my lads and lasses, how are you all? Where's Blackey, who has stood near London Bridge these five-and-twenty years, with a painted skin to represent disease?—Here he is, Mr. Field!—How are you, Blackey?—Jolly, sa!—Not playing the fiddle to-night, Blackey?—Not a night, sa! A sharp, smiling youth, the wit of the kitchen, interposes. He an't musical to-night, sir. I've been giving him a moral lecture; I've been a talking to him about his latter end, you see. A good many of these are my pupils, sir. This here young man (smoothing down the hair of one near him, reading a Sunday paper) is a pupil of mine. I'm a teaching of him to read, sir. He's a promising cove, sir. He's a smith, he is, and gets his living by the sweat of the brow, sir. So do I, myself, sir. This young woman is my sister, Mr. Field. *She's* getting on very well too. I've a deal of trouble with 'em, sir, but I'm richly rewarded, now I see 'em all a doing so well, and growing up so creditable. That's a great comfort, that is, an't it, sir?—In the midst of the kitchen (the whole kitchen is in ecstasies with this impromptu "chaff") sits a young, modest, gentle-looking creature, with a beautiful child in her lap. She seems to belong to the company, but is so strangely unlike it. She has such a pretty, quiet face and voice, and is so proud to hear the child admired—thinks you would hardly believe that he is only nine months old! Is she as bad as the rest, I wonder? Inspectorial experience does not engender a belief contrariwise, but prompts the answer, Not a ha'porth of difference!

There is a piano going in the old Farm House as we

approach. It stops. Landlady appears. Has no objections, Mr. Field, to gentlemen being brought, but wishes it were at earlier hours, the lodgers complaining of ill-convenience. Inspector Field is polite and soothing—knows his woman and the sex. Deputy (a girl in this case) shows the way up a heavy broad old staircase, kept very clean, into clean rooms where many sleepers are, and where painted panels of an older time look strangely on the truckle beds. The sight of whitewash and the smell of soap—two things we seem by this time to have parted from in infancy—make the old Farm House a phenomenon, and connect themselves with the so curiously misplaced picture of the pretty mother and child long after we have left it,—long after we have left, besides, the neighbouring nook with something of a rustic flavour in it yet, where once, beneath a low wooden colonnade still standing as of yore, the eminent Jack Sheppard condescended to regale himself, and where, now, two old bachelor brothers in broad hats (who are whispered in the Mint to have made a compact long ago that if either should ever marry, he must forfeit his share of the joint property) still keep a sequestered tavern, and sit o' nights smoking pipes in the bar, among ancient bottles and glasses, as our eyes behold them.

How goes the night now? Saint George of Southwark answers with twelve blows upon his bell. Parker, good night, for Williams is already waiting over in the region of Ratcliffe Highway, to show the houses where the sailors dance.

I should like to know where Inspector Field was born. In Ratcliffe Highway, I would have answered with confidence, but for his being equally at home wherever we go. *He* does not trouble his head as I do, about the river at night. *He* does not care for its creeping, black and silent, on our right there, rushing through sluice-gates, lapping at piles and posts and iron rings, hiding strange things in its mud, running away with suicides and accidentally drowned bodies faster than midnight funeral should, and acquiring such various experience between its cradle and its grave. It has no mystery for *him*. Is there not the Thames Police?

Accordingly, Williams leads the way. We are a little late, for some of the houses are already closing. No matter. You show us plenty. All the landlords know Inspector Field. All pass him, freely and good-humouredly, wheresoever he wants to go. So thoroughly are all these houses open to him and our local guide, that, granting that sailors must be entertained in their own way—as I suppose they must, and have a right to be—I hardly know how such places could be better regulated. Not that I call the company very select, or the dancing very graceful—even so graceful as that of the German Sugar Bakers, whose assembly, by the Minories, we stopped to visit—but there is watchful maintenance of order in every house, and swift expulsion where need is. Even in the midst of drunkenness, both of the lethargic kind and the lively, there is sharp landlord supervision, and pockets are in less peril than out of doors. These houses show, singularly, how much of the picturesque and romantic there truly is in the sailor, requiring to be especially addressed. All the songs (sung in a hailstorm of halfpence, which are pitched at the singer without the least tenderness for the time or tune—mostly from great rolls of copper carried for the purpose —and which he occasionally dodges like shot as they fly near his head) are of the sentimental sea sort. All the rooms are decorated with nautical subjects. Wrecks, engagements, ships on fire, ships passing lighthouses on iron-bound coasts, ships blowing up, ships going down, ships running ashore, men lying out upon the main-yard in a gale of wind, sailors and ships in every variety of peril, constitute the illustrations of fact. Nothing can be done in the fanciful way, without a thumping boy upon a scaly dolphin.

How goes the night now? Past one. Black and Green are waiting in Whitechapel to unveil the mysteries of Wentworth Street. Williams, the best of friends must part. Adieu!

Are not Black and Green ready at the appointed place? O yes! They glide out of shadow as we stop. Imperturbable Black opens the cab-door; Imperturbable Green takes a mental note of the driver. Both Green and Black then open, each his flaming eye, and marshal us the way that we are going.

The lodging-house we want is hidden in a maze of streets and courts. It is fast shut. We knock at the door, and stand hushed looking up for a light at one or other of the begrimed old lattice windows in its ugly front, when another constable comes up—supposes that we want "to see the school." Detective Sergeant meanwhile has got over a rail, opened a gate, dropped down an area, overcome some other

Upon the whole, it was the dragon, Pauperism, in a very weak and impotent condition ; toothless, fangless, drawing his breath heavily enough, and hardly worth chaining up.

When the service was over, I walked with the humane and conscientious gentleman whose duty it was to take that walk, that Sunday morning, through the little world of poverty enclosed within the workhouse walls. It was inhabited by a population of some fifteen hundred or two thousand paupers, ranging from the infant newly born or not yet come into the pauper world, to the old man dying on his bed.

In a room opening from a squalid yard, where a number of listless women were lounging to and fro, trying to get warm in the ineffectual sunshine of the tardy May morning —in the " Itch Ward," not to compromise the truth— a woman such as HOGARTH has often drawn, was hurriedly getting on her gown before a dusty fire. She was the nurse, or wardswoman, of that insalubrious department—herself a pauper—flabby, raw-boned, untidy—unpromising and coarse of aspect as need be. But, on being spoken to about the patients whom she had in charge, she turned round, with her shabby gown half on, half off, and fell a crying with all her might. Not for show, not querulously, not in any mawkish sentiment, but in the deep grief and affliction of her heart ; turning away her dishevelled head : sobbing most bitterly, wringing her hands, and letting fall abundance of great tears, that choked her utterance. What was the matter with the nurse of the itch-ward ? Oh, "the dropped child " was dead ! Oh, the child that was found in the street, and she had brought up ever since, had died an hour ago, and see where the little creature lay, beneath this cloth ! The dear, the pretty dear !

The dropped child seemed too small and poor a thing for Death to be in earnest with, but Death had taken it ; and already its diminutive form was neatly washed, composed, and stretched as if in sleep upon a box. I thought I heard a voice from Heaven saying, It shall be well for thee, O nurse of the itch-ward, when some less gentle pauper does those offices to thy cold form, that such as the dropped child are the angels who behold my Father's face !

In another room were several ugly old women crouching, witch-like, round a hearth, and chattering and nodding, after the manner of the monkeys. " All well here ? And enough to eat?" A general chattering and chuckling; at last an answer from a volunteer. "Oh yes, gentleman! Bless you, gentleman! Lord bless the Parish of St. So-and-So! It feed the hungry, sir, and give drink to the thusty, and it warm them which is cold, so it do, and good luck to the parish of St. So-and-So, and thankee, gentleman!" Elsewhere, a party of pauper nurses were at dinner. "How do *you* get on?" "Oh pretty well, sir! We works hard, and we lives hard—like the sodgers!"

In another room, a kind of purgatory or place of transition, six or eight noisy madwomen were gathered together, under the superintendence of one sane attendant. Among them was a girl of two or three and twenty, very prettily dressed, of most respectable appearance, and good manners, who had been brought in from the house where she had lived as domestic servant (having, I suppose, no friends), on account of being subject to epileptic fits, and requiring to be removed under the influence of a very bad one. She was by no means of the same stuff, or the same breeding, or the same experience, or in the same state of mind, as those by whom she was surrounded; and she pathetically complained that the daily association and the nightly noise made her worse, and was driving her mad—which was perfectly evident. The case was noted for inquiry and redress, but she said she had already been there for some weeks.

If this girl had stolen her mistress's watch, I do not hesitate to say she would have been infinitely better off. We have come to this absurd, this dangerous, this monstrous pass, that the dishonest felon is, in respect of cleanliness, order, diet, and accommodation, better provided for, and taken care of, than the honest pauper.

And this conveys no special imputation on the workhouse of the parish of St. So-and-So, where, on the contrary, I saw many things to commend. It was very agreeable, recollecting that most infamous and atrocious enormity committed at Tooting—an enormity which, a hundred years hence, will still be vividly remembered in the bye-ways of English life, and which has done more to engender a gloomy discontent and suspicion among many thousands of the people than all the Chartist leaders could have done in all their lives—to find the pauper children in this workhouse looking robust and well, and apparently the objects of very great care. In the Infant School—a large, light, airy room at the top of the

PRINCE BULL. A FAIRY TALE

ONCE upon a time, and of course it was in the Golden Age,
and I hope you may know when that was, for I am sure
I don't, though I have tried hard to find out, there lived in
a rich and fertile country, a powerful Prince whose name
was BULL. He had gone through a great deal of fighting,
in his time, about all sorts of things, including nothing ;
but had gradually settled down to be a steady, peaceable,
good-natured, corpulent, rather sleepy Prince.

This Puissant Prince was married to a lovely Princess
whose name was Fair Freedom. She had brought him a
large fortune, and had borne him an immense number of
children, and had set them to spinning, and farming, and
engineering, and soldiering, and sailoring, and doctoring,
and lawyering, and preaching, and all kinds of trades. The
coffers of Prince Bull were full of treasure, his cellars were
crammed with delicious wines from all parts of the world,
the richest gold and silver plate that ever was seen adorned
his sideboards, his sons were strong, his daughters were handsome, and in short you might have supposed that if there
ever lived upon earth a fortunate and happy Prince, the
name of that Prince, take him for all in all, was assuredly
Prince Bull.

But appearances, as we all know, are not always to be
trusted—far from it ; and if they had led you to this conclusion respecting Prince Bull, they would have led you wrong
as they often have led me.

For this good Prince had two sharp thorns in his pillow,
two hard knobs in his crown, two heavy loads on his mind,
two unbridled nightmares in his sleep, two rocks ahead in
his course. He could not by any means get servants to suit
him, and he had a tyrannical old godmother, whose name
was Tape.

She was a Fairy, this Tape, and was a bright red all over.
She was disgustingly prim and formal, and could never

bend herself a hair's breadth this way or that way, out of
her naturally crooked shape. But she was very potent in
her wicked art. She could stop the fastest thing in the
world, change the strongest thing into the weakest, and the
most useful into the most useless. To do this she had only
to put her cold hand upon it, and repeat her own name,
Tape. Then it withered away.

At the Court of Prince Bull—at least I don't mean literally at his court, because he was a very genteel Prince, and
readily yielded to his godmother when she always reserved
that for his hereditary Lords and Ladies—in the dominions
of Prince Bull, among the great mass of the community
who were called in the language of that polite country the
Mobs and the Snobs, were a number of very ingenious men,
who were always busy with some invention or other, for
promoting the prosperity of the Prince's subjects, and aug-
menting the Prince's power. But, whenever they submitted their models for the Prince's approval, his godmother
stepped forward, laid her hand upon them, and said "Tape."
Hence it came to pass, that when any particularly good
discovery was made, the discoverer usually carried it off to
some other Prince, in foreign parts, who had no old godmother who said Tape. This was not on the whole an
advantageous state of things for Prince Bull, to the best of
my understanding.

The worst of it was, that Prince Bull had in course of
years lapsed into such a state of subjection to this unlucky
godmother, that he never made any serious effort to rid
himself of her tyranny. I have said this was the worst of it,
but there I was wrong, because there is a worse consequence
still, behind. The Prince's numerous family became so downright sick and tired of Tape, that when they should have
helped the Prince out of the difficulties into which that evil
creature led him, they fell into a dangerous habit of moodily
keeping away from him in an impassive and indifferent
manner, as though they had quite forgotten that no harm
could happen to the Prince their father, without its inevitably affecting themselves.

Such was the aspect of affairs at the court of Prince Bull,
when this great Prince found it necessary to go to war with
Prince Bear. He had been for some time very doubtful of
his servants, who, besides being indolent and addicted to
enriching their families at his expense, domineered over him

dreadfully; threatening to discharge themselves if they were found the least fault with, pretending that they had done a wonderful amount of work when they had done nothing, making the most unmeaning speeches that ever were heard in the Prince's name, and uniformly showing themselves to be very inefficient indeed. Though, that some of them had excellent characters from previous situations is not to be denied. Well; Prince Bull called his servants together, and said to them one and all, "Send out my army against Prince Bear. Clothe it, arm it, feed it, provide it with all necessaries and contingencies, and I will pay the piper! Do your duty by my brave troops," said the Prince, "and do it well, and I will pour my treasure out like water, to defray the cost. Who ever heard ME complain of money well laid out!" Which indeed he had reason for saying, inasmuch as he was well known to be a truly generous and munificent Prince.

When the servants heard those words, they sent out the army against Prince Bear, and they set the army tailors to work, and the army provision merchants, and the makers of guns both great and small, and the gunpowder makers, and the makers of ball, shell, and shot; and they bought up all manner of stores and ships, without troubling their heads about the price, and appeared to be so busy that the good Prince rubbed his hands, and (using a favourite expression of his), said, "It's all right!" But while they were thus employed, the Prince's godmother, who was a great favourite with those servants, looked in upon them continually all day long, and whenever she popped in her head at the door said, "How do you do, my children? What are you doing here?" "Official business, godmother." "Oho!" says this wicked Fairy. "—Tape!" And then the business all went wrong, whatever it was, and the servants' heads became so addled and muddled that they thought they were doing wonders.

Now, this was very bad conduct on the part of the vicious old nuisance, and she ought to have been strangled, even if she had stopped here; but she didn't stop here, as you shall learn. For a number of the Prince's subjects, being very fond of the Prince's army who were the bravest of men, assembled together and provided all manner of eatables and drinkables, and books to read, and clothes to wear, and tobacco to smoke, and candles to burn, and nailed them up in great packing-cases, and put them aboard a great many ships, to be carried out to that brave army in the cold and inclement country where they were fighting Prince Bear. Then up comes this wicked Fairy as the ships were weighing anchor, and says, "How do you do, my children? What are you doing here?"—"We are going with all these comforts to the army, godmother."—"Oho!" says she. "A pleasant voyage, my darlings.—Tape!" And from that time forth, those enchanted ships went sailing, against wind and tide and rhyme and reason, round and round the world, and whenever they touched at any port were ordered off immediately, and could never deliver their cargoes anywhere.

This, again, was very bad conduct on the part of the vicious old nuisance, and she ought to have been strangled for it if she had done nothing worse; but she did something worse still, as you shall learn. For she got astride of an official broomstick, and muttered as a spell these two sentences, "On Her Majesty's service," and "I have the honour to be, sir, your most obedient servant," and presently alighted in the cold and inclement country where the army of Prince Bull were encamped to fight the army of Prince Bear. On the sea-shore of that country, she found piled together a number of houses for the army to live in, and a quantity of provisions for the army to live upon, and a quantity of clothes for the army to wear: while, sitting in the mud gazing at them, were a group of officers as red to look at as the wicked old woman herself. So, she said to one of them, "Who are you, my darling, and how do you do?"—"I am the Quarter-master General's Department, godmother, and I am pretty well."—Then she said to another, "Who are you, my darling, and how do you do?" —"I am the Commissariat Department, godmother, and I am pretty well." Then she said to another, "Who are you, my darling, and how do you do?"—"I am the Head of the Medical Department, godmother, and I am pretty well." Then she said to some gentlemen scented with lavender, who kept themselves at a great distance from the rest, "And who are you, my pretty pets, and how do you do?" And they answered, "We-aw-are-the-aw-Staff-aw-Department, god-mother, and we are very well indeed."—"I am delighted to see you all, my beauties," says this wicked old Fairy, "—Tape!" Upon that, the houses, clothes, and provisions, all mouldered away; and the soldiers who were sound, fell sick; and the soldiers who were sick, died miserably: and the noble army of Prince Bull perished.

When the dismal news of his great loss was carried to the Prince, he suspected his godmother very much indeed; but he knew that his servants must have kept company with the malicious beldame, and must have given way to her, and therefore he resolved to turn those servants out of their places. So he called to him a Roebuck who had the gift of speech, and he said, "Good Roebuck, tell them they must go." So the good Roebuck delivered his message, so like a man that you might have supposed him to be nothing but a man, and they were turned out—but not without warning, for that they had had a long time.

And now comes the most extraordinary part of the history of this Prince. When he had turned out those servants, of course he wanted others. What was his astonishment to find that in all his dominions, which contained no less than twenty-seven millions of people, there were not above five-and-twenty servants altogether! They were so lofty about it, too, that instead of discussing whether they should hire themselves as servants to Prince Bull, they turned things topsy-turvy, and considered whether as a favour they should hire Prince Bull to be their master! While they were arguing this point among themselves quite at their leisure, the wicked old red Fairy was incessantly going up and down, knocking at the doors of twelve of the oldest of the five-and-twenty, who were the oldest inhabitants in all that country, and whose united ages amounted to one thousand, saying, "Will *you* hire Prince Bull for your master?—Will *you* hire Prince Bull for your master?" To which one answered, "I will if next door will;" and another, "I won't if over the way does;" and another, "I can't if he, she, or they, might, could, would, or should." And all this time Prince Bull's affairs were going to rack and ruin.

At last, Prince Bull in the height of his perplexity assumed a thoughtful face, as if he were struck by an entirely new idea. The wicked old Fairy, seeing this, was at his elbow directly, and said, "How do you do, my Prince, and what are you thinking of?"—"I am thinking, godmother," says he, "that among all the seven-and-twenty millions of my subjects who have never been in service, there are men of intellect and business who have made me very famous both among my friends and enemies."—" Aye, truly ? " says the Fairy.—" Aye, truly," says the Prince.—" And what then ? " says the Fairy.—" Why, then," says he, " since the regular old class of servants do so ill, are so hard to get, and carry it with so high a hand, perhaps I might try to make good servants of some of these." The words had no sooner passed his lips than she returned, chuckling, " You think so, do you? Indeed, my Prince ?—Tape ! " Thereupon he directly forgot what he was thinking of, and cried out lamentably to the old servants, " O, do come and hire your poor old master ! Pray do ! On any terms ! "

And this, for the present, finishes the story of Prince Bull. I wish I could wind it up by saying that he lived happy ever afterwards, but I cannot in my conscience do so ; for, with Tape at his elbow, and his estranged children fatally repelled by her from coming near him, I do not, to tell you the plain truth, believe in the possibility of such an end to it.

A PLATED ARTICLE

PUTTING up for the night in one of the chiefest towns of
Staffordshire, I find it to be by no means a lively town. In
fact is as dull and dead a town as any one could desire not
to see. It seems as if its whole population might be imprisoned in its Railway Station. The Refreshment Room
at that Station is a vortex of dissipation compared with the
extinct town-inn, the Dodo, in the dull High Street.

Why High Street? Why not rather Low Street, Flat
Street, Low-Spirited Street, Used-up Street? Where are
the people who belong to the High Street? Can they all
be dispersed over the face of the country, seeking the unfortunate Strolling Manager who decamped from the mouldy
little Theatre last week, in the beginning of his season (as
his play-bills testify), repentantly resolved to bring him back,
and feed him, and be entertained? Or, can they all be
gathered to their fathers in the two old churchyards near
to the High Street—retirement into which churchyards
appears to be a mere ceremony, there is so very little life
outside their confines, and such small discernible difference
between being buried alive in the town, and buried dead in
the town tombs? Over the way, opposite to the staring
blank bow windows of the Dodo, are a little ironmonger's
shop, a little tailor's shop (with a picture of the Fashions in
the small window and a bandy-legged baby on the pavement staring at it)—a watchmaker's shop, where all the
clocks and watches must be stopped, I am sure, for they
could never have the courage to go, with the town in
general, and the Dodo in particular, looking at them. Shade
of Miss Linwood, erst of Leicester Square, London, thou
art welcome here, and thy retreat is fitly chosen! I myself was one of the last visitors to that awful storehouse of
thy life's work, where an anchorite old man and woman
took my shilling with a solemn wonder, and conducting
me to a gloomy sepulchre of needlework dropping to pieces
with dust and age and shrouded in twilight at high noon,

left me there, chilled, frightened, and alone. And now, in ghostly letters on all the dead walls of this dead town, I read thy honoured name, and find that thy Last Supper, worked in Berlin Wool, invites inspection as a powerful excitement!

Where are the people who are bidden with so much cry to this feast of little wool? Where are they? Who are they? They are not the bandy-legged baby studying the fashions in the tailor's window. They are not the two earthy ploughmen lounging outside the saddler's shop, in the stiff square where the Town Hall stands, like a brick and mortar private on parade. They are not the landlady of the Dodo in the empty bar, whose eye had trouble in it and no welcome, when I asked for dinner. They are not the turnkeys of the Town Jail, looking out of the gateway in their uniforms, as if they had locked up all the balance (as my American friends would say) of the inhabitants, and could now rest a little. They are not the two dusty millers in the white mill down by the river, where the great water-wheel goes heavily round and round, like the monotonous days and nights in this forgotten place. Then who are they, for there is no one else? No; this deponent maketh oath and saith that there is no one else, save and except the waiter at the Dodo, now laying the cloth. I have paced the streets, and stared at the houses, and am come back to the blank bow window of the Dodo; and the town clocks strike seven, and the reluctant echoes seem to cry, "Don't wake us!" and the bandy-legged baby has gone home to bed.

If the Dodo were only a gregarious bird—if he had only some confused idea of making a comfortable nest—I could hope to get through the hours between this and bed-time, without being consumed by devouring melancholy. But, the Dodo's habits are all wrong. It provides me with a trackless desert of sitting-room, with a chair for every day in the year, a table for every month, and a waste of side-board where a lonely China vase pines in a corner for its mate long departed, and will never make a match with the candlestick in the opposite corner if it live till Doomsday. The Dodo has nothing in the larder. Even now, I behold the Boots returning with my sole in a piece of paper; and with that portion of my dinner, the Boots, perceiving me at the blank bow window, slaps his leg as he comes across

the road, pretending it is something else. The Dodo ex-
cludes the outer air. When I mount up to my bedroom,
a smell of closeness and flue gets lazily up my nose like
sleepy snuff. The loose little bits of carpet writhe under
my tread, and take wormy shapes. I don't know the ridiculous man in the looking-glass, beyond having met him
once or twice in a dish-cover—and I can never shave *him*
to-morrow morning! The Dodo is narrow-minded as to
towels ; expects me to wash on a freemason's apron without
the trimming : when I asked for soap, gives me a stony-
hearted something white, with no more lather in it than
the Elgin marbles. The Dodo has seen better days, and
possesses interminable stables at the back—silent, grass-
grown, broken-windowed, horseless.

This mournful bird can fry a sole, however, which is
much. Can cook a steak, too, which is more. I wonder
where it gets its Sherry ? If I were to send my pint of
wine to some famous chemist to be analysed, what would
it turn out to be made of ? It tastes of pepper, sugar, bitter-
almonds, vinegar, warm knives, any flat drinks, and a little
brandy. Would it unman a Spanish exile by reminding
him of his native land at all ? I think not. If there really
be any townspeople out of the churchyards, and if a caravan
of them ever do dine, with a bottle of wine per man, in
this desert of the Dodo, it must make good for the doctor
next day !

Where was the waiter born ? How did he come here ?
Has he any hope of getting away from here ? Does he ever
receive a letter, or take a ride upon the railway, or see anything but the Dodo ? Perhaps he has seen the Berlin Wool.
He appears to have a silent sorrow on him, and it may be
that. He clears the table ; draws the dingy curtains of the
great bow window, which so unwillingly consent to meet,
that they must be pinned together ; leaves me by the fire
with my pint decanter, and a little thin funnel-shaped wine-
glass, and a plate of pale biscuits—in themselves engendering
desperation.

No book, no newspaper ! I left the Arabian Nights in the
railway carriage, and have nothing to read but Bradshaw,
and "that way madness lies." Remembering what prisoners
and shipwrecked mariners have done to exercise their minds
in solitude, I repeat the multiplication table, the pence table,
and the shilling table : which are all the tables I happen to

know. What if I write something? The Dodo keeps no pens but steel pens; and those I always stick through the paper, and can turn to no other account.

What am I to do? Even if I could have the bandy-legged baby knocked up and brought here, I could offer him nothing but sherry, and that would be the death of him. He would never hold up his head again if he touched it. I can't go to bed, because I have conceived a mortal hatred for my bedroom; and I can't go away, because there is no train for my place of destination until morning. To burn the biscuits will be but a fleeting joy; still it is a temporary relief, and here they go on the fire! Shall I break the plate? First let me look at the back, and see who made it. COPELAND.

Copeland! Stop a moment. Was it yesterday I visited Copeland's works, and saw them making plates? In the confusion of travelling about, it might be yesterday or it might be yesterday month; but I think it was yesterday. I appeal to the plate. The plate says, decidedly, yesterday. I find the plate, as I look at it, growing into a companion.

Don't you remember (says the plate) how you steamed away, yesterday morning, in the bright sun and the east wind, along the valley of the sparkling Trent? Don't you recollect how many kilns you flew past, looking like the bowls of gigantic tobacco-pipes, cut short off from the stem and turned upside down? And the fires—and the smoke—and the roads made with bits of crockery, as if all the plates and dishes in the civilised world had been Macadamised expressly for the laming of all the horses? Of course I do!

And don't you remember (says the plate) how you alighted at Stoke—a picturesque heap of houses, kilns, smoke, wharfs, canals, and river, lying (as was most appropriate) in a basin —and how, after climbing up the sides of the basin to look at the prospect, you trundled down again at a walking-match pace, and straight proceeded to my father's, Copeland's, where the whole of my family, high and low, rich and poor, are turned out upon the world from our nursery and seminary, covering some fourteen acres of ground? And don't you remember what we spring from:—heaps of lumps of clay, partially prepared and cleaned in Devonshire and Dorsetshire, whence said clay principally comes—and hills of flint, without which we should want our ringing sound, and should never be musical? And as to the flint, don't you recollect that it is first burnt in kilns, and is then laid under the four iron feet of a demon slave, subject to violent stamping fits, who, when they come on, stamps away insanely with his four iron legs, and would crush all the flint in the Isle of Thanet to powder, without leaving off? And as to the clay, don't you recollect how it is put into mills or teazers, and is sliced, and dug, and cut at, by endless knives, clogged and sticky, but persistent—and is pressed out of that machine through a square trough, whose form it takes—and is cut off in square lumps and thrown into a vat, and there mixed with water, and beaten to a pulp by paddle-wheels—and is then run into a rough house, all rugged beams and ladders splashed with white,—superintended by Grindoff the Miller in his working clothes, all splashed with white,—where it passes through no end of machinery-moved sieves all splashed with white, arranged in an ascending scale of fineness (some so fine, that three hundred silk threads cross each other in a single square inch of their surface), and all in a violent state of ague with their teeth for ever chattering, and their bodies for ever shivering! And as to the flint again, isn't it mashed and mollified and troubled and soothed, exactly as rags are in a paper-mill, until it is reduced to a pap so fine that it contains no atom of "grit" perceptible to the nicest taste? And as to the flint and the clay together, are they not, after all this, mixed in the proportion of five of clay to one of flint, and isn't the compound—known as "slip"—run into oblong troughs, where its superfluous moisture may evaporate; and finally, isn't it slapped and banged and beaten and patted and kneaded and wedged and knocked about like butter, until it becomes a beautiful grey dough, ready for the potter's use?

In regard of the potter, popularly so called (says the plate), you don't mean to say you have forgotten that a workman called a Thrower is the man under whose hand this grey dough takes the shapes of the simpler household vessels as quickly as the eye can follow? You don't mean to say you cannot call him up before you, sitting, with his attendant woman, at his potter's wheel—a disc about the size of a dinner-plate, revolving on two drums slowly or quickly as he wills—who made you a complete breakfast-set for a bachelor, as a good-humoured little off-hand joke. You remember how he took up as much dough as he wanted, and, throwing it on his wheel, in a moment fashioned it into a teacup—caught up more clay and made a saucer—a larger dab and whirled it into a teapot—winked at a smaller dab and converted it into the lid of the teapot, accurately fitting by the measurement of his eye alone—coaxed a middle-sized dab for two seconds, broke it, turned it over at the rim, and made a milkpot—laughed, and turned out a slop-basin—coughed, and provided for the sugar? Neither, I think, are you oblivious of the newer mode of making various articles, but especially basins, according to which improvement a mould revolves instead of a disc? For you *must* remember (says the plate) how you saw the mould of a little basin spinning round and round, and how the workman smoothed and pressed a handful of dough upon it, and how with an instrument called a profile (a piece of wood, representing the profile of a basin's foot) he cleverly scraped and carved the ring which makes the base of any such basin, and then took the basin off the lathe like a doughy skull-cap to be dried, and afterwards (in what is called a green state) to be put into a second lathe, there to be finished and burnished with a steel burnisher? And as to moulding in general (says the plate), it can't be necessary for me to remind you that all ornamental articles, and indeed all articles not quite circular, are made in moulds. For you must remember how you saw the vegetable dishes, for example, being made in moulds; and how the handles of teacups, and the spouts of teapots, and the feet of tureens, and so forth, are all made in little separate moulds, and are each stuck on to the body corporate, of which it is destined to form a part, with a stuff called "slag," as quickly as you can recollect it. Further, you learnt—you know you did—in the same visit, how the beautiful sculptures in the delicate new material called Parian, are all constructed in moulds; how, into that material, animal bones are ground up, because the phosphate of lime contained in bones makes it translucent; how everything is moulded, before going into the fire, one-fourth larger than it is intended to come out of the fire, because it shrinks in that proportion in the intense heat; how, when a figure shrinks unequally, it is spoiled—emerging from the furnace a mis-shapen birth; a big head and a little body, or a little head and a big body, or a Quasimodo with long arms and short legs, or a Miss Biffin with neither legs nor arms worth mentioning.

G 3

And as to the kilns, in which the firing takes place, and in which some of the more precious articles are burnt repeatedly, in various stages of their process towards completion,—as to the kilns (says the plate, warming with the recollection), if you don't remember THEM with a horrible interest, what did you ever go to Copeland's for? When you stood inside of one of those inverted bowls of a pre-Adamite tobacco-pipe, looking up at the blue sky through the open top far off, as you might have looked up from a well, sunk under the centre of the pavement of the Pantheon at Rome, had you the least idea where you were? And when you found yourself surrounded, in that dome-shaped cavern, by innumerable columns of an unearthly order of architecture, supporting nothing, and squeezed close together as if a pre-Adamite Samson had taken a vast Hall in his arms and crushed it into the smallest possible space, had you the least idea what they were? No (says the plate), of course not! And when you found that each of those pillars was a pile of ingeniously made vessels of coarse clay—called Saggers—looking, when separate, like raised-pies for the table of the mighty Giant Blunderbore, and now all full of various articles of pottery ranged in them in baking order, the bottom of each vessel serving for the cover of the one below, and the whole kiln rapidly filling with these, tier upon tier, until the last workman should have barely room to crawl out, before the closing of the jagged aperture in the wall and the kindling of the gradual fire; did you not stand amazed to think that all the year round these dread chambers are heating, white hot—and cooling—and filling—and emptying—and being bricked up —and broken open—humanly speaking, for ever and ever? To be sure you did! And standing in one of those kilns nearly full, and seeing a free crow shoot across the aperture a-top, and learning how the fire would wax hotter and hotter by slow degrees, and would cool similarly through a space of from forty to sixty hours, did no remembrance of the days when human clay was burnt oppress you? Yes. I think so! I suspect that some fancy of a fiery haze and a shortening breath, and a growing heat, and a gasping prayer; and a figure in black interposing between you and the sky (as figures in black are very apt to do), and looking down, before it grew too hot to look and live, upon the Heretic in his edifying agony—I say I suspect (says the plate) that some such fancy was pretty strong upon you when you went out into the air, and blessed God for the bright spring day and the degenerate times!

After that, I needn't remind you what a relief it was to see the simplest process of ornamenting this "biscuit" (as it is called when baked) with brown circles and blue trees—converting it into the common crockery-ware that is exported to Africa, and used in cottages at home. For (says the plate) I am well persuaded that you bear in mind how those particular jugs and mugs were once more set upon a lathe and put in motion; and how a man blew the brown colour (having a strong natural affinity with the material in that condition) on them from a blowpipe as they twirled; and how his daughter, with a common brush, dropped blotches of blue upon them in the right places; and how, tilting the blotches upside down, she made them run into rude images of trees, and there an end.

And didn't you see (says the plate) planted upon my own brother that astounding blue willow, with knobbed and gnarled trunk, and foliage of blue ostrich feathers, which gives our family the title of "willow pattern"? And didn't you observe, transferred upon him at the same time, that blue bridge which spans nothing, growing out from the roots of the willow; and the three blue Chinese going over it into a blue temple, which has a fine crop of blue bushes sprouting out of the roof; and a blue boat sailing above them, the mast of which is burglariously sticking itself into the foundations of a blue villa, suspended sky-high, surmounted by a lump of blue rock, sky-higher, and a couple of billing blue birds, sky-highest—together with the rest of that amusing blue landscape, which has, in deference to our revered ancestors of the Cerulean Empire, and in defiance of every known law of perspective, adorned millions of our family ever since the days of platters? Didn't you inspect the copper-plate on which my pattern was deeply engraved? Didn't you perceive an impression of it taken in cobalt colour at a cylindrical press, upon a leaf of thin paper, streaming from a plunge-bath of soap and water? Wasn't the paper impression daintily spread, by a light-fingered damsel (you *know* you admired her!), over the surface of the plate, and the back of the paper rubbed prodigiously hard—with a long tight roll of flannel, tied up like a round of hung beef—without so much as ruffling the paper, wet as it was? Then (says the plate), was not the paper washed away with

OUR HONOURABLE FRIEND

WE are delighted to find that he has got in! Our honourable friend is triumphantly returned to serve in the next
Parliament. He is the honourable member for Verbosity—
the best represented place in England.

Our honourable friend has issued an address of congratulation to the Electors, which is worthy of that noble con-
stituency, and is a very pretty piece of composition. In
electing him, he says, they have covered themselves with
glory, and England has been true to herself. (In his preliminary address he had remarked, in a poetical quotation
of great rarity, that nought could make us rue, if England to
herself did prove but true.)

Our honourable friend delivers a prediction, in the same
document, that the feeble minions of a faction will never
hold up their heads any more ; and that the finger of scorn
will point at them in their dejected state, through countless
ages of time. Further, that the hireling tools that would
destroy the sacred bulwarks of our nationality are unworthy
of the name of Englishman ; and that so long as the sea
shall roll around our ocean-girded isle, so long his motto
shall be, No surrender. Certain dogged persons of low
principles and no intellect, have disputed whether anybody
knows who the minions are, or what the faction is, or which
are the hireling tools and which the sacred bulwarks, or what
it is that is never to be surrendered, and if not, why not ?
But, our honourable friend the member for Verbosity knows
all about it.

Our honourable friend has sat in several parliaments, and
given bushels of votes. He is a man of that profundity in
the matter of vote-giving, that you never know what he
means. When he seems to be voting pure white, he may
be in reality voting jet black. When he says Yes, it is just
as likely as not—or rather more so—that he means No.
This is the statesmanship of our honourable friend. It is in

this that he differs from mere unparliamentary men. *You* may not know what he meant then, or what he means now; but our honourable friend knows, and did from the first know, both what he meant then, and what he means now; and when he said he didn't mean it then, he did in fact say that he means it now. And if you mean to say that you did not then, and do not now, know what he did mean then, or does mean now, our honourable friend will be glad to receive an explicit declaration from you whether you are prepared to destroy the sacred bulwarks of our nationality.

Our honourable friend, the member for Verbosity, has this great attribute, that he always means something, and always means the same thing. When he came down to that House and mournfully boasted in his place, as an individual member of the assembled Commons of this great and happy country, that he could lay his hand upon his heart, and solemnly declare that no consideration on earth should induce him, at any time or under any circumstances, to go as far north as Berwick-upon-Tweed; and when he nevertheless, next year, did go to Berwick-upon-Tweed, and even beyond it, to Edinburgh, he had one single meaning, one and indivisible. And God forbid (our honourable friend says) that he should waste another argument upon the man who professes that he cannot understand it! "I do NOT, gentlemen," said our honourable friend, with indignant emphasis and amid great cheering, on one such public occasion. "I do NOT, gentlemen, I am free to confess, envy the feelings of that man whose mind is so constituted as that he can hold such language to me, and yet lay his head upon his pillow, claiming to be a native of that land,

> Whose march is o'er the mountain-wave,
> Whose home is on the deep!"

(Vehement cheering, and man expelled.)

When our honourable friend issued his preliminary address to the constituent body of Verbosity on the occasion of one particular glorious triumph, it was supposed by some of his enemies that even he would be placed in a situation of difficulty by the following comparatively trifling conjunction of circumstances. The dozen noblemen and gentlemen whom our honourable friend supported had "come in" expressly to do a certain thing. Now, four of the dozen said, at a certain place, that they didn't mean to do that thing, and had never meant to do it; another four of the dozen said, at another certain place, that they did mean to do that thing, and had always meant to do it; two of the remaining four said, at two other certain places, that they meant to do half of that thing (but differed about which half), and to do a variety of nameless wonders instead of the other half; and one of the remaining two declared that the thing itself was dead and buried, while the other as strenuously protested that it was alive and kicking. It was admitted that the parliamentary genius of our honourable friend would be quite able to reconcile such small discrepancies as these; but there remained the additional difficulty that each of the twelve made entirely different statements at different places, and that all the twelve called everything visible and invisible, sacred and profane, to witness that they were a perfectly impregnable phalanx of unanimity. This, it was apprehended, would be a stumbling-block to our honourable friend.

The difficulty came before our honourable friend in this way. He went down to Verbosity to meet his free and independent constituents, and to render an account (as he informed them in the local papers) of the trust they had confided to his hands—that trust which it was one of the proudest privileges of an Englishman to possess—that trust which it was the proudest privilege of an Englishman to hold. It may be mentioned as a proof of the great general interest attaching to the contest, that a Lunatic whom nobody employed or knew, went down to Verbosity with several thousand pounds in gold, determined to give the whole away —which he actually did; and that all the publicans opened their houses for nothing. Likewise, several fighting men, and a patriotic group of burglars sportively armed with life-preservers, proceeded (in barouches and very drunk) to the scene of action at their own expense; these children of nature having conceived a warm attachment to our honourable friend, and intending, in their artless manner, to testify it by knocking the voters in the opposite interest on the head.

Our honourable friend being come into the presence of his constituents, and having professed with great suavity that he was delighted to see his good friend Tipkisson there, in his working-dress—his good friend Tipkisson being an inveterate saddler, who always opposes him, and for whom he has a mortal hatred—made them a brisk, ginger-beery sort of speech, in which he showed them how the dozen noblemen and gentlemen had (in exactly ten days from their coming in) exercised a surprisingly beneficial effect on the whole financial condition of Europe, had altered the state of the exports and imports for the current half-year, had prevented the drain of gold, had made all that matter right about the glut of the raw material, and had restored all sorts of balances with which the superseded noblemen and gentlemen had played the deuce—and all this, with wheat at so much a quarter, gold at so much an ounce, and the Bank of England discounting good bills at so much per cent. ! He might be asked, he observed in a peroration of great power, what were his principles ? His principles were what they always had been. His principles were written in the countenances of the lion and unicorn ; were stamped indelibly upon the royal shield which those grand animals supported, and upon the free words of fire which that shield bore. His principles were, Britannia and her sea-king trident ! His principles were, commercial prosperity coexistently with perfect and profound agricultural contentment ; but short of this he would never stop. His principles were these,—with the addition of his colours nailed to the mast, every man's heart in the right place, every man's eye open, every man's hand ready, every man's mind on the alert. His principles were these, concurrently with a general revision of something—speaking generally—and a possible readjustment of something else, not to be mentioned more particularly. His principles, to sum up all in a word, were, Hearths and Altars, Labour and Capital, Crown and Sceptre, Elephant and Castle. And now, if his good friend Tipkisson required any further explanation from him, he (our honourable friend) was there, willing and ready to give it.

Tipkisson, who all this time had stood conspicuous in the crowd, with his arms folded and his eyes intently fastened on our honourable friend : Tipkisson, who throughout our honourable friend's address had not relaxed a muscle of his visage, but had stood there, wholly unaffected by the torrent of eloquence, an object of contempt and scorn to mankind (by which we mean, of course, to the supporters of our honourable friend) ; Tipkisson now said that he was a plain man (Cries of " You are indeed ! "), and that what he wanted to know was, what our honourable friend and the dozen noblemen and gentlemen were driving at?

Our honourable friend immediately replied, "At the illimitable perspective."

It was considered by the whole assembly that this happy statement of our honourable friend's political views ought, immediately, to have settled Tipkisson's business and covered him with confusion; but that implacable person, regardless of the execrations that were heaped upon him from all sides (by which we mean, of course, from our honourable friend's side), persisted in retaining an unmoved countenance, and obstinately retorted that if our honourable friend meant that, he wished to know what *that* meant?

It was in repelling this most objectionable and indecent opposition that our honourable friend displayed his highest qualifications for the representation of Verbosity. His warmest supporters present, and those who were best acquainted with his generalship, supposed that the moment was come when he would fall back upon the sacred bulwarks of our nationality. No such thing. He replied thus: "My good friend Tipkisson, gentlemen, wishes to know what I mean when he asks me what we are driving at, and when I candidly tell him, at the illimitable perspective, he wishes (if I understand him) to know what I mean?" "I do!" says Tipkisson, amid cries of "Shame" and "Down with him." "Gentlemen," says our honourable friend, "I will indulge my good friend Tipkisson by telling him both what I mean and what I don't mean. (Cheers and cries of "Give it him!") Be it known to him then, and to all whom it may concern, that I do mean altars, hearths, and homes, and that I don't mean mosques and Mohammedanism!" The effect of this home-thrust was terrific. Tipkisson (who is a Baptist) was hooted down and hustled out, and has ever since been regarded as a Turkish Renegade who contemplates an early pilgrimage to Mecca. Nor was he the only discomfited man. The charge, while it stuck to him, was magically transferred to our honourable friend's opponent, who was represented in an immense variety of placards as a firm believer in Mahomet; and the men of Verbosity were asked to choose between our honourable friend and the Bible, and our honourable friend's opponent and the Koran. They decided for our honourable friend, and rallied round the illimitable perspective.

It has been claimed for our honourable friend, with much appearance of reason, that he was the first to bend sacred matters to electioneering tactics. However this may be, the fine precedent was undoubtedly set in a Verbosity election : and it is certain that our honourable friend (who was a disciple of Brahma in his youth, and was a Buddhist when we had the honour of travelling with him a few years ago) always professes in public more anxiety than the whole Bench of Bishops, regarding the theological and doxological opinions of every man, woman, and child in the United Kingdom.

As we began by saying that our honourable friend has got in again at this last election, and that we are delighted to find that he has got in, so we will conclude. Our honourable friend cannot come in for Verbosity too often. It is a good sign ; it is a great example. It is to men like our honourable friend, and to contests like those from which he comes triumphant, that we are mainly indebted for that ready interest in politics, that fresh enthusiasm in the discharge of the duties of citizenship, that ardent desire to rush to the poll, at present so manifest throughout England. When the contest lies (as it sometimes does) between two such men as our honourable friend, it stimulates the finest emotions of our nature, and awakens the highest admiration of which our heads and hearts are capable.

It is not too much to predict that our honourable friend will be always at his post in the ensuing session. Whatever the question be, or whatever the form of its discussion ; address to the crown, election petition, expenditure of the public money, extension of the public suffrage, education, crime ; in the whole house, in committee of the whole house, in select committee ; in every parliamentary discussion of every subject, everywhere : the Honourable Member for Verbosity will most certainly be found.

OUR SCHOOL

WE went to look at it, only this last Midsummer, and found that the Railway had cut it up root and branch. A great trunk-line had swallowed the playground, sliced away the schoolroom, and pared off the corner of the house: which, thus curtailed of its proportions, presented itself, in a green stage of stucco, profilewise towards the road, like a forlorn flat-iron without a handle, standing on end.

It seems as if our schools were doomed to be the sport of change. We have faint recollections of a Preparatory Day-School, which we have sought in vain, and which must have been pulled down to make a new street, ages ago. We have dim impressions, scarcely amounting to a belief, that it was over a dyer's shop. We know that you went up steps to it; that you frequently grazed your knees in doing so; that you generally got your leg over the scraper, in trying to scrape the mud off a very unsteady little shoe. The mistress of the Establishment holds no place in our memory; but rampant on one eternal door-mat, in an eternal entry long and narrow, is a puffy pug-dog, with a personal animosity towards us, who triumphs over Time. The bark of that baleful Pug, a certain radiating way he had of snapping at our undefended legs, the ghastly grinning of his moist black muzzle and white teeth, and the insolence of his crisp tail curled like a pastoral crook, all live and flourish. From an otherwise unaccountable association of him with a fiddle, we conclude that he was of French extraction, and his name *Fidèle*. He belonged to some female, chiefly inhabiting a back-parlour, whose life appears to us to have been consumed in sniffing, and in wearing a brown beaver bonnet. For her, he would sit up and balance cake upon his nose, and not eat it until twenty had been counted. To the best of our belief we were once called in to witness this performance; when, unable, even in his milder moments, to endure our presence, he instantly made at us, cake and all.

Why a something in mourning, called "Miss Frost," should still connect itself with our preparatory school, we are unable to say. We retain no impression of the beauty of Miss Frost—if she were beautiful; or of the mental fascinations of Miss Frost—if she were accomplished; yet her name and her black dress hold an enduring place in our remembrance. An equally impersonal boy, whose name has long since shaped itself unalterably into "Master Mawls," is not to be dislodged from our brain. Retaining no vindictive feeling towards Mawls—no feeling whatever, indeed— we infer that neither he nor we can have loved Miss Frost. Our first impression of Death and Burial is associated with this formless pair. We all three nestled awfully in a corner one wintry day, when the wind was blowing shrill, with Miss Frost's pinafore over our heads; and Miss Frost told us in a whisper about somebody being "screwed down." It is the only distinct recollection we preserve of these impalpable creatures, except a suspicion that the manners of Master Mawls were susceptible of much improvement. Generally speaking, we may observe that whenever we see a child intently occupied with its nose, to the exclusion of all other subjects of interest, our mind reverts, in a flash, to Master Mawls.

But the School that was Our School before the Railroad came and overthrew it, was quite another sort of place. We were old enough to be put into Virgil when we went there, and to get Prizes for a variety of polishing on which the rust has long accumulated. It was a School of some celebrity in its neighbourhood—nobody could have said why —and we had the honour to attain and hold the eminent position of first boy. The master was supposed among us to know nothing, and one of the ushers was supposed to know everything. We are still inclined to think the first-named supposition perfectly correct.

We have a general idea that its subject had been in the leather trade, and had bought us—meaning Our School— of another proprietor who was immensely learned. Whether this belief had any real foundation, we are not likely ever to know now. The only branches of education with which he showed the least acquaintance, were, ruling and corporally punishing. He was always ruling ciphering-books with a bloated mahogany ruler, or smiting the palms of offenders with the same diabolical instrument, or viciously drawing a pair of pantaloons tight with one of his large hands, and caning the wearer with the other. We have no doubt whatever that this occupation was the principal solace of his existence.

A profound respect for money pervaded Our School, which was, of course, derived from its Chief. We remember an idiotic goggle-eyed boy, with a big head and half-crowns without end, who suddenly appeared as a parlour-boarder, and was rumoured to have come by sea from some mysterious part of the earth where his parents rolled in gold. He was usually called "Mr." by the Chief, and was said to feed in the parlour on steaks and gravy; likewise to drink currant wine. And he openly stated that if rolls and coffee were ever denied him at breakfast, he would write home to that unknown part of the globe from which he had come, and cause himself to be recalled to the regions of gold. He was put into no form or class, but learnt alone, as little as he liked—and he liked very little—and there was a belief among us that this was because he was too wealthy to be "taken down." His special treatment, and our vague association of him with the sea, and with storms, and sharks, and Coral Reefs occasioned the wildest legends to be circulated as his history. A tragedy in blank verse was written on the subject—if our memory does not deceive us, by the hand that now chronicles these recollections—in which his father figured as Pirate, and was shot for a voluminous catalogue of atrocities: first imparting to his wife the secret of the cave in which his wealth was stored, and from which his only son's half-crowns now issued. Dumbledon (the boy's name) was represented as "yet unborn" when his brave father met his fate; and the despair and grief of Mrs. Dumbledon at that calamity was movingly shadowed forth as having weakened the parlour-boarder's mind. This production was received with great favour, and was twice performed with closed doors in the dining-room. But it got wind, and was seized as libellous, and brought the unlucky poet into severe affliction. Some two years afterwards, all of a sudden one day, Dumbledon vanished. It was whispered that the Chief himself had taken him down to the Docks, and re-shipped him for the Spanish Main; but nothing certain was ever known about his disappearance. At this hour, we cannot thoroughly disconnect him from California.

Our School was rather famous for mysterious pupils. There was another—a heavy young man, with a large double-cased silver watch, and a fat knife the handle of which was a perfect tool-box—who unaccountably appeared one day at a special desk of his own, erected close to that of the Chief, with whom he held familiar converse. He lived in the parlour, and went out for his walks, and never took the least notice of us—even of us, the first boy—unless to give us a deprecatory kick, or grimly to take our hat off and throw it away, when he encountered us out of doors, which unpleasant ceremony he always performed as he passed—not even condescending to stop for the purpose. Some of us believed that the classical attainments of this phenomenon were terrific, but that his penmanship and arithmetic were defective, and he had come there to mend them; others, that he was going to set up a school, and had paid the Chief "twenty-five pound down," for leave to see Our School at work. The gloomier spirits even said that he was going to buy us; against which contingency, conspiracies were set on foot for a general defection and running away. However, he never did that. After staying for a quarter, during which period, though closely observed, he was never seen to do anything but make pens out of quills, write small hand in a secret portfolio, and punch the point of the sharpest blade in his knife into his desk all over it, he too disappeared, and his place knew him no more.

There was another boy, a fair, meek boy, with a delicate complexion and rich curling hair, who, we found out, or thought we found out (we have no idea now, and probably had none then, on what grounds, but it was confidentially revealed from mouth to mouth), was the son of a Viscount who had deserted his lovely mother. It was understood that if he had his rights, he would be worth twenty thousand a year. And that if his mother ever met his father, she would shoot him with a silver pistol, which she carried, always loaded to the muzzle, for that purpose. He was a very suggestive topic. So was a young Mulatto, who was always believed (though very amiable) to have a dagger about him somewhere. But we think they were both outshone, upon the whole, by another boy who claimed to have been born on the twenty-ninth of February, and to have only one birthday in five years. We suspect this to have been a fiction—but he lived upon it all the time he was at Our School.

The principal currency of Our School was slate pencil. It had some inexplicable value, that was never ascertained, never reduced to a standard. To have a great hoard of it was somehow to be rich. We used to bestow it in charity, and confer it as a precious boon upon our chosen friends. When the holidays were coming, contributions were solicited for certain boys whose relatives were in India, and who were appealed for under the generic name of "Holiday-stoppers,"—appropriate marks of remembrance that should enliven and cheer them in their homeless state. Personally, we always contributed these tokens of sympathy in the form of slate pencil, and always felt that it would be a comfort and a treasure to them.

Our School was remarkable for white mice. Red-polls, linnets, and even canaries, were kept in desks, drawers, hat-boxes, and other strange refuges for birds; but white mice were the favourite stock. The boys trained the mice much better than the masters trained the boys. We recall one white mouse, who lived in the cover of a Latin dictionary, who ran up ladders, drew Roman chariots, shouldered muskets, turned wheels, and even made a very creditable appearance on the stage as the Dog of Montargis. He might have achieved greater things, but for having the misfortune to mistake his way in a triumphal procession to the Capitol, when he fell into a deep inkstand, and was dyed black and drowned. The mice were the occasion of some most ingenious engineering, in the construction of their houses and instruments of performance. The famous one belonged to a company of proprietors, some of whom have since made Railroads, Engines, and Telegraphs; the chairman has erected mills and bridges in New Zealand.

The usher at Our School, who was considered to know everything as opposed to the Chief, who was considered to know nothing, was a bony, gentle-faced, clerical-looking young man in rusty black. It was whispered that he was sweet upon one of Maxby's sisters (Maxby lived close by, and was a day pupil), and further that he "favoured Maxby." As we remember, he taught Italian to Maxby's sisters on half-holidays. He once went to the play with them, and wore a white waistcoat and a rose: which was considered among us equivalent to a declaration. We were of opinion on that occasion, that to the last moment he expected Maxby's father to ask him to dinner at five o'clock, and therefore neglected his own dinner at half-past one, and finally got none. We exaggerated in our imaginations the extent to which he punished Maxby's father's cold meat at supper; and we agreed to believe that he was elevated with wine and water when he came home. But we all liked him; for he had a good knowledge of boys, and would have made it a much better school if he had had more power. He was writing master, mathematical master, English master, made out the bills, mended the pens, and did all sorts of things. He divided the little boys with the Latin master (they were smuggled through their rudimentary books, at odd times when there was nothing else to do), and he always called at parents' houses to inquire after sick boys, because he had gentlemanly manners. He was rather musical, and on some remote quarter-day had bought an old trombone; but a bit of it was lost, and it made the most extraordinary sounds when he sometimes tried to play it of an evening. His holidays never began (on account of the bills) until long after ours; but in the summer vacations he used to take pedestrian excursions with a knapsack; and at Christmas time he went to see his father at Chipping Norton, who we all said (on no authority) was a dairy-fed pork-butcher. Poor fellow! He was very low all day on Maxby's sister's wedding-day, and afterwards was thought to favour Maxby more than ever, though he had been expected to spite him. He has been dead these twenty years. Poor fellow!

Our remembrance of Our Schools presents the Latin master as a colourless doubled-up near-sighted man with a crutch, who was always cold, and always putting onions into his ears for deafness, and always disclosing ends of flannel under all his garments, and almost always applying a ball of pocket-handkerchief to some part of his face with a screwing action round and round. He was a very good scholar, and took great pains where he saw intelligence and a desire to learn: otherwise, perhaps not. Our memory presents him (unless teased into a passion) with as little energy as colour—as having been worried and tormented into monotonous feebleness—as having had the best part of his life ground out of him in a Mill of boys. We remember with terror how he fell asleep one sultry afternoon

with the little smuggled class before him, and awoke not
when the footstep of the Chief fell heavy on the floor; how
the Chief aroused him, in the midst of a dread silence, and
said, "Mr. Blinkins, are you ill, sir?" how he blushingly
replied, "Sir, rather so;" how the Chief retorted with
severity, "Mr. Blinkins, this is no place to be ill in" (which
was very, very true), and walked back solemn as the ghost
in Hamlet, until, catching a wandering eye, he caned that
boy for inattention, and happily expressed his feelings
towards the Latin master through the medium of a
substitute.

There was a fat little dancing-master who used to come in
a gig, and taught the more advanced among us hornpipes
(as an accomplishment in great social demand in after life);
and there was a brisk little French master who used to come
in the sunniest weather, with a handleless umbrella, and to
whom the Chief was always polite, because (as we believed),
if the Chief offended him, he would instantly address the
Chief in French, and for ever confound him before the boys
with his inability to understand or reply.

There was, besides, a serving man whose name was Phil.
Our retrospective glance presents Phil as a shipwrecked
carpenter, cast away upon the desert island of a school, and
carrying into practice an ingenious inkling of many trades.
He mended whatever was broken, and made whatever was
wanted.   He was general glazier, among other things, and
mended all the broken windows—at the prime cost (as was
darkly rumoured among us) of ninepence, for every square
charged three-and-six to parents.   We had a high opinion
of his mechanical genius, and generally held that the Chief
"knew something bad of him," and on pain of divulgence
enforced Phil to be his bondsman.   We particularly remember that Phil had a sovereign contempt for learning:
which engenders in us a respect for his sagacity, as it implies
his accurate observation of the relative positions of the Chief
and the ushers.   He was an impenetrable man, who waited
at table between whiles, and throughout "the half" kept
the boxes in severe custody.   He was morose, even to the
Chief, and never smiled, except at breaking-up, when, in
acknowledgment of the toast, "Success to Phil! Hooray!"
he would slowly carve a grin out of his wooden face, where
it would remain until we were all gone.   Nevertheless, one
time when we had the scarlet fever in the school, Phil

nursed all the sick boys of his own accord, and was like a mother to them.

There was another school not far off, and of course Our School could have nothing to say to that school. It is mostly the way with schools, whether of boys or men. Well! the railway has swallowed up ours, and the locomotives now run smoothly over its ashes.

> So fades and languishes, grows dim and dies,
> All that this world is proud of,

—and is not proud of, too. It had little reason to be proud of Our School, and has done much better since in that way, and will do far better yet.

OUR VESTRY

WE have the glorious privilege of being always in hot water if we like. We are a shareholder in a Great Parochial British Joint Stock Bank of Balderdash. We have a Vestry in our borough, and can vote for a vestryman—might even *be* a vestryman, mayhap, if we were inspired by a lofty and noble ambition. Which we are not.

Our Vestry is a deliberative assembly of the utmost dignity and importance. Like the Senate of ancient Rome, its awful gravity overpowers (or ought to overpower) barbarian visitors. It sits in the Capitol (we mean in the capital building erected for it), chiefly on Saturdays, and shakes the earth to its centre with the echoes of its thundering eloquence, in a Sunday paper.

To get into this Vestry in the eminent capacity of Vestryman, gigantic efforts are made, and Herculean exertions used. It is made manifest to the dullest capacity at every election, that if we reject Snozzle we are done for, and that if we fail to bring in Blunderbooze at the top of the poll, we are unworthy of the dearest rights of Britons. Flaming placards are rife on all the dead walls in the borough, public-houses hang out banners, hackney-cabs burst into full-grown flowers of type, and everybody is, or should be, in a paroxysm of anxiety.

At these momentous crises of the national fate, we are much assisted in our deliberations by two eminent volunteers; one of whom subscribes himself A Fellow Parishioner, the other, A Rate-Payer. Who they are, or what they are, or where they are, nobody knows; but whatever one asserts, the other contradicts. They are both voluminous writers, indicting more epistles than Lord Chesterfield in a single week; and the greater part of their feelings are too big for utterance in anything less than capital letters. They require the additional aid of whole rows of notes of admiration, like balloons, to point their generous indignation; and they sometimes communicate a crushing severity to stars. As thus:

MEN OF MOONEYMOUNT.

Is it, or is it not, a * * * to saddle the parish with a debt of £2,745 6s. 9d., yet claim to be a RIGID ECONOMIST?

Is it, or is it not, a * * * to state as a fact what is proved to be *both a moral and a* PHYSICAL IMPOSSIBILITY?

Is it, or is it not, a * * * to call £2,745 6s. 9d. nothing; and nothing, something?

Do you, or do you *not* want a * * * TO REPRESENT YOU IN THE VESTRY?

Your consideration of these questions is recommended to you by

A FELLOW PARISHIONER.

It was to this important public document that one of our first orators, MR. MAGG (of Little Winkling Street), adverted, when he opened the great debate of the fourteenth of November by saying, "Sir, I hold in my hand an anonymous slander"—and when the interruption, with which he was at that point assailed by the opposite faction, gave rise to that memorable discussion on a point of order which will ever be remembered with interest by constitutional assemblies. In the animated debate to which we refer, no fewer than thirty-seven gentlemen, many of them of great eminence, including MR. WIGSBY (of Chumbledon Square), were seen upon their legs at one time; and it was on the same great occasion that DOGGINSON—regarded in our Vestry as "a regular John Bull:" we believe, in consequence of his having always made up his mind on every subject without knowing anything about it— informed another gentleman of similar principles on the opposite side, that if he "cheek'd him," he would resort to the extreme measure of knocking his blessed head off.

This was a great occasion. But our Vestry shines habitually. In asserting its own pre-eminence, for instance, it is very strong. On the least provocation, or on none, it will be clamorous to know whether it is to be "dictated to," or "trampled on," or "ridden over rough-shod." Its great watchword is Self-government. That is to say, supposing our Vestry to favour any little harmless disorder like Typhus Fever, and supposing the Government of the country to be, by any accident, in such ridiculous hands, as that any of its

authorities should consider it a duty to object to Typhus
Fever—obviously an unconstitutional objection—then, our
Vestry cuts in with a terrible manifesto about Self-government, and claims its independent right to have as much
Typhus Fever as pleases itself.   Some absurd and dangerous
persons have represented, on the other hand, that though
our Vestry may be able to "beat the bounds" of its own
parish, it may not be able to beat the bounds of its own
diseases; which (say they) spread over the whole land, in
an ever-expanding circle of waste, and misery, and death,
and widowhood, and orphanage, and desolation.   But our
Vestry makes short work of any such fellows as these.

It was our Vestry—pink of Vestries as it is—that in
support of its favourite principle took the celebrated ground
of denying the existence of the last pestilence that raged in
England, when the pestilence was raging at the Vestry doors.
Dogginson said it was plums; Mr. Wigsby (of Chumbledon
Square) said it was oysters; Mr. Magg (of Little Winkling
Street) said, amid great cheering, it was the newspapers.
The noble indignation of our Vestry with that un-English
institution the Board of Health, under those circumstances,
yields one of the finest passages in its history.   It wouldn't
hear of rescue.   Like Mr. Joseph Miller's Frenchman, it
would be drowned and nobody should save it.   Transported
beyond grammar by its kindled ire, it spoke in unknown
tongues, and vented unintelligible bellowings, more like an
ancient oracle than the modern oracle it is admitted on all
hands to be.   Rare exigencies produce rare things; and
even our Vestry, new hatched to the woful time, came forth
a greater goose than ever.

But this, again, was a special occasion.   Our Vestry, at
more ordinary periods, demands its meed of praise.

Our Vestry is eminently parliamentary.   Playing at Parliament is its favourite game.   It is even regarded by some of
its members as a chapel of ease to the House of Commons:
a Little Go to be passed first.   It has its strangers' gallery,
and its reported debates (see the Sunday paper before
mentioned), and our Vestrymen are in and out of order,
and on and off their legs, and above all are transcendantly
quarrelsome, after the pattern of the real original.

Our Vestry being assembled, Mr. Magg never begs to
trouble Mr. Wigsby with a simple inquiry.   He knows better
than that.   Seeing the honourable gentleman, associated in

their minds with Chumbledon Square, in his place, he wishes to ask that honourable gentleman what the intentions of himself, and those with whom he acts, may be, on the subject of the paving of the district known as Piggleum Buildings? Mr. Wigsby replies (with his eye on next Sunday's paper) that in reference to the question which has been put to him by the honourable gentleman opposite, he must take leave to say, that if that honourable gentleman had had the courtesy to give him notice of that question, he (Mr. Wigsby) would have consulted with his colleagues in reference to the advisability, in the present state of the discussions on the new paving-rate, of answering that question. But, as the honourable gentleman has NOT had the courtesy to give him notice of that question (great cheering from the Wigsby interest), he must decline to give the honourable gentleman the satisfaction he requires. Mr. Magg, instantly rising to retort, is received with loud cries of "Spoke!" from the Wigsby interest, and with cheers from the Magg side of the house. Moreover, five gentlemen rise to order, and one of them, in revenge for being taken no notice of, petrifies the assembly by moving that this Vestry do now adjourn; but is persuaded to withdraw that awful proposal, in consideration of its tremendous consequences if persevered in. Mr. Magg, for the purpose of being heard, then begs to move, that you, sir, do now pass to the order of the day; and takes that opportunity of saying, that if an honourable gentleman whom he has in his eye, and will not demean himself by more particularly naming (oh, oh, and cheers), supposes that he is to be put down by clamour, that honourable gentleman—however supported he may be, through thick and thin, by a Fellow Parishioner, with whom he is well acquainted (cheers and counter-cheers, Mr. Magg being invariably backed by the Rate-Payer)—will find himself mistaken. Upon this, twenty members of our Vestry speak in succession concerning what the two great men have meant, until it appears, after an hour and twenty minutes, that neither of them meant anything. Then our Vestry begins business.

We have said that, after the pattern of the real original, our Vestry in playing at Parliament is transcendantly quarrelsome. It enjoys a personal altercation above all things. Perhaps the most redoubtable case of this kind we have ever had—though we have had so many that it is difficult to decide—was that on which the last extreme solemnities passed between Mr. Tiddypot (of Gumption House) and Captain Banger (of Wilderness Walk).

In an adjourned debate on the question whether water could be regarded in the light of a necessary of life; respecting which there were great differences of opinion, and many shades of sentiment; Mr. Tiddypot, in a powerful burst of eloquence against that hypothesis, frequently made use of the expression that such and such a rumour had "reached his ears." Captain Banger, following him, and holding that, for purposes of ablution and refreshment, a pint of water per diem was necessary for every adult of the lower classes, and half a pint for every child, cast ridicule upon his address in a sparkling speech, and concluded by saying that instead of those rumours having reached the ears of the honourable gentleman, he rather thought the honourable gentleman's ears must have reached the rumours, in consequence of their well-known length. Mr. Tiddypot immediately rose, looked the honourable and gallant gentleman full in the face, and left the Vestry.

The excitement, at this moment painfully intense, was heightened to an acute degree when Captain Banger rose, and also left the Vestry. After a few moments of profound silence—one of those breathless pauses never to be forgotten—Mr. Chib (of Tucket's Terrace, and the father of the Vestry) rose. He said that words and looks had passed in that assembly, replete with consequences which every feeling mind must deplore. Time pressed. The sword was drawn, and while he spoke the scabbard might be thrown away. He moved that those honourable gentlemen who had left the Vestry be recalled, and required to pledge themselves upon their honour that this affair should go no farther. The motion being by a general union of parties unanimously agreed to (for everybody wanted to have the belligerents there, instead of out of sight: which was no fun at all), Mr. Magg was deputed to recover Captain Banger, and Mr. Chib himself to go in search of Mr. Tiddypot. The Captain was found in a conspicuous position, surveying the passing omnibuses from the top step of the front-door immediately adjoining the beadle's box; Mr. Tiddypot made a desperate attempt at resistance, but was overpowered by Mr. Chib (a remarkably hale old gentleman of eighty-two), and brought back in safety.

Mr. Tiddypot and the Captain being restored to their

places, and glaring on each other, were called upon by the chair to abandon all homicidal intentions, and give the Vestry an assurance that they did so. Mr. Tiddypot remained profoundly silent. The Captain likewise remained profoundly silent, saving that he was observed by those around him to fold his arms like Napoleon Buonaparte, and to snort in his breathing—actions but too expressive of gunpowder.

The most intense emotion now prevailed. Several members clustered in remonstrance round the Captain, and several round Mr. Tiddypot; but both were obdurate. Mr. Chib then presented himself amid tremendous cheering, and said, that not to shrink from the discharge of his painful duty, he must now move that both honourable gentlemen be taken into custody by the beadle, and conveyed to the nearest police-office, there to be held to bail. The union of parties still continuing, the motion was seconded by Mr. Wigsby—on all usual occasions Mr. Chib's opponent—and rapturously carried with only one dissentient voice. This was Dogginson's, who said from his place "Let 'em fight it out with fistes;" but whose coarse remark was received as it merited.

The beadle now advanced along the floor of the Vestry, and beckoned with his cocked hat to both members. Every breath was suspended. To say that a pin might have been heard to fall, would be feebly to express the all-absorbing interest and silence. Suddenly, enthusiastic cheering broke out from every side of the Vestry. Captain Banger had risen—being, in fact, pulled up by a friend on either side, and poked up by a friend behind.

The Captain said, in a deep determined voice, that he had every respect for that Vestry and every respect for that chair; that he also respected the honourable gentleman of Gumption House; but that he respected his honour more. Hereupon the Captain sat down, leaving the whole Vestry much affected. Mr. Tiddypot instantly rose, and was received with the same encouragement. He likewise said—and the exquisite art of this orator communicated to the observation an air of freshness and novelty—that he too had every respect for that Vestry; that he too had every respect for that chair. That he too respected the honourable and gallant gentleman of Wilderness Walk; but that he too respected his honour more. "Hows'ever," added the distinguished Vestryman, "if the honourable or gallant gentleman's honour is never

more doubted and damaged than it is by me, he's all right."
Captain Banger immediately started up again, and said that
after those observations, involving as they did ample concession to his honour without compromising the honour of
the honourable gentleman, he would be wanting in honour
as well as in generosity, if he did not at once repudiate all
intention of wounding the honour of the honourable gentleman, or saying anything dishonourable to his honourable
feelings. These observations were repeatedly interrupted by
bursts of cheers. Mr. Tiddypot retorted that he well knew
the spirit of honour by which the honourable and gallant
gentleman was so honourably animated, and that he accepted
an honourable explanation, offered in a way that did him
honour; but he trusted that the Vestry would consider that
his (Mr. Tiddypot's) honour had imperatively demanded of
him that painful course which he had felt it due to his
honour to adopt. The Captain and Mr. Tiddypot then
touched their hats to one another across the Vestry, a great
many times, and it is thought that these proceedings
(reported to the extent of several columns in next Sunday's
paper) will bring them in as churchwardens next year.

All this was strictly after the pattern of the real original,
and so are the whole of our Vestry's proceedings. In all
their debates, they are laudably imitative of the windy and
wordy slang of the real original, and of nothing that is better
in it. They have headstrong party animosities, without any
reference to the merits of questions; they tack a surprising
amount of debate to a very little business; they set more
store by forms than they do by substances:—all very like
the real original! It has been doubted in our borough,
whether our Vestry is of any utility; but our own conclusion
is, that it is of the use to the Borough that a diminishing
mirror is to a painter, as enabling it to perceive in a small
focus of absurdity all the surface defects of the real original.

OUR BORE

It is unnecessary to say that we keep a bore. Everybody does. But the bore whom we have the pleasure and honour of enumerating among our particular friends, is such a generic bore, and has so many traits (as it appears to us) in common with the great bore family, that we are tempted to make him the subject of the present notes. May he be generally accepted!

Our bore is admitted on all hands to be a good-hearted man. He may put fifty people out of temper, but he keeps his own. He preserves a sickly solid smile upon his face, when other faces are ruffled by the perfection he has attained in his art, and has an equable voice which never travels out of one key or rises above one pitch. His manner is a manner of tranquil interest. None of his opinions are startling. Among his deepest-rooted convictions, it may be mentioned that he considers the air of England damp, and holds that our lively neighbours—he always calls the French our lively neighbours—have the advantage of us in that particular. Nevertheless he is unable to forget that John Bull is John Bull all the world over, and that England with all her faults is England still.

Our bore has travelled. He could not possibly be a complete bore without having travelled. He rarely speaks of his travels without introducing, sometimes on his own plan of construction, morsels of the language of the country—which he always translates. You cannot name to him any little remote town in France, Italy, Germany, or Switzerland but he knows it well; stayed there a fortnight under peculiar circumstances. And talking of that little place, perhaps you know a statue over an old fountain, up a little court, which is the second—no, the third—stay—yes, the third turning on the right, after you come out of the Post-house, going up the hill towards the market? You *don't* know that statue? Nor that fountain? You surprise him! They are not usually seen by travellers (most extraordinary, he has never yet met with a single traveller who knew them, except one German, the most intelligent man he ever met in his life!) but he thought that you would have been the man to find them out. And then he describes them, in a circumstantial lecture half an hour long, generally delivered behind a door which is constantly being opened from the other side; and implores you, if you ever revisit that place, now do go and look at that statue and fountain!

Our bore, in a similar manner, being in Italy, made a discovery of a dreadful picture, which has been the terror of a large portion of the civilized world ever since. We have seen the liveliest men paralysed by it, across a broad dining-table. He was lounging among the mountains, sir, basking in the mellow influences of the climate, when he came to *una piccola chiesa*—a little church—or perhaps it would be more correct to say *una piccolissima cappella*—the smallest chapel you can possibly imagine—and walked in. There was nobody inside but a *cieco*—a blind man—saying his prayers, and a *vecchio padre*—old friar—rattling a money-box. But above the head of that friar, and immediately to the right of the altar as you enter—to the right of the altar? No. To the left of the altar as you enter—or say near the centre—there hung a painting (subject, Virgin and Child) so divine in its expression, so pure and yet so warm and rich in its tone, so fresh in its touch, at once so glowing in its colour and so statuesque in its repose, that our bore cried out in an ecstasy, "That's the finest picture in Italy!" And so it is, sir. There is no doubt of it. It is astonishing that that picture is so little known. Even the painter is uncertain. He afterwards took Blumb, of the Royal Academy (it is to be observed that our bore takes none but eminent people to see sights, and that none but eminent people take our bore), and you never saw a man so affected in your life as Blumb was. He cried like a child! And then our bore begins his description in detail—for all this is introductory—and strangles his hearers with the folds of the purple drapery.

By an equally fortunate conjunction of accidental circumstances, it happened that when our bore was in Switzerland, he discovered a Valley, of that superb character, that Chamouni is not to be mentioned in the same breath with it. This is how it was, sir. He was travelling on a mule—had been in the saddle some days—when, as he and the guide,

Pierre Blanquo : whom you may know, perhaps ?—our bore is sorry you don't, because he's the only guide deserving of the name—as he and Pierre were descending, towards evening, among those everlasting snows, to the little village of La Croix, our bore observed a mountain track turning off sharply to the right. At first he was uncertain whether it *was* a track at all, and in fact, he said to Pierre, " *Qu'est que c'est donc, mon ami ?*—What is that, my friend ? " " *Où, monsieur ?* " said Pierre—"Where, sir ? " " *Là !*—there ! " said our bore. " *Monsieur, ce n'est rien de tout*—sir, it's nothing at all," said Pierre. " *Allons !*—Make haste. *Il va neiger*—it's going to snow ! " But our bore was not to be done in that way, and he firmly replied, " I wish to go in that direction—*je veux y aller.* I am bent upon it—*je suis déterminé. En avant !*—go ahead ! " In consequence of which firmness on our bore's part, they proceeded, sir, during two hours of evening, and three of moonlight (they waited in a cavern till the moon was up), along the slenderest track, overhanging perpendicularly the most awful gulfs, until they arrived, by a winding descent, in a valley that possibly, and he may say probably, was never visited by any stranger before. What a valley ! Mountains piled on mountains, avalanches stemmed by pine forests ; waterfalls, châlets, mountain-torrents, wooden bridges, every conceivable picture of Swiss scenery ! The whole village turned out to receive our bore. The peasant girls kissed him, the men shook hands with him, one old lady of benevolent appearance wept upon his breast. He was conducted, in a primitive triumph, to the little inn : where he was taken ill next morning, and lay for six weeks, attended by the amiable hostess (the same benevolent old lady who had wept over night) and her charming daughter, Fanchette. It is nothing to say that they were attentive to him ; they doted on him. They called him in their simple way, *l'Ange Anglais*—the English Angel. When our bore left the valley, there was not a dry eye in the place ; some of the people attended him for miles. He begs and entreats of you as a personal favour, that if you ever go to Switzerland again (you have mentioned that your last visit was your twenty-third), you will go to that valley, and see Swiss scenery for the first time. And if you want really to know the pastoral people of Switzerland, and to understand them, mention, in that valley, our bore's name !

Our bore has a crushing brother in the East, who, some-how or other, was admitted to smoke pipes with Mehemet Ali, and instantly became an authority on the whole range of Eastern matters, from Haroun Alraschid to the present Sultan. He is in the habit of expressing mysterious opinions on this wide range of subjects, but on questions of foreign policy more particularly, to our bore, in letters ; and our bore is continually sending bits of these letters to the newspapers (which they never insert), and carrying other bits about in his pocket-book. It is even whispered that he has been seen at the Foreign Office, receiving great consideration from the messengers, and having his card promptly borne into the sanctuary of the temple. The havoc committed in society by this Eastern brother is beyond belief. Our bore is always ready with him. We have known our bore to fall upon an intelligent young sojourner in the wilderness, in the first sentence of a narrative, and beat all confidence out of him with one blow of his brother. He became omniscient, as to foreign policy, in the smoking of those pipes with Mehemet Ali. The balance of power in Europe, the machinations of the Jesuits, the gentle and humanising influence of Austria, the position and prospects of that hero of the noble soul who is worshipped by happy France, are all easy reading to our bore's brother. And our bore is so provokingly self-denying about him ! "I don't pretend to more than a very general knowledge of these subjects myself," says he, after enervating the intellects of several strong men, "but these are my brother's opinions, and I believe he is known to be well-informed."

The commonest incidents and places would appear to have been made special, expressly for our bore. Ask him whether he ever chanced to walk, between seven and eight in the morning, down St. James's Street, London, and he will tell you, never in his life but once. But it's curious that that once was in eighteen thirty ; and that as our bore was walking down the street you have just mentioned, at the hour you have just mentioned—half-past seven—or twenty minutes to eight. No ! Let him be correct !—exactly a quarter before eight by the palace clock—he met a fresh-coloured, grey-haired, good-humoured looking gentleman, with a brown umbrella, who, as he passed him, touched his hat and said, " Fine morning, sir, fine morning ! "—William the Fourth !

Ask our bore whether he has seen Mr. Barry's new Houses of Parliament, and he will reply that he has not yet inspected them minutely, but that you remind him that it was his singular fortune to be the last man to see the old Houses of Parliament before the fire broke out. It happened in this way. Poor John Spine, the celebrated novelist, had taken him over to South Lambeth to read to him the last few chapters of what was certainly his best book—as our bore told him at the time, adding, "Now, my dear John, touch it, and you'll spoil it!"—and our bore was going back to the club by way of Millbank and Parliament Street, when he stopped to think of Canning, and look at the Houses of Parliament. Now, you know far more of the philosophy of Mind than our bore does, and are much better able to explain to him than he is to explain to you why or wherefore, at that particular time, the thought of fire should come into his head. But it did. It did. He thought, What a national calamity if an edifice connected with so many associations should be consumed by fire! At that time there was not a single soul in the street but himself. All was quiet, dark, and solitary. After contemplating the building for a minute—or, say a minute and a half, not more—our bore proceeded on his way, mechanically repeating, What a national calamity if such an edifice, connected with such associations, should be destroyed by—— A man coming towards him in a violent state of agitation completed the sentence, with the exclamation, Fire! Our bore looked round, and the whole structure was in a blaze.

In harmony and union with these experiences, our bore never went anywhere in a steamboat but he made either the best or the worst voyage ever known on that station. Either he overheard the captain say to himself, with his hands clasped, "We are all lost!" or the captain openly declared to him that he had never made such a run before, and never should be able to do it again. Our bore was in that express train on that railway, when they made (unknown to the passengers) the experiment of going at the rate of a hundred miles an hour. Our bore remarked on that occasion to the other people in the carriage, "This is too fast, but sit still!" He was at the Norwich musical festival when the extraordinary echo for which science has been wholly unable to account, was heard for the first and last time. He and the bishop heard it at the same moment, and caught each other's eye. He was present at that illumination of St. Peter's, of which the Pope is known to have remarked, as he looked at it out of his window in the Vatican, "*O Cielo! Questa cosa non sara fatta, mai ancora, come questa*—O Heaven! this thing will never be done again, like this!" He has seen every lion he ever saw, under some remarkably propitious circumstances. He knows there is no fancy in it, because in every case the showman mentioned the fact at the time, and congratulated him upon it.

At one period of his life, our bore had an illness. It was an illness of a dangerous character for society at large. Innocently remark that you are very well, or that somebody else is very well; and our bore, with a preface that one never knows what a blessing health is until one has lost it, is reminded of that illness, and drags you through the whole of its symptoms, progress, and treatment. Innocently remark that you are not well, or that somebody else is not well, and the same inevitable result ensues. You will learn how our bore felt a tightness about here, sir, for which he couldn't account, accompanied with a constant sensation as if he were being stabbed—or, rather, jobbed—that expresses it more correctly—jobbed—with a blunt knife. Well, sir! This went on, until sparks began to flit before his eyes, water-wheels to turn round in his head, and hammers to beat incessantly thump, thump, thump, all down his back—along the whole of the spinal vertebræ. Our bore, when his sensations had come to this, thought it a duty he owed to himself to take advice, and he said, Now, whom shall I consult? He naturally thought of Callow, at that time one of the most eminent physicians in London, and he went to Callow. Callow said, "Liver!" and prescribed rhubarb and calomel, low diet, and moderate exercise. Our bore went on with this treatment, getting worse every day, until he lost confidence in Callow, and went to Moon, whom half the town was then mad about. Moon was interested in the case; to do him justice he was very much interested in the case; and he said, "Kidneys!" He altered the whole treatment, sir—gave strong acids, cupped, and blistered. This went on, our bore still getting worse every day, until he openly told Moon it would be a satisfaction to him if he would have a consultation with Clatter. The moment Clatter saw our bore, he said, "Accumulation of fat about the heart!" Snugglewood, who was called in with him, differed, and said, "Brain!" But what they all agreed upon was, to lay our bore upon his back, to shave his head, to leech him, to administer enormous quantities of medicine, and to keep him low; so that he was reduced to a mere shadow, you wouldn't have known him, and nobody considered it possible that he could ever recover. This was his condition, sir, when he heard of Jilkins—at that period in a very small practice, and living in the upper part of a house in Great Portland Street; but still, you understand, with a rising reputation among the few people to whom he was known. Being in that condition in which a drowning man catches at a straw, our bore sent for Jilkins. Jilkins came. Our bore liked his eye, and said, "Mr. Jilkins, I have a presentiment that you will do me good." Jilkins's reply was characteristic of the man. It was, "Sir, I mean to do you good." This confirmed our bore's opinion of his eye, and they went into the case together—went completely into it. Jilkins then got up, walked across the room, came back, and sat down. His words were these. "You have been humbugged. This is a case of indigestion, occasioned by deficiency of power in the Stomach. Take a mutton chop in half-an-hour, with a glass of the finest old sherry that can be got for money. Take two mutton chops to-morrow, and two glasses of the finest old sherry. Next day, I'll come again." In a week our bore was on his legs, and Jilkins's success dates from that period!

Our bore is great in secret information. He happens to know many things that nobody else knows. He can generally tell you where the split is in the Ministry; he knows a deal about the Queen; and has little anecdotes to relate of the royal nursery. He gives you the judge's private opinion of Sludge the murderer, and his thoughts when he tried him. He happens to know what such a man got by such a transaction, and it was fifteen thousand five hundred pounds, and his income is twelve thousand a year. Our bore is also great in mystery. He believes, with an exasperating appearance of profound meaning, that you saw Parkins last Sunday?—Yes, you did.—Did he say anything particular?—No, nothing particular.—Our bore is surprised at that.—Why?—Nothing. Only he understood that Parkins had come to tell you something.—What about?—Well! our bore is not at liberty to mention what about. But he believes you will hear that from Parkins himself,

soon, and he hopes it may not surprise you as it did him.
Perhaps, however, you never heard about Parkins's wife's
sister?—No.—Ah! says our bore, that explains it!

Our bore is also great in argument. He infinitely enjoys
a long humdrum, drowsy interchange of words of dispute
about nothing. He considers that it strengthens the mind,
consequently, he "don't see that," very often. Or, he would
be glad to know what you mean by that. Or, he doubts
that. Or, he has always understood exactly the reverse of
that. Or, he can't admit that. Or, he begs to deny that.
Or, surely you don't mean that. And so on. He once
advised us; offered us a piece of advice, after the fact,
totally impracticable and wholly impossible of acceptance,
because it supposed the fact, then eternally disposed of, to
be yet in abeyance. It was a dozen years ago, and to this
hour our bore benevolently wishes, in a mild voice, on
certain regular occasions, that we had thought better of his
opinion.

The instinct with which our bore finds out another bore,
and closes with him, is amazing. We have seen him pick
his man out of fifty men, in a couple of minutes. They
love to go (which they do naturally) into a slow argument
on a previously exhausted subject, and to contradict each
other, and to wear the hearers out, without impairing their
own perennial freshness as bores. It improves the good
understanding between them, and they get together afterwards, and bore each other amicably. Whenever we see
our bore behind a door with another bore, we know that
when he comes forth, he will praise the other bore as one
of the most intelligent men he ever met. And this bringing us to the close of what we had to say about our bore,
we are anxious to have it understood that he never bestowed this praise on us.

A MONUMENT OF FRENCH FOLLY

It was profoundly observed by a witty member of the Court of Common Council, in Council assembled in the City of London, in the year of our Lord one thousand eight hundred and fifty, that the French are a frog-eating people, who wear wooden shoes.

We are credibly informed, in reference to the nation whom this choice spirit so happily disposed of, that the caricatures and stage representations which were current in England some half a century ago, exactly depict their present condition. For example, we understand that every Frenchman, without exception, wears a pigtail and curl-papers. That he is extremely sallow, thin, long-faced, and lantern-jawed. That the calves of his legs are invariably undeveloped; that his legs fail at the knees, and that his shoulders are always higher than his ears. We are likewise assured that he rarely tastes any food but soup maigre, and an onion; that he always says, "By Gar! Aha! Vat you tell me, sare?" at the end of every sentence he utters; and that the true generic name of his race is the Mounseers, or the Parly-voos. If he be not a dancing-master, or a barber, he must be a cook; since no other trades but those three are congenial to the tastes of the people, or permitted by the Institutions of the country. He is a slave, of course. The ladies of France (who are also slaves) invariably have their heads tied up in Belcher handkerchiefs, wear long earrings, carry tambourines, and beguile the weariness of their yoke by singing in head voices through their noses—principally to barrel-organs.

It may be generally summed up, of this inferior people, that they have no idea of anything.

Of a great Institution like Smithfield, they are unable to form the least conception. A Beast Market in the heart of Paris would be regarded an impossible nuisance. Nor have they any notion of slaughter-houses in the midst of a city.

One of these benighted frog-eaters would scarcely understand your meaning, if you told him of the existence of such a British bulwark.

It is agreeable, and perhaps pardonable, to indulge in a little self-complacency when our right to it is thoroughly established. At the present time, to be rendered memorable by a final attack on that good old market which is the (rotten) apple of the Corporation's eye, let us compare ourselves, to our national delight and pride as to these two subjects of slaughter-house and beast-market, with the outlandish foreigner.

The blessings of Smithfield are too well understood to need recapitulation; all who run (away from mad bulls and pursuing oxen) may read. Any market-day they may be beheld in glorious action. Possibly the merits of our slaughter-houses are not yet quite so generally appreciated.

Slaughter-houses, in the large towns of England, are always (with the exception of one or two enterprising towns) most numerous in the most densely crowded places, where there is the least circulation of air. They are often underground, in cellars; they are sometimes in close back yards; sometimes (as in Spitalfields) in the very shops where the meat is sold. Occasionally, under good private management, they are ventilated and clean. For the most part, they are unventilated and dirty; and, to the reeking walls, putrid fat and other offensive animal matter clings with a tenacious hold. The busiest slaughter-houses in London are in the neighbourhood of Smithfield, in Newgate Market, in Whitechapel, in Newport Market, in Leadenhall Market, in Clare Market. All these places are surrounded by houses of a poor description, swarming with inhabitants. Some of them are close to the worst burial-grounds in London. When the slaughter-house is below the ground, it is a common practice to throw the sheep down areas, neck and crop—which is exciting, but not at all cruel. When it is on the level surface, it is often extremely difficult of approach. Then, the beasts have to be worried, and goaded, and pronged, and tail-twisted, for a long time before they can be got in—which is entirely owing to their natural obstinacy. When it is not difficult of approach, but is in a foul condition, what they see and scent makes them still more reluctant to enter—which is their natural obstinacy again. When they do get in at last, after no trouble and suffering to speak of (for there is nothing in the previous journey into the heart of London, the night's endurance in Smithfield, the struggle out again, among the crowded multitude, the coaches, carts, waggons, omnibuses, gigs, chaises, phaetons, cabs, trucks, dogs, boys, whoopings, roarings, and ten thousand other distractions), they are represented to be in a most unfit state to be killed, according to microscopic examinations made of their fevered blood by one of the most distinguished physiologists in the world, PROFESSOR OWEN—but that's humbug. When they *are* killed, at last, their reeking carcases are hung in impure air, to become, as the same Professor will explain to you, less nutritious and more unwholesome—but he is only an *uncommon* counsellor, so don't mind *him*. In half a quarter of a mile's length of Whitechapel, at one time, there shall be six hundred newly slaughtered oxen hanging up, and seven hundred sheep—but the more the merrier—proof of prosperity. Hard by Snow Hill and Warwick Lane, you shall see the little children, inured to sights of brutality from their birth, trotting along the alleys, mingled with troops of horribly busy pigs, up to their ankles in blood—but it makes the young rascals hardy. Into the imperfect sewers of this overgrown city, you shall have the immense mass of corruption, engendered by these practices, lazily thrown out of sight, to rise, in poisonous gases, into your house at night, when your sleeping children will most readily absorb them, and to find its languid way, at last, into the river that you drink—but the French are a frog-eating people who wear wooden shoes, and it's O the roast beef of England, my boy, the jolly old English roast beef.

It is quite a mistake—a new-fangled notion altogether—to suppose that there is any natural antagonism between putrefaction and health. They know better than that, in the Common Council. You may talk about Nature, in her wisdom, always warning man through his sense of smell, when he draws near to something dangerous ; but that won't go down in the City. Nature very often don't mean anything. Mrs. Quickly says that prunes are ill for a green wound ; but whosoever says that putrid animal substances are ill for a green wound, or for robust vigour, or for anything or for anybody, is a humanity-monger and a humbug. Britons never, never, never, &c., therefore. And prosperity to cattle-driving, cattle-slaughtering, bone-crushing, blood-boiling, trotter-scraping, tripe-dressing, paunch-cleaning, gut-spinning, hide-preparing, tallow-melting, and other salubrious proceedings, in the midst of hospitals, church-yards, workhouses, schools, infirmaries, refuges, dwellings, provision-shops, nurseries, sick-beds, every stage and baiting-place in the journey from birth to death!

These *un*common counsellors, your Professor Owens and fellows, will contend that to tolerate these things in a civilised city, is to reduce it to a worse condition than BRUCE found to prevail in ABYSSINIA. For there (say they) the jackals and wild dogs came at night to devour the offal; whereas, here there are no such natural scavengers, and quite as savage customs. Further, they will demonstrate that nothing in Nature is intended to be wasted, and that besides the waste which such abuses occasion in the articles of health and life—main sources of the riches of any com-munity—they lead to a prodigious waste of changing matters, which might, with proper preparation, and under scientific direction, be safely applied to the increase of the fertility of the land. Thus (they argue) does Nature ever avenge infractions of her beneficent laws, and so surely as Man is determined to warp any of her blessings into curses, shall they become curses, and shall he suffer heavily. But this is cant. Just as it is cant of the worst description to say to the London Corporation, "How can you exhibit to the people so plain a spectacle of dishonest equivocation, as to claim the right of holding a market in the midst of the great city, for one of your vested privileges, when you know that when your last market holding charter was granted to you by King Charles the First, Smithfield stood IN THE SUBURBS OF LONDON, and is in that very charter so de-scribed in those five words?"—which is certainly true, but has nothing to do with the question.

Now to the comparison, in these particulars of civilisa-tion, between the capital of England, and the capital of that frog-eating and wooden-shoe wearing country, which the illustrious Common Councilman so sarcastically settled.

In Paris, there is no Cattle Market. Cows and calves are sold within the city, but the Cattle Markets are at Poissy, about thirteen miles off, on a line of railway; and at Sceaux, about five miles off. The Poissy market is held every Thursday; the Sceaux market, every Monday. In Paris, there are no slaughter-houses, in our acceptation of the term. There are five public Abattoirs—within the walls, though in the suburbs—and in these all the slaughtering for the city must be performed. They are managed by a Syndicat or Guild of Butchers, who confer with the Minister of the Interior on all matters affecting the trade, and who are consulted when any new regulations are contemplated for its government. They are, likewise, under the vigilant superintendence of the police. Every butcher must be licensed: which proves him at once to be a slave, for we don't license butchers in England—we only license apothecaries, attorneys, post-masters, publicans, hawkers, retailers of tobacco, snuff, pepper, and vinegar—and one or two other little trades, not worth mentioning. Every arrangement in connexion with the slaughtering and sale of meat, is matter of strict police regulation. (Slavery again, though we certainly have a general sort of Police Act here.)

But, in order that the reader may understand what a monument of folly these frog-eaters have raised in their abattoirs and cattle-markets, and may compare it with what common counselling has done for us all these years, and would still do but for the innovating spirit of the times, here follows a short account of a recent visit to these places:

It was as sharp a February morning as you would desire to feel at your fingers' ends when I turned out—tumbling over a chiffonier with his little basket and rake, who was picking up the bits of coloured paper that had been swept out, over-night, from a Bon-Bon shop—to take the Butchers' Train to Poissy. A cold, dim light just touched the high roofs of the Tuileries which have seen such changes, such distracted crowds, such riot and bloodshed; and they looked as calm, and as old, all covered with white frost, as the very Pyramids. There was not light enough, yet, to strike upon the towers of Notre Dame across the water; but I thought of the dark pavement of the old Cathedral as just beginning to be streaked with grey; and of the lamps in the "House of God," the Hospital close to it, burning low and being quenched; and of the keeper of the Morgue going about with a fading lantern, busy in the arrangement of his terrible waxwork for another sunny day.

The sun was up, and shining merrily when the butchers and I, announcing our departure with an engine shriek to sleepy Paris, rattled away for the Cattle Market. Across

the country, over the Seine, among a forest of scrubby trees
—the hoar frost lying cold in shady places, and glittering
in the light—and here we are at Poissy! Out leap the
butchers, who have been chattering all the way like madmen,
and off they straggle for the Cattle Market (still chattering,
of course, incessantly), in hats and caps of all shapes, in
coats and blouses, in calf-skins, cow-skins, horse-skins, furs,
shaggy mantles, hairy coats, sacking, baize, oil-skin, anything
you please that will keep a man and a butcher warm, upon
a frosty morning.

Many a French town have I seen, between this spot of
ground and Strasburgh or Marseilles, that might sit for your
picture, little Poissy! Barring the details of your old
church, I know you well, albeit we make acquaintance,
now, for the first time. I know your narrow, straggling,
winding streets, with a kennel in the midst, and lamps
slung across. I know your picturesque street-corners,
winding up-hill Heaven knows why or where! I know
your tradesmen's inscriptions, in letters not quite fat enough;
your barbers' brazen basins dangling over little shops; your
Cafés and Estaminets, with cloudy bottles of stale syrup in
the windows, and pictures of crossed billiard cues outside.
I know this identical grey horse with his tail rolled up in
a knot like the "back hair" of an untidy woman, who
won't be shod, and who makes himself heraldic by clattering
across the street on his hind-legs, while twenty voices shriek
and growl at him as a Brigand, an accursed Robber, and
an everlastingly-doomed Pig. I know your sparkling town-
fountain, too, my Poissy, and am glad to see it near a cattle-
market, gushing so freshly, under the auspices of a gallant
little sublimated Frenchman wrought in metal, perched
upon the top. Through all the land of France I know this
unswept room at The Glory, with its peculiar smell of
beans and coffee, where the butchers crowd about the stove,
drinking the thinnest of wine from the smallest of tumblers;
where the thickest of coffee-cups mingle with the longest of
loaves, and the weakest of lump sugar; where Madame at
the counter easily acknowledges the homage of all entering
and departing butchers; where the billiard-table is covered
up in the midst like a great bird-cage—but the bird may
sing by-and-by!

A bell! The Calf Market! Polite departure of butchers.
Hasty payment and departure on the part of amateur Visitor.

Madame reproaches Ma'amselle for too fine a susceptibility in reference to the devotion of a Butcher in a bear-skin. Monsieur, the landlord of The Glory, counts a double handful of sous, without an unobliterated inscription, or an undamaged crowned head, among them.

There is little noise without, abundant space, and no confusion. The open area devoted to the market is divided into three portions: the Calf Market, the Cattle Market, the Sheep Market. Calves at eight, cattle at ten, sheep at mid-day. All is very clean.

The Calf Market is a raised platform of stone, some three or four feet high, open on all sides, with a lofty overspreading roof, supported on stone columns, which give it the appearance of a sort of vineyard from Northern Italy. Here, on the raised pavement, lie innumerable calves, all bound hind-legs and fore-legs together, and all trembling violently—perhaps with cold, perhaps with fear, perhaps with pain; for this mode of tying, which seems to be an absolute superstition with the peasantry, can hardly fail to cause great suffering. Here they lie patiently in rows, among the straw, with their stolid faces and inexpressive eyes, superintended by men and women, boys and girls; here they are inspected by our friends, the butchers, bargained for, and bought. Plenty of time; plenty of room; plenty of good humour. "Monsieur François in the bear-skin, how do you do, my friend? You come from Paris by the train? The fresh air does you good. If you are in want of three or four fine calves this market morning, my angel, I, Madame Doche, shall be happy to deal with you. Behold these calves, Monsieur François! Great Heaven, you are doubtful! Well, sir, walk round and look about you. If you find better for the money, buy them. If not, come to me!" Monsieur François goes his way leisurely, and keeps a wary eye upon the stock. No other butcher jostles Monsieur François; Monsieur François jostles no other butcher. Nobody is flustered and aggravated. Nobody is savage. In the midst of the country blue frocks and red handkerchiefs, and the butchers' coats, shaggy, furry, and hairy: of calf-skin, cow-skin, horse-skin, and bear-skin: towers a cocked hat and a blue cloak. Slavery! For *our* Police wear great-coats and glazed hats.

But now the bartering is over, and the calves are sold. "Ho! Gregoire, Antoine, Jean, Louis! Bring up the carts, my children! Quick, brave infants! Hola! Hi!"

The carts, well littered with straw, are backed up to the edge of the raised pavement, and various hot infants carry calves upon their heads, and dexterously pitch them in, while other hot infants, standing in the carts, arrange the calves, and pack them carefully in straw. Here is a promising young calf, not sold, whom Madame Doche unbinds. Pardon me, Madame Doche, but I fear this mode of tying the four legs of a quadruped together, though strictly à la mode, is not quite right. You observe, Madame Doche, that the cord leaves deep indentations in the skin, and that the animal is so cramped at first as not to know, or even remotely suspect that he *is* unbound, until you are so obliging as to kick him, in your delicate little way, and pull his tail like a bell-rope. Then, he staggers to his knees, not being able to stand, and stumbles about like a drunken calf, or the horse at Franconi's, whom you may have seen, Madame Doche, who is supposed to have been mortally wounded in battle. But what is this rubbing against me, as I apostrophise Madame Doche? It is another heated infant with a calf upon his head. "Pardon, Monsieur, but will you have the politeness to allow me to pass?" "Ah, sir, willingly. I am vexed to obstruct the way." On he staggers, calf and all, and makes no allusion whatever either to my eyes or limbs.

Now, the carts are all full. More straw, my Antoine, to shake over these top rows; then, off we will clatter, rumble, jolt, and rattle, a long row of us, out of the first town-gate, and out at the second town-gate, and past the empty sentry-box, and the little thin square bandbox of a guardhouse, where nobody seems to live: and away for Paris, by the paved road, lying, a straight straight line, in the long long avenue of trees. We can neither choose our road, nor our pace, for that is all prescribed to us. The public convenience demands that our carts should get to Paris by such a route, and no other (Napoleon had leisure to find that out, while he had a little war with the world upon his hands), and woe betide us if we infringe orders.

Droves of oxen stand in the Cattle Market, tied to iron bars fixed into posts of granite. Other droves advance slowly down the long avenue, past the second town-gate, and the first town-gate, and the sentry-box, and the bandbox, thawing the morning with their smoky breath as they come along. Plenty of room; plenty of time. Neither man nor beast is driven out of his wits by coaches, carts, waggons, omnibuses, gigs, chaises, phaetons, cabs, trucks, boys, whoopings, roarings, and multitudes. No tail-twisting is necessary —no iron pronging is necessary. There are no iron prongs here. The market for cattle is held as quietly as the market for calves. In due time, off the cattle go to Paris; the drovers can no more choose their road, nor their time, nor the numbers they shall drive, than they can choose their hour for dying in the course of nature.

Sheep next. The sheep-pens are up here, past the Branch Bank of Paris established for the convenience of the butchers, and behind the two pretty fountains they are making in the Market. My name is Bull: yet I think I should like to see as good twin fountains—not to say in Smithfield, but in England anywhere. Plenty of room; plenty of time. And here are sheep-dogs, sensible as ever, but with a certain French air about them—not without a suspicion of dominoes —with a kind of flavour of moustache and beard—demonstrative dogs, shaggy and loose where an English dog would be tight and close—not so troubled with business calculations as our English drovers' dogs, who have always got their sheep upon their minds, and think about their work, even resting, as you may see by their faces; but dashing, showy, rather unreliable dogs: who might worry me instead of their legitimate charges if they saw occasion—and might see it somewhat suddenly.

The market for sheep passes off like the other two; and away they go, by *their* allotted road to Paris. My way being the Railway, I make the best of it at twenty miles an hour; whirling through the now high-lighted landscape; thinking that the inexperienced green buds will be wishing, before long, they had not been tempted to come out so soon; and wondering who lives in this or that château, all window and lattice, and what the family may have for breakfast this sharp morning.

After the Market comes the Abattoir. What abattoir shall I visit first? Montmartre is the largest. So I will go there.

The abattoirs are all within the walls of Paris, with an eye to the receipt of the octroi duty; but they stand in open places in the suburbs, removed from the press and bustle of the city. They are managed by the Syndicat or Guild of Butchers, under the inspection of the Police. Certain

cleansing and scalding calves' heads and sheep's feet—
a place for preparing tripe—stables and coach-houses for
the butchers—innumerable conveniences, aiding in the
diminution of offensiveness to its lowest possible point, and
the raising of cleanliness and supervision to their highest.
Hence, all the meat that goes out of the gate is sent away
in clean covered carts. And if every trade connected with
the slaughtering of animals were obliged by law to be
carried on in the same place, I doubt, my friend, now
reinstated in the cocked hat (whose civility these two francs
imperfectly acknowledge, but appear munificently to repay),
whether there could be better regulations than those which
are carried out at the Abattoir of Montmartre. Adieu, my
friend, for I am away to the other side of Paris, to the
Abattoir of Grenelle! And there I find exactly the same
thing on a smaller scale, with the addition of a magnificent
Artesian well, and a different sort of conductor, in the
person of a neat little woman with neat little eyes, and
a neat little voice, who picks her neat little way among the
bullocks in a very neat little pair of shoes and stockings.

Such is the Monument of French Folly which a foreigneer-
ing people have erected, in a national hatred and antipathy
for common counselling wisdom. That wisdom, assembled
in the City of London, having distinctly refused, after
a debate of three days long, and by a majority of nearly
seven to one, to associate itself with any Metropolitan
Cattle-Market unless it be held in the midst of the City,
it follows that we shall lose the inestimable advantages of
common counselling protection, and be thrown, for a market,
on our own wretched resources. In all human probability
we shall thus come, at last, to erect a monument of folly
very like this French monument. If that be done, the
consequences are obvious. The leather trade will be ruined,
by the introduction of American timber, to be manufactured
into shoes for the fallen English; the Lord Mayor will be
required, by the popular voice, to live entirely on frogs;
and both these changes will (how, is not at present quite
clear, but certainly somehow or other) fall on that unhappy
landed interest which is always being killed, yet is always
found to be alive—and kicking.

The Lamplighter

CHARACTERS

THE ASTROLOGER, a crazy old man, who has spent fifteen years in fruitless experiments in attempting to discover the philosopher's stone.

MISS FANNY BARKER, niece to the astrologer.

EMMA, daughter of the astrologer.

GALILEO ISAAC NEWTON FLAMSTEAD, Christian names of the son of the astrologer.

TOM GRIG, a lamplighter.

MR. MOONEY ("The Gifted"), a learned but very absent-minded philosopher.

THE LAMPLIGHTER

"IF you talk of Murphy and Francis Moore, gentlemen," said the lamplighter who was in the chair, "I mean to say that neither of 'em ever had any more to do with the stars than Tom Grig had."

"And what had *he* to do with 'em?" asked the lamplighter who officiated as vice.

"Nothing at all," replied the other; "just exactly nothing at all."

"Do you mean to say you don't believe in Murphy, then?" demanded the lamplighter who had opened the discussion.

"I mean to say I believe in Tom Grig," replied the chairman. "Whether I believe in Murphy, or not, is a matter between me and my conscience; and whether Murphy believes in himself, or not, is a matter between him and his conscience. Gentlemen, I drink your healths."

The lamplighter who did the company this honour, was seated in the chimney-corner of a certain tavern, which has been, time out of mind, the Lamplighters' House of Call. He sat in the midst of a circle of lamplighters, and was the cacique, or chief of the tribe.

If any of our readers have had the good fortune to behold a lamplighter's funeral, they will not be surprised to learn that lamplighters are a strange and primitive people; that they rigidly adhere to old ceremonies and customs which have been handed down among them from father to son since the first public lamp was lighted out of doors; that they intermarry, and betroth their children in infancy; that they enter into no plots or conspiracies (for who ever heard of a traitorous lamplighter?); that they commit no crimes against the laws of their country (there being no instance of a murderous or burglarious lamplighter); that they are, in short, notwithstanding their apparently volatile and restless character, a highly moral and reflective people: having among themselves as many traditional observances as the Jews, and being, as a body, if not as old as the hills, at least as old as the streets. It is an article of their creed that the first faint glimmering of true civilization shone in the first street-light maintained at the public expense. They trace their existence and high position in the public esteem, in a direct line to the heathen mythology; and hold that the history of Prometheus himself is but a pleasant fable, whereof the true hero is a lamplighter.

"Gentlemen," said the lamplighter in the chair, "I drink your healths."

"And, perhaps, Sir," said the vice, holding up his glass, and rising a little way off his seat and sitting down again, in token that he recognised and returned the compliment, "perhaps you will add to that condescension by telling us who Tom Grig was, and how he came to be connected in your mind with Francis Moore, Physician."

"Hear, hear, hear!" cried the lamplighters generally.

"Tom Grig, gentlemen," said the chairman, "was one of us; and it happened to him, as it don't often happen to a public character in our line, that he had his what-you-may-call-it cast."

"His head?" said the vice.

"No," replied the chairman, "not his head."

"His face, perhaps?" said the vice. "No, not his face."
"His legs?" "No, not his legs." Nor yet his arms, nor his hands, nor his feet, nor his chest, all of which were severally suggested.

"His nativity, perhaps?"

"That's it," said the chairman, awakening from his thoughtful attitude at the suggestion. "His nativity. That's what Tom had cast, gentlemen."

"In plaister?" asked the vice.

"I don't rightly know how it's done," returned the chairman. "But I suppose it was."

And there he stopped as if that were all he had to say; whereupon there arose a murmur among the company, which at length resolved itself into a request, conveyed through the vice, that he would go on. This being exactly what the chairman wanted, he mused for a little time, performed that agreeable ceremony which is popularly termed wetting one's whistle, and went on thus :

"Tom Grig, gentlemen, was, as I have said, one of us ; and I may go further, and say he was an ornament to us, and such a one as only the good old times of oil and cotton could have produced. Tom's family, gentlemen, were all lamplighters."

"Not the ladies, I hope?" asked the vice.

"They had talent enough for it, Sir," rejoined the chairman, "and would have been, but for the prejudices of society. Let women have their rights, Sir, and the females of Tom's family would have been every one of 'em in office. But that emancipation hasn't come yet, and hadn't then, and consequently they confined themselves to the bosoms of their families, cooked the dinners, mended the clothes, minded the children, comforted their husbands, and attended to the house-keeping generally. It's a hard thing upon the women, gentlemen, that they are limited to such a sphere of action as this ; very hard."

"I happen to know all about Tom, gentlemen, from the circumstance of his uncle by his mother's side having been my particular friend. His (that's Tom's uncle's) fate was a melancholy one. Gas was the death of him. When it was first talked of, he laughed. He wasn't angry ; he laughed at the credulity of human nature. 'They might as well talk,' he says, 'of laying on an everlasting succession of glow-worms ;' and then he laughed again, partly at his joke, and partly at poor humanity.

"In course of time, however, the thing got ground, the experiment was made, and they lighted up Pall Mall. Tom's uncle went to see it. I've heard that he fell off his ladder fourteen times that night, from weakness, and that he would certainly have gone on falling till he killed himself, if his last tumble hadn't been into a wheelbarrow which was going his way, and humanely took him home. 'I foresee in this,' says Tom's uncle faintly, and taking to his bed as he spoke —'I foresee in this,' he says, 'the breaking up of our profession. There's no more going the rounds to trim by daylight, no more dribbling down of the oil on the hats and bonnets of ladies and gentlemen when one feels in spirits. Any low fellow can light a gas-lamp. And it's all up.' In this state of mind, he petitioned the government for—I want a word again, gentlemen—what do you call that which they give to people when it's found out, at last, that they've never been of any use, and have been paid too much for doing nothing?"

"Compensation?" suggested the vice.

"That's it," said the chairman. "Compensation. They didn't give it him, though, and then he got very fond of his country all at once, and went about saying that gas was a death-blow to his native land, and that it was a plot of the radicals to ruin the country and destroy the oil and cotton trade for ever, and that the whales would go and kill themselves privately, out of sheer spite and vexation at not being caught. At last he got right-down cracked; called his tobacco-pipe a gas-pipe; thought his tears were lamp-oil; and went on with all manner of nonsense of that sort, till one night he hung himself on a lamp-iron in Saint Martin's Lane, and there was an end of *him*.

"Tom loved him, gentlemen, but he survived it. He shed a tear over his grave, got very drunk, spoke a funeral oration that night in the watch-house, and was fined five shillings for it, in the morning. Some men are none the worse for this sort of thing. Tom was one of 'em. He went that very afternoon on a new beat: as clear in his head, and as free from fever as Father Mathew himself.

"Tom's new beat, gentlemen, was—I can't exactly say where, for that he'd never tell; but I know it was in a quiet part of town, where there were some queer old houses. I have always had it in my head that it must have been somewhere near Canonbury Tower in Islington, but that's a matter of opinion. Wherever it was, he went upon it, with a bran-new ladder, a white hat, a brown holland jacket and trousers, a blue neckerchief, and a sprig of full-blown double wall-flower in his button-hole. Tom was always genteel in his appearance, and I have heard from the best judges, that if he had left his ladder at home that afternoon, you might have took him for a lord.

"He was always merry, was Tom, and such a singer, that if there was any encouragement for native talent, he'd have been at the opera. He was on his ladder, lighting his first lamp, and singing to himself in a manner more easily to be conceived than described, when he hears the clock strike five, and suddenly sees an old gentleman with a telescope in his hand, throw up a window and look at him very hard.

"Tom didn't know what could be passing in this old gentleman's mind. He thought it likely enough that he might be saying within himself, 'Here's a new lamplighter—a good-looking young fellow—shall I stand something to drink?' Thinking this possible, he keeps quite still, pretending to be very particular about the wick, and looks at the old gentleman sideways, seeming to take no notice of him.

"Gentlemen, he was one of the strangest and most mysterious-looking files that ever Tom clapped his eyes on. He was dressed all slovenly and untidy, in a great gown of a kind of bed-furniture pattern, with a cap of the same on his head; and a long old flapped waistcoat; with no braces, no strings, very few buttons—in short, with hardly any of those artificial contrivances that hold society together. Tom knew by these signs, and by his not being shaved, and by his not being over-clean, and by a sort of wisdom not quite awake, in his face, that he was a scientific old gentleman. He often told me that if he could have conceived the possibility of the whole Royal Society being boiled down into one man, he should have said the old gentleman's body was that Body."

"The old gentleman claps the telescope to his eye, looks all round, sees nobody else in sight, stares at Tom again, and cries out very loud:

"'Hal-loa!'

"'Halloa, Sir,' says Tom from the ladder; 'and halloa again, if you come to that.'

"'Here's an extraordinary fulfilment,' says the old gentleman, 'of a prediction of the planets.'

"'Is there?' says Tom. 'I'm very glad to hear it.'

"'Young man,' says the old gentleman, 'you don't know me.'

"'Sir,' says Tom, 'I have not that honour; but I shall be happy to drink your health, notwithstanding.'

"'I read,' cries the old gentleman, without taking any notice of this politeness on Tom's part—'I read what's going to happen, in the stars.'

"Tom thanked him for the information, and begged to know if anything particular was going to happen in the stars, in the course of a week or so; but the old gentleman, correcting him, explained that he read in the stars what was going to happen on dry land, and that he was acquainted with all the celestial bodies.

"'I hope they're all well, Sir,' says Tom,—'everybody.'

"'Hush!' cries the old gentleman. 'I have consulted the book of Fate with rare and wonderful success. I am versed in the great sciences of astrology and astronomy. In my house here, I have every description of apparatus for observing the course and motion of the planets. Six months ago, I derived from this source, the knowledge that precisely as the clock struck five this afternoon a stranger would present himself—the destined husband of my young and lovely niece—in reality of illustrious and high descent, but whose birth would be enveloped in uncertainty and mystery. Don't tell me yours isn't,' says the old gentleman, who was in such a hurry to speak that he couldn't get the words out fast enough, 'for I know better.'

"Gentlemen, Tom was so astonished when he heard him say this, that he could hardly keep his footing on the ladder, and found it necessary to hold on by the lamp-post. There *was* a mystery about his birth. His mother had always admitted it. Tom had never known who was his father, and some people had gone so far as to say that even *she* was in doubt.

"While he was in this state of amazement, the old gentleman leaves the window, bursts out of the house-door, shakes the ladder, and Tom, like a ripe pumpkin, comes sliding down into his arms.

"'Let me embrace you,' he says, folding his arms about him, and nearly lighting up his old bed-furniture gown at Tom's link. 'You're a man of noble aspect. Everything combines to prove the accuracy of my observations. You have had mysterious promptings within you,' he says; 'I know you have had whisperings of greatness, eh?' he says.

"'I think I have,' says Tom—Tom was one of those who can persuade themselves to anything they like—'I've often thought I wasn't the small beer I was taken for.'

"'You were right,' cries the old gentleman, hugging him again. 'Come in. My niece awaits us.'

"'Is the young lady tolerable good-looking, Sir?' says Tom, hanging fire rather, as he thought of her playing the piano, and knowing French, and being up to all manner of accomplishments.

"'She's beautiful!' cries the old gentleman, who was in such a terrible bustle that he was all in a perspiration. 'She has a graceful carriage, an exquisite shape, a sweet voice, a countenance beaming with animation and expression; and the eye,' he says, rubbing his hands, 'of a startled fawn.'

"Tom supposed this might mean, what was called among his circle of acquaintance, 'a game eye;' and, with a view to this defect, inquired whether the young lady had any cash.

"'She has five thousand pounds,' cries the old gentleman. 'But what of that? what of that? A word in your ear. I'm in search of the philosopher's stone. I have very nearly found it—not quite. It turns everything to gold; that's its property.'

"Tom naturally thought it must have a deal of property; and said that when the old gentleman did get it, he hoped he'd be careful to keep it in the family.

"'Certainly,' he says, 'of course. Five thousand pounds! What's five thousand pounds to us? What's five million?' he says. 'What's five thousand million? Money will be nothing to us. We shall never be able to spend it fast enough.'

"'We'll try what we can do, Sir,' says Tom.

"'We will,' says the old gentleman. 'Your name?'

"'Grig,' says Tom.

The old gentleman embraced him again, very tight; and without speaking another word, dragged him into the house in such an excited manner, that it was as much as Tom could do to take his link and ladder with him, and put them down in the passage.

"Gentlemen, if Tom hadn't been always remarkable for his love of truth, I think you would still have believed him when he said that all this was like a dream. There is no better way for a man to find out whether he is really asleep or awake, than calling for something to eat. If he's in a dream, gentlemen, he'll find something wanting in the flavour, depend upon it.

"Tom explained his doubts to the old gentleman, and said that if there was any cold meat in the house, it would ease his mind very much to test himself at once. The old gentleman ordered up a venison pie, a small ham, and a bottle of very old Madeira. At the first mouthful of pie and the first glass of wine, Tom smacks his lips and cries out, 'I'm awake—wide awake;' and to prove that he was so, gentlemen, he made an end of 'em both.

"When Tom had finished his meal (which he never spoke of afterwards without tears in his eyes), the old gentleman hugs him again, and says, 'Noble stranger! let us visit my young and lovely niece.' Tom, who was a little elevated with the wine, replies, 'The noble stranger is agreeable!' At which words the old gentleman took him by the hand, and led him to the parlour; crying as he opened the door, 'Here is Mr. Grig, the favourite of the planets!'

"I will not attempt a description of female beauty, gentlemen, for every one of us has a model of his own that suits his own taste best. In this parlour that I'm speaking of, there were two young ladies; and if every gentleman present, will imagine two models of his own in their places, and will be kind enough to polish 'em up to the very highest pitch of perfection, he will then have a faint conception of their uncommon radiance.

"Besides these two young ladies, there was their waiting-woman, that under any other circumstances Tom would have looked upon as a Venus; and besides her, there was a tall, thin, dismal-faced young gentleman, half man and half boy, dressed in a childish suit of clothes very much too short in the legs and arms; and looking, according to Tom's comparison, like one of the wax juveniles from a tailor's door, grown up and run to seed. Now, this youngster stamped his foot upon the ground and looked very fierce at Tom, and Tom looked fierce at him—for to tell the truth, gentlemen, Tom more than half suspected that when they entered the room he was kissing one of the young ladies; and for anything Tom knew, you observe, it might be *his* young lady—which was not pleasant.

"'Sir,' says Tom, 'before we proceed any further, will you have the goodness to inform me who this young Salamander'—Tom called him that for aggravation, you perceive, gentlemen—'who this young Salamander may be?'

"'That, Mr. Grig,' says the old gentleman, 'is my little boy. He was christened Galileo Isaac Newton Flamstead. Don't mind him. He's a mere child.'

"'And a very fine child too,' says Tom—still aggravating, you'll observe—'of his age, and as good as fine, I have no doubt. How do you do, my man?' with which kind and patronising expressions, Tom reached up to pat him on the head, and quoted two lines about little boys, from Doctor Watts's Hymns, which he had learnt at a Sunday School.

"It was very easy to see, gentlemen, by this youngster's frowning and by the waiting-maid's tossing her head and turning up her nose, and by the young ladies turning their backs and talking together at the other end of the room, that nobody but the old gentleman took very kindly to the noble stranger. Indeed, Tom plainly heard the waiting-woman say of her master, that so far from being able to read the stars as he pretended, she didn't believe he knew his letters in 'em, or at best that he had got further than words in one syllable; but Tom, not minding this (for he was in spirits after the Madeira), looks with an agreeable air towards the young ladies, and, kissing his hand to both, says to the old gentleman, 'Which is which?'

"'This,' says the old gentleman, leading out the handsomest, if one of 'em could possibly be said to be handsomer than the other—'this is my niece, Miss Fanny Barker.'

"'If you'll permit me, Miss,' says Tom, 'being a noble stranger and a favourite of the planets, I will conduct myself as such.' With these words, he kisses the young lady in a very affable way, turns to the old gentleman, slaps him on the back, and says, 'When's it to come off, my buck?'

"The young lady coloured so deep, and her lip trembled so much, gentlemen, that Tom really thought she was going to cry. But she kept her feelings down, and turning to the old gentleman, says, 'Dear uncle, though you have the absolute disposal of my hand and fortune, and though you mean well in disposing of 'em thus, I ask you whether you don't think this is a mistake? Don't you think, dear uncle,' she says, 'that the stars must be in error? Is it not possible that the comet may have put 'em out?'

"'The stars,' says the old gentleman, 'couldn't make a mistake if they tried. Emma,' he says to the other young lady.

"'Yes, papa,' says she.

"'The same day that makes your cousin Mrs. Grig will unite you to the gifted Mooney. No remonstrance—no tears. Now, Mr. Grig, let me conduct you to that hallowed ground, that philosophical retreat, where my friend and partner, the gifted Mooney of whom I have just now spoken, is even now pursuing those discoveries which shall enrich us with the precious metal, and make us masters of the world. Come, Mr. Grig,' he says.

"'With all my heart, Sir,' replies Tom; 'and luck to the gifted Mooney, say I—not so much on his account as for our worthy selves!' With this sentiment, Tom kissed his hand to the ladies again, and followed him out; having the gratification to perceive, as he looked back, that they were all hanging on by the arms and legs of Galileo Isaac Newton Flamstead, to prevent him from following the noble stranger, and tearing him to pieces.

"Gentlemen, Tom's father-in-law that was to be, took him by the hand, and having lighted a little lamp, led him across a paved court-yard at the back of the house, into a very large, dark, gloomy room: filled with all manner of bottles, globes, books, telescopes, crocodiles, alligators, and other scientific instruments of every kind. In the centre of this room was a stove or furnace, with what Tom called a pot, but which in my opinion was a crucible, in full boil. In one corner was a sort of ladder leading through the roof; and up this ladder the old gentleman pointed, as he said in a whisper:

"'The observatory. Mr. Mooney is even now watching for the precise time at which we are to come into all the riches of the earth. It will be necessary for he and I, alone in that silent place, to cast your nativity before the hour arrives. Put the day and minute of your birth on this piece of paper, and leave the rest to me.'

"'You don't mean to say,' says Tom, doing as he was told and giving him back the paper, 'that I'm to wait here long, do you? It's a precious dismal place.'

"'Hush!' says the old gentleman. 'It's hallowed ground. Farewell!'

"'Stop a minute,' says Tom. 'What a hurry you're in! What's in that large bottle yonder?'

"'It's a child with three heads,' says the old gentleman; 'and everything else in proportion.'

"'Why don't you throw him away?' says Tom. 'What do you keep such unpleasant things here for?'

"'Throw him away!' cries the old gentleman. 'We use him constantly in astrology. He's a charm.'

"'I shouldn't have thought it,' says Tom, 'from his appearance. *Must* you go, I say?'

"The old gentleman makes him no answer, but climbs up the ladder in a greater bustle than ever. Tom looked after his legs till there was nothing of him left, and then sat down to wait; feeling (so he used to say) as comfortable as if he was going to be made a freemason, and they were heating the pokers.

"Tom waited so long, gentlemen, that he began to think it must be getting on for midnight at least, and felt more dismal and lonely than ever he had done in all his life. He tried every means of whiling away the time, but it never had seemed to move so slow. First, he took a nearer view of the child with three heads, and thought what a comfort it must have been to his parents. Then he looked up a long telescope which was pointed out of the window, but saw nothing particular, in consequence of the stopper being on at the other end. Then he came to a skeleton in a glass case, labelled, 'Skeleton of a Gentleman—prepared by Mr. Mooney,'—which made him hope that Mr. Mooney might not be in the habit of preparing gentlemen that way without their own consent. A hundred times, at least, he looked into the pot where they were boiling the philosopher's stone down to the proper consistency, and wondered whether it was nearly done. 'When it is,' thinks Tom, 'I'll send out for sixpenn'orth of sprats, and turn 'em into gold fish for a first experiment.' Besides which, he made up his mind, gentlemen, to have a country-house and a park; and to plant a bit of it with a double row of gas-lamps a mile long, and go out every night with a French-polished mahogany ladder, and two servants in livery behind him, to light 'em for his own pleasure.

"At length and at last, the old gentleman's legs appeared upon the steps leading through the roof, and he came slowly down: bringing along with him, the gifted Mooney. This Mooney, gentlemen, was even more scientific in appearance than his friend; and had, as Tom often declared upon his word and honour, the dirtiest face we can possibly know of, in this imperfect state of existence.

"Gentlemen, you are all aware that if a scientific man isn't absent in his mind, he's of no good at all. Mr. Mooney was so absent, that when the old gentleman said to him, 'Shake hands with Mr. Grig,' he put out his leg. 'Here's a mind, Mr. Grig!' cries the old gentleman in a rapture. 'Here's philosophy! Here's rumination! Don't disturb him,' he says, 'for this is amazing!'

"Tom had no wish to disturb him, having nothing particular to say; but he was so uncommonly amazing, that the old gentleman got impatient, and determined to give him an electric shock to bring him to—'for you must know, Mr. Grig,' he says, 'that we always keep a strongly charged battery, ready for that purpose.' These means being resorted to, gentlemen, the gifted Mooney revived with a loud roar, and he no sooner came to himself than both he and the old gentleman looked at Tom with compassion, and shed tears abundantly.

"'My dear friend,' says the old gentleman to the Gifted, 'prepare him.'

"'I say,' cries Tom, falling back, 'none of that, you know. No preparing by Mr. Mooney if you please.'

"'Alas!' replies the old gentleman, 'you don't understand us. My friend, inform him of his fate.—I can't.'

"The Gifted mustered up his voice, after many efforts, and informed Tom that his nativity had been carefully cast, and he would expire at exactly thirty-five minutes, twenty-seven seconds, and five-sixths of a second past nine o'clock, a.m., on that day two months.

"Gentlemen, I leave you to judge what were Tom's feelings at this announcement, on the eve of matrimony and endless riches. 'I think,' he says in a trembling voice, 'there must be a mistake in the working of that sum. Will you do me the favour to cast it up again?'—'There is no mistake,' replies the old gentleman, 'it is confirmed by Francis Moore, Physician. Here is the prediction for to-morrow two months.' And he showed him the page, where sure enough were these words—'The decease of a great person may be looked for, about this time.'

"'Which,' says the old gentleman, 'is clearly you, Mr. Grig.'

"'Too clearly,' cries Tom, sinking into a chair, and giving one hand to the old gentleman, and one to the Gifted. 'The orb of day has set on Thomas Grig for ever!'

"At this affecting remark, the Gifted shed tears again, and the other two mingled their tears with his, in a kind—if I may use the expression—of Mooney and Co.'s entire. But the old gentleman recovering first, observed that this was only a reason for hastening the marriage, in order that Tom's distinguished race might be transmitted to posterity; and requesting the Gifted to console Mr. Grig during his temporary absence, he withdrew to settle the preliminaries with his niece immediately.

"And now, gentlemen, a very extraordinary and remark-able occurrence took place; for as Tom sat in a melancholy way in one chair, and the Gifted sat in a melancholy way in another, a couple of doors were thrown violently open, the two young ladies rushed in, and one knelt down in a loving attitude at Tom's feet, and the other at the Gifted's. So far, perhaps, as Tom was concerned—as he used to say— you will say there was nothing strange in this: but you will be of a different opinion when you understand that Tom's young lady was kneeling to the Gifted, and the Gifted's young lady was kneeling to Tom.

"'Halloa! stop a minute!' cries Tom; 'here's a mistake. I need condoling with by sympathising woman, under my afflicting circumstances; but we're out in the figure. Change partners, Mooney.'

"'Monster!' cries Tom's young lady, clinging to the Gifted.

"'Miss!' says Tom. 'Is *that* your manners?'

"'I abjure thee!' cries Tom's young lady. 'I renounce thee. I never will be thine. Thou,' she says to the Gifted, 'art the object of my first and all-engrossing passion. Wrapt in thy sublime visions, thou hast not perceived my love; but, driven to despair, I now shake off the woman and avow it. Oh, cruel, cruel man!' With which reproach she laid her head upon the Gifted's breast, and put her arms about him in the tenderest manner possible, gentlemen.

"'And I,' says the other young lady, in a sort of ecstasy, that made Tom start—'I hereby abjure my chosen husband too. Hear me, Goblin!'—this was to the Gifted—'Hear me! I hold thee in the deepest detestation. The maddening interview of this one night has filled my soul with love—but not for thee. It is for thee, for thee, young man,' she cries to Tom. 'As Monk Lewis finely observes, Thomas, Thomas, I am thine, Thomas, Thomas, thou art mine: thine for ever, mine for ever!' with which words, she became very tender likewise.

"Tom and the Gifted, gentlemen, as you may believe, looked at each other in a very awkward manner, and with thoughts not at all complimentary to the two young ladies. As to the Gifted, I have heard Tom say often, that he was certain he was in a fit, and had it inwardly.

"'Speak to me! Oh, speak to me!' cries Tom's young lady to the Gifted.

"'I don't want to speak to anybody,' he says, finding his voice at last, and trying to push her away. 'I think I had better go. I'm—I'm frightened,' he says, looking about as if he had lost something.

"'Not one look of love!' she cries. 'Hear me while I declare——'

"'I don't know how to look a look of love,' he says, all in a maze. 'Don't declare anything. I don't want to hear anybody.'

"'That's right!' cries the old gentleman (who it seems had been listening). 'That's right! Don't hear her. Emma shall marry you to-morrow, my friend, whether she likes it or not, and *she* shall marry Mr. Grig.'

"Gentlemen, these words were no sooner out of his mouth than Galileo Isaac Newton Flamstead (who it seems had been listening too) darts in, and spinning round and round, like a young giant's top, cries, 'Let her. Let her. I'm fierce; I'm furious. I give her leave. I'll never marry anybody after this—never. It isn't safe. She is the falsest of the false,' he cries, tearing his hair and gnashing his teeth; 'and I'll live and die a bachelor!'

"'The little boy,' observed the Gifted gravely, 'albeit of tender years, has spoken wisdom. I have been led to the contemplation of woman-kind, and will not adventure on the troubled waters of matrimony.'

"'What!' says the old gentleman, 'not marry my daughter! Won't you, Mooney? Not if I make her? Won't you? Won't you?'

"'No,' says Mooney, 'I won't. And if anybody asks me any more, I'll run away, and never come back again.'

"'Mr. Grig,' says the old gentleman, 'the stars must be obeyed. You have not changed your mind because of a little girlish folly—eh, Mr. Grig?'

"Tom, gentlemen, had had his eyes about him, and was pretty sure that all this was a device and trick of the waiting-maid, to put him off his inclination. He had seen her hiding and skipping about the two doors, and had observed that a very little whispering from her pacified the Sala-mander directly. 'So,' thinks Tom, 'this is a plot—but it won't fit.'

"'Eh, Mr. Grig?' says the old gentleman.

"'Why, Sir,' says Tom, pointing to the crucible, 'if the soup's nearly ready——'

"'Another hour beholds the consummation of our labours,' returned the old gentleman.

"'Very good,' says Tom, with a mournful air. 'It's only for two months, but I may as well be the richest man in the world even for that time. I'm not particular, I'll take her, Sir. I'll take her.'

"The old gentleman was in a rapture to find Tom still in the same mind, and drawing the young lady towards him by little and little, was joining their hands by main force, when all of a sudden, gentlemen, the crucible blows up, with a great crash; everybody screams; the room is filled with smoke; and Tom, not knowing what may happen next, throws himself into a Fancy attitude, and says, 'Come on, if you're a man!' without addressing himself to anybody in particular.

"'The labours of fifteen years,' says the old gentleman, clasping his hands and looking down upon the Gifted, who was saving the pieces, 'are destroyed in an instant!'—And I am told, gentlemen, by-the-bye, that this same philosopher's stone would have been discovered a hundred times at least, to speak within bounds, if it wasn't for the one unfortunate circumstance that the apparatus always blows up, when it's on the very point of succeeding.

"Tom turns pale when he hears the old gentleman expressing himself to this unpleasant effect, and stammers out that if it's quite agreeable to all parties, he would like to know exactly what has happened, and what change has really taken place in the prospects of that company.

"'We have failed for the present, Mr. Grig,' says the old gentleman, wiping his forehead. 'And I regret it the more, because I have in fact invested my niece's five thousand pounds in this glorious speculation. But don't be cast down,' he says, anxiously—'in another fifteen years, Mr. Grig——'

"'Oh!' cries Tom, letting the young lady's hand fall. 'Were the stars very positive about this union, Sir?'

"'They were,' says the old gentleman.

"'I'm sorry to hear it,' Tom makes answer, 'for it's no go, Sir.'

"'No what!' cries the old gentleman.

"'Go, Sir,' says Tom, fiercely. 'I forbid the banns.' And with these words—which are the very words he used— he sat himself down in a chair, and, laying his head upon the table, thought with a secret grief of what was to come to pass on that day two months.

"Tom always said, gentlemen, that that waiting-maid was the artfullest minx he had ever seen; and he left it in writing in this country when he went to colonize abroad, that he was certain in his own mind she and the Salamander had blown up the philosopher's stone on purpose, and to cut him out of his property. I believe Tom was in the right, gentlemen; but whether or no, she comes forward at this point, and says, 'May I speak, Sir?' and the old gentleman answering, 'Yes, you may,' she goes on to say that 'the stars are no doubt quite right in every respect, but Tom is not the man.' And she says, 'Don't you remember, Sir, that when the clock struck five this afternoon, you gave Master Galileo a rap on the head with your telescope, and told him to get out of the way?' 'Yes, I do,' says the old gentleman. 'Then,' says the waiting-maid, 'I say he's the man, and the prophecy is fulfilled.' The old gentleman staggers at this, as if somebody had hit him a blow on the chest, and cries, 'He! why he's a boy!' Upon that, gentlemen, the Salamander cries out that he'll be twenty-one next Lady-day; and complains that his father has always been so busy with the sun round which the earth revolves, that he has never taken any notice of the son that revolves round him; and that he hasn't had a new suit of clothes since he was fourteen; and that he wasn't even taken out of nankeen frocks and trousers till he was quite unpleasant in 'em; and touches on a good many more family matters to the same purpose. To make short of a long story, gentlemen, they all talk together, and cry together, and remind the old gentleman that as to the noble family, his own grandfather would have been lord mayor if he hadn't died at a dinner the year before; and they show him by all kinds of arguments that if the cousins are married, the prediction comes true every way. At last, the old gentleman being quite convinced, gives in; and joins their hands; and leaves his daughter to marry anybody she likes; and they are all well pleased; and the Gifted as well as any of them.

"In the middle of this little family party, gentlemen, sits Tom all the while, as miserable as you like. But, when everything else is arranged, the old gentleman's daughter says, that their strange conduct was a little device of the waiting-maid's to disgust the lovers he had chosen for 'em, and will he forgive her? and if he will, perhaps he might even find her a husband—and when she says that, she looks uncommon hard at Tom.   Then the waiting-maid says that, oh dear! she couldn't abear Mr. Grig should think she wanted him to marry her; and that she had even gone so far as to refuse the last lamplighter, who was now a literary character (having set up as a bill-sticker); and that she hoped Mr. Grig would not suppose she was on her last legs by any means, for the baker was very strong in his attentions at that moment, and as to the butcher, he was frantic.   And I don't know how much more she might have said, gentle-men (for, as you know, this kind of young women are rare ones to talk), if the old gentleman hadn't cut in suddenly, and asked Tom if he'd have her, with ten pounds to recom-pense him for his loss of time and disappointment, and as a kind of bribe to keep the story secret.

"'It don't much matter, Sir,' says Tom, 'I ain't long for this world.   Eight weeks of marriage, especially with this young woman, might reconcile me to my fate.   I think,' he says, 'I could go off easy after that.'   With which he embraces her with a very dismal face, and groans in a way that might move a heart of stone—even of philosopher's stone.

"'Egad,' says the old gentleman, 'that reminds me—this bustle put it out of my head—there was a figure wrong. He'll live to a green old age—eighty-seven at least!'

"'How much, Sir?' cries Tom.

"'Eighty-seven!' says the old gentleman.

"Without another word, Tom flings himself on the old gentleman's neck; throws up his hat; cuts a caper; defies the waiting-maid; and refers her to the butcher.

"'You won't marry her!' says the old gentleman, angrily.

"'And live after it!' says Tom.   'I'd sooner marry a mermaid with a small-tooth comb and looking-glass.'

"'Then take the consequences,' says the other.

"With those words—I beg your kind attention here, gentlemen, for it's worth your notice—the old gentleman wetted the forefinger of his right hand in some of the liquor from the crucible that was spilt on the floor, and drew a small triangle on Tom's forehead.   The room swam before his eyes, and he found himself in the watch-house."

"Found himself *where?*" cried the vice, on behalf of the company generally.

"In the watch-house," said the chairman. "It was late at night, and he found himself in the very watch-house from which he had been let out that morning."

"Did he go home?" asked the vice.

"The watch-house people rather objected to that," said the chairman; "so he stopped there that night, and went before the magistrate in the morning. 'Why, you're here again, are you?' says the magistrate, adding insult to injury; 'we'll trouble you for five shillings more, if you can conveniently spare the money.' Tom told him he had been enchanted, but it was of no use. He told the contractors the same, but they wouldn't believe him. It was very hard upon him, gentlemen, as he often said, for was it likely he'd go and invent such a tale? They shook their heads and told him he'd say anything but his prayers—as indeed he would; there's no doubt about that. It was the only imputation on his moral character that ever *I* heard of."

To be Read at Dusk

CHARACTERS

CAROLINA, maid to the young bride.

CLARA, a young bride, on her wedding-trip.

SIGNOR DELLOMBRA, a dark, remarkable-looking, accomplished man, of a secret and reserved air.

AN ENGLISH GENTLEMAN, Clara's husband.

GIOVANNI BAPTISTA, a Genoese courier.

JAMES, a bachelor in business with his brother.

JOHN, twin-brother to James.

A NEAPOLITAN COURIER.

A SWISS COURIER

WILHELM, a German courier.

TO BE READ AT DUSK

ONE, two, three, four, five. There were five of them.

Five couriers, sitting on a bench outside the convent on the summit of the Great St. Bernard in Switzerland, looking at the remote heights, stained by the setting sun, as if a mighty quantity of red wine had been broached upon the mountain top, and had not yet had time to sink into the snow.

This is not my simile. It was made for the occasion by the stoutest courier, who was a German. None of the others took any more notice of it than they took of me, sitting on another bench on the other side of the convent door, smoking my cigar, like them, and—also like them—looking at the reddened snow, and at the lonely shed hard by, where the bodies of belated travellers, dug out of it, slowly wither away, knowing no corruption in that cold region.

The wine upon the mountain top soaked in as we looked ; the mountain became white ; the sky, a very dark blue ; the wind rose ; and the air turned piercing cold. The five couriers buttoned their rough coats. There being no safer man to imitate in all such proceedings than a courier, I buttoned mine.

The mountain in the sunset had stopped the five couriers in a conversation. It is a sublime sight, likely to stop conversation. The mountain being now out of the sunset, they resumed. Not that I had heard any part of their previous discourse ; for indeed, I had not then broken away from the American gentleman, in the travellers' parlour of the convent, who, sitting with his face to the fire, had undertaken to realise to me the whole progress of events which had led to the accumulation by the Honourable

Ananias Dodger of one of the largest acquisitions of dollars ever made in our country.

"My God!" said the Swiss courier, speaking in French, which I do not hold (as some authors appear to do) to be such an all-sufficient excuse for a naughty word, that I have only to write it in that language to make it innocent; "if you talk of ghosts —— "

"But I *don't* talk of ghosts," said the German.

"Of what then?" asked the Swiss.

"If I knew of what then," said the German, "I should probably know a great deal more."

It was a good answer, I thought, and it made me curious. So I moved my position to that corner of my bench which was nearest to them, and leaning my back against the convent wall, heard perfectly, without appearing to attend.

"Thunder and lightning!" said the German, warming, "when a certain man is coming to see you, unexpectedly; and, without his own knowledge, sends some invisible messenger, to put the idea of him into your head all day, what do you call that? When you walk along a crowded street—at Frankfort, Milan, London, Paris—and think that a passing stranger is like your friend Heinrich, and then that another passing stranger is like your friend Heinrich, and so begin to have a strange foreknowledge that presently you'll meet your friend Heinrich—which you do, though you believed him at Trieste—what do you call *that?*"

"It's not uncommon, either," murmured the Swiss and the other three.

"Uncommon!" said the German. "It's as common as cherries in the Black Forest. It's as common as maccaroni at Naples. And Naples reminds me! When the old Marchesa Senzanima shrieks at a card-party on the Chiaja—as I heard and saw her, for it happened in a Bavarian family of mine, and I was overlooking the service that evening—I say, when the old Marchesa starts up at the card-table, white through her rouge, and cries, 'My sister in Spain is dead! I felt her cold touch on my back!'—and when that sister *is* dead at the moment—what do you call that?"

"Or when the blood of San Gennaro liquefies at the request of the clergy—as all the world knows that it does regularly once a year, in my native city," said the Neapolitan courier after a pause, with a comical look, "what do you call that?"

"*That!*" cried the German. "Well, I think I know a name for that."

"Miracle?" said the Neapolitan, with the same sly face.

The German merely smoked and laughed; and they all smoked and laughed.

"Bah!" said the German, presently. "I speak of things that really do happen. When I want to see the conjurer, I pay to see a professed one, and have my money's worth. Very strange things do happen without ghosts. Ghosts! Giovanni Baptista, tell your story of the English bride. There's no ghost in that, but something full as strange. Will any man tell me what?"

As there was a silence among them, I glanced around. He whom I took to be Baptista was lighting a fresh cigar. He presently went on to speak. He was a Genoese, as I judged.

"The story of the English bride?" said he. "Basta! one ought not to call so slight a thing a story. Well, it's all one. But it's true. Observe me well, gentlemen, it's true. That which glitters is not always gold: but what I am going to tell, is true."

He repeated this more than once.

Ten years ago, I took my credentials to an English gentleman at Long's Hotel, in Bond Street, London, who was about to travel—it might be for one year, it might be for two. He approved of them; likewise of me. He was pleased to make inquiry. The testimony that he received was favourable. He engaged me by the six months, and my entertainment was generous.

He was young, handsome, very happy. He was enamoured of a fair young English lady, with a sufficient fortune, and they were going to be married. It was the wedding-trip, in short, that we were going to take. For three months' rest in the hot weather (it was early summer then) he had hired an old place on the Riviera, at an easy distance from my city, Genoa, on the road to Nice. Did I know that place? Yes; I told him I knew it well. It was an old palace with great gardens. It was a little bare, and it was a little dark and gloomy, being close surrounded by trees; but it was spacious, ancient, grand, and on the seashore. He said it had been so described to him exactly, and he was well pleased that I knew it. For its being a little bare of

furniture, all such places were. For its being a little
gloomy, he had hired it principally for the gardens, and
he and my mistress would pass the summer weather in
their shade.

"So all goes well, Baptista?" said he.

"Indubitably, signore; very well."

We had a travelling chariot for our journey, newly built
for us, and in all respects complete. All we had was
complete; we wanted for nothing. The marriage took
place. They were happy. *I* was happy, seeing all so bright,
being so well situated, going to my own city, teaching my
language in the rumble to the maid, la bella Carolina, whose
heart was gay with laughter: who was young and rosy.

The time flew. But I observed—listen to this, I pray!
(and here the courier dropped his voice)—I observed my
mistress sometimes brooding in a manner very strange; in
a frightened manner; in an unhappy manner; with a cloudy,
uncertain alarm upon her. I think that I began to notice
this when I was walking up hills by the carriage side, and
master had gone on in front. At any rate, I remember that
it impressed itself upon my mind one evening in the South
of France, when she called to me to call master back; and
when he came back, and walked for a long way, talking
encouragingly and affectionately to her, with his hand
upon the open window, and hers in it. Now and then, he
laughed in a merry way, as if he were bantering her out of
something. By-and-by, she laughed, and then all went well
again.

It was curious. I asked la bella Carolina, the pretty little
one, Was mistress unwell?—No.—Out of spirits?—No.—
Fearful of bad roads, or brigands?—No. And what made
it more mysterious was, the pretty little one would not look
at me in giving answer, but *would* look at the view.

But one day she told me the secret.

"If you must know," said Carolina, "I find, from what
I have overheard, that mistress is haunted."

"How haunted?"

"By a dream."

"What dream?"

"By a dream of a face. For three nights before her
marriage, she saw a face in a dream—always the same face,
and only One."

"A terrible face?"

"No. The face of a dark, remarkable-looking man, in black, with black hair and a grey moustache—a handsome man except for a reserved and secret air. Not a face she ever saw, or at all like a face she ever saw. Doing nothing in the dream but looking at her fixedly, out of darkness."

"Does the dream come back?"

"Never. The recollection of it, is all her trouble."

"And why does it trouble her?"

Carolina shook her head.

"That's master's question," said la bella. "She don't know. She wonders why, herself. But I heard her tell him, only last night, that if she was to find a picture of that face in our Italian house (which she is afraid she will) she did not know how she could ever bear it."

Upon my word, I was fearful after this (said the Genoese courier) of our coming to the old palazzo, lest some such ill-starred picture should happen to be there. I knew there were many there; and, as we got nearer and nearer to the place, I wished the whole gallery in the crater of Vesuvius. To mend the matter, it was a stormy dismal evening when we, at last, approached that part of the Riviera. It thundered; and the thunder of my city and its environs, rolling among the high hills, is very loud. The lizards ran in and out of the chinks in the broken stone wall of the garden, as if they were frightened; the frogs bubbled and croaked their loudest; the sea-wind moaned, and the wet trees dripped; and the lightning—body of San Lorenzo, how it lightened!

We all know what an old palace in or near Genoa is—how time and the sea air have blotted it—how the drapery painted on the outer walls has peeled off in great flakes of plaster—how the lower windows are darkened with rusty bars of iron—how the courtyard is overgrown with grass—how the outer buildings are dilapidated—how the whole pile seems devoted to ruin. Our palazzo was one of the true kind. It had been shut up close for months. Months?—years!—it had an earthy smell, like a tomb. The scent of the orange trees on the broad back terrace, and of the lemons ripening on the wall, and of some shrubs that grew around a broken fountain, had got into the house somehow, and had never been able to get out again. There was, in every room, an aged smell, grown faint with confinement. It pined in all the cupboards and drawers. In the little rooms of communication between great rooms, it was stifling. If you turned a picture

—to come back to the pictures—there it still was, clinging to the wall behind the frame, like a sort of bat.

The lattice-blinds were close shut, all over the house. There were two ugly grey old women in the house, to take care of it; one of them with a spindle, who stood winding and mumbling in the doorway, and who would as soon have let in the devil as the air. Master, mistress, la bella Carolina, and I, went all through the palazzo. I went first, though I have named myself last, opening the windows and the lattice-blinds, and shaking down on myself splashes of rain, and scraps of mortar, and now and then a dozing mosquito, or a monstrous, fat, blotchy, Genoese spider.

When I had let the evening light into a room, master, mistress, and la bella Carolina, entered. Then we looked round at all the pictures, and I went forward again into another room. Mistress secretly had great fear of meeting with the likeness of that face—we all had; but there was no such thing. The Madonna and the Bambino, San Francisco, San Sebastiano, Venus, Santa Caterina, Angels, Brigands, Friars, Temples at Sunset, Battles, White Horses, Forests, Apostles, Doges, all my old acquaintances many times repeated?—yes. Dark handsome man in black, reserved and secret, with black hair and grey moustache, looking fixedly at mistress out of darkness?—no.

At last we got through all the rooms and all the pictures, and came out into the gardens. They were pretty well kept, being rented by a gardener, and were large and shady. In one place there was a rustic theatre, open to the sky; the stage a green slope; the coulisses, three entrances upon a side, sweet-smelling leafy screens. Mistress moved her bright eyes, even there, as if she looked to see the face come in upon the scene; but all was well.

"Now, Clara," master said, in a low voice, "you see that it is nothing? You are happy."

Mistress was much encouraged. She soon accustomed herself to that grim palazzo, and would sing, and play the harp, and copy the old pictures, and stroll with master under the green trees and vines all day. She was beautiful. He was happy. He would laugh and say to me, mounting his horse for his morning ride before the heat:

"All goes well, Baptista!"

"Yes, signore, thank God, very well."

We kept no company. I took la bella to the Duomo and

Annunciata, to the Café, to the Opera, to the village Festa, to the Public Garden, to the Day Theatre, to the Marionetti. The pretty little one was charmed with all she saw. She learnt Italian—heavens! miraculously! Was mistress quite forgetful of that dream? I asked Carolina sometimes. Nearly, said la bella—almost. It was wearing out.

One day master received a letter, and called me.

"Baptista!"

"Signore!"

"A gentleman who is presented to me will dine here to-day. He is called the Signor Dellombra. Let me dine like a prince."

It was an odd name. I did not know that name. But there had been many noblemen and gentlemen pursued by Austria on political suspicions, lately, and some names had changed. Perhaps this was one. Altro! Dellombra was as good a name to me as another.

When the Signor Dellombra came to dinner (said the Genoese courier in the low voice, into which he had subsided once before), I showed him into the reception-room, the great sala of the old palazzo. Master received him with cordiality, and presented him to mistress. As she rose, her face changed, she gave a cry, and fell upon the marble floor.

Then I turned my head to the Signor Dellombra, and saw that he was dressed in black, and had a reserved and secret air, and was a dark remarkable-looking man, with black hair and a grey moustache.

Master raised mistress in his arms, and carried her to her own room, where I sent la bella Carolina straight. La bella told me afterwards that mistress was nearly terrified to death, and that she wandered in her mind about her dream, all night.

Master was vexed and anxious—almost angry, and yet full of solicitude. The Signor Dellombra was a courtly gentleman, and spoke with great respect and sympathy of mistress's being so ill. The African wind had been blowing for some days (they had told him at his hotel of the Maltese Cross), and he knew that it was often hurtful. He hoped the beautiful lady would recover soon. He begged permission to retire, and to renew his visit when he should have the happiness of hearing that she was better. Master would not allow of this, and they dined alone.

He withdrew early. Next day he called at the gate, on

horseback, to inquire for mistress. He did so two or three times in that week.

What I observed myself, and what la bella Carolina told me, united to explain to me that master had now set his mind on curing mistress of her fanciful terror. He was all kindness, but he was sensible and firm. He reasoned with her, that to encourage such fancies was to invite melancholy, if not madness. That it rested with herself to be herself. That if she once resisted her strange weakness, so successfully as to receive the Signor Dellombra as an English lady would receive any other guest, it was for ever conquered. To make an end, the signore came again, and mistress received him without marked distress (though with constraint and apprehension still), and the evening passed serenely. Master was so delighted with this change, and so anxious to confirm it, that the Signor Dellombra became a constant guest. He was accomplished in pictures, books, and music; and his society, in any grim palazzo, would have been welcome.

I used to notice, many times, that mistress was not quite recovered. She would cast down her eyes and droop her head, before the Signor Dellombra, or would look at him with a terrified and fascinated glance, as if his presence had some evil influence or power upon her. Turning from her to him, I used to see him in the shaded gardens, or the large half-lighted sala, looking, as I might say, "fixedly upon her out of darkness." But, truly, I had not forgotten la bella Carolina's words describing the face in the dream.

After his second visit I heard master say:

"Now, see, my dear Clara, it's over! Dellombra has come and gone, and your apprehension is broken like glass."

"Will he—will he ever come again?" asked mistress.

"Again? Why, surely, over and over again! Are you cold?" (she shivered).

"No, dear—but—he terrifies me: are you sure that he need come again?"

"The surer for the question, Clara!" replied master, cheerfully.

But he was very hopeful of her complete recovery now, and grew more and more so every day. She was beautiful. He was happy.

"All goes well, Baptista?" he would say to me again.

"Yes, signore, thank God; very well."

We were all (said the Genoese courier, constraining himself to speak a little louder), we were all at Rome for the Carnival. I had been out, all day, with a Sicilian, a friend of mine, and a courier, who was there with an English family. As I returned at night to our hotel, I met the little Carolina, who never stirred from home alone, running distractedly along the Corso.

"Carolina! What's the matter?"

"O Baptista! O, for the Lord's sake! where is my mistress?"

"Mistress, Carolina?"

"Gone since morning—told me, when master went out on his day's journey, not to call her, for she was tired with not resting in the night (having been in pain), and would lie in bed until the evening; then get up refreshed. She is gone!—she is gone! Master has come back, broken down the door, and she is gone! My beautiful, my good, my innocent mistress!"

The pretty little one so cried, and raved, and tore herself that I could not have held her, but for her swooning on my arm as if she had been shot. Master came up—in manner, face, or voice, no more the master that I knew, than I was he. He took me (I laid the little one upon her bed in the hotel, and left her with the chamber-women), in a carriage, furiously through the darkness, across the desolate Campagna. When it was day, and we stopped at a miserable post-house, all the horses had been hired twelve hours ago, and sent away in different directions. Mark me! by the Signor Dellombra, who had passed there in a carriage, with a frightened English lady crouching in one corner.

I never heard (said the Genoese courier, drawing a long breath) that she was ever traced beyond that spot. All I know is, that she vanished into infamous oblivion, with the dreaded face beside her that she had seen in her dream.

"What do you call *that*?" said the German courier, triumphantly. "Ghosts! There are no ghosts *there!* What do you call this, that I am going to tell you? Ghosts! There are no ghosts *here!*"

I took an engagement once (pursued the German courier) with an English gentleman, elderly and a bachelor, to travel through my country, my Fatherland. He was a merchant who traded with my country and knew the language, but

who had never been there since he was a boy—as I judge,
some sixty years before.

His name was James, and he had a twin-brother John,
also a bachelor. Between these brothers there was a great
affection. They were in business together, at Goodman's
Fields, but they did not live together. Mr. James dwelt in
Poland Street, turning out of Oxford Street, London ;
Mr. John resided by Epping Forest.

Mr. James and I were to start for Germany in about a
week. The exact day depended on business. Mr. John came
to Poland Street (where I was staying in the house), to pass
that week with Mr. James. But he said to his brother on
the second day, "I don't feel very well, James. There's not
much the matter with me ; but I think I am a little gouty.
I'll go home and put myself under the care of my old housekeeper, who understands my ways. If I get quite better, I'll
come back and see you before you go. If I don't feel well
enough to resume my visit where I leave it off, why *you* will
come and see *me* before you go." Mr. James, of course,
said he would, and they shook hands—both hands, as they
always did—and Mr. John ordered out his old-fashioned
chariot and rumbled home.

It was on the second night after that—that is to say, the
fourth in the week—when I was awoke out of my sound
sleep by Mr. James coming into my bedroom in his flannel-
gown, with a lighted candle. He sat upon the side of my
bed, and looking at me, said :

"Wilhelm, I have reason to think I have got some strange
illness upon me."

I then perceived that there was a very unusual expression
in his face.

"Wilhelm," said he, "I am not afraid or ashamed to tell
you what I might be afraid or ashamed to tell another man.
You come from a sensible country, where mysterious things
are inquired into and are not settled to have been weighed
and measured—or to have been unweighable and unmeasur-
able—or in either case to have been completely disposed of,
for all time—ever so many years ago. I have just now seen
the phantom of my brother."

I confess (said the German courier) that it gave me a little
tingling of the blood to hear it.

"I have just now seen," Mr. James repeated, looking full
at me, that I might see how collected he was, " the phantom

of my brother John. I was sitting up in bed, unable to sleep, when it came into my room, in a white dress, and regarding me earnestly, passed up to the end of the room, glanced at some papers on my writing-desk, turned, and, still looking earnestly at me as it passed the bed, went out at the door. Now, I am not in the least mad, and am not in the least disposed to invest that phantom with any external existence out of myself. I think it is a warning to me that I am ill; and I think I had better be bled."

I got out of bed directly (said the German courier) and began to get on my clothes, begging him not to be alarmed, and telling him that I would go myself to the doctor. I was just ready, when we heard a loud knocking and ringing at the street door. My room being an attic at the back, and Mr. James's being the second-floor room in the front, we went down to his room, and put up the window, to see what was the matter.

"Is that Mr. James?" said a man below, falling back to the opposite side of the way to look up.

"It is," said Mr. James, "and you are my brother's man, Robert."

"Yes, Sir. I am sorry to say, Sir, that Mr. John is ill. He is very bad, Sir. It is even feared that he may be lying at the point of death. He wants to see you, Sir. I have a chaise here. Pray come to him. Pray lose no time."

Mr. James and I looked at one another. "Wilhelm," said he, "this is strange. I wish you to come with me!" I helped him to dress, partly there and partly in the chaise; and no grass grew under the horses' iron shoes between Poland Street and the Forest.

Now, mind! (said the German courier) I went with Mr. James into his brother's room, and I saw and heard myself what follows.

His brother lay upon his bed, at the upper end of a long bed-chamber. His old housekeeper was there, and others were there: I think three others were there, if not four, and they had been with him since early in the afternoon. He was in white, like the figure—necessarily so, because he had his night-dress on. He looked like the figure—necessarily so, because he looked earnestly at his brother when he saw him come into the room.

But, when his brother reached the bed-side, he slowly

raised himself in bed, and looking full upon him, said these words :

"JAMES, YOU HAVE SEEN ME BEFORE, TO-NIGHT—AND YOU KNOW IT !"

And so died !

I waited, when the German courier ceased, to hear something said of this strange story. The silence was unbroken. I looked round, and the five couriers were gone : so noiselessly that the ghostly mountain might have absorbed them into its eternal snows. By this time, I was by no means in a mood to sit alone in that awful scene, with the chill air coming solemnly upon me—or, if I may tell the truth, to sit alone anywhere. So I went back into the convent-parlour, and, finding the American gentleman still disposed to relate the biography of the Honourable Ananias Dodger, heard it all out.

Sunday under Three Heads

DEDICATION

TO THE RIGHT REVEREND THE BISHOP OF LONDON

My Lord,

You were among the first, some years ago, to expatiate on the vicious addiction of the lower classes of society, to Sunday excursions ; and were thus instrumental in calling forth occasional demonstrations of those extreme opinions on the subject, which are very generally received with derision, if not with contempt.

Your elevated station, my Lord, affords you countless opportunities of increasing the comforts and pleasures of the humbler classes of society—not by the expenditure of the smallest portion of your princely income, but by merely sanctioning with the influence of your example, their harmless pastimes and innocent recreations.

That your Lordship would ever have contemplated Sunday recreations with so much horror, if you had been at all acquainted with the wants and necessities of the people who indulged in them, I cannot imagine possible. That a Prelate of your elevated rank has the faintest conception of the extent of those wants, and the nature of those necessities, I do not believe.

For these reasons, I venture to address this little Pamphlet to your Lordship's consideration. I am quite conscious that the outlines I have drawn, afford but a very imperfect description of the feelings they are intended to illustrate ; but I claim for them one merit—their truth and freedom from exaggeration. I may have fallen short of the mark, but I have never overshot it : and while I have pointed out what appears to me to be injustice on the part of others, I hope I have carefully abstained from committing it myself.

I am, My Lord,
Your Lordship's most obedient, humble Servant,
TIMOTHY SPARKS.

June, 1836.

SUNDAY UNDER THREE HEADS

I

AS IT IS

THERE are few things from which I derive greater pleasure, than walking through some of the principal streets of London on a fine Sunday, in summer, and watching the cheerful faces of the lively groups with which they are thronged. There is something, to my eyes at least, exceedingly pleasing in the general desire evinced by the humbler classes of society to appear neat and clean on this their only holiday. There are many grave old persons, I know, who shake their heads with an air of profound wisdom, and tell you that poor people dress too well now-a-days ; that when they were children, folks knew their stations in life better ; that you may depend upon it, no good will come of this sort of thing in the end,—and so forth : but I fancy I can discern in the fine bonnet of the working-man's wife, or the feather-bedizened hat of his child, no inconsiderable evidence of good feeling on the part of the man himself, and an affectionate desire to expend the few shillings he can spare from his week's wages, in improving the appearance and adding to the happiness of those who are nearest and dearest to him. This may be a very heinous and unbecoming degree of vanity, perhaps, and the money might possibly be applied to better uses ; it must not be forgotten, however, that it might very easily be devoted to worse : and if two or three faces can be rendered happy and contented, by a trifling improvement of outward appearance, I cannot help thinking that the object is very cheaply purchased, even at the expense of a smart gown, or a gaudy riband.   There is a great deal of very unnecessary cant about the over-dressing of the common people. There is not a manufacturer or tradesman in existence, who would not employ a man who takes a reasonable degree of pride in the appearance of himself and those about him, in preference to a sullen slovenly fellow, who works doggedly on, regardless of his own clothing and that of his wife and children, and seeming to take pleasure or pride in nothing.

The pampered aristocrat, whose life is one continued round of licentious pleasures and sensual gratifications; or the gloomy enthusiast, who detests the cheerful amusements he can never enjoy, and envies the healthy feelings he can never know, and who would put down the one and suppress the other, until he made the minds of his fellow-beings as besotted and distorted as his own;—neither of these men can by possibility form an adequate notion of what Sunday really is, to those whose lives are spent in sedentary or laborious occupations, and who are accustomed to look forward to it through their whole existence, as their only day of rest from toil, and innocent enjoyment.

The sun that rises over the quiet streets of London on a bright Sunday morning, shines till his setting, on gay and happy faces. Here and there, so early as six o'clock, a young man and woman in their best attire may be seen hurrying along on their way to the house of some acquaintance, who is included in their scheme of pleasure for the day; from whence, after stopping to take "a bit of breakfast," they sally forth, accompanied by several old people, and a whole crowd of young ones, bearing large hand-baskets full of provisions, and Belcher handkerchiefs done up in bundles, with the neck of a bottle sticking out at the top, and closely-packed apples bulging out at the sides,—and away they hurry along the streets leading to the steam-packet wharfs, which are already plentifully sprinkled with parties bound for the same destination. Their good humour and delight know no bounds—for it is a delightful morning, all blue over head, and nothing like a cloud in the whole sky; and even the air of the river at London Bridge is something to them, shut up as they have been, all the week, in close streets and heated rooms. There are dozens of steamers to all sorts of places—Gravesend, Greenwich, and Richmond; and such numbers of people, that when you have once sat down on the deck, it is all but a moral impossibility to get up again—to say nothing of walking about, which is entirely out of the question. Away they go, joking and laughing, and eating and drinking, and admiring everything they see, and pleased with everything they hear, to climb Windmill Hill, and catch a glimpse of the rich corn-fields and beautiful orchards of Kent; or to stroll among the fine old trees of Greenwich Park, and survey the wonders of Shooter's Hill and Lady James's Folly; or to glide past the beautiful meadows of Twickenham and Richmond, and to gaze with a delight which only people like them can know, on every lovely object in the fair prospect around. Boat follows boat, and coach succeeds coach, for the next three hours; but all are filled, and all with the same kind of people—neat and clean, cheerful and contented.

They reach their places of destination, and the taverns are crowded; but there is no drunkenness or brawling, for the class of men who commit the enormity of making Sunday excursions, take their families with them: and this in itself would be a check upon them, even if they were inclined to dissipation, which they really are not. Boisterous their mirth may be, for they have all the excitement of feeling that fresh air and green fields can impart to the dwellers in crowded cities, but it is innocent and harmless. The glass is circulated, and the joke goes round; but the one is free from excess, and the other from offence; and nothing but good humour and hilarity prevail.

In streets like Holborn and Tottenham Court Road, which form the central market of a large neighbourhood, inhabited by a vast number of mechanics and poor people, a few shops are open at an early hour of the morning; and a very poor man, with a thin and sickly woman by his side, may be seen with their little basket in hand, purchasing the scanty quantity of necessaries they can afford, which the time at which the man receives his wages, or his having a good deal of work to do, or the woman's having been out charing till a late hour, prevented their procuring over-night. The coffee-shops too, at which clerks and young men employed in counting-houses can procure their breakfasts, are also open. This class comprises, in a place like London, an enormous number of people, whose limited means prevent their engaging for their lodgings any other apartment than a bedroom, and who have consequently no alternative but to take their breakfasts at a coffee-shop, or go without it altogether. All these places, however, are quickly closed; and by the time the church bells begin to ring, all appearance of traffic has ceased. And then, what are the signs of immorality that meet the eye? Churches are well filled, and Dissenters' chapels are crowded to suffocation. There is no preaching to empty benches, while the drunken and dissolute populace run riot in the streets.

Here is a fashionable church, where the service commences at a late hour, for the accommodation of such members of the congregation—and they are not a few—as may happen to have lingered at the Opera far into the morning of the Sabbath; an excellent contrivance for poising the balance between God and Mammon, and illustrating the ease with which a man's duties to both may be accommodated and adjusted. How the carriages rattle up, and deposit their richly-dressed burdens beneath the lofty portico! The powdered footmen glide along the aisle, place the richly-bound prayer-books on the pew desks, slam the doors, and hurry away, leaving the fashionable members of the congregation to inspect each other through their glasses, and to dazzle and glitter in the eyes of the few shabby people in the free seats. The organ peals forth, the hired singers commence a short hymn, and the congregation condescendingly rise, stare about them, and converse in whispers. The clergyman enters the reading-desk,—a young man of noble family and elegant demeanour, notorious at Cambridge for his knowledge of horse-flesh and dancers, and celebrated at Eton for his hopeless stupidity. The service commences. Mark the soft voice in which he reads, and the impressive manner in which he applies his white hand, studded with brilliants, to his perfumed hair. Observe the graceful emphasis with which he offers up the prayers for the King, the Royal Family, and all the Nobility; and the nonchalance with which he hurries over the more uncomfortable portions of the service, the seventh commandment for instance, with a studied regard for the taste and feeling of his auditors, only to be equalled by that displayed by the sleek divine who succeeds him, who murmurs, in a voice kept down by rich feeding, most comfortable doctrines for exactly twelve minutes, and then arrives at the anxiously expected "Now to God," which is the signal for the dismissal of the congregation. The organ is again heard; those who have been asleep wake up, and those who have kept awake, smile and seem greatly relieved; bows and congratulations are exchanged, the livery servants are all bustle and commotion, bang go the steps, up jump the footmen, and off rattle the carriages: the inmates discoursing on the dresses of the congregation, and congratulating themselves on having set so excellent an example to the community in general, and Sunday-pleasurers in particular.

Enter a less orthodox place of religious worship, and observe the contrast. A small close chapel with a whitewashed wall, and plain deal pews and pulpit, contains a closely-packed congregation, as different in dress as they are opposed in manner, to that we have just quitted. The hymn is sung—not by paid singers, but by the whole assembly at the loudest pitch of their voices, unaccompanied by any musical instrument, the words being given out, two lines at a time, by the clerk. There is something in the sonorous quavering of the harsh voices, in the lank and hollow faces of the men, and the sour solemnity of the women, which bespeaks this a stronghold of intolerant zeal and ignorant enthusiasm. The preacher enters the pulpit. He is a coarse, hard-faced man of forbidding aspect, clad in rusty black, and bearing in his hand a small plain Bible from which he selects some passage for his text, while the hymn is concluding. The congregation fall upon their knees, and are hushed into profound stillness as he delivers an extempore prayer, in which he calls upon the Sacred Founder of the Christian faith to bless his ministry, in terms of disgusting and impious familiarity not to be described. He begins his oration in a drawling tone, and his hearers listen with silent attention. He grows warmer as he proceeds with his subject, and his gesticulation becomes proportionately violent. He clenches his fists, beats the book upon the desk before him, and swings his arms wildly about his head. The congregation murmur their acquiescence in his doctrines: and a short groan occasionally bears testimony to the moving nature of his eloquence. Encouraged by these symptoms of approval, and working himself up to a pitch of enthusiasm amounting almost to frenzy, he denounces sabbath-breakers with the direst vengeance of offended Heaven. He stretches his body half out of the pulpit, thrusts forth his arms with frantic gestures, and blasphemously calls upon the Deity to visit with eternal torments those who turn aside from the word, as interpreted and preached by—himself. A low moaning is heard, the women rock their bodies to and fro, and wring their hands; the preacher's fervour increases, the perspiration starts upon his brow, his face is flushed, and he clenches his hands convulsively, as he draws a hideous and appalling picture of the horrors preparing for the wicked in a future state. A great excitement is visible among his hearers, a scream is heard, and some young girl falls senseless on the floor. There is a momentary rustle, but it is only for a moment—all eyes are turned towards the preacher. He pauses, passes his handkerchief across his face, and looks complacently round. His voice resumes its natural tone, as with mock humility he offers up a thanksgiving for having been successful in his efforts, and having been permitted to rescue one sinner from the path of evil. He sinks back into his seat, exhausted with the violence of his ravings; the girl is removed, a hymn is sung, a petition for some measure for securing the better observance of the Sabbath, which has been prepared by the good man, is read; and his worshipping admirers struggle who shall be the first to sign it.

But the morning service has concluded, and the streets are again crowded with people. Long rows of cleanly-dressed charity children, preceded by a portly beadle and a withered schoolmaster, are returning to their welcome dinner; and it is evident, from the number of men with beer-trays who are running from house to house, that no inconsiderable portion of the population are about to take theirs at this early hour. The bakers' shops, in the humbler suburbs especially, are filled with men, women, and children, each anxiously waiting for the Sunday dinner. Look at the group of children who surround that working man who has just emerged from the baker's shop at the corner of the street, with the reeking dish, in which a diminutive joint of mutton simmers above a vast heap of half-browned potatoes. How the young rogues clap their hands, and dance round their father, for very joy at the prospect of the feast: and how anxiously the youngest and chubbiest of the lot lingers on tiptoe by his side, trying to get a peep into the interior of the dish. They turn up the street, and the chubby-faced boy trots on as fast as his little legs will carry him, to herald the approach of the dinner to "Mother" who is standing with a baby in her arms on the doorstep, and who seems almost as pleased with the whole scene as the children themselves; whereupon "baby" not precisely understanding the importance of the business in hand, but clearly perceiving that it is something unusually lively, kicks and crows most lustily, to the unspeakable delight of all the children and both the parents: and the dinner is borne into the house amidst a shouting of small voices, and jumping of fat legs, which would fill Sir Andrew Agnew with astonishment; as well it might, seeing that Baronets, generally speaking, eat pretty comfortable dinners all the week through, and cannot be expected to understand what people feel, who only have a meat dinner on one day out of every seven.

The bakings being all duly consigned to their respective owners, and the beer-man having gone his rounds, the church bells ring for afternoon service, the shops are again closed, and the streets are more than ever thronged with people; some who have not been to church in the morning, going to it now; others who have been to church, going out for a walk; and others—let us admit the full measure of their guilt—going for a walk, who have not been to church at all. I am afraid the smart servant of all work, who has been loitering at the corner of the square for the last ten minutes, is one of the latter class. She is evidently waiting for somebody, and though she may have made up her mind to go to church with him one of these mornings, I don't think they have any such intention on this particular afternoon. Here he is, at last. The white trousers, blue coat, and yellow waistcoat—and more especially that cock of the hat—indicate, as surely as inanimate objects can, that Chalk Farm and not the parish church is their destination. The girl colours up, and puts out her hand with a very awkward affectation of indifference. He gives it a gallant squeeze, and away they walk, arm in arm, the girl just looking back towards her "place" with an air of conscious self-importance, and nodding to her fellow-servant who has gone up to the two-pair-of-stairs window, to take a full view of "Mary's young man," which being communicated to William, he takes off his hat to the fellow-servant: a proceeding which affords unmitigated satisfaction to all parties, and impels the fellow-servant to inform Miss Emily confidentially, in the course of the evening, "that the young man as Mary keeps company with, is one of the most genteelest young men as ever she see."

The two young people who have just crossed the road, and

are following this happy couple down the street, are a fair specimen of another class of Sunday-pleasurers. There is a dapper smartness, struggling through very limited means, about the young man, which induces one to set him down at once as a junior clerk to a tradesman or attorney. The girl no one could possibly mistake. You may tell a young woman in the employment of a large dress-maker, at any time, by a certain neatness of cheap finery and humble following of fashion which pervade her whole attire; but unfortunately there are other tokens not to be misunderstood —the pale face with its hectic bloom, the slight distortion of form which no artifice of dress can wholly conceal, the unhealthy stoop, and the short cough—the effects of hard work and close application to a sedentary employment, upon a tender frame. They turn towards the fields. The girl's countenance brightens, and an unwonted glow rises in her face. They are going to Hampstead or Highgate, to spend their holiday afternoon in some place where they can see the sky, the fields, and trees, and breathe for an hour or two the pure air, which so seldom plays upon that poor girl's form, or exhilarates her spirits.

I would to God, that the iron-hearted man who would deprive such people as these of their only pleasures, could feel the sinking of heart and soul, the wasting exhaustion of mind and body, the utter prostration of present strength and future hope, attendant upon that incessant toil which lasts from day to day, and from month to month; that toil which is too often protracted until the silence of midnight, and resumed with the first stir of morning. How marvellously would his ardent zeal for other men's souls diminish after a short probation, and how enlightened and comprehensive would his views of the real object and meaning of the institution of the Sabbath become!

The afternoon is far advanced—the parks and public drives are crowded. Carriages, gigs, phaetons, stanhopes, and vehicles of every description, glide smoothly on. The promenades are filled with loungers on foot, and the road is thronged with loungers on horseback. Persons of every class are crowded together, here, in one dense mass. The plebeian, who takes his pleasure on no day but Sunday, jostles the patrician, who takes his from year's end to year's end. You look in vain for any outward signs of profligacy or debauchery. You see nothing before you but a vast number of people, the denizens of a large and crowded city, in the needful and rational enjoyment of air and exercise.

It grows dusk. The roads leading from the different places of suburban resort, are crowded with people on their return home, and the sound of merry voices rings through the gradually darkening fields. The evening is hot and sultry. The rich man throws open the sashes of his spacious dining-room, and quaffs his iced wine in splendid luxury. The poor man, who has no room to take his meals in, but the close apartment to which he and his family have been confined throughout the week, sits in the tea-garden of some famous tavern, and drinks his beer in content and comfort. The fields and roads are gradually deserted, the crowd once more pour into the streets, and disperse to their several homes; and by midnight all is silent and quiet, save where a few stragglers linger beneath the window of some great man's house, to listen to the strains of music from within, or stop to gaze upon the splendid carriages which are waiting to convey the guests from the dinner-party of an Earl.

There is a darker side to this picture, on which, so far from its being any part of my purpose to conceal it, I wish to lay particular stress. In some parts of London, and in many of the manufacturing towns of England, drunkenness and profligacy in their most disgusting forms, exhibit in the open streets on Sunday a sad and a degrading spectacle. We need go no farther than St. Giles's, or Drury Lane, for sights and scenes of a most repulsive nature. Women with scarcely the articles of apparel which common decency requires, with forms bloated by disease, and faces rendered hideous by habitual drunkenness—men reeling and staggering along—children in rags and filth—whole streets of squalid and miserable appearance, whose inhabitants are lounging in the public road, fighting, screaming, and swearing—these are the common objects which present themselves in, these are the well-known characteristics of, that portion of London to which I have just referred.

And why is it that all well-disposed persons are shocked, and public decency scandalised, by such exhibitions?

These people are poor—that is notorious. It may be said that they spend in liquor, money with which they might purchase necessaries, and there is no denying the fact; but let it be remembered that even if they applied every farthing of their earnings in the best possible way, they would still be very, very poor. Their dwellings are necessarily uncomfortable, and to a certain degree unhealthy. Cleanliness might do much, but they are too crowded together, the streets are too narrow, and the rooms too small, to admit of their ever being rendered desirable habitations. They work very hard all the week. We know that the effect of prolonged and arduous labour is to produce, when a period of rest does arrive, a sensation of lassitude which it requires the application of some stimulus to overcome. What stimulus have they? Sunday comes, and with it a cessation of labour. How are they to employ the day, or what inducement have they to employ it in recruiting their stock of health? They see little parties, on pleasure excursions, passing through the streets; but they cannot imitate their example, for they have not the means. They may walk, to be sure, but it is exactly the inducement to walk that they require. If every one of these men knew that by taking the trouble to walk two or three miles he would be enabled to share in a good game of cricket, or some athletic sport, I very much question whether any of them would remain at home.

But you hold out no inducement, you offer no relief from listlessness, you provide nothing to amuse his mind, you afford him no means of exercising his body. Unwashed and unshaven, he saunters moodily about, weary and dejected. In lieu of the wholesome stimulus he might derive from nature, you drive him to the pernicious excitement to be gained from art. He flies to the gin-shop as his only resource; and when, reduced to a worse level than the lowest brute in the scale of creation, he lies wallowing in the kennel, your saintly lawgivers lift up their hands to heaven, and exclaim for a law which shall convert the day intended for rest and cheerfulness, into one of universal gloom, bigotry, and persecution.

II

AS SABBATH BILLS WOULD MAKE IT

THE provisions of the bill introduced into the House of Commons by Sir Andrew Agnew, and thrown out by that House on the motion for the second reading, on the 18th of May in the present year, by a majority of 32, may very fairly be taken as a test of the length to which the fanatics, of which the honourable Baronet is the distinguished leader, are prepared to go. No test can be fairer; because while on the one hand this measure may be supposed to exhibit all that improvement which mature reflection and long deliberation may have suggested, so on the other it may very reasonably be inferred, that if it be quite as severe in its provisions, and to the full as partial in its operation, as those which have preceded it, and experienced a similar fate, the disease under which the honourable Baronet and his friends labour, is perfectly hopeless, and beyond the reach of cure.

The proposed enactments of the bill are briefly these:—All work is prohibited on the Lord's day, under heavy penalties, increasing with every repetition of the offence. There are penalties for keeping shops open—penalties for drunkenness—penalties for keeping open houses of entertainment—penalties for being present at any public meeting or assembly—penalties for letting carriages, and penalties for hiring them—penalties for travelling in steam-boats, and penalties for taking passengers—penalties on vessels commencing their voyage on Sunday—penalties on the owners of cattle who suffer them to be driven on the Lord's day—penalties on constables who refuse to act, and penalties for resisting them when they do. In addition to these trifles, the constables are invested with arbitrary, vexatious, and most extensive powers; and all this in a bill which sets out with a hypocritical and canting declaration that "nothing is more acceptable to God than the *true and sincere* worship of Him according to His holy will, and that it is the bounden duty of Parliament to promote the observance of the Lord's day, by protecting every class of society against being required to sacrifice their comfort, health, religious privileges, and conscience, for the convenience, enjoyment, or supposed advantage of any other class on the Lord's day"! The idea of making a man truly moral through the ministry of constables, and sincerely religious under the influence of penalties, is worthy of the mind which could form such a mass of monstrous absurdity as this bill is composed of.

The House of Commons threw the measure out certainly, and by so doing retrieved the disgrace—so far as it could be retrieved—of placing among the printed papers of Parliament, such an egregious specimen of legislative folly; but there was a degree of delicacy and forbearance about the debate that took place, which I cannot help thinking as unnecessary and uncalled for, as it is unusual in Parliamentary discussions. If it had been the first time of Sir Andrew Agnew's attempting to palm such a measure upon the country, we might well understand, and duly appreciate, the delicate and compassionate feeling due to the supposed weakness and imbecility of the man, which prevented his proposition being exposed in its true colours, and induced this Hon. Member to bear testimony to his excellent motives, and that Noble Lord to regret that he could not—although he had tried to do so—adopt any portion of the bill. But when these attempts have been repeated again and again; when Sir Andrew Agnew has renewed them session after session, and when it has become palpably evident to the whole House that

> His impudence of proof in every trial,
> Kens no polite, and heeds no plain denial—

it really becomes high time to speak of him and his legislation, as they appear to deserve, without that gloss of politeness, which is all very well in an ordinary case, but rather out of place when the liberties and comforts of a whole people are at stake.

In the first place, it is by no means the worst characteristic of this bill, that it is a bill of blunders: it is, from beginning to end, a piece of deliberate cruelty, and crafty injustice. If the rich composed the whole population of this country, not a single comfort of one single man would be affected by it. It is directed exclusively, and without the exception of a solitary instance, against the amusements and recreations of the poor. This was the bait held out by the Hon. Baronet to a body of men, who cannot be supposed to have any very strong sympathies in common with the poor, because they cannot understand their sufferings or their struggles. This is the bait, which will in time prevail, unless public attention is awakened, and public feeling exerted, to prevent it.

Take the very first clause, the provision that no man shall be allowed to work on Sunday—"That no person, upon the Lord's day, shall do, or hire, or employ any person to do any manner of labour, or any work of his or her ordinary calling." What class of persons does this affect? The rich man? No. Menial servants, both male and female, are specially exempted from the operation of the bill. "Menial servants" are among the poor people. The bill has no regard for them. The Baronet's dinner must be cooked on Sunday, the Bishop's horses must be groomed, and the Peer's carriage must be driven. So the menial servants are put utterly beyond the pale of grace;—unless indeed, they are to go to heaven through the sanctity of their masters, and possibly they might think even that rather an uncertain passport.

There is a penalty for keeping open houses of entertainment. Now, suppose the bill had passed, and that half-a-dozen adventurous licensed victuallers, relying upon the excitement of public feeling on the subject, and the consequent difficulty of conviction (this is by no means an improbable supposition), had determined to keep their houses and gardens open, through the whole Sunday afternoon, in defiance of the law. Every act of hiring or working, every act of buying or selling, or delivering, or causing anything to be bought or sold, is specifically made a separate offence—mark the effect. A party, a man and his wife and children, enter a tea-garden, and the informer stations himself in the next box, from whence he can see and hear everything that passes. "Waiter!" says the father. "Yes, Sir." "Pint of the best ale!" "Yes, Sir." Away runs the waiter to the bar, and gets the ale from the landlord. Out comes the informer's note-book—penalty on the father for hiring, on the waiter for delivering, and on the landlord for selling, on the Lord's day. But it does not stop here. The waiter delivers the ale, and darts off, little suspecting the penalties in store for him. "Hollo," cries the father, "waiter!" "Yes, Sir." "Just get this little boy a biscuit, will you?" "Yes, Sir." Off runs the waiter again, and down goes another case of hiring, another case of delivering, and another case of selling; and so it would go on *ad infinitum*, the sum and substance of the matter being, that every time a man or woman cried "Waiter!" on Sunday, he or she would be fined not less than forty shillings, nor more than a hundred; and every time a waiter replied, "Yes, Sir," he and his master would be fined in the same amount: with the addition of a new sort of window duty on the landlord, to wit, a tax of twenty shillings an hour for every hour beyond the first one, during which he should have his shutters down on the Sabbath.

With one exception, there are perhaps no clauses in the whole bill, so strongly illustrative of its partial operation, and the intention of its framer, as those which relate to travelling on Sunday. Penalties of ten, twenty, and thirty pounds, are mercilessly imposed upon coach proprietors who shall run their coaches on the Sabbath; one, two, and ten pounds upon those who hire, or let to hire, horses and carriages upon the Lord's day, but not one syllable about those who have no necessity to hire, because they have carriages and horses of their own; not one word of a penalty on liveried coachmen and footmen. The whole of the saintly venom is directed against the hired cabriolet, the humble fly, or the rumbling hackney-coach, which enables a man of the poorer class to escape for a few hours from the smoke and dirt, in the midst of which he has been confined throughout the week: while the escutcheoned carriage and the dashing cab may whirl their wealthy owners to Sunday feasts and private oratorios, setting constables, informers, and penalties, at defiance. Again, in the description of the places of public resort which it is rendered criminal to attend on Sunday, there are no words comprising a very fashionable promenade. Public discussions, public debates, public lectures and speeches, are cautiously guarded against; for it is by their means that the people become enlightened enough to deride the last efforts of bigotry and superstition. There is a stringent provision for punishing the poor man who spends an hour in a news-room, but there is nothing to prevent the rich one from lounging away the day in the Zoological Gardens.

There is, in four words, a mock proviso, which affects to forbid travelling "with any animal" on the Lord's day. This, however, is revoked, as relates to the rich man, by a subsequent provision. We have then a penalty of not less than fifty, nor more than one hundred pounds, upon any person participating in the control, or having the command of any vessel which shall commence her voyage on the Lord's day, should the wind prove favourable. The next time this bill is brought forward (which will no doubt be at an early period of the next session of Parliament) perhaps it will be better to amend this clause by declaring, that from and after the passing of the act, it shall be deemed unlawful for the wind to blow at all upon the Sabbath. It would remove a great deal of temptation from the owners and captains of vessels.

The reader is now in possession of the principal enacting clauses of Sir Andrew Agnew's bill, with the exception of one, for preventing the killing or taking of "*fish, or other wild animals,*" and the ordinary provisions which are inserted for form's sake in all acts of Parliament. I now beg his attention to the clauses of exemption.

They are two in number. The first exempts menial servants from any rest, and all poor men from any recreation: outlaws a milkman after nine o'clock in the morning, and makes eating-houses lawful for only two hours in the afternoon; permits a medical man to use his carriage on Sunday, and declares that a clergyman may either use his own, or hire one.

The second is artful, cunning, and designing; shielding the rich man from the possibility of being entrapped, and affecting at the same time, to have a tender and scrupulous regard for the interests of the whole community. It declares, "that nothing in this act contained, shall extend to works of piety, charity, or necessity."

What is meant by the word "necessity" in this clause? Simply this—that the rich man shall be at liberty to make use of all the splendid luxuries he has collected around him, on any day in the week, because habit and custom have rendered them "necessary" to his easy existence; but that the poor man who saves his money to provide some little pleasure for himself and family at lengthened intervals, shall not be permitted to enjoy it. It is not "necessary" to him: —Heaven knows, he very often goes long enough without it. This is the plain English of the clause. The carriage and pair of horses, the coachman, the footman, the helper, and the groom, are "necessary" on Sundays, as on other days, to the bishop and the nobleman; but the hackney-coach, the hired gig, or the taxed cart, cannot possibly be "necessary" to the working-man on Sunday, for he has it not at other times. The sumptuous dinner and the rich wines are "necessaries" to a great man in his own mansion: but the pint of beer and the plate of meat degrade the national character in an eating-house.

Such is the bill for promoting the true and sincere worship of God according to his Holy Will, and for protecting every class of society against being required to sacrifice their health and comfort on the Sabbath. Instances in which its operation would be as unjust as it would be absurd, might be multiplied to an endless amount; but it is sufficient to place its leading provisions before the reader. In doing so, I have purposely abstained from drawing upon the imagination for possible cases; the provisions to which I have referred, stand in so many words upon the bill as printed by order of the House of Commons; and they can neither be disowned nor explained away.

Let us suppose such a bill as this to have actually passed both branches of the legislature; to have received the royal assent; and to have come into operation. Imagine its effect in a great city like London.

Sunday comes, and brings with it a day of general gloom and austerity. The man who has been toiling hard all the week, has been looking towards the Sabbath, not as to a day of rest from labour, and healthy recreation, but as one of grievous tyranny and grinding oppression. The day which his Maker intended as a blessing, man has converted into a curse. Instead of being hailed by him as his period of relaxation, he finds it remarkable only as depriving him of every comfort and enjoyment. He has many children about him, all sent into the world at an early age to struggle for a livelihood; one is kept in a warehouse all day, with an interval of rest too short to enable him to reach home, another walks four or five miles to his employment at the docks, a third earns a few shillings weekly as an errand boy, or office messenger ; and the employment of the man himself, detains him at some distance from his home from morning till night. Sunday is the only day on which they could all meet together, and enjoy a homely meal in social comfort ; and now they sit down to a cold and cheerless dinner : the pious guardians of the man's salvation having, in their regard for the welfare of his precious soul, shut up the bakers' shops. The fire blazes high in the kitchen chimney of these well-fed hypocrites, and the rich steams of the savoury dinner scent the air. What care they to be told that this class of men have neither a place to cook in—nor means to bear the expense, if they had ?

Look into your churches—diminished congregations, and scanty attendance. People have grown sullen and obstinate, and are becoming disgusted with the faith which condemns them to such a day as this, once in every seven. And as you cannot make people religious by Act of Parliament, or force them to church by constables, they display their feeling by staying away.

Turn into the streets, and mark the rigid gloom that reigns over everything around. The roads are empty, the fields are deserted, the houses of entertainment are closed. Groups of filthy and discontented-looking men are idling about at the street corners, or sleeping in the sun ; but there are no decently-dressed people of the poorer class passing to and fro. Where should they walk to ? It would take them an hour, at least, to get into the fields, and when they reached them they could procure neither bite nor sup without the informer and the penalty. Now and then a carriage rolls smoothly on, or a well-mounted horseman, followed by a liveried attendant, canters by ; but with these exceptions, all is as melancholy and quiet as if a pestilence had fallen on the city.

Bend your steps through the narrow and thickly-inhabited streets, and observe the sallow faces of the men and women who are lounging at the doors, or lolling from the windows. Regard well the closeness of these crowded rooms, and the noisome exhalations that rise from the drains and kennels ; and then laud the triumph of religion and morality, which condemns people to drag their lives out in such stews as these, and makes it criminal for them to eat or drink in the fresh air, or under the clear sky. Here and there, from some half-opened window, the loud shout of drunken revelry strikes upon the ear, and the noise of oaths and quarrelling—the effect of the close and heated atmosphere—is heard on all sides. See how the men all rush to join the crowd that are making their way down the street, and how loud the execrations of the mob become as they draw nearer. They have assembled round a little knot of constables, who have seized the stock-in-trade, heinously exposed on Sunday, of some miserable walking-stick seller, who follows clamouring for his property. The dispute grows warmer and fiercer, until at last some of the more furious among the crowd rush forward to restore the goods to their owner. A general conflict takes place; the sticks of the constables are exercised in all directions; fresh assistance is procured; and half a dozen of the assailants are conveyed to the station-house, struggling, bleeding, and cursing. The case is taken to the police-office on the following morning; and after a frightful amount of perjury on both sides, the men are sent to prison for resisting the officers, their families to the workhouse to keep them from starving: and there they both remain for a month afterwards, glorious trophies of the sanctified enforcement of the Christian Sabbath. Add to such scenes as these the profligacy, idleness, drunkenness, and vice, that will be committed to an extent which no man can foresee, on Monday, as an atonement for the restraint of the preceding day; and you have a very faint and imperfect picture of the religious effects of this Sunday legislation, supposing it could ever be forced upon the people.

But let those who advocate the cause of fanaticism reflect well upon the probable issue of their endeavours. They may by perseverance, succeed with Parliament. Let them ponder on the probability of succeeding with the people. You may deny the concession of a political question for a time, and a nation will bear it patiently. Strike home to the comforts of every man's fireside—tamper with every man's freedom and liberty—and one month, one week, may rouse a feeling abroad which a king would gladly yield his crown to quell, and a peer would resign his coronet to allay.

It is the custom to affect a deference for the motives of those who advocate these measures, and a respect for the feelings by which they are actuated. They do not deserve it. If they legislate in ignorance, they are criminal and dishonest; if they do so with their eyes open, they commit wilful injustice; in either case, they bring religion into contempt. But they do NOT legislate in ignorance. Public prints, and public men, have pointed out to them again and again the consequences of their proceedings. If they persist in thrusting themselves forward, let those consequences rest upon their own heads, and let them be content to stand upon their own merits.

It may be asked, what motives can actuate a man who has so little regard for the comfort of his fellow-beings, so little respect for their wants and necessities, and so distorted a notion of the beneficence of his Creator. I reply, an envious, heartless, ill-conditioned dislike to seeing those whom fortune has placed below him, cheerful and happy— an intolerant confidence in his own high worthiness before God, and a lofty impression of the demerits of others— pride, selfish pride, as inconsistent with the spirit of Christianity itself, as opposed to the example of its Founder upon earth.

To these may be added another class of men—the stern and gloomy enthusiasts, who would make earth a hell, and religion a torment: men who, having wasted the earlier part of their lives in dissipation and depravity, find themselves when scarcely past its meridian, steeped to the neck in vice, and shunned like a loathsome disease. Abandoned by the world, having nothing to fall back upon, nothing to remember but time mis-spent, and energies misdirected, they turn their eyes and not their thoughts to Heaven, and delude themselves into the impious belief, that in denouncing the lightness of heart of which they cannot partake, and the rational pleasures from which they never derived enjoyment, they are more than remedying the sins of their old career, and—like the founders of monasteries and builders of churches, in ruder days—establishing a good set claim upon their Maker.

III

AS IT MIGHT BE MADE

THE supporters of Sabbath Bills, and more especially the extreme class of Dissenters, lay great stress upon the declarations occasionally made by criminals from the condemned cell or the scaffold, that to Sabbath-breaking they attribute their first deviation from the path of rectitude; and they point to these statements, as an incontestable proof of the evil consequences which await a departure from that strict and rigid observance of the Sabbath, which they uphold. I cannot help thinking that in this, as in almost every other respect connected with the subject, there is a considerable degree of cant, and a very great deal of wilful blindness. If a man be viciously disposed—and with very few exceptions, not a man dies by the executioner's hands, who has not been in one way or other a most abandoned and profligate character for many years—if a man be viciously disposed, there is no doubt that he will turn his Sunday to bad account, that he will take advantage of it to dissipate with other bad characters as vile as himself; and that in this way he may trace his first yielding to temptation, possibly his first commission of crime, to an infringement of the Sabbath. But this would be an argument against any holiday at all. If his holiday had been Wednesday instead of Sunday, and he had devoted it to the same improper uses, it would have been productive of the same results. It is too much to judge of the character of a whole people by the confessions of the very worst members of society. It is not fair to cry down things which are harmless in themselves, because evil-disposed men may turn them to bad account. Who ever thought of deprecating the teaching poor people to write because some porter in a warehouse had committed forgery? Or into what man's head did it ever enter, to prevent the crowding of churches because it afforded a temptation for the picking of pockets?

When the Book of Sports, for allowing the peasantry of England to divert themselves with certain games in the open air, on Sundays, after evening service, was published by Charles the First, it is needless to say the English people were comparatively rude and uncivilised. And yet it is extraordinary to how few excesses it gave rise, even in that day, when men's minds were not enlightened, or their passions moderated, by the influence of education and refinement. That some excesses were committed through its means, in the remoter parts of the country, and that it was discontinued in those places in consequence, cannot be denied: but generally speaking, there is no proof whatever on record, of its having had any tendency to increase crime, or to lower the character of the people.

The Puritans of that time were as much opposed to harmless recreations and healthful amusements as those of the present day, and it is amusing to observe that each in their generation advance precisely the same description of arguments. In the British Museum there is a curious pamphlet got up by the Agnews of Charles's time, entitled "A Divine Tragedie lately acted, or a Collection of sundry memorable examples of God's Judgements upon Sabbath Breakers, and other like Libertines in their unlawful Sports, happening within the realme of England, in the compass only of two yeares last past, since the Booke (of Sports) was published, worthy to be knowne and considered of all men, especially such who are guilty of the sinne, or archpatrons thereof." This amusing document contains some fifty or sixty veritable accounts of balls of fire that fell into church-yards and upset the sporters, and sporters that quarrelled and upset one another, and so forth: and among them is one anecdote containing an example of a rather different kind, which I cannot resist the temptation of quoting, as strongly illustrative of the fact, that this blinking of the question has not even the recommendation of novelty.

"A woman about Northampton, the same day that she heard the booke for sports read, went immediately, and having 3. pence in her purse, hired a fellow to goe to the next towne to fetch a Minstrell, who coming, she with others fell a daucing, which continued within night; at which time shee was got with child, which at the birth shee mur-thering, was detected and apprehended, and being convented before the justice, shee confessed it, and withal told the occasion of it, saying it was her falling to sport on the Sabbath, upon the reading of the Booke, so as for this treble sinfull act, her presumptuous profaning of the Sabbath, w^h. brought her adultory and that murther. Shee was according to the Law both of God and man, put to death. Much sinne and misery followeth upon Sabbath-breaking."

It is needless to say that if the young lady near Northampton had "fallen to sport" of such a dangerous description, on any other day but Sunday, the first result would probably have been the same: it never having been distinctly shown that Sunday is more favourable to the propagation of the human race than any other day in the week. The second result—the murder of the child—does not speak very highly for the amiability of her natural disposition; and the whole story, supposing it to have had any foundation at all, is about as much chargeable upon the Book of Sports, as upon the Book of Kings. Such "sports" have taken place in Dissenting Chapels before now; but religion has never been blamed in consequence; nor has it been proposed to shut up the chapels on that account.

The question, then, very fairly arises, whether we have any reason to suppose that allowing games in the open air on Sundays, or even providing the means of amusement for the humbler classes of society on that day, would be hurtful and injurious to the character and morals of the people.

I was travelling in the west of England a summer or two back, and was induced by the beauty of the scenery, and the seclusion of the spot, to remain for the night in a small village, distant about seventy miles from London. The next morning was Sunday; and I walked out towards the church. Groups of people—the whole population of the little hamlet apparently—were hastening in the same direction. Cheerful and good-humoured congratulations were heard on all sides, as neighbours overtook each other, and walked on in company. Occasionally I passed an aged couple, whose married daughter and her husband were loitering by the side of the old people, accommodating their rate of walking to their feeble pace, while a little knot of children hurried on before; stout young labourers in clean round frocks; and buxom girls with healthy, laughing faces, were plentifully sprinkled about in couples, and the whole scene was one of quiet and tranquil contentment, irresistibly captivating. The morning was bright and pleasant, the hedges were green and blooming, and a thousand delicious scents were wafted on the air, from the wild flowers which blossomed on either side of the footpath. The little church was one of those venerable simple buildings which abound in the English counties ; half overgrown with moss and ivy, and standing in the centre of a little plot of ground, which, but for the green mounds with which it was studded, might have passed for a lovely meadow. I fancied that the old clanking bell which was now summoning the congregation together, would seem less terrible when it rung out the knell of a departed soul, than I had ever deemed possible before—that the sound would tell only of a welcome to calmness and rest, amidst the most peaceful and tranquil scene in nature.

I followed into the church—a low-roofed building with small arched windows, through which the sun's rays streamed upon a plain tablet on the opposite wall, which had once recorded names, now as undistinguishable on its worn surface, as were the bones beneath, from the dust into which they had resolved. The impressive service of the Church of England was spoken—not merely *read*—by a grey-headed minister, and the responses delivered by his auditors, with an air of sincere devotion as far removed from affectation or display, as from coldness or indifference. The psalms were accompanied by a few instrumental performers, who were stationed in a small gallery extending across the church at the lower end, over the door : and the voices were led by the clerk, who it was evident derived no slight pride and gratification from this portion of the service. The discourse was plain, unpretending, and well adapted to the comprehension of the hearers. At the conclusion of the service, the villagers waited in the churchyard to salute the clergyman as he passed ; and two or three, I observed, stepped aside, as if communicating some little difficulty, and asking his advice. This, to guess from the homely bows, and other rustic expressions of gratitude, the old gentleman readily conceded. He seemed intimately acquainted with the circumstances of all his parishioners ; for I heard him inquire after one man's youngest child, another man's wife, and so forth ; and that he was fond of his joke, I discovered from overhearing him ask a stout, fresh-coloured young fellow, with a very pretty bashful-looking girl on his arm, "when those banns were to be put up?"—an inquiry which made the young fellow more fresh-coloured, and the girl more bashful, and which, strange to say, caused a great many other girls who were standing round, to colour up also, and look anywhere but in the faces of their male companions.

As I approached this spot in the evening about half an hour before sunset, I was surprised to hear the hum of voices, and occasionally a shout of merriment from the meadow beyond the churchyard; which I found, when I reached the stile, to be occasioned by a very animated game of cricket, in which the boys and young men of the place were engaged, while the females and old people were scattered about: some seated on the grass watching the progress of the game, and others sauntering about in groups of two or three, gathering little nosegays of wild roses and hedge flowers. I could not but take notice of one old man in particular, with a bright-eyed grand-daughter by his side, who was giving a sunburnt young fellow some instructions in the game, which he received with an air of profound deference, but with an occasional glance at the girl, which induced me to think that his attention was rather distracted from the old gentleman's narration of the fruits of his experience. When it was his turn at the wicket, too, there was a glance towards the pair every now and then, which the old grandfather very complacently considered as an appeal to his judgment of a particular hit, but which a certain blush in the girl's face, and a downcast look of the bright eye, led me to believe was intended for somebody else than the old man,—and understood by somebody else, too, or I am much mistaken.

I was in the very height of the pleasure which the contemplation of this scene afforded me, when I saw the old clergyman making his way towards us. I trembled for an angry interruption to the sport, and was almost on the point of crying out, to warn the cricketers of his approach; he was so close upon me, however, that I could do nothing but remain still, and anticipate the reproof that was preparing. What was my agreeable surprise to see the old gentleman standing at the stile, with his hands in his pockets, surveying the whole scene with evident satisfaction! And how dull I must have been, not to have known till my friend the grandfather (who, by-the-bye, said he had been a wonderful cricketer in his time) told me, that it was the clergyman himself who had established the whole thing: that it was his field they played in; and that it was he who had purchased stumps, bats, ball, and all!

It is such scenes as this I would see near London on a Sunday evening. It is such men as this who would do more in one year to make people properly religious, cheerful, and contented, than all the legislation of a century could ever accomplish.

It will be said—it has been very often—that it would be matter of perfect impossibility to make amusements and exercises succeed in large towns, which may be very well adapted to a country population. Here, again, we are called upon to yield to bare assertions on matters of belief and opinion, as if they were established and undoubted facts. That there is a wide difference between the two cases, no one will be prepared to dispute; that the difference is such as to prevent the application of the same principle to both, no reasonable man, I think, will be disposed to maintain. The great majority of the people who make holiday on Sunday now, are industrious, orderly, and well-behaved persons. It is not unreasonable to suppose that they would be no more inclined to an abuse of pleasures provided for them, than they are to an abuse of the pleasures they provide for themselves; and if any people, for want of something better to do, resort to criminal practices on the Sabbath as at present observed, no better remedy for the evil can be imagined, than giving them the opportunity of doing something which will amuse them, and hurt nobody else.

The propriety of opening the British Museum to respectable people on Sunday, has lately been the subject of some discussion. I think it would puzzle the most austere of the Sunday legislators to assign any valid reason for opposing so sensible a proposition. The Museum contains rich specimens from all the vast museums and repositories of Nature, and rare and curious fragments of the mighty works of art, in bygone ages: all calculated to awaken contemplation and inquiry, and to tend to the enlightenment and improvement of the people. But attendants would be necessary, and a few men would be employed upon the Sabbath. They certainly would; but how many? Why, if the British Museum, and the National Gallery, and the Gallery of

Practical Science, and every other exhibition in London, from which knowledge is to be derived and information gained, were to be thrown open on a Sunday afternoon, not fifty people would be required to preside over the whole : and it would take treble the number to enforce a Sabbath bill in any three populous parishes.

I should like to see some large field, or open piece of ground, in every outskirt of London, exhibiting each Sunday evening on a larger scale, the scene of the little country meadow. I should like to see the time arrive, when a man's attendance to his religious duties might be left to that religious feeling which most men possess in a greater or less degree, but which was never forced into the breast of any man by menace or restraint. I should like to see the time when Sunday might be looked forward to, as a recognised day of relaxation and enjoyment, and when every man might feel, what few men do now, that religion is not incompatible with rational pleasure and needful recreation.

How different a picture would the streets and public places then present ! The museums, and repositories of scientific and useful inventions, would be crowded with ingenious mechanics and industrious artisans, all anxious for information, and all unable to procure it at any other time. The spacious saloons would be swarming with practical men : humble in appearance, but destined, perhaps, to become the greatest inventors and philosophers of their age. The labourers who now lounge away the day in idleness and intoxication, would be seen hurrying along, with cheerful faces and clean attire, not to the close and smoky atmosphere of the public-house, but to the fresh and airy fields. Fancy the pleasant scene. Throngs of people, pouring out from the lanes and alleys of the metropolis, to various places of common resort at some short distance from the town, to join in the refreshing sports and exercises of the day—the children gambolling in crowds upon the grass, the mothers looking on, and enjoying themselves the little game they seem only to direct ; other parties strolling along some pleasant walks, or reposing in the shade of the stately trees ; others again intent upon their different amusements. Nothing should be heard on all sides, but the sharp stroke of the bat as it sent the ball skimming along the ground, the clear ring of the quoit, as it struck upon the iron peg : the noisy murmur of many voices, and the loud shout of mirth and delight, which would awaken the echoes far and wide, till the fields rung with it. The day would pass away in a series of enjoyments which would awaken no painful reflections when night arrived; for they would be calculated to bring with them only health and contentment. The young would lose that dread of religion, which the sour austerity of its professors too often inculcates in youthful bosoms; and the old would find less difficulty in persuading them to respect its observances. The drunken and dissipated, deprived of any excuse for their misconduct, would no longer excite pity but disgust. Above all, the more ignorant and humble class of men, who now partake of many of the bitters of life, and taste but few of its sweets, would naturally feel attachment and respect for that code of morality, which, regarding the many hardships of their station, strove to alleviate its rigours, and endeavoured to soften its asperity.

This is what Sunday might be made, and what it might be made without impiety or profanation. The wise and beneficent Creator who places men upon earth, requires that they shall perform the duties of that station of life to which they are called, and He can never intend that the more a man strives to discharge those duties, the more he shall be debarred from happiness and enjoyment. Let those who have six days in the week for all the world's pleasures, appropriate the seventh to fasting and gloom, either for their own sins or those of other people, if they like to bewail them; but let those who employ their six days in a worthier manner, devote their seventh to a different purpose. Let divines set the example of true morality: preach it to their flocks in the morning, and dismiss them to enjoy true rest in the afternoon; and let them select for their text, and let Sunday legislators take for their motto, the words which fell from the lips of that Master, whose precepts they misconstrue, and whose lessons they pervert —"The Sabbath was made for man, and not man to serve the Sabbath."

THE END